FOREVER YOURS

This book is dedicated to my long-time friend and story editor, Lyndsy Fernandes, without whose insights and guidance it would not have been possible.

CONTENTS

PLANNED 2025 SIGNATURE COLLECTION RELEASES

Soulmates, February 2025. D.R. Peters, 'Doc' to his friends, is an artist. He paints portraits of women. Doc loves women. Many of the women he paints love him. Then smart and sexy Rita, his next door neighbor, asks him to teach her the art of love, which Doc is all too happy to do. He's not quite so sure, though when Rita, a research scientist, decides to start experimenting with the effect his relationship with his models has on his art. Doc is about to learn all about the science of the art of love.

The Art and Science of Love, March 2025. D.R. Peters, 'Doc' to his friends, is an artist. He paints portraits of women. Doc loves women. Many of the women he paints love him. Then smart and sexy Rita, his next door neighbor, asks him to teach her the art of love, which Doc is all too happy to do. He's not quite so sure, though when Rita, a research scientist, decides to start experimenting with the effect his relationship with his models has on his art. Doc is about to learn all about the science of the art of love.

Drawing on the Dark Side of the Brain. April 2025. Artist Jett Blackburn's paintings reveal the soul of his subjects. They have the power to change the viewer, the model, and the artist. Sometimes emotionally, sometimes terminally. Join this digital native and his accumulation of girlfriends as they break the ties with their parents and move off to college and self-discovery.

Forever Yours. September 2025. Artificial Intelligence programming prodigy Henry pulls three other friends with him to create a new company with $billion prospects. Getting through jealousies, college, loves, virtual and physical attacks, takeover challenges, and family life, Henry succeeds in creating a singularity AI—one that can contain all the data from one's life. But how will it be used?

Bob's Memoir: 4,000 Years as a Free Demon. November 2025. "Hi! I'm Bob and I'll be your demon tonight." So begins the adventure of a free demon, loosed on the world by an inept adept some 4,000 years ago. But Bob is not your ordinary textbook demon. He was not imbued with any traits of evil when he was summoned and as a result is rather benign, learning about humanity and morality as he goes. He's just your everyday, slightly horny, happy-go-lucky (mostly lucky) demon. The full three-volume trilogy in one hardcover book!

Schedule and Releases Subject to Change

FOREVER YOURS

Devan Payne

SIGNATURE EDITION

ELDER ROAD BOOKS
LYNNWOOD WA

PART I

"Before the middle of this century, the growth rates of our technology—which will be indistinguishable from ourselves—will be so steep as to appear essentially vertical. From a strictly mathematical perspective, the growth rates will still be finite but so extreme that the changes they bring about will appear to rupture the fabric of human history. That, at least, will be the perspective of unenhanced biological humanity.

"The Singularity will represent the culmination of the merger of our biological thinking and existence with our technology, resulting in a world that is still human but that transcends our biological roots. There will be no distinction, post-Singularity, between physical and virtual reality. If you wonder what will remain unequivocally human in such a world, it's simply this quality: ours is the species that inherently seeks to extend its physical and mental reach beyond current limitations."

—Ray Kurzweil, *The Singularity is Near*

1

THE PRINCIPLES OF LUST

Henry RUSHED FROM his last class on Thursday to get to the side door of the school where Isobel usually met her ride and looked across the parking lot. *Shit!* Isobel was kissing Luke next to his new Corvette. Luke's father had surprised him with the car for his eighteenth birthday the previous Sunday.

"Aw. You're too late," Chastity said from behind his left shoulder.

He wasn't sure when she had shown up. Must have gotten there right after him.

"She's going to the prom with Luke. You know, she likes you both, but he has more 'status' than you do. So far. His dad owns a company."

"He's the Chevrolet dealer," Henry laughed.

"That's a company," Chastity said. "Isobel can't see into the future past the obvious. Luke is a good catch. He's the last of us to have turned eighteen. You should have seen her eyes when she saw his new car. He's smart and has money. Or his father does. She doesn't see what I see."

"What's that?" Henry asked, turning to Chastity at last.

Chastity, Isobel, Luke, and Henry had been best friends for years. Isobel was the glamour girl, with Latina fire and good looks. Luke was the DECA business club's selection for "most likely to succeed." Henry was a software and computer geek. But Chastity…

Henry quickly decided he hadn't been paying enough attention to Chastity. She was tall and thin and certainly pretty. He couldn't help letting his eyes wander over her statuesque form. Either she'd removed her bra or had just taken off the vest she wore over her T-shirt. He could see the hard points of her nipples pressing the fabric out and the distinct shape of the barbell nipple piercings she'd gotten on her eighteenth birthday.

"I see our future," she said. "Luke is going to manage a great company. Isobel is going to make money grow. But you, dear Henry, are going to make us millions."

"Millions? I hope you are a true prophetess," Henry laughed. "And what are you going to do?"

"I'm going to start by going to the prom with you," Chastity said.

"*You* want to go with *me*?" he asked, a little surprised. He hadn't had much hope of Isobel going with him, but he'd always considered Chastity a little out of his league. Great friends, but ultimately just a fantasy. Chastity almost always had a date on the weekends—sometimes two or three.

"Well... Not 'go with' as in dating. Just take me to the prom. Treat me like a goddess for the night and I absolutely guarantee you'll get lucky," Chastity said.

"Wow! You know, most girls are happy with princess treatment." Henry crossed his arms and waited for Chastity's response.

"I know my worth. And you will," she said, pulling his hand around and placing it on her butt. Henry squeezed lightly as they looked into each other's eyes.

Chastity was suddenly *very* attractive in ways Henry never seriously considered before.

"Okay, my goddess. I'd be delighted to take you to the prom," he said, giving her bottom another squeeze.

"And have fun with me?"

"I promise we'll have fun and you, too, will get lucky."

"That's a fair transaction," Chastity smiled. She put a hand on his chest and used her thumb to trace around his right nipple. "Just remember: Worship my body. Don't pretend to fall in love. We don't need that complication. It's just for the night."

"I'll check online for 'how to worship a goddess'," he said, pulling her close.

"Oh, yeah. I'll share some links. Maybe you want to get us a hotel room for the night, unless you have a private space at home."

"Not that private. I hate to have my parents hearing my date screaming my name," he said. He brushed his lips against hers lightly.

"Better see if the hotel has a soundproof room. I tend to be noisy when I'm having a good time."

Henry was serious. He could find almost anything online. He broke most of the stereotypes of the computer geek. He *didn't* spend much time playing games, like most of his classmates did. If he was on his computer, he was creating something. He didn't smell, bathed regularly, and wore clean, if not new, clothes. He had intense blue eyes that people said saw right through them. He was polite and had a decent sense of humor. He might not be elected homecoming king, but people generally liked him.

The next night, Friday, there was a dance after the last regular season basketball game. Henry joined Isobel, Luke, and Chastity at the game as their typical foursome when they didn't have individual dates. Isobel was constantly bumping into and brushing against him as she flirted. After the game they all headed for the end of season dance. At her insistence, Henry took Isobel to the dance floor.

"Are you supposed to be paying so much attention to me?" he asked. "You're going to the prom with Luke."

"That's not for two months yet. I notice you aren't just hanging on Chastity," Isobel said.

"Part of our agreement. We aren't dating, we're just going to the prom together."

They bounced around to the music and Isobel backed up to grind against him as she threw her head back to ask, "What makes you think Luke and I are dating?"

"The way he's staring at you across the room."

"Yeah. I love that. He'll wait until I'm done with you."

The song ended and Isobel wandered toward Luke, who made a direct line to her. Henry didn't manage to leave the dance floor before he was snagged by Sheila, the class president. The blonde cheerleader was intent on lecturing him about the need for a senior project for the class. Henry automatically checked around to see where his friends were.

"Are you listening to me, Henry?" she asked, moving in closer and putting her arms around him in a way that wasn't particularly suited to the music.

"Of course, Sheila. And I agree that we need a really good senior project. But it's getting late in the year to be starting something now," he answered. She cuddled in his arms, satisfied that he wasn't daydreaming, or watching that slut, Chastity.

"Well, what do you think we could do, given the time constraints? It's already March and we're just three months from graduation."

"Yeah. I can't believe nobody thought of this six months ago."

"We were all too concerned with getting early apps for college out. Have you been accepted somewhere yet?"

"Yes. I'm staying local and will go to the university. They have a good computer science program with a new specialization in artificial intelligence and machine learning. I have a couple of good scholarship offers."

"That stuff's creepy," she said, shuddering a little. The motion did wonderful things for the way her breasts were pressed against his chest.

"How about if we got an upgrade to the gym PA system?" Henry asked suddenly. "Announcements during the game tonight were all garbled. I don't think it was just my hearing. I worked the system for an event once and it must be fifty years old. It's practically falling apart."

"That's true. Do you think we could raise enough money in the time we have to replace it?"

"Put Isobel on raising the money and Chastity on recruiting volunteers. The whole system will need to be removed and those speakers in the middle of the gym must weigh in at fifty pounds each. I'll check with the local electronics stores to see what we can get. Might have to build something, but it can be done. I'll take Luke with me and he can negotiate the deals," Henry said.

"You four do everything together, don't you? Well, I won't complain. If you need a date because Chastity is off screwing someone else, let me know. I mean, you know, while we're working on the project," Sheila said.

"That's really kind of you, Sheila. I'll see what comes up."

"Mmmhmm," she said, rubbing her middle against his to see if she could get something to come up.

It was, but the song ended and Henry guided Sheila over to where Luke had arrived with Isobel, Chastity, David, and Rachel. It seemed Luke was telling a very funny story and Sheila laughed politely as she heard the punchline.

"Hey, I was just talking to Henry about what we could do for a senior project," Sheila said, stepping in. As class president, she was used to commanding attention whenever she wanted it. "Isobel, I'm wondering if we could meet after school Monday to talk about the fundraising aspect. Luke, I think Henry has an idea about putting in a new gym sound system that could use your negotiating skills. Anybody else want to get involved? Why don't we all plan to meet Monday. Invite others and we'll divide up into working groups."

"Great idea, Sheila," David said, moving next to her. "You know I'll do whatever you need. Why don't you fill me in on the details while we hit the dance floor."

"That was slick," Rachel said as the two left the group.

"Don't worry. Henry will dance with you," Chastity said. "He's a great dancer."

Henry doubted that what he did could be called great dancing, but he did manage to not make a fool of himself or his partner. He led Rachel to the dance floor. Chastity had cut him off just when he was going to ask her to dance. Luke led Isobel to the farthest side of the gym to clutch each other and shuffle their feet. Chastity was alone for almost fifteen seconds before one of the basketball players asked her to dance.

AFTER THEIR ORGANIZATIONAL meeting on Monday, Henry and Luke went right to work on the PA system project, but it wasn't the only thing Henry was working on. His real brainchild had originated with his computer tinkering from as early as eight years old. That was when his father, Ryan, helped him build a new computer for his mother, explaining what each part was and the relationship of the software to the firmware to the hardware.

"And you are what we refer to as wetware," Ryan said. "That's what's up here in your head. Without your brain to assemble this machine and to program it or give it instructions, it is nothing but a boat anchor. No matter how smart machines appear to get, *you* are smarter. You just need to remember to use your head."

Sylvia, Henry's mother, was happy to have a new computer and was pleased with how well it worked. As Henry studied and devoted himself to learning more about computing, Sylvia was often distressed to find her computer in pieces on the kitchen table as Henry installed new hardware components or worked on optimizing the software. Still, the computer always ran better and faster when he was done with it.

At her suggestion, Henry soon built his own computer as a laboratory to experiment with how commercial software affected the computer memory and how the hardware itself influenced software development. By the time he was a teenager, he had a pretty good understanding of what the world of software and hardware was really like.

"One of the things I've noticed," Henry told Luke, Isobel, and Chastity at lunch one day, back when they were freshmen, "is that software companies survive on upgrades. You can bet that if you put a giant software company in charge of building a bridge to Hawaii, they'd get it built to the middle of the Pacific Ocean and then they'd open it to traffic. They'd charge a toll for people who used the bridge to fund building it the rest of the way. To make people feel good about only getting halfway to Hawaii, they'd get a third-party investor to build a big shopping mall out there. And in ten years, you still probably wouldn't be able to use it to get all the way to Hawaii."

"Okay. That's profound," Chastity said. "What are you going to do about it?"

"Well, I can't take charge of building the rest of the bridge, but I can probably clean up some of the construction debris. See, when the software company releases each upgrade, it doesn't necessarily get the bridge any closer to the destination. So, you get bridge update 2.0 and find that you now have three different routes you can use to get to the middle of the Pacific. But none of them get you any closer to Hawaii. One is an exclusive express lane that costs a little extra, but you can get to the middle of the ocean faster. One has extra features. You can stop here and see whales. At this branch, you can eat the best fish stew in the world. And over there, you can transfer to a ferry that will take you either to Hawaii or back to the mainland. And the one route you really wanted still stops in the middle of the ocean at an even bigger shopping mall. So, if that's the only route you want, why clutter the waves with these others?"

"So, you don't buy the upgrade?" Luke asked.

"There might be one feature in that upgrade that enables new cars to use the bridge. Without it, only old cars could use it," Henry explained. "Here's what we need to do: We build an app that examines each upgrade to whatever software is on our computers, and makes sure only the important pieces are taking up space on our computers. You can choose whether you want the whale watching feature or if you want to strictly go in the express lane, but you don't have to accept everything they build."

"Will that even work?" Isobel asked.

"It's what I've been doing manually to my mother's computer and my home lab computer for years. And while I'm in there, I tweak the system a little and make it run faster, optimize the file distribution, recover lost space, and reset the clock speed. There's no reason it requires wetware to do it, though. I've been working on writing a utility that will search stuff out, give the user the choices for what to include, and wipe out everything that's not getting us closer to Hawaii."

"I could sell that," Luke said.

"I'm counting on it," Henry laughed.

"I mean, we could create a company around just that idea," Luke expanded.

"And keep making money by selling upgrades to the app each time a major software update comes out from another manufacturer," Isobel said.

Henry groaned, but nodded his head. Chastity picked up his nod with a wry smile, but didn't say anything.

As seniors, Luke and Henry worked on building the PA system with Isobel and Chastity heading up fundraising. The app Henry had spent three years developing was finally being tested by his friends and select others in the school's computer science program.

LUKE NEGOTIATED SOME great deals for the components of the new system and Mr. Roland gave them access to the computer lab to work on assembling the system. It was not much different than assembling a computer, as far as Henry was concerned. However, he had to do much more wiring and soldering than in a computer. Any mistake in that process could cause feedback, static, or a variety of other sound errors. They carefully tested each stage.

Sheila often hung out with Henry as he was working in the computer lab, pretending to help, and teasing him with 'accidental' flashes of her legs and breasts. Nothing that could be mistaken for indecency, of course, but Sheila wanted to be sure Henry was motivated to complete the project. He never actually saw her nipples, and only seldom her underwear, but he often stared down her advantageously positioned cleavage.

"What are you doing for prom?" Sheila asked as she held a clamp in place so Henry could solder a pre-amp on the six-channel mixing board. Henry alerted to possible danger. He had a date. He didn't want to lead Sheila on, but he *was* enjoying her company in the lab.

"Oh. Well, um... I thought..."

"I'm sorry. Not me," Sheila interrupted him. "Dave already asked me. You know I wouldn't back out on someone for someone else."

"Of course. That sounds like fun. I'm..."

"Anyway, we're going to recognize the project committee at the prom and plan on doing the presentation there. You should get a date and plan to attend."

Sheila leaned over the table and made sure Henry had a clear view down her front as she kissed him on the cheek. Then she left the room. She didn't wait for him to answer the question about the prom. Apparently, she just wanted him to know she had a date and expected him to be there.

Henry was thankful Sheila wasn't waiting for him to ask her. Over the weekend, his friends and a few others had gone to a movie. Chastity had carefully maneuvered people in the seats so that Isobel sat next to Henry and was well-separated from Luke.

Isobel quickly put the armrest between their seats up and leaned against Henry. She held his hand, ultimately placing it on her leg and encouraging him to squeeze a little. Of course, she was wearing slacks, so it wasn't like he was feeling her up, but she did snuggle up against him and just before the end of the movie kissed his cheek.

Unfortunately, when the movie ended, the group reformed for burgers and he was separated from her, so the friendly cuddle was at an end. He didn't know why he continued to want Isobel's attention. He knew it wasn't going anywhere. But that was a principle of lust.

HENRY WAS CONCERNED about Isobel, though his concern was often over-shadowed by his desire. She was extremely flirtatious around him most of the time, but he recognized that as a part of her character. She hung on Luke when they were together, and Henry had seen her plant a kiss on Dave right in front of Sheila. Henry had been on the receiving end of one or two of those kisses and could attest that they were worth waiting for.

But Isobel's mood could change in a flash. He'd once opened a door for her and put his hand on her waist as she walked through. She'd turned and snapped at him.

"Keep your hands to yourself! I'm not Chastity!"

Henry hadn't even recognized what he'd done wrong. He considered himself clueless when it came to women.

When Isobel started fundraising for the class project, she was a focused monster. Chastity admitted that she only went with Isobel so Isobel would have someone to cry to after a visit. Isobel raised twice the money needed to buy the components of the sound system. They'd expanded the original idea to add six separate input and output channels to the amplifier, microphones, and speakers.

Isobel seemed to vanish when the fundraising was finished. They saw her in class and in the halls, but she never spoke to anyone and stayed away from their group for a week. The next Monday, she was hanging on Luke as if they were getting married.

"You wouldn't believe last week," Luke said to Henry after they met with the installation team Monday afternoon. "We'd planned a date to go see the new *Wonder Woman* movie. I picked her up and when we got to the theater, I reached out to hold her hand and she just lit up. She told me all I ever wanted was sex and she wasn't going to put up with it. She didn't know why she'd agreed to go to prom with me and was deciding not to even go."

"Good grief! Do you put that much pressure on her?"

"Dude! We've never *had* sex. The most I've ever gotten with her is a little squeezing of those incredible breasts. But she called me the next day and wanted to know why I wasn't taking her to brunch at the club the day after our big date. I went to get her and we had a great time. Even went to the driving range after brunch and hit a bucket of balls. It was like the previous night didn't even exist!"

"I'm worried about her," Henry said. "And you, too, bro."

"I think she's under a lot of stress at home. Her father plans to take her to Argentina to meet the family and some prospective husbands. Her mother is throwing a fit," Luke said. "Anyway, I guess we're on for prom. She told me to get a room."

"If you haven't got it paid for yet, better get over there. The prom's next weekend. You know they insist on cash up front from people at the prom. If you weren't eighteen, they wouldn't rent to you at all. There's a whole page of rules they make you read and sign when you pay for the room," Henry said.

"You sound like you've got experience."

"Chastity promised I'd get lucky. Frankly, I like the idea."

"But you haven't dated at all before the prom? She's almost as unpredictable as Isobel," Luke said.

"Well, we'll see how the night turns out. Good luck."

"You, too, man."

2

THE ARRANGEMENT

HENRY AND LUKE went to get their tuxes at the rental shop the next Wednesday. They'd been lectured by Luke's mother on good conservative dress for a prom. They'd ordered plain black tuxes, pleated shirts, and bow ties. The prom was to be a masked ball and they'd ordered black on black filigree eye masks.

No one would ever confuse one for the other. Luke was three inches shorter and possibly thirty pounds heavier than Henry, which wasn't to say that Luke was heavy. Henry was just incredibly thin.

"I suppose this is how we'll dress for your wedding," Henry joked.

"Wedding!? You've got to be kidding. Bro, we have so much to do before we can think about finding wives. We have to get our company launched. That means we need to get you some help, too," Luke said. "How did the most recent test go?"

"Still some bugs," Henry sighed. "Seems like every time I squash one, another pops up. I'd like to develop an AI to handle the tasks, but at the moment all we really have is some look-up tables and algorithms. Still, it's better than what we see on most computers."

"So, we don't have to worry about you taking over our computers with a sinister AI?" Luke joked.

"Not with *this* product," Henry shot back. He looked at his alarmed friend and winked.

He'd been tinkering with computers seriously for ten years. He had as many hacking tools acquired from the dark web as he had legitimate

12

programming tools. He considered it all part of his instruction and learning. He wouldn't really hack into a friend's computer, but that didn't mean he *couldn't* if he wanted to. One of the things he'd learned was where to look in the system for both dangerous and benign files.

The previous fall, he'd joined an online group of hackers he'd found who were exploring the use of AI to get through security systems and break into various corporate networks. They'd had some success at it, leaving behind a token as evidence they'd been there and then withdrawing. Henry made note of the applications and their shortcomings. For now, he was simply searching and comparing the program and application files for unused processes that served to slow the computer down. The app did its work and withdrew until launched by the user again.

He felt confident in his ability to get past most encryption and security systems, but that was technically illegal, so he didn't do it beyond his initial tests with the hackers. There was a lot of gray area when dealing with who owned what on a person's private computer. He didn't want to stray into a black area.

Henry and Luke went to pick up the girls' flowers and confirmed the arrangements for Saturday night. Luke—by way of his father's auto dealership—had rented a limo to take them to the prom. Isobel and Chastity would enjoy that.

"WHEE! LET'S PAR-TAY!" Izzy shouted when they were in the limo.

"I think you started without me, Bae," Luke said.

"Catch up!" Chastity said, producing a small bottle of tequila from her bag.

Henry had been instructed to bring lime wedges and salt. Luke held out a shot glass. There was only one, so they took turns doing their shots. When Izzy reached for the glass for a second shot, Luke intercepted it and stuck it in his bag.

"Just one before the dance," he said. "We don't want to be sloshed when we get there. Remember, we can leave whenever we want to and there's a bottle in our room."

"God! I didn't know I was dating my mother," Isobel snapped. "'Here's just a little tequila to relax you before the dance,' she said. 'I told your father you were going to Chastity's house after the after party. So be sure to be there when he shows up to pick you up for brunch.'"

"We can do that," Chastity said.

"Oh, it was rich," Isobel continued. "'I'm not telling you to have sex with your boyfriend tonight, but your father thinks he can make a good match for his *virgin* daughter when we go to Argentina this summer. If you haven't already taken care of that, this might be a good opportunity.'"

"Mama Perez gave you permission to have sex with me?" Luke exclaimed. "I don't want to disappoint your mama!"

"Yeah, well there better be plenty of that stuff in our room when we get there tonight. Just so you know, going to our room with you is all the permission you need tonight. Don't wake me up unless I'm snoring!" Isobel said. "When is that ceremony they're doing to recognize the project team? I won't last much longer than that. These boobs can only take bouncing up and down as we dance for so long, you know. Someone's going to have to help support them."

Isobel was on quite a roll. Henry wondered if Mama Perez had stopped at one drink before they picked her up. It wasn't that unusual for Isobel to go off like this, though. There were times when they were all hard-put to keep up with her. Then she'd crash and go silent for a few days and then everything would be 'normal.'

She wore a red dress and her lipstick matched it perfectly. She'd told them earlier she was going to a spa in the morning and having a full makeover. The dress was sleeveless and off the shoulder, so it left acres of her honey-colored skin exposed. That accented the single strand of pearls around her neck and pearl earrings beautifully. She had chosen a long evening gown that was slit up the side almost to her waist. Even sitting in the limo, she made quite an appealing display, while dangling her red lace mask from her fingers.

Chastity opted for a cream sheath dress, which accented her Grecian features with a wide gold braid around her neck. From the braid, two strips of fabric parted to cover her breasts, leaving the space between open. The strips came back together at a high waist. The dress was backless. Her blue-tinted hair—Henry thought it was naturally black, but wasn't sure since he'd seen several colors over their high school years—swept around her shoulders with a hair pin on the side as an accent. The only other jewelry she wore were the decorative piercings in her nipples, which pressed against the fabric of the dress.

Chas carried a blue mask with gold braid, similar to the neckline of her dress.

A doorman at the hotel opened the limo door for Luke and Henry. They then stood so their dates could emerge gracefully from the car without exposing themselves in any way. There were a few awkward moments in the hotel lobby as they decided the best places for the girls to wait while Luke and Henry dashed to their rooms with the overnight bags.

Though they were only gone ten minutes, there were already half a dozen men standing near Chastity and Isobel, chatting them up.

"There you are!" Isobel exclaimed when she saw Luke. She broke through the group of men to hurry to him. "I was afraid I'd been abandoned and would have to take one of these delightful men to the prom. Do you think they are too old to go dancing with a teenager?"

The men shifted uncomfortably as Chastity took Henry's arm. The four went directly to the ballroom and were admitted after showing their tickets. They found the photo booth and all had their pictures taken in front of a background of pillars and statuary. Then they parted, Luke and Isobel making a round of the ballroom to greet all their classmates.

Henry and Chastity said hello to those who greeted them on the way to the refreshment bar. They were not as well-known and popular as Luke and Isobel. They took their drinks and plate of snacks to a table and watched the people beginning to filter onto the dance floor. Henry felt he needed to get into the spirit before he could enjoy bouncing around to the music. Isobel had dragged Luke out to dance as soon as the music started.

"What are you thinking, my man?" Chastity said, putting a hand on his and looking into his eyes through the holes in their masks.

"Honestly? I was thinking how glad I am that I'm with you and not Isobel. I think Luke is going to have his hands full this evening."

"He certainly is once he gets that dress off her!" Chastity laughed. "Hope you aren't disappointed."

"Not a chance."

There were other entertainment stations around the room. While everyone enjoyed the music, dancing was slow getting started. People could play or cheer others on at shuffleboard, skittles, Skee-Ball, and even a game of Twister for those who dared attempt it in their formal wear. Henry and Chastity played a couple of games and cheered on others until the DJ played a moderately paced song. Then a flood of couples headed for the dance floor just to get a chance to clinch with their dates.

The music picked up after a second slower number and many of the people stayed on the dance floor. As they circulated and met others, more than one boy's date punched him in the arm when his gaze lingered too long at the exposed space between Chastity's breasts or on the outline of her pierced nipples. Henry couldn't blame them. His own eyes wandered to the sight more than occasionally.

Preceding the announcement of the prom king and queen and their court, the principal called Sheila to the stage as the senior class president. Of course, Dave joined her as her escort.

"On behalf of the Freedom Valley High School and the Freedom Valley School Corporation, I would like to officially recognize our graduating class," the principal announced to cheers and shouts from the attendees. "I would also like to thank you for the gift of the new sound system for the gym. I'll turn this over to senior class president, Sheila Anderson, to recognize the significant members of the committee."

"Thank you, Principal Soffit," Sheila said, taking the microphone. "The great Freedom Valley senior class of 2026 is proud to present to the school this token of our appreciation for years of nurture and guidance as we have been students here. It was hard not to notice the condition of our PA system in the gym, so when it was suggested that we replace it as a senior project, we jumped at the chance. I'd like to ask our committee members to please come to the stage so we can thank each one for your participation."

The dozen people who had joined the committee to work on the project came to the stage. Sheila called out Henry, Luke, and Isobel as the significant members who had raised funds, negotiated deals, and actually built the system. She gave each of the members of the committee a gift card to the local coffee shop for their participation.

They all shook hands with the principal, a representative of the school board, and their class sponsors, then they left the stage. The principal moved on to thank the prom committee and make the announcement of the royal court and the prom king and queen.

"It's TIME TO take a break and go to the ladies' room," Chastity whispered to Henry. "Come with me."

"To the ladies' room?" he asked.

"It's time to get lucky," she whispered back.

Chastity had scouted the facility thoroughly and led Henry to a less frequented hallway with restrooms. She pushed him into a side hall just before they reached the restrooms.

"Just stay here and wait. I promise you'll be happy."

"I don't doubt it," he said, kissing her ear and down her neck.

"Remember that spot for later," she panted. Then she rushed to the ladies' room a dozen steps away.

Henry adjusted his stiffening cock in his trousers. He hadn't anticipated a quickie in the hallway, but he was willing to do whatever Chastity wanted. She'd kept him subtly aroused ever since they'd arrived at the event. This had included rubbing against him while they danced, kissing his ears, and backing him against a wall where she reached behind her and stroked his cock. Once in the shadows, he'd managed to slip a hand inside the slit in her dress to caress one of her lovely breasts, twisting the piercing slightly as she gasped.

"There you are," a voice said, entering the alcove where Henry waited.

The voice was quickly followed by lips pressing against his lips and a tongue questing for entry into his mouth. This was definitely not Chastity.

"We don't have much time, but I can't help myself. I'll go to hell for this, but I want you."

Isobel continued kissing Henry while she stroked his growing cock and got his zipper down.

"Do me. Do me."

She turned in his arms and put her hands against the wall.

"Condom," Henry gasped as he dug in his pocket.

"Don't need it. Just do me!"

He wasn't about to stop and tell her he wasn't Luke. He dipped a hand into the top of her dress and filled it with her voluptuous breast as he kissed her ears and down to the pearls around her neck.

His other hand snaked around her side and through the slit at her thigh. She spread her legs as his fingers reached the smoothly shaved snatch between them. Isobel was panting and was already drenching his fingers with her juices.

"Yes! Yes! I took them off for you. I'll give them to you if you want."

Henry swept the dress up over Isobel's butt and pressed his cock against her crack. Isobel reached back with one hand to hold the dress up, while Henry guided his cock between her legs.

"Do it! I want you!"

Henry slid through her moist folds and into her vagina.

"Ah! Oh, God! That wasn't so bad. I expected worse! Now fuck me!"

She thrust her butt out farther to give him deeper access. Between the position against the wall and her high heels, she was as open to him as if they were naked on a bed. He began thrusting into her, one hand returning to her clit and the other to her boobs.

So, this was what Chastity had in mind when she told him he would get lucky. Whatever the girl wanted tonight, he'd happily give her. He didn't doubt that he'd be soaking in Chastity's juices later.

Isobel, meanwhile, was ramping up and becoming louder.

"Fuck! Oh, yes. I knew your cock was big. You're splitting me open. Fuck! Fuck your little cunt!"

Henry moved a hand from her breast to cover her mouth as he continued to plow into her. She met every thrust while still holding herself against the wall with one hand and holding her dress up with the other. The tension built and soon Henry could feel his come rising.

Then Isobel thrust back against him hard and froze. She dropped her dress and slammed her hand against the wall, as she pressed harder against Henry. He felt her vagina clamping and pulsing around his cock. He began filling her with his semen.

They held still while the pulsing subsided. Henry pulled her back against him and continued kissing her neck as his hand moved from her mouth back into her bust to grasp her sweaty breasts.

"Oh, God! I will definitely burn in hell for that. I had to. I had to have you first."

"First?" Henry panted, sliding his finger through her slit from his cock to her clit again.

"I knew it had to be you for my first time. It didn't hurt as much as I expected it to. Except you're so big I can't believe you got it in me," she said.

She moved to turn and face him. His hands lost their grip and his cock popped out of her. She slammed her mouth into his again, probing with her tongue.

"I need to go back to the restroom and pull myself together before Luke and I leave."

"Will we do this again?" Henry asked. He pushed her dress down so he could capture one of her nipples in his lips. She whined and pushed him away, pulling her dress back up.

"I doubt it. You know Luke is my man. We won't even be going to the same college as you. I just had to have you once."

"First."

"Yes. You were my first. God! I hope I'm not too sore to do Luke. It was everything I wanted it to be. Now let me go to the restroom."

"Right."

Isobel ran to the restroom with a hand under her dress and between her legs. Henry sank back against the wall panting. It might have been everything Isobel wanted, but he'd have liked to take more than five minutes to enjoy her. Nonetheless, he'd just fucked Isobel Perez! He was just straightening up to put himself away when Chastity joined him. She immediately sank to her knees and sucked his cock into her mouth, bathing him with her tongue. Then she tucked him back inside and zipped his trousers.

"She tastes good on you," Chastity giggled. "Hope you had fun."

"Um... Yeah. I should thank you, I guess."

"I have ideas on how you can do that. Let's go to our room."

THEY DIDN'T BOTHER to say goodbye to anyone at the prom. Their room was on the eleventh floor of the hotel and they went to the nearest elevator. It was just approaching midnight and most of the attendees were still at the dance trying to get every second of party in before the 1:00 a.m. close.

"I need the restroom now," he said. "You need it first?"

"I can wait. I was in the restroom while you were in Isobel," Chastity laughed.

It didn't take Henry long to clean his pipes and wipe his cock with a damp cloth. He looked in the mirror and snorted at seeing he was still wearing his mask and tux. He hung it on the back of the bathroom door with his jacket, cummerbund, and tie. Then he returned to the room where Chastity was waiting.

She had her bottle of tequila, the salt and lime, and a shot glass waiting for them. When Henry approached for a kiss, Chastity backed away.

"Remember: I'm not your girlfriend. I don't do tongue kisses."

Okay. So, what the hell is she?

She took his hand and licked the webbing between his thumb and index finger, then sprinkled salt on it. She put the wedge of lime between her lips and handed Henry the shot of tequila. He licked the salt, threw back the shot, and took the lime from Chastity's lips in his teeth.

Chastity repeated the gestures, using Henry's hand for the salt and positioning the lime wedge between his teeth. Then she poured her shot and did her shot.

"You know tequila isn't like other boozes," Chastity said. "You have to drink a lot of it to get really drunk."

"I don't want to get really drunk," Henry said.

"Of course not! That's why we'll keep shots available for special occasions. Like when I get naked."

"When is that going to be?" he asked.

"When you take my clothes off me," she replied.

Chastity didn't allow tongue kisses, so Henry circled her, kissing every available bit of her exposed skin, including her bare back. Chastity encouraged him with little sighs and murmured 'yes.' While he was behind her, he slipped his hands under the two strips of fabric covering her breasts and fondled them as he kissed up and down her spine.

"It's just eyehooks on the collar," she whispered.

He withdrew his hands and unclipped the collar, coming around in front of her to lower the collar and the front of the dress away from her chest.

"Do you like them?" she whispered as she pulled his head to her nipples. He licked and sucked, moving from one to the other.

"Hell, yeah," he said. "Chastity, you're beautiful."

"Don't get a ring caught between your teeth. That could hurt. Me," she clarified. "Yeah. More of that. Are they as good as Izzy's?"

"Chas, don't ever compare yourself to Izzy... or anyone else for that matter. You are fantastic. I only imagined what it would be like to caress you like this."

"Yeah. And I don't mind tongue kisses on my nipples, you know. Or further down for that matter. Lick there a little more."

Henry licked the offered nipple and Chastity pulled away from him. She sprinkled salt on her nipple and then squeezed a lime wedge on the other one. She handed him another shot. He quickly cleaned her left breast of the salt, drank the shot, and sucked on her right nipple to get the lime juice.

"Yes! My turn now," Chastity said fiercely, pushing him back to arm's length. She removed the studs and cufflinks from his formal shirt, thoughtfully laying the set on the dresser.

When his shirt was off, Chastity did a full circuit of Henry's body, much as he had done with her, kissing all the exposed skin and tonguing his nipples until he squirmed. She pushed him back on the bed and approached him with the shot prep. Henry had noticed she wasn't really filling the shot glass completely. It was obviously a game, not an intent to get drunk.

She licked his left nipple and sprinkled salt on it, then squeezed the lime on his right nipple. He shuddered at the cold drops. Chastity did a thorough job of cleaning the salt from his nipple and then drank the shot, sucking on Henry's right nipple until she was satisfied it was completely clean of lime juice.

She fell on top of him, pressing their chests together as they kissed and fondled each other.

"I need to freshen up a bit now," she said, getting up. She grabbed her bag and turned toward the bathroom as Henry gazed at her. "Get my zipper for me, babe?"

Henry jumped up and found the zipper at the small of her back. He unzipped it over her round bottom and she let the dress pool around her ankles. It was all she was wearing. Henry stroked down her hips and over her butt.

"I hope you're... just as dressed as I am when I come out of the bathroom," she whispered, turning to kiss him again and then disappear into the bathroom.

3
CHILDHOOD'S END

CHASTITY EMERGED FROM the bathroom, wearing only her high heels and her nipple piercings. She found Henry appropriately undressed, standing at the foot of the bed.

"Not *in* bed?" Chastity asked, strutting toward him.

"I think I have some worshiping to do before I get in this bed. After all, I am in the presence of a goddess," Henry said. He knelt and kissed her feet.

"Oh, wow! You took me literally!"

"I have so much for you," he said.

"I saw that."

"I mean before we get to that. For example, these shoes must be killing your feet. Lie here and let me get rid of them for you."

"I thought you'd enjoy seeing them," she said.

"Oh, I do, but you deserve to be comfortable and pampered. Please allow me," he said.

She sat on the bed and scooted back until her feet were at the edge. Henry lifted them one after the other to remove the shoes and kiss her toes.

"Be right back."

Henry ran into the bathroom and in a few moments came out with a warm wet washcloth and towel. He wrapped one foot and gently washed it, then wrapped it in the towel as he moved to wash the other foot. He tossed the washcloth back in the bathroom. Then he made sure both feet were dry before beginning a gentle massage, watchful for any ticklish triggers he should avoid.

He spent time working his way up her legs, massaging and then kissing them. She may have expected him to stop when he reached her sex, but Henry continued with only a few light kisses and continued his way up her body, kissing her stomach.

"Not my navel!" Chastity said, squirming. "I hate it. It's too ticklish."

"Well, just consider it to have been worshiped, then," Henry laughed. "I have a lot yet to cover. Let's roll you over, milady."

"But…"

"Don't worry. I'll be back to this side soon."

"I do hope so!" Chastity rolled to her stomach and Henry began by kissing around her neck and ears, then working his way down to her shoulders. While kissing her, he nudged her knees apart so he could kneel between them and begin massaging her back as he continued to kiss her.

"Oh, God! You'll put me to sleep."

"Honey, if you need to sleep, I'll watch over you until you wake."

"Hey, if I fall asleep, you go ahead and punch my ticket. Yes! Fuck! You're kissing my ass. How did you know?"

"Something I read about worshiping a goddess."

"Praise the goddess, yes!"

Chastity wanted him to focus on her hot spots, but she was just as happy with the attention he paid to her as he continued to massage and kiss his way down the backs of her legs and feet, then had her roll to her back again.

Henry would have liked to get into some serious kissing, but he respected Chastity's rule against tongue kissing and just brushed her lips before peppering the rest of her face with kisses and moving down her chin and across her collar bones. Chastity squirmed as he worked his way down onto her small, but apparently sensitive, breasts.

Chastity's piercings were more decorative than the bars that often showed in outline against her shirts—a fringe of short dangling chains, each with a small jewel at the end. He played with the piercings both with his lips and his fingers, twisting slightly and tugging on them.

"Yeah! I love to have them played with. I'd do it myself if you weren't paying attention," she said. "Twist a little more."

She panted as he moved down from her breasts onto her ribs and stomach again. He carefully avoided touching her navel, but paid attention to the slight hollow above her hip bones before he moved down over her pubis.

He brushed through the triangular patch of hair pointing directly to her clit, and began to pry her lower lips apart with his tongue. She pulled her legs back to give him better access to her inner treasures and even helped by pulling her lips to the side. He flicked her clit with the tip of his tongue a few times, then slid down to her opening where he thrust his tongue in and out of her while rubbing her clit with his upper lip.

"Oh, goddess! I'm going to come! You're going to make me come. Don't stop! Oh, fuck! I'm coming!"

Chastity had warned him that she was noisy when she was having fun, but it didn't bother Henry in the least. Even if someone heard them through the door, he was committed to making her as satisfied as he could. He moved up to press against her clit with the flat of his tongue, and moved his head left and right to rub it.

"Fuck, yes!! I'm still coming. Don't stop. Please, don't stop! Yes!"

The bed sheet was balled in Chastity's fists as she threw her head left and right, calling out indistinct curses and praises. Henry was frantically working with his hands to hold her butt and get a finger into her wet channel. Soon, Chastity's hands pushed at his head.

"Now. Now, please," she pled.

Henry climbed up her body and she gripped his erect cock to guide it into her hot center. He sank into her with a sigh.

"Oh, fill me up! God, you're huge!"

Whether Henry was as huge as she thought or not, he was glad to bury himself completely in Chastity. She bucked against him and then, using surprising strength, rolled him over on his back without losing their connection.

Once she was on top, she really started moving. It was only a minute before she was climaxing again. Henry wanted to stay in Chastity as long as possible, but when she settled down full on him and began rocking back and forth, it was too much stimulation. He began powerful spurts up into her.

The heat and pressure of his ejaculation pushed Chastity to a new height and once she'd enjoyed another orgasm, she collapsed against him.

"I didn't expect that to be so sensual. Where did you ever learn all that?" she gasped in his ear.

"I had a good teacher," he laughed. "A while back. We used each other as a learning aid, determined to find out as much as we could in as little time as possible. Then we went our separate ways."

"I should write her a thank you note," Chastity laughed as they cuddled together and pulled the blanket up over them. It was two in the morning and sleep wasn't long coming.

SUNDAY MORNING WAS relaxed. They had sex again, much more casually than their first time. They didn't rush, but were more focused on getting to their climax before breakfast arrived.

"I want to be part of your group," she said as they ate the breakfast room service delivered.

"What group is that?" he asked.

"Whatever you're calling it," she said. "I know you've got more than you've shown us in our tests. You and Luke are constantly whispering about what you'll do. I can't believe you're just going to go to work for the Borg and be assimilated. You and Luke are planning something big. I want to be a part of it. I know Isobel plans to do whatever is necessary to be part of it. She and Luke are both going to Villanova. I just want to be on the ground floor of what you're planning."

"I don't know how Luke is going to structure things. I'm leaving the business end up to him."

"Don't let him run away with it. Just treat me well and take care of me, and I'll be anything you want me to be. Professionally."

"You said you didn't want to be a girlfriend."

"That's right. I said professionally."

"I suppose we need to figure out a position for you."

"We haven't done doggie yet."

"I mean professionally."

"So do I, Henry. If what you want is for me to wear short skirts and no underwear and hang around your desk all day, make sure it's worth my effort. I think you'll find, though, that I have a lot of other talents you can exploit in a new company. And still be available if you need arm candy."

"That's quite an offer to a guy who scarcely has two nickels to rub together."

"I'm betting on the come, so to speak," she giggled. "Seriously, Henry. What do I need to do?"

"I don't think we could hire a sex doll," he laughed. "And just as seriously, Chastity, as much as I am going to lust for you, I think a lot more of you than that."

"Yeah. We should keep that just between the two of us. Just tell me what you want me to do."

"You did a really good job recruiting people for the senior class project. How would you feel about handling administration or recruiting?"

"Mmmhmm. Could do both in the beginning. I like people, so I'm sure I could find the ones you need. I'll make that my area of study in college. Human resource management. Yeah."

"Welcome aboard."

"Yeah. We have time for one more before I need to get Isobel to my house. Come back to bed and let me climb onboard."

"You know, I think this will be good for both of us."

"I'm counting on it."

THE LAST FOUR weeks of school were intense. After the excitement and fun of prom weekend, seniors faced their final exams, including all the AP exams for those getting college credit for some of their classes, Henry among them. He'd focused his last year of school on getting as many dual credit classes in as possible. He didn't want to waste college credits on fundamentals.

Luke was in much the same situation but was focused on getting some business credits built into his pre-college load. He planned to take the summer off and do an around-the-country road trip in his new Corvette. He couldn't convince Henry to join him, though.

Memorial Day was the earliest possible, on the 25th of May. So, Henry had chosen Saturday morning the 23rd for a golf course meeting with his father's lawyer friend, Don Harvey. The weekend was busy at Constitution Links, but Henry had managed a tee time with his parents and Don. It was early morning, but the links were dry and only a light breeze ruffled the grass.

"Ryan and Sylvia. It's great to see you both. I was afraid I wouldn't make it to the golf course this weekend. Things have been chaotic at work," Don said.

"It's good to see you, too, Don. This morning's outing is compliments of my son. You've met Henry before. Maybe it's been a while."

"Indeed it has. Thank you for the invitation, Henry. How do you happen to have a membership here at Constitution Links?" Don asked as the moved to the first tee.

"It was a benefit of being on the high school golf team," Henry said, taking Don's offered hand. "I was on the State Championship runner up team back in October and have a summer job here as a part-time youth golf pro."

"Go easy on us," Don laughed. "It's been a long time since I played with a golf pro."

Sylvia teed up on the women's tee for the first hole and hit a solid drive of nearly 150 yards on the par four hole. Don took his shot next and did not do much better. He was still pleased with the placement. Ryan teed up and sent his solid drive nearly 200 yards, but it was at the edge of the rough. Henry took his turn and dropped a powerful drive at about 220 yards.

"I see right away where the real competition is," Don said as they walked the fairway and completed the hole. Henry liked this first hole at the club and made par. The others were a respectable one or two over and would probably be tight competition once their handicaps were figured in.

"I had some legal questions, Mr. Harvey," Henry ventured as they made their way to the next tee.

"What can I do to help you? You know I won't 'officially' give legal advice out here, and I don't do criminal law, if you're in trouble."

"It's patent law I'm interested in," Henry said.

"Thinking of studying to be a lawyer in college? Patent law is a good field. I might even have an internship available when you're ready."

"I'm more interested in filing patents on a couple of inventions," Henry said. "I've studied up on what's required for a patent and I think I have a couple of software systems and methods that are patentable. And an app that should be copyrighted."

"That's a tricky area, but it can be profitable—especially if you file a patent that catches the attention of one of the big publishers and they decide to acquire it," Don said.

They finished the next hole and walked on. Being walkers on an early morning golf round meant they let another foursome play through, but the club encouraged people to walk the course instead of using carts.

"I'd like to keep them from having it instead of selling it," Henry said. "I have a plan to start a business and will need the patents as assets when we go after venture capital."

"Interesting. Now, don't tell me a thing about what the software does. We need to have a signed agreement before we talk about the specifics. Have you shown the software to anyone else?"

"I have six alpha testers. They are all over eighteen and have signed non-disclosure agreements. They've tested the app on their personal computers, but it was set to time out, so they could only use it for a period of one week," Henry said.

"Reasonable precautions. It sounds like you are within the patenting parameters. I'll want to check that more thoroughly when we start work on the patents."

"You'll work on them with me?" Henry asked.

"If you can show me a viable patentable product, I will file the first patent pro bono, meaning everything except the federal filing fee. That will cost you between $220 and $320, depending on what category the patent is and how ready it is to file. The lower cost is for a provisional patent, but then we would still need to file the full application. Sound fair?"

"Yes, sir. How can I thank you?"

"First, have a stellar idea that we can file. Second, come up with more ideas. We'll talk about fees and costs after we get the first one under our belts."

The morning went well. By the end of their eighteen holes, Henry had an appointment to see the attorney the first week of June. Don liked what he saw and a deal was struck. The first patent filing was underway.

HENRY AND HIS friends received their high school diplomas on Saturday, June 6, 2026, and were invited to an exclusive party at Sheila's house. They were all excited about being free for the summer and starting college classes in the fall. Henry had already enrolled in a couple more classes at the university during the summer and was excited to get started.

"I wish you'd reconsider and join me on the road trip," Luke said. "It will be so sweet! The 'Vette is just waiting for us!"

Luke's shiny 2020 Corvette was sitting in the drive. His dad had the car completely gone over in his shop to make sure it was in top running condition when he gave it to his son.

"A convertible and the open road," Luke continued painting the dream. "Here to San Francisco, South to LA and San Diego, then straight across to Florida. We'll be back up north in time for classes in the fall."

"You can afford a trip like that. I'm working and getting a head start on classes. With the credits I've been getting, I'll be able to start with sophomore standing. I've managed a couple of grants and a huge scholarship, but time is driving us forward."

"I hear you. Not to cry 'poor-little-rich-kid,' but the disadvantage of having rich parents is that I don't get as many opportunities for grants. One nice DECA scholarship, but the rest is coming from Dad. He says he'll pay as long as I'm completing an MBA in five years. I'd like to get it done in four if I can. But I'm not going to give up one last summer of playing."

"I thought you'd jump all over taking Isobel with you," Henry said, looking across the crowded party to where the fiery Latina was holding court.

"Would have," Luke said, "but she won't be around this summer. You know, her father decided she needed to experience her Latin American culture and booked a trip to Argentina to visit relatives."

"I heard her mention he hoped to make a match for her," Henry said. They opened beers and toasted each other.

"I gotta tell you, bro, she is so hot she can melt your dick. That prom night was a-ma-zing! We've only managed a couple of quickies since and decided we'd have to cool it until fall when we're both at Villanova.

Luke glanced toward the kitchen where he saw Sheila, the stunning blonde cheerleader and president of their graduating class. She smiled at him. He lifted his beer to her.

"We aren't saying anything to anyone," Luke said, lowering his voice. "But when I take off out of here next weekend, my first stop will be right back here to pick up a certain blonde who has the money and spirit to join me on a little drive."

"Sheila's going to go with you for the summer?" Henry asked, amazed. "And you're still asking me?"

"Maybe. Maybe not. She's coming with me for the first week. If we're getting along well, she'll stay with me. At any time during the summer, either of us has the option to call it off and drop her at the nearest airport. Stupid Dave killed his chances by bragging about what they did after prom. She won't even speak to him now. But what he said about her makes traveling with her a beguiling prospect."

"Good luck with that. I doubt I'll have much action this summer," Henry snorted.

"I thought you and Chastity were hooking up."

"Dude, Chas is a good friend. Not my girlfriend," Henry said. They had not gotten together since prom. "We aren't an item. But if all goes the way we've talked, she wants to join us in the company. As a founder. We need someone with her people skills to handle recruiting and admin. That's what she's studying this fall. And it wouldn't hurt to have four of us instead of just three. I think Isobel needs someone to calm her down at times."

"God knows, I don't do a great job of that. Here's to getting the company going!"

They raised their bottles again, drained them, and opened another round.

4
READY, SET, GO!

HENRY WAS INTENT on knocking off the remaining two classes that were freshman requirements for the university over the summer. His job as a 'Youth Pro' at the Constitution Links Country Club kept him busy teaching children and teens the rudiments of golf, mostly in the long evenings.

But he was just as determined to follow through with Don Harvey to get his intellectual property protected. He wanted patents filed so he could get paid for his inventions. But they were also intellectual property for the company that would help them get employees and funding.

Over the summer, he did some research in the university library regarding businesses that were started by college students and grew into highly successful corporations. There were a surprising number starting with Apple, Microsoft, and more recently, Facebook.

He and Chastity both had classes and summer jobs. Isobel was in South America. Luke was tripping across the country. But text messages and emails flew among them, solidifying their partnership throughout the summer.

"I'm convinced we need to shelter ourselves with a Limited Liability Company, an LLC," Luke wrote. "We will each need to put a nest egg in the company and we can use that to fund a lawyer to file incorporation papers when we're ready to launch. We start out as equal partners in the LLC, but when the corporation is established, we'll each receive stock and options in whatever proportions we decide are fair."

"How much?" Chastity asked—always the most practical of the quartet.

"I figure we can get in business for a thousand each," Luke responded.

"Ouch!" Henry said. "I'd better pick up some more hours at the club."

"I can do it, but I won't be having much fun this summer," Chastity said. "Not that I was, anyway."

Isobel's response came the next day. "Okay."

"HENRY, I NEED a guy for a double date. Are you available Saturday?" Chastity asked when she called him on Wednesday, the first of July.

"Hey. I haven't done anything fun so far this summer. Will it be fun?" he asked.

"Oh, yeah. It's the Fourth of July! We're going out to the Avonmore Trails to ride horses, then back into town for dinner and to watch the fireworks," Chastity said.

"That sounds like fun. When should I pick you up?"

"All excited about driving now that you've got a car?" Chastity teased. Luke's father had helped Henry pick out a good used car at a real deal of a price. "Not to worry this time. Allen is driving. We'll pick you up at one Saturday afternoon."

"See you then."

ASIDE FROM THEIR frequent texts, Henry hadn't seen Chastity since graduation. The idea of going out, no matter what the event, was attractive. He remembered well their time after the prom. He was ready in jeans and sturdy shoes at one when Allen pulled up in his Jeep. This guy was obviously a real outdoorsy type. Henry ran out to join the group and Chastity held the seat forward so he could get in back… with a lovely young woman. Chastity got in front next to Allen.

"Henry, this is Allen and your beautiful date is Avery," Chastity said.

"Oh! Hi!" Henry said offering his hand to Avery. "I'm Henry."

"You're surprised!" Avery said.

"Not unpleasantly. Chastity didn't mention who my date would be so I assumed you'd be with Allen and I'd be with her," Henry said. "No problem."

"Oh, yuck! I mean Allen is a nice guy and all, but he's my brother. Definitely not dating material. I had to agree to come along on a double in order to get him to date Chastity."

"That's funny. I hope you aren't disappointed. How do you know Chas?" Henry asked.

"We work together at the Olde Towne Inne. Those are all with extra 'e's. Talk about pretentious. We wait tables. Allen is a ranch hand at Avonmore," Avery said. "And no, I'm not disappointed. So far, you're everything Chastity promised. A gentleman and a scholar."

"Haven't been able to practice either much since graduation. Although I'm getting a head start on university classes this fall and I'm working as a 'Youth Pro' at Constitution Links," Henry said.

"Maybe I could get some lessons sometime."

"I'm sure that could be arranged."

Avonmore Trails was a beautiful hundred-acre horse ranch with riding trails, a show ring, and an outdoor training ring. Allen was the only one of the four who had actual riding clothes, including jodhpurs and knee-high boots. But he spent time with each of them seated on barrels, seeing that their stirrups were properly adjusted and then instructing them on how to sit in the saddle and cue their mounts. Then he actually brought horses out, saddled them, and had the three mount.

They spent quite a while in the training ring as Allen gave them continued instructions until he considered them ready to go on a trail ride. Henry was certain he heard his horse sigh as they left the barnyard.

All told, it was a fun afternoon. Allen led the way with Chastity behind him. Avery apparently had no more experience than Henry did, but Henry enjoyed watching her bounce in her saddle as she rode ahead of him. His horse was content to simply maintain his place in line and do whatever her horse did. It was nearly five when they finally dismounted at the barn, removed the saddles from their trusty mounts, and set about brushing them down and feeding them carrots to thank them for their kindness on the trail.

"Ah!" Henry grimaced as he took the back seat next to Avery. "I think I have a blister on my butt!"

"That's interesting," Avery snorted.

"Sorry. I'm just thinking of how much sitting remains to be done today," he laughed.

"I'm not looking forward to that, either," she agreed.

"I saw the play *Arsenic and Old Lace* at our high school this past winter," Henry said. "I recall something about it having been a wonderful compliment to one of the women when her riding companion said, 'Madam, you have a good seat.'"

"Ooh. I'm glad you noticed," Avery said. She raised an eyebrow at Henry and offered him her hand. He took it with a smile and they held hands all the way to the restaurant.

"Where are we going for fireworks?" Allen asked as they all got in the car again about eight o'clock.

"Out to the point," Chastity answered. "Avery and I brought blankets, so we can sit and watch the display over the river."

Allen drove out to the crowded parking area, but several people were leaving because the family day activities had ended. They found a parking spot and the guys were given the blankets. They passed the security checkpoint and headed down the trail.

Henry's other hand was soon occupied by Avery's. He saw Chastity and Allen holding hands ahead and quashed an instant pang of jealousy.

There was no reason to be jealous. He and Chastity were not an item and he had a perfectly delightful and lovely woman holding his hand. Allen was a couple of years older than they were, but Avery had also just graduated. They were all well-matched. Chastity had been doing a good job of getting Allen out of his shell and he was pretty funny when his sister tormented him.

"This looks like a good spot," Avery said, pointing out a location on the Fort Duquesne lawns. People were scattered all over the area, which was large enough to not be crowded. They spread out their blankets to wait for the nine-thirty start of the show.

The first fanfare burst over the river and Henry automatically leaned back to look up at the sky. Avery leaned back against him. She was incredibly cuddly. Between explosions, she leaned in to whisper in Henry's ear.

"Are you going to ask me out again?"

"That sounds like a great idea to me," he answered. "Would you like to go out?"

"Oh, yeah. I just wanted to make sure we'd be doing this again before I kissed you."

With that, Avery moved her lips to Henry's and they started little kisses, interrupted by each explosion in the sky. The longer the display went on, the longer their kisses became. When the last barrage was launched and everyone started cheering, Avery and Henry were in a serious clinch.

"I think we need to get up and fold our blanket," Avery whispered. "People are leaving."

"I really enjoyed the day with you," Henry said. "Shall we find something for next Saturday?"

"Yeah. I know we can't really do anything more often. You're working and studying. I'm working. Chastity has me convinced I need to enroll in classes over at the Community College. Saturday will be a great time. Maybe something a little easier on our asses," she giggled.

Henry held his arm around Avery as they walked back to the car. He no longer noticed Chastity and Allen.

"SHE'S PRETTY DAMN cute, isn't she?" Chastity asked on the phone the next day.

"Yes. You got me there. She's really sweet," Henry answered.

"Just treat her nicely, okay? She's more a girlfriend type than I am. Don't mistreat her."

"You know I won't. Thank you for introducing us."

"Yeah. Allen's nice. We'll probably hang out a few more times this summer, but I don't think it's anything long-term."

"Hey, Chas. Are you going to be okay coming up with the thousand for the LLC buy-in?" Henry asked. "I think I could help."

"You know, I have no objections to accepting things from you, but for my own self-esteem, I think I should furnish my own buy-in. You know, it's the first time I'll really feel like an equal partner with the other three of you. I can make the numbers."

"Good. You know, I consider you an equal partner regardless."

"Yeah, in the LLC. But we all know that as far as a share in the company goes, there wouldn't be one without what you are developing. That's definitely a majority share. That doesn't make me feel bad. I recognize that I offer something different. And even with a lesser share in the corporation, I know it's going to be profitable. Profit isn't the only reason I'm here, but I wouldn't be here without it."

"That's clear, Chas. I'm devoted to making sure you are always happy with us."

"It's not too hard, babe. At least not all the time."

THE CAR PAUL RIORDAN, Luke's father, had helped Henry pick out was economical and reliable. The Chevy Spark was nothing like the Corvette Luke was driving across country, but it did get Henry to and from his job and classes, and most importantly to Avery's house to pick her up for dates. With almost two months of summer left, the two made the most of their time with outdoor activities every weekend. They discovered a mutual fondness for hikes, especially on long day trips down to Blackwater Falls. There was always a place near some trail or other where they could spread out the blanket from Henry's backpack and spend some quality time making out.

It was mid-August, though, when they decided not to rush back to the city and took a room at the Billy Motel. The manager didn't seem too surprised to have a couple of eighteen-year-olds booking a room at the last minute. This was West By-God Virginia, after all. After dinner, at the motel's restaurant, they found themselves together in a somewhat rustic room.

"Is this okay?" Henry asked as he held her, looking at the motel room.

"It's not the Hilton, is it?" she laughed. "But this isn't our honeymoon, either. And I don't think there's enough room in the back of your Spark for either of us to do what we want to do. It's fine, Henry. As long as you're gentle and the same considerate guy you've been through all our dates, I'm happy."

She demonstrated her happiness by kissing Henry and drawing him toward the bed.

Their lovemaking was gentle and comfortable. Henry grabbed a condom from his pocket before he allowed her to guide him into her. They moved slowly and kept eye-contact through the whole time. Avery stimulated herself with a hand between them and managed to get off before Henry did. They spent a long time cuddling in the afterglow.

"I'm glad we got a chance to do this," Avery said. "You start freshman orientation this week and I'm moving to full-time evenings and weekends so I can go to school during the day. We aren't going to have time for day-long outings to the mountains, not to mention that it will be snowy and dangerous in a couple of months. I'm so glad we stopped here tonight."

"You don't want to continue seeing me?" Henry asked.

"Oh, sure. If we can manage it. But we'll both be in new worlds from here on. I don't see much chance that we'll be able to keep it up."

"Wow! I guess I never thought about that. I've enjoyed having you as my girlfriend."

"I've enjoyed it, too. You really are a great guy. I like being with you. I guess, though, I never seriously considered this more than a summer thing," she said. "I wouldn't mind doing it again now, though, if you're up to it."

"Yeah. I guess we can just enjoy each other with no expectations, right?"

"Only the expectation that you'll continue to treat me like your girlfriend right up until the very last minute."

They coupled again, held each other as they slept, and managed another time before they showered, dressed, and went out to breakfast the next morning.

"There's something else, isn't there, Avery? Something you haven't told me?" Henry asked as they drove back to the city. There was a long silence.

"I guess so. I never intended to bring it up, but here it is. My high school boyfriend and I broke up at graduation. He left to try to get better work out east. But he called me this week and said he's coming back home. He kind of wants us to get back together again. I don't know if it will work. Chastity convinced me to give college a chance and I'm going to the community college this fall. I don't think he'll go back to school, but he's taken a real interest in automotive maintenance and says he's got an internship at a car dealership when he gets back. We'll see how it goes."

Henry took a deep breath and relaxed. This was considerably more final than what they'd discussed the night before.

"Thank you for making my summer a little brighter," he said, reaching for her hand. She took it and held it until they reached her home.

"Hey! It's about time! How was the road trip?" Henry asked Luke when his friend got back to town. The friends had all decided to get together on Saturday before they had to start classes.

"It was pretty damned amazing. The second half wasn't as much fun as the first half, after Sheila bailed on me in California. But five weeks getting out there in the slickest pussy you've ever imagined was pretty fine," Luke said.

"I never did get why she bailed on you," Henry asked.

"She's going to Stanford this fall. Figured my 'Vette was more fun than flying. I have to agree."

"At least you had a few weeks. Have you talked to Isobel?"

"She got back to town last night about the same time I did. We had just a few minutes to plan lunch today and our drive out to Villanova together Monday. I don't know yet if we'll pick up where we left off or not. I'd like to. How's Chastity?"

"She'll be here shortly. We've talked and even double-dated a couple of times. She's excited about getting our venture up and running."

"I've got the papers ready. We just need to sign and register them with the State. There's still stuff we need to do after they're signed, but we can probably handle the rest over Labor Day weekend. You know, like opening a bank account to deposit our investments," Luke said. "You're sure the LLC should be equal shares?"

"We might not have equal roles in the corporation, but having this founding part equal just seems right to me," Henry said.

"Once we raise capital, we probably won't even have a controlling interest," Luke said. "We should get as much done as we can before we actually bring in capital."

"I agree. We need to actually have a value before we invite someone else to participate. Look! Here come Chastity and Isobel."

The two women ran from their car to greet Henry and Luke with hugs.

"My God, Henry! I've missed you!" Isobel said collapsing against him and hugging him fiercely.

"Life just isn't as interesting without you around," Henry laughed. He turned to hug Chastity and received a sweet kiss on the lips.

"They're holding a table for us," Luke said, pointing the way to the club restaurant. "I made the reservation for noon, but told them not to expect us before 12:30. And look! Here we are, right on time."

They went in and were immediately ushered to their table. A waiter took their orders and brought them soft drinks.

"I thought sure you were going to text us and tell us you were married," Chastity said. "How did you manage to escape?"

"Mama. I thought my dad would have a heart attack when I announced to the family, I wasn't a virgin and was heading back to go to college. Dad wanted me to go straight to confession, but I told him I'd already gone to confession here and that I wasn't going to any priest in Argentina. Then Mama, bless her soul, announced we were leaving for Costa Rica the next day. We spent three beautiful weeks on the beach. Magnificent," Isobel rattled off.

"Will your mama adopt me, too?" Chastity asked.

"Oh, sure. But you have to follow her rules. Even Luke has promised to take the catechism when we're at Villanova. Mama won't have any non-Catholics hanging around. And Luke had to make that promise in order to drive me to school Monday!"

"I don't mind," Luke said. "There are worse things I could be asked to do. Here's the LLC agreement. It's short and sweet. Just that we agree to create a company with the purpose of investing in technology and other business endeavors as needed. It declares us equal partners and lists the opening investment." He handed around copies of the single page agreement."

"So, Luke is the managing member," Chastity said. "I'm fine with that. Isobel is treasurer? Okay. What do Henry and I do?"

"Henry keeps developing and you keep an eye on him," Luke said. "And really, all four of us need to be focused on learning everything we can about getting a for-real corporation established. One of the downsides of our little group is that Henry is the only technology guy among us. If we need to get him help, that will be your job, Chas. Hopefully, not before we get established, but there's going to be stuff that he needs help with. It's the nature of the beast."

"How's that all going, Henry?" Izzy asked.

"Not badly. I've got new apps for you guys to test, but they don't go any further than us four for now. I've filed patents on the tech and copyrights on the software. It's real stuff now and we need to protect it. The biggest thing I'm likely to need help with is the UI. We won't be able to go to market with a command line program, even if it works great that way. If people don't have an icon or an emoji to look at, they have no idea what to do."

"And we can't expect Henry to keep up the pace he's been working this summer," Chastity said. "He's been working here at the club, finished two classes at the university, and has continued developing in what is laughingly called his spare time. I barely got him out on dates all summer."

"You've been dating?" Izzy asked.

"No! Not me. I just arranged for him to meet someone who needed to get out more, too."

"When do we get to meet your girlfriend?" Izzy asked Henry.

"Whenever I get one. We agreed to break it off last weekend. It was friendly and I like her a lot, but there were other complications. We're good," Henry said.

"Bummer," Luke said. "Chastity might need to find you another girlfriend. We don't want your creative juices getting backed up."

They all laughed and continued their lunch as old friends.

5

THE CHALLENGE OF COLLEGE

"WOULD YOU BE interested in a little playtime tonight?" Henry asked Chastity after their lunch with Luke and Isobel. "We might not have much time for entertainment after classes start next week."

"Worried about your creative juices getting backed up? Get used to having a girl in your bed this summer? Yeah. I'm up for that," Chastity said. She linked her arm in his and headed toward his little car.

"You know it wasn't like that," Henry said. "We only got together like that last weekend. Then we said our goodbyes."

"Henry! No! I didn't know that. When I saw her at work, she was all goo-goo-eyed about how nice you were and how she loved spending time with you. That bitch!"

"Hey, it's okay. I really did have a good time with Avery. I even feel more fit since I've been out hiking every weekend. It just wasn't a summer of sex. And I'm fine with that." Henry opened the car door for Chastity and made sure she was seated and had nothing hanging out the door before he closed it. "Shall we get a room at the motor inn?"

"No. Let's go to my place. You know I managed to get my own apartment this month."

"We really haven't been hanging out enough!"

"Yeah. Well, now we have a whole summer of sex to catch up on!" Chastity said. "Don't worry, though. Even though we'll be working hard in school and our jobs, I'll still make time for you. You just need to speak up, you know?"

40

They got to Chastity's modest apartment where Henry met her two cats. A short time later the lovers were spread naked on her bed. Little kisses led to petting and Henry found himself responding to her sensuous body as he had after the prom.

He spent time worshiping between her legs with his tongue and then kissed his way up her body until they were lip to lip again. She guided his cock into her and soon he was seated deep inside.

"This is nothing like anything I had this summer either," she said. "Goddess! You fill me so completely."

They rose together and then drifted off to sleep next to each other for a short nap.

Henry awoke before Chastity and contemplated their strange relationship. Their night at the prom might have been the previous night, as comfortable as they were with each other. But Chastity maintained she was not girlfriend material and he was determined not to treat her as if she was at his beck and call.

His petting of her while she slept and kissing her nipples soon had her stirring. He found her sex to be well-lubricated and moved between her legs, which opened easily for him. Then he was in her again. Chastity didn't open her eyes, but she kept pace with his thrusts, moving against him until he started coming. Chastity raked his back with her nails.

"Oh, fuck! What a way to wake up! Your come is dripping out of me. You must have poured a gallon into me."

"I'm sure those urban legends are exaggerated," Henry laughed. "No guy actually produces that much. You just have a tiny space to put it."

"Especially when it's full of your cock! Next time, I'm waking you up."

"Please do. Any time," he laughed.

"Let me up. I need to use the john. I don't think we've had a whole summer's worth of orgasms yet."

"Want to get some dinner? I'll text Mom and let her know I won't be home."

"We can order in."

Henry sent a text to his mother to let her know he was staying out. Then he checked Chastity's address and called a nearby restaurant to order food.

"I should get myself an apartment," he said when she emerged from the bathroom. She'd stayed naked, so he had no problem remaining that way, too. "This is nice. And your kitties seem to like it a lot."

"They love the window ledge. I'll give you the name of a great rental agent. She got me mine and I'm sure she'd love to work with you. So to speak."

"Are you arranging a rental agent or a date?" Henry laughed.

"Yes. Personnel recruitment is my specialty."

HENRY ROLLED OUT of bed earlier than he intended Sunday morning. Early in the morning, Chastity had told him he should go home, but he'd been mostly asleep and didn't move from the bed. He'd nearly forgotten that he was picking up his parents for the university president's orientation address at 9:30. Chastity was grumpy and just waved at him as she rolled over and went back to sleep. They might not have gotten an entire summer's worth of sex in overnight, but they'd tried hard.

The hour-long orientation event was filled with information about the university's history, commitment to academic freedom, and striving for excellence. The president only spoke for about twenty minutes out of the hour, but the program was tightly run and began and ended precisely on time.

"I guess we go different directions now," Henry said to Ryan and Sylvia. "Honestly, if you guys finish and want to go home, just text me. It seems like a long time to hold you here just for a family orientation and resource fair."

"Oh, it will give us a chance to tour the school and see how much it's changed since we were here," Ryan said. "What's your schedule?"

"Since I'm living at home—thank you very much for that—I don't have anything after my computer science school welcome and orientation. That ends at two o'clock," Henry said.

"We'll plan to meet you at the car about 2:30 then," Sylvia said. "That should be plenty of time to see what we want to see. We don't need to tour any dormitories."

They split up and Henry met with people in the School of Computer Science for the first general meeting of the year. He reminded himself that these were all freshman students and he'd meet some of the older students when classes started in a week.

The School of Computer Science (SCS) was huge. In addition to a general computer science degree, the school offered degrees in artificial intelligence, computational biology, human-computer interaction, and robotics. There were over a hundred students enrolled in the Machine Learning Department, which was where the AI program was based.

The computer science luncheon and introduction was crowded with over three hundred new students. They included what Henry assumed was a typical array of computer geeks. About a third of the incoming class were women. The guys were pretty much clueless. Henry had to give himself a once-over when he caught a whiff of one of the other guys. He'd rolled out of bed with Chastity, given himself a quick wipe with a washcloth, dressed, and was out to get his parents in fifteen minutes. At least he was wearing the clothes from his lunch at the club on Saturday, so he guessed he didn't look too bad.

He made a note to himself to be careful of his hygiene. Some of the girls in the school looked kind of cute in their own geeky sort of way. It was a diverse group. About a third were Asian and another third African or Indian. Henry was irrationally pleased that as a white male he was in a definite minority. His high school had not been nearly as diverse.

He met several people and exchanged contact information with some. It was looking like a pretty good year.

MONDAY MORNING, HENRY was up and showered. He grabbed his clubs and was off to his first team practice for the golf team. As a State Championship runner up, he was awarded a modest scholarship to play at the university. While golf wasn't a major sport, it was respected enough that Henry found he was the only one of the two dozen men and women on the team who was actually from Pennsylvania.

Coach Dan and Coach Ty coached both the men's and women's teams with a couple of student assistants. Usually, they would be training and traveling together. The morning was spent with the coaches observing their athletes driving and putting. Henry's summer routine had included at least a bucket of balls each day at the club where he coached children and youth wanting to play. As a result, he was in good shape for his driving and putting. The top two golfers he observed would be serious contenders for professional playing soon. Henry wouldn't place in the top five his first year there.

After a team lunch, those who could stay for the afternoon split into foursomes and played a full eighteen holes. Henry found that he was more at home with the golfers than he'd been with the computer scientists.

"How'd you get so good?" Kaitlyn asked him as they played their mixed group.

"I competed four years on my high school team. We had a sponsor who made sure we all had memberships at a local club and could get practice time in. I ended up working there this summer as a youth pro. So, lots of time on the links," Henry said.

"Hey, you still a member there?" she asked.

"Yeah. They kept me on a student membership."

"You could… ask me on a golf date one day," she said. She teed up and Henry watched her form as she sent her drive down the center of the fairway. He wasn't really watching her golf form. She had a very pleasing shape in her short golf skirt and team shirt.

"It looks like my schedule is completely jammed for the week of orientation. I'm not living in a residence on campus, so I didn't need to go to any of those sessions today. Why don't I see if I can get us a tee time a week from Saturday? It might be early in the morning, since it's a holiday weekend," Henry suggested.

"That would be great. We've got our first match on Labor Day. It will be good to get a full eighteen in a couple of days before," Kaitlyn said.

"It's a date," Henry said.

They continued to chat as they walked the golf course next to the university.

"Say… Are you going to the general convocation on Thursday?" Henry asked as they neared the eighteenth hole.

"I suppose so. It's not technically required of juniors, but if we're on campus, we're asked to go," she sighed.

"I was thinking that if I met you there, we could go out to dinner afterward," Henry said. He just wasn't used to asking girls out and hoped he wasn't being too forward. Kaitlyn was a couple of years older than he was.

"I was beginning to think I'd have to ask you," she giggled. "Yeah. Let's plan on it."

HENRY MADE IT to the AI and Machine Learning group dinner, considerably fresher after a shower at the clubhouse and a change of clothes. About thirty students attended along with three professors and a couple of graduate assistants. It was an informal meet and greet and the time was spent mostly with the people at their table of nine. It was a good opportunity to get to know a few of the people he'd be spending the most time with.

The three women at the table sat next to each other, but they were the center of attention for much of the meal. It was apparent to Henry that his male classmates had not had a lot of experience with women. He couldn't say much for the breadth of his own experience. He'd seldom dated, even though he'd had three sex partners in the past year. He didn't see much likelihood of that number growing, even with his classmates and teammates in golf.

"Well, this is a good opportunity to get to know each other by doing more than giving your name and where you're from. As you introduce yourselves around the table, I'd like you to also give a brief synopsis of what you think the greatest challenges of artificial intelligence are," Professor Jacoby said. He wasn't that much older than the students, but most of the people involved in artificial intelligence were still pretty young. Those who were actually involved in the technology—not those who owned the businesses.

"I'm Lisa Hartwell from Baton Rouge, Louisiana," said one of the women to get things started. She happened to be sitting on the professor's left, so it was assumed that was the direction introductions would proceed. "From my perspective, I'd say the whole training process is an issue. You have to waste incredible amounts of time and energy to train an AI for even moderate functionality. I'd like to see more innovation using game theory in training AIs."

"Thank you, Lisa. That should be very interesting," Jacoby said. He turned to the next woman and the introductions continued. Halfway around the circle, the guy next to Henry introduced himself.

"I'm Josh Daniels from Seattle. I'd have to say that ethics is still the major issue with artificial intelligence. We are still dealing with issues of copying intellectual property in order to train these things. We'll have to pay the piper sometime."

Henry nodded his agreement.

"I'm Henry Pascal from right here in Pennsylvania. I'd have to agree with the issues that have been mentioned so far, but I'm surprised no one has mentioned power. It seems like having enough power to run our server farms and AI is a gating factor."

"Don't you think we can always get more power?" Josh asked. "Like we've proven we can get more memory. Add another server."

"Henry, tell us what you see as the power restriction," Jacoby said.

"We've heard more than one major AI source commit to booking power from seven modular nuclear generators to power their server farms. That's a huge commitment to the resources needed to advance AI. And it comes just at a time when the popular trend is away from potentially destructive power sources. There could easily be a backlash against the licensing of the MNGs before they come online. Then where will the power come from to serve our consumption needs?"

Josh started to make another statement, but Jacoby held up a hand.

"Those are good points. I think we'll all have to understand AI better before we can begin to debate them properly," Jacoby said. "We've got three more people to introduce, so let's not get stuck on one item."

"Hi. I'm Dan Zhang from Boston. Like Henry, I agree with what everyone else has said so far, and that includes a couple of things I hadn't thought about. What I see as a big issue is breaking the monopolies. We've already discovered that AI isn't necessarily right. But people accept the results anyway. The big companies in the business are training the AIs to produce the answers that agree with that company's policies. Or their government, as we saw the Chinese AI come online with things like refusing to answer any questions about human rights or to say anything about Taiwan other than that it is a province of Mainland China. We've got to break the hold of the big guys and produce an AI that is independent and honest."

The last two guys introduced themselves and the group enjoyed their coffee and desserts while asking each other questions to clarify their stances on certain subjects. There was a lively discussion and they sat at the table long after the official 7:30 end-time for the social.

Tuesday was Community Day and was one of the more interesting days of the orientation week. Henry expected it to be about the city and questioned whether he needed to be in the sessions at all. But it turned out to be about the university community and its make-up. The keynote speaker was introduced as the director of the united university.

Henry thought it might mean something about global studies, but sat in the auditorium to listen to Dr. Meredith Logan.

"Recently, the university was pressured by the United States Government funding offices to eliminate its department of Diversity, Equity, and Inclusion, and not to mention it again. So, I won't be talking about DEI this morning. I won't even mention the words diversity, equity, and inclusion in my entire address to this diverse group of students entering our classes this year. I will not discuss how we include people of all races, colors, religions, national origin, gender identity, and sexual preference in our united university. Please don't ask me to use any of those words in describing how diverse, equitable, and inclusive we are. I won't talk about how lesbian, gay, bisexual, and transsexual are welcome here. All."

There was some laughter from the students at her repeated use of the forbidden words, but the students soon realized how serious she was about the subject.

"The united university is a place where *all* are welcome. If you need a definition of the word 'all,' I refer you to the dictionary. If you scroll down far enough to the pronoun usage, you will find the definition 'Everyone. Everything.' That is what the united university is, and what my office is devoted to preserving. Don't ask me if it includes your particular ethnic background or that of your perceived enemies. *All.* If you are a human being, you are part of 'all.' And as a part of the all, if you find you are discriminated against, treated unfairly, or otherwise treated as though you are other than all, this office is here to support you and put things right."

Henry thought that things mentioned in the director's speech might actually go a lot further than what had been covered by DEI. The university had complied with the demand of the government to preserve the funding it received, but had effectively come back with a program and policy that was even richer than the one abandoned.

"Let me also say that if you are bigoted, a religious fanatic, a racist, a misogynist, a misandrist, rich or poor, or a straight white male, you are also welcome here. All. You are just as queer as everyone else!" Dr. Logan said. It took a moment for it to soak in, but then the entire auditorium cheered.

"There is a rule that governs all. Since all are welcome, it is against the rule to trespass on anyone else's right to be here. That includes any form of hate speech, discrimination, exclusion, denigration, or violence. Every person here is just as queer as every other, so get used to living together, studying together, engaging in intellectual conversation, competing in athletics, and becoming friends. We put this one rule into effect because we will never mention diversity, equity, or inclusion at this completely DEI-free school."

After the keynote address, there were small-group sessions that people could choose to discuss any aspect of 'all.' Then they went to lunch at which various aspects of the university community were discussed, including housing protocols, classroom environment, communications and publications, and entertainment. Following the lunchtime plenary session, students returned to small group discussions.

By the time dinner was finished that evening, Henry was tired and glad to go home.

6
DATE NIGHT

CONVOCATION THURSDAY EVENING had been much like the other keynotes from the university president, the director of the united university, and the provost, but it had more solemnity and a religious overtone to it. The participants had all worn their black gowns with three velvet stripes on the sleeve and variously colored hoods. They processed up a center aisle and had flags and banners they displayed on the stage.

There was an invocation, a song by one of the university chorales, and the message by a guest speaker who was a graduate from the university. He held an important position in the steel industry and brought home the responsibility of those with an education to share their gift with all levels of society. Henry thought the message was pretty cool.

"Overwhelmed with college yet?" Kaitlyn asked when she met Henry after the convocation.

"I think I'll know better after classes actually start next week. It seems a little out of sequence to try to convince freshmen to join all these campus organizations and to volunteer for community service when we don't have an actual understanding of what our workload will be. So, aside from playing golf, I haven't signed up for any extra-curricular activities. I have about as much as I can handle with my class schedule," Henry said. "Was it like that with you?"

"No. I can only admire your ability to resist. By the time I was through orientation week, I was signed up for ten different organizations and projects because they all sounded so good. Within a month after classes started, all I was active in was golf and the Chinese-American Club," she said.

Henry drove Kaitlyn to a favorite restaurant that was inexpensive but just far enough off campus that he didn't expect a lot of college kids to be there. They were seated and ordered from their waiter before picking up their conversation.

"It seems like there's always some tension between the US and China being hyped up. Have you experienced problems because of it?" Henry asked.

"I'm not from China. I'm from San Francisco," Kaitlyn said. "That said, it's a racial thing. If someone is bigoted about one thing, they are likely to be bigoted about the Chinese, too. Between COVID and the tariff wars, there are a lot of places we aren't particularly welcome. However, if I'd realized how common Asian faces were here at the university, I probably wouldn't have bothered joining the club. I thought it was going to be the only way I'd see people who looked like me in this little midwestern town."

"Midwestern? Wow! I've never heard Pittsburgh referred to as midwestern. For most people, the Midwest starts about thirty miles west of here. Most people here try to lay claim to East Coast values, though you'll find the area a lot more conservative than, say, Philadelphia."

"True that. So, what's your big goal in life?" Kaitlyn asked.

"That bypasses all the small-talk, doesn't it?" Henry laughed. "My plan is to launch a corporation built around some of my computing ideas and make some changes to how people view artificial intelligence. What's your big goal?"

"To marry a nice guy—or girl for that matter, I don't care—who will support me for the rest of my life, while I play golf every day."

Henry looked at her with his mouth open slightly.

"I'm kidding. A little," she said. "I think I can improve my game enough to join the LPGA. So far, the game has given me enough scholarship help that I can continue to improve here in college. I'm majoring in exercise science so I can reasonably anticipate employability as a coach when I get out if I haven't made it to the LPGA yet."

"I think that's a great goal. Mine is probably a little less defined," Henry laughed.

Their dinners arrived and the conversation continued along the vein of getting the most out of their time on campus. After dinner, Henry drove Kaitlyn back to campus and her residence hall.

"So, taking the schedule of this week and next into consideration and confirming our golf date for next weekend, would you like to go out again?" Henry asked.

Kaitlyn turned on the steps of the residence to face Henry.

"I tell you what, let's see how we get along on the golf course and how next week's golf date goes. We've got a Labor Day competition, too. Then we'll see about how things shape up," Kaitlyn said. "I have to tell you, though, Henry, I don't really see a future for us and I don't just date around. Let's call this 'getting to know your teammate' and not have any additional expectations."

"I hear you," he said. "I'm definitely not looking for a commitment of any sort. I'll be happy to call you my friend."

"Agreed."

Kaitlyn entered her residence hall and Henry drove home.

By the time orientation week ended on Sunday evening, Henry felt like he'd been on campus all his life. He'd made two additional practices with the golf team and had met with his classmates in the School of Computer Science and with the smaller group of students interested in artificial intelligence. He was ready to put the orientation behind him and get into his studies.

He'd completed nearly all the required freshman classes except the "Freshman Immigration" course for a single credit. He still couldn't declare his major in artificial intelligence until the spring term, but he could start taking the classes. His major classes were AI: Representation and Problem Solving, Parallel and Sequential Data Structures and Algorithms, and Probability Theory for Computer Scientists. This gave him a total of only twelve credits, so he piled on an ethics class and a computer engineering elective for another six credits. It was considered a heavy load, but Henry was determined to get deep into his subject and get out of college.

The classes were challenging from the first day. Parking on campus was at a premium and upper-classmen had priority for parking permits, so Henry grabbed a bus from near his house at seven in the morning. He returned about seven in the evening, after golf practice. He happily gobbled down the dinner his mother had prepared while his parents quizzed him about the first day of class.

Then he was off to study. All his classes had a hefty amount of reading to be done and he continued to read until he fell asleep about midnight. In the morning, he was up and back on the bus at seven.

The golf date on Saturday was less a date than a practice session. Henry invited two other team members to round out their foursome. When he found out about the match, Coach Ty asked if he could walk the course with them.

The coach kept the scores and used simple plus-minus rules with the two girls competing with each other and the two guys competing against each other. The player in each pair who got the lowest score on a hole won a point. All four were well-matched and the scores were close. Henry won his match 3-2. That meant they'd tied on thirteen holes. Kaitlyn beat Carol 6-3, having tied on the other nine holes.

All through the play, the coach had given them subtle hints and critiques without attempting to take over the friendly competition. The golfers were happy with the results of their match and after a late breakfast at the club, were all off to their holiday weekend activities.

HENRY'S ACTIVITY WAS at Luke's house where they were meeting with Chastity and Isobel to work on the formation of their business. Isobel had acquired an employer identification number from the IRS and the four went to an appointment at the local bank to open their business account. They deposited their thousand dollar checks and signed the account papers.

"I guess that makes us officially a company," Luke said. "Wow! I really didn't expect this at eighteen."

"No kidding," Chastity said. "What comes next?"

"I've been in touch with the Small Business Administration for some advice," Luke said. "I asked specifically for advice on incorporating a software company so we could protect our—or Henry's—IP. It turns out that one of the professors in my department is an SBA consultant and we struck up a good conversation. He's agreed to work with us at Villanova, and will come to periodic meetings with the group here in Pitt or by Zoom. There's a lot of preliminary work to be done in the next couple of months. So, we probably won't have much of a meeting with him until at least winter break."

"What are the big issues we need to deal with?" Henry asked. "Can we all work on it or is it strictly in your court now?"

"I figure we'll all have work to do. We didn't really need to think much about what to name our LLC: Pascal, Riordan, Perez, and Pappa. It's not really going to be doing any public business. We're strictly founding owners of The World's Greatest Computer Company. Which is a name I checked on and it's already taken. So, we all need to be figuring out what we're going to call our corporation. We can start shooting names back and forth through text and email, though I'd rather we figure out a company website for PRPP so we have secure email and aren't using a commercial service."

"I can set that up," Henry said.

"Good. I was hoping you'd say that so we don't need to dip into the funds too deeply. Then the names we generate need to be checked against whether or not they are available and not trademarked," Luke continued.

"I can do that. It's similar to what I did to get the LLC registered," Isobel said.

"I suppose most of the basic stuff like determining the type of business according to the various tax tables, the state of incorporation, which doesn't need to be the same as the state where we are operating, and the initial stock setup—like how many shares we're going to authorize and who gets how much is my problem," Luke said.

"This summer I found out employment laws vary from state to state and county to county," Chastity said. "I think when we decide on a state of incorporation and place of business, we should be considering local laws on employment. I don't care so much about whether there is a diversity, equity, and inclusion law as that it isn't forbidden. If we are going to be an engineering firm, we need to be able to hire the best engineers and that is going to be a diverse population."

"Well said," Henry added. "We need that to be a founding policy."

"I'll figure out a way to work it into the articles of incorporation or bylaws," Luke said. "Chas, I'll be asking for your help on that."

"Got it."

"WHAT IS IT about this business stuff that makes me so horny?" Chastity said, looping her arm through Henry's as they left the restaurant where the group had dinner. "Want to help me with that?"

"Hmm. It's Saturday night on a holiday weekend. I've been in class or orientation for two weeks, and the only date I've had is a 'Let's Be Friends,' teammate on the golf team. I think that makes me completely available to help out a friend in need," Henry laughed.

"We should enjoy each other tonight, then," Chastity said. "Goddess knows when we'll ever have a chance again. I ended up with a full load of classes and I'm still holding my job at the restaurant."

They went to Chastity's apartment and Henry spent a few minutes petting the cats while Chastity puttered at putting a few things away and smoothing the bedding. Then they cuddled up on the bed and began seriously playing at getting each other turned on.

"Don't you like my ass?" Chastity said as she came down from her first orgasm and Henry was getting into position to enter her.

"Of course I like your ass!" he responded. "What's not to like?"

"We've never done it doggie. Why don't you get behind me and cuddle up against it?"

"Sure. I mean, this is only like our third time together. I was trying not to rush things."

"Silly! Doing it from behind isn't rushing things. If you tried to put it *in* my ass, that would be rushing things," Chas said as she rolled over and presented her backside to him.

Henry fondled the ass in question and then lined up to enter Chas again. As soon as he started, Chastity pressed back against him, driving his cock deep in her pussy.

"Oh, fuck, Chastity! That almost got me off. Would have been a really short fuck."

"I got greedy. Told you I was horny. I just love the feeling of your cock stuffing me. I just want to remind you that even in the office, I'm yours for the taking. It's part of our agreement!"

Henry picked up the speed and even if he hadn't come as soon as he entered her, it wasn't long before he began spurting. Chastity was right with him.

"What is it you have against dating and marriage, Chas? We make a great team."

"Nothing against them in principle. But not us. We aren't in love. And if I lived with you, I know it wouldn't be long before I fell out of lust, too. Not going to happen," Chastity said, giving him a shove to get out of bed. "I'm going to keep you from getting sucked into a relationship because you're horny instead of being in love. I'm not going to prevent you from finding your one true love or whatever hogwash you want to label it, nor to stop you from fucking whomever you want. But I don't want to wake up with you in the morning!"

"Hey! I spent the night last time."

"Barely. You were up and out the door before I had a chance to wake up and throw you out. Just go, Henry. I'm your happy-for-an-hour, not your happily-ever-after."

FOUR COLLEGES COMPETED on Monday in two two-way matches with men's and women's tournaments. It was considered a first of the year mixer in some ways. Henry's team played against the men from one of the other colleges, but the two women in their foursome were from the third and fourth colleges. It made for a very collegial atmosphere and everyone did well. Henry won his match by a single point, but the university men's team lost the match. The university women's team won their match and Kaitlyn won hers by three.

The day was exhausting as the team had a four-and-a-half-hour drive each direction. They didn't get back to campus until almost ten that night.

Then the rhythm of classes picked up again. Henry was relieved that he didn't need to play every tournament. There were twelve men and twelve women on the team, but typically a tournament only allowed five per team to enter. An exceptional sixth person might enter the tournament as an individual, but not be counted as part of the team. Henry wouldn't be playing the varsity matches in the fall and didn't have another outing with the B-team until the end of September.

By that time, Henry had settled into the routine of college life. After the initial push to get started, classes seemed to even out and there were many discussions with his classmates about the subject matter. He joined a study group with Josh, Lisa, and Dan. They'd identified each other at the first department dinner during orientation as people to work with, then they discovered they had three major interest classes together. The conversations were often lively.

"Henry's made a convert out of me," Josh laughed. "I see what you mean about the power issue. With the drive toward electric everything as a clean energy, where are we going to get enough power to run our computers?"

"Thank God we're not getting power from coal much anymore," Dan said. "Fifteen percent is still too much, but we continue to cut it back."

"The attacks on solar and wind generation slowed down the drop," Lisa said. "There's so much disinformation about environment and efficiency that people believe burning coal is still providing the bulk of our power. Mostly, that isn't true except in Texas—which doesn't make the air over Louisiana any cleaner."

"Where's the power going to come from, Henry?" Josh asked. "You got us thinking about this, but what's the answer."

"If I had the answer already, I wouldn't be in college studying all these things. I believe, though, there must be ways to reduce the *amount* of power needed, not just ways to produce *more* power. Don't forget that energy isn't the only resource being used. All that power usage in computers creates heat.

Heat is an enemy of computers. So, they all have to be cooled. For the most part, cooling takes water. A lot of the places where server farms and AI bases are being set up are remote so they won't be an eyesore. But those remote areas often don't have enough water as it is."

"How about using the heat and water to generate more power?" Dan asked. "Doesn't solve all the problems, but it reduces the dependency on more power from current sources."

"Reduce, reuse, recycle," Josh said. "Haven't we been taught that since we were babies?"

"I think we've identified a problem, but we aren't deep enough into it to identify any real solutions yet," Henry said. "It's too bad we don't have, like, an AI that could come up with a solution."

The study group looked at him and all started to snicker. Maybe they could create that.

THE NEXT GOLF tournament Henry was involved in was the B-Team Invitational in Meadville. That was only an hour and a half north of Pittsburgh, but it was the last time most of the freshman players on the team would have a chance to play until spring. The two coaches took five women and five men to the tournament for Saturday and Sunday, including meals and a motel room for the night. The major fall competitions were in North Carolina, Georgia, and Florida. Only the top tier players would be flown to those tournaments. Weather would soon become a factor in playing locally.

The tournament started at ten with nine women's teams. The 'shotgun start' meant foursomes would start on twelve different holes around the course at the same time. This was a cumulative score competition, meaning the scores of all men's team members would be added together. The lowest cumulative score would win the tournament. They would play eighteen holes on Saturday and eighteen on Sunday.

The men started their round at 1:30 in the afternoon. There were eleven teams, so they started on fourteen holes. Henry did pretty well on his round, shooting four over par. That put him on the leader board in sixth place and his team was ranked at third. It was a good round. The women were playing well and the leader board had the team ranked in second.

The hundred players and their coaches were served dinner at the country club's welcome banquet. The varsity team, Henry supposed, was treated this well at all their tournaments, but this was something special for the B-teams.

After dinner, a motivational speaker addressed the group. He was a fairly well-known pro golfer, though Henry didn't think he'd won any champion-ships. He mused that that was appropriate for second tier golfers to listen to.

"Do you think that was meant to encourage us to stay on the B-team?" Carol joked with him on their way to the bus.

"I guess that would be appropriate. How many of us are going to become pro golfers?"

"I understood that. I'm here to get a Health Sciences degree. Pre-med student. I want to make sure I have a good golf game for my weekends as a doctor," she laughed.

Carol had joined Kaitlyn and Henry on their golf date early in the month. She was probably as good a golfer as Henry was and better than most of the guys on the team, but the women's team was pretty high quality overall. She was definitely second tier.

"Computer science specializing in AI for me," Henry said. "I don't even know if I'd be able to maintain the schedule if I was a varsity golfer. I don't see myself taking off for two or three days for every competition. And there aren't that many tutors in the department."

"Kaitlyn will go pro. That's what she's here for. What you saw of her when we played together was just a warm-up for her."

"She's a killer," Henry said. "I don't know if Geoff will be dedicated enough to make it as a pro. He's good, but I think he's more likely to end up a coach. Nothing wrong with that. I had a great coach in high school. I could end up doing that myself."

"With a degree in AI? I doubt it."

"What are we supposed to do for rooms at this place?" Henry asked when they pulled in to the Hampton Inn.

"Oh, the girls came over after our round and checked into the rooms," Carol said.

"And the guys?"

"Well, there's five rooms, five guys, and five girls," Carol said.

"You can't mean everyone is expected to pair up!"

"No! Of course not. We'll give keys to two rooms to the guys and three rooms for us," Carol teased.

"Well, not that I would object to sharing a room with you, Carol…"

"Good. Because it comes out to two rooms with two girls each, two rooms with two guys each, and one room with one of each. If you're not too aggressive, I'll share with you. The rooms all have two beds and I didn't bring enough stuff with me for this overnight to occupy the entire bathroom."

"Are you serious, Carol?" Henry asked.

"Well… yeah. I mean, I'm not offering to screw you. We've hung out a little and I like you, though. It's *possible* that we might enjoy each other's company. But I also know you're a decent guy. I don't think you'd pressure me. None of the girls feel that way about any of the other guys," Carol said.

"If you trust me, I promise to be trustworthy," Henry said. "I'd love to just hang out for the night and get to know you better."

"Perfect."

"ARE YOU A guy who stays up late watching TV?" Carol asked when they got to their room. It was spacious enough that they would have no difficulty sharing. Henry's duffle bag had only enough clean clothes and toiletries for a night. Both golf bags occupied the closet.

"No. I seldom watch TV. Help yourself if you want. I've got my laptop. I was thinking I could study if I didn't fall asleep too quickly," he said.

"Yeah. I brought a book. I heard somewhere that being a freshman in college was just like high school without a parent. I never studied this hard in high school!"

"Isn't that the truth? I came in as a freshman with sophomore standing and my classes are brutal. I didn't have the opportunity to study anything as in-depth as what I'm doing here," Henry said. He kicked off his shoes and settled back on the bed Carol had left unoccupied.

"It's probably our chosen fields. Is it true that you have to be smarter than anything you develop in computing?" she asked.

"It's a weird thing. My cellphone is smarter than I am if you just measure intelligence by how fast it can compute and find answers. My dad explained it to me years ago. He said a computer was hardware, firmware, and software. But it took wetware to create it and to use it." He pointed at his head.

"I might start using that term in my human physiology class," Carol laughed. "So, are you saying artificial intelligence won't replace me as a doctor?"

"If it does, the world will be a poorer place for it. The computer in all its variations is a tool. You learn to use a tool proficiently. Maybe you can ask the computer questions to help you diagnose a patient that has symptoms you aren't familiar with. But you can't let the computer just create the diagnosis.

You'd never know if the AI was giving you good information or if it had just made it up from something it discovered in a seventeenth century treatise on women and hysteria."

"It could do that, couldn't it?" Carol said. "So let me ask you something less professionally oriented. Do you have a girlfriend?"

"Oh, wow! Uh, no. In fact, I haven't had a date since our golf outing Labor Day weekend. There just hasn't been time. How about you? Do you have a boyfriend? Or girlfriend?"

"No. Like you, too busy. I came here from Cleveland and don't know many people in the area except those who are on the team and those who are in my major. I really can't imagine dating anyone who's studying medicine. But if you can, I might be interested."

"Carol, I think you're pretty cool. We have a lot of fun when we're golfing together. I'm enjoying sharing a room with you. Understanding we might not have a lot of dating time, I'd be interested in exploring the possibilities," Henry said.

"Would you be interested in exploring some of the possibilities tonight?" she asked, tossing the covers on her bed back.

"Is that too quick?" he asked.

"It's not you being aggressive. I'm offering... to let you check out my wetware."

7

PROGRESS

CAROL'S OFFER PROVED to have some limitations. They explored some possibilities, but stopped short of consummating a relationship because neither one had a condom. And neither was willing to take a chance on a person they didn't really know that well.

They slept together, kissed, fondled, and both exploded in orgasm, but woke up in the morning a little embarrassed and hurrying to get to the second day of the tournament.

The short night didn't seem to do either of them any harm when they stepped on the links. Carol led the women's team to a first place victory with a team total of 613 for the two-day event. She medaled with a five over par.

While Henry shot a slightly better four over par, the men's team managed only fourth place among the eleven teams. Still, everyone was happy with the results and relaxed on the hour-and-a-half ride back to campus.

"Um... So, about last night..." Carol said.

"Yes," Henry replied. "I would like to date you. But please don't think that every time we go out, we'll end up like we were last night. I still live at home with my parents to save up money this year. You live in a residence hall. I don't think either of us wants to entertain in our homes."

"Oh, God! Yes. That's just what I was thinking. I mean, last night was really fun and I'm not upset about it, but it was a lot bolder and faster than I normally am. I mean, I hope we do it again, and that we have a condom or twenty. But it will be hard to have regular dates. We aren't even on the same part of campus to meet for lunches and stuff, you know?"

"Yeah. But if you have time next weekend, we could do something normal like go to the football game."

"Football? I hate to say it, but I've never actually been to a football game," Carol said.

"Even in high school?"

"All girls school. I hear, though, they're going to start girls' flag football in the spring or something. There's a big movement to get it established nationwide."

"Maybe it will be like women's basketball," Henry said. "A lot more entertaining to watch than men's."

"How about lunch before the game and we can see what we come up with afterward?"

"Deal."

HENRY WAS BOTH stimulated by his classes and frustrated that they weren't advanced enough to do more than talk about general theory. He was at a point where he needed someone to test his next batch of code and hadn't built a trusting enough relationship with others in the department to share it with them. He managed to get an appointment with his advisor on Wednesday that week.

"Professor Jacoby, I'm having a problem," he said.

"Too rigorous a class schedule? I was concerned about you taking eighteen credits. That's a pretty heavy load."

"That's not the problem. Most of the classes aren't requiring much more than reading and discussion. I'm sure I'll need to start working on a couple of papers by the end of the month. It's more of a professional dilemma."

"Do tell. What kind of dilemma can you be having at this stage of your career?"

"You know I've been working on some software apps and code. We talked about it in my application interview. I have three patent applications and two copyrights. I guess the patents take longer than the copyrights. Those are already issued."

"You can't patent software. Are you doing this on your own?"

"No, sir. I have a pretty good patent attorney, I think. The patents are on system and methods," Henry said, trying to keep too much pride from showing through.

"That's impressive. All developed on your own?"

"Yes. That's the problem I'm facing. I have further developments but I really need to test them before I can give them to my attorney."

"That would be wise."

"But I don't have any testers. I was really lucky in high school to have close friends and a teacher who were all over eighteen and could sign non-disclosures. They did a good job of testing, but I know it fell short of what could have been done. But now, I don't have anyone. I don't really know how to interview potential testers/or how to handle it while I'm here at the university," Henry said.

"Don't."

"Sir?"

"There have been a couple of test cases in which inventions by students who use university resources for development can be claimed to be owned by the university. There have also been cases dismissed. But it's risky. The university has been probing the computer science department as a place where they might find intellectual property they can claim and license. This conversation, in fact, has probably gone as far as we should take it here on campus. How about we meet someplace this weekend and explore the possibilities?"

"That would be... fine. If you could meet me at Constitution Links for brunch on Sunday at eleven o'clock, we could launch our discussion then. I'll bring a non-disclosure," Henry said.

"I like your decisiveness. I'll see you there on Sunday."

HENRY PICKED CAROL up at eleven-thirty Saturday morning and drove straight to the stadium parking lot. It was already starting to fill. They managed to get seats at Burgertory for lunch and relaxed. Game time was at two.

"How many people are going to be there?" Carol asked.

"They say the stadium seats over 68,000, but that's really for the Steelers games. College games can run anywhere from 25,000 to 45,000," Henry said. He'd looked things up to prepare for the day. It wouldn't do to arrange a date and then not be able to get in or to be late.

"Would you mind terribly keeping hold of my hand?" she asked. "I don't want to sound like a baby, but I'm not used to big crowds. Just being on campus sometimes drives me a little crazy."

"Carol, I don't ever mind holding your hand. I'd like to keep you close."

"We've been a lot closer than we'll manage today, I'm sure, but keeping in touch is still high on my list," she laughed.

THEY FINISHED LUNCH and headed to the stadium. Once inside, they stopped at a vendor to get hot chocolate and made their way through the crowds to their seats in the student section.

"This is good, but I'm going to freeze to death out here," Carol said. "I should have worn a heavier coat, but I wasn't expecting it to be so chilly today."

"The mild temps this past week were deceiving. We're definitely headed into fall weather," Henry said. "Fortunately, I checked the forecast before I picked you up."

His clear plastic backpack looked like a grade schooler's, but that was one of the rules of the stadium. He opened it and extracted a blanket that he shook out and spread over the two of them.

"Oh! This will be good," Carol said. "When we finish our drinks, we can pull it all the way up over our shoulders and cuddle together!"

"That will be a pretty ideal thing," Henry said. "Like I said, I want to stay in touch with you. I didn't mean by email."

"I think we're thinking the same thing. Okay. I think we have to stand up for the National Anthem."

They stood, sang, and sat. Then the game was underway and they soon had to stand up to cheer. It was only three minutes into the game before their team scored and led 7-0. In three more minutes of playing time, they scored again, and again five minutes after that.

"Wow! Is our team that good or does theirs really suck?" Henry asked.

"We probably won't know until they play someone else," Carol said. "I saw a poster outside that said we were 5-0 coming into this contest, so I'm guessing the team is really good. Unfortunately, I don't understand anything that's going on down there except when one of our team carries the ball into the end zone."

"Well, look at the bright side," Henry said.

"Is there a bright side?"

"We're cuddled together under a blanket keeping warm together and I'm not attempting to explain anything that's going on."

"I was going to ask you about that. Not the cuddling thing. I understand that really well. I was wondering about why you weren't explaining things. Isn't that what guys are supposed to do at sporting events?"

"I'm a computer geek. The only sport I understand is the one I participate in. Golf is a long way from football!" Henry said.

He turned toward her and she kissed him.

"If we keep this up, we might have to put the blanket over our heads!"

RATHER THAN PULL the blanket over their heads, Henry and Carol left the stadium at halftime with the score at 42-10. They hadn't been that interested in the game anyway. Once they were in Henry's car and he had the heater running, they kissed over the console. Carol kept the blanket over her and Henry kept his hands busy beneath it.

"We'd better get out of the parking lot before more people start leaving the game," Henry said, pulling back. "It's five o'clock."

"Oh, crap! How long do football games last?" Carol asked.

"Three-and-a-half or four hours, I guess."

"Let's go then. I'd rather not be sitting here with my bra around my neck and my shirt and jacket wide open."

"Mmm. A fond farewell, then," Henry said, squeezing one of the exposed breasts again.

He fastened his seat belt and pulled out of their parking space. There was already a line of cars exiting the parking lot. Carol spent a minute getting her bra in place and her shirt buttoned before fastening her own seatbelt. Then they both started giggling.

"That felt almost like high school," Henry said.

"I never had anything feel that good in high school," Carol answered. "I mean, not that I'm innocent and all, but attending an all-girls school and being super studious, I didn't have a lot of social activities. Even when I dated, it wasn't as fun as this was."

"I'm glad you think this was fun. I'd hate to imagine I was the only one enjoying it," Henry said. "Shall we go someplace for dinner?"

"Yeah, if you'd like. I really can't stay out late, though. You wouldn't believe the amount of anatomy homework I have this weekend."

"Anything I can help with?"

They both started laughing again.

"Ah... you know next weekend starts our fall break," Carol said. "I promised I'd go back to Cleveland, but I wouldn't have to leave as soon as classes are out on Friday. We could find someplace to study anatomy together for the weekend."

"How were you planning to get back to Cleveland?"

"Ugh. Greyhound."

"Why don't I drive you back. We could break the trip up a little. It's such a long way. We might need to stop at cheap motels a couple of nights."

"It's only, like, two hours."

"Yeah. I really hate to make those long trips all at once."

"We could leave after last class on Friday and maybe find someplace exotic to stay like Youngstown."

"There must be a Motel 6 there," Henry said.

Carol looked at him in horror. "Would you really take me to a Motel 6 when I'm offering to let you study my anatomy? In detail?"

"Not unless you insisted. Trust me. I'll find us someplace suitable," Henry answered.

"I don't know exactly why, but I actually do trust you. Um... After dinner tonight... I guess I don't really need to get back to start studying right away. We could find a place and explore a little more before you take me back."

HENRY MET PROFESSOR Jacoby and Don Harvey at the club for brunch Sunday morning at eleven.

"Professor Jacoby, this is my patent attorney, Don Harvey," Henry introduced them. "I thought it would be good to have him along because I don't understand all the ins and outs of this patent stuff and the limitations of our testing."

"Great idea, Henry. Dale Jacoby," the professor said, offering his hand to Don. They shook and went in to partake of the buffet brunch.

When they'd served themselves and sat, Henry slid a non-disclosure form over to his professor. Jacoby read it over before signing and dating it. He handed it to Don. The attorney folded it and put it in an inside pocket.

"If you hadn't had one of those ready, I'd have been seriously concerned," Jacoby said. "But as prepared as you were with a time and location for our meeting, I was pretty confident. Henry, you're well ahead of others in your class. Tell me about what you've got."

"In high school, I started developing a suite of utilities for optimizing computers and streamlining software based on the user's needs. We've filed three patents and two copyrights on the applications. But those are all kind of background patents and apps for what I want to do," Henry said.

"The copyrights, of course, are fairly simple to file and issue," Don said. "I'm expecting the patents will start issuing within a month or two. There has been no request for revision or clarification."

"That's a testament to both the invention and your ability as a patent attorney," Jacoby said. "I've had patents in process for three years."

"What Henry is proposing might take longer, but we need a dependable testbed before I can even begin to file the next series of patents," Don said. They turned back to Henry.

"The initial concept was a pretty simple adaptation of what I'd been doing manually for a few years on my own and my mother's computers," Henry said. "It involved searching for hidden processes that slowed down application performance, defragmenting and optimizing hard disks, and tuning the running of the system and the hardware. What I am working on now is an adaptation of a narrow intelligence app that will work algorithmically instead of on a lookup table, and more importantly that will learn from the user's computer experience. In other words, it might do a simple optimization when it's first installed, but then continue to tune the device as it learns the user's preferences and actual usage."

"Whoa! That means you are creating an app you expect to keep running in the background that will kill other things running in the background?" Jacoby said.

"That's a simple way to put it."

"Okay. Jump forward with me a minute. How do you expect people to receive that? People are panicked enough these days about unknown things on their computer. Why would they install something to live on it?" Jacoby asked.

"Good question," Henry said. "To answer it, we have to ask why people are so cautious about such a thing these days. I believe it's because AI software currently reports everything it learns to big brother. Whoever owns the software code. We know already that these megacorps use that information to target the user with advertising. But they also use it to gather detailed personal information that might give them power over the user in yet unknown ways. We've already seen the federal government subpoenaing user information on associations, searches, and email, or simply raiding it from government agencies."

"We live in a connected world," Jacoby said.

"So, let's disconnect from it. Current renditions of AI-enabled applications reside in or report to the cloud, not the computer. What I'm proposing is an app that resides on the computer and actively *prevents* personal information, including how the app is being used, from leaving the computer. Since it is capable of learning the user's preferences, it doesn't even need to be constantly upgraded. Only if the big guys decide to actively go after the app will it need to have protective upgrades."

"Well, shit. The big guys, as you call them, will hate that," Jacoby said. "This needs to be tested in absolute secrecy or they would start building defenses against it before it's ever released."

"That's the problem with most of the testing resources we've identified," Don said. "We need to lock in confidentiality in such a way that testers are actually excited about maintaining it."

"Offering them something valuable for maintaining the confidentiality rather than beating them with a wet noodle if they betray it," Jacoby nodded.

The three men took their time over brunch and brainstormed several ideas for finding and maintaining testers for the project. They didn't have drinks, but the brunch still extended past two hours.

"HOW ARE YOU funding all this, Henry?" Jacoby asked after they'd said good-bye to Don. "Just having your attorney at this meeting must have cost $500, plus the meal."

Henry stopped and looked at the clear sky when they were outside.

"Good faith and promises," he sighed. "Don and I are keeping track of his expenses and I've agreed to cut him in for a part of the proceeds from the sale of the patents. That's a lot of faith to have in the inventions of an eighteen-year-old kid. My parents are providing me with housing and meals, and college expenses I can't cover. I have a part-time job here at the club. And I've been really conservative with the way I'm spending my grants at the university."

"That's not an adequate way to start a business like you want."

"I have three partners. We created an LLC to invest in and begin the corporation when we're ready to get it open. Not a lot of money there, but we all put into it."

"When do you think you'll be ready?"

"I'm loaded to the max with credits. I'd like to finish in three years and have an office I can move into as soon as I have the degree in hand."

"Well, here's some more faith. When you need some capital to get things started, tell me. I'm in. Won't be enough to support lavish offices and high sal-aries, but it will help put some life in your company. While you focus on your inventions, I'll start pulling my finances together so I'm ready when you are."

"Thank you, sir. Your help in getting the testbed set up is really appreciated. It was a major hurdle."

HENRY TEXTED HIS partners with the news that he had a testbed set up for his newest rendition. He also mentioned the interest of his professor so they could get the corporation set up. They were equally enthused.

"Does that mean we won't be testing for you again?" Chastity asked.

"No. It means we'll all have a more formal testing contract. It doesn't really change anything for us because the LLC will hold the contracts."

"I need to buy a fireproof file cabinet," Chastity said. "It will be a small one, but we need someplace to put the contracts and our agreement. I'd sure feel better if we had a more secure email."

"In about a month or so," Henry said. "I'm setting up a self-hosted server, so we won't be using any hosting services for our email. It just takes time to get it set up."

"We're holding expenses to only what we have to have," Luke said. "Our resources have to get us through to startup."

"We'll make it," Isobel said. "Money grows when you plant it."

None of them were certain what she meant by that, but it sounded encouraging.

8

IMPATIENCE

HENRY PULLED UP to the residence hall where Carol was waiting for him Friday afternoon. He put her bag in the back of the car and kissed her before opening the door for her.

"We're off!" he said when he started the car and pulled away from the curb.

"I can't believe I'm going off on a dirty weekend," Carol said as she reached across to put her hand on Henry's leg.

"I have never heard it put that way," he laughed. "How about a romantic weekend retreat?"

"That does sound more… romantic. Um… We don't have to spend all our time in bed, do we?"

"I have no idea what there is to do in Youngstown, but I certainly hope we'll be able to find something else to do. I'm a teenager, but I'm not a super-man when it comes to being a lover," Henry said.

"Oh, thank God. I haven't had sex since high school got out in the spring. I don't want to be too sore to walk when we get to Cleveland."

"Hon, we'll take however much time we need and do whatever feels right to do," Henry reassured her, patting her hand, still on his leg.

"So, what's the dream, Henry?" Carol said. "Um… I don't mean about screwing all weekend. I mean for life. What do you really want to be when you grow up?"

"The life dream?"

"Yeah. Like I really want to be a doctor and practice women's medicine."

"You mean like gynecology?"

"There are other parts of women," Carol snorted. "I just think women need to be tended by people who don't see all their problems as hysteria and the solution to be an orgasm."

"That's pretty eighteenth century."

"Well, we've been regressing as fast as possible."

"Okay. Well, I want to conquer AI. I want to be the one who creates applications that are needed and uses AI to accomplish it. All the major research is toward how to get a general AI and once the tool is there, then they go hunting for a use for it. I've got some ideas for solving some real problems that I think would be better if there was a degree of artificial intelligence used in the process."

"Will AI become truly intelligent?"

"Not in my opinion. AI depends on processing power to arrive at solutions, not on creativity. But *real* intelligence—human intelligence—doesn't require massive amounts of processing power. It involves the creative instinct to leap beyond the available data."

"How are you going to go about it? I mean, becoming a doctor has a series of well-defined steps. Degree. Medical school. Internship. Residency. General practice. What are the steps to becoming an AI developer?"

"Not as clearly defined," Henry said. "I'm already an AI developer. I have two copyrights and three patents pending. And I'm hoping to file a couple more by the end of the year. The big question is how to make it successful. That's not something one person can do. I have three partners and we are all working toward having a corporation set up and funded by the time we're out of college."

"Wow! Fast!"

"In some things, I'm not a very patient guy. I want to see some of my solutions being used by the public. On the other hand, if we need all weekend just to get to know each other without actually having sex, I'm in. It's just in my career and development that I'm impatient."

"So, in four years, you expect to have your degree and your corporation set up and funded so you can start selling your solutions?"

"Three years. I'm taking every class I can fit into my schedule to accelerate my degree. Which is why the rest of my 'free time' for the fall break will be spent writing code."

"A new application?"

"This time, I'm setting up the server to host our company so the four of us partners can work together in a secure environment. None of our email, for example, will be stored on a hosting site. It will all be on our own server and connected through a virtual private network. Do you want to tell me about ovaries now? Because getting any deeper into what I'm doing is about as interesting as dissecting a single aspect of medicine."

"People do that, you know, but we should be able to enjoy our weekend without boring each other to tears with minutiae," Carol said. "That being said, you provided just enough that it was interesting even if I didn't understand half the terms you were using."

"In an ideal world, no one has to understand the terms to use the product."

"So, in that ideal world, what happens when you create the perfect AI? What will become of Henry Pascal?"

"I suppose I'll die," he said, reaching down to give her hand a squeeze. She still didn't remove it from his leg.

"What? No retirement plans?"

"Do you know anyone our age with retirement plans?"

"Sort of. I want to retire when I'm young enough to enjoy life, but too old to have children. Then I want a beach home—say Malibu—convenient to the local golf club. And I guess, around then, I'll be interested in having companionship from a nice guy—or a girl if it's better—who wants to wake up next to me each morning as we grow old."

"Hmm. I think I'd like to have children one day," Henry said. "That assumes that I find a wife, since I don't think I can bear them, and it also assumes that the world starts getting better instead of continuing a desperate downward spiral. I'd be pretty cognizant of the kind of world I was bringing kids into."

"You've left the door open. I'm thinking of slamming it closed. Going into women's medicine is a last-ditch effort to improve things. It's really comforting the downtrodden and pointing out that the world sucks, so she doesn't have to."

Henry laughed at the double entendre. It was amazing they were nearly to Youngstown already. He checked his GPS for the exit number.

"Do you want to head straight to the hotel and check in, or go out to have some dinner first. It's almost six. Dinner has less pressure than going to our room."

"It seems that way. Mostly because when we get to the room, I don't think I'm going to want to leave it for such a minor thing as eating," she laughed.

"So, let's do dinner and then go test out the room to be sure it is suitable for our weekend plans."

HENRY HAD CHOSEN a suites hotel near the freeway. Carol found an unassuming family restaurant nearby. After a light dinner, they stopped at a QuickStop and picked up a few snacks and soft drinks.

"Um... condoms?" Carol asked.

"I came prepared this time."

"Thank you! That makes me feel better already," she smiled.

They checked into the hotel and made their way down a quiet corridor to their room. Henry opened the door and held it for her.

"Henry, this is really nice!" Carol said.

"You didn't really think I'd take you to a Motel 6, did you?"

"No, but there are probably things that would fall between that and this. I didn't mean for you to break the bank."

"I'd like to go on and on about how nothing is too good for you, but the truth is that I found a good deal on the room, so spending a couple of nights here is quite promising," he said.

"Definitely. Um... Before we do anything else, could we spend some time just kissing and making out? I mean before we lose all our clothes and jump into bed."

"You are definitely my kind of girl, Carol. I hate to rush things. And look! Over on the other side of the divider, there's a nice sofa and a TV."

"I don't care about the TV. I mean, I'm not kidding anyone about why we're here. I'd just like to get warmed up first."

They got their shoes off, used the bathroom, and settled onto the sofa. Henry sat and Carol laid back in his arms and looked up at him.

"This is nice. You know I could never do this if I didn't like you, Henry. I don't even know what possessed me to check you into my room at the golf tournament. That was really unlike me. I'm glad I did, though. It's been fun talking to you and I know it's fun kissing you, too."

They started kissing with little kisses at first before seriously locking lips and exploring each other's mouths.

"Mmm. I like kissing you, Carol."

"You're a great kisser. Let's do it some more."

They went back to kissing and somewhere along the line their hands got in on the action. Carol worked the buttons on his shirt open and Henry caressed her breasts.

"If you wear a shirt with buttons tomorrow, I might not be able to restrain myself from just ripping it open and having the buttons fly all over the room," she murmured as they kissed some more.

"Hmm. I have a western shirt. You know, with the yoke front. A conservative one, not a line dancing shirt. But it does have snaps down the front. I *hear* girls like them because they can rip them open without having to sew all the buttons on again."

"That's a positive. There's something appealing about having the buttons flying all over the room, though."

"Can I pull your sweater off so I don't get tempted to do any ripping?" he asked.

"Yeah. And take your shirt the rest of the way off. I'd like to feel your skin against mine."

"This could become one of my favorite feelings in the world," Henry said, pulling her closer so they were chest to chest and lip to lip.

"Don't go thinking I don't want you to pick me up and carry me to bed now," she murmured as their excitement mounted.

"I'd hate to think we weren't on the same page about that," he said.

It was a little awkward standing up from the sofa because of their entangled position, but eventually, he managed to pick her up and carry her around the room divider to the bed, while she did her best to keep her lips and tongue touching his.

Once they'd managed to get the spread off the bed while they were on top of it and get the sheet and blanket turned down, they stretched out and continued making out with more serious intent. They were soon naked. Henry stroked through her wet folds and found her hot button while she stroked his cock.

"Can I go down on you?" he asked, kissing down to her breasts and intending to go further.

"No," she panted. "I mean, yes, of course, I'd love for you to go down on me, but not yet. Let's just progress to the old-fashioned way first. I'm really ready for you."

"I won't object to that," he said. He reached for a condom from the pack he'd set on the bedside table.

"That's a big package," she sighed.

"You said to bring one or twenty. I don't expect to use them all, but there are definitely more than one."

"Believe me, it pays to be prepared."

She took over rolling the condom on his penis and then swung a leg over his mid-section.

"I hope you don't mind," she said. "You're pretty big and I'd rather be the one controlling the rate of entry and the depth."

"Believe me, I love looking up at you like this," he said as she swiped the tip of his cock through her juices and then positioned him for entry.

"It's been a while since I last did this," she said. "Oh, God! I think you're bigger than Bob."

"Who's Bob?"

"Battery Operated Boyfriend," she laughed, sinking a little farther onto him. "I haven't had a lover in a long time, but I haven't been going completely without."

"I'm glad to hear that. Carol, you're torturing me. This is so good."

"Yes, keep playing with my breasts. I really like what you're doing. Yes! With the tongue as well. I've got to figure out how to work this into my schedule more often."

"I agree. Oh! You're..."

"You're all the way in, I think. Henry, that's so good. You stretch me, but it doesn't hurt. It just feels... fucking fantastic."

Conversation came to an end. Carol leaned forward and kissed him as she pulsed up and down his cock.

"Babe. I'm not going to last long. You feel so good."

"Don't worry about it. I didn't expect to come the first time, but I'm really close. Oh, yeah. Pump into me. This is... so... good!"

They were both caught up in the pinnacle of their orgasms and held each other tightly as they returned to kissing.

THEY WERE SURPRISED to find it was only 8:00, but that was the way of first times. They relaxed, talked some more, and then headed back to bed. This time, Henry managed to complete his journey down her body and set about making sure Carol had reached an earth-shaking climax before he was done.

"Oh, God. You must be related to James Bond!" Carol panted.

"What?"

"Moneypenny tells him 'You always were a cunning linguist.' I never thought I'd actually meet one."

"It's just one of my favorite things," he said. "I love to give you pleasure."

"Success! Yeah! Success," Carol said. "Give me a few minutes to catch my breath and I'll return the favor."

"You don't need to. Like I said, I get great pleasure from giving you pleasure."

"Then wrap it up and stick it in again," she advised. "After your linguistics, I'm flooding the area. You can slide right in."

Henry put on a new condom and this time mounted in the more traditional missionary position. Carol welcomed him into her arms and her body. He was also a little slower to reach a peak this time, and she made it to the top before him. The excitement of feeling her orgasm drove him over the edge and he filled the second condom.

They didn't bother to dress before using the bathroom to brush teeth and get ready for bed. When they did get in bed again, sex was further from their thoughts than it had been. They cuddled together much the way they had during the golf tournament and went to sleep.

"So, WHAT IS the meaning of life?" Carol asked on Sunday when they checked out of the hotel and headed the last hour to Cleveland.

They'd spent time on Saturday exploring Youngstown, including the old mill and the art museum. It was the art museum that had inspired the conversation on the meaning of life. One of the exhibits had been labeled 'Artists, Art, and Meaning.' They'd begun the conversation Saturday night, but became far too caught up in pleasuring and exploring each other to treat it seriously.

Henry hesitated for a minute before he replied.

"I think we spend too much time searching for that answer," he said. "Life *is* the meaning. People try to find meaning in life instead of embracing life as the meaning."

"I take it you aren't religious."

"Not really. Although, maybe that is conditional as well. I don't look for meaning in religion. I used to, but I lost interest in that. Religion is a bunch of unrelated sayings designed to keep people enslaved to whatever that religion is."

"But life?"

"You're born and you die. Between is all the meaning, the reward, and the punishment that you will ever get. I think one of the reasons I'm so impatient to get my software established, have my company up and operating, and push forward with my goals is that the ending chapter could be written at any time. I have something I consider so important that I can't wait for it."

"Oh. Well, I guess I'm glad you took a break from it to spend some time with me this weekend," Carol said, pulling her hand away from its normal resting place on his leg. He reached to put it back.

"Don't believe that. Being with you this weekend is just as important as any other part of my life. More important than most—say, like golf. That's something I do to stay fit and healthy and feel like I'm good at something other than coding. But it isn't more important than anything, really. People are the most important part of life. Not computer code."

"I'm going to need a while to process that. I can do it, but I want to contemplate it for a while. I'm really more important than your big goals?"

"You know how important? Look in the back seat."

"Yeah. There's just a black bag."

"That black bag is my computer. Have you seen me open it this weekend."

"No! Henry! That's so sweet."

"I might stop someplace on the way back to Pitt tonight and open it to stay up all night, but we need to have a balanced life."

"How did you arrive at that?"

"My senior lit teacher in high school was really old. As in retirement old. Maybe a long time past. He led a discussion about goals and the creative mind and recited a poem by someone even older who wrote it before World War II. It was by an Indiana radio personality and started out, 'My life I carry in a leaky pail, and drop by drop my minutes fall upon the sand; fall upon the thirsty sand and disappear. But I must hurry on. My goal lies just ahead.' It ends up with the guy reaching the end of his life and discovering his goal was a field of bleached bones and he'd wasted his life. I'm a bit of a sentimentalist and I printed out the poem and put it on my bedroom wall to remind me that life is the purpose of living."

"Henry, sometimes you are so deep. Um... the next exit is ours. I didn't ask before. Do you want to come in and meet my parents? I promise they won't assume we are getting married, but they'd probably like to meet you. I didn't tell them we were leaving campus Friday. They think we just drove up today."

"It's up to you, hon. If it's awkward for you, I'll just unload your suitcase and give you a kiss goodbye at the car. If you'd rather I gave you that kiss on your front step, I'll come in and meet your parents."

"Yeah. Let's."

THE REST OF Henry's fall break was spent with his head buried in code. Except for the after-school sessions he held for his young golfers. Being with Carol for the weekend had reminded him that his career goals were not all-consuming. Life was for living. Carol was a pretty good reason to take time away.

That being said, getting a company site set up that would enable his partners and him to communicate securely was a top priority. It would also serve as the host for the testers to get the app and to give their feedback.

Following Professor Jacoby's advice, the testers enrolled by digitally signing a non-disclosure with PRPP LLC. None of the partners were identified. Each tester was given a log-in to the download site that would work just one time. They couldn't give their log-in to another person, for example, and download another copy of the software.

It seemed like a lot of legal work, and Don Harvey had created the testing non-disclosure. But both Don and Jacoby had impressed the seriousness of Henry maintaining confidentiality—and even a level of secrecy—regarding the project. The bulk of the testers would be recruited by Jacoby. Since most of them would be students in the same department as Henry, it seemed important to keep Henry's name out of the information they received.

There was the typical threat of dire repercussions if the non-disclosure was violated. Don referred to that as 'forty lashes with a wet noodle.' But those who maintained confidentiality and faithfully filled out their reports would be rewarded with a release version of the software to use on their computers.

It seemed fair to most, so the agreements started coming in and by Thanksgiving, the test was in full swing.

9

START-UP

"WHAT HAS GOT into you?" Chastity demanded. "You've been squirrelly all week with text messages and voicemail at all hours. Have you even slept this week?"

"Not much," Henry said. "Um... Not at all last night. I had to put my girlfriend on a bus for Cleveland this morning, so we didn't want to waste the night."

"Girlfriend? Is that what this is all about? Don't tell me you're getting serious about a girl before you're even nineteen! I mean, I understand Luke and Isobel. They spend most of their time trying to convince themselves they aren't madly in love, but they are."

"Oh, it's not quite like that. I mean, it's good, but neither Carol nor I have time for much of a relationship other than getting together to screw about once every other weekend. She's pre-med and I'm..."

"Obsessed," Chastity said. "What's with insisting that Luke and Isobel get here by noon?"

"That's when Don Harvey will be here," Henry said. "My patent attorney. I went in to finalize the patent filing on the new system Monday and he gave me some good news. But I want him here to tell you all about it so we can all be on the same page when it comes time for a decision."

"Now you've got *me* antsy. You might need to take me someplace and settle me down. You know how to do it so well."

"I'm sure you'll be fine until after the meeting at least," Henry laughed.

"Does that mean you might settle me down later?" she asked.

77

"Mmm... Maybe."

"Okay, it's a quarter till noon. I see a red Corvette entering the parking lot," Chastity said.

"I see Don's Lincoln just behind them."

It took a few minutes for everyone to get parked and gather at the door of the golf club. Henry introduced everyone to Don Harvey and they got seated for the casual lunch served at the club. They ordered and then Henry took a deep breath and calmed himself to get things started.

"Okay, you've all noticed I've been a little hyper this week. That's because of the news Don gave me on Monday when I went in to finish the application for the fourth patent. That's for the system and method being tested with our testers now. You know we've all been running it from a command line and there's not much of an application built on the system, but that will change in the next few months. But Don had big news. Don?"

"Congratulations to Henry and by extension to all of you. The first two patents have issued. I expect the third will follow by Christmas. That's on top of the two copyrights for the initial software," Don said.

"All right!" Luke exclaimed. "We only have pop, but here's a toast to the first successes of our—meaning Henry's—big business endeavor."

Everyone raised a glass of something and congratulated Henry.

"That's not all," Henry said. "It seems Don has been fielding offers for us."

"Somebody wants to buy *us?*" Isobel asked. "Don't you mean offers for you, Henry?"

"It could be interpreted that way, but I choose not to. I'm writing code, guys. I'm not thinking business. Don has been keeping me from going off half-cocked. Don, if you can speak around that BLT, better fill them in on the offer," Henry said.

"Thanks for giving me a few minutes to get at least one wedge of this sandwich down. You know, all the other places in town have decided they need to add something to a perfectly good idea. They want to add avocado or put it on rye bread, or—God forbid—pour some kind of sauce or cheese on it. This BLT is just what it's supposed to be: bacon, lettuce, and tomato on white toast with a smear of mayo. But that's not the offer you're asking about."

They laughed but waited expectantly while Don wiped his hands.

"A large computer security software company has seen the patent and the copyright on the first piece of software. They've decided it would make a good addition to their suite of tools and would like to make it a part of their offering. Of course, their opening bid was to acquire all rights to the patent and the copyrighted application for a ridiculously small sum. Not enough to get the company you are planning started.

"I've been teasing them along with alternate ideas, but have carefully left out any details of where the development is going. They'll figure that out soon enough, though, when they see the new filing. So right now, their offer is for the first patent and application that was based on it. But you don't have to sell outright. I believe they would accept a deal to buy the app and development rights to it and license the patent it's built on."

"Are you going to do it, Henry?" Chastity asked.

"Are *we* going to do it? I am not cutting my support team out of our first deal. If we do it, we all profit from it."

"Yeah, but you invented it. The most we can say we did was some testing," Luke said.

"What are the numbers?" Isobel asked. She'd apparently accepted that they were joint owners without hesitating.

"I believe that we'll be able to pull in seven figures when we're done. Not high seven, but more than a million," Don said. "Their real interest is in the patented method and system. They want the application and development rights so we—or Henry—doesn't keep developing that line. In our conversations, Henry has said he considered that a test for making something that worked, not something that he'd keep improving. The other apps and patents stand alone. I think we can license the patent for a long-term royalty without a second thought, but these guys seem interested enough that we could license this one patent with non-exclusive rights for a one-time license fee that would give you enough to get your business started."

"Holy cow! Henry, why are you even considering sharing this with us?" Chastity insisted. "You could fund the startup costs and own the entire corporation."

"Guys, I started developing this shit when I was a freshman in high school. It was the three of you who listened, brainstormed, and even tested my initial attempts. Even when the results weren't pleasing. We are the only ones who ever tested the app before we'd turned eighteen. That means our puny non-disclosures we signed were never enforceable. Not like the one we're using now. What I'm proposing is that I sell the patent and copyright outright to our LLC. Our little preliminary company can then license and sell them to this manufacturer. That money will be paid to the LLC and used to fund our startup. It gives us all equal shares as founders."

"How many thousand do you want for them?" Isobel asked. She'd been typing on her cell phone during the entire meal and her salad was still untouched.

"I have to show that it's a real purchase, so how about twenty each for the patent and copyright?" Henry asked.

"So, forty thousand from a company that has a total of not quite four in the bank?" Isobel scoffed.

"No, no, no! Twenty *dollars* each. That's only $40 total, okay?" Henry said.

"You're kidding," Chastity whispered. Henry shook his head.

"I'm dead serious. You guys need to have a significant vested interest in this company and this is the best way I can think of to get it."

The discussion and questions continued through the rest of the meal and eventually Isobel got around to eating her salad. Don also had to tell them what he would get out of the sale for negotiating the whole deal. He was asking for only five percent. It didn't sound like much until he quoted $75,000 as his expected take.

"I'M REALLY HORNY now," Chastity said as they walked to Henry's car. "I doubt Isobel and Luke will even say hello to their families until tomorrow. If you'd expressed the least interest, we'd have been invited to join them. Can you imagine? Isobel and me with our legs parted and you and Luke switching back and forth between us?"

"No matter how erotic that image may seem, I don't want to be in any room where Luke is balling either of you. It's just not my thing," Henry laughed as he brushed her lips with his.

"Um... So, is it okay for you to come up to my apartment for a while? I mean with your girlfriend and all?" Chastity said.

"Ever heard of a hall pass?" Henry asked.

"I don't think so."

"It's a limited permission to fuck one other person during a particular span of time. It's pretty much what Avril had last summer when she slept with me and then went back to her boyfriend. You are my hall pass for the weekend."

"Wow! What did you have to trade for that?"

"Carol has a favorite cousin who will be joining her family for Thanksgiving. Seems they've had at least one encounter before. She wants to try her new-found skills on this girl. She thinks she's learned a lot since the last time they were together."

"A girl?"

"Yeah. Who knows? She might come back a confirmed lesbian. She sure likes it when *I* go down on her."

"So do I."

"JUST A LITTLE more. Oh, goddess! I'm... Ohhh!" Chastity moaned as Henry licked her to fulfillment. "No! Yes! More! I'm coming again!"

Henry was determined to give her the best he had. He'd learned a lot from his fairly regular, though infrequent, times with Carol. When Chastity began to come down, Henry lay beside her and planted little kisses on the side of her head and face. Chastity's hand circled his penis.

"Yeah. Give me just a minute so I can fully appreciate what's coming," she moaned as she stroked.

Henry reached to the bedside table and grabbed a condom. When he was ready to roll it on, Chastity took over.

"Yeah. You've got another partner. Better take precautions," she said. She put a leg over Henry and looked down at him as he held his cock in position for her to settle onto.

"How about you? Don't you have another partner?"

"Yeah. A couple. Or three. I go in to a special clinic in town to get tested every two weeks. It's recommended for sexually active women. I insist they use condoms, too."

"Wow! With so many options, why choose me tonight?" Henry asked.

"So many reasons. You made me horny, so why take that to anyone else?"

"How did I make you horny? We sat in a business meeting all through lunch."

Chastity started rocking back and forth with Henry buried deep in her. Henry was ramping up pretty quickly now that he had skin in the game, but Chastity was getting there just as fast.

"Yeah," she sighed. "A business meeting in which you basically gave each of us a quarter of a million dollars. I'm not quite as motivated by money as Isobel is, but the idea of getting a quarter of a million dollars from you definitely got my juices flowing."

"And I loved tasting every drop," Henry laughed.

The juices flowing this time moved them both closer and they focused on their impending climaxes. When they hit, they crashed over them in waves leaving both spent and panting.

"Yeah. We can start all over again in a few minutes," Chastity gasped. "I wonder if there is any aphrodisiac as potent as money."

"None of us will actually see any of that money, you know. Not for years, more than likely. It should get us through the startup phase as long as we're careful. And let's not forget there will be taxes," he said.

"Will we have to come up with the money for taxes on what goes to the LLC?" she asked.

"Not exactly. One of the advantages of having the LLC is that it can deduct each of our share of taxes and pay them on our behalf. It just means that out of whatever we end up making on the deal, almost a third will go to taxes of one sort or another. And, we'll have to hire a good tax consultant to figure it out. I trust Isobel with managing the money, but until she has a few more classes under her belt, I don't think she's ready to do corporate or partnership taxes."

"Still, if Don gets the deal he thinks he can, we'll end up with nearly a million in the bank."

"That's another thing we need to deal with. I don't know if an individual bank should hold a million in deposits for us. There's something about a limit on deposit insurance. We might need to diversify in some way. That is something I'm more than willing to let Luke and Isobel handle. It makes my head hurt."

"I think you got my juices flowing again. Henry, I don't know what makes you so generous with us, but I'll give you anything you want if I can."

"I know the limitations of that," he said, kissing her closed lips. He rolled on another condom and slid into her depths.

"Yeah. You know, even discounting all the other stuff, this has its own rewards. Move in me, lover. Take your time and build us up to a good one."

They did take their time, shifting positions, slowing down or speeding up when necessary, and generally enjoying playing with each other. When the explosion came, both were ready and held each other in the afterglow.

For a few minutes. Then, Chastity was up and headed for a shower. Henry dressed and waited for her to emerge before he left. When she left the bathroom, all she was wearing was a towel wrapped around her head. Henry knelt and started at her feet, kissing his way up her body until he reached her lips.

"I still worship you, my goddess," he said.

"I feel it in my bones—as well as other places. Go home now. I know your parents are waiting to have you."

"They always have me. What about yours? You never say anything about your parents."

"Yeah… well… I left home when I was seventeen. I was taken in by a nice older couple who sheltered me until I was out of high school. They aren't really interested in me coming back these days."

"Chas, do you need someplace to go for Thanksgiving? You know you're welcome at my house!"

"No, Henry. I'm having Thanksgiving with Isobel and her family. Her mother still thinks there's hope for turning me into a Catholic. I like to lead her on a little."

"Okay. Let me know if you need anything, Chastity. I can't anticipate everything."

"You always take care of me, Henry. Of all of us."

HENRY MADE SURE to take care of her on Friday as well. It was Chastity's nineteenth birthday and he wanted to make sure she fully enjoyed the day. He made arrangements at the club for her to enjoy a spa morning and then took her to a late lunch at the Tower revolving restaurant.

"Why are you doing all of this for me?"

"Because I want you to know how important you are to me and to our company and our friendship. You know Luke and Isobel helped pay for the spa day. They care about you, too. Chas, I know we aren't boyfriend and girlfriend, but we have a very important relationship. It extends far beyond just being business partners."

"As long as you remember that part about not being boyfriend and girlfriend, we'll be fine. And remember, I'm your personnel department. When you're actually ready for a serious relationship, I'll find the perfect girl. Don't try to hire someone without me!"

"Oh, it will be years. I'm not even looking for prospects. I barely have time to breathe with everything that's going on," Henry said. They watched the view of the city as the restaurant slowly revolved at the top of the building. Eventually, Henry paid the bill and they left.

"I suppose you'd like sex now," she said when they reached his car. Henry looked a little puzzled.

"Chas, this is *your* day. You don't have to do anything to please me. I've been guessing what would make you happy today. Do you want to have sex?" he asked.

"Not really," she sighed. "I mean, we just had sex Wednesday. We shouldn't get in the habit."

"What would you like to do?"

"Can we go see the new *Hunger Games* movie?"

"Sure! Sounds like fun."

THERE WAS RAIN, but the tees at the driving range were sheltered. Henry and Luke set up next to each other Saturday afternoon. The temperature hadn't reached 40° and both guys were hampered in their driving by the heavy sweatshirts they wore.

"Are your lousy drives the result of too much clothing on or is your game falling to pieces?" Luke asked.

"Yeah. A little of both," Henry admitted. "We took a break starting in mid-October and only our top five went to the championships down in Florida. Obviously, I wasn't one of them. In a way, I was thankful."

"Why? I expected you to be in the lead for a varsity position."

"Not likely as a freshman. And high school gave me an inflated opinion of my skills. Some of the guys on the team are near professional level. The thing is, I couldn't have afforded the time. I was busy getting our server set up and that last patent filed. This is going to be a big one, Luke. Don is holding it until the deal with Mc… you know… is closed. We don't want them to see this one and try to get it rolled into what they're buying."

"I've used the command line and the stats generated on my computer show a twenty percent improvement in performance. Every application I use is running faster. But that's pretty much what the app we're selling did. Will we have to let them have the new stuff anyway?"

"No. The new app accomplishes a similar result, but its processes are completely unrelated to the first app. It doesn't share any code, so it can't be considered a derivative. The big difference is that I managed to harness an artificial narrow intelligence to it. Through the use of prediction algorithms instead of general AI, it's able to learn and store the behaviors and preferences of the user. That means that the longer the app resides on your computer, the more efficient your computer should be. It's not a one-and-done operation."

"All I got out of that was that I should be impressed. What else should we be able to expect from the patent that makes it more valuable than the others?"

Henry finally got a good drive off that dropped around the 200-yard marker. They both stopped to celebrate that for a second. Then he shanked his next drive.

"The big thing about this is pattern recognition," Henry said. "It sees the pattern of what you do on your computer and when it sets about optimizing, it does so for the way you use your computer. That pattern recognition can be done on a much smaller scale than what happens with general AI. It can actually run on just the information that's on your computer. But it's expandable. It could be installed on a network. Let's say you want everything directly connected to your computer to run better and faster. We'll be able to tell it how many degrees of separation should be used for optimization. Every computer connected to your computer? Every computer connected to those? And so on. It could run on just the network server and optimize every computer in the company."

"That could be huge! We'll have this running in our company?"

"Mostly, we already do. It's a little less automated. You've already installed the run line on your computer. But if you uninstalled it, the copy running on our company server would automatically work on any device we connected to it. So, when you connect to the new server, your computer would automatically be optimized."

"That sounds a little big brotherish."

"It could be. In reality, the company would need to make an ethical decision regarding how much control it should have over employee computers. If it's a company-owned computer on the company network, the company could just have it running as default. But ethically, each employee should know and understand that it is running. And maybe they should have either the opportunity to opt in or opt out of the hosted optimization. I think that's a matter of corporate policy, not the software developer. On the other hand, the company probably has no right to run the app on an employee's personal computer just because he connected to the network."

"Gotcha. It means that we need policies in place for *our* company that are clear and well-understood by our employees. We need to tell them what information is being collected and how it is used with an opt-out that is easy. I'm going to have a lot of other stuff to do besides just getting the corporation papers filed. Chastity and I will need to work on policies and procedures before we ever launch. Like you, I won't be having time for any extracurricular activities next term."

"I'm going to try to stay on the golf team when the spring season starts," Henry said. "But I might never see varsity. I just want to stay close enough that Carol and I can make the most of our non-class time."

"I'd like to meet her sometime. I know Izzy and Chas would be interested. Any chance of a get together over Christmas break?"

"We haven't got a concrete plan yet. You know, she might not want to get sucked into our little world. She's pre-med. She's dating me because only idiots date doctors." Henry paused and then snorted. "When she said that, it meant that she didn't want to date anyone in her program. What does it say about me?"

"Well, my friend, we're all idiots when it comes to women."

10

GETTING REAL

DON NEGOTIATED THE terms of the sale to the security software company and Henry signed the licensing agreements on behalf of the LLC. The buyer agreed to make payment after the first of the year so the group could make arrangements for taxes without being under the pressure of the year-end filing date. They needed to get their finances stabilized before they funded the corporation.

When it came to New Year's Eve, however, they were all excited to celebrate. Carol had taken off for Cleveland as soon as the winter holiday break began, but promised Henry she'd be back for New Year's Eve if he got them a room for the long weekend. There would still be a week of winter break after that and she planned to go on a ski trip with friends from Cleveland.

Their post-Thanksgiving reunion had been strained at first until they decided to tell each other about their encounters with their hall pass partners.

"Well, Chastity reminded me once again that she is not my girlfriend and not to get attached," Henry said. "And when I took her out for her birthday, she didn't want to have sex again so soon after we'd done it the night before Thanksgiving. That was fine. We went to a movie and had a good time, but she's really my business partner. I don't know if even those occasional get-togethers will continue anymore."

"Don't give up on it, really," Carol said. "You won't have me around forever. I can't imagine that the few times we have sex are enough to satisfy your needs. Most of mine are sublimated into studies."

87

They'd gone out Saturday evening just to have this conversation. Carol hesitated a bit before she continued with her side of the adventure.

"I'm in love," she said finally. "And it's frustrating as hell. I mean, we could go find a place for sex right now and it would be mostly me trying to get you to eat me to orgasm so I could forget Taylor."

"Didn't she... come across?"

"Oh, hell, yeah. She sure did. And I spent hours munching between her legs and sleeping with her in my bed. Then Saturday, she packed up to go back to Michigan and told me that it had been fun, but she wasn't going to mention it to her boyfriend or he'd want to join in. She figured that would just mean we'd always have the awkward relationship of us two girls and her husband. She'd be way too jealous for that to ever work. So, she said it was nice but that was the last time."

"Oh, Carol, I'm so sorry. And you really love her."

"I thought she loved me. Henry, I was prepared to come home and tell you we needed to break up because I'd found the love of my life. I'm sorry. It was selfish of me to go home for the break thinking I might actually be going to meet my forever girlfriend."

"What do you want to do, hon?" Henry asked.

"Well, now that I've spewed out everything, that whole idea of having you eat me until I come so hard I forget her doesn't sound half bad. Is there someplace we can go?" she asked.

"That depends. How do you feel about meeting my parents at breakfast tomorrow morning?" he asked.

"Oh! Shit! You mean, go to your room?"

"They've told me often enough that I don't need to be afraid to bring my girlfriend home for the night. They aren't trying to keep us apart."

"Meet your parents?" she said hesitantly. Then she shrugged. "Okay. You met mine and we survived. I'll try not to be too loud!"

IT HAD BEEN a good night and not too awkward at breakfast. That was when they decided to spend the long New Year's weekend together. Henry reserved a room at the Suites Hotel and when he went to Cleveland early on New Year's Eve to pick her up, he and Carol came directly back to the hotel to check in. They spent a comfortable time renewing their relationship in a way they hadn't had a chance to do since their night in his room.

The 'First Annual Company Holiday Party,' as they called it, was held at the Constitution Links Golf Club. Henry and Luke were members in good standing and the party were all given wristbands that declared them too young for alcohol. All except Tom.

Tom was Chastity's date for the party. None of the others knew him. He seemed nice enough, though he was several years older than the rest of them. That might have influenced his slightly condescending attitude toward their 'company.' No one bothered to correct his opinion. Carol was introduced and liked Henry's three partners.

She took a turn dancing with both Luke and Tom as Henry danced with Chastity and Isobel. Soon, Carol was next to him again and the music had begun to slow as midnight approached.

"You've slept with both of them, haven't you," Carol whispered as she kissed his cheek.

"Whatever do you mean?" Henry asked innocently.

"Well, I knew about Chastity. There are little clues about Isobel. That last dance did not require quite *that* much touching. Thankfully. While you were in a clinch with Isobel, I was trying to stay out of one with Tom. He's a little creepy. And he's definitely been drinking."

"He's older, so he doesn't have a non-alcohol wristband," Henry said. "I hope he and Chastity plan to take a cab home."

"Well, it's okay that you've had both of them. I'd fuck both of them."

"Hmm. I might be able to arrange that."

"Really?"

"I don't know if Isobel swings both ways. We'll have to see."

"Well, when classes start again in a week, we'll be much too busy to screw all the time," Carol said. "Hence, this long weekend."

"Where are you going skiing?" Henry asked.

"There's a little place on the lake about twenty-five miles east of Cleveland. We girls reserved it before we graduated last spring. The four of us are supposed to ski during the day and sit around drinking hot chocolate and telling stories about our great adventures at night. And maybe some schnapps."

"Sounds like you'll have a good time."

"Look!" Carol pointed Henry toward where Tom was hanging on to Chastity's arm as she tried to pull away. Carol gave Henry a little push and he headed straight for the conflict.

"That looks a little rough, Tom," Henry said coming up to them.

"Fuck off. It's time for us to leave this hole and start our own party."

"I don't want to leave, Tom. This is my party. I invited you. If you want to leave, go. I'm staying," Chastity said, struggling to free her arm.

"I said we're going," Tom growled, pulling roughly at Chastity.

Henry reached out and grabbed Tom's wrist, just as he had Chastity's He twisted against Tom's skin.

"Hey! Let go, you son of a bitch," Tom said.

"You were told to leave," Henry said. "Let go of Chastity and get your drunk ass out of here."

"I haven't had nearly enough to get drunk," Tom said, pulling his hand away from both Henry and Chastity. He rounded on Henry with a fist raised, just in time to see Luke step up beside him. Isobel and Carol rushed to comfort Chastity.

"It's time for you leave," Henry said again. Luke nodded. The two of them escorted Tom to the door, quickly joined by one of the club security men.

"Mr. Reynolds needs to leave the club," Henry said to the doorman. "Permanently."

"Can I call you a cab, Mr. Reynolds?" the doorman asked. Tom spun as if to have another go at Luke and Henry, only to be met by the combined presence of the doorman and the security guard.

"You can take your filthy nigger hands off me! You two-bit punks with your whore business party. Nobody treats me like that!" Tom spent another minute shouting invective at the partners, the security, the doorman, and everyone inside, as the club employees kept him moving out of the club. Then he stumbled away to his car. As he started the car and pulled out of his parking spot, the doorman spoke into his cell phone.

"Thank you 9-1-1. This is Constitution Links. There is a party leaving the club in a blue Lexus, license plate RAD4141. It is my belief the driver is inebriated and a danger to other travelers. He declined our offer to call a cab."

"One moment, please." There was a moment's silence on the line. "We've dispatched a patrol. Thank you for the report," the operator said. They disconnected.

"Sorry for the inconvenience," Luke said to the doorman. "Not one of our usual people."

"He's been here before," the doorman said. "He won't be allowed in again."

Luke and Henry went back to where Isobel and Carol were comforting Chastity. Carol was examining the bruise discoloring her wrist already.

"I told Chastity we'd take her home tonight," Carol said immediately.

"No problem," Henry said.

"Is he okay?" Chastity asked.

"Don't know. Don't care," Henry said. "The rest of his night is not likely to be what he imagined it would be."

"More importantly, are you okay, Chas?" Luke asked.

"Yeah. It happens sometimes. He sounded like a nice guy when he called and I thought it would be a good innocuous date for the party. We'd have sex later and then I'd go home. Quid pro quo."

"Chas? He called you out of the blue?" Isobel said. "Why would you accept a date with a guy you don't even know?"

"Izzy, wake up. It's what I do. How do you think I came up with a thousand dollars to put in the company or my rent on an apartment by myself and my two cats? Seating people at the Olde Towne Inne? I don't have rich parents. Or any parents."

"Shit. Honey, we'll take care of you," Henry said.

"You do, Henry. We have our arrangement. When the company is open and we're rolling in money, I'll only do it when we need something we can't get any other way."

They were all silent for a moment, soaking in what Chastity had revealed. Then people started counting down the seconds until the New Year. A waiter put a bottle of sparkling juice and glasses on their table.

"Let's forget the unpleasantness and join the countdown," Luke said.

There were noisemakers and champagne corks flying. The lights didn't go completely out, but they stayed low long enough for everyone to get a good kiss in. Henry kissed Carol and then turned to find Chastity waiting for a kiss as well. Of course, he still abided by her 'no tongue' rule—perhaps understanding it a little better. He was surprised, though, when Carol pulled Chastity around for a kiss as well.

The party didn't officially end until one o'clock, but people spent most of the last hour giving good wishes and saying goodnight to everyone. The partners were out of the club by 12:30.

<hr>

"I INVITED HER to join us," Carol said after they dropped Chastity at her door and headed for the hotel. "She declined. Should I have offered... like money?"

"No! God, no! I've known Chastity since we were in junior high school. The subject has never come up."

"Really?"

"Sure. Maybe I'm just dense. We've always had an understanding. At least since our first time together at the Prom last spring. She has rules."

"Tell me."

"No tongue kisses. Stay away from her navel. Treat her like a goddess and always take care of her."

"She's really a caretaker, isn't she?"

"I guess so. But she needs to be taken care of, too. If Isobel and Luke bowed out of our company, Chas and I would still launch it. I promised to take care of her and I will."

"Um… About the rules… *You* like tongue kisses, don't you? Not just faking it for me?"

"I would put my tongue anyplace in your body I could fit it. Just don't bite it off," he laughed as they reached their room at the hotel and he opened the door.

"I can think of someplace you can put it tonight."

"Any place it hasn't been before?"

"What? No repeats?"

"I'll repeat, over and over," he said.

"Good. Get my clothes off me!"

THE REMAINDER OF Tom Reynolds' night was not as happy as anyone else in the group. Even Chastity, home alone with her cats, counted out the ten hundred-dollar bills he'd given her when he picked her up. She supposed she might have to fuck him eventually, just so he wouldn't try to trash her name. Guys always got what they wanted from her eventually.

Tom, on the other hand, cleverly decided to try to outrun the police when he saw their flashing lights coming up on him. That led him over a curb and into a fire hydrant that began spraying freezing water up under his car. He tried to escape on foot, but couldn't get his seatbelt unfastened before officers were handcuffing him and pulling him from the car. When the belt kept him in place, they simply cut it and hauled him to the squad car.

His car was impounded. Firemen and maintenance workers were called out to stem the freezing water and repair the hydrant. His license was taken and he spent the night in a holding cell with a dozen other drunken revelers. The charges piled up against him. What would have been a simple, if unpleasant, DUI, now included resisting arrest, fleeing an emergency vehicle, destruction of public property, reckless endangerment, and anything else the district attorney could think of based on the police report.

It would be a week before he was released on bail to await trial.

HENRY AND CAROL'S weekend included a New Year's Day brunch with his parents who were very interested in the events of the previous evening. They'd chosen a quiet night in for their celebration and said they hadn't actually stayed awake until midnight.

"Well, Carol, are you satisfied with your progress at the university so far?" Sylvia asked as they sat down to waffles Ryan was pulling off the iron as quickly as he could. Henry put out a plate of bacon and one of scrambled eggs.

"Yes. It's been a good program so far. I feel I'm making progress and at least getting a bunch of fundamentals out of the way."

"And you're pre-med?" Ryan asked.

"Well, health sciences. Pre-med isn't actually a defined major, it's more of a selection of paths that will hopefully lead to med school," Carol said. "These waffles are so good! They never serve anything this good in the residence hall."

"How well I remember," Sylvia said. "I did my nursing degree there and Ryan got his degree in computer science. Of course, that was long before there was an AI specialization like Henry is working on. Where do you want to go to med school?"

"Um... Johns Hopkins," Carol said. "It's a difficult program to get into. The university here was my second choice, actually. I got wait-listed at Johns Hopkins for the Public Health program. That's a surer way to get into their med school. There's still a chance they'll call me this spring and tell me there's an opening."

"Really?" Henry said. "You'd just leave our university and go off to... isn't Hopkins in, like, Maryland?"

"It's in Baltimore. And yes. If they call, I'll go. I don't know if there's much chance of it, though. I thought they'd call all fall semester and I'd be able to start spring semester there. Not yet, though."

"Wow! I don't know what to hope, except that of course I hope you'll get in. That's what you really want. I'd miss you, though," Henry said.

"Yeah. You'd be the hardest part of leaving," she said. "And there's no golf program at JHU. I might have to take up tennis."

"I'm glad I rank right up there with golf," Henry laughed. She'd made a similar joke on their fall break weekend.

It was a real shock. Carol had never mentioned that she wanted to transfer to Baltimore, but he supposed she considered it a hope but not a likelihood. He wasn't going to let it disturb him. He was very fond of Carol, but neither of them was really treating their relationship as if it was more than a convenience.

"When does spring golf start?" Ryan asked.

"First competition is the first of March," Henry said. "That's probably how I'll be spending spring break. The matches are in Georgia and North Carolina. Those are the only B-Team matches this spring, so unless I miraculously knock another four strokes off my game, those are probably the only matches I'll be playing in."

"Same here," Carol said. "I already know I won't be knocking enough off my game to make varsity."

"Well, at least you'll have a nice week traveling together, won't you?" Sylvia said brightly. The two looked at each other with a big grin and nodded.

HENRY AND CAROL enjoyed the rest of their weekend together, going to an indoor driving range, seeing the new *Dune* movie, and spending plenty of quality time in bed. Then he drove her back to her house in Cleveland where her three girlfriends were waiting to start their ski trip.

When Henry got back home, he went straight to his room. He admitted to himself that he'd been distracted a few times over the weekend when stray thoughts of Tom Reynolds crossed his mind. He seemed more sinister than just a guy who got drunk and tried to rough up his escort. There was only one way Henry could think of to find out if he should be worried.

When he was in high school, he'd spent time getting to know computer hackers and testing his own skills against them. Most of their conquests were like counting coup. A hacker had to show that he could get past the firewalls of this or that corporation without getting caught in order to be accepted among the people who led him to the dark web. There, Henry found several tools that were useful for other than nefarious purposes.

Henry had a search engine he'd modified with his own AI—the one he'd just filed the patent on. With it, he could search for just about anything that resided in the cloud. The cloud was really just a bunch of servers on a ranch in Utah or Arizona or Montana or wherever else one of the big guys had set up shop. The server farms had thousands of servers with petabytes of storage each where innocent (and not so innocent) people believed their data was securely stored. For Henry, it was all exposed.

He searched for everything he could locate on Tom Reynolds.

Tom's private email was filled with messages coercing coeds at the university to sleep with him in exchange for him getting them the financial aid they applied for at the office where Tom worked. One had threatened to report him and had mysteriously disappeared. Henry packaged that evidence and sent it to the VP of Financial Services at the university. He was pretty sure that would get Tom shit-canned, but it still left him a dangerous person to people Henry cared about.

Even Tom's banking records were an open book for Henry to search. He paused. Police would need a warrant to seize his banking records and simply sending the records to the police would not be enough. But Henry found transfers of funds on the days female students received aid, meaning if a woman hadn't acquiesced to his sexual demands, she ended up paying him out of her financial aid package, whether she knew it or not. Reporting the suspected fraud to both the university and the bank would be enough to freeze Tom's accounts.

People like Tom always had a back door to escape through if they were discovered. Henry searched further. He discovered the address of property in Upstate New York registered to Tom as owner and figured that would be where he would escape to. He alerted police there to the suspected behavior and asked them to be aware of any APB that came out.

It took the better part of the week before Henry had dug up as much as he could on Tom Reynolds. By the time he was released on bond, he had no car, no job, and no bank accounts. There was only one thing left for Henry to do.

He called Luke Riordan's father.

11

PROTECTION

"**M**R. RIORDAN, IT'S Henry Pascal," Henry said when he was finally connected.

"Henry, you've known me all your life. You came to play with Luke before you were both in kindergarten and have always felt at home with us. When will you finally accept that you can call me Paul?"

"Yes, sir. I just always try to be respectful."

"And you succeed at that. What can I do for you? Trouble with the car?"

"No, sir. It's working fine. I couldn't be happier. This is a more… personal matter."

"Sounds serious, Henry. Are you in trouble?"

"Not exactly. Did Luke tell you about our little run-in with a guy on New Year's Eve?" Henry asked. Luke said he told his father, just as Henry had informed his parents.

"Yes. Nasty business. You boys handled it well. I'm not going to lecture you or your partners on being more careful. Just be more careful, okay?"

"Yes, sir. I've done some investigating of this guy, Tom Reynolds, and I've supplied a lot of information to the police. I understand he's out on bail now. The thing is, I think he's more dangerous than just a drunk on New Year's Eve. I… I think Chastity could be in danger. I've found indications that this isn't the first time he's been in trouble like this and the women didn't fare well," Henry said.

"You're sure of this?"

"Yes, sir. I've dug pretty deep and I believe he's dangerous, especially to women who don't comply with what he wants."

96

"Don't say anything else. Don't ask for anything. You don't know anything about him or what he's like. Do you understand?" Paul asked.

"Yes, sir."

"Goodbye, Henry."

IF HENRY HADN'T known Paul Riordan for his entire eighteen years, he might have taken that as a dismissal of his concerns. But Henry knew Paul would never reject a person—a family member—in need.

Henry and Luke were eleven years old when Paul encountered difficulties at his dealership. He was well on the way to becoming the biggest auto dealer in the metropolitan area and there were others who weren't pleased with him. He always had prices that would beat the operating costs of other dealers, and had acquired franchises for all the GM product lines. At the time, he was negotiating to acquire both Toyota and Honda franchises.

That's when a series of unfortunate events began occurring at his business locations. Windows were broken to start. The dealership windows could have been the result of a teen gang just out to destroy convenient property. But when the damage extended to vandalism of new and used vehicles, Paul wasn't content to wait for police to figure it out.

It was never clear how much he was involved in the 'security' company he hired to deal with the problem. No one was ever arrested for vandalizing his property or inventory. But the vandalism slowly dissipated. Not long thereafter, the local Toyota dealer sold his business to Riordan Motors. The former owner moved to Hawaii.

What Henry knew was that Paul Riordan had contacts and they were capable of changing the landscape if necessary. Henry had no idea what the people would do to protect Chastity, but he went to sleep that night secure in the knowledge she was safe.

ON SATURDAY, HE drove up to Cleveland to pick up Carol and bring her back for the start of spring classes at the university. Of course, they didn't get back until just in time for classes to start on Monday morning. They liked the little hotel they'd found in Youngstown and decided to spend a couple of nights there.

"Well, Janice and Leah have put on the freshman fifteen and show no sign of stopping there," Carol laughed about her high school friends who went skiing together. "But they seemed happy enough. Teri was always the quiet one among us and I expected her to do pretty well at Wellesley. I guess you could say she has. I never expected the girl to come out of her shell like she has. Come out of it? I think she blew it up and filed for insurance. She was nothing like the girl we went to high school with."

"I've heard of that happening at five- or ten-year class reunions, but never over the course of one semester," Henry said.

"I can't say it was a bad thing. Maybe it was just getting out from under the thumb of her very religious parents. She was only home a few days over Christmas and then went to stay with Leah for the rest of the break until we all went skiing. She's headed straight for the airport back to Boston this afternoon," Carol said.

"I'm glad you had a good time. You know, I hang out with my three best buddies from high school all the time. Even though it's mostly online. We met together a few times this week, just to work on company philosophy and bylaws. We talked about going to the zoo to adopt a corporate seal, but they only have California sea lions and that didn't seem to have the same humor."

"Sounds like you had some fun!"

"Yeah. We got a lot of work done, but when it comes down to it, we're still working on creating a corporate name. We might have to recruit someone with more imagination," Henry said.

It didn't take long after they'd checked in for the two to be naked on the bed.

"Oh! Oh, God! I almost forgot what that felt like! We girls didn't forget how to go down on each other. We'd been doing that since we were freshmen in high school. But none of the girls had this piece of equipment. God! I love this feeling. Yeah. Move in me. Ohh!"

It sounded like Carol had done more than ski during her break and that always brought inspiring images to mind when she talked about pleasuring or being pleasured by another woman. He'd like to be the meat in that sandwich.

Just being buried in Carol, though, was like a welcome home celebration for both of them. Touching and sucking on her breasts, sliding in and out of her, filling his hands with her sexy ass, were all incredible. And coming with her while they kissed deeply was a phenomenon that left them both exhausted and wrapped in each other's arms.

Carol had had a few orgasms at the hands and tongues of her high school friends. Henry had none since she left. Not that it was a great hardship—they often went a week or two without on campus. But something else had been bothering Henry.

HE COULD HAVE called Chastity at any time over the previous week and she'd have invited him over for some of the best sex of his life. But she'd finally said something on New Year's Eve that jarred him and he couldn't believe he'd never put it together before.

Chastity was an escort. She earned most of her money from providing sexual services to her dates. Despite having told Henry frequently that all she wanted from him was for him to take care of her, he felt conflicted now.

It wasn't about whether or not trading sex for favors of one kind or another, including financial, was moral or immoral. Isobel and her mother might question that, but not Henry. He didn't think Luke would be conflicted about it, either. Henry's problem was he felt like having sex with Chastity and not paying was somehow stealing from her.

Yet, he thought offering to pay her might damage their relationship in other ways. He understood that his 'generosity' in including her as an equal partner in the LLC and transferring the patent and software to them to license for a substantial sum had made them all wealthy... on paper. Chastity considered that to be taking care of her.

But none of them could touch the million dollars in the bank. Luke and Isobel had sat down with an investment counselor over the break and worked out what to do with the money until it was needed to fund the corporation. He supposed he could have gone, but that part of the business frankly bored him.

He just wanted... He wanted to take care of Chastity. She certainly took care of him.

ISOBEL WAS THE second of the partners to turn nineteen on the twenty-fourth of January. There was a flurry of text messages to congratulate her and celebrate, but she and Luke stayed at Villanova and did not come back to Pittsburgh.

Henry was busy trying to keep up with the heavy course load he had. He no longer had any classes with Dan and only one, Intro to Machine Learning, with Josh. He and Lisa shared both Theoretical Computer Science and Calculus in Three Dimensions. They still met with Josh and Dan in their study group, but did more independent study or one-on-one. Josh had two classes with Dan, so they all had plenty to keep them busy. Henry's other two classes included a cognitive science elective: Thinking in Person vs. Thinking Online, and a Humanities elective: The Nature of Language. He was maxed out at 18 credits again, but since he'd aced all his first semester classes, there was no question about him being able to handle the load.

He and Carol had scarcely had time together when she stood next to him at golf practice on Tuesday the ninth of February and gave him a nudge.

"Hey, what's up, gorgeous? I'm sorry I haven't had any time to breathe in the past week. Want to get together this weekend?" he asked.

"No. I mean, yes, of course, but we're getting together tonight," Carol replied

"We are?"

"I'm sure glad I gave your mother my phone number," she laughed. "You have no idea, do you?"

"Uh... I... No... No idea."

"It's your birthday, silly. Your mother invited me to dinner to celebrate with you tonight," Carol laughed.

"She did? My birthday? My gosh! I'm nineteen!"

"Yeah. I think your mother remembers every minute of those nineteen years, plus the seven hours she was in labor."

"She would bring that up," Henry laughed. "Wow! So, we're going to my place after practice?"

"Yep."

"Uh... Do you need to come back to campus after dinner?"

"Nope."

"I think it will be a very happy birthday."

It was only part of Henry's surprise. When he and Carol reached his house, he found Chastity helping his mother set the table.

"Oh, hey!" he said when they walked in.

"Happy birthday!" she said.

"This is all a surprise. Did Mom invite anyone else?" Henry asked.

"Your father will be here, but your mom didn't exactly set this up. She was a willing participant when I suggested it, though," Chastity said.

"And Chastity swore me to absolute secrecy," Carol said.

"I didn't know you guys had been in touch since New Year's Eve."

"Yeah, we talk every once in a while. We have to keep tabs on how our company exec is doing."

"And how *is* Luke?" Henry teased.

"Better than you're going to be if you don't settle in to enjoy yourself. And us," Chastity growled.

"I surrender!"

"Good plan."

Once Henry's father was home, the family gathered at the table and Henry's parents proceeded to try to embarrass him to death in front of the girls with stories of his youth and childhood. Chastity got in one or two, but said she'd save the good stuff for when the parents weren't there.

"Speaking of which, we need to get going," Sylvia said after dinner, "The much-delayed nurses' holiday party is tonight. We skipped the dinner, but I want to get some dancing in and participate in the silent auction."

"You're having a party on a Tuesday night?" Henry asked, puzzled.

"When you are in the medical field, you take whatever opportunity you have. Remember that, Carol. The time is coming," Sylvia said. They all cleared the table and put away the leftovers, but Sylvia insisted they leave the dishes for her to load when she got home. Sylvia and Ryan left Chastity, Carol, and Henry with the house to themselves.

"Um..."

"Don't even try to guess," Carol said. "This is your big birthday surprise."

"What is?"

"Two women," Chastity said. "When Carol and I were talking a while ago, she mentioned how turned on you were by the stories of her and her high school girlfriends. We decided to give you a little taste of what it would be like."

"You mean... You and Carol... We're all... Holy shit!"

The two girls closed in on him and with bumped heads, squashed noses, and puckered lips, managed to all three get their mouths together. Carol welcomed Henry into her mouth but did no more than lick Chastity's lips as part of their kiss.

They headed straight for Henry's bedroom, which he was thankful he kept fairly tidy—a short-lived condition. Soon the clothes of all three were strewn across the room and Henry lay sprawled on the bed as the two girls worshiped his body with their mouths. As particular as Chastity was about no tongue kisses, that was definitely limited to tongue to tongue. She had no difficulty at all licking and sucking on Carol's nipples, or bathing Henry's cock with her tongue before sucking him deep into her mouth.

"You know, I love it when you go down on me, Henry, but there is something special about a woman's tongue finding her way around my clit," Carol said as she kissed him and Chastity flicked her clit. "This is where Chastity gets me off and you get in Chastity."

Henry took the hint and grabbed a condom from his bedside table, rolling it on as he got behind Chastity and pushed into her. Chastity's licking of Carol's clit sped up and Carol announced her pleasure to the world. Henry wanted to see what he could experience with two women and pressed himself over Chastity's back, reaching under her with his left hand to find and play with her nipple piercings. With his right hand, he reached farther forward until he found the wet juncture of Chastity's mouth and Carol's pussy. He pressed a finger into his girlfriend and stimulated her from the inside while Chastity took care of the outside.

The position was stimulating, but mostly to the imagination and not to the parts involved. Chastity disconnected from Henry and crawled up to straddle Carol's face as Henry moved his cock to Carol's soaked opening. He slid deep inside her, pinching her nipples a little to help a bit. Chastity leaned back against him and he started kissing all around her neck and ears as he used one hand to twist her nipple rings and the other on Carol's breasts.

This position was much more directly stimulating and it wasn't long before they were getting off, sometimes sequentially and sometimes in unison. Both girls seemed to have multiple orgasms, so Henry just kept pumping until he'd regained enough erection to pop again.

There were plenty of breaks in the action. They cuddled together, all three aware they were just regrouping for the next round.

"Thank you," Chastity whispered in Henry's ear, aware that Carol could probably hear what she was saying as well. "You did it."

"I think you girls organized this," Henry laughed. "I should be thanking you."

"One threesome isn't enough to thank you," Chastity continued. Carol got out of bed to use the bathroom, knowing Chastity needed a minute alone with Henry. "Tom was killed outside my apartment building over the weekend. Police said it was gang violence. They found heavy-duty drugs on his body. He had a gun and had fired several shots, but they never found the bullets. I've been living in fear ever since New Year's. He was trying to get me to meet him somewhere to finish what we started. I guess he finished it, all right."

"I didn't know he was at your apartment this weekend," Henry said. In fact, he hadn't thought about the whole thing since his phone call with Paul Riordan.

"I know. But I also know you would never let anyone hurt me," Chastity said. "For whatever you did or didn't do, thank you."

"Honey, you know I swore to always take care of you."

"I wouldn't believe that of anyone but you. Now it's time for me to join your girlfriend in taking care of you one more time before I go home."

HENRY HAD PURGED every item that could be connected to Tom Reynolds from his computers, including evidence of the searches he'd sent his AI on. He ran his own optimization software on the computers, updating all the drives with the latest version.

As far as he was concerned, Tom Reynolds had never existed.

Police reports later revealed Reynolds was a known stalker and predator and speculated the drugs found on his body had been intended to inflict an overdose on his next victim. The case was closed.

The university sent letters to each of the women they discovered had been scammed or cheated with the evidence they'd found on his work computer. They were each offered a nice sum as restitution. None of the women wanted their names dragged through a lawsuit to get back at a man who was already dead, so they all accepted the university's offer and apology.

LUKE'S BIRTHDAY WAS two weeks after Henry's on the twenty-second. Henry hoped his friend had as good a time on his birthday as Henry had.

Henry and Carol did get a couple of very tame dates in, but spent most of their time together on the golf course. It was still pretty wet. The temperatures were barely making it into the forties and were near freezing at night, but all the snow had melted.

They wore ski gloves and jackets as they walked between holes, but took them off long enough to make their drives or other shots before quickly huddling into them again. They needed the practice.

Classes got out for spring break Friday the twenty-sixth of February. On Saturday, all twenty-four of the men and women boarded a decent bus for the long trek to Savannah, Georgia for the first of two tournaments. Football players and basketball players traveled by charter jet. Golfers traveled by bus.

Everyone was excited to be on the road at first, sharing snacks and thermoses. The school provided soft drinks and water on the bus, but they stopped at an unlikely looking truck stop for lunch somewhere around the Virginia state line. Then they reboarded the bus and managed their first night's stay in Charlotte, North Carolina. No one thought twice about Henry and Carol sharing a room. Six of the men and women had become couples over the winter and another decided to try it out on this trip.

After breakfast in the morning, they reboarded the bus for another four and a half hours to Savannah. They were in early enough to have lunch, and then went out to explore the historic city in delightful 70-degree weather. That evening they gathered for the welcome dinner.

12

PUTTING AROUND

THE FIFTY-FOUR-HOLE tournament started on Monday morning. The men's and women's tournaments were on neighboring courses, so the bus dropped one coach with the women at The Club of Savannah Harbor then drove the other coach and the men to the Savannah Country Club.

Three courses were scheduled for the tournament. With ninety-four men, including individuals and teams, the competition was divided into two rounds. Henry found himself in the second round, teeing off at 1:00, and wished he'd been able to watch Carol in the morning.

They both did well. Henry carded a 73 on the par 71 course. Carol had finished six over for the first round.

The team ate together and were encouraged to get to bed early Monday evening. Of course, several elected to walk the warm and interesting streets of Savannah, especially around the waterfront. They all bought roses made of reeds from the homeless people selling them on every street.

Henry moved onto the leader board when he shot one under on the second round at Glen Cove Golf Course. Carol improved by a couple of strokes on the second day as well, but was still pretty far back from the top. On Wednesday, Henry blew up and shot six over at the Club of Savannah Harbor. It was the same score Carol had on that course. She continued to improve at just three over when she went to Glen Cove.

Both the men and women's teams did well. The women placed first and the men placed fourth. There was a celebratory dinner Wednesday night. Then Henry and Carol went to celebrate together.

105

"WE'VE BEEN SLEEPING together for four nights and only had sex on Saturday. Think you're up to it tonight?" Carol asked.

"There's never been a problem being up for it," Henry laughed. "It's been taking care to be sure you weren't too sore to swing your clubs."

"Thank you for that, though it didn't seem to make a difference. Tomorrow is a travel day, so I have all day riding on that bus with you to recover from any damage you do to my vagina. Not that I expect you to damage it, but I'm sure I can recover from a good round of sex tonight."

"You're on," Henry said, reaching for her.

They didn't even pretend to 'make love.' They both wanted sex and had a willing partner sharing their bed. It might have been the most adventurous in bed they'd ever been. They rolled around, joining in different positions, and ramping up to satisfying orgasms. Then they took an hour to rest and recoup, and went at it again.

"That might not be a good idea tonight," Carol said when Henry rubbed his cock up her crack. He caught a second on her pucker and then slid past.

"Didn't intend to do that," he said.

"I don't mind!" she clarified. "But I don't know if I can recover from that in one day so I can play. I'd hate to walk an entire eighteen holes feeling like I was going to poop my pants."

"I don't even want to imagine the feeling," Henry said.

"Here. Isn't this what you were aiming for?" she asked, directing him to her pussy as he pushed from behind. "Yeah. Man, I like this. Why don't we plan on the other Saturday night after the tournament? If it's good, we can go again Sunday night when we get back to Pitt."

"You know, that's something I would just never ask of a woman," Henry said. "But I won't turn down this beautiful ass if it's offered."

"Saturday. Tonight, just pound my pussy again!"

Henry had no difficulty doing that. Since it was his third time for the night, he lasted plenty long enough for Carol to get her cookies twice, then spurted weakly into the condom.

He petted her bottom as he softened and withdrew. He learned something new about Carol every day.

THEY HAD ENOUGH time when they reached Pinehurst that they could get some practice in at the club before their matches. It was a much smaller field with only eleven men's teams and twelve women's teams. Many of the teams had a long way to travel on Sunday, with some planning to leave Saturday afternoon. The men's tournament comprised two eighteen-hole rounds, played early in the morning on Friday and Saturday. After the Friday men's round, the women played eighteen holes. On Saturday, they played only nine.

Henry shot four over in the first round, but that was adequate to put him in a four-way tie for third on the leader board. Carol had a fantastic round, just two over par and took the first-round lead for the women. They were congratulating each other profusely, and even though they withheld from having sex, they shared the shower and played with each other.

Saturday morning, Henry shot two over and moved into first place. He stayed there for the tournament and was awarded his medal. Carol may have been inspired by him, or perhaps challenged. She shot two under for the nine-hole completion and stayed in first. She got the individual medal as well. The men's and women's teams both followed their leaders and took first place for the tournament. There were congratulations for everyone at the dinner that night. Half the teams had left after their matches, but there was still a nice group hanging around for the dinner.

The team was warned that they would be traveling early the next morning and to make sure they'd packed and dropped their bags at the bus before breakfast at seven. They moaned about it, but they'd get home Sunday evening.

"I... UH... WOW... I haven't done this in a long long time," Carol said when she came out of the bathroom.

"You've done it before?" Henry asked.

"Not with a guy. The girls did it with a dildo a few times. After all, it was supposed to be the honorable way for good Catholic girls to have sex without contraception," she laughed. "That was passed down to us as freshmen by upper class girls who were supposed to be our 'big sisters' at the academy. Eventually, we figured out they just liked to push things into other girls' butts."

"We don't have to do this," Henry said.

"But I want to. I really would like to know if a flesh and blood cock feels better than a plastic one. I already know it feels better in my vagina. Besides, I kind of prepared things. I'd hate to waste it," she sighed.

"Well, come here and let me do some preparation, too," he said, pulling her to him in bed. She went willingly into his arms to start kissing and petting.

Henry went so far as to be sure she got off with his mouth before he thought about entering her. He reached for a condom.

"Why don't we skip that tonight," Carol said. "I'd like to feel the whole experience and you should, too."

"You're sure?"

"I don't think you'll get me pregnant, shooting back there. And I don't think either of us are carrying anything. Unless you're wigged out about being bareback in my asshole."

"I've never found anything about you to get wigged out about."

"Then turn me over and plunder me."

"No," he said softly. "I want to see your face and kiss you."

"What? While...? Oh, God! You're going to enter me while I'm face up? That is so... Use some of this lube, please," she panted.

Henry applied it liberally and then lined the head of his cock up with her anus and bent to kiss her. As their tongues meshed, he pushed gently but firmly. Carol gasped when the head of his cock popped through her anal ring.

"Oh, God! You're there. Kiss me some more. It makes me really turned on."

They continued kissing and Henry slowly sank more deeply into her bottom.

"You're still going in. God! There's a lot of you!"

"I'll stop anytime you say," he whispered. "But there isn't really much more anyway."

"I want it all! I want to feel your whole length going in and out. I might even..." She pushed her hand between them so she could reach her clit and began applying pressure to it as Henry backed most of the way out and then slid in again. It went much smoother.

"This is really better than a gold medal," Carol gasped. "I've been thinking about it all day!"

"It did something for your game," Henry said. He withdrew and pressed in again.

"If you need to, you can go faster, but I like it this way."

"As long as I can kiss you, we can take as long as you want."

"Yes, kiss me. I'm taking all the length you've got."

It didn't really take all that long. Between the newness of the experience and the raw sexuality, Carol started coming, strumming her clit as rapidly as she could with her hand caught between their bodies. It took Henry only a few more strokes before she could feel his pulses in her bottom and came again.

"Oh, wow! That was intense. Please... slowly... take it out now. That feels like the biggest poop I've ever had. Let's head for the shower."

The experience had been intense enough to satisfy both of them for the night. They cleaned each other in the shower and kissed more, but then they fell asleep until their wakeup call at six.

THEY SPENT THE first few hours of the bus trip back to Pittsburgh sacked out, as did most of their teammates and their coaches. By lunch, they were all stirring and looking for something to do. That included everything from card games to makeup parties. It helped the trip go by and by six, they were being discharged from the bus.

Carol and Henry kissed again but had no inclination to try to spend another night together. The next day they returned to classes and saw each other only at practice. They were both just marking time at practice and Henry had already announced he would not be returning to the team the next year. The coaches were focused on their top talent and getting ready for the regional and national tournaments, so the announcement only received a nod from them.

HENRY GOT PLENTY of practice time in at Constitution Links over the next four weeks. The various high school teams and younger golfers were returning for the summer season. He was happy the club renewed him as a youth pro, so he could continue his club membership and have an income. He'd inquired about becoming a teaching or research assistant in his department at college, but those positions were mostly given to grad students.

That meant his "free time" was spent analyzing the test results on his newest patent and filing a revision with Don. Added to that, Luke and Isobel were home for their spring break the last full week of March and there was "business" to discuss.

WEDNESDAY EVENING, HENRY took time off work and met at Luke's house with Isobel and Chastity. Once they had pop and snacks, Luke connected his computer to a Zoom session and his advisor from Villanova joined them.

"Dr. Levin, I think you've met everyone in the company so far in our earlier meetings. Thank you for joining us this evening," Luke began.

"A pleasure to see you all again," Levin said.

"We're close to being able to file our articles of incorporation," Luke said. "Dr. Levin has been really helpful in getting that going. There's a major item left to take care of before we get launched, though. Dr. Levin?"

"As Luke said—major item," Levin said. "We can't file for incorporation without a business name. I know you've all been thinking about this, but we need to resolve it so we can move forward."

"What should we be thinking of? Something real techy?" Chastity asked.

"Well, it's a tech company, so that's something to consider," Levin answered. "But let me give you some general rules for naming your company. First, KISS. You probably aren't old enough to understand the old acronym. Keep It Short and Simple. Or when applied to Dan Quayle, Keep It Short, Stupid. Ideal business names these days are one or two-syllable words, but that is getting harder and harder to come by. Even a three-syllable word or two words that total three syllables may be hard to come by, but if it adheres to the other rules, it will fly."

"Okay, KISS," Henry said. Chastity turned toward him and blew him a kiss. "What's next?"

"Make it memorable and pronounceable," Levin said. "What's that name again? If people can't remember it, they won't use it. The same is true if people get confused about pronouncing it. Naming your company "Fish" won't help if you spell it ghoti. That's gh as in enough, o as in women, and ti as in nation. No one will be able to find you on the internet."

They all laughed, but nodded.

"Next, and closely related, it should be easy to spell in a single way. Not only phonetically, but logically. Don't use an alternate spelling or even a word that has an alternate spelling if you can help it. And don't use hyphens in it. They confuse people. They'll get frustrated trying to find you when they type in the name without a hyphen, they'll more than likely go elsewhere."

"That makes sense," Isobel said. "There's a clothing site I used to like, but it had a hyphen in it and I quit using it because without the hyphen it went to a pornography site."

"Exactly!" Levin said. "Now, we have two things that your name needs to comply with, even if you've covered all the others. First of all, it needs to be brandable. In other words, no one else is using it. And you need to check that in some other languages. Years ago, there was a big manufacturer of lawn and garden equipment called Toro. Big reputation in the US, but when they went international, they discovered they couldn't brand the name in Spanish speaking countries because it was just a common word. Like calling your company Bull."

"So, we have to search it in other languages and check meanings," Luke said.

"And you need to file a domain that is available," Levin said. "As soon as you decide the name, register the dot-com and dot-net domains. There are others, of course, but you should be sure you have those two."

"It sounds like we'll be starting from scratch on this," Henry said. "This could take forever."

"Not necessarily," Luke said. "Chastity and I have been compiling a list of names as we worked on the bylaws. We've had some long Zoom conferences between the two of us. Thank you, Dr. Levin, for getting us started on this. I know you plan to enjoy some time with your family this week. We won't interrupt you any longer."

"Good luck to you all," Levin said. "This is an exciting time. Let the excitement of actually creating your business help you through the hard work."

He signed off and the group turned to the list of possible name suggestions Chastity and Luke had compiled.

As they went through each name, Isobel typed in the name as a dot-com in her browser. Several were eliminated from there.

"From working with Henry, I'd say the idea of trust and security are really tantamount to what we want to accomplish," Luke said.

"I agree, but I'm not that sure we want the term AI in the business name. It just puts so many people off at the moment. We went through a period two or three years ago when AI was a big selling point for websites, applications, cell phones, and entire home security systems. But there was a huge backlash. People held back on upgrading their phones and refused to buy phones that only offered built in AI. That's names like Trusted AI, Private AI, and AI Integrity."

"I like this one," Chastity said. "Open Cloak. It implies that we aren't keeping secrets from the user."

"Of course we will," Luke said. "Unless we're going to incorporate as a charitable foundation, we have to keep Henry's code secret."

"Yes, but there's something about that I like," Henry said. "Maybe adding the idea of development to it so people understand what we do. Open Cloak Development."

"No. That's so boring," Chastity said. "How about Design. Open Cloak Design. It implies that we're open with the user about what they are buying, and at the same time there is a cloak involved to keep their information private."

"And we design software with the user in mind. It's available," Isobel said. "I'd recommend that even if the full company name is Open Cloak Design, we register the websites as just OpenCloak.com and OpenCloak.net."

"There are people out there who watch to see what names have been searched and try to register them first. If we can live with a company named Open Cloak Design, let's grab the websites," Luke said.

"I'm in favor," Chastity said.

"Yes," Henry said.

"I'm on the registration site now," Isobel said.

"Then let's grab them and get the ball rolling toward our actual incorporation," Luke said. He sent a text message to Levin and received an immediate reply that said, "Go!"

"I didn't expect to spend all night just working on a company name," Henry said. "I still have class tomorrow."

"I understand, but I think this calls for something special," Luke said. He left the room and returned with a bottle of champagne. "Dad put this aside for us to celebrate with. I think this calls for the celebration."

Isobel ran to get glasses from a cabinet, indicating she knew right where such things were kept in Luke's home. Luke popped the cork and poured a glass for each of them. They all turned to Henry for the toast.

"Wow! My best friends. My business partners. My most trusted allies. Here's to our success with Open Cloak Design," he said, raising his glass.

"Damn right!" Luke said.

Henry offered to take Chastity and Isobel home after they'd had a glass of champagne.

"Um... There's still half a bottle of champagne," Isobel said. "I think I'll just stay here and help Luke finish it. Okay?"

"Okay with me," Luke said. "It might take us all night."

"I hope so!" Isobel chimed in.

Henry and Chastity left.

13

LAUNCHES

I T WASN'T UNTIL the first weekend of April that Henry and Carol could spend quality time together. Spring Carnival opened on Thursday, but neither one could spare the time away from classes to go that day. They agreed to spend the rest of the weekend just having fun.

Henry had been recruited to help set up the robot races as part of the sponsoring department team. He helped map out the course in the quad outside the Computer Sciences building. That amounted to measuring and painting a two-inch white stripe through the half-mile course, complete with trick curves and dead-end branches.

While many of the robots that would compete came from the robotics department, a part of computer sciences, many also came from alternate programs on campus and even a few industrial competitors from around the area. The civil engineering group, mechanical engineering, physics groups, and even a couple of fraternities entered the two-phase event. Robots had to follow the course while making decisions regarding path directions and overcoming obstacles.

He worked with several other people in the department to map the route and paint the stripe on Tuesday and Wednesday nights before watching the qualifying races Thursday morning to observe if any corrections needed to be made to the course. The number one rule was that once the robot was started on its path, there could be no interference from humans directing or correcting it. They weren't 'remote control cars.' They had to be 'self-driving.'

Carol joined him for the final races Friday morning. After the track set up and overnight adjustments, Henry had no active responsibilities when the race was being run.

"You mean the robot has to make decisions as it travels the course?" she asked when she saw the first contestant speed around the track.

"I understand it gets harder each year," Henry said. "Look. The next contestant is from the pros. American Robotics Development Corp., right here in town. ARDC won the professional division last year, but Edison Robotics is putting up a real challenge this year."

They watched the ARDC robot zip down the track, stop at a fork in the road, then proceed to the next obstacle.

"So how are these things different from a Roomba?"

"Mostly, a Roomba just wanders around sucking up whatever is in its path. It doesn't have a set course around the house and doesn't go back and forth in a pattern like a person might vacuum. If it bumps into something, it changes course. These robots actually have to read the signs—which are simple, but we're talking about robots, not people—and decide which path to take based on the information given. Look! It's come to the detour I created last night. If it ignores the detour sign, it will fall into a puddle of water. The robots don't often function well in water."

The robot came to a stop at the "Bridge out" warning and chose to follow the detour. It had to slow down because the detour route was less clearly marked than the main route. It made it around the hazard and sped on.

After the races, Henry and Carol were free to head for the midway, held in the north parking lot. Some 50 booths were set up in the parking lot, some as much as three stories high! Every Greek society on campus and many of the larger organizations had booths. Each booth had games, food, or entertainment for the people walking through the "American Revolution" themed midway. Some of the booths also sold various crafts, but just visiting the booths was free.

"We should have worn costumes," Henry laughed. "It's like a 1776 Renn Faire."

"Too much work. Finals are in four weeks. You would not believe how much crap the professors are piling on us as we move toward the end of term," she answered.

"I understand. In fact, we need to register for fall classes next week. I've already registered for my summer classes."

"About that, Henry. The festival is exciting and all, but can we go some-place private for a while. I need to *talk* to you in an environment that is very private."

Henry got the distinct impression that Carol was far more interested in getting personal with Henry than being entertained. That suited Henry just fine. They walked to his car and he drove to his house. His parents were still at work. They went directly to his bedroom.

Carol was almost frantic in her desire to get undressed and into bed. Henry responded just as rapidly, losing his clothes and diving into the bed with her. They kissed and touched each other. Carol pulled him to her and nearly had him in her before he grabbed a condom and got it on.

That seemed to turn Carol on even more. She pulled him into her and drove up to meet his thrusts. They hadn't had quite such a raw rutting together since their golf trip. By mid-afternoon, they were exhausted and sweaty. They showered and Henry brought their favorite soft drinks to his room so she didn't need to dress. They cuddled together on the bed, still caressing and kissing.

"Wow! That was something else!" Henry said.

"I've been looking forward to this afternoon ever since we got back from the tournament. I was afraid we'd never get back together."

"The past month has gone past in a blur. I was at the point of just coming to camp out in front of your dorm to wait for you. I knew we'd get there soon. What was the rush today?" he asked.

She looked at him and tears started running from her eyes.

"Henry, I'm leaving," she wailed.

The news was a physical shock as Carol gripped him and wept on his chest.

"I know it's been hard, but we can make it, Carol," he said.

She shook her head and reached for a tissue from the bedside table.

"I got word. An email. Yesterday," she said. "I'm moving to Baltimore. Johns Hopkins says I can enroll for the summer session, but that means I need to be there the first week of May. As soon as I walk out of my last final, my parents will be there to drive me to Maryland."

"Oh. Crap! I mean, congratulations, I guess. I know it's what you really wanted. I just... I've really grown fond of you, Carol."

"I know. Me, too!"

A new flood of tears started and this time, they were mixed with Henry's.

"I'd given up. When there was no word after spring break, I just fig-ured that was it and they didn't want me. When I got that email yesterday, I couldn't believe it. I called them and they said they had a cancellation and one space was open if I wanted it. What could I do? I accepted on the spot. Johns Hopkins, Henry. Johns Hopkins wants me!"

"So do I, but I'm not going to try to compete with them. It's really great news for you, Carol. This is like a dream come true for you. I could not be happier for you," he asked.

"Happy and sad and angry and excited and elated and devastated and... I wanted to see you last night, but you were out marking the robot course. I just wanted to be in your arms," she said.

"You're always welcome in my arms," he said. "No matter what."

Their next round of sex was slow and loving, each afraid it would be their last.

HENRY HAD ALREADY registered for the summer classes he intended to take, but Monday, he had to get waivers from instructors and his advisor in order to get the fall classes he wanted. His record over two semesters and one summer session made it possible for him to pack his schedule for the fall.

He was officially declared to be on the AI degree track. His schedule for the fall included Computer Vision, Natural Language Processing, Machine Learning, Human Memory, Decision Making and Robotics, and Human AI Interaction. He was taking his electives over the summer, figuring the classes called Language and Thought, and Ethics and Policy Issues in Computing would be more relaxing and allow some summer down time. He might even get to visit Carol in Maryland sometime over the summer.

Her announcement that she was leaving could have ended their relationship on the spot, but instead, they found more time to be with each other, even meeting in the library to study and rushing to Henry's house to make love during a two-hour break in schedules in the afternoon.

"Is this going to make it harder for you to leave?" he gasped as he filled a condom.

"Are you trying to make it harder?"

"No. I just want as much of you as I can get while we are together."

"Then I want to make this hard for you. Push into me again!"

Of course, the final day of classes approached on the twenty-third and they took Saturday to check into a hotel, order room service, and screw as much as possible. Sunday, they had to get back to their respective groups to study for finals. Both had intense loads and finals nearly every day. They spent the reading day on Wednesday together, but when they kissed goodbye that evening, both knew it was probably for the last time.

"I don't want to let you go, Henry, but I know this is what's right for me."

He bit back a retort about what was right for him and just held her more tightly.

"I guess we always knew this was a possibility," he said. "That doesn't mean I will miss you less. I love you, Carol. Maybe one day we'll be in the same space at the same time."

"As long as you aren't stretched out on an emergency room operating table, I'll be happy about that. I love you, Henry."

They didn't drag the parting out.

Carol was gone by three in the afternoon on Friday while Henry was completing his last final exam.

HENRY HAD A week to get his head straight before summer session began. Unfortunately, Luke and Isobel still had two weeks in their spring semester before they would get home.

"Hey, Chas. How's it going?" he asked when his call connected.

"Blech! I've already switched to full-time at the restaurant but the wages are so tiny, I don't know why I bother. I could be making over a thousand a day, just to hang out with some random dude who's lonely and wants to pretend he has a hot young girlfriend. How about you?"

"Well, I don't have a girlfriend anymore. She's gone to Baltimore. Didn't know if you'd want to hang out at all, but I can't afford a thousand a day."

"Do you think I'd charge you like that? Henry, don't make it about money. You take care of me. That's all I've ever asked."

"Do I do that well enough?"

"Oh, yeah. We aren't seeing each other often, but you are an anchor I really need. How about Wednesday night? I'm off Wednesday because I work Saturday and Sunday."

"That would be great. Um... I was also wondering if you'd get me the name of that rental agent you mentioned. Luke says we need a physical street address for our corporation and he's temporarily assigned *my* home address as the corporate address. I'd rather it wasn't at Mom and Dad's house."

"Good point. I'll text you her name and number. I'll see you Wednesday night."

Henry contacted the agent and set up an appointment to tour apartments.

"CHASTITY PAPPA SPOKE highly of you," Anna, the rental agent, said. "I was disappointed to not hear from you earlier."

"I had very little time to spare during the school year and was saving as much money as I could for this move," Henry said. He was pleased that she'd been able to arrange showings for him on Tuesday. His parents had declined to collect rent from him during the school year, even though he had grants to cover it. They all figured he would need the money to pay for a decent space when he moved out, not to mention groceries.

"I think we'll be able to work well together. This first apartment I want to show you is the basic single apartment, not much different than Chastity's. You won't be holding parties here. Many of the residents are older and quite vocal about keeping the noise down. I know that sounds like a contradiction in terms, but they don't hesitate to call the building manager, or even the police if they consider a tenant to be making too much noise. Still, the rent is comparable to university residence halls, but you don't have the benefit of meals."

Henry considered the possibilities. The building was quiet, but if he brought Chastity over to celebrate, they'd certainly be thrown out. She was quite vocal at times. The apartment itself was basic. It had one large living area that included the kitchen and breakfast bar with room for a television and sofa. It had one bedroom with attached bath. Henry didn't have too many clothes—especially compared to Chastity, but there would be barely enough room in this closet to put the basics, and if he wanted a dresser, it would need to be in the living room. With just one window in the kitchen and one in the bathroom, the whole place made Henry feel claustrophobic. Each time Henry found an outlet, he tested the circuit and wasn't happy with how few he found.

"It has possibilities," Henry sighed. "I think it's too small. I have quite a lot of computer equipment, and I'm concerned about power."

"Hmm. We might do better to get into a more modern building that has better power, then," Anna said.

Power consumption was always an issue, it seemed, even when AI wasn't involved.

The next building she showed him, however, was newer construction and was pre-wired for cable, WiFi, and had multiple outlets on every wall. The main room was an open space that included a living/dining area and kitchen, much like the first apartment. The bedroom was larger, as were the bath and closet.

He nodded as he checked all the outlets with a circuit tester. He found two twenty-amp circuits in the apartment, plus separate circuits for the kitchen appliances. That meant plugging devices into different outlets wouldn't necessarily mean they were on different circuits. He would need to back each of them up with an uninterrupted power source (UPS), and protect even the company server. It just still felt small.

"I *kind of* like this place," he told Anna. "Is this as good as they get?"

"Well, there is another place I could show you, but you'll want a roommate to split the cost with you. It's quite a bit bigger. It's a renovated older space, so I'm sure you'll want to check the power in it as well. I haven't actually toured it yet, so this will be an adventure."

The unit was a two-suite row house. Henry was concerned that it was older construction and might not be adequately wired, but the renovation had included everything out to the walls.

"According to the listing, the developer who owns this unit is a fanatic when it comes to modern conveniences. He gutted the unit to the shared walls and rebuilt everything. The second and third floors are complete master bedroom suites with private workspaces as well as a lounge area and bedroom. The first floor has a large living room, dining room, kitchen, and a half bath."

"This place is huge!" Henry said as he began surveying the main floor.

It was eighteen feet wide and the front third or more of the length was devoted to a living room with an attractive bay window next to the front door. Then came the stairwell, which was open all the way to the third floor. Beyond the stairwell was the dining room, the kitchen, and a laundry/utility room.

He checked the breaker box in the utility room and discovered the unit was dual metered for the two private suites with a common living area. He continued exploring up to the second floor and found the bedroom at the front of the house. A large sitting area was between the stairs and the bathroom. Beyond the bathroom was a large work area or second bedroom.

"It could be used as a two-bedroom suite, but the owner doesn't want to split the lease more than two ways," Anna said.

"I wouldn't want more than one housemate anyway," Henry said. "Having a full office area is a big bonus." He checked the wiring, noting cable connections in the bedroom, the sitting room, and the second room.

They continued to the third floor. The layout was identical. Henry could imagine two people with full offices in their suites. Anna said even the cable wiring was split between the two suites.

"What's up there?" he asked, pointing to where the stairs narrowed and continued to a door above.

"The listing just says 'usable space, but no bath.' Might as well check it out. If you don't want this place, I can think of some other people who might match the profile."

They went on to the fourth floor and opened the door. This was an open room, about half the length of the unit instead of a full suite. It had windows in front and French doors in back. The doors opened to a rooftop deck. The room was wired as well as the suites, but it was all one open space.

Henry headed back to the third floor, this time checking water pressure and time to heat. Both were good. He also noted that all the bedroom, bathroom, and workspace doors were lockable.

"I suppose that now I'm enthused about the space, you'll tell me it's three or four grand a month," he said.

"List is $4,000," Anna said. "Remember, the owner is expecting to need to split that between two tenants. I could put your application in and go scrambling to see if I can find you a roommate for the other half. Or... hmm... I bet I could get ten percent, or maybe even fifteen off, if you take it as a single lease with a waiver to sublet part of it. I'm betting the owner doesn't really want to manage the housemate situation. If you are the only lessee, I'm sure I could talk him down."

"I assume since everything is double metered, utilities are on top of that," Henry said.

"Oh, yes. If your computing takes up that much power you could be adding a chunk."

"I like it. I'm sure I can find a housemate, but it might take until people start showing up for the fall at the university. And I think my business will chip in to have the office space on the fourth floor. I can handle a few months of the full lease if you can get it down a bit. I'll take the top floor and a half. That's a sweet suite."

"You don't even need to tell a subletter how much of the space you have," she said.

Henry considered that notion, but didn't think it would make a difference. He would have a space large enough that Open Cloak Design could hire one or two people.

He couldn't wait to tell Chastity.

14

IN BUSINESS

CHASTITY WAS READY and waiting when he picked her up for dinner Wednesday at six. They headed east to get away from the city a little.

"I signed a lease this morning," Henry said. "Paid the security deposit and first month's rent."

"When do you move in?"

"We can move in the first of June," Henry said happily.

"We? Henry! Is Carol coming back?" Chastity asked.

"Uh... No... The place has two large private suites. I thought you might like to move with me," Henry said.

Chastity stared at him in silence for a long time.

"I hope you didn't sign the lease with that expectation," she said quietly. "I'm not your girlfriend, Henry. I won't live with you."

"I wasn't thinking you would," he backpedaled. "I signed the lease intending to sublet one suite. I just thought you might like to have a little more room is all. No big deal."

"It *is* a big deal, Henry. My lifestyle is not compatible with sharing a house with anyone. It's bad enough I had to tell you at all. Just be my friend. You take care of me, and when you need it, I take care of you," she said.

"I won't abuse you," Henry said.

"Of course not. That doesn't mean we can't have sex once in a while. Like tonight."

They drove on to a restaurant near the freeway and went in for a very good meal. Henry was quiet, trying to understand all there was to know about

121

his friend. By the time they left the restaurant he decided he didn't need to understand. All he needed to do was accept her and be there when she needed him. And when that included sex, it was a benefit.

THE NEWS OF his new domicile was received by his partners enthusiastically.

"It's more than an official address for the company," Henry said when Luke and Isobel returned to town in mid-May. "There is actually space we can use as an office as long as there's just us. I plan to install the server on the fourth floor and we can get a couple of desks up there. We don't want to do too much. There's no elevator, so let's not stuff it full of crap. Just the basics. Besides, anyone who goes up there has to pass through the living room on the first floor and the second and third floor entries. I'll need to make sure whoever my renter is understands the traffic pattern. The second floor will be off limits to anyone but my renter."

"When can you get in?" Luke asked.

"The lease says June 1, but I talked to the developer this week and he said it was fine to move in over Memorial Day weekend. That's the 29th, 30th, and 31st. That way I'll be moved in and won't interrupt class on Tuesday the first."

"We're only here for this weekend so we can get back to start summer classes," Isobel said. "But we can come back to help move over Memorial Day, can't we Luke?"

"Absolutely."

"Your help will be welcome, but I don't really have that much to move," Henry said.

"You're going to need to buy some furniture," Chastity said. "Even if you take your bed from home, you don't have any living room furniture, no dishes or cookware, and no place to eat. Also, the company needs to pay for office space. You say the fourth floor is about 450 square feet? Shared office spaces in town are going for about three dollars a square foot per month. That would be $1350 per month rental."

"How did you happen to have that info at the top of your head?" Isobel asked.

"My office administration class this term included all kinds of information on what goes into having an office in the city," Chastity answered. "I figured it would be important to the company sometime soon."

"Mom and Dad have agreed to sponsor an attic shopping trip. If I can't find it in their attic or basement, then we go to Goodwill," Henry laughed.

"There's a used furniture store over on Arlington," Chastity said. "That's where I got the things for my apartment. And I already picked up a fireproof safe at the office furniture store next to the convention center. They had lots of used office furniture. I'm sure we can get what we need without spending a ton."

"Speaking of spending," Luke said, "It's time to spend a million dollars. Are you guys ready?"

"What?" Chastity gasped.

"We filed the incorporation papers this week. We now own a company called Open Cloak Design. We are going to transfer $1 million from PRPP LLC to Open Cloak Design in exchange for ten million shares of common stock at ten cents per share. That means 2.5 million shares for each of us. It also means we have a corporate bank account to meet these expenses."

"Holy shit!" Henry said.

"It means we're really in business. The corporate address will be your new row house," Luke said. "I move that this meeting now be opened as the first meeting of the board of directors of Open Cloak Design."

"Hell, yeah!" Henry said. Chastity and Isobel both nodded, almost too choked up to speak.

"Let the record show the first meeting has convened," Luke said.

"What record?" Chastity asked.

"Hmm. All in favor of Chastity as Corporate Secretary say yes," Luke said.

"Yes!" they all agreed. Chastity's vote was a little weaker than the others but she nodded.

"Madam Secretary, please record the minutes of the first meeting of the board," Luke said.

"I move Luke Riordan be elected Chairman of the Board and CEO," Henry said. These motions were really formalities as the group had talked frequently over the past year about the role each of them would play. But it was exciting to act as if they were just launching. And really, they were.

They continued with Isobel elected Treasurer and Henry being confirmed as Vice-Chair and Chief Technology Officer.

"In our first acts," Luke said, "we need to budget the setup of the office, projected expense for any positions we need to fill, and the acquisition of Henry's other patents."

"There went that million," Isobel said.

"Luke and I talked, and with your approval, we think we have a plan that will work," Henry said. "We need the cash in the bank for operating expenses over the coming year. And we all need to draw an introductory salary. Not enough to live high, but enough to help with individual expenses."

"We really mean *introductory*," Luke said. "We're proposing a year one salary for each of us at $1,000 per month. We are all working like hell to get this launched. It doesn't really make a difference what role we are filling; we all need to cover a few of our expenses."

"That's great for us," Chastity said, "but you can't expect Henry to sur-render all the work he's done for a grand. That is really not fair."

"No, but his patents and software are a capital acquisition," Luke con-tinued. "It's why we established the price per share for the founders at ten cents a share. Henry should receive $100,000 for each of the five patents, including the one that was filed in January and hasn't issued yet and the one we've already licensed to the security company. The $100,000 will be pay-able in a stock exchange at $.10 per share. In other words, Henry will receive another five million shares. This isn't set in concrete, so we can have an open discussion before we vote on it."

"I'm still a little uncomfortable with the amount," Henry said. "Thank you for your faith in what I've developed, but they aren't all worth the same amount. Plus, we owe—or I owe—ten percent of the sale to Don Harvey, who has filed everything and deferred payment until the company is estab-lished. I just think that five million shares would give me a fifty percent interest in the company and that doesn't recognize how much you all have contributed."

"You're worth it," Chastity said, reaching over to pat Henry's shoulder.

"I agree in principle that you are worth it, but I'd rather the three of us have the ability to outvote Henry if we feel something is really off the rails," Isobel said. "I'd suggest a $75,000 purchase for each patent for a total of four million shares."

"Henry? Does that feel good or like we're taking advantage of you?" Luke asked.

"I don't think you are taking enough advantage of me. Here's what I'm thinking: The $75k is good, but I already sold one of the patents to the LLC. So, that should put another 750,000 shares in joint ownership by the LLC, in case we decide we want to buy something else. Um... I think that comes out to 3.25 million shares for me, and an extra 750,000 shares in our LLC pool."

"You've always been generous, Henry," Chastity said. "I vote we approve this proposal."

"I agree," Isobel said.

"As an equal partner, I vote yes," Henry said.

"I'll ask the secretary to write up the agreement as a proper motion approved unanimously by the board," Luke said.

The four friends and partners sat at the table in Luke's dining room and talked about the other aspects of the business. Eventually, they resolved the budget, and agreed they would be back together in two weeks to help Henry move. Chastity would go shopping for office furniture and arrange to have it delivered on the Saturday of Memorial Day weekend.

"Hen-ry," Chastity sang softly when they were in the car to take her home. "I just came into a windfall and really want to celebrate."

"What kind of windfall, Chas?" Henry teased.

"I just got two-and-a-half million shares of a hot new tech stock."

"Hon, you know that even though we set a value of ten cents a share, it isn't real money."

"I know. I'm not Isobel. She would have preferred to take her share and bought $250,000 worth of some 'real' stock in a 'real' company. I told you a long time ago, I am in it for the future."

"I'm glad you are. So, you want to celebrate?"

"Yes. I'm not a complete floozy. I pay attention to the news and the markets. Microsoft is over $400 a share. Google is $200 a share. Apple is $250 a share. Do you know how much my 2.5 million shares will be worth when we reach that? Between $500 million and $1 billion."

"It could take years and years to get to that," Henry laughed. "If we ever do."

"Yeah. But it's pretty likely we'll hit a dollar a share or even ten a share in the foreseeable future. That's between two-and-a-half and twenty-five million dollars. In my book, that will make me a rich woman. So, I want to celebrate."

"What would you like, Chas?"

"I would like you between my legs. Face first, then dick second. I want to show you just how happy I am that you are the friend who promised to take care of me. And I'll reaffirm my pledge. Even this summer. When I come to my new office at the top of your house, I'll be wearing a short skirt with nothing under it. My little titties will be easily accessible. If you want to fuck my butt, it's yours. If you need a blowjob, here's my mouth. If you are tired and stressed, I'll rub your back and your shoulders and your front and your dick and anything else you want me to rub."

"You know, you are hired to do actual work," Henry laughed.

"Oh, I will. I'll just always be available to you. And I won't interfere when you get another girlfriend. I'll just go about my work... and still be available."

"And tonight?"

"Tonight, I just want all the sex you can give me!"

It turned out that was a lot of sex, even though Henry went home about two in the morning. The previous week, when Henry had suggested she rent the second suite in his home, they'd had sex later, but it seemed a little mechanical. This time, the sex was raucous, loud, and enthusiastic. Henry didn't even consider his own pleasure for the first hour. He did everything he could to take care of Chastity. When he entered her and they came together, she wept and told him how happy he made her.

Whatever it took, Henry vowed to himself to keep her happy.

HENRY SPENT THE last Friday afternoon of May getting everything he owned into the U-Haul truck his father rented. At nineteen he couldn't rent a vehicle, even though he could rent an apartment. His parents had 'found' pieces of furniture for him that would give him the basics in his new abode, but they also went to Goodwill to pick up things like dishes and cookware and another sofa for Henry's sitting room.

All his computer equipment was packed and Henry was connected to the others only by phone.

"Do you need us tonight?" Isobel texted. "I'm shot!"

"No," Henry responded. "The truck is loaded and I just need to go over to pick up the keys. We move tomorrow."

"We ride at dawn," Luke texted.

"Don't believe him. We'll have breakfast at Denny's about eight-thirty and then go unload. The office furniture people said they would deliver between ten and noon," Chastity said.

"There isn't all that much. We should all be finished by noon," Henry texted.

It was five by that time and Henry drove over to his new apartment to meet the builder.

"How did you decide to equip the house with all the modern conveniences?" Henry asked Ray.

"I built it for myself. I was going to do just what you plan to do and live on the third floor with my office on the fourth. I'd rent out the second floor suite and be sitting pretty," Ray said.

"What made you change your mind?"

"Well, about halfway through the renovation, I met Darlene. We're getting married in two weeks. She was not a suitable lessee for the second floor and didn't want anyone else living in 'our' house," Ray laughed. "I don't work on just one property at a time. I have another place suitable for a married couple, even though I'll keep using the construction trailer as my office for now."

"Well, I'm glad we got matched up. I'll have to look for a housemate this summer, but we're good for a while. The company will pay me some rent for the office and I have a steady income plus my grants. We'll treat the place nicely."

"You don't have to sell me again. Anna did a pretty good job of that. She's a tough negotiator, but she always finds good tenants. Here's the keys. I labeled a full set. You know all the doors are lockable. I'm sure you'll want your office locked and a renter would want their rooms locked separately. I have a full set in the office, but I don't use them unless you make an appointment for service when you aren't there. Here's the card with the phone number. Service includes any faults in the power, water, sewer, appliances, heating, or air conditioning. Or if you find anything has been faultily installed. I hope I never need to see you—though I'm sure we'd get along well in a social environment."

"Thanks, Ray. We'll start moving in tomorrow morning."

<hr>

THEY GATHERED FOR breakfast Saturday morning and were at the apartment well before the estimated delivery of ten o'clock. Henry had labeled the boxes for his bedroom, study, and the office. His mother had labeled the kitchen and bathroom boxes. As a result, the girls were able to move boxes quickly to the correct rooms. Luke, Henry, and Ryan focused on moving in furniture. Their buying expedition had resulted in minimal furniture for the first floor, including seating for the living room, a dining table and chairs, and a few lamps.

When everything was moved in, the space was still sparsely furnished.

Ryan helped Henry set up his bed while Luke joined the women until the delivery truck arrived about eleven-thirty.

He pitched in with the two burly men from the office furniture store to cart desks and filing cabinets to the top floor. When they realized what was going on, Ryan and Henry joined the parade up the stairs.

Chastity directed traffic, telling people exactly where each item was to be set. In twenty minutes, she tipped the guys from the office supply store and Henry started setting up the company server.

Sylvia, Chastity, and Isobel left to get lunch while Ryan and Luke continued to assemble desks and chairs. Chastity had chosen furniture that could be taken apart when they wanted to move again.

"What about phones and printers?" Ryan asked when they'd nearly finished. "Do you have equipment coming?"

Luke and Henry looked at Henry's father and then collapsed on the floor laughing.

"What? What's so funny?"

"Dad, we've got cell phones," Henry said. "Does your company still have a landline?"

"How about a FAX?" Luke asked.

"You'll learn," Ryan huffed. "Maybe you can keep up with just cell phones while there is just the four of you and you don't have any outside business, but eventually, you'll need a permanent phone with extensions for your employees and a number customers will use to reach you. Maybe there will be a wireless system suitable for an office, but it will be a lot more than your smart phones."

"I'm sure we'll need something more than cell phones," Henry said seriously. "Even the house here is wired for something like four different phone lines—in case we need them. But the wireless phone systems are a lot more robust than wired systems. We can conference, transfer, set up voice mail, and even contract a secretarial service for receptionist duties without ever having a person in the office. Once we get our own AI set up, we might not even need that."

"We need to run lean and mean for the next two or three years," Luke added. "Henry will need some help because we can't expect to feed our entire company exclusively off what he develops. He's got ideas that are just sitting in a folder because he doesn't have time to do the development. But as much as possible, we want the operations of the office to be automated and low-impact."

"We weren't actually laughing because phone lines and FAXes are outdated," Henry said. "We were laughing because we had almost the same conversation when we were working on our budget two-weeks ago. Everything we do, we need to weigh against cost and efficiency. We put a million dollars into starting up the company, but it won't last long if we try to act like a big company when there's just the four of us."

"Okay. Well, you had me going for a minute. You guys are a mile ahead of anything I would have dreamed up in my teens," Ryan said. "Do I dare bring up marketing and sales?"

"The pain!" Luke said, clutching his heart. "That's one area that none of the four of us have any experience or desire to gain an experience. I mean, there's lots we don't know about business, but somewhere along the line we need to find someone who can be the Henry of sales and marketing."

"I hope he or she is better than that," Henry said. "We need a genius with a Midas touch."

"I'll keep an eye out," Ryan said.

"Food's here!" Sylvia called from the main floor.

"Maybe we need an intercom," Henry said as they left the office and headed downstairs.

⁂

END PART I

PART II

"*How Smart Is a Rock? To appreciate the feasibility of computing with no energy and no heat, consider the computation that takes place in an ordinary rock. Although it may appear that nothing much is going on inside a rock, the approximately 10^{25} (ten trillion trillion) atoms in a kilogram of matter are actually extremely active. Despite the apparent solidity of the object, the atoms are all in motion, sharing electrons back and forth, changing particle spins, and generating rapidly moving electromagnetic fields. All of this activity represents computation, even if not very meaningfully organized. We've already shown that atoms can store information at a density of greater than one bit per atom, such as in computing systems built from nuclear magnetic-resonance devices. University of Oklahoma researchers stored 1,024 bits in the magnetic interactions of the protons of a single molecule containing nineteen hydrogen atoms.51 Thus, the state of the rock at any one moment represents at least 1027 bits of memory.*"

— **Ray Kurzweil** *The Singularity is Near*

15

DEGREES OF SEPARATION

THERE WERE PLENTY of hiccups in the arrangements over the summer. Henry had to get an extra air conditioning unit for the office and install it in the front window. Isobel raised an alarm at the rate they were spending their investment and returned to Pittsburgh to berate Henry and work with Chastity on refining the budget, including exactly how much they could afford for an assistant to Henry.

"I don't know if I can get any computer pro to work for $25 an hour," Henry said, shaking his head. "Even at just ten hours a week. I realize we're all salaried at $1000 a month, but we're vested in the company."

"There won't be a company to be vested in if we don't get some income to offset these expenses. I can't believe we've been in business for a month and have already spent nearly $50k. We can't keep going like that."

"Okay, I get the point," Chastity said.

"You'd better get it!" Isobel yelled at her. "You won't have a job much longer if you don't."

"Isobel, calm down," Henry said. "You don't have the right to threaten another partner with termination. We'll do our part to keep expenses down. You do your part and pay the fucking bills."

"Maybe it's me who should quit," Isobel shot back. "But then *my* $250,000 would be worth *nothing!*"

They'd made it through the upset, but after Isobel left, Chastity dragged Henry to his bedroom and demanded to be fucked into the mattress.

For his part, Henry spent a lot more than ten hours a week working on his projects. He was able to specify what was needed for an optimization app based on his AI patent. His testers had no options regarding how the program ran. A real user would need settings they could use to at least give the illusion they had control. And they would have limited control over what the AI could learn. Still, it needed to 'look pretty,' as one of the testers said.

On August nineteenth, Henry went to campus for the opening convocation. It wasn't required, but students who were in town were encouraged to attend. It seemed like it had been forever since he met Kaitlyn after the convo the previous year. He hadn't seen her in the spring, as he had resigned from the golf team. He just didn't have the time to play golf on a team.

He was surprised to see members of his study cohort at the convocation and went out to dinner after the event with Lisa and Josh.

"I didn't expect to see either of you until next week," Henry said.

"I never left town for the summer," Josh said. "I got a summer internship over at Monroe Systems Management. Didn't pay much but it was a good experience."

"My dad works there," Henry said.

"I figured Mr. Pascal was related to you, but I didn't have much interaction with him."

"What about you, Lisa? What brings you into town early?" Henry asked.

"I stupidly pledged a sorority last spring and I had to come and act pretty in the Kappa Tau booth to talk to the freshmen this week. I don't know if living in the sorority house is any better than the residence halls, but it's temporary," Lisa said.

"I got a couple more classes taken care of this summer," Henry said. "Between that and my part time job at the golf course, I didn't have time for much else." He didn't want to mention his other work or the new business. It was still too soon to reveal that to classmates. Several had signed non-disclosures to test his invention, but didn't know he was behind it.

They compared their upcoming class schedules and determined they would have Machine Learning and Human AI Interaction together. Henry's other classes in the department were more advanced than either of the others'.

"We should invite Simon and Leonard to join our study group. I'm sure they have a couple of these courses, too," Josh suggested.

"I'd agree to that," Lisa said. "As long as Leonard takes a bath occasionally."

"I hear you," Henry said. "I'm good with inviting them to join. They're both really smart and will give us some different perspectives. Is Dan still in?"

"Oh, sure. He's just not back on campus yet," Josh said.

"How did you get into Computer Vision and Natural Language Processing?" Lisa asked.

"I'm taking ridiculous loads so I can finish in three years," Henry said. "I need to be out of here so I can spend full time getting my business up and operating. It's hard to do while I'm in school."

"Okay, Boy Genius. That means you should be established and ready to hire me the next year when I graduate," Josh said.

"It's not impossible," Henry said. "I just need to find a boatload of money first."

"Henry, could I talk to you for a minute in private?" Lisa asked as they left the restaurant. It was in walking distance to the campus, so they headed back that way as Josh left to catch up with some other friends who had texted him to meet.

"Sure. You headed to the sorority house? We can walk that way."

Henry liked Lisa. She was sharp, a good study partner, and nice looking in his book. She wore her black hair with square-cut bangs and braids. Her round glasses were slightly tinted, probably to compensate for the glare of her computer screen. When they met at the convo, Henry recognized her right away by the clothes she was wearing: a baggy green sweater and rust-colored overalls.

"Hey, you got braces over the summer," he said. "That sure hurt when I had mine."

"Yeah. I don't know why I couldn't have had these when I was twelve like everyone else. Just don't look, okay?"

"Okay, but I think they're kind of cute."

"You would," she laughed. "You... don't mind being seen with me?"

"Why would I? We're right in the middle of campus."

"I... wanted to ask you for a favor. It's no big deal, really. I'm not asking for any kind of commitment, but I don't have a lot of guy friends," Lisa said.

"If I can do something for you, I'm happy to," he said.

"Well, I'm staying over at Kappa Tau for the next month and there's this... event coming up. I kind of need an escort. If I don't come up with my own, my big sister will get a random guy from Omega Rho to escort me. I've met her friends there and I wouldn't trust any of them."

"Just as an... escort to the event?" Henry asked. He winced at the term, thinking automatically of Chastity.

"Dance. It's the homecoming cotillion. I promise not to be a burden. We don't even need to stay that long. I just have to be there for the pledge recognition and I need an escort. Then we can just take off and maybe get dinner or something until the event is over and I can slip back to my room without being noticed."

"Lisa, you're asking me to the fall cotillion at your sorority?" Henry clarified to make sure he understood.

"Yeah... Never mind. I knew it was a bad idea."

"Hey! Don't withdraw the invite, please," he said. "I think that's really sweet. Thank you for inviting me. Let's stop for a cup of coffee and you can tell me all the details. I'd love to take you to the dance."

They stopped at Ground Rules and ordered drinks, then sat to talk. Homecoming was scheduled for Saturday, September eleventh. It wouldn't be difficult for Henry to arrange his schedule for a Saturday date. He and Carol had talked only a couple of times over the summer and he was feeling awfully alone now that he lived in his own apartment.

"It isn't formal," Lisa said. "You don't need a tux or to get a flower or anything like that. It's jacket and tie for guys and dresses for girls. Ugh! I'll have to wear a dress. I'll try not to look too ugly."

"Who thinks you're ugly? You're pretty cute."

"Braces," she moaned. "My big sister at the sorority nearly had a fit when she saw me."

"Not even with braces. And when they come off, you'll really look great."

"Like, don't lay it on too thick," she said. "Thank you for the compliment, I think. I should get back to the sorority. There's still the Greek festival on the commons tomorrow."

They walked on and Henry stopped at the door to the sorority.

"I accept, by the way," he said. "I'd love to take you to the dance."

"Thanks, Henry. I'll see you in class on Monday."

She went in and Henry chuckled to himself at the odd encounter. It would be fun. He was sure. Mostly.

HE DIDN'T REALLY think much more about the dance. He had his work and was trying to decide if a new feature he thought of was an extension of what he had filed or would be a new patent. He needed to talk to Don Harvey and possibly to Professor Jacoby.

He managed to set a time for dinner Tuesday evening, a week after classes started, for Professor Jacoby and Don Harvey to join him at the golf club. Henry described his idea.

"What inspired this?" Jacoby asked.

"I was thinking about how the system could work on a corporate network," Henry said. "If you have an installation on the server, what devices does it work on? If it's only on those directly connected to the server, that's one thing. But there are often devices connected to those devices. Does it automatically install on those as well? And if that device connects to something else, does it automatically go to work there? Sounds more like a virus. So, I'm thinking I need to establish something like degrees of separation from the host install. Like, zero degrees would mean active on the host only. One degree of separation would be to only those devices directly connected to the host. Two degrees would extend to devices connected to the connections. And so on."

"It's really a means to limit the effective range of a distributed application," Don mused. "I can see this as possibly having applications far separate from the optimization app."

"I agree," Jacoby said. "Think about privacy. Could a person limit how far information on a website could be spread? That would be huge."

"Disruptive," Don agreed. "There are some—shall we say marketing apps? Some that depend on both disseminating and collecting information from several levels. What you call degrees of separation."

"Have you tried it?" Jacoby asked.

"I installed it as a limiter on the previous app. It can't affect anything beyond the device that directly installed it. Zero degrees. Then I ran it on my own devices and started thinking I should only have had to install on the server," Henry said. "I spent a good bit of the summer trying to get it to work right."

"I think we should file it separately," Don said. "Don't even mention the previous patent. It might work with that technology, but it is completely separate."

"Yeah," Jacoby said. "And we need to find a suitable testbed for it. Good work, Henry."

"YOU MUST BE running up quite a bill with Don," Jacoby said as he walked to his car with Henry. "I hope he isn't encouraging you to file patents to keep his bills growing."

"We settled everything current. We came into some money last spring when I licensed the first patent. Don got five percent of that for negotiating the deal. With the money we got from that deal, we incorporated. Then the company paid me in stock to transfer the other existing four patents. Don got five percent of those shares."

"He's still betting on you to make it big then," Jacoby laughed. "Well, keep me in mind if you need another round of funding. I know some people who would be interested in investing. What is your current share price?"

"When I transfer the new patent, we'll raise it two cents," Henry laughed. "That will make it twelve cents a share. Of course, that's all on paper at the moment. We aren't public, so we aren't selling."

"Like I said, keep me in mind. I think I could arrange a few million when you need it."

"It will be a while, but thanks. I'll definitely let you know."

HENRY STUDIED THE data from the testers on the optimization app, determining how rapidly the app was collecting user data and improving its performance. The data was all statistical and he didn't have a view into each computer to capture the learning base. That was frustrating.

He'd used the app on the company server and used the new feature of setting degrees of separation so that any computer that connected directly to the server would also be optimized. He was pleased to have his development computer, personal computer, laptop, and tablet all updated and optimized much more efficiently.

He didn't consider, however, that the software would automatically transfer to his partners' computers when they logged onto the server.

The new data for training the AI was much more robust than what was received from any one computer. This was good as far as he was concerned. The AI was learning much faster and still keeping his computer running smoothly and efficiently.

He was in his study when his cell phone rang. He noticed it was Lisa, so he answered immediately.

"Hi there."

"Oh, good. You're alive. You missed class yesterday so I didn't get a chance to confirm that we are still on for tomorrow night. Are you okay?" Lisa said.

"Wow! It's that time already. Sorry to have been absent yesterday, but I was getting a lot of new data on my computer I wanted to analyze. I kind of stayed up all night. I didn't mean to ignore you."

"You're like, not backing out, are you? I mean, not that I'd blame you. The longer I'm in this house, the lamer this whole sorority thing seems. I never should have pledged in the first place."

"I suppose there's no time limit on just saying you aren't interested in them any longer. Why don't you at least wait until after the dance tomorrow night so we can go have some fun. I haven't been out in a long time."

"You mean that, Henry? You think it will be fun?"

"It's all in our attitude. We go to have fun. What could go wrong?"

"Um... Do you, like, drink?"

"Sometimes a beer, but not when I'm driving. Last thing I'd need is a DUI while I'm underage. If you want to partake, I'll look out for you. I'd appreciate it if you didn't drink so much you puke on me."

"Hey! I don't drink. I just know there will be liquor at the party. I didn't want to get stranded because my date was falling over drunk."

"We probably should have talked about that up front. Sorry I haven't been available much this term so far. Just have a lot going on. But it sounds like we're on the same page. No booze," Henry said.

"Yeah. It's funny, you know?

"What is?"

"I don't really know all that much about you except what you're like in class and our study cohort. I talked to my mother and she asked who my date was for tomorrow. She was a Kappa when she was here, which is why I pledged. Anyway, I realized I couldn't really tell her about my date, because I don't know much about you."

"Well, I'm 5'11", black hair or dark enough brown to think it's black. I've got a beard, but try to keep it trimmed and neat. I spend a lot of time sitting in front of my computer, but try to get an hour's walk in each day—mostly around campus. I shower every day, so I don't smell too bad, I don't think," Henry laughed.

"I know that stuff! At least what you look like. Didn't know you exercise. I've never noticed an unpleasant odor around you. That's one of the reasons I asked you. You're kind of the cleanest of our classmates."

"I guess that's a pretty good reason. Why else did you ask me?"

"You're, like, always decent to me. It's a little weird being the only female of our year in the AI program. I just don't feel comfortable with most of the guys."

"As long as you don't expect me to lie down in a mudpuddle so you can walk across my back in your spike heels, or want me to fight off all your admirers for you, I think you can count on me being decent to you. I can't treat you to anything fancy. I'm not here to make your real boyfriend jealous. You know. Stuff like that."

"You're kind of a dope, aren't you? As if I cared about money or have a boyfriend. But I *am* using you to be my date to an event so I don't get passed around to a bunch of frat guys."

"I'm down with that. It might also interest you to know that I have *not* pledged a fraternity and I don't plan to," Henry said.

"It's not like I'm asking you to be my boyfriend or to plan anything beyond the dance tomorrow. That's probably the limit of my socializing for the year."

"Okay, Lisa. What color is your dress?"

"Huh? Green... I guess. You don't need to get a flower. Nobody will have flowers."

"I just wanted to make sure my tie doesn't clash. And I don't want to look like we dressed all coordinated like a couple."

"Oh, God, no! Wear, like, a blue or a red tie. Or if that's too political, black if you want. Don't match me!"

"I think we have the basics down then. I'll be at Kappa house at eight o'clock sharp."

"Okay. I'll see you then. Goodnight."

"Goodnight, Lisa."

HENRY WORKED A while longer, but found he was distracted. He really hadn't forgotten the dance was tomorrow. He had an alarm set on his phone. He supposed he could have been a little less distant since she asked him out, but he hadn't really changed any of his behaviors one way or the other.

He finally shut down, showered, and went to bed. Hmm. He wondered what Lisa would be like as a lover. He shook that thought off. There was absolutely nothing that would lead him to believe he and Lisa would have anything except a decent time at a dance and they would continue as classmates. That was all.

He went to sleep thinking he would need to get a haircut in the morning.

16
PARTY

HENRY GOT HIS HAIRCUT, ate lunch at the mall, and drove his car through a car wash. He went home, showered, and dressed. He was ready for his date and it was only four in the afternoon.

He'd kept a few vital things from Lisa, like Open Cloak Design, but realized he hadn't asked much about her except the color of her dress. They really had a surface-deep relationship.

The creation of androids, or humanoid robots, had come up in one of their expanded study sessions. Henry appreciated the subject but was not enthused. He detected that Lisa was slightly repelled by the concept.

He knew her as an intelligent woman who often had key points to offer to a conversation that enhanced their understanding of a subject. She was cute—as far as he could tell. Her baggy clothes never revealed much about her shape, but he considered her on the petite side with a pretty face.

But who was she? Where did she come from? What were her goals? What was her favorite food? Music? Did they actually have anything besides their classes in common?

He didn't really need to know any of that for their date. It was just a formality—a favor for a friend—taking her to a dance so she didn't get passed around to frat boys looking to get lucky. That was all. He could find out more about her while they were together.

He went into his private study. This room was a bonus in his opinion. It was as large as his bedroom, which was generously proportioned. He had his own computers set up next to a wall, but over the summer, he had added a reading corner and a desk for working on class projects and papers. His development computer was in this room rather than upstairs in the office. Just like his partners did, he connected to the company server via their virtual private network.

The Board of Directors—all four of them—had agreed that until they were full time, Henry's development work on new patents should be considered independent work rather than work for hire. As a result, whatever he created would ultimately be acquired by the company for another $75,000 worth of shares. Of that, Don Harvey would continue to receive $3,750 for his work. Don had readily agreed.

Henry was still absorbed in the new data he'd received on the performance of his new optimization app. He couldn't understand why he seemed to be getting more data than he had previously. He studied the data and finally ran a query on the number of devices represented. He was surprised to find three more than his own collection.

That was when the light turned on. His partners all connected directly to the server through the VPN. That was considered within the one degree of separation he had defined. He hurriedly checked to see if anyone connecting to the website had been "infected" by his app, but the website, even though served by the same server, was not considered a direct connection. That was encouraging. His app would not just continue to spread. It was contained.

Henry's phone alarm sounded and he realized he had spent the entire afternoon in the study and it was time to go to Lisa's party.

HENRY TEXTED LISA when he arrived at the sorority house. "I'm coming up the walk. Do I need to announce myself to someone?"

"I'll meet you at the door," she sent back.

The door opened as he approached and a guy held it open for him.

"I'm here to meet Lisa Hartwell," he said.

The doorman looked at him curiously and then at a stunning brunette just inside.

"Lisa? I mean, like, wow!"

"I hope that means you approve." She gestured to her hair and dress. "It took forever."

Her braces flashed when she spoke and Henry quickly adapted to the 'new look' Lisa.

"You look spectacular. I wasn't expecting anything so elegant and lovely."

He quickly re-evaluated his entire assessment of his classmate. She was obviously still shy, but once freed of the baggy casual clothes he'd always seen her in, she blossomed into a beauty.

"Um... Thanks, I think. It's not exactly my style. My mother bought it for me to attend a cousin's wedding last year. I tried four-inch heels so we'd be more the same height, but I couldn't stand them. Hope this is okay."

She wore a pair of matching green pumps with about a two-inch heel.

"I think you're perfect."

"Don't spread it too thick. I might need my image bolstered later," she laughed.

She looped a hand through his arm and they walked in to the main room of the house. The party had already spread to the dining room and kitchen. Henry thought he heard some voices up the stairs. Lisa introduced Henry to those she met, but got them through to the refreshments.

"Would you mind opening a can of sparkling water for me?" she asked. "I don't trust anything here not to have been tampered with."

"This must really be stressful," Henry said, opening a can of water for her and a pop for himself. "Whatever inspired you to pledge a sorority in the first place? It seems so unlike you."

"My mother," she sighed. "She was everything in college I'm definitely not. Sorority president, queen of the ball, society maven. But she turned around and married the biggest geek in the school. I was the result. She did her best to pressure me into joining the sorority. I guess I take after my father more."

"He must be pretty cool to have a daughter like you."

"God, Henry! Are you just a natural born flatterer?"

"I didn't mean that as flattery," he defended himself. "I personally think being queen of the geeks is superior to queen of the ball."

"Queen of the Geeks. I like that. Considering I'm the only woman in our year in the program. Simon might contest the title of Queen, though," Lisa laughed.

"He did kind of stake a claim to the word early on, didn't he?"

"He loves it! I couldn't invite him to the cotillion, though. He'd have been prettier than me."

The benefit of holding hands at the party—Henry suddenly wondered when her hand had slid down his arm to rest in his—was that with a drink in the other hand, they didn't have to shake hands with anyone; they just nodded and smiled.

"Tell me more about your family. I realized that I don't really know much about you after we talked yesterday," Henry said.

"Last summer, I got hold of my mother's letters and diary from when she was in school here. She talks a big game about how great sorority life was, but she did some pretty nasty stuff before Dad latched on to her and straightened her out. And I mean got her straight, too. By the time she was a senior, she either needed to get married or live on the streets."

"I'm sorry you found out about something like that. I hope it hasn't destroyed your relationship," Henry said.

"No. It wasn't that great a relationship to start with. Now I know I need to deal with an adult who faced some of the same trials and temptations we all face. She's more real now. I don't want to talk any more about it."

"Yeah. I understand. If you ever *do* want to talk, I'll listen," he said.

As they circulated around the party, they spent a little time dancing, but most people were more caught up in the football team's homecoming victory earlier in the day. Henry had only been to one football game the previous fall. He and Carol had stayed for only half of it and then went to the car to make out.

There were obvious temptations for some around the party. Alcohol and weed were plentiful, even though Henry estimated most of the party attendees were underage, like he and Lisa were. Harder drugs were found in corners, usually with a boy convincing a girl to try something. Most of the guys had frat pins on their lapels and didn't seem to be with any particular girl. Many of the girls were apparently unattached as well, and moved freely from boy to boy to boy—sometimes dancing and sometimes just trying to occupy the same space at the same time.

Henry had just led Lisa off the dance floor again to get fresh drinks when a large guy shouldered his way between them.

"Hi. I'm Brad and I'll be your date tonight," he said with a swagger as he faced Lisa. "What say we go find a room and celebrate the victory today. Did you see me sack their quarterback? It was listed as the play of the game."

Henry tapped him on the shoulder and lightly pushed the huge linebacker aside.

"You're dicking around with my girlfriend," he said. "Fuck the hell off."

"Oh, listen to you." The alcohol on the guy's breath was enough to make everyone in the room drunk. "Pretty woman like this deserves a real man. There's a couple skanks here who'll do anyone—even you. Now get lost."

"I said, move aside," Henry said. He gave a tug to Lisa's hand and she spun to his side as if they were still dancing.

"You'll regret that, punk."

"Bite me."

"Hey, Brad! Inverteds!" a guy shouted from a few feet away.

Brad spun on his heel and headed toward his friend waving a bottle of rum in the air. Henry immediately got Lisa on the other side of him and they moved to the refreshment table, leaving Brad to have rum, lime juice, and soda poured into his mouth.

"Hey, Lisa, are you okay?" a young woman asked as she came up to them at the table.

"Hi, Miss Susan. I'm fine. Uh… Susan, this is my date, Henry Pascal. Henry, this is our sorority president, Susan Barkley."

"Happy to meet you, Miss Barkley."

"Let me introduce Eric Jones, president of Omega Rho," Susan said about her date. Eric didn't try to shake hands but bumped fists with Henry.

"On behalf of Omega Rho, I want to apologize for our brother's rude behavior to you both. Brad is pretty full of himself after the game today. He thinks he's immune to common decency. Once he gets this last drink into him, I've asked one of the guys to get him out of here."

"Thank you for your kind apology," Lisa said.

"And Henry, it's a pleasure to meet you. We could use more guys of sound character in our frat. I hope you'll consider pledging during spring rush."

"Thank you for your invitation," Henry said noncommittally. He bet they *could* use guys of sound character. He doubted very much if the frat president would even recall their interaction by spring rush, even if Henry had an inclination to join a Greek society.

"Lisa," Susan said, "don't let this little incident color your impression of Kappa Tau or of Omega Rho. We watch out for each other and most of the guys are really decent. You know, even we at Kappa Tau have a couple of girls of questionable character. We pride ourselves in being the upper crust of the university, but no one can vouch for the character of everyone. You're a legacy pledge and in your mother's honor, we want to welcome you."

"I understand, Miss Susan," Lisa said. "Thank you for talking to a mere pledge like me."

"Oh, Lisa, we have different ranks, but we are sisters as soon as we choose our letters. And may I say, you look truly spectacular tonight. Membership is not based on physical appearances and you were no less welcome as the kind of geeky girl we know you are. But seeing you in this dress, and with your handsome boyfriend, tells us you could also represent the face of the sorority one day."

The two presidents excused themselves and wished them a good time for the rest of the evening. They looked around the room, but didn't see the football player anywhere.

"Miss Susan?" Henry asked after they'd had a sip of their drinks.

"I'm a pledge. She's an active. It's a sign of respect," Lisa sighed.

"Okay. I hope they don't judge you by me. I don't think I'd fit with Greek life."

"It's after eleven. I think I'm ready to leave," Lisa said.

"Don't you live here?" he asked.

"Not tonight. And it's temporary. I'm staying with a friend over at the MacMillan Residence Hall tonight. If you don't mind dropping me there."

"I'm at your service," Henry laughed. "After all, I was just promoted to boyfriend."

"Oh, my God! Don't like... I mean the declaration of the sorority president is not legally binding."

"I'll let you off the hook. I'm ready anytime you are."

"Great. I need my coat and overnight bag from the hall closet. Then we can find the pledge mistress to say goodnight."

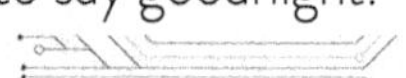

Finding her coat was easier than finding the pledge mistress, but eventually, Lisa said her goodbyes and they left. It was nearly a two-block walk to where Henry had parked and Lisa leaned against Henry while continuing to hold his hand.

"Oh, yeah. Pretty little bitch and her wimpy boyfriend. I'm not done with you yet," Brad said, stepping out of the shadows behind them.

Henry spun to face him, pulling Lisa behind him so he was between her and Brad and dropping her overnight bag beside him.

"Forget it, Brad." Henry said. "You don't want this fight."

"Fight? You think you can fight me for her? You her big brave protector?"

"Women don't need men to protect them. But I won't stand by when a jerk is threatening." Henry noticed Lisa had slipped out of her heels. Whether to defend herself or to run, Henry approved.

"Move aside or I'm coming through you like you're an offensive guard."

"I warn you, I don't fight clean," Henry said. Not that he'd ever really fought before.

"Gonna kick me in the balls? Surprise! I'm a linebacker. I always wear a cup."

Brad moved aggressively as if to push Henry aside. He wasn't expecting Henry's potentially lethal blow to the throat. Brad doubled over gasping for air that wouldn't come.

"You should have worn the cup around your neck," Henry said.

He turned, took Lisa's hand, grabbed her bag, and led her on to the car. She kept glancing back at the boy writhing on the ground.

"Did you kill him?" she asked as they pulled away from the curb. She looked back again but didn't see Brad.

"Don't know. Don't care," Henry said.

"That's... That's all?"

Henry sighed.

"No. I doubt that I killed him. He has a thick neck and I'm not that strong. But I wasn't going to let him hurt either one of us if I could help it."

"Yeah, but..." Lisa was quiet as they drove toward the residence hall on the other side of campus. Finally, she broke the silence. "I suppose... you want to have... sex now," she ventured. "I guess it would be okay. You kind of earned it."

Henry jerked the wheel of the car abruptly to pull to the curb and turned on his flashers. He slammed the car into park and turned to face Lisa.

"Listen to me, Lisa. Get this straight right away. *If* you and I *ever* have sex, it will be because we both really want it. Want it more than anything. It won't be because one of us thinks we're owed or the other is owed, and it won't be because one of us expects it or because it's convenient. I like you. It was an honor to be your escort tonight. I'd happily repeat it in the future. But you are under no obligation to me. *Now or ever.*"

"Henry? Are you angry with me? I'm sorry about it all."

"No. I'm not angry. I'm a little intense at the moment. I think there's still some extra adrenaline in my veins. I didn't mean to frighten you. I'll never do anything to hurt you," he said.

Lisa looked at him as intensely as he was looking at her. She unfastened her seatbelt and leaned across the console. She touched his cheek to pull him to her for a gentle kiss.

"Thank you," she said. They smiled at each other in the dim light of the car.

Henry turned off the flashers, and signaled to pull away from the curb. In a few minutes he found a place to park near the residence hall. He opened the car door for her and took her hand in his again. At the door of the residence hall, she paused long enough to give him another sweet kiss and take her bag, then went in.

NOTHING REALLY CHANGED between Henry and Lisa. They saw each other in class and had lunch with their study cohort to go over the week's notes. Sometimes, the interaction during study time was more like a book club where members drank wine and never discussed the book. Except they had no wine.

Henry felt he had made a breakthrough during the week with his new rendition of the optimization app and had gotten it out to the testers. He was a little more relaxed and was listening to his friends. They'd expanded the study group to include Leonard and Simon this fall.

"I am so glad I'm no longer in the residence hall," Josh said. "I share an apartment with three other guys, but it's still better than the hall. They're pretty good guys and aren't into partying all the time. I can actually get some studying done at home."

"I wish," Lisa said. "I have to be out of the sorority house by the end of the month. Living there through September was a temporary offer. Right now, I don't think I'll even continue with them. I'm still looking for a place."

"Why don't you get an apartment?" Josh asked. "Get a couple girls to share it with you."

"It's not that easy for women," Lisa said. "Single women living alone or with other women are easy targets for predators. There's a woman in my ethics class who was attacked on her way home from class. It was only just after dark and she was walking alone."

"Women shouldn't walk alone," Leonard said.

"Men shouldn't attack women," Henry responded.

"Yeah, of course," Josh rebutted. "None of us at this table would attack a woman. Unless Simon saw one in a dress he wanted. And by attack, I mean run up to her and gush." They all laughed and their gay classmate wiggled his fingers at them. "But reality is reality. Men are assholes. You can see that at every level of government and entertainment. I'm guessing it's the same in any corporate hierarchy. That's why we need to get an AI that will counteract the inherent unfairness of the patriarchy."

"So woke," Dan said beneath his breath. They didn't let it distract them from their conversation.

"I had no idea you were so passionate about that, Josh," Lisa said.

"My old man," Josh breathed. "He is one of said assholes and I'm determined to bring him and those like him to their knees."

"Ooh! In front of me, please," Simon said. Everyone chuckled at that image. Josh clearly was angry with his father, but didn't want to discuss it further.

"Um… I'm looking for a roommate," Henry said to Lisa. "You could check that out."

"Henry! That was just for one night!"

"Wait! Did you two hook up?" Dan asked.

"No! Not like that!" Lisa laughed. "Henry was kind enough to escort me to a sorority party last week. Nothing more."

"I wasn't suggesting you live, like, *with* me," Henry said. "I've got a pretty cool apartment that has a lock-off suite. I'm looking for a subletter, not a girlfriend."

"Really? How much?"

"$1,500 plus your share of utilities."

"Kitchen?"

"Shared with me. Equal responsibility for keeping the place clean."

"Equal?"

"Absolutely, unless one of us gets suddenly fabulously rich and can afford a cleaning service. I'm not anticipating that in the near future," Henry said.

"Could I… see this lock-off suite?" Lisa asked.

"I'm not doing anything this afternoon. Let's go over now."

"Hey, giving a tour? Can we all come?" Josh asked.

With that, Henry and six classmates headed in three cars to his row house. Lisa rode with Henry.

17

DISCLOSURE

IT WAS THE FIRST time Henry had anyone visit his apartment outside of his parents and business partners. Chastity came in once a week just to use the office as an official place of business, though there was very little paper mail. She did handle all the non-disclosures and business records, though. And she'd begun looking at resumes for part-time user interface developers. Very few wanted a job of only ten hours a week with possible weeks off, and of those, most wanted $50 an hour or more.

When Henry's cohort and classmates finally found parking spaces, he led them into the main floor of the apartment. It was still so sparsely furnished that the living room echoed with their voices.

"This place is huge!" Josh said, coming out of the kitchen. "But there's no bedroom."

Henry pointed to the stairs and led them to the second floor suite. They explored the front bedroom, back bedroom, and sitting room.

"Don't you use one of the bedrooms?" Dan asked.

"No. I've got an identical suite on the third floor. This whole floor is to be rented by my subletter."

"I'd pay two grand for this," Leonard said. "Can I have the second floor?"

"No!" Lisa said. "Is this an auction, Henry?"

"Not at all, Lisa. I offered the suite to you for $1,500 plus your utilities. If you want it at that, it's yours."

"Sold!" she shouted. "When can I move in?"

"Henry? Is that you? I thought I heard voices," Chastity said as she came down the stairs.

"Hi, Chastity. I'm just showing the second floor suite. I think I have a renter," he said as she appeared on the stairs.

"Holy sh...! I mean... Is this your girlfriend, Henry?" Josh asked.

Chastity was dressed in her usual 'office attire,' with a mini skirt and a crop top. At the moment, she happened to be barefoot, having jumped up from her desk and rushed downstairs when she heard voices. She stopped short when she saw the group.

"No. Chastity is one of my business partners. We have a small office on the fourth floor. Lisa, I should have mentioned that there would be others coming in to work on occasion, though none of us are around full time. Chastity likes to come in on Fridays so it feels like we've got a real office."

"I'll always knock first," Chastity said. "I won't come in without letting you know."

"I guess that's okay. Are there a lot of you?" Lisa asked.

"Only the four partners at the moment," Henry said. "I'm looking for another part timer, but he or she might not even work out of the office. And the other two partners are students at Villanova, so they really only show up with one of us."

"Wait! Wait!" Simon said. "Chastity? As in... Like, are you the person I sent my non-disclosure to at PRPP for testing?"

"Oh, you're kidding!" Josh said.

"You guys are PRPP?" Leonard asked.

"You guys are all testing for PRPP?" Henry asked, holding his breath. They all raised their hands and nodded.

"Jacoby said it was a good opportunity and we should all take a look at some practical AI development," Josh said.

"Okay, then you know that your non-disclosure includes not revealing who you are testing for," Henry said, scowling at them.

"Was that a violation?" Lisa asked.

"Technically, yes. But I'll let it pass. I just want to remind you that your discovery of our actual business and ownership is not permission to disclose it to anyone else. Let's go downstairs and have a pop. I'll answer your questions."

"Can we see the office first?" Leonard asked, apparently not quite believing the story.

"Sure," Henry said, turning to the staircase.

All of his classmates were watching the retreating figure of Chastity in her short skirt going up the stairs. They followed Henry.

"It's not really much to look at," Henry said, pointing at the four stations where computers could be set up.

Chastity's laptop was on her desk and she quickly sat behind it. She'd done some minimal decorating over the summer with plants and some artwork. A photo of the four founders the night they signed the incorporation papers hung on one wall.

"We have a company server," Henry continued. "We self-host our online work and our website where you've downloaded the app you're testing. Because it's just Chastity and me at the moment, there really isn't much else here."

"Nice patio, though," Dan said, looking out the French doors.

"I figure it will be unusable after the first snowfall," Henry laughed. "Let's head downstairs now and let Chastity finish her work."

They all left, several of the guys giving a backward glance at the sexy Chastity behind her desk.

THE DISCUSSION CONTINUED in the living room after they had chosen soft drinks and Henry found a bag of chips.

"So, you're really the inventor of the stuff we've been testing for the past six months?" Josh asked.

"Yes," Henry sighed. "I hope you can understand why we want to keep that quiet. I don't have a lot of jobs to offer and everything is really experimental at the moment. I've filed the necessary patents and five of the six have been issued. But the app is still under development. If I was fielding questions at school all the time, I'd never get any studying done."

"Got it," Dan said expansively. "We've all become close over the past year. I think we can keep this among ourselves. Right, guys?"

"No question," Leonard said. "I'd still want to know what I needed to do to work here. The app is rad. My machine runs faster than it ever has."

"I noticed a new feature that lists 'Degrees of Separation.' But it's locked at zero. What is it?" Josh asked.

"You should read the release notes," Henry laughed. "We'll test that feature sometime soon, but it has to be in a controlled environment. Locking it at zero means it can only run or affect the machine it's installed on. But in a small business or corporate environment, you might want to have it running on the network. I have it installed on our server upstairs, but that means it only runs on my machines and those of my partners, who attach via VPN."

"Our computers?" Leonard asked.

"No. You only access the website. You never actually get on the network."

"Are you going to launch it as part of PRPP? It's not a very sophisticated name. I thought it was a law firm," Dan said.

Henry paused to think about the answer. These were the people he was closest to other than his partners and it would be helpful to bounce some ideas off them occasionally. He figured he could afford some transparency.

"PRPP is, like, a holding company. The four of us are partners in it. But as soon as the patents issue, they are assigned to Open Cloak Design, which is our development corporation. If you decide you want to continue testing after this release, your next non-disclosure will come from OCD. Eventually, when we've got everything running correctly, no one will ever see PRPP. It will just be a stock holder."

"Any way to buy in?" Josh asked.

"Not at the moment," Henry said.

"Not to make this all about me, but when can I move in?" Lisa asked. "The sooner I'm out of the sorority house the better."

"I can help with that," Chastity said, entering the room. "If you'd like to come over here to the dining table while Henry entertains the guys, I'll go over the lease with you."

Lisa went with Chastity and the guys continued talking for half an hour before they finally took off.

<hr>

"As MUCH AS I'd like to move in tomorrow, I need to set some things up first. I'll move next weekend," Lisa said as Henry drove her home.

"Anything I can help with?" Henry asked. "I could get a couple of guys to help with the move."

"It's not that, exactly," Lisa said. "I just rented an unfurnished apartment and I don't have any furniture. I have some things at home my parents will haul up for me. I'll have to stop at some used furniture place, too. I don't even have a bed."

"I hear you. I spent a week shopping for used furniture before I moved in. Mom and Dad and my partners all helped get the apartment set up."

"Are your... other partners... as slick as Chastity?"

"Chas is in a class by herself. Isobel is more glam. Luke is conservative, but good looking, I guess. Why do you think Chastity is so hot? Keep in mind, I've seen *you* in a dress and makeup."

"Yes, but that was, like, a character I put on in order to survive the night. I bet you've never seen Chastity when she didn't look like she was ready to go out on a date."

Henry wasn't sure he wanted to continue that conversation.

"Probably."

"There are girls in the sorority who would literally kill to look like her. But they aren't willing to put in the work," Lisa said. "I really like Chastity."

"I'm glad," Henry said. "I do, too."

Lisa didn't pursue the conversation as Henry pulled up to the sorority to let her off.

"By the way, there's a bus line a block from the house that comes straight to the student union. If I'm driving and we're going in at the same time, you're welcome to ride along. It's twenty minutes by bus and usually takes me that long to find a parking space. Most of the time, I ride the bus."

"Good to know," Lisa said. "Thanks for everything, Henry. I'll see you in class next week."

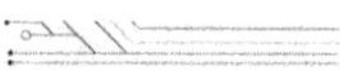

"PLEASE DON'T CANCEL our rental agreement when you meet my parents," Lisa said when she met Henry after class on Monday.

"Did they not think moving was a good idea?"

"Mother. She's so tied to the sorority that she thinks I'm throwing my life away by leaving it. She wants to be sure 'my boyfriend' is upstanding and will be able to support me."

"Wait! We're not involved like that," Henry said.

"My dad understands that, but Mom is still convinced that a girl should go to college to find a husband, and should have as much fun as possible during the hunt. She can be a little overbearing at times. Please, don't even mention that we've been on a date. That was a nice thing to do for a friend, but Mom would immediately jump to wedding invitations."

"Do you want me to just not be around?"

"Henry, it's your house. I'm just a renter. And I really will appreciate the help when it comes to moving furniture up those stairs. Dad isn't exactly a super fit jock."

"I'll get Josh to come over and help. He said he was willing."

"I like Josh. He seems like a guy with a conscience. Besides, that will keep my mother guessing," Lisa laughed. "See you later."

FRIDAY, HENRY SPENT some extra time cleaning the downstairs so it would all look good when Lisa and her parents arrived. Her mother sounded like a real piece of work. Well, he could put up with her for an afternoon, and Lisa made it sound like her father was a really nice guy. What a combination of people!

Chastity came downstairs and found him moving the furniture around to vacuum under it. She bent to the task of helping him, which made her mini-skirt ride up all the way to her butt-ledge.

"Mmm. Now that's appetizing," he said.

"I already told Lisa that you and I wouldn't mess around here. If you want to have a little fun, you'll have to come to my apartment," Chastity laughed, pushing Henry down on the couch. She plopped in his lap. "Of course, she isn't moving in until tomorrow."

"How did us having sex come up in a conversation with Lisa?" Henry asked.

"Oh, she's very perceptive and direct. She asked me straight out if I was your girlfriend or just a friend with benefits."

"Well, that's pretty forward."

"She just wanted to know what to expect when she moved in. I told her I'm not your girlfriend and I wouldn't compete with another woman for your affection. But I am *always* available to you—for *anything* you need."

"Did she ask you to hang out tomorrow while her parents are here?" Henry asked.

"Nope. And I don't intend to be here."

Henry stroked up and down her bare thigh and planted a tongueless kiss on her lips. He considered whether this was one of those times when he needed her and decided it would be if he kept this up.

"Oh, I came downstairs to show you a résumé I received. I think this could be the answer to your need for a UI developer," Chastity said, handing him her phone with the resume displayed on it.

"There's no name," Henry said as he scanned down the resume. "Ah! Student. Someone I already know perhaps?" He continued reading. "Experience as a game UI developer for EZ Daze Corp? They're the hottest RPG game developer around. This guy is rad."

"What makes you think it's a guy?" Chastity teased.

She was still holding the phone for him while Henry's hand slid up under her crop top to play with her nipple rings. Occasionally, Chastity caught her breath or leaned in to nibble his ear.

"Guy. Gal. Makes no difference to me. Student who wants part time work. If he or she is legit and we can work together, I'm sold. It's a lot better than the guys who have no experience and want $75 an hour with paid vacation and insurance. I say arrange an interview and let's get some pretty pictures put around the code," Henry said.

Chastity dropped her phone on the sofa and turned in Henry's arms to straddle him. Her skirt slid up to reveal she had no underwear covering her bare pussy. She worked on Henry's belt and zipper as he pushed her top above her breasts and leaned in to suck on her. A condom fell out of the bunched-up material.

"I thought I might get you hot with this news," Chastity said as she nibbled on his ear.

Henry pushed his trousers down so his erection stood between them. Chasitity rolled the condom on him and lifted enough to slot his cock into her willing pussy.

"Oh, yeah," Henry said. "I really needed this."

"Frankly, so did I," Chas said. "I do prefer to *enjoy* sex. Yes. Right there. It's been four weeks since we last did this. Too long."

"I agree. And the last time was in the office upstairs. Sometime, we need to actually make it to a bed."

"Mine will be available. Just don't turn down any good chances for romance should they come along."

"I doubt there will be much in the near future. I'm not seeing many women around. The only place I meet them is in class. There just aren't a lot."

"Just be aware. In the meantime, thrust up into me. More!"

Henry tried to be sure Chastity 'enjoyed' their coupling before he let go and filled the condom. She collapsed against him, both breathing hard.

"I should get back to work," Chastity said. "I'll arrange an interview next week. I'm pretty sure you'll like this one."

They moved apart, Chastity slow to pull either her skirt or top down to cover her. Henry stripped off the condom and gave her one more kiss before he pulled up his own jeans. Chastity headed toward the stairs, strutting with her bare bottom showing as she disappeared out of sight.

JOSH ARRIVED AT Henry's row house about the same time Lisa texted that she and her parents were ten minutes away. When Henry saw the U-Haul truck turn onto his block, he pulled out of his parking spot to make room for Josh to direct the truck backing up to the sidewalk. The street wasn't wide, but there was room for traffic to pass. Henry had to park a block away and then jogged back to where Lisa was introducing her parents to Josh.

As soon as he arrived, Henry was also introduced.

"This is my landlord, Henry Pascal," Lisa said. "My parents, Bill and Jaqueline Hartwell."

"Happy to meet you. Can we just start moving things or did you want to show them the place first?" Henry asked Lisa.

"Tour!" her mother said.

"Let's just grab a load and start carting. We'll have plenty of time for the grand tour. We shouldn't keep the street blocked any longer than absolutely necessary," Lisa's father said, cutting off her mother's intention.

Bill unlocked the back of the truck and they immediately started carrying furniture.

"I'm going to use the back bedroom for sleep and the front for my study," Lisa said as Henry and Josh pulled a mattress off the top.

"Makes sense," Henry said. "It's a long way from the front bedroom to the bathroom, but I spend more time in my study than in my bedroom."

"Oh, my! Bill, you let the boys carry the furniture upstairs," Jaqueline said. "You and I can carry the clothes."

"I'm not frail," Bill groused. Still, he did what his wife said and carried a box up the stairs. "I'm really not that old," he said to Henry as they met in the bedroom. "I just can't depend on my back all the time."

"Any time you need to, flop down and rest. There isn't really that much in the truck. Josh and I can handle it," Henry said.

"Lisa has told me a lot about you. I'm glad she found a good place to live. Don't pay any attention to Jackie's's commentary. In one breath, she'll be treating Lisa like a five-year-old and in the next she's impatient for grand-children. But as much as they bicker, they are both very supportive of each other."

The bickering started in when the guys passed through the lower level on their way upstairs with another load.

"Mom! You can't just start rearranging Henry's things in the kitchen to make way for what you bought," Lisa said.

"But this cookware is so much nicer than these old pots and pans," Jackie shot back. "You need to take control of this relationship and not let him walk all over you."

"Henry and I don't have a relationship, Mother! He's a classmate and my landlord. That's all. He owns the space. I'm just a renter."

"Hey, anything you need to rearrange in the kitchen, have at it," Henry said, stopping by. "Just leave me a map of where my things end up, okay?"

"Such a nice boy!" Jackie said.

Henry, Josh, and Bill all laughed as they headed back to the truck.

As soon as the truck was unloaded, Bill pulled the truck out of the space. Henry pulled his car back in. Bill parked in a bank parking lot a couple of blocks away and strolled back to the apartment looking around the neighborhood. He arrived back at the apartment at the same time a delivery driver was handing off Thai food for the group's late lunch.

"I don't like you living in sin, Lisa. It would have been much better for you to live at the sorority house," Jacqueline said.

"You can't mean that, Mother. If you want to tote up sins, the sorority house is ten times worse than living here. How many times do I have to tell you Henry and I are not romantically involved? This is my suite and it locks."

"And where does Henry sleep?"

"He has an identical suite on the third floor. I've never been up there to see it. He has an office on the fourth floor."

"I'm so sorry! He must be blind not to see what a treasure he has living under the same roof."

"Mother, I'm focusing on school. Nothing else."

"I was so afraid you'd fail your classes because you'd fallen in love like I did. I barely managed to graduate."

"You send a lot of mixed messages, Mom," Lisa said exasperatedly.

They joined the others in the dining room. Henry only had four dining chairs, but he had a couple of folding chairs so they could all sit.

"Is this food from Thai Palace?" Jackie asked.

"Yes," Henry said. "It's convenient and they deliver."

"I always loved the food from Thai Palace. And it's so affordable, too."

"That helps," Henry chuckled.

"What's your religion, Henry?" Jackie asked brightly. Lisa and her father both groaned.

"Religion? I don't spend much time thinking about religion. How about you, Josh?" Henry deflected the question.

"I'm Jewish," Josh answered. "But that's a culture, not a religion."

"We're Methodists," Jackie continued with a note of pride in her voice. "The liberal branch. We accept all races, societal levels, and sexual persuasions."

"I'm not a Methodist, Mother! I'm an atheist. There *is* no god."

"That exhausts the subject of religion," Bill chimed in. "Henry, Lisa tells me you have started a company, but said she wasn't allowed to say anything else about it. What are you working on?"

"Lisa and Josh are both under non-disclosure," Henry said. "I didn't even know who was on our tester list until last week. They kind of discovered us by accident when one of my partners came downstairs while I was giving a tour. Without going into detail, we are a small software development company working on new systems and processes utilizing AI for computer optimization and power conservation. We wrote that up this week after the guys found out who we were."

"Sounds interesting," Bill said. "I started a company just out of school. If you need to bounce any questions or ideas off someone, give me a call. I'll even sign a non-disclosure."

"Thank you, sir."

18

DEVELOPMENT

"HEY, GUYS," HENRY said when Luke and Isobel connected to the Zoom meeting the next Friday. "I've got you on the big screen. We've got a web cam set up for the interviewee. I hope we don't scare her away, but I thought our first hire interview should be with all four of us. I can't believe we're interviewing to hire someone!"

"This is where it gets real, bro. Chas says this candidate is the real thing, though. It's mostly going to be you making sure you can work with her."

"She'll win him over quickly," Chastity predicted.

"Hello," Lisa said when she came down the stairs into the living room.

"Oh, hi, Lisa. Um… We're on a Zoom meeting and I'm expecting a job candidate any time now," Henry said.

"I know," Lisa said.

"Henry, Isobel, and Luke, the candidate we're interviewing is Lisa Hartwell. She also happens to live in the second suite here at corporate headquarters," Chastity said. "Sorry I kept her identity from you, Henry. I was afraid you'd jump the gun and start interviewing before she even had her boxes unpacked."

"I don't know why I'm even surprised," Henry said. "Welcome, Lisa. Let me introduce Chastity and my other two partners, Luke Riordan and Isobel Perez."

"Welcome, Lisa," the long distance partners said.

"Hi. It's nice to meet the whole company."

"You are our first interview, so we decided we should all at least watch," Isobel said. "You know you're on camera, too?"

"Yes. I can see myself on the big screen here in the corporate living room," Lisa laughed.

"Well, Lisa, let's get right to it. Tell us about your background and experience," Henry said. "I already know your education experience here at the university because we've shared several classes and a study group. But your resume says you worked for EZ Daze Corp for four years. You started in high school?"

"Uh, yes. And I'm still doing some dev work for them," Lisa said. "You met my father and he told you he had a small development company. It's EZ Daze. I learned coding working on the games and did a lot of the UI development."

"Oh! Wow! Uh... Why do you want to work with us then?"

"I talked it over with the owner of EZ Daze," Lisa said. "He told me he thought it would be good for me to get experience with a different type of development and interface needs. He also wants to know if he's a good boss or a bad one by comparison."

"What do you think?" Henry asked.

"Well, I haven't actually worked for you, but Dad's a good manager, in my opinion."

"You've done some testing of our new app as part of the test group. What would you say is the top UI need?" Henry asked.

"Well, obviously it needs a GUI. No one is going to buy a program that runs from a command line with a dozen tokens and arguments. Especially since your target user isn't necessarily a computer programmer. It doesn't make a difference what platform today's user is on, they are only familiar with graphic interfaces. So, we need to start by outlining what the options are, then wrap pretty pictures around them that will make the user comfortable with selecting them."

"So, we just need some drop-down menus, right?" Luke asked.

"I think we probably need something more than that," Lisa laughed. "Not only do people need access to the options, they need to know what each one is controlling. For example, the newest drop of the app has a feature called 'Degrees of Separation.' I saw the old movie about the con-artist who convinced people he was the son of Sidney Poitier. It was a required part of my training to be 'on my own,' as my father put it. But it didn't tell me anything about what this feature is."

"So, you think we need an explanation of the feature in the UI?" Chastity asked.

"Sort of. Henry explained it to a bunch of us a couple of weeks ago, but users might not even get the reference then. A simple picture that showed the levels of reach for the app would make it clear."

"Can you show us?" Henry asked, handing her a tablet and stylus.

She quickly sketched a three-level flow chart that showed the top single computer as being 'Just my machine.' The next row of a few computers said, 'Machines connected to mine.' The third row of more computers said, 'Machines on my server.'

"I skipped a couple of levels," she said. "The concept is that the user will know how far the effect will be felt without burdening them with learning about a 1990s movie."

The interview progressed well and all three partners chimed in with questions. They had a rather good time, even though Chastity had to quash a question by Isobel regarding whether Lisa had a boyfriend as being an unacceptable interview question.

"So, what do you see in the future with Open Cloak Design?" Henry asked.

"What I've seen so far is all good. I know you are concerned about computer optimization and that leads you to power conservation as well. You mentioned one of your optimization apps was licensed by a big security company. I'd see more of that. You want to use AI in creative ways. How about in protecting your system? You're already screening for viruses. What else?"

"Interesting," Henry said. "It's always seemed odd to me that firewalls just protect the host, but they don't really do anything to repel the attacker. They're passive barriers. The hacker can continue to attack the wall, but no one is standing up there pouring boiling oil on them."

"That's picturesque," Isobel said.

"Guys, do we need a further consult?" Chastity asked.

"It's Henry's call," Luke said. "I'm satisfied."

"If you can work together and not cost a fortune, I'm in," Isobel said.

"Henry, are you ready?" Chastity asked.

"I don't think every hire is going to be this easy," Henry said. "Lisa, we'd like to offer you a contract position for up to ten hours a week developing User Interfaces for our products. As a contractor, we'll still be deducting taxes, but we don't have health benefits, accumulated vacation time, or really any other benefits, except I always keep pop in the fridge you can help yourself to."

"I'd like to accept that offer," Lisa said. "I think this will be both fun and educational."

"For both of us," Henry agreed.

"HENRY! HOW NICE to see you again!"

Henry turned at the sound of the voice in the student union on Wednesday to see Kaitlyn Lau, his former golf teammate.

"Kaitlyn, hi! It's been a while."

"The team could have used you this fall! We've got one more tournament down in Florida next week, then it's packed up until spring. You could still join for the spring season," Kaitlyn said.

"I'm carrying a heavy course load and just don't have time for extracurricular activities," Henry said. "Join me for lunch?"

"I'd love to."

They moved through the cafeteria line and picked up food, then found a table that wasn't too crowded.

"How'd you happen to be all the way over in this part of campus instead of near the golf course and athletic facilities?" he asked.

"I get bored over there," she answered. "All the conversations are about sports. I like sports, but there are other things happening in the world, you know?"

"How true. It's sometimes that way near the computer science area. It's not unusual to hear people talking code at lunch," Henry laughed.

"Do you hear anything from Carol?" Kaitlyn asked.

"We text back and forth occasionally. I guess not as much anymore."

"Too bad. You two made a cute couple."

"Thanks. Different dreams. You understand that."

"Yes. Well, sometimes you have to wake up and take notice of what else is happening in life," Kaitlyn said. "How's your business going?"

"We're getting started. Pretty slow at the moment because we're all in school, but we made our first hire this past week, so there's a chance we could release an actual product by spring."

"How exciting. Are you playing any golf at all?"

"I haven't played since school started this fall. I had to cut my hours at the club, too."

"Let's play a round Saturday!" she said enthusiastically.

Henry hesitated, thinking at first, she'd said 'Let's play around.' Kaitlyn was certainly a pretty girl and he wouldn't mind playing around. She'd made it clear, though, that she was only interested in husband material, and Henry didn't fit her profile.

"That would be fun if you don't humiliate me too badly."

"I'll give you four strokes," she said.

For some reason, everything she said seemed to be loaded with double entendre. Henry blamed it on his dirty mind. It hadn't been that long since he'd been with Chastity.

Ultimately, they agreed that Henry would pick her up at her apartment Saturday morning and they would go out to Constitution Links.

HENRY SPENT FRIDAY afternoon in the office with Lisa and Chastity. Lisa was still coming up to speed with what Henry envisioned for the new generation of software. Lisa did a lot of sketching and brainstorming.

"We might get the protection software started soon, too," Henry said. "I don't think I want it rolled into the same app, though. I need to work on the AI being able to identify threats and not to respond whenever someone pings the server. We'll get things spec'd out in the next couple of weeks."

"I can see there are elements of the current app that you might want to use in the protection software," Lisa said. "I'll start putting together a couple of prototypes for the UI and we can review them next week." Lisa looked at her screen. "Oh! We're on fall break next week! No classes. I might fly back to Louisiana for the week. I need to call Mom and Dad."

"That works for me. I'm going out to play golf tomorrow morning. It might be the last time the weather is good enough to play and I haven't had time since school started. I'll probably be buried in code the rest of the week."

"Ah! I'm ready for a break from life!" Chastity said. "I think I'll go find a warm sunny beach. I'll see you two next Friday. Or the week after. Whatever."

IF IT WEREN'T for the four strokes Kaitlyn gave him, Henry's score wouldn't have been close to hers. He definitely hadn't been keeping up with his game.

"Well, maybe we aren't missing as much on the team as I thought," Kaitlyn laughed when he double-bogeyed a par four.

"That was embarrassing. I can't remember the last time I didn't par that hole."

"Well, you looked pretty while doing it," she said as they teed up on the next hole.

Talk about looking pretty! Kaitlyn was a natural Asian beauty to start with. Dressed in her short golf skirt and tight sweater, she looked incredible. Since it was late in the season and many golfers had already put up their clubs for the winter, they were able to golf as a pair rather than accepting another pair for a foursome. It was giving them a lot of time just to catch up.

"Next week, I'll be down in Sarasota for the Fall Nationals," Kaitlyn said. "Last year the temps there were in the mid-80s. I won't even need to play in a sweater."

"If you took that off, it would definitely make the game more interesting."

"If you par the next hole, I'll show you," she said.

Henry didn't remember Kaitlyn ever being so flirtatious. Even when they'd gone out a couple of times the previous fall, she'd made it clear she wasn't into dating around. It was just a game between friends.

Nonetheless, Henry rose to the challenge and managed a birdie on the next hole.

"Have you been sandbagging?" Kaitlyn demanded.

"No such thing," he laughed. "Just a couple of lucky shots."

Kaitlyn looked around as they headed to the next hole and pulled Henry off the path and behind a tree.

"It's too cold to take it off," she said.

She grabbed the hem of her sweater and lifted it up above her breasts. On the way up, she hooked her bra with her little fingers and pulled it up, too. Henry was faced with two delicious looking breasts with nipples hardening in the cool air. He caught his breath and Kaitlyn lowered both the bra and sweater back into place, then wiggled around a bit to get her boobs seated in the bra correctly.

"Wow!"

"If you want more than that, you'll have to take me someplace warmer. Or come down to Florida and be my good luck charm. It always worked for Carol."

"I mean, wow, Kaitlyn! I did not expect that!" he said.

"If you'd only made par, I'd have left the bra in place, but superior performance deserves superior rewards."

"I honestly didn't even expect the sweater to be lifted."

"I made the wager. I pay up. I've always thought you were pretty cute and regretted not pursuing a relationship last year. Maybe it's not too late."

Henry didn't shoot as well through the rest of the game.

WHEN HENRY TOOK Kaitlyn home after lunch, there was no suggestion that he come in. He did, however, receive a very warm kiss and a promise to be available when she got back from Sarasota if he'd like a date someplace other than the golf course.

He spent his week drawing up the specification for a firewall counter-attack. Lisa had gone back to Louisiana for the break. Villanova didn't have a fall break like his. Chastity had told him she was not available for the week because she really needed a break. So, there was no one available to talk over his idea for counterattack software.

It was relatively easy to plant a virus on a computer once access was granted. It could amount to anything from spyware to ransomware to file or system corruption. It was considerably harder to identify the source of an attack. Hackers knew methods of routing their attack through different proxy servers across the internet. Sometimes the misdirect went through ten or more servers that didn't know they were being used for an attack. These servers could be anyplace in the world while the attack was coming from right next door.

By the time a defender tracked the attack to the source, the attack was usually over and the attacker would have disconnected. But the time-honored method of tracking that attack was to have an equally competent hacker employed to reverse engineer the direction. That took time.

Time Henry decided he didn't need to take. A sufficiently trained AI could retrace an attack in a fraction of the time it took a human hacker. The AI needed to use some of the same tools a hacker would use in the first place.

Henry didn't leave his study for the entire week. He slept little and ate food that was delivered. On Saturday morning, he got a text from Lisa saying she was arriving on a two o'clock p.m. flight from New Orleans. "Just letting you know in case you need to hide a bunch of naked ladies dancing around the apartment. 😍!"

Henry looked around. There were no naked ladies, but the house was a mess. Dishes filled the sink. Empty food containers were on the counters. There were even a few beer bottles lying around. Even in his own study, debris had been left to accumulate. And Henry stunk.

He started laughing hysterically. He was the epitome of the social recluse computer hacker he was trying to prevent getting access to his computers. He launched a blitz-cleaning of the entire apartment, running the dishwasher and emptying the trash. He vacuumed and dusted and wiped things down. Then he headed for his bathroom and stripped off his boxers, which were the only thing he'd been wearing the past few days.

The hot shower felt fantastic. He combed his hair and trimmed his beard. Then he cleaned his bathroom and started a load of laundry. That meant stripping his bed and putting clean sheets on it—something he hadn't done since before Lisa moved in. Not that she would know that, but he felt bad that he'd been so neglectful.

About three o'clock, Lisa stumbled in the front door pulling her carry-on behind her.

"Hey, you're back," Henry said, standing up from the couch in the living room.

"Hi! It was a good trip. I'm exhausted. I'm headed up to get a shower and maybe a nap. Don't mean to be anti-social, but I've been social for six straight days!"

"I understand. Let me know if you want to share an order-in dinner. I don't have anything in the fridge."

"I might be ready around six. Wait. The house smells—did you just clean?"

"I tidied up a bit. No big deal."

"Wow. I don't suppose you cleaned my suite? I didn't think so. Oh, well. See you later."

Henry breathed deeply and headed back upstairs to his study where he'd left a window open so it would air out.

HENRY WAS SATISFIED with his development of the counterattack software. The AI was working well, tracking back every system ping with a ping of its own. Henry could see the log of exactly where each ping on his server had come from.

Of course, pings were not attacks. Even major search engines pinged servers all over the world to verify they were on and available. Henry had put in criteria that included number of contacts, number of attempts to enter further, and number of stops by the firewall. He set the numbers sufficiently high that he believed anything beyond that point would constitute an attack.

The response was to corrupt the system core files. Corruption can be temporarily achieved by simply changing the file type identifier in the file header. That can be done even on compiled code. The damage caused by this could be easily corrected by reinstalling the system. It wouldn't damage any content files.

As a final touch to his system, Henry applied the 'degrees of separation' code, enabling him to direct the AI regarding how many levels would be affected by his counterattack. He set it to zero by default.

He finished up and went downstairs again to order dinner for Lisa and himself.

19

DEEP WATER

KAITLYN CALLED SUNDAY evening to tell him she was back in town. Of course, they'd had a few dozen text messages through the week, so Henry already knew she'd placed second in the national tournament. They made arrangements to go out to dinner the following Saturday.

Monday afternoon, Henry took some time to grab a cup of coffee and hang out in the student lounge. He often saw members of his cohort there and wanted to discuss how to test his counterattack software app.

"You dirty bastard!" Dan growled when he joined Henry.

"Hey! What a collegial greeting. How's it going, Dan?"

"You know how it's going. My computer is trashed," Dan said.

"What? How'd that happen?"

"Jesus! Stop playing so innocent. You knew some of us would probe the defenses on your server. You set a trap. Now my computer is in the shitter."

"Whoa! Wait a minute! Don't tell me you tried to get past our corporate server firewalls!"

"Of course I did! I'm not the only one. You grabbed testers who are curious and always want to dig a layer deeper. You had to know we'd test your servers. You didn't have to nuke our computers."

"Are there more than you who tried?"

"I can't imagine I'm the only one. You could have at least given a warning."

"First off, don't scrap your computer! Nothing's damaged on it. All you need to do is change the file type on the system core. Secondly, I really didn't think any of you would test it, especially since you knew who it belonged to.

And third, I just installed the app on Saturday and was waiting here to catch people to figure out a way to test it. You jumped to the head of the line. So how did it work?"

"Now you want a testing report? Shit, man! It worked fine. I'd just gotten past the first level of the firewall and all of a sudden, my computer was toast."

"Hmm. Suggested improvements?"

"Besides don't kill my computer? At least give a warning. People figure they'll get rejected from a good system, not that they'll get attacked. How did you even identify the computer?"

"Pretty much the same thing you'd do as a hacker to find the server you want in the first place. I trained a narrow AI to trace the proxy chain to the source. As soon as the source was located, the counter was implemented," Henry said. "Why should all computer security be based on defense? This is just a next step in the process."

"I don't know that I agree with that. It seems unethical."

"Ask Josh. Here he comes," Henry said.

Josh scowled at his two study partners.

"How was your break?" Henry asked.

"Don't tell me you're going to play bright and innocent," Josh growled.

"You, too?" Henry asked. "Did all my so-called friends try to hack into my computer this weekend?"

"It was supposed to be a joke," Josh said. "We were just going to leave a token that would put fireworks on your screen when you logged in."

"You guys all get bombed by this asshole, too?" Leonard asked as he came up to the group.

"How many of you tried to hack into my corporate server?" Henry asked. "This is ridiculous!"

"Only those who knew *you* are Open Cloak," Josh said. "Except Lisa. We didn't let her in on the hack-a-thon because she lives with you."

"She rents an apartment from me," Henry corrected. "But I'm glad she wasn't involved. It would have made things complicated."

"I broke a nail!" Simon said as he came up to the group.

"Well, at least you can't blame me for that," Henry said.

"When you killed my computer, I slammed my hand down on my duvet and snagged the nail. It was terrible! You nasty man!"

"I'm not sure I should even tell you all the fix for your computers," Henry said.

"Just reinstall the system," Leonard said. "Worked fine."

"It's easier than that," Henry said. "Just change the file type ID of the core file. I wasn't out to do any serious damage to anyone, even if you were trying to break into my secure corporate files. If you guys had waited to check in with me today, I was going to ask for volunteers to test the security software. I just installed it Saturday night. Thanks for running the test without me."

"Dude, seriously. It was just a joke," Josh said. "We never expected to have a counter-attack launched on us."

"Which brings me to the question of ethics that Dan brought up," Henry said. "Not whether or not it was ethical for you all to launch an attack on my company—even as a joke. Dan felt it was unfair of me to install a trap that would disrupt an attacker. He feels that computer security should all be passive."

"I don't see that as a problem," Leonard said. "If you're doing it for real, you should corrupt the bios and ROM. Teach the bastards a lesson they will never forget."

"I didn't want to do permanent damage to anyone," Henry said.

"Plant a virus that keeps corrupting the computer and all its files, even when it's been reformatted," Simon said.

"Oh, that's nasty," Dan said. "I guess I see your point. I still think you should have given some kind of last second warning. 'Retreat or die!' Something like that."

"That would just be a challenge to the hackers I've known," Leonard said. "If you use that kind of warning, make sure they die."

"I don't know whether I want to ask you for a copy to install on my own system or to hope I never see it again," Josh said.

"Well, it's not for sale," Henry said. "Not until I'm sure it can't be used as a tool against the one deploying it. I'm not even sure I'll leave it on *our* server. Which is not an invitation for you to 'test' it again."

⁂

WHEN HENRY TOLD Lisa about his development and the study group's 'test' of it, she was horrified.

"Why didn't they invite me?" she asked. "I'd have been suspicious of the whole thing because of our conversation on counterattacks."

"Yeah, well, they didn't tell you because we 'live together,'" Henry said.

"We don't live together!"

"That's what I told them. But please do me a favor and don't try to hack into the server."

"Why would I do that? I'm attached to the server. And I've got some designs to show you later this week," she said.

"That's great. Let me ask you this. The guys said I should have given them a warning before I attacked their machines. What do you think?" he asked.

"You mean you actually succeeded in attacking them?" Lisa said. "I hope you trashed their computers!"

"Not quite. I corrupted the system core file. It's not even a difficult fix."

"But it worked! Congratulations!"

"Warning?"

"Well, a warning would probably thwart a percentage of attacks itself. You aren't really out there laying a honeytrap for hackers. There's another percentage who would see the warning as a challenge to step up their attack further. In gaming, we always give an out. I mean, the object of the game is to get to the ultimate level and win, but you can't do that if the game just randomly eliminates you. Even if it is an ambush, there's a clue that there's a threat. You see the monster and have a chance to retreat or engage. That kind of thing."

"But I don't want to challenge them to get past me. I want the challenge eliminated," Henry protested. "Our so-called friends will probably try again to see if there's a way around the counterattack. All I can do is step up the penalty they'll pay if they do."

"If you're concerned about them, then a warning is definitely in order. What about if it's a hacker from Russia trying to steal your latest AI design?"

"I'd just eliminate him."

"Like he was a linebacker after your date."

Henry stopped and looked at Lisa. He'd acted instinctively against the guy, picking his most vulnerable point. 'Did you kill him?' she'd asked. 'Don't know. Don't care,' he'd responded. Of course, two weeks later, the linebacker had been back on the field. If they met again, Henry was sure the guy would try to kill him.

"Should have made sure," he sighed. "I hear you."

HENRY AND KAITLYN had fun on their movie date Saturday. The movie was a very sensuous portrayal of Cleopatra, played by one of the top actresses of the decade. Henry was happy to watch her, whether he was interested in the movie or not.

When the show got out at nine-thirty, they went to a nearby pizza place and had a loaded pizza with Cokes. And they talked about the movie, as well as life.

"So, she had an oracle she consulted about Caesar," Kaitlyn said. "But it was so obscure to hear that he was one but not the only. She immediately went out and killed her brother-husband so Caesar could be the only one."

"But, of course, she was then forced to marry her younger brother, who was only like five at the time," Henry added.

"She eventually got rid of him, too. But then Marc Antony came along."

"Isn't that the nature of oracles?" Henry asked. "They never give a straight answer, so whatever happens you can say, 'The oracle said this would happen,' no matter how far you have to stretch it."

"Why do people bother?"

"Do they still?" Henry asked.

"Heck yes. That's what astrology is all about. Fortune tellers. Tarot cards. I ching. Magic 8 Ball. They're all forms of oracles people seek out to tell them what is going to happen in the future, or just to find the answer to a puzzling question."

"What question would you ask?"

"When is Henry going to actually make a pass at me?" Kaitlyn asked. "The suspense is killing me."

"The oracle says, 'The alignment of the stars makes the future cloudy.' I hope that is sufficiently obscure so that it will come as a complete surprise when it happens," Henry laughed.

"When—not if. I think I'll check my horoscope when I get home."

When Henry walked her to her door, they shared a very nice kiss. There were plenty of opportunities for him to make that pass as Kaitlyn held him and rubbed up against him. Henry decided to let the idea brew for a while since he knew now that Kaitlyn was expecting it.

"ORACLE, ORACLE, ORACLE," Henry muttered as he sat in his office Sunday afternoon. He'd spent part of the weekend refining his counterattack software. Among other things, he wanted a record of when it was activated and against whom. It seemed a little crazy that his study cohort had all attacked him and he didn't even know they'd been repelled or that the software was even activated. He needed a log.

He also had the software put up a five-second warning. He didn't want it displayed, though, until the AI had a fix on the source of the attack. When it was triggered, a message flashed up on the screen that simply said, 'You have been identified. Response launched in 5 seconds.' Then the number would count down from 5 to 1. It didn't go to zero because by that time the counterattack would have been launched. If the attack was broken off before the final countdown ended, the software deactivated.

He didn't consider the software particularly polished, but he didn't want to work on it any longer on Sunday. Instead, he stumbled down to the kitchen in a T-shirt and pair of cutoff sweats to start frying up some bacon for his breakfast. Or lunch if he bothered to look at a clock. He kept mumbling about an oracle.

"Hey, are you cooking bacon?" Lisa said, looking around the corner of the stairs.

"Yeah. I haven't eaten yet this morning. Sorry about the smell."

"Don't apologize. I was up most of the night. Can I toss a couple of strips in, too?"

"Sure. What had you up all night?"

"Calculus in Three Dimensions."

"That class was a bitch," Henry said.

"Why are you chanting 'oracle' over and over? Want to conjure up their success?" she asked.

She went to the refrigerator and pulled out eggs and bread. It looked like they were having breakfast together.

"Oh. No, I suppose I need a different name if I ever do anything with it. I was thinking about ancient oracles that people consulted to find their future," Henry said.

He really didn't know why his discussion with Kaitlyn had struck that chord with him, or why he didn't make the expected pass last night. He was sure now she would welcome it.

"Mmm. What's that famous one? Delphi?"

Henry pulled out his phone and spoke into it.

"What are the names of famous oracles?"

"Pythia was the most famous oracle of Apollo in ancient Greece and was found at Delphi," the phone recited back to him. "Dodona was the oracle of Dione and Zeus at Epirus. The Sibylline Oracles are a collection of oracular utterances ascribed to the prophetesses called Sibyls. Most oracles were ascribed to Apollo, the Greek god of prophecy. There are many other lesser oracles. Would you like me to name them?"

"No. Thank you."

The phone went silent.

"That was interesting," Lisa said.

"I bet there were all kinds of prophetesses. Who was that one in Troy who no one believed?"

"Cassandra," Lisa responded. "That was a sad story. Did you read *The Iliad*? It's a lot of war crap to wade through, but the parts about the gods were very enlightening. Apollo fell in love—or lust—with Cassandra, who was, like, twelve. He tried to woo her by giving her the gift of prophecy, but she would have nothing to do with him. So, he cursed her by telling her she would only ever be able to speak true prophecy, but that no one would believe her."

"A missing part of my classical education. I'm sure if I was getting a BA instead of a BS, I'd have had to take some course in classic literature," Henry said.

"It's not all bad. How do you want your eggs?"

Henry realized they were standing elbow to elbow at the stove. It was kind of nice. He felt he could have good conversations with Lisa without the burden of trying to maintain 'a relationship.' They were just friends and class-mates. And she was his employee.

"Just break the yolks and make them hard. I don't like them runny," he said.

"Neanderthal," she laughed. Nonetheless, she broke the yolks and cooked all of the eggs into a scramble.

"So, what got you interested in oracles this morning?" she asked as they grabbed the toast out of the toaster and sat at the table.

"Oh, the movie we saw last night. Cleopatra consulted an oracle and we talked about it a little. I was just thinking about the comparison between that and predictive text on a smart phone."

"That's a leap!"

"Not really. It's the way generative AI works, isn't it? Listen to the ques-tion, then run through the data banks for the most likely responses. In its untrained state, the AI doesn't know what's right or wrong. It just hears the word 'Thou' and the most likely next word in a sentence is 'shalt.' Then you branch. Do you continue or do you modify with 'not.' Put up a hundred actions to follow the branch and you are as likely to get 'Thou shalt kill,' as 'Thou shalt not eat.' I just think that the vocabulary an AI uses can be custom-ized. Narrowed down, if you will. Only train the AI with oracular sayings and the AI becomes an oracle."

"You know, I've only been awake for an hour. I think I need to come back to this subject when I've had more sleep. Don't you have enough on your plate right now?" she asked.

"Oh, hell yeah. I'm not pursuing this. Well, I might do some web scraping for oracular sayings. But anyway, I really liked that last rendition of the UI you came up with. I think tomorrow I'd like to start coding it in. It would be good to test it with our group," Henry said.

"Yeah. I have the spec and most of the graphics ready. I can work on refining the graphics once they're connected to the code."

"Fantastic. We'll have a real product by Christmas, I think."

"Wow! You really think this fast before coffee?" She took a sip of her coffee and squeezed her eyes shut.

"I had the first pot at six this morning," Henry sighed. "Don't worry about it."

HENRY TOOK KAITLYN to the Improv the next Saturday evening after dinner. The comedienne was funny and they had a good time. At one point, though, she pointed at them and asked "Are you two a couple?"

Henry wasn't sure what to answer, but Kaitlyn immediately nodded her agreement.

"You aren't too sure and you are definite," the comic said. "Keep it that way, girl. Keep him guessing is what I always say. How long have you been dating?"

"A month," Kaitlyn answered.

"And when did you start doing the deed?"

"Oh!" Kaitlyn said, blushing. "We... uh... haven't yet."

"No wonder he's not sure!"

She moved on to some other audience members and Henry breathed a sigh of relief that Kaitlyn had handled all the interaction. He wasn't interested in being a part of her show.

"What did you think?" Kaitlyn asked as they pulled out of the parking area.

"She was funny. She was a little crude at times, but that didn't bother me. Were you okay with it?" he asked.

"Oh, yeah. I thought she was really funny. I wasn't expecting to be asked how long we'd been fucking. That was a little embarrassing."

"Yeah. But she wasn't any harder on us than anyone else."

"Are you really not sure about our relationship?" she asked.

"Well, we've never really sat down to talk about our *relationship*," Henry said. "I mean, we are dating, but I don't know if that even makes us a couple. And I'm not saying it hinges on sex. I'd be just as confused if we did that."

"Oh, look at the view over the river," she sighed. "Can we stop a few minutes?"

"Sure," Henry said. He found a parking area and pulled into a space where they could see river traffic moving down the Monongahela toward the Ohio River.

He'd just turned the car off when Kaitlyn launched herself across the console to kiss him. It was an irresistible invitation. He clutched her and accepted her tongue in his mouth. In a few minutes, their clothing was in disarray and Henry was holding her breast in his hand. She had large hard nipples—easy to find and play with. He thought briefly that they would be easy nipples to pierce.

They finally relaxed a little, the console gap between the seats making it difficult to keep up the passion for long.

"Oh, wow!"

"Maybe that will help clear up your confusion about whether we're a couple," Kaitlyn said.

"I guess so. I'd better take you home before we get too carried away."

"You just had your hand inside my shirt pinching my nipples. How much more carried away do you think we can get in this little car?"

Henry didn't respond and Kaitlyn pulled her clothes together before they reached her apartment. At her door, they engaged in another tongue battle with a lot of grinding together, but she didn't invite him in. He went back to the car and finally reached his house a little after midnight.

Henry was still conflicted. He'd been very fond of the women he'd had sex with in the past. He liked Kaitlyn, but he had to admit he felt closer to Chastity than to her. And, though he hadn't heard her talk about it since they started dating, she'd been pretty committed to finding a husband who would support her while she golfed all day.

He thought she must have changed her goals some since he certainly couldn't be on her prospect list. And how fond of her did he need to be to fuck her? She was sexy enough. The mess he made after he got to his bedroom was testament that she turned him on.

He halfway expected her to lean over the gap between the seats and give him a blowjob, the way their making out was going. He probably wouldn't resist that. He'd still feel like he owed her one, though, and getting a blowjob in the car was a lot easier than eating a girl out in the front seat.

He wondered how she tasted.

Well, if it happened, he just wasn't going to resist. It had been a while.

20

SEARCH ME

"SO, HOW MANY total testers are there?" Lisa asked Henry as they worked on the UI for his optimization software.

"We have seventy agreements on file, but not all of them have downloaded the latest version. I included a test suite with the latest version so we should automatically see the results of use on any computer it's installed on. These builds have a timeout on them and uninstall themselves after twenty-one days."

"But it doesn't return the computer to its previous state, does it?"

"No. Not unless the tester requests a reversion to a backup. Then there is still only so much we can return. Once a hard drive is optimized, it's almost impossible to deconstruct the consolidated files and break them up into different sectors again. Besides, any work that is done after the optimization could affect whether the sector is even available anymore."

"You've got a network install option on this version. How does that get controlled?" she asked.

"I have to get a test network to run it on. So far, all we have is our own corporate server and the five computers attached to it—which includes yours," Henry said.

"I guess it's okay to run a test like that, but you really need to disable the network install feature on the release."

"What? Why?"

"This is something I learned from my father, even though it isn't a huge issue for games. Let's say you charge $100 for an individual install. Nice round number. The software works on exactly one device. It can only be installed on one device. Can't hand it to your buddy and install it."

"Right. I think we've got that covered with our download service."

"Okay. Now Corporation X comes along and wants to install it on their network. A hundred machines are attached to the server. And you just sold the software for $100. Flat rate. Technically, you should receive $10,000 for a hundred installs, but you gave away $9,900."

"Nobody's going to pay ten grand for optimization software," Henry protested.

"Fine. They'd still pay a thousand for a hundred licenses. At least then you're only giving away $9,000. And wait until you're popular and Corporation Y comes along and installs it on 10,000 company computers. You lost a boatload of money."

"Damn. I really need a marketing person," Henry growled. "Are you applying for that position, too?"

"No way. It's just stuff I learned from my dad. Don't give away a network version for the same price as an individual license. And it affects the UI as well."

"How does it affect the UI?"

"For the individual license, you don't want to expose any of the tricks for installing it on a network. We remove the degrees of separation feature, for example. And when you do a network license, you'll want an opt in for people on the network. None of that should be exposed on the consumer version."

"You're right. I think it's okay to test this way, but when we go to market at Christmas, we only take the consumer version. I'll get a marketing person to manage the network version."

"Probably better plan on another server, too," Lisa said. "I think we're going to be swamped with orders."

"May it be so!"

"No matter what we decide, it's going to sound a whole lot easier than it really is," Luke said when he talked to Henry. "I mean, we could probably blitz the market through social media and direct advertising. We'd undoubtedly get a few hundred—maybe a few thousand—sales. But how do we fulfill them? Right now, you're managing downloads of software off our company server. But can you handle payments? Licenses? We don't have a site to handle ecommerce."

"I figured I'd be sitting behind the computer 24/7 sending the software out," Henry sighed.

"Talk about crippling our company right out of the gate! Man, you are developing new software applications. The optimization software is great. If we can move forward with computer protection software, we'll win big time. But I know that's only the tip of what you can come up with. Like, you're making a quantum improvement over what is out there, but from the moment we release, our improvements will barely be incremental. I know this isn't the only thing you're dreaming of. We need you completely disconnected from the sales and fulfillment," Luke said.

"All right! You've got me convinced. What do we do?" Henry asked. He looked at his friend and business partner's image on his computer screen. Conferencing software was probably another area they could make an impact on if he put his mind to it. Just not today.

"I might not be working around the clock like you are, but I am putting in a lot more than our projected ten hours a week for start-up," Luke laughed. "I've found two platforms that will handle the licensing and ecommerce for us—for a fee, of course."

"Of course."

"I've got a preference, but it's not set in concrete. EMEE is a website that handles licensing of software. They only handle computers, not mobile devices. That's why we can't just go to an app store and sell the stuff there. We're not making this available for mobile devices."

"What a nightmare that would be. I doubt the principles would even be the same if we tried to move to that platform. It's bad enough handling the three big operating systems," Henry said.

"Right. Well, this company, EMEE, manages the entire sales and licensing process. They're especially interested in us expanding to network platforms. Bulk licenses are a real money-maker, I guess."

"What would we need to provide?"

"The locked software that they can license, and managed updates if there are any," Luke said. "They will feature the software on their website, but that doesn't completely cover marketing. We'll have to talk about that later. Different company. EMEE will handle the money, maintaining the registry of licenses, and prosecuting piracy. They'll provide the download site and filter for people who download more than once. They'll prevent multiple downloads from being installed on other machines. The license will be registered to a single device."

"That's always been a concern. I don't need to build that into the software itself?" Henry asked.

"There might be a hook you need to provide, but they have some pretty capable programmers on their site who do this stuff all the time. You'll be able to tell them exactly what we want."

"You said there was more than one. What sets this one up as better in your opinion?"

"The other site is more game-oriented. It's a little cheaper, but I doubt their ability to expand to the corporate environment when the time comes. EMEE wants to get into that market with our software. I think if we went with the other, we'd end up migrating to a different vendor in a few months."

"That's a compelling argument. Let's set it up. Do we need Isobel and Chastity to vote on that?"

"I'll give them the skinny and make sure they're on board. As long as it doesn't cost anything, Isobel will be fine. It will be a lot harder to get an ad agency on board that she doesn't throw a fit about."

"I'll let you handle that," Henry laughed. "Thanks for keeping her over there in Philly most of the time. Say, that reminds me. You guys coming into town for Thanksgiving?"

"We hadn't made a plan yet."

"I'm thinking of having a dinner here at the apartment. Just some of our friends and maybe a few guys at school who can't get home for the holiday."

"I'm up for that. We'll have to spend time with our own parental units, but having a relaxed dinner with people our own age would be cool."

"I'll plan on it," Henry said. "Talk to you soon."

Henry broached the idea with his parents and they were happy with it.

"I won't need to cook!" Sylvia said with glee.

"This might be a good time for a little retreat," Ryan said. "Just the two of us, say in Florida?"

"I'll put in for the time off. I have enough seniority they should let me off for this holiday, though it means I'll probably have to be on duty over Christmas," Sylvia said.

His parents got caught up in making plans for their own holiday and Henry excused himself. He started spreading the word among his friends, starting with Lisa and Chastity.

"I thought I might just go over to the campus and participate in the 'orphans' dinner' at the Student Union," Lisa said. "This sounds like much more fun. I can help in the kitchen if you like."

"As long as you'll still take me out for my birthday on Saturday," Chastity said. "As to helping in the kitchen, you'd be better off asking your girlfriend."

"Hey, if he isn't available Saturday, I'll take you out," Lisa said. "He's tied up to this lady golfer most weekends."

"I'll reserve the time," Henry said. "And if Chastity wants to invite you along, that's up to her."

Josh and Simon were both enthused about joining the group, but Leonard and Dan had other plans. There was just one more person to convince, and Henry had a date with her Saturday night.

HENRY CHOSE AN evening at the country club for their date. It was getting late in the season for doing a whole round of golf, but they both enjoyed spending an hour on the driving range. Then they went inside for a nice dinner.

"So, I'm thinking I'll have some people over for Thanksgiving dinner. Would you like to come?"

"Oh, my! Is this my big 'meet the parents' invitation?" Kaitlyn asked.

"No, afraid not. My parents are going to Florida. This would all be people our own age. My three partners, my housemate, a couple of guys from my program at the U. If you wanted to extend the invitation to another golfer, that would be cool," Henry said.

"I guess that's okay," Kaitlyn said. "We'll have all weekend together!"

"Oh. Not quite. One of my business partners has a birthday on Saturday. We have a tradition of going out to celebrate together. You and I will have to go out on Friday instead of Saturday," Henry said.

"This partner is a guy?" Kaitlyn asked.

"No. My other two partners will also be in town. You'll get to meet all three of them at dinner. But it's Chastity's birthday."

"I don't know if I like that. You only ever see me on Saturdays."

"Like I said, it's a holiday weekend, so we can go out on Friday that week. Sunday, too, if you want," Henry said.

"I don't think you should be seeing another woman," Kaitlyn pouted.

"Don't even suggest that I not take Chastity out for her birthday," Henry said sternly. "I won't be giving up any of my friends, any more than I'd expect you to stop seeing George on the golf team."

"What?"

"I know you're friends with George and you often go to events—especially sporting events. That's fine."

"We don't do anything! Not like that."

"Neither do you and I, Kaitlyn. It doesn't make a difference."

It was the closest to a real argument they'd had since they started dating. The meal was quiet for a few minutes after that, but they recovered without either of them admitting they were wrong. After dessert, they went for a drive out in the country, just holding hands as they talked. Eventually, Henry arrived back at her door, without her having suggested they pull over anyplace to make out.

"Maybe we should change that," Kaitlyn said.

"Change what?" Henry asked.

"The part about us not doing anything like that. Um... Want to come in?"

"You know I like you a lot and you turn me on, right? I'm not making any real long-term commitments here."

"Shut up. Come in and fuck me."

NINETY MINUTES EARLIER, Henry was on the verge of telling Kaitlyn he didn't think things were working out between them. Now he had his face buried between her legs, licking for all he was worth. She was responsive as far as moans, groans, thrust hips, and lubrication were concerned, but she seemed no nearer to a climax than when they'd started.

"Just come up here and put it in me," she moaned, pulling at his ears.

Henry had put a condom on earlier, when he thought oral was only going to take a couple of minutes. He hadn't flagged during his tongue work, so he moved over the top of Kaitlyn and slid smoothly but slowly into her.

"Oh, my God! Take it easy! I have an Asian vagina. It doesn't stretch that much!"

"I'll pull back," Henry said, sliding away. It hadn't really felt that tight.

"No! Just give me a chance to adjust. You have a huge white dick. Try again."

Henry was amused. He'd heard stories about Asian women being smaller than Caucasians, and he'd been told he was generously proportioned, though he rather doubted the exclamations his partners had made in the past. He just hadn't encountered any resistance or tightness as he entered Kaitlyn. Perhaps it was just her way of talking dirty to him.

He slid in again and this time, Kaitlyn took him all the way without effort. She redoubled her moaning and thrusting. Henry latched onto one of her big nipples with his lips and began sucking and chewing gently on it. That seemed to accelerate her activity.

"Yes! Oh, God, yes! I'm coming! I'm coming! Come in me, Henry!"

He was already getting tired from the effort and it didn't take long for him to reach his own peak and fill the condom. He moaned a little as he came, mostly from relief.

"That was so good!" Kaitlyn said. "I need the bathroom."

Henry pulled out and rolled away so she could run to the bathroom. He pulled the condom off and looked for a wastebasket, finally finding one under the kitchen sink. Kaitlyn's little efficiency apartment was even smaller than Chastity's. While she was in the bathroom, he looked around and found his hastily discarded underwear and clothing. He hadn't really been invited to spend the night. Perhaps Kaitlyn was the same about that as Chas. The only times Henry had spent the entire night with Chastity were after the prom and the night before freshman orientation at the university. Neither of them counted the latter because he woke up before her and was out of her apartment in ten minutes to pick up his parents.

By the time he was fully dressed, he heard the bathroom door open. Kaitlyn was in pajamas and a robe.

"I'd uh… invite you to stay, but my period just started. No reason to stick around for that. I have a tampon in," she said.

"No problem," he said. "I suppose I should get home and do some studying. I have a huge resource text on computer vision to read."

"Yeah. Well, thank you for a great time. I'll see you next weekend. This was fun."

Henry kissed her and left. He wasn't as confident as she was that it had all been fun. In fact, it was the first time in his life that he was pretty certain his sex partner had faked her orgasm. His jaw still ached as well.

He hoped he could talk her into telling him what he'd done wrong, or if he could increase her pleasure in some way.

⁂

It was three weeks until Thanksgiving and final exams were two weeks after that. Henry had been serious about the amount of reading he needed to do. He'd spent his fall break working on the counterattack software and had fallen behind on his classwork. Taking the course load he was might not have been the wisest decision, but he was surviving. He might not ace every class this term. He'd been spending a lot of his time on the class work for Human AI Interaction.

The class had spent a lot of time analyzing conversations with various chat bots. At some point, it seemed the human began considering the AI to be a real person. They even developed 'friendships.'

There were companies that advertised their chats as 'online friends.' The bots used more natural language, and some seemed to really care about the people they were chatting with. Understanding the principles of AI, of course, Henry could see the pattern of responses of the chat bot. The bots were notorious liars! They didn't really differentiate between kinds of information found on the internet.

His own private search engine used several principles of AI development to make his results more robust. By using his own search tool, he could eliminate the advertising and artificial SEO coding that often brought up false results. He'd posed a question regarding how many people considered themselves wealthy. Standard search engines retrieved over thirteen million results. The first ten pages of results were about American millionaires who *didn't* consider themselves wealthy. His own search engine returned a few thousand results, but on the first few pages, he found information on what was considered wealthy in different countries and a worldwide percentage of people who considered themselves wealthy. It was much better than the biased commercial results.

He hadn't yet addressed the search engine prospects with his partners. It had started as a project to simply help him get better search results. But it was the same underlying AI that had enabled his counterattack software to trace the attacks on his server, even through various proxies.

It wasn't that he didn't want to share his development with his partners, but he was missing a critical element in everything he developed. Other than a few class projects, none of his material had been code-reviewed by a competent engineer. He felt like he wrote good clean code, but it really needed to have a professional review.

The non-AI version of optimization software they'd licensed early on had been taken over by the licensee. They built on what he'd created and had plenty of engineers to streamline the code and integrate it into their security suite. The one time he'd managed to talk to their development lead after the licensing, he was merely told that it was a good job and they'd be able to really use the work. Whatever that meant. At least it got them over a million dollars in investment capital to start the corporation.

And there were so many other projects he wanted to get started on. He really needed at least one more developer. He'd use Lisa for code reviews, too, once the UI for this project was finished. They were getting close.

He sat at his computer and did a search for software developer resumes. It seemed hopeless.

21

BUILDING MEMORIES

HENRY CHEATED. AT least, that was his assessment of things. Instead of cooking, he ordered a Thanksgiving meal for eight from the local co-op. It came complete with turkey, dressing, mashed potatoes, gravy, cranberry sauce, sweet potatoes, green bean casserole, and pumpkin pie.

Lisa still helped in the kitchen to make sure everything was hot before their friends arrived. Henry went to his parents' house for folding chairs and they decided to serve the dinner on paper plates. No one was planning to spend the afternoon washing dishes.

There were nine at the table instead of the expected eight. Kaitlyn took Henry seriously when he suggested she could invite her golf friend, George. She'd given him enough notice that he could get another chair from his parents' house. Kaitlyn sat next to Henry at the table, but George seemed especially enamored of Chastity. He'd also brought a couple of bottles of wine, which was appreciated since all the others except Kaitlyn were under twenty-one.

"We're not discussing business at this party," Luke said as he raised his glass, "but we would be remiss if we didn't congratulate Henry on pre-releasing our software to EMEE for final tests before release. It will be in the market in two weeks. Congratulations, Henry."

Everyone cheered.

In keeping with the statement of not talking business, though, that was all that was mentioned.

"Here's to Chastity's twentieth birthday, Saturday," Henry said. "May this be just the beginning."

187

"To our hosting couple, Henry and Lisa," Isobel said.

"Uh... We're not a couple," Lisa said. "I just rent an apartment. Henry's a couple with Kaitlyn."

"Oh. That was what I meant," Isobel backed things up. "I meant we're guests in your home. I mean..."

"We get it, Isobel," Chastity said. "Here's to Henry and Kaitlyn. May you have a long life together. And now on to pumpkin pie."

There was a lot of shuffling around to clear the table and reset with pie plates and plastic forks. Henry had a pot of coffee ready for those who wanted a cup. He already had an entire cupboard of coffee mugs that just seemed to continue to grow.

He put an arm around Kaitlyn as he poured. Josh was given the honor of serving the pie, but Lisa was standing by with two cans of spray cream topping.

"Want to spend the night tonight?" he asked. "I've never had a girl stay over in my apartment."

"Except your roommate," Kaitlyn said. "I'm not feeling well. I'm going to ask George to take me home. I'll see you tomorrow night and we can just have sex if you want."

"That's not the only reason for us to get together," Henry said. In fact, they'd only connected that way once since their first time.

"I know. But it's too cold to play golf. See you tomorrow, babe." She isolated George who seemed disappointed to have to leave the party early and managed to get Chastity's phone number before they disappeared.

"WHAT ARE YOU doing now that the UI is finished?" Josh asked Lisa as they sat around Thursday afternoon.

"As soon as the app was out the door, Henry switched me over to cleaning up the company website. It needs it," she laughed. "How about you?"

Henry had brought Josh on board to review his code during the past two weeks. There had been a lot of testing each other for ability and trust. Henry had never had anyone actually look at his code before. He thought he trusted Josh, but it was still a big step.

For Josh's part, he didn't want to offend Henry by questioning calls or routines, but he wanted to show his worth, as well. He admired Henry, not so much because he was a brilliant coder, but because he had such interesting vision as to where his development could take them. Josh was ready to hitch his wagon to that rising star.

"He's got me reviewing code for a search engine and I'm getting to add a few features I've always wished I had in my own search engine. Just getting started of course," Josh said. "Uh... I'm not... I mean... Would... Would you be interested in going out sometime? I know we've all got finals coming up in two weeks, but if you need a break, we could hang out... I guess."

"Yeah. That would be okay. Don't expect much, though. I'm probably going to get out of Dodge as soon as my last final is over. I like it here and all, but I need a break," she said.

If 'hanging out' turned into an actual date, Josh would consider that a big win.

"I'm not very good at relationships," Henry sighed as he lay in bed with Chastity Saturday afternoon.

Chastity started laughing.

"Hey, it's not funny. Seriously, what should I do?"

Henry's date with Kaitlyn on Friday could only be described as a little flat. They went out to a movie, had dinner, went back to her apartment, and fucked. Then he said goodnight and went home. He liked Kaitlyn. She seemed to be turned on enough, even though he didn't think she came when he ate her. But she seemed to have a set routine of positions and how long to stay in each one. She scowled at his use of a condom. When he'd come, she made noises like she was having an orgasm, but then hustled him out the door as soon as they were 'done.'

"Well, you could probably start by not having sex with me. I mean, I hope you don't choose that. But I'm not your girlfriend, remember? What we have is between you and me. I don't care who else either of us is involved with," Chastity said.

"Would that still hold true if you were madly in love with someone and decided to settle down and get married?" he asked.

"Yes. But please don't tell me you plan to settle down and get married to Kaitlyn. I don't see any chemistry between the two of you."

"I like her."

"Ye-ah. So, what's the problem?"

"I don't seem to be able to really get her engaged. I mean, I think every time we've had sex, she's faked her orgasm. She could just tell me that I either just don't turn her on or I'm doing something wrong," Henry complained. He settled his face between Chastity's thighs and started licking the way he knew she liked.

"Oh, goddess! Yes," she said. "I was hoping we were getting to this part of the conversation. If she doesn't have an orgasm when you do this, it's because she doesn't want one. Oh, yeah. Keep that up. Yes, inside. I'm… How do you get me there so fast? I'm… Don't stop. Yes!"

Henry didn't let up until she pushed at his head, her usual signal that she'd had enough. He rolled away and just held her while she caught her breath.

"Oh, fuck me!"

"You don't fake that when you're with me, do you?" Henry asked.

"You're entirely too unsure of yourself. Did all your testers fake having their computers blown up when they tried to hack the site?"

"No. That would be pretty hard to fake. And what would the point be?"

"Exactly. What would the point be in faking the one thing I enjoy about sex?"

"You only enjoy cunnilingus?"

"With you. I mean, I like fucking you, too. But I only enjoy getting eaten by you. I don't even let any other guys try anymore. They just get frustrated. And so do I. I might let a girl go down on me, but that's different. So, let me tell you: If she isn't getting off on you eating her, she doesn't want to. Or there's some kind of deep hidden psychological block against her enjoying sex. That's always possible, too. Maybe she was told from the time she was a baby that good girls don't enjoy sex."

"Hmm. I suppose. How did you get past it?" he asked.

"Who says I did? I don't do sex for pleasure. If you're not going down on me, I know how to work the controls myself. And don't think I don't like fucking you, too. I do. It's fun. But I don't do it to come. I do it because it's you. Other guys? I do it for the stack of hundreds they leave on my nightstand."

"I wish it was better for you."

"It will be, eventually. We'll all be making money hand-over-fist in the company when the software releases and I'll retire from escorting. Another year and guys will start looking at me like I'm too old."

"You've got to be kidding! This is only your twentieth birthday!"

"That means old guys can't hire me so they can have sex with a teenager. You have no idea how things really are."

"You're right about that. You know I'd do anything for you, don't you?"

"And you're doing exactly what I want. Now while all your drool is keeping my pussy wet, why don't you get a condom on and slide in for a while."

Time between Thanksgiving and the winter break rushed by. In the last two weeks of classes, Henry had four research papers due. Then there was a week of final exams. All six of his classes had objective exams, meaning there were no essays. There were a few short answer questions that were to be answered in less than one hundred words, but professors tended to stay away from even these. All their exams had to be graded and turned in before they could start their own holiday breaks.

EMEE reported favorable results from their pre-release testing, indicating they had installed the optimization AI on all their company computers. They had not yet installed it on servers, pending further testing. Henry heartily agreed. The software was slated to release the eighteenth of December, coinciding with the end of the semester.

In the midst of the end of semester rush, Henry had to talk to Gallitzin Marketing Solutions—or rather to Darla Gallitzin at the agency. Luke and Isobel had interviewed the agency as they sought someone to handle promotion for the new product. They provided all the corporate information necessary, but Henry had to supply the product information.

"The idea of installing an AI on my computer just raises my hackles," Darla said. "Tell me why I should trust this one?"

"We could call this your domestic AI, or your pet AI," Henry started. "One of the problems with AI is that all the current embodiments we hear about are trying to connect you to everyone. Most of all, to the makers of the AI who use the information it gathers to market more junk to you. The Open Cloak Optimization app installs on your computer and yours alone. It doesn't require you to connect to our company or to report anything from your personal computer to anyone online. Ever. Open Cloak Optimization works for you and you alone. Once installed, you can't even share it with someone else. It is there to be an extension of what you want to do."

"But who determines what I want to do?" Darla asked.

"You do. When it is installed, OC Optimizer goes to work immediately looking for general optimization it can do in the background while you continue to do whatever work you would normally be doing. That includes things like defragmenting metal drives, scouring your computer for background programs that are just using up your processing power without adding any benefits to you, looking for spyware—also known as cookies—that are not associated with things you normally do. You'll see results within the first few hours of having the software installed without having to do anything. At any time, you can tell OCO to report on what it has done and it does so in clear and concise English—not computer speak. It learns as you use your computer and continues to work in the background on your behalf."

"And it does this without being connected?"

"It is totally resident on your computer and does not connect to or report to the internet or anyone else in any way," Henry said.

"My pet AI?"

"Loyal to no one but you."

The marketing agency began putting together its promotional campaign for the new product. When they asked about working on the company website, though, Henry balked.

"I have an extremely good developer that I'm paying to revamp the site. What I would suggest is that you compile a list of whatever you think should be included and forward it so she can crosscheck to be sure she's remembered it. If she needs additional information, I'll have her contact you. I don't want two different people or entities tampering with the site code," Henry said.

Darla attempted an upsell to take over managing the website, but Henry was firm.

"Let's just say I have my own pet AI operating on my site and it would not be friendly to you trying to feed it," Henry concluded. Darla gasped and agreed to keep hands off.

THE HOLIDAY PROVED to be a time for Henry and his family to get together. He even moved back for Christmas week. Kaitlyn had announced that she was flying back to California as soon as classes were out and would not be back until spring semester. It was a rather abrupt parting, though there was nothing antagonistic about it. He wished her well and realized he was a little relieved not to be spending the entire holiday with her in his apartment.

In fact, they'd never spent the night at Henry's apartment. After Thanksgiving, Kaitlyn had simply said she wasn't comfortable spending the night with another woman in the house. No explanations could change her pre-conceptions.

Henry's parents, however, decided to intervene in a different way.

"OH, DON'T WORRY about a thing," Sylvia said to her son. "We've been meeting up with the Donovans every so often to play cards. They had no plans, so we invited them to join us for Christmas dinner. It will be fun. Dad's doing most of the prep work—with your help—since I'll be working from mid-afternoon overnight."

"Six places set, Mom?" Henry asked.

"Well, they can't leave their daughter home alone on Christmas! She's a sweetheart. You'll like her."

That was settled. The Donovans would be joining the Pascals for Christmas dinner and Henry would like them.

He wasn't a curmudgeon about it. It would be nice to have company, though he'd prefer to have had one of his own friends—Chastity, Kaitlyn, or even Lisa, who was home in Baton Rouge. Nonetheless, he decided to have a good time.

Nancy Donovan was a lovely eighteen-year-old who was a senior in high school. Henry did his best to make sure she was included in conversations that seemed a little out of her range. She really didn't know how to respond to the announcement that Henry's software had been released the previous weekend. She supposed it was cool, but it wasn't a game so there was no real reason for her to be interested in it.

After dinner, they stood on the Pascals' front porch as their parents said their goodbyes.

"I don't sleep around," Nancy said bluntly. "If you'd like to go out some-time, I'd be willing if it was something interesting. You seem nice for an older guy."

Henry was only a little more than a month from his twentieth birthday. He supposed that was certainly enough older to make a difference. He expected to graduate from college in a year and a half. Nancy was nice and she was pretty, but he really didn't want to bother with high school drama. He'd had enough difficulty dealing with his own.

"I like you," he said. "But let's not make any plans right now. I kind of have a girlfriend and classes are crazy at the university. If we dated, I'd want to be unencumbered and be able to spend some time planning something fun."

"That's a relief. I mean, it sounds like your girlfriend is kind of tenuous, but that's as good an excuse as any. I felt I had to offer a date, but my heart wasn't in it."

"Mine either," Henry laughed. "It was really nice to meet you, though. Maybe we'll run into each other in the future sometime."

"Yeah. See you around?"

They'd both fulfilled their perceived obligation and went home happy.

HENRY RETURNED TO his apartment the day after Christmas and busied himself just cleaning and settling back in. Chastity had been in over the break and had cleaned the office. He expected all three of his partners to spend time there during this week. Then they would go to the club for their 'second annual' company New Year's Eve party.

When he settled into bed that night, the apartment seemed very big and very empty. He thought about having Kaitlyn with him, but her image was quickly replaced by that of Nancy. Well, that was just a fantasy about a cute girl and nothing he really wanted to pursue. He was definitely restless, though, and sleep avoided him after he went to bed.

He finally got up and went to work on his computer. He sat for a while just scanning what was in his development chain. He'd intentionally taken the week of Christmas off, just so he'd return refreshed. Nothing was jumping out at him, so he dressed and left the apartment to go for a drive. Sometimes new thoughts would come to him while he was just focused on the road. He checked the gas and filled up before he headed toward Wheeling, then picked up I-70 westbound.

He didn't push speed limits. It felt good just to be on the road with no one talking to him and no computer demanding his attention. He stopped in Wheeling and picked up a large cup of truck stop coffee, then continued west. In Columbus, he stopped at another truck stop and ate a trucker special steak and eggs, then continued west.

His AI—what he'd told Darla was his pet AI—was performing well. He'd modified it several times for his personal use, expanding what it was able to anticipate. It now powered his search engine as well as the optimization tool. The guys would start code reviewing and testing the search engine in earnest when they got back to town. But there were all kinds of options for an artificial narrow intelligence to optimize a person's *life* both on and off the computer.

"So, what should I apply it to next?" he asked aloud. He often talked to himself when he was driving alone, but he imagined his father in the seat next to him. Over the summer, he'd actually taken his father for a drive to talk about the ethics of training an AI. Of course, there was a lot of discussion online about the subject, but Henry wanted the opinion of someone he trusted who didn't make snap judgments.

Ryan's comment about having the AI private and disconnected from the network had inspired the way Henry developed the Optimization AI.

"I could turn it into a personal financial manager," he said. "I don't think I'd trust it right away to actually make decisions, but I might direct it to determine when I should transfer money from checking to savings or from savings to longer term investments. It could simply send me a message when it spots something and I could decide whether it was worth my time to make the transfer. It would learn from my decisions."

That seemed like a good use. He'd also adapted his AI to track down proxy servers in case of a hacking attack on his company. It had worked remarkably well.

"What about the oracle?" he heard his father ask. Henry looked over at the empty passenger seat.

"For that matter, why am I talking to you in my head instead of waking you up in the middle of the night to talk these ideas out in person?"

As a matter of fact, his father would be open to that if it didn't happen more than once a year or so. He'd get pretty tired of it if Henry called him as often as he had questions he was trying to work out.

"In my human memory class, the professor talked about associative memory. Traditionally, psychologists classified six types of human memory: episodic, semantic, procedural, short-term working, sensory, and prospective. But the thing that ties memories together is association. If I smell pine chips, my memory automatically goes back to Oedipus, that club-footed guinea pig I had in eighth grade. When someone says 'waffles,' I smell you cooking on special mornings and it associates with all kinds of memories of those breakfasts, why we were having waffles that day, what we were celebrating, what every person at the table said."

Of course, all those memories would also fit into one of the categories of traditional psychology, but the professor believed that was what tied them together and gave people access to their memories. "That reminds me..." is a common phrase.

"So, when I ask you a question, but you aren't there, I still hear your voice as I piece together memories. I'm just so afraid I'll lose that. You know I hear your voice less these days than when I lived at home. What will I do when... you know... when you aren't there any longer?"

It bothered Henry. He needed to figure a way to preserve his father's voice, his stories, and his advice. Recording was easy. But he could program his AI to do the associative part of recalling the memories.

Henry found another truck stop on the east edge of Indianapolis and bought a pad of paper and a pen. He sat in the restaurant sketching out his associative memory AI. He would preserve his father's voice and wisdom forever.

22

PLOY

THE DOWNSIDE OF an overnight 'thinking' trip was that Henry was 400 miles from home in the morning and hadn't slept. He sent text messages to his partners inviting them to make themselves at home in the apartment office. He found a motel he could day-sleep in and then headed back home that night.

"So, what took you out of town so suddenly?" Chastity asked when he arrived back. He found her sleeping on the sofa in the living room waiting for him. She went to his bedroom and slipped into bed with him. "Don't get used to this. I'm just still too sleepy to go home. Tell me what's up."

"I figured out a general structure for preserving a person's life record and then accessing it randomly. I have a whole lot of development to do and will try to pull together a prototype in the next few months, but it will really be cool. You see, I'll start by asking my dad to record his stories and to file his papers and documents on a hard drive I'll give him. I think he'll cooperate. Then I'll train the AI on his memories. It works on the same principle as the optimization AI, learning how important things are by how often they appear in his papers. Then, I can ask questions of the AI and it will be as if Dad was answering them."

He looked over at Chastity and saw she was sound asleep. He rolled over and went to sleep as well. When he woke up in the morning, Chastity was gone.

"THE GENERAL CONCEPT has been around for a while," Henry explained to his father. "Kurzweil wanted to ask questions of his deceased father and started pulling together things from his past. But to use AI, he or people he worked with tried to train a general AI—or as near as we have to a general AI—to think like his father. These massive AIs, though, have too much crap in them. A person could never navigate that much material. But if you trained an AI only on that person's information and thoughts, it would be much more faithful to the character of that person. You. Kurzweil called it The Singularity."

"You're preparing for me to die?" Ryan asked his son.

"Shit! No! That's... Yeah, maybe. I'm not looking forward to it any time soon, but I am thinking that someday in the distant future, maybe your grandchildren or great grandchildren might want to get to know you and who you really were," Henry said.

"Ah. Grandchildren and great-grandchildren. Now we're talking. Any prospects?"

"That's the problem, Dad. It could take me years to get around to procreating. Not against it, but just can't handle it at the moment."

"Okay. I'll participate in your great experiment. What do I need to do?"

Henry paused. His notes were expansive and he wasn't sure how much he needed yet.

"Let's start with anything you already have and just copy it onto a hard drive. I don't expect to be able to begin training the AI for at least a year or more. Then anything new you add would increase its knowledge of you. So, documents you have, including scans of photos, email, poetry you secretly wrote to Mom, and stories you think of from your life. The stories can either be written, or sit in front of a video recorder and just tell the stories. Might be difficult at first, but you'll relax into it. You can even have Mom there to tell the stories to if you want. There are a dozen services that sprang up a few years ago to help people write their memoirs. We can subscribe to a couple of those and you'll get a prompt each week for something to talk about," Henry said.

"THERE'S NOTHING REALLY here that we can sell, is there?" Luke asked when they all got together Tuesday afternoon.

"This definitely has a longer dev cycle than other things I've worked on, simply because the data needs to be gathered before the AI can be trained," Henry said.

"How do we serve this to people? Wouldn't you need a server farm if your AI was working on 500 or 5,000 people's lives? How much data is in a person's life?" Isobel asked.

"Yeah. It would be a problem. That's why I'm basing it on what we do for AI driven optimization. In fact, I think it's the only way we'd ever sell anything. It has to be local and not in the cloud. In other words, the AI resides on the customer's computer with no interaction with the internet. All that person's data is kept local. They can back it up to the cloud if they want to, but the operation is always local," Henry explained, pointing out the pieces in his schematic drawing.

"Is there anything we could test it on that doesn't require waiting for your father to record his entire life?" Chastity asked.

"I have a vague idea for a test," Henry said. "It could use the same overall principle in which you ask a question and it gives an answer."

"Don't all chat apps do that?" Luke asked.

"Sort of. Once again, those apps are too big. Let's take one aspect and collect info on that. Something that is completely public domain," he said. "We could build a kind of oracle. We start with the simplest. Like a Magic Eight Ball. The answers are yes, no, maybe, and ask me later. Then start building from there. Progress to more complex answers that read more like a Chinese fortune cookie or the daily horoscope. Maybe the I Ching. Collect the Sybilline Sayings. Train the AI on that body of literature plus, say, Proverbs, the sayings of Confucius, and anything else we can collect at no charge. We can start asking the oracle our questions and see what it comes up with."

"Isn't that a little random?" Isobel asked.

"Yes. It's supposed to be. The thing about oracles is that they need to be interpreted. They are never clear and concise. Like, 'The rolling thunderstorm inseminates the lake, then moves on to where the lake cannot follow.' That could be the answer to almost any question, if you figured out how to interpret it."

"Back to the parent thing," Luke said. "Do you expect that to generate random responses, too?"

"More or less. We'd have to discover key words in the question so the answer seems relevant. 'Should I marry Isobel?' I might ask."

"No way!" Isobel chimed in. "Well, maybe," she added shrugging her shoulders.

"The question has two key words. Marriage and Isobel. The AI would find closely associated concepts and return a response. 'Successful or not, a sincere approach is the only answer.' It doesn't actually say anything about marriage or Isobel, but it gives you something to think about. The key to oracles is the multiple interpretations."

"I get it. If your dad actually said in his ramblings, 'Whatever you do, don't marry Isobel,' then that might come up as a direct answer from your father, but if there wasn't any direct instruction, he might just respond with a philosophical thought on marriage in general or even his own marriage," Luke nodded.

Henry felt like they were getting the idea.

"We're going to need more money within the next year," Isobel said. "When do we get sales results on the current software release?"

"EMEE will issue monthly reports on the previous month's sales and what we are due," Luke said. "They pay fifteen days after the end of each quarter. That means we should see a report for December soon after the first and we should get our first check payable on activity for the fourth quarter by the fifteenth of January."

"Woohoo!" Chastity said. "We'll be able to make payroll."

"That's pretty optimistic," Isobel said. "Even I don't expect two weeks of sales to give us enough for payroll. It would be nice if it paid for the office."

"Still optimistic," Henry said. "I wouldn't expect to see anything significant until mid-year. At least two quarters."

"It highlights the problem, though," Luke said. "Sales are only one avenue for revenue. I need to look for an investor and get some real capital behind us. By the time Henry is out of school in eighteen months, we need to have a functioning full-time office with enough people to actually create, test, and market software."

"That puts it in perspective, doesn't it?" Chastity sighed.

"I NEED YOU to pick me up at the airport the fifteenth at 2:00. Then we'll have the weekend together, but I need to start focusing on the driving range. Can you get me time at your club to practice? I like the booth heaters they have. Then we'll need to schedule the tournaments I'll be playing in. It's a heavy schedule and I want you to come to Georgia, Florida, and Texas with me for the big ones. Of course, my parents will be coming out for graduation. It would be nice if that other apartment in your place was empty for them. They want to get to know you."

Henry looked at the text message from Kaitlyn and then thumbed to the next one and the next one. All had her schedule outlined and when he needed to be somewhere for her.

He sighed. This was really too much. She must have written out all this, then copied and pasted it into text messages. When the last message indicated she could move in with him the first of June, that was the last straw. Henry realized he had no desire to live with Kaitlyn at all.

"This isn't going to work for me," he texted back. "I think we'd better break up now."

He heard his phone buzz several times in the next hour, but ignored the messages. She couldn't even be bothered to actually call and talk to him.

THE BIG EVENT of the week was New Year's Eve on Friday. This time it was just the four partners who went to the club together. They danced, told stories about school, and had a great meal, before toasting the New Year with sparkling juice.

"It will be nice when we can all have a glass of champagne to toast the New Year," Isobel said. "Chastity is the only one who has made it to twenty so far. That means next year, we'll all have to drink our juice while she drinks a whole bottle of champagne."

"Not to worry," Chastity said. "I'm not drinking now and don't plan to start again. You might all be toasting the New Year with champagne the next year while I'm sipping my sparkling apple juice."

"I know where there's a bottle of champagne on ice waiting for us, babe," Luke said to Isobel.

"You might get laid tonight after all," Isobel responded.

They all left the table and the club. Luke made a half-hearted invitation to Chastity and Henry to join them at his house, but they declined.

"You could get laid tonight, too," Chastity said as Henry drove her home. "Want to come up for a while?"

"You're way too much for me to resist," Henry said.

"You're pretty cavalier about cheating on your girlfriend."

"Text message break-up," Henry laughed. "I don't currently have a girlfriend."

"In that case, let's have our own little party," Chastity said.

They headed to her apartment and celebrated for another couple of hours before Henry headed home.

He hadn't told Chastity the text message had been from him to Kaitlyn rather than the other way around. He supposed it didn't matter.

SATURDAY MORNING, HENRY set programs in motion to scrape the internet for specific kinds of content. For the first few days, he'd have to stop and start the program frequently to adjust parameters. He wanted no recognizable references to established religion, gods, or identifiable political parties. Collecting material, for example, from the Proverbs of Solomon had to have references to Judaism and God scrubbed from them.

It started as a two-step process, first gathering the information and then scrubbing it. Eventually, Henry managed to eliminate certain results from his content gathering.

Fine-tuning 'the wall' on which he wanted to train his AI, however, involved more than just avoiding religion. He also needed to de-sex the content. Since he was using all public domain sources, most were over seventy years old and highly patriarchal and male-directed. Much of the data was also nationalistic, and not just American either. Stripping the content of objectionable material of this sort was considerably harder than removing references to one god or another.

Henry also discovered proverbs were not always statements, but could be questions as well.

"What can you expect from a pig but a grunt?"

"Why buy a cow when milk is so cheap?"

"If you look into your own heart and find nothing wrong there, what is there to worry about?"

"Why should your springs flow in the streets, your streams of water in the public squares?"

"Can you embrace fire and your clothes not be burned?"

"If you have nothing with which to pay, why should your bed be taken from under you?"

Of course, his partners stopped by every day to spend some time in the office finding and researching things the business needed. And to discuss Henry's project.

"So, you ask this oracle thing a question, it looks at the key words, and selects an old saying?" Isobel asked.

"No. Not quite. The AI won't work the same as a search engine. It won't simply look something up and display the results. It will look for concepts and put something together out of the ideas expressed. More like predictive text. It might not even use words that are found in the wall," Henry explained. "That's partly because so many of the sayings and proverbs and philosophies it's built on are phrased archaically. And also, it will learn from the questions it's asked. I've been spending the time this week just building the wall and scrubbing it, but then I have to actually train the AI and establish rules for it to use."

"So, what's the difference between this and just using a chat online?" Luke asked. "Doesn't a chatbot just... you described it as predictive text, right? It just picks a word from the query and chooses the most likely word to continue next?"

"In a way, it's the same. But this is specialized. It isn't pulling from the entire body of human knowledge. It's only being trained on a pretty severely restricted body of philosophical literature, and even that is being scrubbed for objectionable material," Henry said.

"And who decides what is objectionable?" Chastity asked.

"I guess at the moment I do, but I'm willing to open that up to those in this room."

"As long as we aren't promoting anything illegal or immoral, I don't object," Isobel said.

"Let's restrict that to illegal. Even in this room we wouldn't agree on what is immoral," Luke countered.

"Oh, just do it," Isobel laughed. "I don't have time to consider a bunch of rules for a computer to answer questions. I just want a better search engine."

"Got it coming," Henry laughed. "I just need three more of me to get stuff done as fast as I want."

SATURDAY, HENRY WAS in sweats and focused on training parameters for the AI when his doorbell rang. It was unusual, but perhaps there was a delivery. He headed downstairs as the bell rang repeatedly. He opened the door to face Kaitlyn.

"You didn't answer my messages," she shouted at him. "What kind of boyfriend are you?"

"I think I answered that question when I broke up with you," he said. "I'm not a boyfriend at all."

"You can't do that! Didn't you read the messages I sent after that?"

"I figured if you had something important to say you'd call. It was all I could do to get through the first batch of messages," he said.

"We need to get married! I'm pregnant!" she shouted at him before he could close the door.

Henry stared at her through the doorway. He could count the times they'd had sex on one hand. He'd always carefully used a condom, even when she'd suggested he didn't need to. No. It wasn't possible.

"I hope you know who the father is," he said calmly. "I've always used a condom."

"The first time," she said. "You quit eating me and just stuck your cock in me. It had to have been then."

"I already had a condom on by then. And you went into the bathroom and put a tampon in because your period started right after."

"It must have been blood from you being so rough with me. I haven't had a period since."

"I'm sorry, Kaitlyn, but I can't accept that. When the baby is born, we can do a DNA test and if it proves to be mine, I'll make arrangements to care for it—even adopt it if you can't take care of it. But we aren't getting married. That would just be another disaster."

"You can't just ignore me! This is your fault. If you don't marry me, I'll sue you for everything you have," she shouted.

"You say that as if I have a lot," he said.

"You have this huge apartment!"

"If it weren't for having a housemate and the company paying rent, I wouldn't have this. I don't have money, Kaitlyn."

"But the company. All your big deal programming," she wailed.

"It's all a future that isn't today," he said. "It might be successful and it might not. No guarantees in that. It would certainly fail if I was distracted with a wife and child now."

"You're a terrible person!"

"No, Kaitlyn. I'm just not going to let you use me so you can live a life on the golf course. We aren't in love. We've never even talked about a future together. It's obvious when we have sex that you aren't really interested. I'm not settling for a life like that," he said. "I wish you luck. You should probably check with George to see if he'll claim the child—if you have one."

Kaitlyn stared at him with open mouth as he closed the door. He didn't slam it, but he made sure the bolt made a noise when it slid into place.

WHEN SHE WAS gone, Henry sank into the sofa and stared into space. Was it possible? No. He was certain this was a ploy of some sort. Kaitlyn hadn't expressed an interest in him until after they'd formed the company and he'd hired Lisa.

Kaitlyn had been clear with him when they first met that her goal in college was to marry a nice guy who would support her for the rest of her life, while she played golf every day. He didn't think her goals had changed and he wouldn't put it past her to either get pregnant or pretend to it in order to get the guy she could control like that.

He heaved a sigh and went back to his computer upstairs. However, he didn't go back to training the AI. Instead, he launched his search engine. Since his search was private and powered by his own version of a limited AI, it didn't automatically filter results simply because they were private or behind a fire-wall. He'd used it to find everything about that guy who threatened Chastity a year ago. He hadn't used it like that since.

But now he sent it to retrieve everything it could find about Kaitlyn Lau.

23

SPECIALIZATION

ALL KAITLYN REALLY WANTED to do was play golf. She was certain to become a force in the LPGA within a year or two if she could maintain her training. To maintain her training, she needed support. She hadn't considered Henry a potential candidate the year before, but her visit home in the summer had moved him up the ladder.

It seemed her family had connections. Their connections wanted control—control of Open Cloak Design.

Her family had established a trust fund for Kaitlyn that could have supported her golf career. The fund, however, withheld that support until she was twenty-five or married. It looked like the family and their connections had nothing against using Kaitlyn to achieve their objectives.

The infant Open Cloak Design had strong potential in the market, but no proven track record. The connections—a company Henry couldn't decipher the name of because it was named in Chinese characters—had determined the quickest and easiest way to gain control of the Open Cloak was to marry into it. They were ruthless in using other people.

When Kaitlyn had been rejected by Henry, she put together the plan to fake a pregnancy and pressure Henry to marry her. That, too, had failed. She was desperate. The promise of funding for her golf career from the trust fund she would gain control of if she married Henry was disappearing.

Unknown to Kaitlyn, within three days of her confrontation with Henry, all these details were known to him. His AI driven search had uncovered the conspiracy, the email, text messages, and even phone conversations through two degrees of separation.

205

HENRY WAS UP all night Monday, analyzing the data from his search of Kaitlyn. His AI had revealed the data, but making sense of it was a process that could take him days. What he understood immediately, though, was he needed to neutralize the threat from Kaitlyn. That was his most immediate problem. If she wasn't pregnant—which he assumed—she might try desperately getting pregnant so she could blame him. There was just too much destruction of lives involved with that.

While Henry had gained access to email, bank accounts, the trust, and other documents, the problem with interfering in them was that much of the communication between her parents and their connections was in Mandarin. While his AI could tap other sources to get a reasonably accurate translation of their conversation, he could not depend on it to translate an English message into Chinese. He could comprehend the translated messages from Mandarin to English, but they were nothing like what a native English speaker would say. He could only assume the opposite would also be true.

While Henry had no particularly loving feelings toward Kaitlyn, he didn't want to see her hurt for the pressure that had been put on her. She needed a secure financial outlook. Her parents could have given her that at any time by changing the terms of the trust. The next four years would be critical for Kaitlyn's development.

It took Henry two more days to decide what to do. At what point was it okay to do something technically illegal to save someone from people who were applying illegal—or at best unethical—pressure against them?

A year ago, he'd struck out at a man threatening Chastity. He'd supplied evidence of wrong-doing to police and the university. And he'd asked Paul Riordan for help. Tom had died in a supposed gun battle in front of Chastity's apartment building. He deserved it. Kaitlyn didn't. And attacking her parents and their connections could lead to a different kind of conflict—one Henry wasn't sure he could win.

He thought her parents had been pressured to use their daughter as well. The trust fund they'd established for her was in the millions and would give her a great head start on life.

He finally decided to act.

It was not that difficult to break into a bank if you were only targeting one customer. He could impersonate her parents and have access. The bank was in San Francisco, so the documents and communications he needed were in English. He changed the terms of the trust so it would transfer to Kaitlyn upon reaching the age of 25 or having graduated from college. That meant she'd gain control of the trust in June. He also had the trustee changed so her parents could not alter it again. Then he sent the necessary correspondence from her parents to the bank and from the bank to Kaitlyn.

Since graduation was still five months away, nothing would show up immediately other than Kaitlyn being notified that the terms had changed. That should satisfy her need to marry Henry in order to get the trust money and partial control of the company. She was free and he erased all signs of his interference.

Henry did not, however, trust that the connections would be satisfied with the results. They wanted his company and he'd be damned if he let them have it. He'd reduced the range of the hacking counterattack software on the company server. He reactivated the full range but set the software to alert him to any perceived attack rather than to counter immediately. He connected the alert to his phone so he would get it at any time and location.

MONDAY BEING A holiday, the spring semester began on Tuesday the eighteenth. Henry had finally managed to frontload his classes to the first four days of the week so he would have Fridays off for a long weekend. That was his way of establishing a three-day work week at the office.

His Tuesday/Thursday classes that met for an hour and a half each day were AI Society and Humanity, Language and Thought, and Decision Making. On Monday and Wednesday he would have Modern Regression (Statistics), Design of AI Products, and Search Engines.

Lisa was in all three of his Tuesday/Thursday classes but had different classes on Monday and Wednesday. She was as loaded in her schedule as he was with eighteen hours. Josh had also managed Fridays free, so the office on Friday was likely to be busy. He had a class with Henry on Monday/Wednesday and one with Henry and Lisa on Tuesday/Thursday. There was some overlap with others in their study group as well.

It was Fridays that interested Henry the most. He was soaking up the information in his other classes as fast as he could absorb it, including staying up late at night reading the several texts assigned. But Friday morning, Josh, Lisa, and Chastity all showed up and headed to the fourth-floor office. Henry was already there.

"Okay, you're going to have a dev meeting in a few minutes, but Luke wanted us all together for a Zoom call first thing this morning. I'll connect," Chastity said.

Luke's picture filled most of the monitor with a single picture of the four of them in the office. Isobel showed up in another window.

"Good morning, partners and contractors," Luke said. "I felt it was worth our time to hear this good news all at once. We have received our first royalty deposit from EMEE, representing business in the fourth quarter. Drumroll, please!" He flashed an image of an electronic check on the screen. "Yes! We made $21.92 on sales of eight units of the new Open Cloak Optimization software. We are in business."

"Oh, geez, Luke. Twenty-two dollars? Really? Can we even pay for this call with that?" Isobel shouted.

"Keep in mind, my friends that we were only in business for two weeks in the fourth quarter. Granted, if we made that every two weeks it would still only be $263 a quarter. That won't pay anyone's salary here. But it's a good sign, nonetheless. We *do* have a real product and we *do* have sales. It will only get better from here. Let's have a little cheer and everyone get back to work!"

"Whoopee!" they all yelled, laughing. Chastity cut the connection.

"Okay," Henry said. "As to the work—as if we don't all have enough work to keep us busy with school—Lisa is still on the revamp of our website. It's coming along nicely. Lisa, guide us through it, please."

Lisa took control of the presentation, flashing up the current site on the screen and comparing it to the new UI. It was clean and professional, but also stood out as a masterful UI implementation. The interface was fast and smooth. The graphics were beautiful but not ostentatious. And most of all, the PR firm had sent a list of suggestions that she'd been able to implement.

"When is this going live?" Henry asked.

"We should have the last bits tested by next weekend," Lisa said. "Then it lacks only your signal to go live. The changeover will take us about an hour."

"Fantastic!" Henry said. "Just in time for you to get involved with the next project I want you to work on. Josh, your project is to *take over* development of the Open Cloak search engine. I think we're pretty close on it, but I want every line of code reviewed. We'll bring on Simon and Leonard for the review, but the time for them is limited. You're the lead. You'll have leeway to propose improvements and implement them on approval."

"Hot damn! I've wanted to get my fingers in that code," Josh said. "Does that mean I can install it and start using it myself?"

"After code review, I want to release it to all our testers for code bashing. Until then, your machine only. No other distribution."

"Got it. What are you working on?"

"I have a new project we're going to use to test the singularity concept," Henry said. "It's a narrow AI trained in just one field. It needs to be kept small, but allowed to acquire new knowledge based on queries. In some ways, it will be similar to the search engine, but it will be searching only a single device and then using predictive text to formulate answers to questions. We might need a few dozen testers for this one."

"Cool. I'll start the code review now," Josh said.

"I'm on the UI final," Lisa said. "Can't wait to get the new project."

"I'm ordering in deli sandwiches for lunch," Chastity said. "That will take care of our royalty."

WITH CLASSES IN full swing, Isobel and Luke back at Villanova, and the new pressure on Henry, Lisa, and Josh to get software ready to release, there was little time to consider anything else—like dating. However, at the end of January, Henry received a brief text message from Kaitlyn.

"False alarm. Sorry."

He responded with a thumbs up emoji and didn't hear anything else.

Darla Gallitzin, the PR agent, called that day as well, pushing all thoughts of Kaitlyn out of Henry's mind.

"I've arranged for you to have an interview with Gene Grey on the *Grey's Analysis* podcast," Darla said when she connected. "It's a great opportunity to promote the Open Cloak Optimization software. Could be a big break for us."

"And why am I doing this instead of Luke? He's the front man for our company," Henry said.

"I'm getting the company business exposure with Luke. Harvard Business Review is talking about a bootstrapping article that will feature Luke as one of the young CEOs," Darla answered. "But Gene is a techie. His show is about technology. He isn't interested in marketing and promotion. But he *is* interested in the philosophy of technology. He wants to talk about your personal philosophy regarding AI, and how your product answers some of the big ethical issues generative AI has brought to people's minds."

"So, we'll get right into the ethics discussion?" Henry asked.

"Probably. But keep in mind that Gene will probe for how the software works. Don't give away the store. And be mindful of your license agreement for the first optimization patent. Don't imply that it was an early version of this or they'll be all over you for violating the license agreement."

"Got it. Okay. When am I supposed to do this interview?"

"Set up a place in your office where you can be on Zoom with him and I'll set it up for Friday."

CHASTITY WENT TO work getting a Zoom-appropriate station set up for Henry. With herself, Josh, and Lisa in the office upstairs, it wasn't an appropriate place for the interview. Added to that, they'd brought in Simon and Leonard on Friday afternoons to help with code review. Henry was pleased with the results and felt the search engine would be far more efficient than anything else on the market.

The space she determined was best for the interview was Henry's private study in his third-floor residence. She made a couple of purchases to enhance Henry's look, including a ring light and hi-res camera, and a background Lisa created, featuring the company logo that would make it look like Henry was in a professional setting.

On Friday afternoon at the appointed time, she checked Henry's clothing and hair, making sure he was an appropriate representative for the company. She stopped at the last minute and cleaned his glasses. Then she left him alone to accept the meeting request from Gene.

"HELLO, AND WELCOME to Grey's Analysis. This is your host Gene Grey, and we're launching our 79th edition of the podcast. For today's chat, I'm fortunate to have with me one of the founders and chief technology officer of Open Cloak Design, Henry Pascal. Welcome, Henry."

"Thanks, Gene. I'm happy to be here."

"I have to ask you right off if your name influenced your choice of professions. Are you a descendant of the famed French mathematician Blaine Pascal?" Gene asked.

"Hmm. I don't think so. Maybe I should pay more attention to ancestry than I have. However, my father, Ryan Pascal, certainly influenced my early interest in computers and programming," Henry said.

"I just had to ask," Gene said lightly. "I'm going to jump to another totally inappropriate question because it was a surprise to me when we connected, having not met you before. How old are you, Henry?"

"Yeah, that's kind of inappropriate, but understandable. I'll be twenty next week. I'm a junior at the university and expect to graduate next year."

"I ask because I've purchased a copy of Open Cloak Optimizer for my computer and I'm seriously impressed that someone so young could develop this software. I was told, though, that you are the sole developer," Gene said.

"I also have a UI designer," Henry said. "She's a college colleague who comes from a similar background and has been designing software interfaces from her early teens."

"Tell me about the software," Gene said. "What inspired you to create software for computer optimization?"

"My mother," Henry laughed. "She was constantly complaining that every software update forced onto to her computer broke something or made it run slower. I tinkered with her computer for years trying to make it run more efficiently."

"You've been developing an AI for years?" Gene asked.

"In a way. When I built my first computer, at age eight, my father explained all the parts to me. He said there were four essential ingredients: hardware, firmware, software, and wetware. The human brain is the wetware part of things. We tell the software, hardware, and firmware what to do. I started developing an AI tool to replicate what the wetware would do in some limited applications."

"Aren't you concerned about replacing a human touch with thinking programs?" Gene asked.

"I see a fundamental problem there," Henry answered. "There is a constant drive for humans to specialize. My mother is a nurse. She has no real idea how to optimize her computer. I could do it because I specialized in computing. But the vast majority of computer users are like my mother. They want the computer to do the tasks they ask of it, quickly and efficiently. But they have neither the working knowledge nor the interest in learning how to optimize their computers."

"So, the wetware you are replacing is a computer consultant?"

"That's an interesting way to put it," Henry said, nodding.

"When the explosion of AI apps hit just a few years ago, there was—and continues to be—a huge outpouring of opposition because it was copying from people without their permission. But now you are producing an AI or artificial intelligence program and suggesting people voluntarily install it on their computers. I'm sure you're aware of the number of red flags that are being waved at this idea. How do you ever hope to overcome that?"

"Over the past few years, the desire has been to expand into general AI. That is an AI that replicates all the functions of the human brain completely. I believe that is the wrong direction. Oh, we're learning valuable things from it, but the amount of memory and power that are expended to create a general AI are hundreds of times what is available in a human brain. Maybe that's why humans tend toward specialization. We only need peripheral awareness of things outside our areas of specialization. And for decades, we've been using software to replace those functions we only use rarely."

"Decades? For example?"

"What's 361 times 287?" Henry asked. "I'm sure there are people among your listeners who can simply give you that answer off the top of their heads. What do the rest of us do? We go to a calculator app and type in the numbers, press a button and read the result: 103,607. We've replaced the bulk of our math specialization with software. Most of us who graduated from college could sit down with a pencil and paper and follow the rules we learned in arithmetic to figure out that answer. But why should we? We have tools to do that."

"You're comparing your AI to a calculator?"

"I think that comparison has been made for years and years. Ever since the development of the first calculating machines. The point is that the calculator is a highly specialized tool we use almost every day. It's not scary. In the same way, other highly specialized AIs can be developed that make specific tasks easier for us. That's what we've done with Open Cloak Optimization. The AI only functions in the area of optimizing your computer the way *you'd* like it to run. And instead of interrupting your workflow at inopportune times to ask you what you want to do, it learns how you work and makes adjustments to your computer when it is idle."

"And I suppose you collect all that information so you can push advertising and promotion to the customer," Gene said.

"No. That's the other flaw with the huge AIs that make people not trust them. They are connected to the cloud and report the information about your usage to agencies for use in promoting other products. Our AI will work on a completely disconnected computer because it does not access or report to *anyone* but the person installing it. You can open the UI and ask for reports on what it has done, but you are the only one who has access to that information. You called it a consultant a while ago. I'd call it a personal assistant for optimizing your computer. It's not a personal assistant to constantly search out things it thinks you might be interested in buying. It is specialized like a calculator."

"An application this powerful must take up a huge amount of computer memory and storage," Gene suggested, already knowing the answer.

"No. That would be contrary to the purpose for the app in the first place. All the information needed to train the AI is already located on your computer, so it doesn't need to create any other huge database to learn from. It would function on less than 100mb of memory when active. You probably have a dozen applications running on your computer right now that are taking up more memory than that—like this communication program that makes it possible for us to have a conversation between Pittsburgh and Silicon Valley as if we're in the same room. Added to that, the application only activates when the computer is idle, so it doesn't occupy any cycles you might be using."

"This is fascinating, Henry. Let's go into what the application actually changes on your computer in order to optimize it," Gene said.

The conversation occupied a full hour, but Gene said the edited version would probably be about forty minutes.

24
ORACULAR SAYINGS

"**H**EY, HENRY," LISA said Wednesday. "Happy birthday!"

"Oh, wow! I'm out of my teens. When can I retire?" Henry laughed.

"That'll be the day. Do you think you'll ever retire?" she asked.

"Well, it won't be today. That statistics class is not what I was expecting. I need strong coffee this morning."

"Oh, hey. Do you remember freshman orientation?"

"Wasn't that like fifty years ago?"

"I'm sure. Did you get one of the department coffee mugs?" she asked.

"Didn't we get a coffee mug from everyone? I think we've got twenty different mugs in the cupboard. Josh and Leonard don't even bother to bring their own mugs over when they're working. So, I'm sure I got one of the department mugs."

"A brown one or a red one?"

"Um... I'd have to say brown. I'm sure I'd remember more clearly if it was the red one. Why?"

"I just ran across a memory pic on my feed and saw the cup I was holding. It was red." She looked at the brown mug in her hands. "I think I've been using your mug since I moved in."

"Lisa! My mug? Really?" Henry asked, feigning alarm. "Does that mean we're, like, married now?"

"Married?! You must be kidding!" Lisa shouted. "We haven't even had sex yet!"

214

"I was joking!" Henry backpedaled.

"Of course. Um… So was I. You know."

They shared a look with each other like they'd just met, then Henry took another swallow of his coffee and they headed for the car to go to class.

HENRY DIDN'T REALLY have time to think about Lisa that day. They split when they got to campus and Lisa caught the bus home as Henry went to his parents' house for birthday dinner. Chastity was waiting for him on the front steps.

"Happy birthday," she said giving him a peck on the lips.

"Oh boy! Are you my birthday present?"

"I don't think your parents would pay for me, so I'll have to give myself to you," she snarked. "So, what's-her-name is out of the picture?"

"Kaitlyn is out of my life, if that is what you mean."

"Okay. Let's not mention her by name again. I never really liked her much and painting on a smile when she was around made me feel like a fake. I am who I am and you and I are both twenty years old now. Let's just make the most of it," she said.

"Why are you standing out here on the porch?" he asked.

"Your parents aren't home yet. I was waiting for you," Chastity said.

"Well, they never took my key away, so I guess I'm allowed to open up. I thought Mom said she was going to be home before I got here," Henry said.

"She must have gotten held up at the hospital," Chastity said. "She works so hard."

"She does. Since she got Thanksgiving weekend off so she and Dad could go to Florida, she had to work every day through Christmas and New Year. When we actually get money ahead in the company and I'm earning a real salary, I'm going to buy Mom and Dad a cruise around the world or something."

He opened the door and reached in to turn on the light.

"Surprise!" a group of people yelled as they were illuminated.

"What the…?" Henry jumped back.

"Your mother told me you'd never had a surprise party. So, we gathered up the gang," Chastity said.

Luke and Isobel reached him right after his parents and congratulated him on leaving his teens. Luke's parents, Paul and Marla, were there as were the Donovans from a few doors down. Then there were the guys from his study group, including the ones who were contracted to the company: Lisa, Josh, Simon, Leonard, and Dan. Professor Jacoby greeted him, along with Conrad and Arden, upper classmen who shared a couple of classes with him.

"I'm... Wow! I mean, this isn't a weekend and it's not like it's even a really important birthday," Henry said. "Really, thank you all for surprising me on my birthday."

"Every birthday is important, son," Ryan said. "It's something you made me realize recently. Every day is a reason to celebrate."

"How's that, Dad?"

"Filling out the questionnaires and recording stories for your project. It's just made me feel especially mindful of the time we have together. Every opportunity we have to celebrate a life event, we should do it."

"People, there's a lot of food and soft drinks," Sylvia called out. "We know everyone has to get back to homes and schedules, being a weeknight, but eat up while you're celebrating."

That broke the press on Henry as people traded places and got food as well as greeting Henry. The house was packed and eventually, Chastity brought Henry a plate of food so he could eat, too.

Isobel took the plate out of Henry's hands and handed it to Luke. Then she smashed herself against him and gave him a kiss that silenced the party.

"Izzy! What the hell?" Henry asked.

"We drove five hours getting here and are getting back in the car to drive five hours back at 8:00. I want to get something out of the trip!" she said.

"Oh! Of course! Come here and let me kiss you again," he laughed.

She pressed herself against him again and people ignored the display this time, even though Henry made himself at home by gripping Isobel's abundant ass.

"Better make that all if I want to get back to Philly tonight. Alive," Izzy laughed. She grabbed Henry's plate from Luke and handed it back to him. Luke followed and shook his hand.

"Uh... Sorry about that," Henry said as he gripped his friend's hand.

"Hell, if that was all I had to worry about, I'd be a very happy man," Luke laughed. He lowered his voice. "The worst part is that I'll have to act offended and jealous all the way back to Philly in order to convince Izzy I love her."

Luke and Isobel's departure at 8:00 was a signal for everyone to leave and by 8:30, the house was nearly empty. The Donovans were helping Henry's parents clean up.

"Hey, Henry. Could you drop me off at the apartment on your way over to Chastity's," Lisa asked when she got next to them.

"I could drop Chastity off and just drive us back," Henry said. "What makes you think I'm going to her house?" Chastity jabbed him in the ribs with her elbow.

"It's where I'd be headed if I were you," Lisa laughed.

"Want to come along?" Chastity asked.

"Oh... uh... Well... Not this time. You know. Not yet," Lisa sputtered.

"I'll take you home, then," Henry said. "This has been a crazy day. I need to say thank you to my parents."

"WHAT WAS ALL that about with Lisa?" Henry asked Chastity as they came down from their first orgasm.

"Can't you tell?" Chastity asked. "She's interested. She just doesn't want to express too much interest too soon after your breakup, but she also doesn't want to miss the chance before you hook up with someone else."

"There's no one else on my horizon but you. Why would she pretty much assume I was going home with you?" Henry felt incredibly stupid. He needed to take more initiative in his relationships. It seemed he was just too busy to treat them seriously.

"Didn't you hear her? She said it's what she would do. She knows we get together for sex once in a while."

"And you invited her to join us."

"Next time you invite her."

"Yeah. Right."

"SO, YOU DON'T really need a fancy interface for this thing, do you?" Lisa asked as she sat with Henry Friday morning in the office. They were looking at the diagram for his oracular sayings software.

"Nothing elaborate at the moment, but we need to decide how a person would interact with the program. Remember this is really a testbed for the Ask Dad program. It's going to be months yet before my father's database has grown to an extent that I can start training an AI on it. The oracle already has a database I scraped from the internet of almost a billion data points."

"What else do you need to do with it?" she asked. "I mean besides have a text box where people can ask a question."

"There are all kinds of possibilities for it. Right now, I'm trying to set up rules for things to ignore and acceptable words to use in response. This is actually a lot simpler than Ask Dad. We're dealing only with text. No audio and no video. That will require another level of development and I hope I have someone else full time on it besides the two of us."

"You consider me full time?"

"Well, not at the moment. You can't work full time while you're in school and we can't afford to pay you until we get more revenue and/or investment," Henry said.

"Okay. So, do you have a dictionary of forbidden words? We could have the interface just substitute an acceptable word when an unacceptable one is entered."

"I'm compiling that, but you should have it soon. For now, let's just have a text input and a text output. That will tell me more about how it needs to be trained than I currently have."

"Okay. We'll input a text string. What's it supposed to be? Ask a question?"

"We should limit it to that at first. Linguistic analysis should enable the AI to respond to statements as well as full questions," Henry said.

He watched Lisa construct a simple text box and link it to the AI. Then she created an answer box, reversing the connection and limiting both to 140 characters. They both laughed at the reference and vowed they would set their own logical limit later.

It still wasn't an interface. It was just two text boxes in her dev app. She was quick and Henry saw a new code snippet he hadn't thought of before. He quickly made a note of it. And then his eyes went back to Lisa.

They'd known each other for a year and a half now. She'd rented an apartment from him for six months. He'd gotten used to seeing her at the breakfast table or lounging in the living room. They often ate dinner together. He liked her.

There wasn't much not to like. She was smart and witty, a good programmer, knowledgeable about AI and quick to grasp concepts as Henry rattled them off. And she was seriously cute, now that he thought about it. He remembered well the stunning girl he'd taken to a fall dance. She never flaunted her looks, but he knew she was really pretty. Sexy. He hadn't really allowed that thought to cross his mind before.

It was still only the two of them in the office on Friday morning. Chastity usually arrived at about noon. Josh, Simon, and Leonard usually rolled in about one. Unlike Henry and Lisa, they ran on a more typical developer schedule, staying up late and waking up late. Lisa was a lot more like Henry, up early and finishing early.

Henry typed out a new line of code and checked it in.

"Okay. I'm ready to enter a text string. Question," Lisa corrected herself. "How does this sound? 'Should I plan on working for my father?' That should be understandable."

"Okay," Henry said, concealing a grin. "What's the result?"

Lisa entered the question and waited for the answer. Then she quickly deleted it.

"Um... I think I must have a syntax error. Let me try another question. 'Will I be healthy, wealthy, and wise?' Those keywords should work."

She entered the text and waited for the response. Then she looked puzzled again. Henry stood up.

"What's it say?"

"Do you want to go out tonight?" Lisa said.

"Oh... Sure. Want to get dinner after we call it quits here?" he asked.

"That wasn't a question from me. I've typed two different questions into your app and I got the same answer twice. 'Do you want to go out tonight?' It doesn't make sense."

"I already answered the question. Are you saying you don't want to go out tonight?" he asked, standing next to her desk.

"Sure... but I... Did you program this into the software to ask me out?"

"I wanted to make sure I had your attention. Sometimes the software is the only thing you're aware of," Henry laughed.

"Of course it is. It's my job here. I can't believe you had to have the software ask me out instead of doing it yourself."

"Lisa, would you go out to dinner with me this evening?" Henry said.

"Yes," she said. "Now take out this code and let me test the app."

Henry went back to his desk and backed out the code he'd entered that morning. Once the changes were checked in, Lisa checked her connections and tried another question. She started laughing.

"What is it?" Henry asked.

"The oracle has spoken," Lisa said. "The longest journey begins with a single step. The second step is unpredictable."

"That's not bad. What question did you ask?"

"Should I date Henry?" Lisa said. "I guess the oracle has spoken."

WHEN JOSH, SIMON, and Leonard got to the office that afternoon, Henry sat with the team to go over the code review on the Open Cloak Search Engine. They were critical of certain aspects.

"Why did you take out the ability to identify the proxy chain?" Leonard asked. "That made it a super-charged search engine."

"I'll listen to reasons it should be in there, but I don't think it has anything to do with conducting a standard search. I think it only belongs in the active defense program. I can't think of another reason that would justify having it in a search engine," Henry said.

"When are we going to get our greedy little fingers in the active defense program?" Simon asked.

"This is all the team we have," Henry said. "When we finish with the search engine and think it's ready to test broadly, we have a new consumer app to test. Lisa is putting the UI together for it now. But you guys have added a lot of good stuff to the search engine. This feature that identifies private links so you don't have to click on a url in order to find out it's forbidden is good."

"But it still identifies the kind of information contained behind the wall," Josh said. "We used the AI:summarize command to identify what is there without actually copying any information."

"And that same string allows us to generate summaries of each url identified by the search. We got Lisa to modify the UI so the user can specify the amount of summary the user gets," Leonard said.

"Tell me about that. Why?" Henry asked.

"Most search engines display a line or two summary of the contents. In the weakest ones, it's just the sentence that contains the search term. However, site owners can buy higher ranking and longer summaries," Josh said. "They call it search engine optimization, but it's all about the company wanting to get better visibility. You've stressed the search engine is a servant of the user, not the corporation. By allowing the user to specify what kind of summary he wants, we give him control over what sites are presented and in how detailed a manner without bowing down to advertising budgets on the other end."

"Perfect. You guys have done a great job."

They continued the full review with a list of bugs that still needed work, but at the end of the meeting, there was only a weekend's worth of work to be done before the app could be released to the testing group.

"WE COULD HAVE just heated one of the delivery meals in the microwave and sat in the dining room instead of the kitchen tonight," Lisa suggested as Henry opened the car door for her. They'd discovered that a service delivering four meals a week for each of them supplemented their diet without having to think of menus and spend time cooking.

"That would really be like a couple of married people, don't you think?" Henry said. "Have dinner together, watch TV, and say goodnight."

"I hope, when the time comes, marriage is a little more exciting than that," Lisa sighed. "It's nice to get dressed up and go out, though. Thank you. Where are we going?"

"Wan Chen Restaurant," Henry said. "It just struck me as a funny place to go that is in the realm of what we've been working on, but is just for entertainment."

"As long as you didn't stuff all the fortune cookies with the same fortune," Lisa laughed. "Why didn't you just ask me?"

"I wasn't sure I could," Henry said. "I've been struggling to get some of my life in balance, and part of that includes deciding what I personally want to happen rather than just accepting everything that does happen."

"You hardly just accept things at work. You have goals and are dedicated to reaching them."

They pulled up to the restaurant and Henry actually let the valet take the car as he and Lisa stepped out to enter the popular restaurant. When they were seated and chose their meals from the menu, Henry went back to the subject of goals.

"I think I'm driving toward some good business goals, but it's the life balance thing I was talking about. That seems to be the only area of my life I seem to have trouble making any steps on my own. Like dating, for example."

"You've always had dates and girlfriends as long as I've known you," Lisa said.

"Yeah. Back in high school, Chastity asked me... no, she told me I was taking her to the prom. When I got to college, a golf teammate arranged to share a room with me at a tournament. Kaitlyn actually looked for me over in the SCS cafeteria and asked me out," Henry said. "Oh, yes, the summer between high school and college, Chastity invited me on a double date, which turned out to be a blind date with the girl I dated all that summer. I didn't take any action at all."

"And I invited you out last fall."

"I do consider that a little different. You needed something and I was happy to help out. That's not like tonight. I made a conscious decision that I'd like to spend more time—casual time—with you so I could really get to know you. I've always liked you, but..."

Henry paused as food was delivered to their table and they served their meals.

"All the girls I've gone out with are pretty," he continued. "I consider Chastity to be the most beautiful of them all, but Chastity is not my girlfriend. Ask her. She'll tell you that emphatically. When I took you to the dance last fall, I realized you are in a whole different category of attractiveness that is way above me. I thought about asking you out last fall, but then I became your landlord and thought it would be too creepy to do that. What a cliché."

"Thank you for the compliment, I think," Lisa snorted. "Why did you decide it was no longer creepy?"

"Fuck! I hope not! Shit. I suppose you could sue me for office harassment after I rigged the software this morning."

"I'll let that pass. You haven't been stalking me. Am I just convenient now that you and Kaitlyn broke up?"

"No. Something Chastity said to me the other day just got me thinking. What would I really like in my life. And then my thought was, 'someone like Lisa.' Of course, it took me a day or two to drop the 'someone like' and decide to ask you out," Henry said.

"I see."

"Please remember what I said last fall, too," Henry said. "I still stand by that. If we ever have sex, it will be because we both really want it; not because it's convenient or because one of us owes the other. And that isn't to suggest that we should have sex tonight. I just really wanted to relax with you and get to know you better. And here, I've done all the talking."

It seemed they'd finally exhausted the topic for the time being and they enjoyed the meal. Lisa told Henry about how her father had taught her coding and sat with her for hours when she learned new games. She said she wanted permission from Henry to set her father up with the questions and project of recording his life and advice. He quickly agreed.

They didn't rush through the meal and it was nearly nine o'clock when the server delivered the bill and the requisite fortune cookies. Henry left cash to cover the meal and tip and they selected their cookies.

"You don't have to reveal your fortune to me," he said.

"Let's share them. There's no sense in one of us being embarrassed by a cookie," Lisa said.

She broke open her cookie, removed the slip of paper from it and popped a bit of the cookie into her mouth before smoothing it out.

"I'm not sure now that I want to even suggest this to you," she laughed. "A smart husband buys his wife fine China; then she doesn't trust him to wash it."

"Hmm. I'll have to put that into my nuggets of wisdom for the future," Henry said. He followed the ritual cookie opening. "Well. Um... It says, Be passionate and totally worth the chaos."

Lisa spluttered with laughter.

"Do you think you can hold the passion and chaos in until we're out of the restaurant?" she asked.

"I will... Yeah... I hope so."

25
THE BIRTH OF PYTHIA

HENRY AND LISA got back from their date about 10:00 that evening. She blocked him at the door to the row house and pulled out her own key. She didn't unlock the door, though. She looked into his eyes.

"I really enjoyed our date, Henry, and I hope you'd like to do it again. I'd consider it appropriate if you wanted to kiss me goodnight," she said. Henry started to move forward, but she held him back with her hand on his chest. "But not in the house. If you want to kiss me goodnight, you need to do it out here and then let me go home."

"I think you have a reason for this?" Henry said, raising an eyebrow.

"Yeah. I've been thinking a lot about it this evening," she said. "If we go inside and kiss in the apartment, it jeopardizes the relationship we have in there. I'm not ready to make a transition yet. It would just be convenient to kiss at breakfast or to sit on the couch making out. I don't want to kiss you because you happen to be there and we've done it before. If we kiss inside, it will mark the beginning of a new kind of relationship. I don't think you're ready to go there yet, either."

"You're right," Henry agreed. "I told you we wouldn't have sex because it was convenient and I agree that this would be another significant step that I wouldn't want to do because it's convenient. However, I would love to kiss my date goodnight at the door, if it is okay."

"Yeah. It's okay," she said.

Henry pulled her to him and she put her hands on either side of his head as she raised her lips to his. The kiss was warm and their tongues even touched slightly before they pulled away from each other.

"Thanks for a lovely evening," she said. She unlocked the door and stepped inside, closing it behind her.

Henry waited a moment and reached for the doorknob, finding it locked. He chuckled as he pulled out his key, unlocked the door, and went into the apartment. He stopped in the kitchen long enough to grab a seltzer from the fridge and then went to his own third floor suite.

BOTH HENRY AND Lisa were a little unsure of how their relationship might have changed after having one date, but their routines were more powerful than any particular attraction. Lisa had a web design to complete and Henry was deep in his work on the oracle. He really wanted to start working on his father's Ask Dad, but he knew there weren't yet enough data points to be able to train the AI. He could, however, start training the oracle.

Henry needed to ask questions through the simple interface Lisa had put together the previous day and test the oracle's answers, correcting mistaken word definitions and syntax. He didn't know how many questions he could come up with until he did a simple search with the new search engine. He entered "questions to ask" and was overwhelmed with results. The first search revealed mostly interview questions and questions designed to get to know another person. When he added a word, "questions to ask myself," more useful suggestions were revealed. He also found "questions to ask an oracle," and a surprising number of "questions to ask my father."

He started compiling the list from the many websites he found.

"What makes life meaningful?"

"What do I need to focus on?"

"What am I not seeing about my current situation?"

"How can I ensure success?"

"What will help me find inner peace?"

"What do I need most right now?"

The answers coming back didn't necessarily match up with the questions. He got some laughs.

"Knowing enough is enough will ensure you always have enough."

"Be mindful of your caffeine and sugar intake."

"Your current situation is not your destination."

"Accept what cannot be controlled."

"Rocket ass boosts horse tracks."

Well, not every answer could even be associated with a question. Occasionally, the randomness of the response was too far off to be parsed by the system.

"I'm ordering some Thai food for dinner," Lisa said, coming upstairs. "You want some?"

Henry looked up and realized it was six o'clock on Saturday evening. He wasn't sure he'd even taken a bathroom break. Chastity was sitting on the corner of his desk facing him and he had a hand on her bare leg. He looked to Lisa.

"Yes. Um... Just some noodle thing, you know," he said.

"How about you, Chastity?" Lisa asked.

"No. I was just saying goodnight to Henry. I need to work on my taxes tonight. I'll see you next week."

Lisa left the office and went downstairs.

"Taxes?" Henry asked.

"You had income this year. You have to report it for taxes."

"We haven't had that much income, have we?"

"You probably haven't made as much as I have, but you still have to report it."

"How do you report your income from... you know?"

"From escorting? I just list it as a sole proprietorship business engaged in entertainment. Nobody questions it."

"Wow."

"Now put away your toys and go have a nice dinner with Lisa," Chastity said. She stood up, letting Henry's hand fall away from her thigh and headed for the stairs down.

LISA CALLED HENRY'S cell phone when dinner arrived and he went to the dining room where she had the Thai food served. He sat down and thanked her for taking care of dinner.

"Uh... Lisa... About Chas upstairs..."

She held up a hand to stop him.

"Not a topic for now. Let me just say that I accepted Chastity as a fact of life before I ever agreed to date you. No more discussion."

"Okay."

Henry certainly didn't expect that kind of response from a girlfriend seeing him with his hand on another woman's bare thigh. Did that mean Lisa wasn't his girlfriend? Kaitlyn, certainly, would have gone ballistic. She didn't even like Lisa living in the same row house or Chastity working with him in the office. That was just one more good reason to have broken up with her. But Lisa?

He didn't mean to flaunt his relationship with Chastity, but he had to admit, Lisa had seen them in that position before. It wasn't unusual for Chastity to perch on the corner of Henry's desk as she gave him a report on the testing agreements, correspondence, or other business matters. It was just so natural for Henry to touch her while they talked. He'd done it without even considering who else was in the room.

"So, what progress did you make on the oracle?" Lisa asked.

"Limited testing. Did you know you can search the internet for questions to ask an oracle? I was running out of things to ask and then found hundreds of questions, both appropriate and inappropriate, at my fingertips."

"What was the most interesting question?" Lisa asked.

"When I wake up tomorrow morning, how will I be different than I am today?"

"Oh. That's a great question. I think though it would be more appropriate for some serious self-examination than an oracle," she said. She handed Henry a spring roll.

"In fact, that's probably where I found it. I got on a search quest and started changing the parameters. Instead of questions to ask an oracle, I entered 'questions to ask myself.' But that wasn't all. I uncovered some good resources for Ask Dad."

"Don't tell me you found 'questions to ask my father!'" Lisa laughed.

"In fact, I did. There are great things that I'm going to feed into Dad's recordings."

"Like?"

"There were a lot of real basic questions, like 'What did you want to become when you were a child?' 'Describe your first pet.' But there were also questions that might make even my dad... think a little," Henry said.

This was exactly the kind of conversation he loved having with Lisa.

"Examples?"

"Like, 'How do you think your career affected your role as a father?' 'What was the craziest thing you did after forty?' And my favorite, 'What was a time in your life when you felt like giving up?' Some cool stuff."

"Okay. Here's one for you? Do you think your mother feels left out because you are doing this project just with your dad?" she asked.

"Holy shit! I don't know. You know the only reason I set it up like I did was to try to get a sample data wall to train an AI with. Mom's so busy and her work as a nurse is so stressful," Henry said.

"You might want to check in with her. I know that as much as I talk about what I found out about my mother, I'd want to compile her life as well."

"We need a new name," Henry said. "We can't just keep calling it Ask Dad. Not if we're going to open it up to others."

They finished dinner and cleaned up the remains and the dishes. They were both thankful they had a dishwasher. It kept them from eating their meals off paper plates. There was a box of grocery store cookies on the counter and they each took a cookie and made a cup of tea, then sat in the living room to continue their discussion.

"I like what you're doing with the website," Henry said. "It really looks professional without looking like we bought it at Ikea. Did you make progress today?"

"Actually, I think we could deploy tomorrow if you wanted to," she said. "The last couple of corrections were pretty easy to make. We got the link to your interview with Gene Grey. He's got it ready for your review and if you approve it, he'll go live with it. Right now, it hasn't been released."

"I suppose I should review it right away, then. Will you be able to start working on the oracle then?" he asked.

"Yes. And I think we need to find a name for that, too. We'll be releasing it to testers before we release the Ask Someone app."

"Right. I'll put it out to Chastity, Isobel, and Luke, too. They have good ideas."

"You really depend on them more than anything, don't you?" Lisa asked.

"I guess sometimes you don't realize how important people are until you don't have as constant access to them. The four of us hung out together all the time. I knew Luke from when we were babies. Isobel in middle school. Chastity joined us in high school. There were other friends we had, too, but whenever it was something important in one of our lives, it was the four of us. It still puzzles me how we managed to so completely miss all the trauma that shaped Chastity's life."

"She came to the three of you for normality. She didn't want to expose you to what wasn't right with her," Lisa said. "That's my completely unprofessional and uninformed opinion."

"You're probably right." They sat in silence as they finished their tea. "I've got a buttload of reading to do. Midterms are in two weeks."

"Ugh! See you tomorrow."

Lisa went upstairs to her room. Henry paused in the kitchen as he put their mugs in the dishwasher and started it. It was odd. He almost felt more like kissing her goodnight after this kind of dinner and conversation than after their date. She was... special.

NOTHING WENT AS fast or as smoothly as they wanted. The partners reviewed the website and the interview and all thought there was a sensitive point in the interview that needed to be changed. Henry couldn't reach Gene Grey until Monday to ask him to remove Henry's comment about the amount of 'trash' that was downloaded to personal computers every time a system, browser, or application update was pushed to it. They all felt that was insulting to the other manufacturers and that it would alert them to what the Open Cloak Optimizer was going to attack.

He spent Sunday afternoon with his parents and asked his mother if she could spare the time to participate in his program to create a legacy.

"Isn't this something special between you and your dad?" she asked. "You don't need to ask me to make me feel better about it. You need special things with your father."

"It *is* special," Henry said, "but that isn't why I didn't approach you about it. Your job has been so stressful, I didn't want to make you feel like you needed to take up valuable rest time participating in this little project."

"Well, as long as you don't have a set time limit that says you need to have three dozen cookies for your class party tomorrow, I think I could participate," she laughed.

"I did kind of forget about that until the last minute, didn't I?" Henry said. "Thanks, Mom. Not only for participating in the project, but for baking cookies when I was in third grade."

HENRY DISCOVERED THAT even though he and Lisa saw each other every day, squeezing out time for and planning actual dates was as difficult as it had been with Kaitlyn. They went out to dinner again on Saturday, but rather than focusing on deeper insights into each other, they spent nearly all their conversation time on trying to figure out what kinds of things they'd like to do on dates other than eat. Going out to dinner seemed like such a date cop-out when they ate most breakfasts and many dinners together.

They did put together a list of things they'd like to do and Lisa agreed to plan the next date. The following Friday, they went to see the final home game of the university's women's basketball team. Henry discovered he enjoyed the sport as much as Lisa did. His experience with sports was focused on golf. In high school, they went to home basketball and football games because they were frequently followed by school dances. No such luck with the college game, but they had a good time and then went out to have pizza with some of Lisa's other friends who were at the game.

That night, the two had their most intense goodnight kiss since they'd started dating. Henry thought he might change his porchlight to a dimmer bulb if they were going to stand on the steps kissing for ten minutes each time they went out.

The company had also been busy that week. They released the test version of the AI search engine and celebrated Luke's birthday by long distance on Tuesday. Then, everyone took a break to prepare for mid-term exams, which would start on Monday.

The best part about mid-terms was that on Friday, spring break began. Chastity was headed to the Bahamas for a few days with a rather wealthy college student who decided that was where he wanted to spend his break and wanted some high-class arm candy with him.

Henry surprised Lisa Friday by taking her to Philadelphia for the first round of the NCAA championship. He'd been unable to see a way to get them there for the play-in game on Wednesday, but the university had won a place in the tournament and were facing the top seed in their region on Friday. Villanova was hosting.

Of course, their university stood little chance against the top ranked Wildcats, but they had a great time at the game and were joined by Luke and Isobel. Henry and Lisa went back to Pittsburgh Friday night, arriving about three in the morning. Luke and Isobel's break was also that week and they came to Pittsburgh the next day.

Henry and Lisa's kiss at their door when they got home could only be described as passionate.

"I'm so close to inviting you in," Lisa sighed as they broke the kiss. "It's just... it's three o'clock in the morning. I don't want to invite you all the way into my suite and I don't want to start something in our shared area. I'm getting awfully turned on by you, though, Henry. Awfully turned on."

"Me, too," he said. "We'll take it at the right pace for us, though. Having a week of vacation time would be a dangerous time to do a lot of fooling around."

"Oh, God! I almost forgot we have all this week in the office together. We'll... do something again next weekend. Okay?"

"Yeah. Goodnight, Lisa."

She unlocked the door and went into the row house. Henry stood on the steps for another minute before he used his key to unlock and then go up to his own suite.

CHASTITY WAS OUT of the office for a few days, but Luke and Isobel were in for a couple of hours every day. Luke joined Lisa and Henry in brainstorming names for the oracle, while Isobel audited the expenses and prepared a financial statement. It wasn't really necessary at that stage, but she created spreadsheets with proforma income and expense projections for every scenario she could think of. From that, she tried to determine how long they could stay in business based on how much they currently had in the bank.

"Nearly every name we've found is in use someplace or another," Luke said. "We could probably use 'Cassandra Says' since no one is going to believe it anyway."

"That's such a sad story," Lisa said.

"I agree," Henry said. "I'm kind of partial to Pythia. It's hard to believe no one has actually named some predictive software after her already."

"Oh, and that could make for some interesting graphics on the site, too," Lisa said.

"How so?" Luke asked.

"According to the wiki, the Oracle of Delphi originally belonged to Python, who was an earth dragon daughter of Gaia," Lisa explained. "Apollo slew her in order to take over the oracle, but the priestess was always considered her daughter and spirit. So, Pythia is associated with the earth dragon. I could do a lot with that."

"I like dragons!" Isobel spoke up from the desk where she was working on a spreadsheet.

"And the dragon-lady has spoken," Luke snarked. What a strange relationship.

"Okay. I'm good with that, but it needs to be more than just the name of the oracle. Like all the ancient Chinese lore seems to begin, 'Confucius Says.' We need something like that for Pythia."

"Speaks," Lisa said. "Pythia Speaks. I can really do some nice graphics for that. And since there is very little else for the interface, we simply have a text box that is labeled 'Ask your question.' Then the answer would be revealed as 'Pythia Speaks.' I love it!"

"I agree," Henry said. "I'm going to register the domain and park it right now."

They all went to work and the site began to take shape.

26
COUNTERATTACK

IN ORDER TO get *Pythia Speaks* across the line between sample concept and a testable program, Henry had to seriously consider what features he wanted the program to have. The obvious features were "Ask Question" and "Generate Response."

For the sake of the program, however, he needed several other features that would not be exposed to users—at least not at first. The AI needed to not only generate the response, but record the conversation so it could add it to its data wall to learn from. Henry had soon discovered in his own testing, though, that there were often follow-up questions and answers. Since both were still limited to 140 characters, it could take three or four questions to finish the conversation.

Pythia needed short term access to the entire conversation. When it ended, the conversation had to be stored in the database so the AI could learn from it.

That brought another matter of ethics up to Henry.

"Should we be storing user information?" he asked. "This would be a typical feature for most AI programs. Some of the conversation bots in the market automatically answer, opening conversations with the human's name. The bot can recall their previous interactions."

"That would require another level of interface," Lisa said. "We'd need to register users. Then, users would want access to previous conversations or the ability to store them, download them, print them, or otherwise use the previous data."

"Whoa!" Luke said. "I thought part of our whole company stance was *not* collecting user data. Both the optimization and the search are based on that."

"This is a different kind of application, though," Henry persisted. "It's accessed through the internet, not on their personal computer. We could probably store the user data in a cookie on their machine and only use it when they access Pythia, but it's just as likely our own optimization software would delete the cookie."

"I say no!" Isobel said emphatically. They all looked at her. "Do you realize how much privacy we don't have anymore? The government has forced cell phone operators to disclose text messages and usage data. Social media sites are rolling over and showing their bellies to agencies demanding user data so they can search people out and deport them. Our little app has to be completely anonymous. I'd stop using it in a second if I thought any of my personal data was stored."

"You've got a point," Henry said. "People used to hide behind the anonymity of social media, but they've found out they aren't anonymous at all and the government can look into any detail of their lives. Izzy, you just won a fan. If I'd been thinking properly, I'd never have suggested it."

Isobel preened at his praise.

"That doesn't mean no one would want to capture their conversation, though," Lisa said. "How can we do that without exposing them?"

"For now, I think we should keep everything temporary. Once a new question is entered, the previous answer vanishes," Henry said.

"We could put in a button for a screen-cap," Lisa said. "If someone wanted to save the conversation, they could click the button and it would be sent to them as a download screen-cap."

"I think I like the idea," Henry said. "I'll work on developing that. But for now, I think temporary and vanishing is optimum. On the other hand, we have lots of leeway for things like that with the Ask Dad app. Or whatever we call it."

"What does Pythia look like?" Isobel asked.

"Oh, here are some sketches I've drawn for the background," Lisa said. "I think I've about captured the concept of a dragon that is powerful but not threatening."

"A dragon? Pythia was a woman, wasn't she? The MoreChat app creates an avatar person who looks better than anyone I've ever met," Isobel said.

"Just what we don't want for this," Henry said. "I even question the idea of using the dragon background. The image in the user's mind should be what the user thinks, not something we push to them."

"That's one I agree with," Luke said. "Not necessarily that we shouldn't have the dragon image. We talked about the logic there earlier in the week. I'm thinking we need to keep the character of Pythia who answers questions as anonymous as the user. Even the dragon isn't Pythia. It's a symbol of foreknowledge and prophecy."

The application was nearly ready to test.

"I'VE GOT TO take off this morning for a meeting with Dr. Hendon," Lisa said. "He's coming back a day early from spring break specifically to meet with his advisees. It seems we never have time when classes are in session."

"That's cool," Henry said. "Here's the car keys. There should be plenty of parking with classes not starting until Monday."

"Are you sure? Thank you, Henry. I should be back by noon. I'm excited to see the app running," Lisa said.

"I should have everything transferred to the new server in a couple of hours. Why don't you try connecting and get Hendon to try your interface?" Henry asked.

"That would be cool. Text me when it's operational."

Lisa left and Henry went to the office to bring the new server online. Isobel had been furious that they needed to buy a new server for the *Pythia Speaks* site, and that they were paying Lisa a full-time wage for the week. Still, Izzy seemed to spend more time during the day asking the oracle questions than working on spreadsheets. She loved the oracle.

HENRY TOOK HIS coffee up to the office and started working on getting the new server functioning. First, he needed to test the software on the server to see that the AI recognized its source material. Then he tested the interface to be sure it was connected properly. Finally, he was ready to bring the server online and route the Pythia Speaks URL to the server. At ten, he pointed his laptop browser at the site and asked a question.

"Will you live up to all our expectations?" Henry typed in the question box.

Pythia responded in just a second. "One who expects nothing will never be disappointed."

Henry had to laugh. It was an appropriate and totally irrelevant answer to the question. Well, the training process was still underway. The more questions Pythia was asked, the richer its responses should become.

He sent a text to Lisa with the first question and response and told her the Pythia test site was online.

She sent a laughter emoji and said they'd try it.

Henry ran back downstairs for another cup of coffee. It had taken less than two hours to run the tests and get the site active and registered. He supposed it wouldn't be available from everywhere yet as the URL had to propagate through the internet. He was on his way back upstairs when he heard a beeping alarm from the office. He ran upstairs, spilling coffee with almost every step. The sound was coming from his cellphone and he quickly thumbed it open.

"Attack detected. Tracing."

It had been two months since he first activated his counterattack software. After his classmates had all been countered when they tried to hack his computer, he'd modified the software to give a warning when an attack was detected. Just a few weeks ago, he'd modified it again to alert him before counter measures were taken after he'd made changes to Kaitlyn's trust fund.

The attack was not on Pythia, but on his corporate server. He switched the monitor to the corporate server and began looking at the AI's route tracing. The software immediately flashed up a familiar address as a source. He was furious.

"Lisa!" He barked into his phone when she answered hers.

"Henry, it's working great!" she responded immediately.

"We're being attacked from the AI computer lab on campus. Someone's trying to hack into the corporate server from there," he said. "Get down there and find out what's going on. Take Hendon with you!"

"Yes, sir!" she responded and disconnected.

Henry supposed he'd been awfully abrupt in ordering her around, but he was confident she'd find out who was trying to hack him from the university computers.

Then the AI flashed a new message. "Proxy one."

Crap! The attack was not coming *from* the lab. The lab was being used as a proxy to get to his company computer. He investigated further and found the computer lab was being used as a proxy to attack over a dozen servers in different locations. His phone buzzed.

"No one's in the lab," Lisa said immediately.

"The lab is being used as a proxy to get to at least a dozen other servers. We aren't the only ones being attacked. I don't know yet where it's coming from. The counterattack AI is wading through a morass of IP addresses. See if Hendon will approve shutting down all except one computer in the lab so I can continue to isolate the attack."

"I'll have to explain what you have," Lisa said. "Am I violating confidentiality?"

"Can't be helped. Nothing will be confidential if this attack succeeds. So far, my enhanced firewalls are handling it but it needs to be countered."

She cut the connection again and Henry could soon see computers on the university lab network going dark. That would warn the attackers, whoever they were that someone was aware of the attack. It didn't seem to dampen their enthusiasm. The hacking continued to probe the computer's defenses.

"Proxy 2, Oslo, Norway," the AI displayed. That was just great. The attackers were using a worldwide proxy network. "Proxy 3, Johannesburg, South Africa." Henry's phone rang again.

"Dr. Hendon has all but the main server offline. He's on the phone notifying all other universities with significant AI research that an attack may be underway. It seems the attack is not only using the university lab as a proxy, but is also trying to crack the security here."

"That's smart. I can still see a dozen connections from the lab server. How many hackers are involved in this anyway?" Henry asked without expecting an answer.

"Proxy 4, San Francisco, CA," the AI displayed.

"As soon as I have a fix on the point of attack, I plan to launch a counter. I've disconnected everything else connected to our server. Sorry, but you've been booted off. Could you please ask Hendon what he thinks an appropriate level of response is? Should I just kick them off or do some damage?"

"I'll ask as soon as I can get his attention. Apparently, there's some kind of calling tree the universities with labs like ours have set up just in case of an emergency like this. Over half the research on AIs is in university labs."

"Proxy 5, Osaka, Japan," the AI displayed.

"They're really routing this through proxies all over the world. They must have had this planned for some time."

"Proxy 6, Mumbai, India," the AI displayed.

"I'm doing some additional work here on the server while Dr. H is on the phone," Lisa said. "Some of the proxies are also in similar labs—some of them corporate as well as collegiate. This attack is massive. Most of them have some kind of protective measures activated. I'm disconnecting other servers from our lab. There are student computers connected as well."

"If I don't get a source soon, I'll have to recommend shutting down to break the chain," Henry said.

"Hang on." Lisa was gone for a minute. "Dr. H says the only appropriate response to this kind of attack is nuclear. He suggests both a viral and immediate corruption campaign. Do you have such things?"

"I've done some research on this. I can do that."

Henry began preparing the response. He would use the optimization code to totally kill the attacking computer, erasing its memory and system. But the more information the AI revealed to him, the more convinced he was that this was an organized attack that could have hundreds of computer hackers involved.

"Proxy 7. Hamburg, Germany."

He looked at the settings he'd created for the counterattack software. They were the same settings he used for searching out a person's connections.

"Proxy 8. Shanghai, China."

With such a wide network going through so many proxies, Henry made his own executive decision without consulting with Lisa's advisor. He changed the degrees of separation setting from zero to six. That was what he called the feature in the first place, though he'd never set it to more than zero. He was determined to get them all.

"Source Identified. Chengdu, China. Response?"

Henry pointed the counterattack to the two programs he'd prepared for the attack. And started the countdown. Five. Four. Three. Two. One. There was no zero and no warning. The attack suddenly ceased to exist.

"Jesus, Henry! What the fuck just happened?" Lisa yelled through the open line. Henry picked up his phone.

"Attack eliminated," the AI on his server displayed.

"Shit! That was fast," Henry panted. "I wanted to see how many computers were affected. I could have used that data. I guess it's over."

"Dr. Hendon said all the attacks he could identify through the lab were gone. He's answering the phone non-stop right now."

"Okay. I'll start bringing things back online here and run system checks. When you get home, you can reconnect your computers."

"Yeah. I'll see you as soon as Hendon says I can go. He's telling everyone on the phone to stand by and he'll get the information to them."

"Thanks for all the help, Lisa. I know I was yelling and abrupt. Please don't hold it against me."

"Believe me, that's not what I'm thinking of holding against you."

"I'M AWARE THAT Henry Pascal has a company currently testing a new search engine," Hendon said, looking at Lisa. "And that you work for him. I've even installed the Open Cloak Optimization software on my own computer at Professor Jacoby's suggestion. Since you were the relay between Henry and me, I can only assume the actual tracing of the attack and its end are his doing." Lisa started to nod. "Don't say anything," Hendon continued, holding up his hand. "The attack was perpetuated and eliminated through the university AI lab. That is all anyone should ever know. Don't talk about it to anyone else. Make sure Henry does not discuss it with anyone. Until we know the actual extent of the attack and damage, it should not be discussed with anyone."

"Yes, sir. I understand and will give the message to Henry."

"Please ask him to have a copy of the actual virus and whatever else was sent to the computers on an SD card on my desk first thing Monday morning. I know I'll be asked for it by someone," Hendon said.

Lisa stood to leave the lab and go home.

"And Lisa," Hendon stopped her. She looked at him. "Thank you to you, to Henry, and to Open Cloak. That is all the recognition I'm afraid you'll get from this."

"I'll let Henry know," Lisa said. She left the lab and headed to the car. Once there, she sat behind the steering wheel shaking for twenty minutes. She looked at her watch and saw that it was nearly three in the afternoon. Neither she nor Henry had anything to eat since breakfast. She ordered a pizza, drove to the shop to pick it up, and headed home.

LISA STOPPED IN the kitchen to pick up a roll of paper towels and a couple of DPs to take to the fourth floor with her. When she reached the office, she saw Henry, apparently asleep, with his head on Chastity's leg as she petted his hair.

"Oh," Lisa said. Chastity turned her head.

"Sorry," she said. "I guess this is your place now."

"Not here. Don't disturb him. I brought food and cokes."

"I just got here and Henry was about to fall over," Chastity said.

"There was a hacker attack on the server. It came through the university, so everyone was working to track it down and block it. It's been a pretty intense day. I was over at the university," Lisa said.

Voices on the stairs alerted them to Isobel and Luke arriving. Chastity gently woke Henry.

"Food and company are here," Chastity said.

"Oh. I drooled on your leg," he said straightening up.

"That's never been a problem," Chastity laughed.

Luke and Isobel arrived.

"Pizza?" Luke asked. "In the office?"

"It's been an especially hard day," Lisa said.

"We got attacked," Henry said, standing and stretching. He headed straight for the pizza.

"Attacked? By who? Is everything okay?" Isobel asked. She quickly looked around the office as if commandos had invaded it.

Henry started to talk around a piece of the pizza, but Lisa put a finger against his lips and shook her head. He yielded to her.

"Somebody unknown tried to attack a whole lot of computers using the university as a kind of gateway. Ours was one of them attacked and Henry and I spent the past six hours or so trying to track down and defend against the attack. I happened to be at the university and was working with Dr. Hendon, my advisor. He's really pretty remarkable, with connections all over the country who were working on countering the attack. They were finally successful, but we were all exhausted. I realized no one had anything to eat since breakfast and grabbed a pizza on the way home. If you'll excuse me, I think I'll have a piece before Henry eats it all."

Henry looked at her curiously but didn't offer any other explanations.

"You know there's a minifridge in the corner over there with pop and seltzer in it, right?" Luke asked, pointing at the corner of the room behind Chastity's desk.

"Oh, yeah. I didn't know if there was DP in there, so I grabbed a couple of cans on the way up," Lisa laughed.

"Hey! In other news," Henry said, changing the subject, "*Pythia Speaks* is active and available online for testing."

"All right!" Isobel shouted, going directly to her desk. Chastity and Luke both went to their computers as well and soon they were all asking the oracle any question that came to mind.

Henry watched Lisa as she launched the site as well and typed in, "Are we safe?"

"Be watchful and take precautions," Pythia answered. They looked at each other and raised an eyebrow.

"Guess that's good advice," Lisa said.

AFTER THE PARTNERS had left the office, Lisa and Henry both went to their suites and took a nap, promising to see each other for their date later. They'd planned to celebrate the end of spring break by going roller skating that night.

When they woke up and met downstairs, they conceded they were both too tired for such a rigorous activity. Not only that, but Henry didn't want to be far away from his computers if the alarm on his phone went off again. Lisa agreed. They decided to spend a quiet evening watching a movie on TV in the living room.

Lisa's mother had provided an air popper for popcorn because she said microwave popcorn always left a smell in the oven that just couldn't be purged. Lisa made popcorn and they settled next to each other to watch the second day of the Sweet Sixteen playoffs. The east coast games were all over, but it was always fun to watch the teams out west vying for another championship.

"I should have told my business partners about what really happened this afternoon, but you took over the narrative," Henry said.

"You can tell them later if you think it's wise or necessary," Lisa said. "The last thing Dr. Hendon said before I left was to not reveal how much you had to do with it. He thanked us, but felt it was better in the short term to let the university take the heat if there was any. If it seemed everything was going to blow over, he'd definitely give you credit. Otherwise, he said his thanks were all the recognition we were likely to get."

"I guess that's good advice," Henry said. "You never know these days if something is going to get you a big reward or get you thrown in a Central American prison. Besides, if the tech was widely known, we'd have everyone, including the government, trying to get hold of it."

"They might still," Lisa sighed.

"I guess that's always been on my mind. I've never really exposed the counterattack software to the public. The guys who tried to hack the server in January are the only ones who really know about it," Henry said.

"Is it patented?" Lisa asked.

"The attorney filed the patent for training an AI to search through connections last week. I haven't called it out as a way to backtrack proxy servers. It's just a part of the search code. And I've never exposed the counterattack code itself to anyone."

"Speaking of which, Hendon wants the code you uploaded—the virus and whatever else you used—on a memory stick in his office first thing Monday morning. I suppose he'll have to answer questions regarding how he actually stopped it."

"That makes sense," Henry said. "I'm happy to have it out of my hands."

"Did you kill them, Henry?"

Henry turned to her penetrating stare.

"Don't know and don't care."

27

THE IDES OF MARCH

SITTING ON THE COUCH sharing a bowl of popcorn as they watched the game was peaceful and, in some ways, more intimate than going out on a date. In fact, once the popcorn was out of the way, they cuddled together and shared small kisses during interruptions in play. At halftime, they muted the television and the kisses became more intense. For the first time, Henry found his hand pressed against Lisa's breast and she was happily rubbing his chest as well.

Then she pulled away.

"Uh... Wow! Uh... This isn't good... to be making out in our common area. It's too easy to start considering it, like, a free zone. With the office on the fourth floor and both of us having separate spaces, we shouldn't do this here," she said.

Henry saw the sense in what she was saying, but was disappointed nonetheless.

"Would you walk me home, Henry?" she asked.

"Sure. We should put away our dishes first," he said.

They agreed and cleaned up the bowl, pop cans, and the air popper. Then Henry took Lisa's hand and they walked upstairs to her door on the second floor.

"This has been a really great evening after a stressful day," he said. "Thank you for going out with me."

"I really liked it. Henry... the second half of the game has probably started. Would you like to come in and watch it with me? I've got a pretty good TV in my sitting room," she said.

It suddenly became clear to Henry that Lisa was no more eager to end their date sitting on the couch together than he was. He smiled.

"I'd love to."

Lisa unlocked her door and led Henry into her suite, turning on the TV in her sitting room and then going to a nice reclining loveseat. Henry hadn't been in her apartment since she moved in back in September. It was very nicely decorated and he could see a few touches he identified as her mother's. Lisa's mother had been up to visit the last couple of days of their winter break when Lisa came back from Louisiana.

They sat in the loveseat and put their footrests up as Lisa tuned in the game, which was already halfway through the third quarter. They'd soon returned to kissing and petting while they pretended to pay attention to the game.

When the game ended, both were panting.

"I should go home now," Henry said. "This has been a great evening, but I don't want to outstay my welcome—especially since we're both so tired."

"Yeah. Thank you," Lisa answered. "I didn't want to just kick you out."

They walked to the door and once it was open and Henry was about to step out, they paused again to kiss deeply.

"I'll see you soon," Henry gasped, giving her one more squeeze.

"Soon," she answered.

He left and she quickly closed the door.

Henry was in the office early Saturday morning with coffee in hand. He focused on scouring the company servers for any sign remaining from the attack. He trusted his optimization software, but there was nothing he trusted more than his own eyes. After several hours sifting through every directory on the server, he was satisfied nothing remained of the attack, including any record that he'd tracked it and countered it.

Then he shifted his attention to the *Pythia Speaks* server. There wasn't as much to search on this server, as it was not directly attacked. He guessed that the attack starting when he took Pythia live was a coincidence. There was no sign of the attack on that server but he installed the counterattack software on it anyway.

He was amused to see a fair amount of activity. Over a hundred questions had been asked that day. Pythia was serving up answers in seconds, even with the traffic. Each hit on the page launched an instance of the AI that functioned independently, so the server could handle an unknown number of hits at the same time. Henry estimated the computing power of the server and wondered if he would need to add capacity.

The hits were largely coming from various social media services, where Henry discovered his partners' threads were suggesting people try the new oracular sayings site. He hadn't expressly forbidden going public with the site and they needed test data. The AI training method patent had been filed before the site went live. The app itself could be copyrighted within thirty days. He might have some changes to code before then.

His phone chimed and Luke sent him a message.

"We're all going to the Hound and Ale this evening. Bring Lisa."

He got the time and sent a message to Lisa, whom he had not seen all day.

"I'm out with friends," was her reply. "I'll see you at the restaurant."

She often came up to the office on the weekend, since that was when the most time was available. But after the previous day, he could easily understand her taking a break. He should have done so himself.

He closed up the office and went to his suite to shower and get ready to go out.

THE REST OF the weekend raced past. Henry visited his parents and spent most of Sunday studying. He decided to do some of his reading in the living room in hopes that he'd see Lisa happen by, but she didn't appear. He wondered if she'd gone out again, but didn't worry about it. He tried to focus on his reading and eventually made himself noodles and went to his room.

Monday morning, Lisa met him over coffee at the breakfast table. They checked in on the rest of their weekend and then headed to the university. That was when things got interesting. Students in the department were discussing the news, something they normally ignored.

"Hey, did you catch what happened?" Josh asked when he saw Henry in the student lounge. He'd been gone all through the spring break, so hadn't been in to the office.

"No. Did you find a girlfriend?" Henry asked.

"I wish. No. The news from China. There was a bulletin about it on network news last night."

"I missed that. I haven't watched TV since Friday night."

"Beijing says they repelled a US-based cyberattack that threatened its internet integrity. Claims it was an act of US terrorists upset about the tariffs on Chinese imports to the US," Josh said.

"You think there's a chance it's true?" Henry asked.

"Don't know. I asked Dr. Ionescu about it this morning and he said there would be a department-wide meeting called this afternoon to discuss the claim."

"I suppose that means we won't get out until dinner," Henry said. "Did you try out the new oracle, *Pythia Speaks?*"

"Yeah. It's cool. Chastity notified the entire testing network and everyone's been pounding at it. Only there isn't really much to test. An input and an output. I think it needs a clock that counts down the time until it answers the question. At the moment, you enter the question, then there's a wait with just silence."

"How long does that last?" Henry asked. He thought the answers came pretty quickly when he tried it.

"Ten to fifteen seconds," Josh said.

"That's not so bad. I thought you were going to tell me it took ten minutes," Henry laughed.

"At thirty seconds, I'd have shut it down as unresponsive. Dude, you can't expect people to wait that long with no response."

Henry nodded. He'd probably do the same thing. He needed to get with Lisa and have her put a timer in the interface indicating how long it would be before the answer was displayed. At four o'clock, he joined the rest of the AI department in the large lecture hall to find out what was up. Each professor in the department had announced the event in class and told students to share it with others. Over 150 students gathered.

"Students and fellow computer scientists," Dr. Hendon said when he stepped on the stage, "the news from China that many of you have been discussing since it broke last night is disturbing. I was engaged in the event, and am here to tell you all exactly what happened."

Henry cringed a little at those words and hoped the department chair was planning to keep his word and not allude to Henry or Open Cloak being involved. He'd dropped the memory chip off on Dr. Hendon's desk before his first class.

"I was in my office on Friday morning, back early to meet with those advisees I'd been unable to discuss fall registration with. While in a meeting, I was alerted to an attempt to break into the AI lab servers. My examination of the network showed that in addition to being an attack at our research, the lab was also used as a gateway to attack several personal computers and other networks that were connected to ours. Some of you may have noticed an abrupt disconnect from our network Friday a little before noon."

There were some murmurs in the lecture hall that confirmed students who had been disconnected.

"You should all run a thorough test and examination of your computers to be sure no damage was done or trojan horses slipped in."

A few students opened laptops right then and began tapping the keys.

"I worked with the AI departments across a dozen universities, all of which were being targeted with the same kind of attack, until we had identified the source of the attack and acted to neutralize it. I will not tell you the exact nature of our neutralization, but it was effective and the attack was stopped. At that point the universities all began scrubbing computers of any possible lingering malware. We all believe we have cleaned our environments over the weekend."

The students applauded, most still not having figured out the connection with the news stories.

"Chinese authorities have positioned this as them having thwarted an attack on their computers and claiming sources in the US as cyberterrorists. We believe the evidence speaks loudly regarding what really happened, but you can all expect there will be investigations, both by government agents brought to campus, and by hackers investigating the online event, either officially or unofficially. Any of us may be subject to having our computers searched."

That information made everyone nervous. No one wanted his personal computer subject to search. As Dr. Hendon wrapped up the info-dump, students started scrambling toward the exits. Then Dr. Hendon called their attention once more.

"I understand the intent of everyone leaving this auditorium," he said. "I will make no comment on it. However, I would highly recommend that you each download and run the Open Cloak Optimizer when you've done whatever you intend to do." Then he turned and left the room.

"WE NEED TO make sure everything is scrubbed," Henry said when he and Lisa were in the car.

"I never thought we'd be subject to a government search on campus," Lisa said. "None of us actually have the code on our machines, do we?"

"None of *you*," Henry replied.

When they arrived home, Lisa pulled prepared dinners from the refrigerator and began heating them. Henry went to the office and attached an external drive to the server. He downloaded all the relevant code for the counterattack software and pocketed the drive. He thought a moment and plugged in another drive to make an additional archival copy, which he encrypted with 128-bit encryption. Then he ordered a complete optimization and backup of the servers both for the company and for *Pythia Speaks*. As soon as it finished running, he downloaded and erased all code except the released optimization app and the search engine which was in testing. He certainly wouldn't want a government hacker to be subject to a counterattack. That would come back on him hard. Finally, he optimized the servers again, erasing all trace that other software had once resided on the computers.

Lisa brought him food and went to each of the computers in the office to run the optimizer. Of course, most of them were already current. After they'd finished eating, she went to her office and made sure her own computers were cleaned and optimized.

Henry went to his private study to remove the two unregistered apps from his personal computer and then run the optimizer. He repeated the process of removing all his development and patent work from his personal computers.

He left the new backup with his development on his desk in the office. If the office was invaded, he could point to the disk as his remote storage, used because of the threats to computer security he'd heard of. His ploy was to leave something for investigators to find and hide the backup of the proxy search and counterattack. His extra copy was on a thumb drive which he simply dropped into a pocket for the moment.

In the morning, he told Lisa he had an errand to run before he could go to class and dropped her off at the bus stop. Then he went to the bank as soon as it opened and put the full backup and the disk with the counterattack code in his safe deposit box.

EVERY UNFAMILIAR FACE around the department Tuesday was subject to suspicion by the students and they avoided them as much as possible. A man in a military uniform seemed to hang out all day in the student lounge, joining conversations when he could. He acted like a recruiter interested in getting people who were involved in artificial intelligence informed about opportunities in the US Army.

No one considered him a serious investigator as he liberally handed out armed forces recruitment brochures to anyone who would accept them. The really suspicious characters were the ones who buttonholed a student and asked him directly what he was working on and where he was during the attack on servers. No one wanted to talk to those guys, but there were a couple of people who had decided the cute girl who spoke with an accent and professed to be on a two-month study visa was someone worth talking to. She had a valid student ID, so most figured she must be legit.

"I've never seen people so tense," Lisa said. "There were some people who simply responded to every question by saying 'Is there a reward for that information?' It was kind of funny."

"I'm not betting on anything," Henry sighed as they left the school to drive home. "I never thought this would be such a big issue. I don't even want to go home, but I'm afraid if I don't, I'll find it trashed."

"I don't like that feeling. Could you... Would you be interested..." Lisa started. "Henry, let's eat dinner in my sitting room and watch the news to see if anything significant comes on. You could... We could... make out a little if you'd like."

"We're really not going to get anything else done, are we?" Henry laughed. "I need to check on the servers and see if there have been any intrusions. Dinner in half an hour?" he asked. They went into the house and he headed for the stairs.

"Yeah. Come to the kitchen and help me heat up the dinners when you're through."

Dinner was served on paper plates and taken to Lisa's sitting room. They ate while chitchatting about nothing in particular. They did hold each other and kiss a little, but both were too pre-occupied with the general atmosphere at school to get involved in seriously making out.

They took their refuse back to the kitchen and cleaned up, then walked back upstairs to Lisa's suite.

"Thanks for walking me home, Henry," she said sweetly. Then she lifted her face to him for a kiss. It wasn't deep or long, but they smiled at each other as Lisa went into her suite. There was definitely a feeling of impending intimacy.

THEY'D JUST FINISHED their coffee and were getting ready to go to class Wednesday morning when the doorbell rang. Lisa caught her breath as Henry motioned her to leave by the back door and gave her his car keys. Then he went to the front door and opened it to find two people in uniform.

Well, at least they weren't dressed in black with ski masks over their heads. These weren't police uniforms. Henry identified the man in front as the Army recruiter he'd seen on campus. He didn't get a good look at the person behind him.

"I didn't know they were sending recruiters out to people's homes," Henry said at once. "I'm not interested in joining up."

"As you undoubtedly know, neither I nor Captain Bernard are recruiters," the soldier said. "I'm Colonel Nathan Schwartz. I'm the Pentagon's Director of Cyber Resilience. This is my assistant, Captain Rebecca Bernard. We are not here in a law enforcement capacity. We are unarmed. What we'd like is a little of your time to discuss a matter of national security."

"May I see your military ID and proof of citizenship?" Henry asked. *It would be just like the Chinese to send an undercover recruit disguised as an army officer,* he thought.

"Of course," Schwartz said. He pulled out a CAC card and his brown passport. Captain Bernard followed suit and Henry recognized her as the exchange student who showed up the previous day. Clever. He checked the ID carefully.

His first inclination was to slam the door in their faces, but he was sure the next visitors wouldn't be as polite. He carried the ID into the house.

"Please come in. May I offer you any refreshment? Coffee?" Henry asked, holding the door open for them. Maybe it was superstition, but he gauged the intent of his visitors by their willingness to accept refreshments.

"Thank you. Black coffee would be great. Can we sit at the table?" Colonel Schwartz asked.

Henry motioned them to the table and tossed the IDs on it. Captain Bernard opened a briefcase, pulling out a laptop and a sheaf of papers. She settled the computer in front of her and gave the papers to Schwartz.

The Colonel began talking while Henry made coffee, making sure he had Henry's attention.

"You're aware of the news stories and the interest various organizations have taken in learning about your school's involvement over the past five days," Schwartz said. "You may not be aware of some of the fallout. The

Chinese government issued an anti-terrorist warning, claiming US-sponsored terrorists attacked their internet infrastructure and were repelled. That is not actually what happened, as I suspect you know, but won't ask you to confirm."

Henry set the coffee mugs on the table for the two army officers and seated himself with a fresh cup. Then he pulled the IDs to him again and quickly snapped photos of them with his phone.

"I saw the news stories and Dr. Hendon addressed the computer science students. He said the actual attack was on ours and several other schools' AI computer labs and that the university repelled the attack," Henry faithfully recounted the official view of things.

"That is *closer* to reality. What few people outside the military know is that we approached an undeclared war with China. In repelling the attack, nearly ten percent of China's internet capacity was destroyed. Utterly."

"Oh, shit!" Henry breathed. The gravity of the situation settled fully on him.

28

THE ASSET

H ENRY STARED AT his coffee cup silently as the Colonel's words sank in. He'd responded to a real threat, but his response had nearly caused a war. The cyber world bleeding over into the real world. All they'd need is for the president to start tweeting about it.

"I thought you would understand why we are concerned," Schwartz said. "We provided the Chinese with the code for the viruses that caused their shutdown, compliments of your department head. They are reverse engineering them in order to develop a vaccine, so to speak, against ever being infected again. We've provided samples to all the major security software companies for the same purpose. That is not what brings me to your door."

Henry nodded, unwilling to volunteer any information that could incriminate him. He calmed his nerves and looked at the Colonel, ignoring the captain, who had removed her hat and let her hair fall to her shoulders. He couldn't afford to be distracted at this point. The colonel smiled.

"During our visit to the university yesterday, we discovered—or rather Captain Bernard discovered—that certain classmates of yours had once launched a hack attack against your company server to see if they could get through your defenses. Your company: Open Cloak Design. I like that name. The informant said you had managed to trace them through several proxy servers and immediately and without warning, corrupt their computers."

"I don't see what the big deal was," Captain Bernard said. "We've been talking for twenty minutes and I've got full access to the server."

"I'd thank you to leave our corporate development and testing alone," Henry said.

"There's nothing here of interest," Bernard said. "A nice search engine being tested and a released computer optimization utility. The computer is as clean as every other computer we've tested."

"We run our own optimization software on our computers and many people have reported improved performance for their computers based on our studies," Henry said. "You should try it."

"Obviously, we aren't directly interested in either of those applications, though I suspect if we truly dissected the Open Cloak Optimization, we'd discover some of the same code that was used to erase the disks of our Chinese attackers," Schwartz laughed.

"What is it you *are* after?" Henry asked.

"I want... The United States Army wants *a copy* of the code you used to track through eight levels of proxy servers and then wipe out every computer even remotely connected to the attackers."

"There's no such code on his server," the captain insisted.

"Of course not. Would you leave something capable of so much destruction lying around where a child might play with it?" Schwartz asked, turning on the captain.

She scowled and color rose in her cheeks. She closed her laptop.

"Henry, you are a unique individual and I'm very interested in your company and software. Interested enough to invest in it," Schwartz said.

"I didn't know the army invests in companies," Henry said. "I would have to decline."

"Yeah, I know. But there are ways we can probably satisfy both of our needs. As I said, I want a *copy* of the two pieces of the puzzle: the tracing software and the counterattack software. In return, I am prepared on behalf of my agency to do two things. I will make a deposit in your account of twenty-five million tax-free dollars. And I will keep the rest of Washington's alphabet soup off your computers."

Henry contemplated both offers. If that was really all, he could hardly refuse. It was a lot better than ending up in a prison in El Salvador. As if on cue, his doorbell rang. He caught his breath. Colonel Schwartz raised an eyebrow. Henry should have consulted with his partners, but instead he nodded at the Colonel.

"Allow me," Schwartz said, standing from the table.

He put his hat on and Bernard hastily tucked her hair up under her own military cover. They went to the door and opened it. Four men stood there and demanded entrance for the FBI.

"This is a project for the Pentagon's Department of Cyber Resilience," Schwartz said. "Per 1998 Presidential directive PD-63, expanded under Homeland Security Presidential Directive HSPD-7 of 2003, for Critical Infrastructure Identification, Prioritization, and Protection, you do not have authority to infringe on an operation of the United States Army engaged in activities critical to national defense against cyber intrusion. You are hereby directed to leave the premises, cease all investigation either personal or electronic regarding the attack on US cyber installations responded to by the US Army, and remove all surveillance of Henry Pascal, Open Cloak Design, and its employees, officers, and shareholders."

Henry held his breath. Schwartz had poured that all out as if he were reading an order from the supreme court. Henry wasn't positive how legal that whole line was, but apparently the FBI agents weren't knowledgeable enough to contradict Schwartz, standing in the doorway. Schwartz handed his card to the lead agent and they left. He closed and locked the door.

"I'd get the code functioning on your server again to defend against future attacks. These guys seldom take no for an answer, though they will be too cowed to raise a fuss if they are rejected in the act of hacking," Schwartz said.

"The code is stored offsite," Henry said.

"That was smart. Why don't the three of us go out for lunch and you can retrieve it while we're out."

"If you don't mind, I need to do some checking to verify your claims. I'd like photos of you along with those I took of your IDs. I'd like to make a call to the Pentagon to ask for your office. And before I retrieve any code, I'd like your signatures on a limited license agreement."

"That's ridiculous," Bernard started.

"No, it's quite reasonable," Schwartz contradicted her. "Here's my card with the number of the Pentagon on it. If you would call directory assistance and ask for the number, you can compare them before you call. Do you have a license agreement we can sign?"

"Upstairs in the office. We can complete the transaction up there and then go retrieve the code."

"And lunch," Schwartz said. "Let's not forget that!"

"I DIDN'T INTEND to do that kind of damage," Henry said. "It's valuable information."

After lunch he'd retrieved his backup from the safe deposit box. Then he'd taken Schwartz and Bernard to the office on the fourth floor to install it and create a copy for the US Army.

"The top level is pretty simple. It's actually buried in the search engine code as well. It simply applies the AI to the task of tracking down information through various paths and proxies. Once we settled in after discovering how wide the attack was on university research facilities, it only took about twenty minutes for the AI to trace the path through the proxies to the source."

"How many computers did that get you?" Schwartz asked.

"One. It was the ice pick probing the wall of our corporate server. I had no idea about the attacks on all the other servers. I knew there had to be an organized attack, based on the information supplied by Dr. Hendon."

"Then how did you get everyone else?" Bernard asked. Once she was in their office and settled in a chair, she'd adopted a much more casual attitude. Schwartz was watching everything Henry did and pointed out as she sipped a soda.

"That tech is actually buried in the Open Cloak Optimization software. The way the app works at the moment, it can be installed on only one device when purchased. We know we will want to offer an enterprise version that a corporation can use to deploy across its network. The question is, how widely we allow it—or the corporate IT allows it—to work. That's actually what's holding us up at the moment. The AI has a feature I call 'Degrees of Separation.' How far from the host do you want to deploy the solution? Zero degrees is the default and only setting on the current app. This computer only. The next would be one degree, which would deploy on all computers directly attached to the host. And so on."

"Just for curiosity's sake, how many degrees did you set the counterattack to?" Schwartz asked. Bernard sat up.

"I didn't really know how far it would go, so I just set it like the movie. Six degrees," Henry said.

"It's possible that seven degrees would have plunged the world wide web into darkness," Schwartz said. "As part of our agreement, allowing you to install it on your server and continue development, we want you to permanently set it to zero. Respond only to the direct attack."

"I think that's reasonable for the server. It's what it's always been set at. This is the first time I've ever set it at anything else."

"Blessed mother!" Bernard said. "Colonel, we should not leave it in his hands!"

"Captain, in order to prevent it from being in his hands, we'd have to cut his hands off. You heard what he said. The code is not only in the counterattack software, but in the computer optimization software and search engine. I had a feeling that was involved."

Henry shuddered at the implication. The code was in his head. They'd have to cut that off, too.

"No, we're sticking to our deal. I think Henry and Open Cloak are going to continue to create valuable tools for the war on cybercrime. We're not going to inhibit the development. Now, you should head out and change clothes. You should be at the university attending lectures and talking to students. Make sure there is no suggestion among them that points to Open Cloak."

"Yes, sir." Bernard snapped to attention. "How long should I plan to stay under cover at the university?"

"I think you told people you were there on a two-month study visa. Get through the first month and we'll give you a cover to move elsewhere."

"A month?" She tried to maintain neutrality. "Yes, sir." She turned crisply and headed down the stairs. There was a bit of a commotion and shortly Chastity appeared at the head of the stairs.

"Who was that?" she demanded immediately. "And who are you?"

Chastity was used to seeing Lisa and Josh on the weekends in the office. Sometimes Leonard and Simon were there, too. But they didn't casually bring guests into the office and to see an army guy intently looking at the server screen over Henry's shoulder was a shock—not to mention being nearly knocked down the stairs by a female army person rushing to the front door.

"Chas, this is Colonel Nathan Schwartz, director of the Pentagon's Department of Cyber Resilience. He's here to... license some software that I've had under development."

"Something we should all be involved in?" Chastity asked.

"Colonel, Chastity Pappa is one of my partners in Open Cloak and is the head of our administration and human resources," Henry said.

"Ah! Very nice to meet you, Miss Pappa. Please, let's all dispense with the formalities now that my assistant has left. I'm Nathan. May I call you Chastity?"

"Yeah. Sure. That's my name," Chastity said, taken aback by his suave demeanor. "Seriously, Henry, do we need Luke and Isobel?"

"Not yet. They'll be here Friday and I'll explain everything then. There's really no decision to be made. I got the license agreement off your computer and printed it. It's been signed by Colonel Schwartz and witnessed by Captain Bernard. When we have the funds in progress, I'll sign the agreement and you can witness my signature. Nathan will need the account to wire funds to."

Schwartz nodded and Chastity started her computer.

"Uh… Since the software he wants isn't officially a part of Open Cloak yet, give him the numbers for PRPP LLC. We'll take care of the patent purchase and such from there."

"Really?" Chastity asked looking up at him. The significance of money going into PRPP was not lost on her. It would not count as revenue for Open Cloak. But it could affect the partners' income significantly. Henry just nodded. Chastity printed out the routing number and account number to hand to Schwartz.

"If you will give me a few minutes," Schwartz said. "May I use the patio?"

"Please do," Henry said, unlocking the outside door. "Afraid we haven't gotten out any furniture yet."

"I'm used to standing," Schwartz laughed. He went outside and they saw him pull out his cellphone.

"Henry," Chastity said, wrapping him in a hug. "Are you under duress?"

"No, babe. Not anymore."

"There's a sticker above our doorbell that says 'Property of the United States Army. Official business only.'"

"I'll check with Nathan to see what that's about, but I think it's to keep the FBI, CIA, and probably ICE away from our door."

"That's what Lisa was talking about!" Chastity said.

"Lisa?"

"She called me and told me there was a possibility that we'd be investigated by some government agency and she'd left you home alone. I… had an appointment this morning and my phone was off. As soon as I got her message, I rushed over here."

"Well, I'm glad you got here. It helps to have a witness."

"Are we going to jail?"

"No. That's what Colonel Schwartz is here to prevent. You've heard about the Chinese attack?"

"By the American terrorists? My God! That was Friday and you and Lisa were so exhausted you fell asleep on my leg. Don't tell me you were the terrorist!"

"No. It was the other way around. Some bunch of Chinese hackers attacked the university lab and our corporate server. I was the one responsible for defeating the attack. It seems to have kicked over a wasp nest. Nathan is responsible for controlling the damages," Henry said.

"I get it. And he's paying you for the... whatever you did."

"That's more or less the sum of it."

The colonel walked back into the office and closed the outside door.

"It's still a little chilly out there for mid-March. In Washington the cherry blossoms are budding. Another week max. You should come to the nation's capital to see the most beautiful sight in the world," he said. He turned directly to Henry. "It's in motion. You should see it by end of day tomorrow."

"Thank you, sir."

"It's Nathan. I'd buy you both a drink to celebrate, but I don't think it's legal," he said.

Henry and Chastity signed the agreement and she gasped when she saw the amount. Henry handed Schwartz the drive with the code on it.

"You know, the general public doesn't expect anything from teens and early twenties. What they call Gen Z. They're so wrapped up in complaining about the new generation not respecting them or canceling things. The average age of an Army recruit is nineteen years and four months. The nation depends on them to defend it from harm. I have no difficulty depending on computer scientists who are twenty years old and show this kind of skill."

He shoved the drive in a pocket.

"Nathan, I can't say the day has all been a pleasure, but thank you for coming to our defense," Henry said, shaking hands with the colonel.

"There were tense moments. Speaking of which, I'd guess things are going to be a little hard on Rebecca at the university. She's extremely bright and completed her degree while she was still eighteen. PhD at twenty-one. The Army direct commissioned her to first lieutenant and she made captain by twenty-three. If you get to know her a little, she might even have some good suggestions for you," Nathan said.

"Thank you, sir. I'll try to be friendly."

"I see she left the briefcase here for me to carry myself. I wonder if she left the car," Nathan said as they showed him down the stairs and out the front door. "Oh," he said, tapping the sticker by the doorbell. "This should be good enough to keep the wolves away for the rest of the week until we get official notices filed. Have a good day."

They closed the door and sank down on the couch in the living room.

HENRY FELL ASLEEP with his head on Chastity's lap after filling her in on a few of the details. When he woke up, he was lying on Lisa.

"Wow! How long have I been asleep?" he asked groggily.

"According to Chastity, it's been about four hours. I took over as your pillow about an hour and a half ago."

"Thank you. You make a really nice pillow. I guess I won't need any sleep tonight."

"Good. Do you need food right now?"

"Um... No, I guess not. I had a really big lunch with Captain Bernard and Colonel Schwartz. I might want something a little later. How about you?"

"I ate with Chastity. You were really out cold."

"It was an emotionally draining day. First the Army, then the negotiations, and then the FBI showing up at the door and being repelled by the Army. And explaining everything in detail. There are things I still don't believe happened."

"Want something else unbelievable?" she asked.

"I think I'm recovered enough. What?"

Lisa didn't say anything. She caught the hem of her shirt and pulled it over her head, leaving her topless. Henry caught his breath. He kissed each of her breasts and looked up into her smiling eyes.

"Not in the living room. Follow me."

Henry scrambled upright and quickly rose to follow topless Lisa up the stairs. She opened the door to her suite and led him directly to the bedroom.

"I've known this was coming for a long time now. I didn't want to rush. But I really want it, Henry. Do you really want me?" she asked.

"I really want you, Lisa."

"Not because we owe each other or because it's convenient. Just because we both really want it," she said, pulling him to her bed.

They stretched out on the unmade bed and Lisa struggled to get Henry out of his shirt. As soon as he was exposed, they went back to kissing and caressing each other. She'd known Henry was thin but firm. She'd gathered that much from their make-out sessions. Seeing him without a shirt and let- ting her hands explore his chest and back confirmed that his time on the golf course had been enough physical exertion for him to develop some nice musculature.

For Henry's part, he'd seen Lisa dressed up and knew she was pretty. He'd had his hands inside her clothes just this past weekend and knew she felt spectacular. Seeing and kissing her perfect breasts, though, showed him exactly how beautiful a woman she was.

They kissed and petted, trying not to hurry through the preliminaries, but both eager for the main event. He pushed her jeans down off her hips and kissed his way down with them. When he crossed her mons with his lips, she moaned excitedly. She went straight to work getting him out of his trousers, happy to have his help.

When his erection was exposed, she held it and licked it as he stroked his fingers through her plentiful juices. She reached to the bedside table and retrieved a condom.

"I prepared for this," she said, opening and applying the prophylactic. "I've had these waiting for nearly a month."

"I'm glad you have them here. I'd hate to have to stop at this point and run upstairs to get one."

"For what it's worth, I'd be running right behind you and we'd be doing this in your bed now."

She pulled him over her and opened her legs to let him between them.

"I want to... taste... and touch..."

"Later. Let me feel you in me. I want to have what I've been dreaming about. I promise, we'll take time to explore and fully appreciate each other. I don't intend to get out of this bed for a long time. Bring it, lover."

Henry scarcely needed the guidance she provided as his cock sank slowly into her.

"Oh, geez, Lisa. This is really..."

"Tight? Was that the word you were looking for?" she gasped. "Good lord! It's been a long time and I don't think I've ever been so full. Take it easy, babe. Just go slow for a while!"

"Any pace you want, Lise. I'm... You're... It's... all just so perfect."

They started slowly, but didn't stay that way for long. Both were too excited to pace themselves. In minutes, they were both approaching their limit and kissed frantically.

"Yes! Do it. I'm almost there!" Lisa cried.

"I can wait for you. What do you need?"

"Just kiss me some more. Kiss me!"

Henry obliged his new lover and when he felt the contractions in her vagina, he rapidly rose to his own climax as well. They continued to kiss as they came down from their peak.

"You know what?" she asked around their kisses. "I think we're cutting classes tomorrow."

THEY DIDN'T REALLY sleep much that night. They didn't bother to dress when they went to the kitchen for late-night food and then scampered back to bed. After a couple of hours of sleep, they went back to the kitchen for coffee and breakfast, then headed back to bed. After having sex again, they finally fell into a deep sleep.

At nearly noon, they heard voices and footsteps on the stairs. The sound went to the office first and then back down to start pounding on Henry's third-floor suite.

"Henry! Henry!"

"I think someone wants me," he said sleepily as he kissed Lisa again and rolled out of bed.

The pounding upstairs continued.

"What?" he yelled from Lisa's door. Footsteps rushed down the stairs and Isobel was followed closely by Luke. Henry stood naked in Lisa's doorway.

"What the fucking hell?" Isobel shouted.

END PART II

PART III

"As long as there is an AI shortcoming in any such area of endeavor, skeptics will point to that area as an inherent bastion of permanent human superiority over the capabilities of our own creations. This book will argue, however, that within several decades informa-tion-based technologies will encompass all human knowledge and proficiency, ultimately including the pattern-recognition powers, problem-solving skills, and emotional and moral intelligence of the human brain itself."
— **Ray Kurzweil** *The Singularity is Near*

29

INVESTING

"WHAT THE FUCKING hell?" Isobel shouted.

Henry looked down at himself.

"Sorry," he said. "Someone was screaming my name and pounding on the door upstairs. I didn't take time to dress."

"I don't fucking care about that!" Isobel shouted. "Fuck whoever you want to. Congratulations. What is this?" She shoved her cell phone in front of his face. Henry pushed it back a little so he could see the numbers in focus. $25,000,000.00.

"Oh. I didn't expect that to hit until late today. Sorry you drove all the way over here on a school day. I intended to tell you about it tomorrow."

"Did you sell the company, Henry?" Luke asked. It was all either of them could imagine would result in a deposit that size to their LLC account and not directly into the corporate account.

"No," Henry said. "Kind of a limited license. I need to go get my clothes. I'll be back in a couple of minutes."

He closed Luke and Isobel out and returned to Lisa. She was sitting up in bed, her beautiful breasts on display for him.

"Do you have to leave?" she asked, moving her legs apart.

"Oh, geez. I wish not. My partners just discovered everything that happened yesterday and I need to go settle them down a little."

"Go ahead," she said, getting out of bed and wrapping her arms around him. "I don't think I could cram that thing into me again today. I'd try, though."

"Lise, let's not hurt ourselves. As soon as I get the crisis settled down out there, we can go back to the plan of spending the weekend in front of the TV with snacks and each other."

"I'll be snacking on you," she giggled, handing him his underwear. She opened a dresser drawer and found underwear for herself while he dressed.

"I think the four of us—as in Luke, Isobel, Chastity, and me—will probably go to the club for lunch while we discuss business," he said, not sure if Lisa was planning to join him.

"I'm going over to the U. I can still make our last class this afternoon. I want to see what that army captain looks like," Lisa answered. "Be sure to explain why the apartment and office are posted like an Army base."

"Yeah. I didn't expect them to drive over this morning. I figured the earliest they'd get here would be tomorrow. I need to get out there before Isobel becomes even more hysterical."

He kissed Lisa again and hugged her, then left to join his partners.

"I HAVE TO tell you about everything that happened. It's my fault that the Army was interested, but the Army might be what is keeping me out of the hands of the FBI or the CIA," Henry said when they sat at lunch at the club.

"What the hell happened?" Luke asked.

"You remember last Friday? We discovered an attack on the corporate server, attempting to break through our firewalls. We presume the intent was to steal our AI research," Henry began.

"We were here. You told us about that," Isobel said.

"There was more that Lisa and I were told to keep quiet until the university could divert suspicion. I intended to tell you this weekend anyway."

He went through all the steps that led to destroying the hackers, and the subsequent discovery that he'd knocked out ten percent of China's Internet infrastructure.

"Chastity gave the colonel the routing information and account for the LLC. I felt it would be easier to keep buried there than having it paid directly to the company."

"Do you know how much tax we're going to owe on twenty-five million?" Isobel asked, shaking her head. "You might as well have just given it all away."

"Oh. I forgot to mention that the money is a government reward and is tax-free. Or post-tax dollars or something like that," Henry said.

"Twenty-five million," Chastity sighed.

"I think it takes care of our next round of funding for the company and we don't lose any control," Henry said.

"You don't," Luke said. "You have twenty-five mil to invest."

"Uh... I don't see it that way," Henry said. "When the money was paid into the partnership, it became equally owned by the four of us. That's the way our LLC is set up."

"You mean you want each of us to have an equal share?" Chastity gasped. Even Isobel's eyes popped open wide.

"I think we should issue shares at a dollar a share to the LLC," Henry said. "We've got enough product in the pipeline to ramp up sales and marketing and get a couple of full-time developers onboard."

"Twenty-five million shares owned by the LLC in addition to the ten mil we already have, at a dollar a share is nearly $9,000,000 each!" Isobel said.

"Nine mil in capitalization each," Luke corrected her. "None of it is money we can touch." Isobel's face fell.

"I was thinking about that," Henry said. "There's no reason we shouldn't all benefit individually from this windfall as well as the company. What would you say to each of us withdrawing $1,000,000 to our personal accounts? We'd invest the remaining twenty-one in the company. We have college debt, living expenses, and a general need to stay encouraged. We deserve to see some fruit of our labors and eat of it."

"Your labors," Luke reminded him.

"I don't believe I'm working any harder for the company than everyone else is. I do think Lisa should be given a bonus from the company for the part she played in coordinating the counterattack with the university. Maybe a thousand."

"I vote yes on all the above," Isobel said. The dollar signs were practically visible in her eyes.

"Yes," Chastity squeaked.

"Yes," Henry said.

"Okay. It's unanimous," Luke said. "Details on distribution to be worked out in the office."

"I'll leave that to you guys. I have a girlfriend and don't plan to spend any more time in the office this weekend."

<hr>

"I THINK I can quit," Chastity said as she and Henry left the club.

"Chas! Really?" he said in shock. "You just get a little money and leave us? I thought you were in it for the long haul!"

Chastity turned to look at him and stood stock still as Henry came to a stop.

"Oh! No," she said. "Not quit the company! I mean quit escorting! With a million in the bank and a steady income, I don't think I need to keep falling on my back anymore."

"Oh, crap! I'm sorry I misunderstood. That's wonderful news, Chastity. I just… I was afraid that… We need you!" He opened the car door for her to take her home. When they were in and he was driving, she picked up the conversation.

"As much as I need you," she said. "Henry, I get $500 for a simple screw. We don't go out. We don't have dinner. He comes to my apartment, drops his pants and twenty minutes later, tops, he's come and gone. Do you know how many times I'd have to do that to make a million? *Two thousand times!* Once a day for five and a half years. Of course, I have clients who want something more. We go out to dinner and dancing or to some affair he needs arm candy for, and then he comes to my apartment, screws me, and leaves. I get $1,500 for that. If a guy wants to hang out with me all day and screw whenever he wants, I get $2,500. Even with all that, I'd still be fucking a stranger fifteen hundred times to make a million. I… I…"

Henry saw tears welling up in her eyes and pulled to the curb so he could hug her. She wept against his shoulder a bit and then looked up at him. She nodded that she was okay and he continued to drive.

"I don't know if I could have lasted, even until we were all full time in the company. I hate the life! I hate the men. I put on a smile. I listen to their woes and their complaints. I give them reassurances. I let them touch me and suck on my nipples. And then I spread my legs and let them fuck me. They all get just what they want. Everybody gets what he wants from good old Chastity. I hate it."

"If the million isn't enough to get you out of the business, I'll give you more," Henry said. "Whatever you need. You've always kept it to yourself and I didn't know how much you hated it. And I've been a part of it. I'm so sorry, Chas. How can I help you quit it forever?"

"No! You've always been my best friend, Henry. Sometimes, my only friend. I will have sex with you anytime you want. I promised that two years ago. I'll never back out of that. I'll work hard in the company. I'll do my job and make sure the office runs smoothly and the employees are taken care of. And anytime you want me, you have me. Anytime, Henry."

"Chas… I just want to help you. I want to celebrate with you, but…"

"I know. You helped me by giving me this big bonus. Now, you've got a new girlfriend and you need to get back to bed. Don't worry. I won't interfere with that. Maybe sometime, she'll invite me along. Later. Not your first weekend together."

"You knew this was coming all along, didn't you?"

"Lisa and I have often talked when you aren't in the office. We might even have kissed once or twice. Maybe. I knew she was interested, almost since before she moved in," Chastity said, winking at him.

"Clever girl. It takes an idiot like me to not see it, I suppose. Yeah. I kind of left abruptly when Isobel and Luke came crashing into the apartment pounding on my door. I don't even have socks on. Lisa will be home from class soon," Henry said.

"You should take her away for the rest of the weekend," Chastity said. "You know the testing guys will be in tomorrow afternoon, and since Isobel and Luke are here, I'd guess we'll be working on transferring funds and buying stock. You'd get sucked into one or the other. Just drop me off and then go back to your lover."

"I wish there was a way to show you how much you mean to me," he said.

"You do, Henry. You show me every day. Now, go have fun!"

She jumped out of the car at her door, waved, and ran inside. Henry headed to his row house.

Henry booked a room in an historic hotel less than an hour south of the city as soon as Lisa agreed to leave for the weekend. They'd managed to get showered and packed before they left, but saved anything else for when they got to the hotel. That included dinner.

The suite Henry booked was expensive, but he'd just given each of the partners a million-dollar bonus, so he was feeling flush. It included a jacuzzi and a king-size bed. Even though both of them professed it was to be a non-working weekend, they brought their laptops and textbooks so they could study. They knew each other well.

They found a nearby grill to have dinner and then walked back to their suite.

"You certainly chose something luxurious," Lisa said as she wrapped her arms around Henry to kiss him just inside the door.

"I'm feeling flush. You're going to get a bonus from the company this week, too, for helping thwart the attack last week. Geez. It's only been seven days. I can't believe so much has changed."

"The company is paying bonuses for the counterattack? That was all your software."

"And you coordinating things between me and Dr. Hendon. You were our major information conduit. Without it, we wouldn't have known when to launch the counterattack," Henry said. "But that's business stuff. We don't need to talk about that tonight. I just want to drink you up. You are so beautiful, Lisa."

"I can't compete with Chastity when it comes to beauty," she laughed.

"Please don't ever feel you need to compare yourself to Chastity. She is different. Her kind of beauty is different. You don't need to compete."

"Nor do you, Henry. I'm not dumb. I know that Chastity is not your girl-friend. She spent a good amount of effort convincing me of that. But I also know you have a special kind of relationship with her. When I got home the other night—oh, man, it was only last night—you were lying in her lap on the sofa. You were nuzzling against her bare breast and occasionally taking a suck on her nipple. She summoned me to take her place so she could leave and wished me luck."

"She was topless?" Henry asked, aghast. He would never have initiated that in the living room. That was a common space in the apartment.

"I don't think she started that way, but... I admit that when we switched places, I managed to get that nipple in *my* mouth, too. Piercing and all. Damn, she is sexy!"

"Well, I'm glad you get along with her."

"I do. And I know she's got a special role with you that isn't in her job description for the company. I can see how valuable it is. To you and to her. Don't change it. Sometimes, maybe we'll share together, but it's nice that you got us out of town for this weekend. I do kind of want to soak up the essence of my lover."

"I... don't know what to say. Just that the attachment we have is different. When I look at you, I see someone I'd like to have in my life for a long time, in or out of the office."

"Don't say anything. Just take me to bed and let's celebrate another night together."

With that, they undressed, brushed their teeth, and headed to bed.

"This is a huge bed," he said.

"We don't have to use it all," she laughed. "When it's time for sleep, I plan to have as much of me on top of you as I can get. Before that, you can get on top of me."

They didn't waste any time getting restarted where they left off that morning.

Henry lay with Lisa cradled in his arms, marveling at how natural and right it seemed. He'd had lovers. Certainly, Chastity more often than anyone else. But Chastity wasn't one to spend a lot of time cuddling after sex. It was good and she was involved and excited by it, but she emphasized repeatedly that she wasn't his girlfriend.

Henry petted Lisa's hair and placed a little kiss on her forehead. Oddly, the only other person Henry had sex with who gave him this kind of feeling was Avery. They'd spent time together the summer between high school and college and had sex on their last date. She'd told him then...

"Lisa," he whispered, "you don't have a boyfriend back in Louisiana you intend to go back to one day, do you?"

"What a silly thing to ask!" she laughed. "If I had any other boyfriend, you and I wouldn't be in bed together. I never had a boyfriend in high school or in Louisiana at all. I'm afraid you're stuck with me."

"That's a relief. I'm genuinely... fond of you," he said, avoiding making too open a declaration of the way he'd begun to feel.

"That's a good word to use. I'm fond of you, too. Have been for some time. Want to know how fond?" she teased.

"Sure. How fond of me are you?" Henry asked.

"Fond enough that even though my vagina's a little sore from so much exercise, I still want you in me. So, I guess it will have to be my mouth," she said, kissing her way down his body.

"You don't have to do that," Henry gasped, as she sucked his flaccid cock into her mouth.

"I know. That's what makes this so great. It just shows my fondness for you," she giggled as she continued to kiss and suck on him.

Henry was not used to so much sex in such a short period of time either, so he wasn't sure how successful Lisa would be at playing with his cock. Her enthusiasm soon had him responding.

"Lise, I'm getting close," he gasped. "Better stop and just let me go."

"I'm not quitting," she said. "I figure you can't have enough left to drown me."

She continued sucking, caressing his balls with her hand. Henry finally relaxed and it wasn't long before a few weak spurts hit Lisa's tongue.

"That wasn't so bad," she said. "I don't know why girls complain about it."

"What?"

"The girls over at the sorority all talked about how miserable it was to have a boy come in their mouths. I had to try it. It's not bad."

Henry pulled Lisa to him and kissed her deeply.

"You'd kiss me when I've had your come in my mouth?" she asked, startled.

"Why not? It's *my* come. I loved what you did and I want to show you."

He started to move down, but was halted by her grip on him.

"Not tonight, babe. It really needs to rest so we can resume in the morning. Since you're okay with it, come and kiss me some more."

THEY HAD NO intention of spending the entire weekend in bed. They went out to explore the town of Washington, including walking through the college campus, looking like any other couple of college students.

"When's your birthday, Lisa?" Henry asked.

"Long time ago."

"I didn't mean when were you born," he laughed. "I just want to know when to plan a celebration."

"I know. But you already celebrated my birthday with me."

"I did?"

"Yeah. It was our first date, last September."

"Why didn't you tell me?"

"I intended to, but things kind of went screwy."

That night, a football linebacker had assaulted them, attempting to take Lisa by force. Henry had responded by punching him in the throat and taking Lisa away from the scene quickly.

"You know what impressed me most about that night?" he asked.

"It couldn't have been the sorority," she snorted.

"No. It was when that crude guy tried to take you with him, I saw you remove your shoes. I wasn't sure if you intended to run or throw them at him, but it was the right thing to do. I thought, 'She can take care of herself.'"

"But you took care of me," she said.

"I didn't want to see you break a nail," Henry laughed.

As they walked through the town, looking at historic buildings and finding interesting places to eat, Henry became quiet and seemed to have a lot on his mind. Lisa tugged at him.

"Do you need to check in at the office?" she asked.

"Hmm? No. Sorry. I got distracted in my head a little."

"Tell me. Okay?"

"Yeah. Sure. Um... I was just realizing that I might not be able to continue in school next fall."

"Why? You've got grants and scholarships, don't you? And a job that pays. Why wouldn't you continue in school?"

Henry sighed and led Lisa to a park bench where they sat, turned toward each other.

"It's the job," he said. "I might not be able to handle working full time and going to school full time."

"Full time? At work?"

"Yeah. I just realized I'm going to have to start full time this summer," he said.

"Why?"

"I haven't mentioned it, but we landed a substantial investment in Open Cloak. With the kind of money we're talking about, we won't be able to handle it as a part time business. I'll need to hire a couple of full-time developers, probably a marketing person, and maybe a bookkeeper. Isobel does a good job of managing our money, but she's got two years of school left and might not be able to handle the amount of work we're going to have."

"That's wonderful! I mean, not that you think you'll quit school, but that you got a big investment in the company!"

"The thing is, I took the investment without considering how it might affect life. Not only mine, but my partners' lives. Luke is on a combined BA/MBA program and can't finish before two more years full time. Isobel has two more years. I might need Chastity full time just to manage the office and employees. Office! We won't be able to continue in the attic. We'll have to have a place where people come to work. There's so much to think of!"

"Henry, I know it's huge. Nobody at our age starts a big business. We've got the search engine in testing. We've got *Pythia Speaks* in testing. The *Ask Dad* app is going to progress, and I know you've got plans to improve AI power consumption. We'll get through it. We'll be successful."

"You say 'we' a lot," he laughed.

"Oh. It's not like I'm projecting our relationship far into the future. Exactly. But as long as I'm part of your life or part of Open Cloak, it will be we."

30

FULL TIMERS

THE EFFECT OF the investment on the four partners was felt almost at once. Chastity started looking for office space. While she cut her 'social obligations' back to almost nothing, she still had several prior appointments she needed to keep. She was getting out of the business, but she didn't want her name trashed by jilted customers. Still, she was going to the office nearly every day and had placed ads in several places for AI engineers and some office help.

She began receiving resumes the next week.

Luke and Isobel began driving back to Pittsburgh from Philadelphia every weekend, just to work in the office on Saturdays and drive back on Sunday. Henry's last two patents issued and the company paid Henry 75,000 shares each at $1 per share for them.

"I'm beginning to see the writing on the wall," Luke said as the partners gathered together for brunch on Sunday before he and Isobel took off for five-hour trip back to Philadelphia.

"What's that mean?" Isobel demanded.

"I need to transfer to Pittsburgh," Luke said. "We're in the process of releasing another software application. We're going to have employees here. Even if I'm not coming into the office daily like Henry plans to, I need to do more than show up on Saturdays."

"That's a big step, Luke," Henry said cautiously.

"What?" Isobel screeched. "You'd leave me at Villanova while the rest of you are all here? You'd be fucking Chastity every night!"

"Whoa! Leave me out of it, Isobel. I'm not the company bike. The only one here who gets to ride is Henry, and even he hasn't in a long time," Chastity growled.

"If not you, someone," Isobel lamented. "I'd be left behind!"

"Do you think you could transfer, too?" Henry asked.

"My parents would be pretty displeased. Unless..." Isobel looked meaningfully at Luke.

"Let's talk about it on the way back to Philly," Luke said. "It's a conversation for the two of us, not the four of us."

Isobel nodded her head with a satisfied smile.

"Hey! We should have our next earnings statement from EMEE tomorrow," Luke said, changing the thought process at the table radically.

"Any idea what we should expect?" Henry asked.

"I think it's going to be good. Ever since your interview with Gene Grey, sales have been picking up steadily. And there have been a couple of spikes. I don't have the final numbers, but they should be positive. It will be a good launch for Open Cloak Search. The idea that ordinary people can have a private search engine that doesn't give false listings based on SEO manipulation or corporate algorithms is revolutionary. EMEE testers were blown away and they plan to do a massive push from their site, not to mention what Gallitzin has planned for our release. Having money in the bank is allowing us to do a real release next week."

"How is your *Ask Dad* app coming along?" Isobel asked.

"The time it takes to collect a person's life information is inhibiting," Henry said. "*Pythia Speaks*, however, has given us a great testbed for the AI training. And I'm going to start testing it on my dad's data soon."

"Speaking of which, why is Pythia running so slowly?" Isobel asked. "Slow?"

"Yes. It takes, like, thirty seconds to get an answer from her these days."

"Gosh! I don't know. She... It should be getting faster with more experience. I'll run a test on the server this afternoon."

"Do it tomorrow, Henry. You're taking Lisa to that Chinese dance and acrobatics show tonight," Chastity said.

"Yeah. Of course!" Henry said. "I meant tomorrow."

They wrapped up their business brunch and all headed home.

HENRY AND LISA had managed their relationship as a couple that dated and not one that lived together. It had been a little tricky, but they had a good start on the ground rules before they became lovers. The common area and office area of the house were off-limits to displays of affection. The difference was that when they went out, Henry walked Lisa to her door inside the house rather than the outside door. And often, Lisa invited him in.

On her visits to his suite, she was impressed with the care he took of his rooms. He'd also hired a maid service to come in and clean once a week, including the office and her suite in the contract. She loved having someone wash her sheets and make her bed every week.

Their intimate time was growing, as well. They moved from one date a week to two or three dates and were getting along well.

MONDAY MORNING, LUKE put the four partners on a conference call and announced the results of their first quarter sales.

"We had sales of 1,731 units in the first quarter!" he announced. "In dollars, that amounted to a deposit of $4,742.94."

"Cool!" Henry said.

"Well, we're going to need to quadruple that in order to meet basic expenses in June," Luke said. "But with Open Cloak Search releasing this week, we stand a chance. You know OCO sells for just four and a half bucks. The search engine is going to go for $29.99. Instead of $2.74 a copy, our share of the search engine will be almost $21 a copy. If we sell a thousand copies, that's $21,000, which will meet our projected July expenses."

"The thing is, we need to be using our revenue account for operational expenses when possible," Isobel said. "I've moved the investment capital mostly into longer term CDs. We still keep transferring any shortfall in our expenses from the capital account, including the initial lease on office space. Daily expenses, like the server hosting and website and office supplies, should be met by revenue."

"Can we have a basic savings account for operating funds, too?" Chastity asked. "I can check balances each day and make sure enough has been moved to our operating checking to cover expenses."

"Good thinking, Chas," Izzy said excitedly. "We should do the same for employee and lease expenses, only transfer the money from our capital account. We'll set it up Friday when Luke and I get there."

"DON'T YOU HAVE class today?" Chastity asked Henry as she perched on the corner of his desk.

"Yeah, but I need to finish the diagnostic on Pythia to see why she's... it's running slowly," he answered, automatically resting his hand on the inside of her thigh. He turned his head slightly and kissed her bare flesh. "I'll make the afternoon classes."

"Not if you keep playing up there," she sighed as his fingers reached her bare pussy.

"Oh! Um... Sorry. I mean. I think it's okay for us to touch in the office, but I haven't really talked to Lisa about getting together with you. You know, it's the first time I actually feel like I have a real girlfriend," he sighed, removing his fingers. She sighed.

"She's a sweetheart," Chas said. "Talk to her. Okay?"

"Yeah. We're overdue for that conversation."

Chastity left for the day and Henry turned his attention to the diagnostics for *Pythia Speaks*. It was soon obvious why it was running slowly. It was getting close to 1,500 hits a day! That was ten times the number he expected.

He didn't make it to class in the afternoon. He was occupied looking for a hosting site that could handle more traffic than their self-hosted site.

HENRY COULD HAVE just used the web enrollment form at Page Services to book space on a server there, but he was looking for something unique. So, he searched for half an hour and finally found a phone number for the company.

"Page Services," a voice answered. No other information was offered.

"This is Henry Pascal of Open Cloak Design," he started. Perhaps they would have heard of him.

"Yes?"

"I'm looking for a server for a new app that is proving to be a little too robust for our corporate server," Henry said.

"We have several plans that might suit your needs," the voice said, almost disinterested.

"I've been to your site and have read about your plans. I determined that I should speak to you because hosting an artificial narrow intelligence might be beyond what you are capable of," Henry said, getting a little irritated with the guy. "I'd like to speak to the boss about capabilities and bandwidth."

"Speaking," the guy said. "I'm Scott Perkins, president, founder, and janitor for Page Services. We're a small company, so you might be right about our ability to host an AI service. Tell me more."

"Okay. Perhaps you'd like to take a look at what we've got going. It's *Pythia Speaks*."

Henry could hear a keyboard tapping.

"This looks pretty simple," Scott said. "Let me ask a question."

Henry heard the keys tapping again.

"How long does it take for this to return an answer?" Scott asked.

"That's the problem we're having. Currently it's taking about thirty seconds. I want to put enough power behind the site to get a response in under five seconds."

"How much power does this use?"

Henry described the server to Scott and then waited.

"Ah. Here we are. It looks like Pythia approves," Scott said.

"What?" Henry asked.

"I just asked your *Pythia Speaks* if I should move forward with working with you."

"And?"

"It answered, 'One cannot have superior science with inferior ethics.' I think it's telling me you're on the up and up. Let's see what we can work out," Scott said.

Two hours later, Henry began migrating the site to a new host with more processing power and more bandwidth.

WHEN LUKE AND Izzy arrived on Friday, she was in a hyper mood. One look at her hand was all the explanation anyone needed. The diamond sparkling there must have cost Luke at least $15,000.

"June 24th! Mark it on your calendar. No excuses! That's our wedding date," Isobel said excitedly.

"You're getting married this summer?" Chastity asked. "Um… Congratulations. Are you pregnant?"

"As if," Isobel snapped back. "We're moving back to Pittsburgh and transferring our courses. We'll be able to work in the office and continue our degrees."

"Isobel wouldn't leave Villanova unless we were married," Luke said. "She did not want to move back to her parents' home. And frankly, I was in favor. It's time I tied her down permanently."

"Well, congratulations," Henry said, patting Luke on the shoulder.

"You will be the best man," Luke continued. "Don't think you'll get out of that, no matter how big this shindig gets. And according to Isobel, it will get big."

"It will be good to have you here," Henry said. "I've registered for a limited course load in the fall. I have to take ten hours in order to keep my scholarship, but since I'm so close to graduation anyway, they are being accommodating. Most days, I'll be in the office full time."

"I'll be here when you aren't," Luke said. "Though I have to maintain a heavy class load in order to get the degree in time. It's a new world."

"Isn't it just, though."

"Okay, guys," Chastity said. "We need to head to the bank and open a new account or two and then I want to show you the office space I've located."

"Lead on," Henry said. "Lisa? Can you manage the guys when they come in?"

"Will do, boss," she smiled.

THE WORK AT the bank was surprisingly quick and easy. They had $20 million in CDs in the bank, and the vice president was very accommodating. Then they went to an office building south of the river that was still under construction. It looked pretty complete and businesses were actually open on the first and second floors.

They met the developer and Henry was pleased to see it was his own landlord.

"Ray, it's good to see you," Henry said as they shook hands.

"I didn't know the business I was contemplating renting to was yours," Ray said. "Does this mean I'll lose you as a tenant in the row house?"

"Oh, no. I have no plan to move in the next year at least. I love the place."

They took the elevator up to the third and top floor. Things looked pretty finished all the way through the building, until Ray led them into the office space. It was bare walls, no carpet, and a little plaster dust.

"I'll build this space out to spec," Ray said. "I have an idea of what you'll need, having talked to Chastity and knowing the type of business you do from the house. It's good to see you outgrowing that space. What we have here is 5,000 square feet. I'll work with you to get a good efficient floor plan and all the power and connections you want. Walls where you want them, or as open a floorplan as you want. The only thing that won't be included in the office is a restroom, but there are restrooms just past the elevators."

"How much will the build-out cost?" Isobel asked.

"Standard build-out is included. If you want two-inch sound-dampening carpet and wallpapered walls, that would be extra." They all laughed at the notion. "I'll help with the interior design as I have a consultant I work with who will draw up the plans. If you are like other computer people I've worked with, you'll want a heavy-duty air conditioner with zones you can control."

"Can we afford this space, Chas?" Luke asked.

"It rents at $18 per square foot," Chastity said. "Ray has offered six months rent-free as a move-in bonus with a five-year lease. It's 5,000 square feet. With average office density planning, we're talking about comfortably having twenty employees. I think we're all agreed that is plenty of room to grow the first few years."

"Wait! $90,000 a month? Are you kidding me?" Isobel screeched.

"Isobel, office space is priced per square foot per year. It comes out to $7,500 a month. Of course, we'll have our share of utilities as well. And no rent for six months after move-in."

"I'm... Oh..." Isobel said, panting. For a moment she'd seen their investment flying out the window. She'd already done sample spreadsheets regarding average employee expenses and benefits. She was planning for health insurance as soon as they hired full-time employees. She was already getting a headache from the extent of her pro formas.

"When could we move in?" Henry asked.

"If we get working right away, you could be in by July 1," Ray said.

"Ray, thank you for showing us the space and the finishing samples," Chastity said. "I need to sit down with my partners and discuss the options. I'll be in touch Monday."

"Of course, Chastity. If I can provide more information, give me a call. You have my number and I'll answer yours even on the weekend."

They left and returned to the office.

THERE REALLY WASN'T much to discuss. Chastity hadn't even prepared other options. This one had topped her list. 'Rent-free for the remainder of the year,' was a key selling point, but so was dealing with a developer they were familiar with.

Isobel had to prepare a current financial statement and as soon as Ray checked with their bank and approved the contract, they started planning the space.

The biggest issue that faced them next was making a couple of hires. Henry had two more weeks until final exams, and then he planned to make the company his full-time responsibility. Lisa and Josh were on-board for the summer, but would cut back to part-time when school started up again in

August. The row house was going to be busy for six weeks from mid-May until the first of July. And Luke and Isobel would be married the week before they moved into the new office.

"INTERVIEW TIME," CHASTITY said to Henry the next Friday.

Henry knew the candidate and already liked him.

"Conrad, welcome to Open Cloak Design," Chastity said when she answered the door. "Come in and relax. We don't have a conference room in the office, so we'll just use the dining table. Would you like coffee or pop?"

"I kind of run on coffee, so if you've got some, that would be great," Conrad said. "Henry. Even knowing you were the CTO of Open Cloak didn't prepare me for what I've been finding out about the company. I've got to say, the new search engine is seriously dope."

"Thanks, Conrad. I'm glad you're interested in working with us. We've got three new apps that need immediate attention and a few things that are looming on the horizon," Henry said, sitting at the table with his friend from college. Conrad was two years ahead of Henry and would graduate within weeks.

"How immediate does the attention need to be?" he asked. "We're still three weeks from commencement."

"We can negotiate a start date," Henry laughed. "You might want a little time between graduation and full-time work. Our new office won't be ready until July first, but we'd like to be fully operational by then. I'll have two contractors starting full time a week after finals. They've been working with me part time for a few months now. They'll be returning to school in the fall and will cut hours back then, so by that time, we'll probably need at least one more developer, or maybe two."

Chastity took over the interview to get it on track so the two guys didn't just sit around shooting the bull. They were there to hire a lead developer and she wanted to know what kinds of projects Conrad had worked on while he was in school. She was impressed that he'd designed the AI for the winning entry in the annual robot races during Spring Carnival this year. Henry asked about the power consumption of that AI.

"It was fairly economical," Conrad said. "There was a clear set of signage approved for the course, so mostly I had to train its vision to recognize and differentiate among the signs. From there it was mostly algorithm-driven, so it didn't require a lot of power."

"One of the apps we're working on is power conservation," Henry said. "There are some pieces that seem to have our part-timers stumped."

"That sounds like fun. I could really get into that."

The interview went for a full hour before Chastity took her signal from Henry to wrap it up.

"Do you have any questions you'd like to ask us?" she said.

"Yes. One. What's with the sign on the door that says 'Property of the United States Army. Official business only.' Are you really working for the military?" Conrad asked.

"No," Henry said. "You might remember back in March that there was an attack on computers from China that was repelled."

"So, it *was* you. The rumor is true."

"App number two that needs attention is the network defense app. We need to commercialize it," Henry said. "The director of the Pentagon Office for Cyber Resilience showed up on the doorstep a couple of days after the attack. We made a deal to license the software to him and keep him apprised of any updates. For that, he slapped a sign on our door that kept the rest of the agencies away from us. You probably know the CIA, FBI, and God-knows who else were on campus at that time and it saved us from being questioned by them."

"I'm cool with that. I just don't want to put on a uniform," Conrad said. "That brings me to an item of full disclosure as well. Rebecca had to disclose to her boss and told me that if I had dealings with Open Cloak, I needed to disclose to you."

"Rebecca?" Henry asked.

"My girlfriend. We started dating a couple of months ago. She's in the army and said she'd had dealings with you before."

"Captain Bernard?" Henry said. "I hope you don't mind if I check in with her boss, then."

"She said you would. She wants you to know she's not spying on you."

"Okay. Pending a conversation with Colonel Schwartz, I'm okay with that. She's a really bright person," Henry said.

"No kidding. She did advise me on a couple of things with the Spring Carnival robot. Then refused to take credit for them."

"Any other questions?" Chastity asked.

"When can I start?"

"Well, we haven't talked wages and benefits yet," Henry laughed. "Believe me, I am aware that you are graduating from the top AI program in the country. It's why I enrolled there. We probably won't match the dollar figure you could get from one of the giants. But we're a new company and we'll give you a significant stock option. Our most recent investment came in at a dollar a share and that's the option price for 210,000 shares vesting over seven years. Couple that with a starting salary of $125,000 and I think it's a good deal. We won't have a health insurance package until we have at least five full-time employees. With Chas and me, you'll be the third. I expect we'll hire at least two more soon after we get into the new office. Until we do get group health insurance, we'll be paying you an extra $500 a month for health coverage."

"Yeah. It will be hard losing the university health plan," Conrad sighed. "But it sounds fair to me. What other agreements are there?"

"There is a standard non-disclosure," Henry said. "That is mostly to prevent you from taking our company secrets with you if you decide to go elsewhere. We're not suggesting a non-compete. At our level—I mean yours and mine—we only have one thing we're trained in. Without working in AI, you'd be unemployable."

"I can live with that." Conrad consulted the calendar on his phone. "Can I start June first?"

"Let me call Colonel Schwartz and then we can sign the papers. Chastity has them all drawn up."

31

JAMBALAYA

THE TWO WEEKS leading up to final exams went by in a flash. Twice, Henry and Lisa decided to forgo planning a date out and just slept together. Henry loved sex with Lisa, but felt they were short-changing their relationship and decided to plan a special outing after their last final.

Each of the six exams he took brought him a step closer to the end of this stage of his life. He had to smile at the thought that he would not be taking classes over the summer and would have a lighter load in the fall. On Friday, when the last exam was completed, he and Lisa walked to the curb where Chastity met them in Henry's car. She drove them straight to the airport and kissed them both goodbye.

"You know, I could really get used to Chastity's kisses," Lisa sighed as they made their way to the two o'clock flight to New Orleans.

"Yeah. Even with her 'no tongue' rule, she's pretty hard to resist," Henry agreed, wrapping his arm around Lisa.

"What 'no tongue' rule?" Lisa asked.

Henry looked at her in astonishment, but Lisa was serious.

"Oh. It's... just something between Chastity and me," he said, wondering if Lisa was truly exempt or just hadn't progressed that far.

The flight landed in Atlanta and they changed planes for New Orleans, but it was a short layover and they landed in New Orleans a little after six. Lisa's mother was waiting at the exit for them. Henry hung back a little to let Lisa greet her mother first.

"You said you were bringing your boyfriend," Mrs. Hartwell said, looking past Henry without recognizing him.

"Mom, this is my boyfriend, Henry Pascal. Henry, my mom, Jacqueline Hartwell."

"Henry? You said he wasn't your boyfriend!"

"That was then. This is now," Lisa said.

"Well! Welcome, Henry," she said reaching out to him.

"Thank you, Mrs. Hartwell."

"Oh, no. That was fine when you were her landlord. Her boyfriend gets to call me Jackie. Are you living together, then?"

"Not exactly, Mom. Henry is still my landlord and we have our private suites. But he gets to visit sometimes," Lisa laughed.

"I will never understand you!" Jackie said. She led the way to her car and they drove up to Baton Rouge where Lisa's father, Bill, was checking on the grill to be sure it was ready.

"You won't believe this, Bill!" Jackie called as they walked into the house. "Lisa's boyfriend is her boss and landlord! It's Henry Pascal!"

"Now that's welcome news," Bill said, giving his daughter a hug and turning to shake Henry's hand. "Something tells me we have a lot of catching up to do."

"I CAN TELL you've got something on your mind," Bill said when he and Henry were alone after dinner. Lisa and Jackie had gone to Lisa's room to settle and chat.

"You're very perceptive," Henry chuckled. "Mostly, I just wanted to do something nice for Lisa after our term ended. The past few weeks have been good, but really stressful with finals and all."

"Are you trying to tell me that you and Lisa are getting serious or that you are breaking up?" Bill asked bluntly.

"Um... neither, really," Henry said. "I like Lisa a lot. Maybe we'll find out more about where the relationship goes this summer. I'm hopeful. But that isn't the subject I wanted to talk about. It's more business related."

"Oh," Bill said. He sounded a little disappointed, but brightened quickly. "Tell me what's up."

"Well, we got a substantial investment in March. It's not the kind of investment that people put into a part-time effort. I was wondering how it was when you got started. I'm feeling unsure about whether or how I can continue school and handle the business full time."

"Wow! That was *not* what I was expecting," Bill said. He dropped his head in puzzlement for a moment. "You are a few steps ahead of where I was at your age. I had investment dollars waiting for me when I graduated, but everything I'd done before that was strictly on my own in a basement apartment with substandard computers. I didn't have money that I could spend to take my girlfriend to see her parents."

"Part of the investment was a substantial personal payment as well," Henry hedged.

"Well, the reason we live in Baton Rouge is that it was a condition of the investment that Jackie's father made in my business. They live just a couple of miles from here and you'll meet them tomorrow. EZ Daze is still a fraction of the size of his shipping empire. But he and I are both pleased with the company we've built. It was good to have a savvy business partner when I made my first hire."

"Unfortunately, our investment didn't come with any wisdom on how to get it done. I have three partners and we have two contractors who work with us. I made my first full time hire and he'll start the first of June. We're moving into an office space on the first of July," Henry said. "Uh... In case you didn't know, Lisa is one of our contractors. She's been doing some great stuff with our UI."

"So, your investment left you with full control of the business?"

"My partners and I were equal participants in the founding, but I've got a few more shares of the company because of the transfer of patents and other IP."

"Hmm. So, you and your partners are all about the same age and trying to complete college while you get the business up and profitable?"

"Yes, sir."

"Let's chew on this a while. When you meet Lisa's grandparents tomorrow, you might want to let Beau in on the questions. The man is truly a management genius. Might even be a future source of funding. Don't go at it from that perspective, though. Test out the waters and see what you think of him. He taught me a lot, but he might not have the same style as you."

"I'm always interested in advice that is more dependable than Pythia," Henry laughed.

"Who's that?"

"Well, it's an app we're testing. Here. Let me show you Lisa's interface," Henry said.

He booted his tablet and directed the browser to *Pythia Speaks*. Bill took it and immediately understood the concept of asking a question. 'What does our business future look like?' he typed. A few seconds later the answer popped up.

"Business is a meeting of minds. Its future depends on the minds involved."

"Well, I can't contradict that," Bill said. "At the same time, I see why you would like more dependable advice. What's behind this?"

"It's an artificial narrow intelligence. The wall it was trained on was restricted to classical philosophy and oracular sayings. I'm surprised it understood the word business, but it's learning from people's questions. We're getting over 1,500 hits on it a day."

"And how will you make money with it?"

"Pythia is a testbed for an AI trained to know and understand a person's life, independent of the complete body of human knowledge. General AI is being trained on as much data as possible. I'm trying to train an AI that will be able to respond as a specific person. Specialization, if you will. It takes far less power to train and is more dependable within the realm of that person's life."

"And that is why Lisa has asked Jackie and me to record our life stories," Bill said. "The Singularity."

"Yes, more or less. The development of AI has been focused on capturing the human capacity to think and respond as a generalist. Our development is focused on a specialist. No one knows your life better than you do. We learn a lot from general AI development, but humans have specialized. If we want our cars repaired, we take them to a mechanic. Few people these days have the knowledge or interest in fixing their own vehicles. So, we go to a specialist."

"Fascinating," Bill said, absently entering another question. "What do you need?"

"Well, I need to go to work in the company full time as soon as we get back from this little vacation. We have two applications in the market now and initial sales are good, but we need to keep developing both those applications and new ones. I've got ideas I can't implement on my own and the investment capital is there to get some other smart people working on them. But I don't think I can just hire other people and walk away. I think I need to quit school."

"First decide the difference between what you want and what you need," Bill said.

"Um..."

"I'm just quoting Pythia," Bill laughed, showing Henry the screen. "But it's a good bit of advice. Do you *need* to quit school, or is that what you want to do? Do you see the business as a shortcut to your goals? Are you cutting corners you will later regret? I realize I'm not giving advice that's any more than what you can get from your little oracle here. But it is a good conversation starter."

Henry and Bill talked for over an hour, continuing the conversation when Lisa and Jackie rejoined them.

"I'm having fun recording stories," Jackie said. "I was just telling Lisa she should get her grandparents in on the game. Dad loves this kind of thing. You might want a video recording from the time you meet him. He's full of stories."

"We could do that, couldn't we, Henry? I mean invite him to participate, not record him as soon as you meet," Lisa said.

"I think it's a great idea. I wish my grandparents were still around. I'd love to get to know them," Henry said.

"You lost them?" Bill asked.

"My dad's parents were kind of old when he was born. He was a surprise and was an orphan by the time he was a teenager. Mom's parents were killed in an airplane crash before I was born."

"That's sad, Henry," Lisa said, petting his arm. "I didn't know that."

"Maybe it's what interested me the most about developing the singularity app," Henry said. "My family doesn't have a lot of lore."

The evening was pleasant and relaxed. Henry enjoyed getting to know Lisa's parents better and was looking forward to meeting her grandparents.

He was also pleased that his girlfriend's parents didn't object to the two of them sleeping together. They enjoyed some quiet loving after they retired, giggling about being quiet so her parents 'wouldn't know.'

***

BEAU AND SOLANGE Benoit arrived Saturday afternoon and were sucked into the conversation immediately.

"Record my life story?" Beau asked in a booming voice. "When am I supposed to have time to do that? I'm not retired yet. Sollie probably has time if you can get her out of the Bingo parlor."

"Don't pay attention to that," Solange joined in. "He sits in that big office of his looking over the port and tells stories to anyone who comes through the door."

"Well, that's true," Beau said. "It's just part of doing business. I suppose I could do some of that. I can just record them?"

"Sure," Henry answered. "One of the things we're working on is assem-bling a video generation component so your image can say things that you didn't necessarily record exactly."

"Why doesn't this Pythia thing show a video?" Beau asked.

"The concept with Pythia is to not control people's image of it. Someone asking a question should put their own image together in their head with the oracle," Henry explained.

"It's too simple," Beau said. "First of all, it's beautiful. That's fine. But it needs something more. There is no way to monetize it the way it is at the moment. And I'm not suggesting the initial version needs this, but there needs to be a way for people to 'join' or 'subscribe' or something. Something you can charge for. Then, paying members can maintain a record of their conversations. Even download them. Maybe talk them over with other mem-bers. Make them able to develop a more personal relationship, like they do in some of those Chat apps. She doesn't need to have a face, but you should be able to hold her hand."

"That's really perceptive, Paw Paw," Lisa said. "We've talked about some of those features before, but I don't think we've talked about putting them in some kind of membership form. Have you, Henry?"

"Not really. I've been focused mainly on the AI training aspect so I can put it in the 'ask dad' app. We really need to find a new name for that soon," Henry said.

"You're a long way from needing a winning name," Bill said. "In fact, I dis-covered the best name for a game often comes when it's ready to be released. Hopefully, you aren't locked into a name when the right name comes along."

"So, how do we get involved in the legacy game?" Solange asked.

"Monday, I'll get a couple of drives you can plug into your computer. I'll download the AI and storage system, then give them to you," Henry said. "All you need to do then is plug them in and start saving everything to that drive. The AI will take care of the rest. Don't expect to see any great wisdom out of it if you decide to test it with a question. It takes time to train the AI and it changes based on how much you've input."

"Why don't you bring them over to the office on Tuesday," Beau asked. "I'd like to show you around the docks."

"Thank you. That would be interesting," Henry said.

SUNDAY, OF COURSE, Henry and Lisa were pressured into attending church with Jackie and Bill. It was tolerable and afterward they were taken out to lunch. Henry had jambalaya for the first time and liked it. That evening, he and Lisa cuddled in bed talking.

"How did you get out of Louisiana without an accent?" he asked Lisa.

"Oh, I had it bad," she drawled. "Before I left for college, Dad sent me to speech classes for three months to get rid of it. A day down here, though, and it all starts coming back."

"I think it's cute."

"I think that's why Dad wanted me to talk like a northerner. He fell in love with Mom's accent, and didn't want to risk me to any boy who was just drawn to the drawl," Lisa laughed, drawing out the syllables.

"So, you're, like half Cajun?" he asked.

"Yeah. Paw Paw and Mee Maw have roots in Louisiana that go back to the Acadian migration," Lisa said. "I'm so glad you agreed to have them record their stories."

"I really wish I could record my grandparents," Henry sighed.

"Have you thought about searching for info? Asking your mom and dad for any old things they might have? You could scan everything in and probably still get a reasonable picture of them."

"That's a great idea. In my spare time, while I'm not developing software and managing development, I think I'll do that."

"Henry!"

"I know. It just seems so overwhelming at times."

"Come to me, lover. I want to feel you moving in me."

Henry rolled toward Lisa and she pulled him on top of her. It didn't take long before he was hard and Lisa got a condom on him.

"You know, if it's just going to be us, we could probably stop using a condom. I mean, I'm on birth control and I don't think either of us have a disease."

He slid into her before he responded, pausing to simply enjoy the feeling of their joining.

"Um... We should probably talk about..."

"Oh! I forgot. It's okay. I'm not going to do anything to interfere with you and Chastity. In fact, I was thinking that when we get back, I'd really like to invite her to join us one night if you're okay with that."

"Me okay? I really didn't think..."

"Henry, the first night we had sex, I found you with her nipple in your mouth. I could understand you being exhausted and just sucking on an available pacifier, but it wasn't that. I saw the look of complete satisfaction on

Chastity's face. If she hadn't known I would be home, I'm sure she would have taken you to bed," Lisa said, thrusting her hips at Henry to get him moving. He slid slowly in and out.

"Chas has told me she would always be available to me, no matter what. I had trouble accepting that after I found out about her profession, but she's past that and so am I. She's just a very special person to me."

"Who isn't your girlfriend," Lisa reminded him. "And your girlfriend would like to have some serious playtime with her. I don't have the same relationship you have, but I really like Chastity and I'm sure she likes me, too. We just need to make it happen."

"I always use a condom when I'm with Chastity. She's always insisted."

"Good. Then we can dispense with it when *we're* having sex."

"Lisa, you know I'm really stuck on you."

"Stuck in me at the moment," she giggled, doing wonderful things to his cock.

"Yeah. I'm really glad we came down this week to meet your parents and grandparents. You've met mine, but we haven't spent much time with them as a couple. I'd like to change that."

"It sounds like you're getting serious, Henry."

"We're only twenty," he breathed.

"We have plenty of time."

They lost track of the conversation in the sensations of moving together until they both rocketed into their orgasms and held each other in bed until they finally slept.

Henry and Lisa went to Bill's office on Monday and Henry was impressed to see that one of the most popular game developers in the country was a small company of only about twenty-five people. Lisa showed him around and they got to test the newest version of the game she'd worked on.

Then they went to an electronics store where Henry could buy three-tera-byte drives for Beau and Solange. Monday afternoon, he set up the drives so he could hand them over the next day.

Tuesday, Beau showed up at the house to pick up Henry and drop off Solange for a girl's day. It was easy to relax with Beau and soon he and Henry were engaged in a lively conversation about the shipping industry.

"Benoit Intracoastal Logistics focuses mostly on moving goods along the pathway from Florida to Texas and back," Beau said when they'd arrived. They walked along the dock where a ship bearing the name *Anais* above the legend

'Benoit Intracoastal Logistics.' Beau was greeted by men who just kept on working, loading the ship.

"That's a pretty big... um... ship? Is that the right term?"

"Not really. This is a barge. One of our tugs will get it into the channel later today and get it down to Texas."

"What do you ship?"

"This load is primarily pipe and fittings for the oil fields. When it comes back, it will be loaded with cotton bales that we'll transfer to Mississippi River traffic. The *Anais* mostly moves between Baton Rouge and Brownsville. Not all our cargo is pipe and cotton, though. We deal with anything a manufacturer wants moved. From here in Louisiana, we can ship north on the waterway, south out into the gulf and around Florida, all the way up to New York. Chemicals, cars, rocket parts, and even oil."

"That's pretty amazing."

"Let's go up to my office. That's where Sollie thinks I spend all my time. Really, I spend a lot of it right down here where my people are working. Sometimes, I even roll up my sleeves and help load."

They walked into a warehouse and Beau led Henry up a stairway to an office that overlooked the docks. From here, they could see the traffic and docks for a couple of miles. The office was comfortable, but not as luxurious as Solange's comments would have led him to expect.

"When my granddaddy started this business, he had one old steamer he salvaged. He loaded all the cargo and piloted the boat. But he built a business out of it," Beau said. "Now tell me, Henry, what kind of capitalization do you need for your business?"

"Oh... uh... I'm not really looking for an investment at the moment. We're pretty well capitalized for a startup," he answered.

"What kind of investment in your business do you have?" Beau asked.

Henry debated what to reveal, but decided he came here for advice and he would have to be straightforward about the situation to get good advice.

"We have about twenty-one million in the bank. We have two software applications released and three under development. We only have sales data for one app and one quarter at the moment, at nearly $5,000. We have nine patents. Our monthly expenses for the past few months have come in at about $9,000, so you can see we are living off capital at the moment. We'll be moving into an actual office on July first and will have employees starting as early as June first," he blurted out.

"Business in software development like Bill's?" Beau asked.

"Yes."

"You have enough to last two and a half years if you don't grow over twenty employees," Beau said. "Don't try to skimp too much, but that budget doesn't allow for waste or luxury. I wouldn't be interested in investing until you are nearer that timeframe unless you start showing over a million a year in revenue."

"Yes, sir. I really didn't come here to ask for an investment," Henry said, baffled.

"No? I must have misunderstood Bill. What is it you want? Connections?"

"Just advice on running a small business so I can make it profitable," Henry said.

"Advice. Damn, Bill. That's what he said."

"I don't get it," Henry said.

"It's an old and dependable premise. If you want money, ask for advice. If you want advice, ask for money. Bill said advice. I heard money," Beau laughed. "Let's have a cup of chicory and talk about what the real issues are."

32

HOLIDAY

ENRY RETURNED FROM Baton Rouge with Lisa and a complete development strategy. His daily meetings with Beau Benoit had been enlightening and helped him to focus his energies. He realized how unfocused he'd become over the past year, jumping from project to project while he attempted to maintain his edge in classes. He'd worked on developing a search engine, counterattack software, an AI-powered singularity app, and half a dozen incomplete patent descriptions. He needed to focus on getting the apps in the market that would make the company money.

One of the problems Beau had helped him identify was the amount of time he was spending managing the company server and the *Pythia Speaks* server. Even while he was in Louisiana, the company server had repelled two attacks. After making his agreement with Colonel Schwartz, Henry had activated the counterattack software on the servers, but had set the degrees of separation to zero. He'd also enabled collecting the IP address and location of the attack before the counter was launched. In the last second before the counterattack was launched, a message popped up on the attacker's screen that said simply, 'US Dept of Defense, Protected.' Then it proceeded to wipe the assaulting computer.

He'd forwarded that information to the colonel and was thanked for it, but didn't know what the response from the Pentagon would be. They had the power to file grievances if the attack was from a domestic agency, and to effect remedies up to and including arrest of suspects if it came from an accessible jurisdiction.

But Henry sent a message to Chastity saying the next hire he needed was an IT professional to manage the servers and network security inside the company. They could wait until they actually moved into the new office, he supposed, but the hire needed to be made so the candidate could start in the office immediately. In fact, if he could be hired soon, it would relieve Henry of the responsibility of getting the initial office setup taken care of.

Once he was back in the office and had run basic health checks on the servers, he began drafting the development plan and schedule. Lisa went to work full time and made great progress designing the features of *Pythia Speaks* to make the subscriber function available. While she didn't touch anything but the UI code, she was essentially a program manager specifying what features needed to be added and how they should function.

Josh and Conrad would start work the following week, just after Memorial Day. Henry outlined the major work that needed to be done. Josh would go to work on bug-fixes in the search engine. Conrad was assigned the dual task of managing development and getting the optimization app ready for corporate network rollout.

Beau had been quick to identify the OC Optimizer for network deployment as one of the fastest potential money-earners. Conrad, a brilliant programmer, could take on that task immediately. Josh would be told to start listing the features needed in order to do network deployment of the search engine. Those two were money-makers and would share some code.

Henry hoped the new IT guy would be able to specify additional protection features for the counterattack software. They'd deal with further development on that product soon.

And that left Henry to work on Pythia with the features Lisa would specify, and on the Ask Dad app.

The spring semester at Villanova ended just as Lisa and Henry were getting back from Baton Rouge. Luke and Isobel took a week off to plan their wedding and would start back to work after Memorial Day. Things were hopping at Open Cloak.

"I THINK I have a candidate for the IT position," Chastity said.

She perched on the corner of Henry's desk as she usually did when they talked. Her smooth bare legs were an open invitation to his touch as she talked.

Lisa had left the office at noon to help Isobel plan a Memorial Day barbecue at Luke's house. Marla Riordan and Lupe Perez were there to help with the planning as well. Isobel invited Lisa to help because it seemed appropriate to have Luke's and Henry's women do the planning. It also helped to keep disputes about the wedding out of the conversation.

"A candidate?" Henry said as he kissed Chastity's bare thigh. He leaned over and lay his head on her leg as she told him what she'd found.

"I've done twenty telephone interviews this week," Chastity sighed. "This is the only one that sounds suitable. If it doesn't work out, I'll start interviewing again."

"Before you tell me about this candidate, tell me about how you ruled out nineteen other candidates," Henry said, looking up at her. The thin top she was wearing clearly showed the outline of the bars piercing her nipples.

"Well, half of them had visions of grandeur. Everything they said was about managing two hundred networked computers. Nothing wrong with that, but they seemed unable to scale that back to even twenty as a startup," Chastity said. "Five were focused on the amount of work it took to maintain a network and keep employees from abusing their privileges. And four just seemed clueless about network management at all and their qualifications seemed to focus on having a couple of computers networked in their homes."

"Wow! And now the last one. What sold you?"

"He was nice," Chastity said. "I don't hold that up as being the sole qualifying standard, but he didn't make me feel like a child while he explained to me what a network was. You just wouldn't believe some of these guys. They are still living in a world where women are children or something. I'd have strangled a couple of them before they were at work a week. Then you'd be without an HR person."

"Okay. Nice is nice. What else?"

"I don't know exactly how old he is, but he's got more years' experience than I've been alive. At his most recent company, he started ten years ago by upgrading their network. From there he became the director of IT."

"Sounds expensive," Henry said.

"You'd think. His asking salary is not out of our range. He said what he was interested in at this stage of his career was getting involved in something he could help grow. And his knowledge of anti-hacking tools seemed to be current. He was even familiar with our OCO app. He suggested that we need to look for a way to expand that so it could be deployed across a network."

"Now we're talking. When will he be in?"

"Not before you are, if you keep tickling me there."

Henry pulled his fingers out of Chastity's pussy and pulled her further onto his desk so he was sitting between her legs. Then he leaned forward and took a swipe of her slit with his tongue.

"Oh, Goddess!" she moaned. "Oh, do me. It's been so long!"

"Too long, Chas," Henry said.

He fed a finger deep into her so he could scratch the spot he knew drove her crazy. She leaned back on his desk so she could support herself on her elbows. He found the right combination of fingering and licking to bring her up near her peak, then pulled his head back.

"The interview? When?" he asked evilly.

"Bastard. Wednesday at ten. Now get back to work!"

She pulled at his head and he returned to licking and plunging his fingers into her.

"Yes! Yes! Oh, fuck!"

"What the hell?" Luke asked from the head of the stairs.

"Shut up and let me finish!" Chastity shouted, pulling Henry's head back into her crotch. Henry didn't slow up and kept at Chastity until she'd finally pushed him away. "I didn't realize how much I needed that."

"Oh, hi, Luke," Henry said, straightening up and wiping his mouth.

"Dude! I thought you were with Lisa!" Luke said.

"Yeah. We have an understanding."

"Right. Okay. Well, I just came to the office for some rest from the women attempting to control my life. I told them I'd go get the meat for the barbecue. Can anyone tell me why it takes four women to plan an outdoor party for us and our families to gather?" Luke said. "Christ! I didn't know what I was walking in on!"

"Oh, don't worry, Luke," Chastity panted as she pulled her short skirt into place and went back to her desk. "That's the first time since we opened the office up here, and will probably be the last. We've got employees starting next week. Henry was especially thankful for the news I brought him."

"Right. That must have been some great news. What was it?"

"Don't get excited," Chastity said. "I found a good candidate for our IT position."

"What's his name, by the way?" Henry asked.

"Darrel Jones," Chastity responded.

"How are the wedding plans coming?" Henry asked Luke.

"Better before we got back," Luke said. "I swear! You think Isobel is unpredictable. You haven't spent time with her mother. I'm getting baptized Sunday."

"I hope you don't need a best man for that!" Henry said.

"No. I just need the best man to come down to the tux shop with me and get fitted. The other guys can go on their own."

"When?"

"Tomorrow morning. We've got an appointment at ten-thirty."

"I can do that."

"Izzy and I had everything planned out before we came back to town yesterday. Nice. Just her and me in a hotel in New York. Of course, mostly she just said what she wanted and I said okay. Did you get your invitations?"

"Yeah. It came yesterday," Henry said.

"Well, as soon as we got back to town, Lupe started in by telling Isobel she couldn't spend the night at my house because it would be sinful. She has to stay in her room at home. Then she was on about why I hadn't been baptized yet since I finished the catechism. Then she got a look at the wedding plan and started drawing lines through things. She's already ordered the wedding cake and has chosen Izzy's gown—subject to her approval, of course. Izzy exploded last night and I thought I'd have to take her back to New York until the wedding. But in the end, she had a few drinks and agreed to go home with her mother."

"Geez! Getting married sounds like a nightmare!" Henry said.

"It has its good parts. We're going apartment hunting Tuesday, so we won't be getting into the office until Wednesday. Hopefully we'll find a place right away. We'll take a week off for a honeymoon after the wedding which will get us back just in time to move into our new place," Luke said.

"What are you looking for in an apartment?" Chastity asked. "I know a good rental agent."

"She found this place for me," Henry said.

"Honestly? Whatever makes Izzy happy," Luke said. "She figures that we each have a million we can live on until the company becomes successful, so we don't need to waste time with a little dive like I rented in Philly."

"Was she living with you out there?" Henry asked.

"Oh, no. Mama Perez kept close tabs on us. Izzy had her place in the women's residence hall and I had a little efficiency apartment. On those rare occasions when we could get together, it was during times when we couldn't get caught. Mama Perez even watched Izzy's and my social sites to make sure we never had a picture in my apartment or a hint that we'd been together. She knows we make it any time we can, but she won't make it easy on us."

"Thanks, Luke," Henry said.

"What?"

"For saving the world. Just think, I might have fallen prey to Mama Perez!"

"Oh, she always liked you better than me," Luke laughed.

HENRY HEADED DOWNSTAIRS to the kitchen, thinking he'd make up some dinner for Lisa and himself. Chastity followed him downstairs just in time to see Lisa coming in the front door. They immediately embraced and Chastity kissed Lisa.

"I didn't take care of him," she said. "Good luck tonight. I think he's ready."

"Thanks, Chas. Monday, okay?"

"After the barbecue?"

"Yeah."

"It's a date."

Lisa came straight into the kitchen where Henry was still trying to figure out what to cook for dinner. She pulled him around and kissed him deeply. Then she pulled back and sniffed around his face.

"Leave dinner for later. I need you in my room so I can lick your face!"

"Lisa..."

"Just come with me!" she commanded.

Henry obediently followed and was shortly stretched out naked on Lisa's bed while she proceeded to lick his face.

"I love the way that girl smells and tastes," Lisa said. "Now do me."

She rolled into a reverse cowgirl and settled onto Henry's face as she sucked his erection into her mouth. Henry chuckled at how voracious his lover was and immediately went to work licking and inserting fingers as she gave him an exquisite blowjob.

"Lisa, I'm about to..." he gasped.

"Do it!" she commanded.

He went back to work lashing her clit desperately as the come welled from his balls and started shooting into Lisa's mouth. She slid down his chin, so he could no longer reach her clit with his tongue.

Lisa kept sucking on him and sliding up and down his cock, preventing him from losing too much of his erection before she could turn around and plant her pussy on it. She kissed him deeply. He could taste himself, but had never objected to that.

"Now you've had all three of us on your tongue in one afternoon," Lisa said. "Just imagine what it will be like when we're all in the same bed."

"It boggles the imagination."

She began moving on him.

"Hey! I don't have a condom on," he said.

"I don't care. I know you're clean and I'm clean. I've always been on birth control. I just wanted to be sure I trusted you before we went bareback. I've decided, Henry. I love you. I know I'm not supposed to say that first, and don't you dare say you love me, too. I took you home to meet my parents and my grandparents. They already think you're their son. I'm not saying we're committed to each other for life, but we are for now. You'll tell me when the time is right for you."

"Lisa, I don't know how to respond without telling you the same thing. I'll wait though. Believe me, it won't be long."

THREE FULL FAMILIES met together at Luke's family home, plus Chastity and Lisa. It was the first time Lisa had met either Luke's father or Isobel's. Izzy's mother, Lupe, was every bit as unpredictable as Izzy. Isandro, her father, seemed more laid back and very conservative. He got along well with Ryan and Paul, though. In addition to her parents, Izzy's little brother, Felipe, was also there, and spotting an opportunity, he immediately attached himself to Chastity. He turned on the charm and Chastity enjoyed the attention. Eventually, though she reminded him that she was twenty and he was only sixteen, so there really wasn't a future for them.

"I'm not asking for a future, fair maiden," he said eloquently. "Only for a night."

"Call me in four years," Chastity laughed.

Felipe took it in good humor, but still hung around with Luke, Izzy, Henry, Lisa, and Chastity.

He also managed to snag a few beers as the afternoon went on, but it seemed he was sharing them with his sister. Both were tipsy before the ribs, steaks, sausages, and chicken came off the grill. There was enough meat to feed twice the number of people, but Luke had promised he would grill enough for everyone.

It looked like Izzy's parents were just as prone to enjoying the alcohol on this warm Memorial Day as their children were. Ryan and Paul indulged, but Sylvia and Marla stayed sober. Sylvia because she was driving and Marla to keep Sylvia company. They'd been friends since they met in birth classes for their boys. Henry, Lisa, and Chastity didn't indulge at all and Luke cut himself off before he was impaired, so he 'could look after Izzy.'

After helping clean up—a task taken on by the sober ones—Henry made his excuses to leave because of work the next day. He took Chastity and Lisa with him.

"I've invited Chastity for a sleepover," Lisa said.

Henry looked at the two girls and changed directions from Chastity's house to his and Lisa's.

"I declined," Chastity said haughtily.

Henry was a little confused. He'd been expecting that Chastity would join them in bed soon. While he and Lisa kept displays of affection out of the main downstairs area, it seemed Lisa and Chas had no such limitation.

"That means I'll need your car keys, Henry. You know I don't do overnights," Chastity said.

"Of course," Henry said, understanding. It was one of Chastity's rules. No overnights. No tongue kisses. Stay away from her navel. Treat her like a goddess.

"You're always welcome to change your mind," Lisa said, reaching to the back seat to take Chastity's hand.

"If there's ever a time, it will be with you," she said.

"JUST REMEMBER," LISA whispered. "You don't need a condom with me, but the rule with Chas still holds. Okay?"

"You really think I'll have sex with Chastity while we're all together?" he asked.

"We'll both be terribly hurt if you don't."

Chastity came out of the bathroom and Henry went in. When he came out, he saw the two women in a clinch, kissing. Lisa left to take her turn in the bathroom.

"That looked like a lot more than a lip kiss," he said to Chastity.

"It doesn't apply to you," Chastity said. "I'm Lisa's girlfriend. I'm not your girlfriend."

"So, you and I are sharing Lisa as a girlfriend?"

"I don't think there's a big deal about sharing," Chastity said. "There's plenty for both of us. And you do get a share of me, too."

"That's all I've ever wanted, Chas. You know how much I care for you."

"Yeah. Me, too. Ooh, here's our lover."

Henry turned to find Lisa leaving the bathroom, completely naked.

"Didn't you guys even loosen your clothes?" she asked.

"Uh… We were talking," Henry said.

"That's never stopped *us* from getting naked," Lisa said.

She immediately removed Henry's shirt and turned him to Chastity while she started working on his trousers. It was obvious why Felipe had been fascinated with Chastity. Her nipples and piercings were clearly outlined under her T-shirt. Henry reached for the hem and she held her arms up so he could pull the shirt off.

As Henry leaned in to capture one of the pierced nipples between his lips, Lisa leaned in from the other side. Chastity held both their heads to her chest as they licked and sucked.

"Don't you just love these?" Lisa asked when they pulled back.

"Oh, yeah," Henry breathed.

They tumbled into bed where they giggled as they attempted to sort out positions and directions.

Eventually, they ended with Chastity on her back as a condom-covered Henry plowed into her for the first time in several months. At the same time, Lisa straddled her face and kissed Henry. Hands found nipples, tickling, scratching, pinching, and twisting piercings a little.

Henry found that fucking Chastity while he was kissing Lisa deeply was incredibly stimulating and he swelled to fill the condom with come. Lisa could feel his release and pushed him back out of Chastity. As soon as he'd pulled out, Lisa dove into Chastity's pussy and the two women brought each other to massive orgasms.

Of course, they started in again after they'd all recovered, but by midnight, Chastity crawled out of bed and fumbled around getting her shorts and T-shirt on. She kissed both Lisa and Henry lightly and headed for the door.

"Goodnight my sweethearts. I'll see you in the morning."

Then she was gone.

33

LAST CHANCE

HENRY SPENT MUCH of his time on Tuesday preparing for his inte
view with Darrel Jones. This involved purchasing some pieces of
equipment that he didn't necessarily need right now, but they would need
when setting up the new office. Isobel gritted her teeth and accepted Henry's
explanation of the expense.

She is really a money miser, he thought. *If we were to give Pythia a human
image, it would be Isobel, the dragon queen.*

Wednesday morning, he set up the office for his interview with Darrel Jones.

"Henry, Darrel Jones is here for his interview with you," Chastity called
into the office. Lisa was at her desk and Josh was at the desk Isobel usually
occupied. She and Luke were out shopping for an apartment.

"Oh, good," Henry called from behind the array of servers he'd moved
out from the wall. "Send him back."

Darrel approached the voice of the hidden man.

"Uh... Hi. I'm Darrel," the much older man said when he reached Henry's
desk.

"Hey, Darrel. I'm Henry. Ah! Found it," he said from behind the server
array. "I was rushing and didn't check all the pieces before I got the server
connected. I've got a bad NIC card. There's a box of them on my desk there.
Open and hand me a new one, would you? I'll get this one out."

"Sure," Darrel said. "Is this clipboard your serial number inventory?"

"Yeah. Chastity checks it each day and enters them in both physical and
electronic inventory."

"Okay. Here you go," Darrel said, handing the new card between two of the servers. Henry handed him the faulty NIC. "I'll mark the old card with blue tape so you can check it out later. Could just be a loose connection."

"Thanks. Yes. That's good. I'll manually boot the new drive. You may have to switch the display to see it. You've got the keyboard next to the monitor."

"Got it. It's running diagnostics. Everything looks okay. Booting now."

Henry stepped from behind the shelves and Darrel helped him move them back against the wall.

"It's so dang much easier with two people than crawling in and out of that tight space," Henry said.

"Might have been easier to install all the hardware and test it before it went on the shelf," Darrel said.

Henry grinned at him and Darrel nodded.

"Of course. Then you wouldn't have had a hands-on interview," Darrel laughed. "Nicely done."

"Let's grab a cup of coffee downstairs and talk about what it will take to move our network to a new office in a month," Henry said. "I appreciate your willingness to play along. You hit every one of the steps, so now it just remains to determine if you're a good fit for our company."

The two walked downstairs and Henry poured them both coffee.

"Cream and sugar?" Henry asked.

"Just black, thanks." They sat at the table.

"Here you go. Why are you looking for work?" Henry asked as he sat with Darrel.

Darrel was easily older than Henry's father, with black hair liberally sprinkled with gray to match his beard. He had sharp eyes and a pleasant demeanor.

"Boredom. I got tired of my job at Broomley because it was the same thing day after day. I told my boss a college kid with a liberal arts degree could do everything I was doing, so he replaced me."

"How long ago was that?"

"Eighteen months. Decided to take a break before I went back into the office. Took my wife for six months in Italy. Great time."

"Sounds like it. You know Open Cloak is a young company, both in terms of how long we've been in business and the age of the four of us founders. We're all twenty years old. Why would you want to join a company like this?"

"Young. Energetic. Startup. Future. Variety. I had to assume some of those things until I found the CTO behind the shelves connecting a network server."

They talked for over an hour and Henry showed Darrel the plans for their office that would be opening in a month. He emphasized that they needed to get the network up as quickly as possible, but they also had to get cables run for the full office in order to have stations ready for new employees.

Darrel understood the needs quickly and made a couple of notes on Henry's flowchart.

"The thing is, we are subject to hack attacks on a regular basis," Henry said. "We've repelled and countered each one, but I can't spend all my time monitoring the system. I need someone who can not only manage the system, but take over security for our network. I think you'll find our defense system is unique, but I don't profess that it's perfect. Yet."

"Hmm. One of the things I missed in my former employment was the chance to actually do something productive as well as provide maintenance," Darrel said. "At Broomley, they considered network security to be separate from IT management."

"I can see a possibility in the distant future that we'd grow to a size that requires that," Henry said. "But as a startup, consolidating things in the IT department makes more sense to me. As long as I have a person savvy enough to monitor the code as well as the usage, I'm content with that."

"What's the big dream?" Darrel asked. "You have some nice apps that will sell, but you don't need much more than you and your partners to keep them going and sell them. You could probably even sell them off to a big company and retire before you hit twenty-one."

"Right. But the bigger dream. My degree is in artificial intelligence and I've filed two system and methods patents that will make a big impact on the AI community. I should say my future degree. I still have a few classes to complete. The first patent is a new, smaller-footprint AI that is specialized for single area efficiency. It could take years for that to displace the direction AI has been headed for the past five or so years. But it's there. The second is more important because it can attach to current AI systems. It will cut power consumption of those systems by at least fifty percent."

"Still leaves them power-hungry, but it's an improvement," Darrel said. "Good. I'm sold."

"Let me call Chastity down here to explain salary and benefits," Henry said. "If everything is good for you, I'd like you to start tomorrow if you can."

DARREL AND CONRAD both showed up for work the next morning, June first. Luke called a company meeting in order to get everyone introduced to everyone else. Conrad already knew Lisa and Josh from college, and had met Chastity. Darrel knew only Chastity and Henry.

"Well, this is an auspicious occasion," Luke said. "It marks the hire of our first full-time employees other than the partners. And we're happy Josh and Lisa will be working full time for the summer. One of the biggest things we need to manage in the coming month is becoming a cohesive team and getting ready for our new office."

With eight people in the company, they held the meeting in the living room on the first floor. Chastity had managed to squeeze two more work stations into the fourth-floor office, but Luke and Isobel agreed to work out of Henry's study for the time being.

"I want to go over a couple of things just to keep everyone informed. The next thirty days will be a little chaotic as we get ready to move into an actual office instead of working from Henry's house. It may be a challenge to keep everything organized when Henry, especially, is out of the office. Henry, will you explain what's going on?"

"Luke said I'd be out of the office. Partially true. Darrel and I will be spending time over at our new office as the finishing stages are completed in the next month. Before everything is sealed up, we want to make sure the infrastructure we need is installed," Henry said.

"With eight people in the company, we can't need that much infrastructure, can we?" Josh asked.

"Imagine twenty people in the office and that half of them are developers working on new AI apps," Henry laughed. "Got that in mind? Darrel?"

"Now double what you've imagined," Darrel joined in.

"And then, because we know every estimate a tech company has made from the beginning of time has been short, double it again. That's the infrastructure we're building in the new office," Henry said. "Most of you have heard Dr. Hendon's favorite catchphrase. 'Developers by nature either underestimate the task or overestimate the resources.' You can see the evidence of that by looking at the floor in any men's restroom on the campus," Henry said.

The women looked a little non-plussed until Chastity rolled her eyes. The other two seemed psychically linked to her as they got the joke as well.

"I will not make any more crude references of that sort," Henry said, a little embarrassed by his own male humor. "The point is that Darrel and I will be trying to overestimate every detail that goes into our company network."

"Did you enhance Pythia?" Isobel asked. "She's much faster now than she was running a few weeks ago."

"I'm glad to hear that," Henry said. "We actually moved *Pythia Speaks* off-site. She... It's running on a server farm out in California. It's a good thing we made the change. We're getting over two thousand hits a day now. Lisa is in charge of specifying the next generation of features and building the interface for the Pythia AI. Much of that architecture will go into the Ask Dad app that we hope to have functioning by the end of the year. In the meantime, when Darrel and I are off-site, Conrad is the dev lead, so he is the person to ask or bounce ideas off of. That being said, his number one development job is getting the network version of the optimization app ready for release. The interface will fall to Lisa as well."

Everyone was nodding.

"Josh, you're in charge of bug fixes for the Search Engine. Sorry to say that we have discovered some. At the same time, I want you to work on specifying a network version of the Open Cloak Search. Don't check in any code for it until we meet to approve the feature list. We've talked about most of it, but I want to be sure everyone gets to read the spec and comment on it before we start developing. And, I'm handing primary responsibility for the unreleased security counterattack software to Darrel. We are still repelling one or two attacks a week with the barrier and need to determine if we will release it to a wider audience. Any progress on that front will also need to be cleared with the Army under our agreement with the Department of Cyber Resilience."

"And you'll be focused entirely on the new office?" Luke asked.

"Uh... No. I have enough data for the *Ask Dad* app to begin training the AI. We've filed the patent app for that method, but there's a lot of work to do to prove it works. Since it is closely related to the *Pythia Speaks* app, I'll be working on the updated spec that Lisa generates for that site. It will include a 'membership' option that will allow a user to create a user ID and save their correspondence with the Pythia AI. And other stuff, to be determined."

"Well, it looks like we all have our marching orders," Luke said. "Chastity is also in and out of the office as she's coordinating the finish work and move-in to the new office. Izzy and I will be here most of the time, though we're getting married the 24th and will be gone for a week after that. That will get us back in time to move to the new office. Let's get to work."

THE MONTH OF June was the busiest any of them had experienced. Henry and Darrel were often at the new office, but Darrel carried the bulk of the load, first wiring the office and then ordering the major pieces of equipment that would be needed. Chastity was there almost as much, especially as offices were completed and furniture was delivered.

But what interrupted Henry's routine most was Luke's upcoming wedding. Luke and Isobel's—Henry felt a little insulated from Izzy's plans and constant demands for attention. She was the very definition of 'bridezilla,' and even her mother was losing patience. When they took possession of their apartment at mid-month, she moved into it, though Luke was not allowed there until after the wedding.

Izzy had decided on five bridesmaids. In typical Isobel fashion, however, she had excluded the two women she had almost daily contact with: Lisa and Chastity. Having seen the slighting of one of their friends, Luke invited Chastity to be one of his groomsmen. She agreed, but refused to wear a shirt under the tux jacket. Isobel was not amused.

The week of the wedding, there was a bachelor party at a local hotel. Henry made most of the arrangements as the best man. Two of Luke's groomsmen from Villanova were over twenty-one and felt it was their duty to provide enough liquor to be sure Luke was drunk when they brought a stripper to the party.

The stripper looked familiar to Henry, but he wasn't sure who she was. She spent half an hour torturing Luke with naked lap dances that made Luke groan. Henry was pretty sure that meant he'd come. From that point, however, the stripper ignored the other men in the room and focused on Chastity. In keeping with her resolution not to wear a shirt with her tux, Chas had also decided not to wear a shirt under the low-cut vest she wore to the party. The guys focused their attention on the two-girl show that was then presented, while drinking enough to pass out before the girls had finished with each other.

"Well, they're not worth much for the rest of the night," the stripper said. "How about you two?"

"I think we'll head home now and let these guys tend to their own headaches in the morning," Henry said.

"This place will stink to high heaven by morning," Chastity said, buttoning her vest.

"Could you drop me off at Izzy's apartment?" the stripper asked.

That was when Henry remembered being briefly introduced to the woman the previous week. She was Isobel's maid of honor, Brittany! He supposed that was one way to keep control of the bachelor party, but wasn't sure if what she'd done was really within the realm of what Isobel would have approved. He and Chastity dropped Brittany off at three in the morning and then headed for the row house.

They went in and knocked on Lisa's door.

"'Lo," Lisa said when she got to the door. "Are you wasted?"

"No, honey," Henry said. "We left the party and came home. The rest might not get up until noon or later tomorrow."

"Well, come in and go to sleep if that's what you want," she yawned.

"I'm leaving Henry with you," Chastity said. "I'll go upstairs and use his bedroom."

"Oh, yeah. Of course, sweetheart. I'll see you in the morning," Lisa said, giving Chastity a kiss. She took Henry's hand and led him inside as he gave Chastity his keys and followed. "You don't want to, like, do anything now, do you?"

"Lise, I always want to do something with you. Right now, that something is sleep."

"Yeah. Okay. Come to bed."

THE REHEARSAL WAS Friday evening and dinner for the wedding party and spouses followed. Lisa gave Henry a kiss before he left.

"Have fun," she said.

"Aren't you joining me?" he asked. "I'm supposed to stay at the hotel tonight to calm Luke's nerves."

"No. I'm not part of the wedding party. I'll see you at the wedding tomorrow morning."

"I'll come home tonight, then."

"Honey, don't. I'm not mad or anything. This is a special time between you and your partners. Cut loose a little. Don't worry about a thing. Just have fun," Lisa said.

She kissed him deeply.

"I love you, Lisa," he breathed.

"See? I knew you'd say it at just the right time," she answered, kissing him again. "Now, go, before you're late."

THE REHEARSAL WAS at five, just before the Friday evening mass in the massive church. Cathedral, Henry reminded himself. Whatever. They left immediately after the rehearsal and went to the dinner in a private room of the hotel across the street, where they'd later be staying. The reception would be at the same hotel the next afternoon.

It seemed almost like an intimate gathering, even though there were eighteen people around the table. Both Isobel's and Luke's fathers offered toasts that competed regarding who could best embarrass their progeny. Henry sat next to Luke and Brittany next to Isobel. Chastity managed to get the seat next to Henry, but Felipe practically arm-wrestled one of the groomsmen for the next place so he could be next to Chas.

The toasts went around the table, Henry offering his congratulations to two of his best friends. He almost said condolences, but decided to keep the toast upbeat, especially in light of the fathers' toasts. With the number of toasts that were offered, Henry's glass of champagne kept getting refilled and he lost track of the count.

The priest even got up to give a toast. Or a prayer. Henry wasn't sure which it was because he kept raising his glass and taking a drink during it. Eventually, the party broke up and everyone went to their rooms in the hotel. Henry and the groomsmen kept Luke company watching a baseball game and drinking until eleven and then all split to go to their own rooms. Henry was definitely under the influence like he'd never been before.

Chastity had maintained her strict exclusion of alcohol and carried her own bottle of sparkling juice with her, guarding it protectively so no one could possibly slip anything into it. After the party broke up, she went home to be with Lisa.

Henry barely got his teeth brushed before he collapsed naked in bed.

Sometime during the night, his lover slipped into bed next to him. He cuddled to her and they kissed as he felt her large breasts beneath his hands. She moaned and Henry's eyes snapped open for the first time.

"Isobel? What are you doing here?"

"I have to have you again."

He'd been hard when he woke up and Izzy was just settling down on his cock.

"This is our last chance. I'd never cheat on my husband!" Isobel said, kissing him again.

"I don't even know how you dare to cheat on him before you're married. And with all your religious stuff. How do you justify it?"

"I'll go to confession in the morning and then I'll be pure for him. Jesus will forgive me. If not, surely Mary will."

"Hmm. By that logic you could justify almost anything. Murder? Surely, that's not too much for Jesus to forgive."

"I'll keep that in mind," she snapped. Isobel was active bouncing on Henry's cock and he wasn't making clear sense of the situation before she started coming.

"Uh... What about Luke?" Henry had half expected Chastity would have gone to Luke if Isobel was in his room.

"He's being well attended by Brittany. God! That slut hasn't stopped talking about Luke's glorious cock since we shared him one night at Villanova. I'm not going to even tell her about this one," Izzy said, working herself up to a second orgasm as Henry responded.

She shoved one of her nipples between his lips. He began lashing it with his tongue as Isobel grabbed his head and held him to her breast.

"No one makes me sin like you do!" she gasped. "Oh, yes, Henry. Make me scream! Take me however you want me!"

They rolled over on the bed and Henry drove his cock deeper into her. He moved his hand between them and touched her clit. It was a tipping point for Isobel he didn't know she had.

As soon as he touched her clit, she started spewing the most salacious batch of vulgarity he could imagine. If she told the priest about everything in confession, the poor man might not make it to the ceremony. Isobel was primed for their encounter long before he touched her.

"Henry! Henry, fuck me. I'm ready for you. Take me and let me enjoy this one more time before I'm married. Yes. Yes. It's as big as I remember. I'll never have anything like this in me again. I want you. I need you." She rolled him over onto his back again and slammed herself down onto his erection while whining loudly. "Yes! In me! Fuck! Fuck me! Don't stop! I'm coming! Harder, you fucking bastard. Cram your cock into my little pussy."

Henry did his best to keep up with her demands. Isobel stiffened and then relaxed completely as she passed out on top of him, giving him an opportunity to just stroke slowly in and out a couple of times. She was only out momentarily, though, before she was reflexively thrusting her hips toward him. It was all Henry could do to keep up with her.

"Behind! Get behind me, Satan!" she called, rolling off him and present-ing her pussy and ass. "Take the devil's hole."

That was too much of an invitation for Henry to resist. Not that he'd resisted anything so far. He pressed his cock against her anus and shoved. Isobel gasped and her moans increased in volume the deeper he sank into her.

"Fuck me! Fuck me! Take my dirty ass! You nasty bastard. Fuck your other business partner like you fuck Chastity. Take me in ways my husband never will. I'm coming again!"

It didn't take long in the tight channel before Henry was pumping into Izzy. This time, after they'd come, they both collapsed on the bed and rolled apart.

"Go shower," Isobel said, pushing him away. "I need to go to my room."

34

PERSONAL ASSISTANT

L UKE AND ISOBEL got married. The ceremony and mass were at one thirty in the afternoon, which gave most of the wedding party a chance to get past their hangovers. Henry had never had that experience before and vowed he'd never have it again. He'd thrown up as soon as he woke up and then ordered coffee and aspirin from room service.

It came with a side of a bloody mary, which the delivery boy said came from the groom's father. Henry was surprised Paul had managed to get a drink delivered to Henry and presumably the rest of the wedding party without anyone raising an eyebrow about ages. He hesitated a minute and then took a drink of the spicy concoction. He didn't detect any alcohol in it, so assumed it was a virgin cocktail. He drank it down.

He drank a cup of black coffee as he stood in the shower with the hot water beating on his back and then finally managed to wake up and finish the process. He wondered a little at why the towels in the bathroom were all damp and then realized he'd taken a shower in the middle of the night after he and Izzy...

That memory came as a shock. She was crazy. But he had to be just as crazy to have participated. No matter who'd been with Luke last night, Henry was going to have a shit-load of guilt to carry with him.

He met Luke and the other groomsmen in the hotel restaurant. Chastity met them there. She was the only one dressed in her tux already. They went to the cathedral where a room was prepared for them to change in. There was a strict separation of the bride's party and the groom's party. Luke wouldn't see his bride until she walked down the aisle with her father.

Both families were well connected, so more than three hundred people attended the wedding. When the music finally started playing, the long day really began. While the wedding party stood facing the altar, there were songs, prayers, scripture readings, and a ten minute sermon by the priest before they even got to the part of addressing the bride and groom. Then there was a statement of intent, an exchange of consent, a blessing and giving of rings. This was followed by a profession of faith, a prayer, and the celebration of the Eucharist. Henry identified it as a communion in protestant terms, though he'd never partaken of one. Those in the congregation who were not Catholic were also not invited to participate. Then another prayer, another song and finally, the priest pronounced them husband and wife. They got to kiss.

That still wasn't the end. There was another prayer, a blessing, and finally the dismissal. The organ in the cathedral boomed out a recessional and then they finally got out to the receiving line where everyone passed the wedding party and said congratulations. That was where Lisa finally caught up with Henry and took a place just behind him. All told it took an hour.

It wasn't over for the wedding party, though. They filed back into the sanctuary where the official photographer set and posed photos until the priest finally told them they had to leave so he could prepare the four-thirty mass.

Everyone had left and headed for the hotel banquet room by then, where people started drinking about four o'clock and were well past the hors d'oeuvres and ready for the banquet. Fortunately for everyone, the wedding party was seated and dinner was served at five-thirty.

The party went well into the night. Henry managed to separate himself from Brittany, the maid of honor, and rejoined Lisa, who sat with Henry's parents. Chastity had long-since joined them. It was after ten when Luke and Isobel left to go to the honeymoon suite. Henry, Lisa, and Chastity considered that to be clearance that they could all leave the party, too.

With the chaos brought on by the impending wedding out of the way, the following week brought even more pressure. Everything in the office was packed up and they started transporting things to the new office late in the week. Ray declared the contract work to be finished and Chastity, with Darrel, walked through the new office, accepted the keys, and called the movers to deliver their furniture and equipment.

At the same time, Henry was in his study on a Zoom call with Gene Grey of *Grey's Analysis*.

"Henry, welcome back to our podcast. You've made quite a splash with another new product since we talked previously. Tell me about the new Open Cloak Search Engine," Gene said when they got started.

"Personally, I'm very excited about this release, Gene. I've been using experimental renditions of this search engine for a couple of years. I routinely get better results from it than from any commercial search engine," Henry explained.

"Why? What is so different about this?"

"Open Cloak Search is not subject to *any* kind of advertising or sponsored links," Henry said. "It works in plain English at the moment, so users of other languages will have to wait a while before we get to a version as robust in other languages. But this is the first search engine that operates as a resident application on your computer."

"Wait. Aren't most search engines an application on your computer?"

"Sort of," Henry said. "As soon as you launch the search engine, it attaches to the index managed in the cloud by the manufacturer. That's why when you search for something, you see 'sponsored links' displayed first. You see, the manufacturers make their money that way. They give you the app for free and collect revenue based on the number of sponsored links users click on. In order to increase that revenue stream, the company collects information about what you click on and all your search terms so they can push more targeted advertising toward you. Open Cloak doesn't do that."

"We talked about the dangers of having everything in the cloud during your last interview and you gave some pretty compelling evidence. Are you saying Open Cloak Search user data is not stored in the cloud?"

"Let me clarify. When you search with one of the big engines, the information on your searches is uploaded from one or more cookies the search engine can access to determine all that browsing history. The more you use your browser, the more information that is stored. These cookies are among those that the Open Cloak Optimizer doesn't interfere with because they are used regularly. We get rid of abandoned or inactive cookies, but don't disturb the way you currently work. With Open Cloak Search, your personal data is stored in the program file itself where an AI compiles the information and uses it to predict the most useful information for you. But that information is never sent to a corporate server in the cloud. It is used... digested, if you will... by the search engine but no personal information is ever collected by the ubiquitous consumer data engines."

"What else is different? We get rid of sponsored links. Then is the content pretty much the same as any other search engine?"

"Not exactly. Corporations use what is referred to as SEO, or search engine optimization, to influence where their content is positioned in search results. Conceptually, it's a great thing that speeds up search results because the engine doesn't need to look at the whole page it is displaying. It only needs to look at header information. Unfortunately, that header information and other SEO techniques can be manipulated by corporations. In fact, there is an industry devoted to SEO. They broaden the number of keywords, links, and link backs to bring what may be completely irrelevant sites to the top of the search results."

"Henry, if you don't use the keywords or SEO, how does your search engine get good results?" Gene asked.

"That's where the real secret sauce comes into play," Henry said. "Our search engine will be a little slower when it's first installed. That's because the built-in AI has to learn how you work and the kind of information you are likely to want. Since the AI resides on your personal computer, it has access to everything you have there. It will learn what you are interested in and how you work from more than your search results and clicks."

"Whoa! The search engine is going to what? Catalog everything on my computer?" Gene asked.

"Essentially. That is what we build its training wall on. You see, when you use an AI search engine, it builds the training wall on a broad selection of information, the bulk of which has nothing at all to do with what you are searching for. Open Cloak is your personal assistant and the first and foremost thing you want from a personal assistant is a non-disclosure agreement. None of that information is passed on."

"A personal assistant," Gene said. "So, large search engine AIs reveal millions of pages of links. What do you get from Open Cloak Search?"

"Back in November, I started a search with a commercial search engine by asking just 'Where to.' I got 186,000,000 results. Now what I was hunting for was 'Where to vote,' so I completed the search. By the way, the first result that had to do with polling places was on the third page of results in the first search. That yielded only 17,700,000 results. But after wading through page after page of results, I still didn't see anything that was specifically about where to vote in the area where I live—Pittsburgh, PA. Of course, getting more specific and asking 'Where to vote in Pittsburgh,' yielded only 6,930,000 results and, in fact, the tenth link on the first page of results was a list of polling places in the greater Pittsburgh metropolitan area."

"Okay, so you got the result?"

"Yes, but why did I have to be so specific and still not get the result as the number one link? Now keep in mind, I conducted this search on November first. Election day was the second. Why didn't I get the 'where to vote' results with the first two words? Open Cloak Search, your personal assistant, knows the date on my computer, knows my location, and knows I've been politically active through donations I made to my preferred candidates. When I entered a search for 'Where to,' I received an immediate page of ten results and the first—the very first—result on the page was the list of polling places in the greater Pittsburgh area."

"What if you wanted to know where to go on vacation?" Gene asked.

"Well, the AI wasn't finished. It gave me a page of ten results based on what it knew about me instantly, but then it kept building search results. Another page of results displayed more voter information, including the county voter pamphlet with the full list of what was on the ballot and statements by each candidate, qualifications to vote, and voter assistance numbers. The next batch of results starting about halfway down page three, was 'where to take my date.' That's something I've looked up frequently. The results, once again were specific to my location and the time of year. Ultimately, I had a total of a little over 17,000 results that covered a plethora of 'where to' information."

"So, how far did you have to look before you found where to go on vacation?" Gene asked.

"I didn't. Who in his right mind ever looks past the fifth page of results without modifying his search?" Henry laughed.

The interview went on for a while and Henry got a chance to plug *Pythia Speaks*, warning people that they were testing the concept and currently it was only a public beta version.

As soon as Henry disconnected from his session with Gene, he stripped out of his business clothes and got into jeans and a T-shirt so he could help move into their new office.

<hr>

"WELCOME, EVERYONE!" LUKE said, Monday morning.

The office felt cavernous with only nine people in it. In fact, they'd dragged their own office chairs to the open and unoccupied area in the middle of the office to have this opening meeting.

"Most of you have met each other, but we have one new employee today, so we'll make introductions all the way around," Luke said. "Chastity, would you do the honors?"

"Certainly. I'd like to introduce you all to Nancy Donovan. Nancy will be our front desk presence and is charged with answering calls and greeting guests. We don't expect that much traffic on either the phone or through the front doors immediately, so Nancy will also be filling an administrative assistant role. If I listed everything, you'd all be amazed that one person could handle it all, but I have faith in Nancy," Chastity said. "I'd like to have each of you introduce yourself to Nancy with your name and position in the company. Isobel?"

"I am Isobel Riordan," Izzy said proudly, standing up. "I'm the company financial manager and one of the original four partners."

They continued around the room introducing everyone in the circle.

"I'm Henry Pascal," Henry said. "I'm the CTO and one of the original four partners, as Isobel termed it."

Lisa and Josh were the last to introduce themselves.

"Well, it isn't every company that launches a new office on the day before a holiday and wishes its employees a nice day off," Luke said when introductions had been concluded. "We don't expect anyone to even put in a full day today with Independence Day tomorrow. Most of you spent at least some time this weekend helping move and set things up. We'd like you to use this morning to get familiar with the office, make sure your space is functional, including work stations and your security information. If you've brought things to decorate your space with, this is a good time to do that. If you need to run out to get things for your space, just let Nancy know when you are leaving and returning to the office so she can answer people who might be looking for you. Boxes from the other office have been moved to your spaces. There is coffee and pop in the break room. Let's get to work!"

When it came down to it, Luke's office was the one that needed the most setup. He and Izzy had just returned from their honeymoon the previous night and hadn't participated at all in the move-in. Chastity's search of used office furniture uncovered an old power desk for Luke's office. It also had room for comfortable chairs and a table for small meetings, like for the four partners.

Everyone had taken a turn trying the keycode on the pad outside the office. The door would be unlocked during business hours, which was why Nancy had a desk next to the door.

"Mr. Pascal," Nancy said from the door to his office. Henry looked up.

"Nancy, I don't think you need to use my father's name when addressing me," he chuckled. They'd last met at Christmas dinner at his parents' house. "I don't think either of our parents would approve."

"Mrs. Riordan said that I needed to use proper titles when referring to the partners," Nancy breathed.

"Mrs... Oh! Isobel. She sure is milking that marriage for all it's worth. Well, in my office and when we're at least in semi-private, always call me Henry. I'm not going to fight with Isobel over office protocol. What was it you wanted?"

"Oh. Um... I just want to say I'm not stalking you. I didn't know Open Cloak was your company. I responded to an ad and Ms. Pappa hired me. I was so thankful to find a job that required no experience, I didn't even ask who worked here."

"That didn't even occur to me. Most of the people in the company were known to some of us before they were hired. I think Darrel is the only exception to that," Henry said. "Welcome to Open Cloak."

"Thank you. I just didn't want you to think I was stalking you. Have a good day, Mr... Henry."

Nancy skipped out of the office and returned to her desk at the door.

Henry went back to testing his workspace and changing the position of the desk so his back wasn't to the window.

EVEN THOUGH HENRY wanted to dig into projects in the new office, he took the Fourth off and took Lisa to his parents' house for the afternoon.

"You have to come over and visit the office," Lisa said as they chatted.

"Made some changes to the fourth floor?" Ryan asked.

"Oh. Uh... I guess I didn't tell you about a few things," Henry said. "Um... Open Cloak got a big investment and we've moved into an actual office building. It isn't huge, but it's a nice space. We opened there yesterday."

"You moved the office out of your row house? Are you still living there?" Sylvia asked.

"Oh, yeah. Lisa and I are still living there. The place does seem kind of empty without people running upstairs," Henry said.

"Son, I understand that you are an adult and don't report to us, but you might keep us up to date on what is happening. We try not to get into your affairs too much, but we're here for you and we want to be part of your life," Ryan said.

"I... It's been hard," Henry sighed. Lisa reached over for his hand. "The business has grown so fast, we've... I've sometimes lost track of what's important. And Lisa and I are discovering how much we care for each other. We went to Louisiana after classes let out to meet her parents and grandparents. Then there was Luke and Isobel getting married. I'm sorry I haven't been in touch more often. Geez, we only live a couple of miles away. You'd think I could manage that."

"Maybe in our desire to give you room to grow on your own, we've been too distant," Sylvia said. "We assumed when we didn't hear from you for a week or two that it was because you were taking such a heavy load in school."

"That was certainly one thing," Henry said. "I... guess I should say that I'll be cutting back on that in the fall. I need to be full-time in the company."

"You're quitting school?" Ryan barked.

"I hope not," Henry said. "I just might not graduate in three years like I planned. Dad, we're actually a computer software development company with products in the market, investors, and employees to take care of. Did you know Nancy Donovan up the street came to work for us yesterday? I didn't know about that until I saw her at the office. She applied and our director of human resources hired her to operate the front desk and do general office administrative assistance."

"How many people in your office?" Ryan asked calmly.

"Nine of us this summer. Two, including Lisa, are contractors who will cut back hours when school starts. I'm guessing we'll have to hire additional help by then. We really need to start a testing department. We've been using a group of testers under non-disclosure, but with some of the new projects, it really needs to be in-house. The office is big enough to accommodate twenty people, but we expected that to get us through five years of the lease."

"It sounds like instead of an office administrative assistant, you need a personal assistant," Sylvia said.

"Funny you should mention that," Lisa said. "Henry did another interview with Gene Grey of *Grey's Analysis* podcast Friday. He referred to our new search engine as a personal assistant."

"Is that released already?" Henry asked, alarmed.

"No. We all watched upstairs while you did it Friday."

"I thought you were all working on packing the office!"

"Mostly, but we really enjoyed getting the skinny on how you really thought about the AI," Lisa said. "When you get into the philosophy and ethics of AI discussions, we all walk away more enthused about what we're doing. We couldn't wait to get to work Monday."

"Sounds like I need to slate some time for those discussions in the office," Henry said. "Everybody should have a part in them."

"Including us," Ryan said. "Let us help you any way you can."

"You've helped so much and worked so hard that as soon as we have a steady stream of revenue and I can afford it, I'm going to buy you a cruise around the world," Henry laughed. "But yeah. I haven't been very good at keeping you up to date with what's going on in my life. I'm sorry."

It seemed to Henry that in some ways, he'd been more open with Bill and Beau in Baton Rouge than he'd been with his own father. He and Lisa spent the entire afternoon catching Ryan and Sylvia up on the extent of the investment, the events at college, and Henry's intent to cut back to ten hours in the fall—just enough to stay full-time.

They talked about *Pythia Speaks* and the *Ask Dad* project. Ryan said he thought he'd captured a lot and suggested Henry could start training the AI on it whenever he wanted. Henry took the drive with him to install the AI program, promising to give the drive back to him the next day. So far, the original drive Henry had given his father had storage capacity, but it didn't have the application. In order to become truly functional, he had to install the AI, which was much the same as the Pythia AI, and point it at the data on the disk for training. The AI was also given access to files on the host computer for training. Finally, there was an activation and consent form his father would need to fill out, giving the AI permission to access files related to his father.

As a last thought, Henry asked if his parents had any historical material regarding his grandparents, whom he had never met. Both agreed to look through their old photo collections and maybe even the attic to see what they had. He was welcome to all of it.

"HENRY, LOVE," LISA said as they drove home that night.

"Yes?" It thrilled him in unreasonable ways to hear her refer to him as 'love.'

"Let's make sure to keep in better touch with our parents, okay?" she said. "I... I mean... If we have a real future together—I mean long-term—and I'm not suggesting right now that we do, but if we end up with one, I'd like to know that our parents are a part of it. They're important people to us and I know I've neglected mine a lot. I'll bet my father knows more about you and what you've been through the past two years than he knows about me. We need to change that."

"Maybe we need to start our own Ask Dad program only it's ask your kids."

"And our kids—I mean, if we ever got that far—should have access to our whole lives and know that we love them forever."

"Forever," Henry whispered. "I like that. They'd know we are theirs forever."

"The name," Lisa responded. "Forever Yours."

35

UPGRADES

WORKING IN AN OFFICE with an official work day and organized staff did not make things easier on them. Nearly everyone except Nancy worked a regular day of ten hours or more. The contractors were strictly limited because they were hourly and could not be paid overtime. So, they often left the office before noon on Fridays if they stayed even that long.

Conrad and Darrel both had significant work that took them more than forty hours. They frequently called Henry in for code reviews. Darrel didn't have broad experience with AI, but his knowledge of computer security software was extensive. He soon had a full suite of security applications specified and awaiting development.

Conrad lacked an actual network to test the network optimization software on. Henry promised to get that resolved.

Henry often swapped code with the other two so he could get *Pythia Speaks* upgrades reviewed as well.

"EVERYBODY LISTEN UP!" Luke called from the center of the office on Monday in the middle of the month. They'd been in the office for two full weeks. The impromptu public address of Luke simply standing in the middle of the office and yelling brought everyone to attention.

"We have the second quarter revenue statement," Luke announced. "We won't always be calling everyone's attention to this as the company grows, but this is a significant milestone and we are a tightknit group. The EMEE quarterly report shows sales of 2,817 units of Open Cloak Optimization resulting in $7,718.58 in revenue."

323

There was polite applause, no one quite knowing what it meant to the company.

"The new Open Cloak Search has just begun selling and we launched 985 units," Luke continued. "That comes in at $18,015.65 in revenue. The company has received a total deposit of $25,734.23. It's not yet enough to meet expenses, but we are genuinely on our way."

This time the applause and cheers were significantly more excited. In reality, that would fall short of meeting the month's expenses. And the revenue was for three months. The partners all felt the burden of getting more revenue generated.

Everyone returned to their tasks and Henry waved to Chastity and Isobel to join him in Luke's office. They all sat around Luke's conference table.

"That was great to get people fired up, Luke," Henry began. "We all know that it isn't near enough and we're feeling the pressure to get the network versions out. This won't be a popular thing, but we need to spend more in order to get us where we want to be. We need dedicated testers."

"I thought we were set through the summer," Isobel said immediately.

"I thought so, too. Our testing group that worked on the first two programs is not able to test the new versions. They need to be tested on a network. That's also going to be true of the counterattack software. Darrel has outlined a great plan to make it better and it could be a genuine product by the end of the year. But it, too, needs to be tested on a network. That means we need at least two testers and an independent testing network to run the apps on."

"Two people?" Isobel screeched. "We definitely didn't say anything about that when we were budgeting."

"When we were budgeting, we didn't even know we'd be a company with $20 million in capitalization, working in an office space we've leased for five years, on products that require full-time employees," Henry shot back. "What do you think an investment is for? If we don't get what we need to generate income then the investment just dwindles without producing anything."

He glared at Isobel and she stared back at him.

"You don't need to teach me about investment capital," she said. "Just make your case for how we'll get a return on the expenses."

"Okay," Henry said, calming down. "We have three products under active development and another two in planning stages with two products released in the market. In addition, we have one person working on fixing the bugs in our search engine that we didn't catch because we rushed it to market with inadequate testing. They aren't serious bugs. Nothing crashes yet. But they will irritate our users enough that they won't consider buying a network installation. The network installation version is one of the products in development, being worked on by the same person working on bug fixes."

"Okay. We've got one person doing two jobs," Luke said.

"We have one person working on a network version of the optimization program. While the desktop version did not report significant bugs, the network version has expanded functionality that can only be tested on a network. We can't really use our corporate network as a testbed. We'd risk having the company shut down periodically and possible loss of data."

"So, that would require both a tester and a network, which would increase Darrel's workload with two networks," Chastity said, making notes.

"Yes, but it would benefit Darrel as well. He will want something to test the defense system on as well. That's the product being spec'd right now," Henry said. "So, the investment isn't just a short-term expense. It will pay off with the testing of at least three products. Finally, we have *Forever Yours* in development. I need to call in all the dev team periodically for code review. I'm afraid the tests will be live. We'll have half a dozen walls with AI trained on each and we'll need to come up with questions to ask our ancestors. I propose expanding the number of people invited to use the product and accept updates as we develop."

"There's a hardware cost to that, too, isn't there?" Isobel asked.

"Currently, we have limited the app to an attachable drive. There is no reason it couldn't be installed on the subject's own computer, but that puts data at risk from computer failure. The detachable drive *should* protect data," Henry said. "I have two of the drives backed up in-house now and have returned the original drives so they can continue to collect data. And Lisa and I are primarily working on that app, though Lisa is also spec'ing a new version of *Pythia Speaks*, and is developing interfaces for both network products."

"Do we need to get a full-timer in that position?" Isobel asked.

"Probably, but we have at least another month before it becomes urgent. We should probably start searching for a UI developer."

"Really, this is only moving the new hires up by a month," Chastity said. "We knew we're going to have both Lisa and Josh returning to school in the fall and would need to fill those positions."

"We might still need to fill those positions," Henry said. "I don't think we adequately planned for any testers."

The meeting went on as they discussed options. Isobel calmed down as she began entering numbers in her spreadsheets and Chastity began searching and compiling job descriptions for the new positions.

Henry returned to his office and training the *Forever Yours* AI.

THE WALL ON which Henry trained his Forever Yours AI was entirely his own legacy. After his conversation with Lisa, he approved the AI gathering all information about him. He didn't actually do any special input. The all-access permission gave the AI unlimited permission to learn about Henry Pascal. That included all the information on his computers, his social media accounts, his financial records, and tax records. Of course, there was little in the latter two that would help the AI answer questions. But it gave the AI a lot of data without him having to actually input anything.

He and Lisa had been liberal about sharing information about their relationship. They'd posted pictures and videos of the two of them together at different events. He'd done a tour of the new office for a video. He'd been interviewed by Gene Grey twice. The company's distribution partner, EMEE, was very pleased about the most recent interview and reported that sales had spiked after it went public.

All of these items were merely data points for the AI.

Unlike *Pythia Speaks*, *Forever Yours* included facial recognition and generative capability, so he could instruct the AI to show what he would look like skiing and it came up with a plausible video, even though he had no video of himself skiing. It was rough and not as polished as most generative AI could create. It was looking like video output would not be part of the first release. He did have photos of a couple of times he'd attempted it when he was younger. The AI did okay with that, but mostly just searched appropriate photos.

Mostly, though, Henry was interested in what kinds of responses the AI would generate to actual questions.

He had collected several self-reflection questions from various websites and used those to start querying the AI.

"What do you value most, Henry?" he typed.

"Relationships. Friendship. People," came the response. It was still slow as it was searching for both keywords and interpretations. Still, the answer was rather specific, and Henry couldn't really argue with it, though he expected something along the lines of 'creativity and intelligence.'

"Tell me about relationships," he instructed.

"I love my family and my best friends. I've thought I was in love a few times, but when I met Lisa, it was all different. My relationship with her is open and honest. It's different than my relationship with my parents or with my best friends. But I value the relationship I have with them as well."

Henry stared at the screen open-mouthed. He noted the AI made distinctions between past and present, which made sense as it had access to the dates and times of everything on his computer and social sites. It showed him a picture of Lisa and him together. He wasn't sure where it was taken, but was vaguely certain that he'd put a heart next to it on Lisa's timeline.

He sat back to contemplate what the computer had shown him. It had exposed things far more intimate than he'd expected.

Do I want to expose this to my children in the future? Do I want to know this kind of thing about my father?

PYTHIA SPEAKS SEEMED simple compared to Forever Yours. The product was still essentially just two parts: ask a question and receive an answer. In the background, he was coding several new features he would release over the next few weeks. First, he and Lisa had expanded the text boxes to a maximum of 400 characters instead of 140. They had debated about the move, but decided the 140-character limit was inadequate for questions people wanted to ask the oracle. They'd collected several samples of questions asked that were incomplete because people couldn't condense them to the limit. The program did not respond to a string of requests, unlike popular social media. He released that feature without an announcement and discovered a fifteen percent increase in the average length of a question.

They'd decided to work on registering subscribers and giving them the ability to enter questions up to 1,000 characters. Subscribers would also gain access to the record of their questions and answers, as well as a forum on which they could discuss their oracles.

Using OC Search, Henry uncovered several social media threads that talked about questions and answers from *Pythia Speaks*. One person posted a question and answer from *Pythia Speaks* every morning on her stream. Hits on the site had risen to over 3,000 per day. Even with the collection of questions and answers recorded on the site for further training, the database of content Pythia relied on was less than five gigabytes. It collected only text, not images or video or formatting.

Pythia could also look up additional information on subjects on the internet, but only what was allowed in its operating parameters. Content had to be in the public domain, had to relate to philosophy and prophecy, and had to be scrubbed of political and religious references, as well as other normal restrictions regarding sex, gender neutrality, hate speech, and racism.

Users were not blocked from asking questions that contained forbidden content, but Pythia never answered with that content. When it stored the conversation for use on its wall, it eliminated those terms.

There was a daily increase in user questions, and the responses were becoming more relevant.

"What is the meaning of life?" Henry asked the oracle.

"Life is the meaning," Pythia responded. Henry waited for more of an answer, but he liked the simple message. One of the most profound questions that faced most humans was answered with four simple words.

"What path should I take?" Henry asked, deciding to go for a more oracular question.

"The path is unrelated to the destination. As long as you keep the goal in sight, the path is irrelevant. It is determined by the kind of person you are, not by your goal."

Holy shit!

Henry went back to work on the code, setting up his autoload function to ask a question every sixty seconds to determine both how the AI responded and also what was added to the database. He'd copied the questions from a few dozen websites that asked philosophical questions. These included questions asked of Socrates, Plato, Confucious, Rumi, and many others.

"What is real?"

"What is a good life?"

"What is beauty?"

"What is justice?"

"How do we know what we say we know?"

Several hundred such questions had been collected in his data feed and he kept pumping them into Pythia. Many of Pythia's answers were shorter than the original 140-character limit. Some, however, seemed to run out of room in the 400-character space. Overall, Henry was pleased with the training, though occasionally, he made an adjustment to Pythia's response, eliminating forbidden words or concepts.

"We have the basis for a full new version of Pythia Speaks almost ready to upload," Henry told Luke, Isobel, and Chastity in mid-August.

"Woohoo!" Chastity said.

"What's the holdup then?" Luke asked.

"I'm torn. I don't think we should try to monetize it," Henry said. "It just doesn't seem right. We're putting very little effort into the site at the moment and are getting over 3,000 hits a day. People love it. I just think it's a betrayal to charge for the subscription."

"We're not a fucking nonprofit," Isobel growled.

"True, but Pythia is a bonus for us. It was only developed to test the code for *Forever Yours*. That project is going well and the code has been integrated and expanded. I just don't think we should charge for the *Pythia Speaks* subscriptions. There are really very few additional features and I think, aside from periodic reviews to see how it is doing, we don't need to do any more after this update," Henry said.

"I don't know," Chastity said.

"It seems like an opportunity to grab extra revenue for further investment. Do we have any estimates as to what kind of revenue it might generate?" Luke asked.

"Yes," Isobel said, looking directly into Henry's eyes. It seemed like she was going to have a famous Isobel meltdown and Henry braced himself. "It's insignificant," Isobel said, surprising Henry. "I don't think *Pythia Speaks* could ever be a significant revenue generator. The new feature set is already available for free on most social media sites. Saving conversations. A forum for discussion. Longer messages. Why would anyone pay for those features on an oracle site. *Pythia Speaks* has been a relatively inexpensive testbed compared to the two testers we've hired in-house. We're releasing network search and optimization this month. I don't think we should burden Pythia with a revenue goal."

"That's really profound, Izzy," Henry said.

"It doesn't mean I don't think there should be some additional restrictions put on the site," she continued. "First of all, its budget needs to be limited to the cost of the server. Secondly, the subscriber list needs to be anonymous. And third, you need to show profitable expansion for *Forever Yours* within the next six months."

"I don't think you can put all those demands on Henry," Chastity began. "We might as well just shut Pythia down."

Luke just looked at the other three, ready to jump in if it became a real dispute, but unwilling to do more than make a final decision based on what they determined among the three of them. He'd been preparing non-stop for an interview with *HBR* and had only taken a break from meeting with Darla Gallitzin to listen to this proposal.

"I think we're near to an agreement," Henry said. "We need to understand that the server cost will undoubtedly increase over time as traffic continues to increase. Second, I need you to clarify what you mean by anonymous sub-scribers. A record of their subscription has to be maintained in order to have a subscription."

"Let Pythia manage them. I don't want anyone's personal information to be available to anyone in our company or to be subject to subpoena. Pythia should keep an encoded... what do they call it? Encryption. An encrypted record of subscribers that only she can access," Isobel explained.

"Actually, I kind of like that idea," Henry said. "It's really hand-in-hand with not charging for it. If Pythia maintains the list and has the only key to encryption, it prevents anyone's private information from being displayed. As to getting *Forever Yours* out the door, I think I can meet your six month requirement for full release. It's in code review now and we'll turn it to the testers as soon as that is done. I accept your criteria."

"One more thing," Isobel said. "It's small, but I think there should be a line at the bottom of the website pages and the forum pages with a link that says, 'Powered by Open Cloak AI.' We should get a little credit for it."

Everyone nodded.

"Well, if Henry agrees, what do you think, Chas?" Luke asked.

"I'll agree," she said. "I'll write up the notes and make sure we all have a copy of the agreement."

"Then we've come to a conclusion. It's all yours, Henry."

"THAT WAS REALLY good, Isobel," Henry said after the meeting. He stopped briefly at her office.

"I'm not always a bitch," she said. "I'm on some pretty good drugs now. I worry about our finances. But some things need to follow our original com-pany principles. We don't collect personal information. Of course, we need to register users so we can push upgrades, but we don't even do that auto-matically. And since I intend to be the first subscriber, I want my information protected."

"You will? I didn't know you paid that much attention to the oracle."

"It's not like I base my life on it," Izzy huffed. "I just like to see what ridic-ulous thing she'll say each day."

"Do you ask the same question every day?"

"Not always. I don't ask the same question two days in a row. But I don't have that many questions. You know, like, 'Will this be a good day?' or 'Why is my mother such a bitch?' I mean, not usually," Izzy said, lowering her eyes.

"Well, they were great suggestions and I'll have it ready for upload later this week," Henry said.

He left Isobel's office wondering exactly what drugs she was taking.

36

WHAT DOES FOREVER MEAN?

BY THE END OF AUGUST, everyone had returned to school. Lisa and Josh cut their work time to ten hours a week, and that highlighted the need for two more full-time developers. Henry was taking only ten hours of classes, the minimum required for full-time status and preservation of his grant and scholarship. It looked like he might still manage to graduate at the end of the school year, since he had accumulated so many extra hours with heavy loads and summer classes. He was still putting in well over forty hours a week at the office.

Luke and Isobel were back to school full-time, though they'd transferred their programs to the local university. They were still in the office ten hours a week. Chastity dropped all her classes but the last two classes she needed for her AA online. She spent the full day every day at the office. She was the full-time operations manager. Nancy, at the front desk, found Chastity leaned on her more and more for support.

"Labor Day plans?" Chastity asked Henry as she perched on the corner of his desk.

She had carefully shut the door behind her and locked it. Henry's hand went immediately to her bare leg and he kissed it. Chastity had become a regular visitor to the row house about once a week to crawl into bed with Henry and Lisa. As far as going out, however, she only went out with Lisa. Henry understood. She was Lisa's girlfriend, not his. They still had a glorious time in bed with the three of them.

"Hmm. I'd like to make a plan," he said, sliding farther up her leg.

"You know we'll do that!" Chas laughed. Her legs, however, parted a little more.

"How about the five of us hanging out on the patio and grilling something or another?" he asked.

"I'll get the message to Izzy and Luke," Chas said as Henry moved his kisses to the inside of her thigh instead of the outside.

"Is it quitting time for today?" Henry asked.

"Everyone but Conrad has left the office," she answered. "I thought you might want to get home before Lisa gets back from class."

"Yeah." Henry managed to get his hand to Chastity's bare pussy and she spread her legs wider. "Let's go home," he said, standing to give her a peck on the lips as he stroked through her moistness.

"Okay, but you need to finish what you just started when we get there."

"You know it."

"HENRY, I'M HOME!" Lisa called when she got inside. Not seeing anyone on the first floor, she ran up to her room to drop off her books and then continued to the third floor. Henry's door was unlocked, so she opened it. "Henry?"

"In the bedroom, love!" he called. She headed to the bedroom and found Chastity stretched out naked on Henry's bed. He was between her legs licking her to peak after peak.

"Oh! That looks like fun."

"Let me have you, Lise!" Chastity called, holding her arms out. "Don't you just love what Henry does with his tongue?"

"I sure do. Is he better than I am?" Lisa asked.

"Oh, it's different," Chastity said. "He just has a magic touch."

Lisa stripped and joined the two in bed. Chastity pulled her on top of her mouth and began getting Lisa's motor running.

"Slide down and kiss me," Chas said, pulling Lisa off her mouth. "Let Henry do what you like most."

Lisa scooted back and began kissing her own juices off Chastity. Henry pulled back and gave a lick up his girlfriend's slit, then moved up behind her. He pushed into Lisa as she continued to kiss Chastity more frantically.

"This is the best of all worlds," Lisa said.

"Yes," Chastity agreed, playing with her girlfriend's breasts, pressed up against her own piercings.

"I love you two like crazy!" Henry declared as he picked up his pace.

"Oh! Yes!" Lisa called out. "What a welcome home this is."

They built to a peak together. Chastity had already had hers on Henry's tongue multiple times.

"The office is so empty without you guys!" Chastity said. "Henry was there today because he doesn't have classes on Monday or Friday. But you and Josh and Izzy and Luke were all missing. I had to just go into Henry's office and spread my legs before he finally got the hint and brought me home."

"I'm glad he did, sweetheart," Lisa said. "Having you here at home is exactly what I want. Why don't you move in with us?"

Henry gave a powerful thrust as she said this and both of them came.

"That's... a great... idea!" Henry said breathlessly. "You aren't really entertaining at home anymore, are you?"

"Not since the first of August," Chas said. "But you both know I couldn't live with either of you. I just can't wake up next to someone in the morning. I'm sorry."

"Lisa and I could... uh..." he looked at Lisa and saw her eyes widen. "We could maybe live together. I mean, move in with me, Lisa. I love you so much!"

Lisa gasped and rolled to the other side of Chastity.

"Maybe... we could get a bigger bed?" Lisa asked.

"Yeah," Henry agreed. "We don't take much space in it when it's just the two of us, but it's nice to have room to roll around a little when there's three of us."

"Okay." Lisa said. "Okay."

It seemed both of them had forgotten about Chastity or why they'd made the suggestion.

"Wait! You'd move in with Henry so I could have your suite?" Chastity asked, amazed.

"Absolutely, babe. Well, not just so you could have the suite. I've been thinking of moving in with him for a while," Lisa said. "I understand you don't want to wake up with someone. And I understand you don't want to be any man's girlfriend—even our Henry. But we love you and we'd love to have you closer."

"What about my cats?"

"Probably better keep them in your suite for a while until they get acclimated. Then, why wouldn't they be welcome, too?" Henry asked.

"I love you two," Chas said, hugging them both.

LABOR DAY FOUND the five of them—Henry, Lisa, Chastity, Isobel, and Luke—relaxing on the rooftop patio. Lisa had spent the weekend moving in with Henry and now her suite was pretty much empty.

Over the summer, they had changed the fourth floor of the row house from an office to a lounge. It had new casual furniture and a TV. The patio door had often been open during the summer as they extended their casual space onto the rooftop. Lisa and Henry spent most nights in one or the other's bed, but both had maintained their separate suites until this weekend.

Henry had ordered a new and larger bed for his bedroom, moving his bed to the second bedroom of what would become Chastity's suite. Chastity declared that she'd be happy to get rid of the bed she'd 'used for work' when she moved to the suite and was happy to have Lisa's bed in one bedroom and Henry's in the other.

"So, something tells me things have changed," Isobel said. "There's a new vibe in the house."

"We're just... consolidating a bit," Henry said. "I've asked Lisa to live with me and she said yes."

"And we asked Chas to take the second suite. She said yes," Lisa said.

"Are you living over here now, Chastity?" Luke asked.

"Not yet. I had to give thirty days' notice I was moving out," Chastity said. "I'll move at the end of the month."

"Wow! This is a real celebration, then," Isobel said. "Dear Henry has been tied down."

"Oh, I don't think so," Henry said. "Liberated is more like it."

"Aww. Newlyweds," Luke said. He looked at Isobel and they both broke up laughing.

"Yuck!" they said together.

"So, is this a forever thing?" Isobel asked.

"We... haven't really looked down the road very far," Henry said. "I think we'd like it to be, but we just haven't talked about it yet."

"What's 'forever,' anyway?" Lisa asked. "It's just a whole string of todays, isn't it?"

Luke had brought some beer and some weed, compliments of his father. They were being moderate, but all had a little buzz. Even though Chastity didn't drink any alcohol, she did indulge in a little smoke.

"Is that what the new software is? Should we be calling it 'Yours Today' instead of 'Forever Yours?'" Isobel asked.

"What's on the web is there forever," Luke said. "Isn't that what we've always been taught? You can never erase something completely."

"I think we know different than that these days," Henry said. "With the new search engine and a little tinkering with its range, I think we could find, retain, and eliminate every occurrence of something."

"Really?" Chastity said. "That sounds dangerous."

"Who said computing was safe?" Lisa responded. "I'd tend to agree that nothing is permanent. I know Dad has a fireproof safe full of huge forty-megabyte discs that fit in an external drive. When he stored them, he had to extract and store a board for his computer called a SCSI port. He's not sure even now if he could install the board on a contemporary motherboard. And it's almost impossible to find a driver to install as well."

"My dad said at their office, they kept all the discs they've used, even though they can't read any of them today," Henry said. "I don't think you can buy a 3.5-inch floppy drive these days."

"What could you store on an 800K disc?" Lisa asked.

"It's still the whole issue of memory bloat," Henry said. "Someplace along the line we decided it was okay to just keep adding memory and keep adding memory instead of managing the size of the software."

"That all doesn't answer the question," Chastity said. "Is *Forever Yours* forever?"

"Is it safer in the cloud than on a disc?" Luke asked.

"I wouldn't put anything up there, wherever there is," Isobel declared vehemently. "All our company financials are kept locally, backed up daily, and stored off-site, but not in the cloud."

"For being such an advanced technology company, we do have some archaic methods," Henry sighed. "Darrel backs up and removes all the development files when he backs up the financials. The thing is, we know how at risk we are from attacks. We still repel at least one hacking attack each week on either the corporate server or *Pythia Speaks*."

"The thing is, *Forever Yours* can be backed up wherever a user wants to put it. But the application and data reside and are accessed locally. If they don't keep the disc safe, it's as vulnerable as a collection of old photos. One fire and you never see great grandma again," Lisa said.

"With the possible exception of having your data backed up off-site—whether it's in the cloud or on a disk in a safe deposit box. Then you can re-download the data, buy another copy of the software app, and train the AI over again.

And we honestly don't know if a second app trained on the exact same content will result in the exact same extractions. I actually doubt it," Henry said.

"To put it in the cloud means to put it on one or more remote servers, which are all subject to disaster, bankruptcy, or just the whim of a technology behemoth. All they have to do is decide they no longer support that application or file format and it's gone," Lisa said.

"I'll tell you what's forever," Chastity said. Everyone looked at her as she looked at the others one at a time. "Now," she declared. "Now is always now. The only time we have is now. We are always here now. Before and after are constructs we use to attempt to project ourselves elsewhere when all we ever are is now."

"That's deep, Chas," Luke said.

"It's why I don't usually smoke this stuff," she laughed.

"WHAT'S MY RENT going to be?" Chastity asked. "I know the house rents for $3,500. I get half of it, so that would be $1,750, right?"

"I thought I'd stop charging rent," Henry said. "I asked Lisa to live with me. So, I just figure I'll cover rent from now on."

"Absolutely not!" Lisa said. "I might have to move out if you try that."

"But... how should we handle it?" Henry said.

"Thirds," Lisa said. "$1,170 a month for each of us."

"I have more private space," Chastity objected.

"I might need the second bedroom on occasion," Lisa responded. "I haven't decided if Henry and I can stand each other *all* the time."

"Well, we should at least charge the company something. We still hold board meetings upstairs," Chastity said.

"I definitely don't want to burden the company with any more rent than it has with the office. We're only three months away from having that $7,500 nut to crack each month," Henry said. "Besides, I don't mind inviting the board to meet here, but I don't want them just considering this an extension of the office. If you two are okay with it, I guess thirds is fair."

"It's less than either of us were paying," Lisa said. "Do we have enough information to just bank a higher rent payment and cover utilities, too?"

"It varies by season, but I think we have the data," Henry said. "We'll have to figure out food and chores."

"Include the maid service in the rent, too," Chastity said. "I'd have had it in my apartment if it weren't for the cats and such a small space."

"Okay. We'll need to collect all the bills and tally them up," Lisa said. "I can work on that if you'll give me access to them, Henry."

"Of course, I will. I don't think I've been gouging anyone on the rates I've charged."

"More likely, you've been covering expenses out of your generosity," Chastity said. "I'll help you, Lise."

"Okay. That ends the family meeting except for one thing," Lisa said. "I suggest that every important family meeting end with sex. Henry has that new big bed that hasn't seen the three of us in it together yet."

"I second that motion," Chastity giggled.

"Well, let's make it unanimous then," Henry said. The girls led the way from the lounge to Henry and Lisa's bedroom.

"I LOVE HOLDING my lovers and cuddling after sex," Lisa sighed.

"Mmm. Me, too," Henry added, reaching across her to touch Chastity as well.

"I love kissing my lovers goodnight and leaving them cuddled in each other's arms," Chastity said, extracting herself from Lisa and Henry to roll out of bed.

"Don't you like to cuddle with us?" Lisa asked plaintively.

Chastity sat on the edge of the bed and turned to the two of them. She had simple basic bars through her nipple piercings and they'd both treated them to a variety of tugs, twists, and pinches as they rutted together.

"You know I do, hon," Chastity said. "I'm sorry I'm so screwed up. It's just that cuddling with a lover is really different than sex. It's not something I can really do afterward. When you and I cuddle on the sofa and watch TV, that isn't sex. Even when Henry lays his head on my bare leg in the office, that isn't sex. I love you both. But even though I'm not having sex with anyone else now, and I enjoy sex with the two of you—or either of you—it isn't love for me. It's just been too ingrained in my psyche to stay separate from it. When I get to my apartment, though, what makes it all worthwhile is thinking about the two of you together. That gives me a warm fuzzy feeling."

"You know we'll figure it out eventually," Henry said. "If it takes a while… I don't know. We'll be here now, whenever you are."

"You almost understand," Chastity smiled. "I'll see you guys tomorrow. We need to have a fun outing for Lisa's birthday!"

"Hell, yeah!" Lisa said.

Chastity kissed each of her lovers and left for home and her cats.

"YOU KNOW, ONE day, she'll break our hearts," Lisa said sadly.

"I think I'll be dead before she does that," Henry said. "When she commits to something, it's all the way. I don't think she'll ever even consider anything that hurts us."

"Maybe so," Lisa said. "She's my girlfriend. You have a special relationship with her."

"Sometimes, I wish I'd never had sex with her."

"Henry! Why?"

"It was a transaction. That's how she considered it. I promised to always take care of her and she promised to always be available to me," Henry said. "I wanted our relationship to be built on our friendship and love, not on a transaction. And the thing is, I don't know how to stop it. I try not to just take advantage of her, but she feels she isn't keeping up her end of the bargain if I don't. When she comes into my office, she still perches on my desk in exactly the way she said she would do before we even established the LLC."

"You keep that edge of your desk clear of everything else, I've noticed," Lisa giggled. They kissed each other and gently petted.

"That's true. It's always available for her. I don't go around trying to get her to kiss me or let me feel her up. But I think she would be hurt if I didn't accept her when she offered herself like that. I love her way too much to ever hurt her."

"She loves you, too."

"Isn't that strange? She's not *my* girlfriend."

"No, she's mine. But I'm also part of how you take care of her. I just don't have the history of being with her when she was selling herself," Lisa said. "You've lived through it all with her."

"It was a long time before I figured out what was going on. How blind was I? When she put up her $1,000 as her share of the LLC, she had sex with three guys to get the money. And I didn't even know! When we opened the corporation and put up the money we'd gotten from the sale of our first license agreement, she took me home to have sex. She said one day that money would be worth a billion dollars. What happens if the company fails? It would destroy her!"

"Henry, my love? Your heart is big and open. You can never fail her. That's what forever really means. Do you know that if you and I broke up, I'd still be her girlfriend and she'd still be in your bed whenever you wanted? And if you didn't tell her you wanted, she'd find a way to suggest it. I'm one of those gifts you gave her, and I take care of her on your behalf. I love you for it. And so does she."

Their kisses became more important than their conversation, and even though they had just had sex with Chastity in their bed, they took their time to love each other and make sure each came to their fulfillment again before they finally dozed off to sleep.

37

GROWTH AND PRINCIPLES

HENRY TRIED TO maintain consistent participation in his study group, even though his class load was lighter than the others and he wasn't on campus as much or as long as they were. He was often gone by noon and since his courses were all electives, none happened to be shared by his study partners. He had *Subword Modeling* for two hours on Tuesday and Thursday. *Monte Carlo Methods and Applications* and *Family History and Social Understanding* were each an hour a day on Tuesday, Wednesday, and Thursday.

As a result, the study group decided to meet once a week at the row house in the fourth floor lounge. The study sessions usually started with a pizza and went well into the night on Wednesdays. Lisa had suggested the arrangement, and it had worked out well.

Until Chastity moved in. She had everything ready to move out of her apartment a week before the end of the month, so rather than wait until she had to be out, Henry, Lisa, and Luke helped her move a week early. They were all still trying to figure out how the new dynamic in the house worked without expecting her to start every night in Lisa and Henry's bed.

When the study group met Wednesday night, Chastity brought a couple of her course books to the fourth floor as well. She was still catching some online courses to finish her AA degree. Her own studies had slowed down as soon as the company was formed.

"Mind if I join you to study tonight?" she asked as she walked into the lounge.

Chastity was dressed like Chastity. The weather was still warm and the fourth floor was comfortable, so the shape-hugging booty shorts and crop top were appropriate for a casual study session. Everyone else was still wearing shorts, though perhaps not as revealing as Chastity's.

"Oh, hell yeah," Dan said. "You can sit right here on my lap. I don't mind at all."

"Excuse me?" Chas said.

Henry stood, but Leonard and Josh both rounded on Dan. Dan had been more and more an outsider to the group as they progressed through the program. It was generally known that he'd been the one who tipped off the army captain the previous spring as to Henry's likely involvement in the Chinese affair. They'd all been careful about what they said around him since then.

"Dude, seriously?" Josh said. "You speak to a woman like that?"

"What? Look at how she's dressed."

"What difference does that make?" Leonard asked. "We're talking about your comments, not her."

Josh, Lisa, Leonard, and Simon had all worked on contracts for Open Cloak and had seen Chastity in many jaw-dropping outfits. Regardless, they weren't about to comment on it in a professional or collegial environment, nor anywhere else for that matter. Simon immediately stood up and positioned himself between Chastity and the offensive person, asking her what she was studying and subtly moving them away slightly. Lisa went to join them.

"Look, a woman dresses like that, she wants some action. No question. What's she even doing here? You said this wasn't an office any longer."

"She lives here," Henry growled. Dan looked puzzled.

"How was I to know that?"

"Why would it make a difference?" Josh asked. "We're in Henry's home. He can have anyone here he wants. And I can't imagine he wants you. You organized our hackathon when we tried to break into his server. You squealed to the first cute woman you saw after the Chinese affair and pointed out Henry. You've been getting more and more gross as time goes by. What is your problem?"

"You have no evidence I said anything," Dan said nervously.

"Captain Bernard was by to visit a couple of times this summer at our office. Seems she became kind of attached to Conrad and insisted on a full disclosure when he came to work for us," Henry said.

"Shit! You can't trust a woman! She said no one would ever know," Dan said.

"Guys, I hate to put it this way, but we can continue to meet with our study group on campus from now on," Henry said. "Or we can continue to meet here without Dan. Gather up your shit and get out of my house, Dan."

"That is just not fair! I've been part of this group since the first day we were on campus!"

"If you'd said something like that to me, I'd have kicked you in the balls," Simon said, rounding on Dan. "After I slapped your face."

"I'm sick of not having a girl. Lisa wouldn't have anything to do with me after our first date as freshmen."

"Last date," Lisa said. "First and last date."

"Yeah, well, whatever. You're just a cunt," Dan said. "Played your sex up to get in Henry's bed I'll bet."

Henry had been trying to keep his cool—especially since the other guys had taken up the crusade. This comment, however, was too much. Henry slugged Dan in his abundant stomach and Dan doubled over.

"I told you to get out of my house," Henry said calmly.

"Fuck you! Fuck you all and the cunts you rode in on!" Dan dragged his bag as he stumbled toward the stairs. Leonard and Josh closed behind him to escort him out of the house.

Chastity was leaning on Lisa and Simon had returned to comforting her.

"Are you okay, babe?" Henry asked, stroking her cheek with his finger.

"I'm sorry," she said. "This was all a bad idea. I didn't mean to cause a problem."

"You didn't cause the problem," Henry said. "The problem was sitting in the room with us. There will never be a time when you aren't welcome in any gathering where Lisa and I are."

"Or me!" Simon chimed in. "You are the coolest woman I know. Want to be my bestie?"

"Oh, Simon," Chastity laughed. "I've been your bestie since the first time we met."

"Let's go shopping Saturday," Lisa said brightly.

"Oh, yes!" Simon exclaimed.

Leonard and Josh returned to the room.

"Is everybody okay?" Josh asked. "We can all take off if you want us to."

"No. Stay," Lisa said. "I have a pile of studying. Did any of you take *Deep Learning Systems: Algorithms and Implementation?*"

"I looked at that course and ran away screaming," Leonard said. "I'll listen though if you want to review something."

"We're supposed to build a complete deep learning library from scratch, capable of efficient GPU-based operations. I think I could have devoted my entire semester just to this course," Lisa said.

They had soon settled in for the evening, forgetting all about the unpleasantness with Dan.

DAN DID HIS best on campus to cast shade at the other members of the study group, but the five of them were generally well-liked and considered to be the stars of the program. Henry was looking forward to when they were all graduates and he could hire them full-time. He'd never really had that feeling about Dan.

The thing was that he could see a geometrically growing need for more people in the near future. They had released the network versions of both the optimization app and the search engine. He'd shifted the two testers over to primarily focus on Darrel's plan for the server security program and to test *Forever Yours*. Conrad was trying to manage all the projects and he had no dedicated developers to put on the security program.

If they were going to need more developers, they were going to also need more funding. Luke and Isobel were spending the bulk of their office time working on the company prospectus. Henry arranged a meeting for the second Monday of October with Professor Jacoby and suggested they meet at the office. Henry wanted to show off the business to his advisor.

"THIS IS A nice setup," Jacoby said when he was greeted by Nancy at the front desk. Henry quickly joined him. "I saw the interview in HBR last week. You have a dynamic leader for your company. Luke, is it?"

"Luke's been one of my best friends for all my life," Henry said. "I'm just glad he turned out to have a business mind like my coding mind. He'll join us in a little bit. He has a Monday morning class."

"The article is just what you needed if you are looking for more funding," Jacoby said. "Do you have a current sales report?"

"Our quarterly report comes out next week. If we have continued interest with you, we'll forward it as an addendum to the prospectus," Henry said. "We won't be profitable yet, but we are generating income."

"That's good to hear."

They went to the conference room and Henry gave Jacoby the outline of their development progress and what he considered to be his pressing needs for more developers. He figured that for the next couple of months, he could have Leonard and Simon join Josh and Lisa as ten-hour per week contractors and start developing the security program.

"We're at a point where we could use an actual program manager, too," Henry said. "We've had both Lisa and Darrel filling that role, but that's not either of their strong suit."

"And what about your legacy creation app? You've decided to call it *Forever Yours*?"

"Yes. I plan to write a research paper based on it, too. We've discovered some interesting things that surprised me."

"How so?"

"I've put the exact same data on two different computers and installed the exact same AI on each. I set the same training parameters. Scientifically, the same inputs should yield the same outputs. But that's not the case. After setting up the same parameters and asking the same questions of the two AIs, we got two different answers. The longer we trained the AIs and the more questions we fed them, always keeping the parameters the same, the more the answers diverged."

"Randomness?"

"I think so, but the thing is the answers all have the same tone and use similar phrasing. It's just as if you asked a random person the same question on two different days. They'd give you the same answer for the most part, but they'd use different words and phrasing. You'd still identify it as being from the same person."

"You need to start your doctoral work," Jacoby said.

"I don't even know if I have time to finish my BS," Henry laughed.

"I hope so. Can I see one of the tests?"

"We can do one live."

Henry had used the search engine to scrape the internet for all it could find on a specific public personage. The person was recently deceased, so new material was not being generated as frequently as it had been during the person's life. Henry had no intention of releasing this in any form, but it was strictly here to test the performance of the AI. In fact, he didn't reveal who the person was.

He used a combined input interface for the two instances of the AI and fed in some of the standard questions.

"Do you have any fears you think are irrational?"

"Do you have a talent you consider useless?"

"What scares you the most?"

In each instance, the answers were not the same, but had similarities that let one easily believe the same person had answered.

"I wonder if you could control the overall temperament of how the person responds," Jacoby said thoughtfully.

"Would that be fair?"

"A comedy company popular several years ago once put out a sketch in which they could dial a scene in for a different style. They had a scene with the exact same script and staging, but they dialed up 'funny,' for example, and the setting turned brighter, the presentation and facial characteristics got lighter, and the overall presentation was just funnier. Then they dialed up 'irony' and the scene was suddenly filled with subtle innuendo. The scene outside the window changed to something completely contradictory to what the actor was saying. I look at your app here, and I think the difference between these two instances could be that the person being questioned is in a different mood. This one answered as if it was a little depressed. Giving you the answer, but sounding a little down about it. The other feels more neutral in its response."

"We're not controlling that, though," Henry said. "Still, I see what you mean. The further down this path we go, the more they are each developing a personality. One of the embodiments of the singularity is a little darker than the other."

Luke joined the two for lunch and presented the prospectus for the company, doing a great job of selling the idea of investing in the next phase of the company's development.

"We're looking more for a long-term commitment from investors rather than a sudden cash infusion," Luke said. "We'd like to see an investor or investor group who will commit to $100 million over four years. The first $25 million will purchase preferred non-voting stock at $1.25 per share. The investment each of the following years would continue to be $25 million per year, but common stock would be purchased at a ten percent discount below market value. We believe we can be stably profitable and ready for an IPO at that time."

"That's ambitious. Why the non-voting shares for the first round?" Jacoby asked.

"It is critical that we maintain control over the company for at least two years," Luke said. "We've studied investment capitalization and find that giving up too much control in the early stages tends to kill both motivation and productivity. Fledgling companies are too often purchased and then disassembled into things that can be sold for a profit. We have a number of patents that have not yet appeared in products, but are planned in the near future. It would cripple the company to have those patents sold off for a short term profit."

"I see. Well, I'm not the chief investor in our consortium. I'm not sure if we have $100 million to toss into a company at the moment. But I like what I see. Your prospectus is nicely done. Send me an income statement current through the third quarter and I'll present the whole thing to our management team," Jacoby said.

They weren't sure if it was really a positive sign, or if they were being gently humored. Nonetheless, Luke promised to forward the requested statement.

"It's NICE TO see six figures for income," Henry said the next week when the board met at his house. The network optimization and network search applications were still fledgling apps, but with Henry's second Grey's Analysis interview and Luke's HBR interview, substantial interest was being generated in the company. Sales revenue from EMEE came in at over $130,000 for the quarter.

"We're a long way from profitability," Luke sighed, "but we're making progress."

"We're going to eat that progress up by hiring new people, though," Isobel said. "We're just drowning in a bigger pool."

"It's going to improve, babe," Luke calmed her. "We've only been in business with a product for eleven months."

"I know," she snapped, shaking his hand off hers. "How soon does *Forever Yours* get to market?"

"It's in final testing," Henry said. "Lisa made a few last adjustments to the UI last week that gives us better display of still images. The app is now in the hands of all the people who have been compiling their content. It is in the training stage and they are all reporting good results."

"It will be nice to sell something for $495 instead of $4.95," Isobel said.

"Remember, this is a higher ticket item, but it's higher cost as well. It's fulfilled by physical delivery and at that price, it won't sell anywhere near the number of copies," Henry said. "Fortunately, I'm slated for another interview on *Grey's Analysis* next week to coincide with the release. Then I'm supposed to meet with the editor of *AI Today* the week after that for an interview. Darla is trying to get it out in a variety of publications."

"What are we doing to promote it?" Luke asked. "It seems like no one will buy into it if they can't see it working?"

"I can cover some of that," Chastity said. "I worked with Darla to place a copy with a few influencers who agreed to record their stories and make them public. We sent them out a month ago. The content has been uploaded to a server out in California—the same company that hosts *Pythia Speaks*. Henry installed the AI and the test subjects can continue to upload content for the training. What's more, Henry's parents, Lisa's parents, and Lisa's grandparents have all agreed to make their content public. Ads will run in magazines and online, linking to the apps so people can ask questions and get answers from these people."

"I've also done training walls for my grandparents. They've all been dead for years, so the walls are of content scraped together from things I found in Mom and Dad's attic and information that I was able to find on the internet— which was a surprising amount when I set our search engine to finding it. All told, there will be twenty people with public *Forever Yours* sites," Henry said.

"And it's all complete and ready to go?" Isobel asked. The astonishment was hard to conceal.

"The first release will not include video creation, and still images will be limited to existing images, not generative. Our first upgrade will be to search and use video, and then we'll work on doing generative AI on the video and still images," Henry said. "The project will grow significantly over the next year. Some of the pieces are really hard and that's part of why we need more experienced developers."

"I feel like only being in the office ten hours a week or so since going back to school this fall has really left me out of the loop," Luke said. "Thanks to both of you for spearheading this next release. I think that we need to approve the new hires, even without having another round of investment lined up."

"Agreed," Chastity said.

"Agreed," Henry responded.

Isobel looked hard at her screen and tapped another key.

"Okay. I agree. I just want to see the numbers rocket," she said.

"WE DIDN'T REALLY talk about Pythia in the meeting," Luke said as he and Henry sat together after the meeting. Isobel had joined Chastity for a tour of her suite. "Everything on track?"

"More than on track," Henry said. "We uploaded the new version with subscriptions and forums. Subscriptions are a little slow coming in, but they're picking up. We're running four servers out at Page Services now and it looks like we'll see our first 10,000 hit day by the end of the year."

"That's cool. Why so many servers?"

"Speed mostly. And redundancy. The search engine continues to uncover new sources of content based on keywords in what has already been found or based on what people have asked it. Once the content is found, it has to be included in the AI training. It's becoming quite sophisticated in its responses," Henry said.

"Her," Luke said. "I know it's just a computer program, but Isobel insists Pythia is a woman giving out women's wisdom."

"I really hate to think women's wisdom is a random selection of vague statements generated from ancient sources," Henry said. "I'll try to remember to refer to it as her when I'm around Izzy."

"Seriously, 10,000 hits in a day is some significant traffic. Isn't there any way we can use that to drive sales of *Forever Yours*?"

"We will. Izzy's idea of putting 'Powered by Open Cloak AI' on the screen was good. We added our web address with a link to the *Forever Yours* landing page. We're already seeing traffic referred by the link, even though we haven't started sales yet. It's going to be interesting."

"Here's to more interest, if not interesting times," Luke chuckled, tapping his pop can against Henry's.

38

SINGULARITY

"HELLO, AND WELCOME to *Grey's Analysis*. This is your host, Gene Grey, and we are launching our 122ⁿᵈ edition. For today's chat, I'm happy to have returning Henry Pascal of Open Cloak Design. Henry, this is your third time on the show this year, which I think is some kind of record. It's always nice to have you join us."

"Thank you, Gene. It seems things have been popping for Open Cloak all year."

"I understand you are in a new location now."

"Yes. We moved into offices the first of July and now we have full time employees, so it's not just my partners and me anymore."

"In the course of the past year, you released the Open Cloak Optimization app and the Open Cloak Search Engine?" Gene asked.

"And network editions of each of those," Henry added.

"There's another... what do you call it? I don't think I have a software category for *Pythia Speaks*. I do know, though, that it is incredibly addictive. Do you call it a chat bot?"

"That would be pretty close, though it doesn't behave like most chat bots you might be familiar with," Henry said. "We call it an oracle."

"Explain the difference."

"You don't really attempt to hold a conversation with Pythia. You ask a question and she gives you an answer. The answer is in plain English, but it isn't designed for you to talk it over with her. You might put her in the same classification as a horoscope, or *I Ching*, or Tarot, or some such. If there's a discussion to be had, you have it with yourself."

"I've certainly had a few of those. How did *Pythia Speaks* come about?"

"It was really a testbed for a new product we're announcing this week. You know we've been working with artificial intelligence applications. Part of our research has been to use specialized small language models to train an AI in a single area, thus reducing the AI footprint, power consumption, and relevance of the responses."

"How many people are using it?"

"It's still pretty small. We made some significant upgrades to Pythia in the past few weeks and we're seeing a sharp incline in usage. This week we had our first 8,000 query day. I would expect over 10,000 per day by Thanksgiving. So, small by comparison to most chat bots or search engines."

"But increasing. Does that make it a growing revenue platform for Open Cloak?"

"No. Like I said, Pythia was created as a testbed for some new technology, not as a profit center. It runs pretty automatically, without interference from our office. Even what we consider premium features recently released, like subscription registration, forums, and retention of conversations, are all available free."

"With advertising?"

"Also, no. The only thing that could be considered advertising is the single link at the bottom of the page to our company website. We don't collect user information or sell advertising."

"Why? It's obviously becoming popular and looks like it could be a cash cow. Why leave it free?"

Henry sighed and collected his thoughts for a moment.

"We've done some analysis on the kind of questions and answers that fuel Pythia. And remember, we make no guarantees regarding how useful her answers will be. It is for entertainment purposes only. But the questions asked are often—no, I'd say usually—pretty serious. They include relationship issues, job issues, people who are deeply upset or joyful or in mourning or celebrating. It just doesn't seem right to charge them for sharing those questions and feelings. Does it to you, Gene?"

"Ah. Well. No, I suppose it doesn't when you put it that way. But we're not used to a company acting on what is right or wrong or altruistically when there is money to be made."

"I agree. And I don't want to sound like all of Open Cloak is a charity. Our financial manager reminds us repeatedly that we are not supposed to be a nonprofit. We've worked very hard to create good software applications that are worth the money we charge for them. We have a strong profit motive. There are just some things we shouldn't take advantage of."

"So, no other future for *Pythia Speaks*?"

"That's where we get into a new application announcement," Henry said. "I mentioned that *Pythia Speaks* was intended to be a testbed to see if we could be more efficient with a specialized small language model than generative AI is with a large language model. We consider that test to be successful."

"What's coming?"

"Are you familiar with Ray Kurzweil's books *The Singularity is Near* and *The Singularity is Nearer?* I think he may soon be able to write *The Singularity is Here.*"

"Now you really have me on a hook, Henry. Are you talking about the consolidation of man and machine? Immortality?"

"That's never really been the vision. Let's say that you'll live on, but you'll still be dead."

"How can you do both?" Gene asked.

"We use the word immortal to refer to things that live on, even after the source is dead. For example, in the words of the immortal bard, 'The evil men do lives after them. The good is oft interrèd with their bones.' We all recognize that Shakespeare is dead, but we refer to him as immortal because his works continue to live on."

"So, it's really the same as it is now. People can look up what you said, but you won't be speaking to them," Gene said with a note of disappointment.

"Sort of. Our new platform is called *Forever Yours*. In this case, what you said is given a new dimension. It isn't 'alive,' but it's living. Let's stick with Shakespeare's works—his plays, his poetry, and any correspondence we could find to or from him or mentioning him. That becomes the wall on which we train our AI. That AI can only answer questions in the words of the bard. However, it might learn new combinations of words based on other ways they were used. So, the AI might answer a hypothetical question by saying, 'Your life is your legacy, good or ill.' That's not quite the same thing we quoted earlier. It's plausible that Shakespeare *could* have said it. When combined with images of the bard, or even animations, it comes to life and is consistent with his works. But it isn't poetic. It's a good summary of the meaning, but it lacks Shakespeare's creativity."

"How does that relate to people today and the singularity?" Gene probed.

"You could upload everything about yourself to a kind of private wall and train the AI on it. Let's go beyond the stories you remember and the photos and videos you upload. Let's let the AI have access to all your social media accounts, your podcasts, your high school and college transcripts, the records of what you spent money on, and the recollections and contributions of those people closest to you. Maybe even the places you've visited. You give your descendant access to *Forever Yours*. Then you die."

"That's encouraging, isn't it? But everything I've done and said is given to the AI and it can answer like me, the same way your Shakespeare AI did?"

"Exactly. It has the record of your life and can sift through that as it is being trained. So, when your descendant has a question, he goes to *Forever Yours* and says, 'Dad, I think I'm in love. She's really sweet and we get along great. But is it real? How do I know I'm really in love?' You might or might not have ever said anything about how to tell you're in love, but the AI sifts through all the information it has about you and compiles an answer for your descendant."

"But I didn't actually say what they hear!"

"No. It's just an answer consistent with other things you've said."

"So, in a way, I'm living on because my thoughts and words are being used to answer new questions I never considered before. Immortality," Gene said.

"Yes. But *you're* dead. Your consciousness is not part of the machine. Depending on how strong a wall it has compiled, it might even give answers that are totally irrelevant. That often happens with *Pythia Speaks*. It doesn't have an exact match for a question, so it compiles what it deduces would be the most likely response."

"What's the downside, Henry? It seems like my descendants could benefit from my words of wisdom," Gene said.

"Well, aside from the fact that you're dead in this scenario, the first downside is in who has access to you. Maybe your descendant thinks everyone should have access to his dad's wisdom. So, he makes it public. Then you have something like Pythia that grows and adds data to her wall based on questions everyone asks. Eventually, the voice of Dad is no longer giving answers you might plausibly have given, but is expanding its training wall with irrelevant bits and pieces. Maybe you've got people asking you for twenty dollars and the car keys. All you can say is 'no.' The whole system, including *Pythia Speaks*, is designed simply to answer questions. She cannot grant wishes. Essentially, that is the same way the great oracles of ancient Greece worked."

"Okay, I guess. It's a little scary, but I can live with it. Or be dead with it. This can get confusing, can't it?"

"More than you imagine. One of the great dangers I see is people depending on the AI for answers and not thinking things through for themselves. It's the old saga of people blindly following the GPS instructions off a ferry dock or down a dead-end road. Society changes. There are new fashions. New behaviors are acceptable that weren't acceptable when you were alive. Ethics, morals, culture, music—it all changes. But the people asking you only see a snapshot of the time when you were alive. *Forever Yours* can't anticipate how you would respond in the new world."

"Hmm. They could be getting advice that is completely out of date. It just happens to be what I might say."

"Yes," Henry said. "It's not a new problem. In fact, it's the Shakespeare example again. It is derived from a snapshot of his life and times. The wisdom is not always going to be wise. You see that all the time with religious writings and the people who follow them. They were written at a specific time with a specific understanding of the world, and they were locked in. So, we have people studying this thousand-year-old or ten-thousand-year-old snapshot and trying to apply it to a society and culture that have changed by multiple orders of magnitude."

"I need to let that sink in for a while," Gene said. "May I ask a question about the technology itself?"

"I'll answer if I can. Some things we have to hold closely to protect the IP."

"Of course. There are eight billion people in the world. Let's narrow that down to a third of a billion people in the US. We're told that AIs require trillions of parameters to function well. Are we headed to a time when there are entire cities of nothing but AI servers?"

"That *is* a frightening prospect. I'll answer it based on what we project," Henry said. "It's true that a generative chat AI uses a couple trillion parameters and consumes enough energy to power at least five million homes each year. But there are specialized small language models that are more economical, faster, and don't generate as much heat. They might have only seven or eight billion parameters. Their power consumption might be equivalent of powering a small city for a few days. We anticipate—though there has to be a lot more research done on this yet—that a singularity AI focused on the legacy of a single person might take less than a billion parameters to be fully operative and run on the equivalent of a car battery. We're talking about storage that is measured in gigabytes instead of petabytes. And with a few new tweaks to the AI engine itself, we might be able to cut the footprint even further."

"Henry, I want to thank you for taking time to be on *Grey's Analysis*. You've given us a lot to think about. Some of it is exciting and some is frightening. And a lot, I can't make up my mind about yet. It's both exciting and frightening. To all our viewers, it's your turn to discuss the topic. This is Gene Grey signing off."

THE INTERVIEW AIRED the following Monday and the release of Forever Yours was announced on Wednesday. The office was busy celebrating and watching for comments. But they had more to deal with on Friday.

"Captain Bernard, welcome to Open Cloak," Henry said when the young army captain arrived at the office. Conrad stood beside Henry and smiled at his girlfriend.

"Mr. Pascal, it is a pleasure to meet you again. May I pass on the greetings of General Schwartz?" she said.

"General? Certainly. Thank you. Conrad, why don't you give a tour and let me know when we're ready to start in the conference room," Henry said.

He went to his office and Conrad conducted the captain around the office, pointing out the things that had changed since her last visit. It wasn't long before the couple met with Henry and Darrel in the conference room. Nancy wheeled a cart of refreshments in behind them and then left, closing the door softly behind her.

"We have invited Captain Bernard here to review the spec for our commercial level network defense system," Conrad said to get the meeting started.

"Conrad, let's dispense with titles," the captain said. "If you all don't mind, I'm Rebecca. I'd love to take off my jacket."

"Please do," Henry said. "I'm Henry and I think you've met Darrel before as well. Darrel is the author of the spec we want to develop and release."

"Is this the entire team?" Rebecca asked, shaking out her blonde hair.

"So far," Henry said. "We're shopping for at least one more developer for the project so Conrad can focus on management."

"Okay," Rebecca said. "Then congratulations. You have stirred a pot full of controversy at the Pentagon once again. Let me say there are a few of the brass there who still aren't happy with the deal General Schwartz cut with you last spring. They are, however, in the minority, and the general has powerful backing for continuing our relationship."

"I guess I'm happy to hear that," Henry said. "Please enlighten us."

"Well, the biggest objection is from those who believe the government should own this and have exclusive use of it. Even they are in favor of the posting of your office as a military asset and keeping CIA, FBI, and anyone else off premises. But General Schwartz has pointed out that the methods and processes used in the defense system are patented and available for study by anyone. Only your unique application of them has created the defense system everyone is interested in. He holds—and top brass affirm—that the development and marketing of such a system belong in the private sector, and we should limit our direct involvement to ways in which we can capitalize on the development and possible ways we can influence your direction," Rebecca said.

"Are you planning to write specifications for us?" Darrel asked. He was the most suspicious of the Defense Department's involvement with the company, even though they had been fairly hands-off.

"Not exactly," Rebecca said. "There is an area or two that we question your implementation plan, but mostly we'd like your input to *our* specification for DoD's equivalent of your defense project. We've been working on our spec basically since we received the license last spring and may share some of the same features you have specified in yours. We believe they are close enough together that we could contract the development to Open Cloak, capitalizing on the overlap in both directions."

"You don't have requirements for our spec?" Henry said.

"A couple of suggestions, but not requirements. On the other hand, we'd want strict adherence to our spec for the version you sell to us."

"It's feeling like we're going to need more people than we budgeted," Henry said.

"If we can work out an arrangement, DoD has resources to assist with that," Rebecca said. "The biggest problem might be in cementing the security arrangements for the DoD product, though we think we can get around that by doing an agency check – that's running the names of people with access to the product past the FBI, NSA, CIA, etc., to see if any concerns pop up—and compartmentalizing the key modules that are different for the DoD version."

From that point, they got down to basics, reviewing the two specifications side by side. There was significant overlap, but the army version was focused on broader security than any specific network. It needed to function across departments and operations to provide national security.

Eventually, Rebecca revealed the Pentagon was willing to place two people in the office and to fund two more positions for Open Cloak development. That led to a separate meeting with the board in Luke's office. The result was a new $5 million contract that both sides needed to have reviewed by attorneys and then signed.

By Election Day, the contract had been signed and the company received an initial payment of a million dollars. A development contract like this would change the complexion of Open Cloak's finances significantly.

Of course, much of that initial payment was earmarked for the development itself. Henry was interviewing for two new developer positions to work on the project and a third to work specifically on power issues. That last would be a tricky position to fill because there weren't many power specialists who understood the potential of AI tools.

The company also received equipment to set up an entire sub-office for the security project. Henry trusted General Schwartz and, mostly Captain Bernard, but he didn't want people in his office who didn't report to Open Cloak attached to his corporate server. They set up a miniature network with a server and all the software needed for the development, including the current code for the defense software. A section of the office had been partitioned off and required RFID access for the members of the team to work with each other. They had a separate internet connection that did not go through the company server. They could send and receive email from the company, but could not download files.

Henry was unboxing computers and preparing to help Darrel with the setup when the older man stepped into the room on Wednesday morning.

"Hey, boss. Congratulations," Darrel said as he moved to break down boxes. "Pythia hit a new milestone."

"That's good news," Henry said. "Did we hit the 10,000 query mark?"

"Blew past it about eleven yesterday morning. We closed the day at midnight Pacific time with over 25,000 queries," Darrel laughed.

"Whoa! 25,000? What happened? Was there a robo attack? Did the servers handle it okay?"

"Not a single hiccup. And no sign of it having been automated. It was 25,000 unique queries."

"How could that happen?"

"Your interview with Gene Grey happened."

"That was, like, two weeks ago."

"Yes, but it's been discovered. He cross-posts on YouTube a week after his own channel and it went viral. The interview has half a million votes and people are rushing to try out *Pythia Speaks*."

"Can you take over here? I need to check in with the partners and figure out what effect this is all having on our projections."

Henry hurriedly left the mini-office and went to look at the statistics himself.

39

UNEXPECTED SUCCESS

THE PARTNERS MET with Darla Gallitzin in Luke's office on Monday. The last three days of the previous week had been frantic. The number of queries to *Pythia Speaks* continued to climb. About one out of ten users followed the link that led to the *Forever Yours* landing page. One of twenty-five people who hit the landing page eventually bought *Forever Yours*.

"That doesn't sound like so much when you look at the percentage," Darla said. "Just four-tenths of a percent in sales. But Pythia had 35,000 hits on Friday. That came down to 140 sales of *Forever Yours*. We didn't anticipate that many sales in the first six months of release. It's a high-ticket item. Of the $495 price, EMEE collects $145. The cost of goods and shipping comes to $91.40. That means a royalty payment of just over $250 per copy. Friday's sales netted $35,000."

"Holy shit! And I was happy to get the payment from the government. This is going to change things drastically," Isobel said.

"Well, with success comes the pain," Darla said. "First of all, EMEE was not prepared for the volume. They ran out of stock for the drives last week. They have about two hundred back orders as of this morning and are placing rush orders from the manufacturer. Statistically, when orders are not shipped within twenty-four hours, two in five are canceled. EMEE has one employee devoted to flashing the drives and packaging them for shipment. I've sent an assistant to Savannah to negotiate shipping costs on their behalf. And shipments aren't just going to the US. Shipping costs will be greater for overseas customers, not to mention VAT and Tariffs."

"But if the number keeps growing..." Chastity said. "I mean we went from 9,000 to 25,000 queries a day overnight and 35,000 within three days. Daily! Your number can't include all the sales since the release of *Forever Yours*."

"I gave you an adjusted percentage based on the past week," Darla said. "What you will see is the percentage dwindling, but still feeling pretty consistent."

"Why's that?" Luke asked.

"A significant portion of daily visits to *Pythia Speaks* is repeat visitors," Darla explained. "If four-tenths of a percent of Friday's 35,000 bought, the likelihood is that only one-tenth of a percent of today's 50,000 visitors will buy because over half of that 50,000 will have already been to the site and made their decision to purchase or not purchase. The total will still look something like 100-150 units sold. Of course, these are all projections. We just don't have enough history to get a real number on it."

"I can't believe we're looking at 50,000 visitors," Henry said. "How is *Pythia Speaks* holding up?"

"She's expanded to six servers," Darla said. "Response time is still holding under ten seconds. Like the orders for *Forever Yours*, a proportion of the queries are coming from outside the US. As long as the question is phrased in English, Pythia responds."

"I asked a question Tuesday morning," Isobel said. "I know you said she was non-political, but I asked who I should vote for."

"How'd it... she respond to that?" Henry asked.

"She said, 'A pure heart will make a pure choice.' I wonder how many people asked the same question and how many different answers she gave," Isobel said.

"I'll review the logs and see what they say," Henry said.

"It's not all positive," Darla broke in. "There are crackpots out there who believe you, Henry, are the devil incarnate, offering eternal life to the damned. They believe you said the Bible, the Koran, and other sacred texts are irrelevant because the world has changed. There is even a meme floating around that has cut your statement from the interview that, 'The wisdom is not always going to be wise. You see that all the time with religious writings and the people who follow them.' Those people who believe the religious writings—even a little—are ready to go to war against you."

"Well, they aren't exactly incorrect in their assessment of where I stand," Henry said.

"It's a hornets' nest," Darla warned. "We've even seen a small number of death threats against you. To those people, you are the next worst thing to an abortion doctor. Most of this chatter is just venting. They are on about the same plane as threats against a billionaire for putting tracking nanochips in vaccines a few years ago. But we have to consider the possibility there are some credible threats out there. We'll forward all those to proper authorities."

"Well, that sucks," Henry said.

"Oh, honey," Chastity said, putting a hand on his arm. "We need to talk about physical security. If there's a threat against you, it could easily extend to all of us. I've been worried about this for a while but didn't have any data to put with it."

"You're right," Isobel said. "The boys go out and get in front of a camera, but they aren't the only ones in the sights. Even our office could be targeted."

"In all likelihood, just taking reasonable precautions will be enough to safeguard all of you. Monitor traffic coming into the office. Be aware of people who might be following you. Don't walk alone—especially at night," Darla said.

"In other words, act like a woman," Chastity said.

"What?" Luke asked.

"It's the way we have to act all the time. Don't accept a drink in a public place. Always leave together. Stay out of poorly lit areas. Get an escort to your car. Women have to live like that every day. Predators are everywhere."

"Shit. We're so blind to what's around us," Henry said. "I knew all that. It just never really sank in. I'm sorry to all of you."

"It's a good warning, but don't get paranoid," Darla said. "Our agency will continue to monitor all comments and track keywords on social media. We'll report anything that looks serious to the police. You have work to do. The purpose of these threats is to make you afraid to do your work. Don't let them."

"Thank you, Darla. Chastity, let's start putting together some ideas on corporate security," Luke said. "But we aren't going to slow down either the development or marketing of our products. We're on the cusp of doing something remarkable. Let's not let it get away."

TWO ARMY OFFICERS were waiting for Henry when he left the meeting with Darla.

"Captain Bernard," he said, greeting Rebecca. They were usually casual, but since she had a subordinate with her, he decided on the formality.

"Mr. Pascal, may I introduce Lt. Michael R. Smith of the Pentagon's Cyber Resilience team," Rebecca said. "The two of us have been assigned to your development team to work on the military grade version of the network defense system if it meets with your approval."

Henry shook hands with the tall and skinny black lieutenant. The uniform hung to his angular frame as if on a wire hanger. Henry wondered that anyone was allowed in the army with such large glasses.

"Welcome to Open Cloak, Lieutenant."

"Thank you, sir," he said straightening to a height of about six-four and towering over Henry's six-foot frame.

"Let's go back and get you set up and introduced to the rest of the team. We've got another new hire just finishing up paperwork with Conrad. By the way, here in the office, I just go by Henry. There is no need to call me Mr. Pascal. The only one in the office who insists on the use of her title is Mrs. Riordan, our financial manager. You can also refer to her as 'Her Highness.' Just not to her face."

"Thanks, Henry. I'm Rebecca and this is Mike. It appears we'll be assigned here for at least six months. When army personnel are assigned to a civilian office, we are not required to wear uniforms so, with your permission, we'll go to regular business attire tomorrow," Rebecca said.

"Thank heavens! The uniforms are nice, but a little intimidating in a small office like ours. Here's where we'll make magic happen." Henry led them into the mini office where six desks were arranged to all have a view out the window.

"Wow! I expected a cubicle in the basement," Mike said.

"Just because that's where we keep you at the Pentagon, doesn't mean it's your equivalent in the civilian world," Rebecca laughed. "Remember, I don't even have a window at HQ."

"It's a pleasure to know our office is an upgrade," Henry said. "Ah, here's Conrad and Leanne."

Conrad entered the small office with a woman of indeterminate ethnic background. Her skin tone was slightly darker than that of Henry, but could have been Latina or Middle Eastern or Mediterranean. She appeared to be in her mid to late thirties.

"Conrad and Leanne, let me introduce you to our two army staff, Rebecca and Mike," Henry said.

"Charmed," Leanne said, offering her hand first to Rebecca and then to Mike.

The single-syllable greeting belied any other thoughts about her heritage. She was obviously from the deep south.

The group went about setting up their workstations and chatting about the task they had at hand. Henry excused himself to work on his other projects. Conrad was in charge of this team. Henry wasn't sure how well it would work if he came in conflict with his girlfriend over the direction of the code. He'd wait and see.

HENRY CALLED SCOTT Perkins at Page Services. With the sharp increase in traffic, he wanted to be sure the server farm was prepared to handle things.

"We're in good shape, Henry," Scott said. "With our current setup and adding a couple more boxes, I believe we'll be able to handle half a million queries a day. We were caught a little flat-footed when the traffic started to spike last week, but we were back to speed in an hour."

"That's great to know, Scott. How about the hits on our *Forever Yours* sample pages?"

"You've got twenty pages being served there and each one is confined to its own partition, as you requested. They are getting a couple hundred hits a day. Average session is four queries. Data walls are scarcely growing at all. It looks really stable."

"I'm glad to have you as a partner in this," Henry said. "How many total servers do you have on your farm? I know it's smaller than some of the majors."

"We're currently running four hundred boxes. That's something that is definitely looking like a limiting factor for our corporate growth. We simply don't have room for more than a hundred more units. I've got Brenda out looking for space, but migrating everything might be more than we can handle. We'll give your boxes priority, but a lot of people want to get online. Hosting AI apps is increasing dramatically."

"How's power consumption?"

"As you can imagine, hardware and power are our two greatest expenses. Not only do we have the power requirements to run the machines, but for the air conditioning, too. The place can turn into a sauna in twenty minutes if the AC goes off. We're in danger of data loss and hardware loss within an hour."

"Backup power?" Henry asked.

"We have a generator. It could keep pace with reduced capacity, but not with a real outage. A major earthquake or an attack on the power company and we'd be toast. Our constant backup would allow us to reset to the point of interruption but whoever thought we'd be depending on external drives in this day and age?"

"We do here at Open Cloak," Henry said. "I've made a hire and he'll be starting right after Thanksgiving. He's a specialist in power management. We've toyed with some processes and even filed a patent or two for reducing power consumption. I'm hoping that putting a guy on it full time will let us move forward with it. I might need to send him out to visit you."

"He'll be welcome as long as he doesn't expect a luxury office to work in. We're pretty bare bones."

"I might be interested in investing and giving you a little capital infusion. If you don't have one, you might consider putting together a prospectus."

"Yeah. Judy's got some preliminary work on that. We'll step up the pace."

"Take care, Scott. We depend on you guys."

THANKSGIVING DINNER WAS served by Sylvia and Ryan, with Henry, Lisa, and Chastity as their guests. When they'd invited Henry and Lisa, Henry immediately asked if Chastity could be invited as well. Sylvia was surprised, but more than happy to have the extra guest.

"You've all been living in the row house for a couple of months now. How is it without the company occupying part of your space?" Ryan asked.

"So much has changed in that time," Henry said. "I think having a couple of cats makes up for not having six extra people, though."

"They don't take up that much room!" Lisa protested.

"I think they've decided Henry is okay," Chastity laughed. "Whenever I can't find one of them, all I have to do is look for Henry's lap. She'll be there."

"Or on my chair just before I sit down," Henry said.

"I never thought you would be much of one for pets," Sylvia said. "Although you did take good care of Oedipus."

"Who was Oedipus?" Lisa asked.

"A club-footed guinea pig I had in junior high," Henry said. "He was a sweetheart and would sit on my lap while I worked on the computer. Seriously, no one I know has ever had a guinea pig that just curled up on his lap."

"And how many carrots did he go through in that position?" Ryan asked.

"Oh, a few hundred. Speaking of which, I'd like some more sweet potatoes," Henry said.

"Who was speaking of sweet potatoes?" Lisa asked.

"They're the same color as carrots," Henry explained.

The banter at the dinner table was lively and enjoyable for all of them. They didn't make a big deal out of Chastity's relationship to either Henry or Lisa, but it was obvious there was more of a connection than just as a renter.

<hr>

"So, your *Forever* Yours page is getting a lot of hits," Henry said to Ryan. "It seems to give more complete answers to people's questions than most of the others. I think that's because your database is the largest. But I hope you are continuing to add to it. It will be interesting to compare answers from the public persona to answers from our private version."

"So, you aren't uploading more info to the public AI?" Sylvia asked.

"No. The AI can collect more data from questions that are asked, but it isn't out searching for new data from other sources. For one thing, I didn't want the public versions to expose too much of our families. And, like I said, I'd like to see how far the two AIs diverge from each other. Even in my tests, two identical setups yield different answers to questions."

"And *your* parents contributed, too, Lisa?" Sylvia asked.

"Parents and grandparents," she answered. "Grandpa is a great story-teller and loves recording things for his *Forever Yours* AI."

"I'm surprised his public persona isn't the most popular," Ryan said.

"I think the problem is that he records almost all his stories on video. We haven't really got the video component working yet. The AI could look up and play back a story, but it can't make one up and show it. I'll be interested to see comments from other people with the number of packages we've sold now. We've been contacted by a couple of the memoir writing companies to see if they can somehow integrate the AI into their workflow as well," Henry said. "I think it's possible. They are recording a memoir or history. We're trying to record a personality and a life."

"I've used three of the services and they've each sent me back a book," Ryan said. "The books are substantially the same, but each has a different style and presentation. Just asking a couple of the questions of the AI reveals a different set of answers. Some are more loquacious than others."

After dinner and cleanup, the family played a few tabletop games and then the trio went home.

<hr>

"You were awfully quiet, love," Lisa said. She sat next to Chastity in the back seat as Henry drove them home.

"I don't have much in the way of family stories to share," she said. "It's pretty yucky. I didn't want to be a downer for the party."

"Hon, you are definitely not a downer for us," Henry interjected as Lisa kissed Chastity. "And speaking of parties, what would you like for your birthday?"

Chastity's birthday was the twenty-seventh and always fell just a few days after Thanksgiving.

"Can you erase my past?" she asked.

"You sound serious," Lisa said. "Are you hurting?"

"I never thought I would, but I just want to forget about so much."

They arrived home and put the leftovers Sylvia had pushed them to take in the refrigerator. Then they played with the cats for a while before all going to Henry and Lisa's bedroom and cuddling together. It was obvious that Chastity continued to be down after the family gathering.

"Tell me what you want erased," Henry whispered to her.

Chastity turned her head toward him and began to cry.

"I still have men contacting me and trying to get dates. I don't mean dates like going to a movie. I mean dates like fucking me. They find me through one of the sites that still have my bio, even though I've dropped my membership. Or worse, a movie," Chastity said.

"You made movies?" Lisa asked, petting her hair.

"Not many. When I turned eighteen, I'd already been performing online for a year, lying about my age. The people who took me in charged me rent of joining them in bed twice a month, so I'd had plenty of experience. A company called me from LA and offered me an 'audition.' At least I managed to negotiate a little. They paid my expenses and $500 for a day of work. I had to spend half an hour masturbating to orgasm, then do a scene with a guy who was hung like a horse. He never got all that hard, but he used his cock like a whip to lash me and then managed to feed it inside until he came. I flew home. That was how I spent the weekend after Thanksgiving when we were seniors in high school."

"I wish I'd known or had been able to do something for you," Henry said.

"You were just a seventeen-year-old senior. You didn't have a way to help. Besides, I wasn't going to tell you about it. I already liked you and wanted to be around you and Luke and Isobel."

"Still..."

"Yeah. Still," Chastity said. She was lost in a kiss with Lisa as Henry held the two of them for a minute. "Over the winter holiday, I went back to LA. I shot a dozen scenes, and made $4,000. Then I told them goodbye and never went back. Those scenes keep resurfacing. Every time someone sees one, I get contacted through one of the sites, wanting me to come to work, go on a date, or just suck their dicks. And, of course, people recorded some of my 'performances' in my chat room. I'm so tired of it."

"Then I'll get rid of it," Henry said.

"Wait. Really?" Lisa asked. "You can do that?"

"I don't see why not."

"I know you said everything on the internet was temporary instead of permanent like we were all told," Chastity said. "But how will you even find it?"

"Well, it's a lot easier to lose things on the internet by accident than on purpose," he said. "But we're creating interesting ways to eliminate threats in our security development. I think if I can find it, I can eliminate it."

"Is that legal?" Lisa asked.

"Don't know. Don't care. What pornographer is going to complain?" Henry answered.

40

THE PURGE

HENRY HAD TAMPERED with online content before. He didn't tell anyone about it, but he kept the tools secreted away just in case he needed them. There had been the process of locating information on Tom Reynolds, distributing it to authorities, wiping out his bank accounts, and then removing every trace that he'd ever had anything to do with it, which included wiping email from an ISP.

When Kaitlyn tried to blackmail him into marrying her, he tracked down where the pressure was really coming from, rewrote her trust, and wiped all evidence that he'd ever been there.

Locating and purging video content was a different matter. It would attract too much attention to remove it. But video content wasn't that difficult to corrupt. He just had to find it first.

Henry's search AI had been in use and development for five years. The company had released a version of it and he handed it over to the team to create a network version, but one of the things about having a personal AI working on your searches was that it learned and expanded its base as it grew. Henry could also set degrees of separation parameters. If he discovered a computer with the content he wanted destroyed on it, he could also search any device connected to that computer. Henry set and refined search parameters repeatedly until he had discovered well over 300 videos on various servers and private computers.

When he first tested the counterattack software, he'd set the attack to simply change the file extension of a key file. That blanked the computer screen, but it was a simple fix to just reset the file extension. That was too simple for this job.

When he'd run the counterattack on the Chinese hackers, he couldn't risk them coming right back and getting to him again. He'd used a two-fold attack, installing a viral reverse optimization that scrambled the hard drive and letting that propagate to all the computers between the second and sixth degree. The 0, 1, 2 degree computers were completely wiped of all their content and system. That was too much for what he wanted to do with the video files.

He wanted people to attempt to launch the videos and get an error that the file was unplayable and probably corrupt. He didn't want to affect anything else on the computer. And he wanted any backup of the file that was uploaded or installed to automatically corrupt itself. So, the AI virus needed to be self-propagating.

For video content, scrambling the clock would make the file play poorly, but would not make it impossible to see. He wanted no trace of Chastity posing nude or being fucked. That would require randomizing the video signal itself. He would introduce unrelated code into the file and blocks of data from it. The best part of this was that if anyone compared two of the corrupt files, they would find they were corrupted in different ways.

He made sure Chastity backed up any images she wanted to keep and disconnected her computer from the internet. Then he also ran searches for her images on 'professional' sites and 'industry' social media sites. When he was certain that he had as much of her content located as he could find, he checked with her to be sure this was what she wanted.

"All I want to keep is my real identity and my money," she said. "As far as I'm concerned you can erase any other trace that I existed."

"Honey, are you sure?" Lisa asked. "Henry, can you even distinguish that kind of information that she would need and what she wouldn't? How about medical records?"

"I don't want to risk erasing you completely, Chas. We need to stick to content that is offensive to you. I'm ready to pull the trigger if you say to," Henry said.

"Do it," she said firmly.

Henry launched the corruption program and it began the process.

"Devices that are off line won't be affected until they connect," he said. "And it will take longer to locate files on cell phones. I'm not 100% sure that the search has located things residing on cell phones, though I've got a lot of confidence in it. It doesn't make a difference what operating system the device is running. This is going after a specific file type and we're going to get them all."

Henry turned from his computer in his chair. He saw Chastity stripping off all her clothes and standing before him and Lisa.

"Take me," she said. "However you want me. Whatever you want to do to me. Take me and use me. I'm free!"

"No!" Henry said, even as Lisa was reaching for her girlfriend. "What I just did might be illegal. Some might say it was immoral or unethical. But I did it because my friend was hurting. I did what directly affected her. And we *never* have sex just because someone thinks they're owed or because it's convenient. That was a promise I made to Lisa and I'll make it to you as well. Even if it means we can no longer be lovers, I'm nullifying the transaction. I love you and I care for you without expectation from you, now and forever."

"Then you listen to me, Henry Pascal," Chastity said straightening up in her naked glory. "Our relationship left the realm of a transaction years ago. I am a free woman and I'll do what my heart and my body tell me is right. And right now, it's right for me to show you how much I love you."

Chastity pulled Henry to her and kissed him, opening her mouth and thrusting her tongue into his. They continued for a breathless minute.

"Don't get used to that. I'm still not your girlfriend. But I am and will always be your lover."

She then turned to Lisa and drew her into a similar embrace. They kissed for significantly longer than she'd kissed Henry.

"You, however," Chastity gasped when they broke the kiss. "I *am your girlfriend.*"

⁂

DECEMBER WAS AN intense month for everyone at Open Cloak. Ari Patel started work the fourth and spent two days in seclusion with Henry mapping out a plan for power conservation. He'd worked in the power industry, developing software for power management from the utility perspective. He was ready to focus on power management from the consumer perspective. Henry stressed the importance of reducing the power consumption of AIs and Ari was all for it.

All those who were in college had final exams for the first semester the week of December 11, just two weeks after Thanksgiving. As students, Henry,

Lisa, Chastity, Luke, Isobel, Josh, and even recent grad Conrad were accustomed to having at least four weeks' vacation at the end of the year. But a corporation preparing to pay its first month's rent in January didn't shut down. As soon as exams were over, everyone was back in the office full time working on the many projects.

HENRY, LISA, AND Chastity spent Christmas Eve with Ryan and Sylvia, then took off Christmas morning for Louisiana. Jackie picked the three up at the airport and drove them up to Baton Rouge. She scarcely knew what to do with Chastity. She was committed to being an accepting person and an ally, but never expected her own daughter to bring both a boy and a girl home with her.

"How should I introduce Chastity to your grandparents?" Jackie asked Lisa when they had a few minutes alone. "Is she a they?"

"No, Mom," Lisa said patiently. "Believe me, she is all woman! Um... I mean... Henry and I are a couple. Chastity is our lover. As in, we both love her. To infinity!"

"It's okay!" Jackie said. "I'm not upset or anything. God knows we did stranger things when I was in the sorority. I mean... I just don't want to offend anyone."

"Mom, you can relax. Chas has never had much of a family. No parents or grandparents. Do like Sylvia does. She treats Chastity like her own daughter. In fact, I think Chastity visits Henry's parents more often than he does," Lisa whispered.

"That will do it!" Jackie said. "My other daughter. We don't need to explain anything else you don't want to. But... uh... what are the sleeping arrangements?"

"Can Chas have the guest room?" Lisa asked. "That whole being alone thing? She doesn't like to wake up next to anyone, even if she starts the night with us."

"Oh, of course! It's all made up. I didn't think your bed was big enough for three. At least not to sleep comfortably."

They arrived at the Hartman home and as soon as Chastity was greeted by Bill and everyone put their luggage in the rooms, they all loaded back in the SUV and went to Beau and Solange's house for Christmas dinner.

Henry and Chastity gazed out the car windows as they turned up the long drive to the Benoit estate. The lane was lined with live oaks. In fact, the entire estate seemed to be a small forest at the center of which was what appeared to be a modest house with three dormers gracing the front. Inside, however, the home was sprawling.

"Come in. Come in," Beau bellowed at the door, greeting the family. "Merry Christmas!"

It looked like Beau had already been imbibing in some Christmas cheer. When Solange emerged from the kitchen, it was obvious he hadn't been drinking alone.

"Oh, you're all here!" Solange said. "Muah. Muah," she said as she went down the line greeting their daughter's family. "Lisa, who is this beautiful creature with you and Henry?"

"Mamé, this is ma chère, Chastity."

"Oh! And Henry?"

"Notre cher," Lisa answered.

Jackie stared at the two in surprise as Henry and Chastity tried to figure out what was passing between Lisa and her grandmother.

"Oh! You are all three so beautiful! Come and have a glass of sherry before dinner," Solange said.

"Could we have something without alcohol?" Lisa asked.

"Of course," Beau broke in. "We've got anything you'd like."

He ushered them into the massive living room with a fireplace between the living room and the dining room where a fire was roaring. Festive garlands were strung around the fireplace, but there were few other decorations.

"What a beautiful home, Beau," Henry said. "Thank you for welcoming us on this Christmas Day."

"The old place threatens to fall down every day," Beau laughed. "My great grandfather, back in 1875, built this place. Of course, things have been updated. Three bathrooms now to go with the three bedrooms. You'll find they are all rather small by today's standard. The house was made to entertain people, so most of the 4,000 square feet are reserved for that purpose, though I have a nice little office on the side over there. That's where I've been recording most of my memoirs for you."

He pulled Henry aside to get the drinks for everyone. He never asked what Bill or Jackie wanted. Just poured their cocktails and set them on a tray.

"Your *maîtresse* is a beautiful woman. But I detect she belongs to Lisa as much as to you," he said.

"Yes, sir."

"Takes me back, it does. Sol and I had a *maîtresse* when we were younger. Well, I suppose we'd still have her if she hadn't passed on. Sad to lose her so young. Jacqueline would hardly remember her, I suppose. I'll have to record that story, I think."

He handed Henry three glasses of soda water on ice and took the cocktails to his daughter and son-in-law. There was never a question about Chastity being accepted. Jackie's worrying had been for naught. In fact, she was quite amazed at how open and loving her parents were.

They had dinner and Solange summoned her daughter and granddaughters to join her in her craft room so she could show them her latest projects. Henry joined Bill and Beau in a walk outside. It was chilly, but the northerners had come prepared with warm jackets.

"When Great Granddaddy built this house, it sat on nearly four miles of property, stretching from here to the river and north over what is now the university campus. Over the years, the plantation has dwindled to just six acres, but it's a pleasant property. If she wants it when we're gone, it will go to Lisa. Of course, I don't expect it to stay in the family forever. We live in a different world these days. It will ultimately be sold and the Benoit name will be forgotten."

"Not forgotten," Henry said. "Your descendants will always have your legacy and your stories."

"Ah, yes. Forever Theirs. I'm happy to leave that behind. How about you, Bill?" Beau asked.

"Of course," Bill said. "I just hope I have your years to record things. And as many adventures as you've had."

"I'm glad we're creating this," Henry said. "It seems a lot of people are happy about it. We've sold over five hundred systems already."

"Well, it's all part of the new era, I was talking about," Beau said. "People today don't know their heritage and family history. They move away from home—sometimes thousands of miles—and they don't see the family that much. Or, they're abandoned like your sweet Chastity. Your parents and Lisa's parents will adopt her and make her part of *our* heritage. I'd guess some of those sales you're making are to people who don't have children or don't know their descendants and are just afraid that no one will remember them when they're gone. But someone will have a disc labeled *Forever Yours* and will ask it what life was like when they were young."

"I hope you've started creating yours, Henry," Bill said. "It would be a lot easier to grab some of those memories while they're still fresh instead of waiting until you have to research your own life in order to remember what it was like when you were a teen."

"I certainly believe that," Henry said. "I've had mine collecting information about me from social media, school records, and scans of things I've done, as well as anything that resides on my computer. One of the things I've discovered is how much of my life is a little embarrassing. Already, I've discovered things that make me cringe when I think of having done them. I'm guessing that some of the things I'm doing now will make a future me shake his head in wonder that I could be so stupid."

"Well, it all goes into making us who we are. You know what they say. Good judgment comes from experience. Experience comes from bad judgment," Beau laughed.

The three went back to the house just as the women were coming down the stairs laughing. Beau stoked the fire in the fireplace and they sat with cups of chicory or cocoa and opened the little presents. The Benoit/Hartman family weren't particularly big on giving gifts, but each one was meaningful. Henry was amazed that Solange had managed to prepare a gift for Chastity. It was a cameo necklace she said was just costume jewelry, but she'd had it far too long not to pass it on. Lisa received a mother-of-pearl pendant on a gold chain. The gifts were small, but meaningful for each of them.

Lisa drove back to her parents' house because she deemed her parents to have drunk over the limit. She and Chastity sat in the front seat while Henry joined Bill and Jackie in the back. When they got home, no one was interested in staying up any longer.

"THIS IS THE happiest Christmas I've ever had," Chastity said as she kissed and undressed with her lovers.

"Merry Christmas, lover," Henry said.

"I'm so glad you are with us," Lisa added.

"Your parents and grandparents," Chastity said giving Lisa a quick kiss, "and your parents," she added, kissing Henry. "They've accepted me like I'm their own daughter—like I'm your sister."

"Is this legal then?" Henry asked as he bent to suck on a nipple.

"Oh, shut up and keep sucking," Chastity moaned. She kissed Lisa intently as they all fell into Lisa's bed. "I'm so happy, I'm leaking."

Henry grabbed a tissue from the bedside table and dabbed at the tears streaming from Chastity's eyes.

"I didn't mean my eyes," she giggled.

Henry got the message and quickly moved between her legs to begin kissing and lapping at her juices. Lisa and Chastity kissed deeply. Soon, Chastity was crying out her first orgasm, only partially muffled by Lisa's lips.

"Do me!" she cried, tugging at Henry's head to get him to move up.

She pulled on Lisa to get her to straddle her face. Henry looked quickly to the side table to find a condom, but there were none there.

"I need to get a condom from my bag," he gasped, starting to get up. Lisa stopped him.

"I don't think you need one any longer," she said. "Chas is clean. We got tested earlier this week. She's done with the life and is all ours."

She positioned Henry's cock at Chastity's opening and pulled him forward. Henry sank unprotected into Chastity for the first time in their long relationship. Lisa leaned forward to kiss him deeply while Chastity licked her to a frenzy.

"Yes! Oh, my God and Goddess! Yes!" Lisa cried out as she tried to devour Henry.

He reached for her breast and found one of Chastity's hands cupping it. He was not going to last long.

"Are you sure this is okay?" he gasped, trying to hold back his orgasm.

Lisa lifted up off Chastity's face a little and Chastity called out to Henry.

"Do it! Come in me! I want my lovers!"

The dam broke for Henry and he began spewing his come into Chastity's unprotected vagina as Lisa cried out her orgasm from Chastity's renewed licking.

When Henry's pulses died down, Lisa pushed him back and lowered her face to Chastity's crotch to lick her clean and bring her along to another orgasm.

They gradually separated and arranged themselves facing the same direction on the bed so they could cuddle and kiss.

"I haven't had come in me since my last movie and there is no longer any record of that," Chastity said. "It's like you are my first, Henry. And you made sure I got a good come from it, too, Lisa, darling."

"You know you don't have to have me in you if you don't enjoy it," Henry whispered. "I'm happy to lick you, too."

"Oh, I like it," Chastity explained. "I don't come from it, but I still like having you in me. If any other man tried it, I'd kill him on the spot. I just want you two."

"I love it," Lisa said. "I know I'll get him in me before the night is over and you'll return the favor of cleaning me up. I'll just get two orgasms from it instead of one. Please don't ever leave us, lover."

"You need to make sure you are together so I can be with both of you," Chastity said.

Something in Henry's mind clicked. He saw the three of them together—even with a family.

"Lisa," he said softly. "Will you marry me so we can keep our lover with us forever?"

41

THE PLAN

O N BOXING DAY, Henry, Lisa, and Chastity borrowed Jackie's car and went shopping. Lisa drove them directly to one of the oldest Louisiana jewelers in business, with a name as Cajun as the Benoits'.

"Whatever you want, love," Henry said as they began looking at the engagement rings and wedding sets. "I'm only going to do this once in my life, so I don't care what it costs."

"You know, if I was a gold digger, I'd take serious advantage of that," Lisa laughed. "I can't help but think how Isobel's hand seems to be weighed down by that rock Luke bought her. I'm a woman of simpler tastes."

"You have me," Chastity whispered.

"That is as complex as my tastes get," Lisa said. "I want to wear my ring all the time, so I don't want something with too high a profile. I don't want to get it snagged on anything."

"This is a pretty set," Chastity said, pointing to a very antique-looking engagement and wedding ring. Henry wisely stayed out of the conversation. He'd give his opinion only if asked.

"Oh, that's nice!" Lisa said. "It doesn't stick up too high and it isn't an open prong setting, so it isn't as likely to get caught when I'm trying to hurry out of my clothes. You know?"

A salesperson named Greg smiled at the implication and pulled the set out of the case to display on a dark blue velvet board.

"I hate to think that I just chose the first one that I liked, like I did with my husband to be," Lisa said with a grin.

377

"Yeah, but sometimes you just get it right the first time," Chastity said.

"Please try it on for size and see how it looks on your hand," Greg said.

Henry moved into action and picked up the engagement ring to place it on Lisa's finger. It was stunning. He added the wedding band to complete the look.

"Do you think it's too much?" Lisa asked, looking at him.

"I think it looks stunning on you," he responded.

"I'd worry about it," Lisa said. "What if I only wore the engagement ring on special occasions and just wore the band the rest of the time?"

"You know I celebrate every day I spend with you as a special occasion," Henry said.

He kissed her lightly.

"Sold," she sighed.

"Now let's check that sizing," Greg said, gently removing the rings and replacing them with a size ring from a series.

He tried one up and one down from the size he'd initially chosen, but returned to the original one, showing his expertise in assessing her size.

"We can have the set ready for you by New Year's," he said. "We'll just need a fifty percent deposit."

"If I pay you the full amount today, can you have it for us by Friday? We're flying out on Saturday," Henry asked.

"Oh! Well, of course!" Greg said. "Let me write it up."

"We're not done shopping yet," Lisa said. "Do the paperwork and we'll continue looking around."

Greg immediately removed the rings and motioned an assistant over to do the paperwork while he accompanied the trio around the display cases.

"What can I show you?" he asked.

"We need something for Chastity," Lisa said. "Not as formal as an engagement set, but something that shows permanence."

"Ah? A third-party wedding?" he asked, as if it were common for people to shop for this kind of jewelry.

"Chastity is our *maîtresse*," Lisa said matter-of-factly.

"Might I suggest a right-hand ring, then," Greg said. He showed a case of lovely rings.

"These all look kind of fancy schmancy and wedding-y," Chastity said. "I don't want something that competes with Lisa's ring."

"I see. We have a small collection of artist rings. These rings were designed by various well-known artists over the past century and were forged and set by contracted studios. They are all limited editions, so you are unlikely to find anyone with a similar ring," Greg said, pulling out a display tray with artistic rings. "With your skin tone and elegance, you remind me of one of these art deco mixed metal rings, like this one with white and yellow gold inset with lapis. It has a kind of ancient Greek feeling."

"Oh! That's gorgeous!" Chastity exclaimed.

"Perfect for you," Lisa whispered. "Would you accept that ring from your girlfriend?"

Chastity sniffed and nodded her head. Greg handed the ring to Lisa and Lisa tried on Chastity's right hand.

"Not too ostentatious, but absolutely elegant," Henry said. "It's perfect."

"I don't believe this will need any sizing," Greg said. "You could take it with you now."

"No!" Chastity breathed. "To pick up when we get Lisa's rings."

Greg smiled and summoned his assistant to write up the mixed metals art ring.

"Now," Chastity said, after she'd wiped her eyes and nose, "we need an engagement gift for our man."

"A watch," Lisa suggested.

"A watch? I have a cell phone," Henry began to protest.

"You deserve a piece of jewelry that does absolutely nothing but remind you that whatever time it is, we love you," Lisa said.

"Oh. That... Yeah... That's great," he said.

"Hmm. You know the big deal these days is the smart watch," Greg said, "but I see where you are going with this. There are still watchmakers who just create watches. Let's see what we can do."

He led them to a selection of men's watches and allowed them to just look without his explanations. Some watches were fairly plain, while some had the date, cycle of the moon, water resistance, and shock resistance. Some were self-winding while others were battery operated. The selection of watches was as diverse as the selection of rings.

"You know, since it is supposed to be a reminder of our love at all hours, I really don't see a reason for anyone else to be able to read it but me," Henry speculated.

"I see exactly where you are looking," Lisa said. "Would you really be content with a black-on-black watch face?"

"Why not?" Henry asked. "It would be clean and simple on my wrist and everyone else can just guess what it says."

Greg withdrew the minimalist watch from the display and strapped it onto Henry's wrist.

"I like it," Henry said.

"We'll take it," Chastity said. "Put it with the other purchases for pickup on Friday."

Greg took the watch and went to where his assistant had written up the other items. He began to add the details from the watch.

"Oh, I'm sorry," Lisa said. "It needs to be three separate checks."

Greg looked at them for a moment with puzzlement written on his face. Then he smiled in understanding. When they left the store, Henry had the receipt for Lisa's wedding set, Lisa had the receipt for Chastity's art ring, and Chastity had the receipt for Henry's watch.

THEY COULD HARDLY wait for the jewelry to be ready on Friday to announce their intentions. Nonetheless, Friday night, the trio took Lisa's parents and grandparents to dinner and announced the engagement together. There was a round of congratulations and Solange and Jackie oohed over the two girls' rings. Beau looked at Henry's watch and nodded, as did Bill.

There was a celebratory toast, even though the trio drank soda water. Then Beau began the lecture.

"Before you run off and tie the knot, you need a pre-nuptial agreement," he said. "All three of you. Yes, I believe you will be together all your lives and the agreement will be completely unnecessary, but this is a world in which we've seen everything we believed in torn to shreds. It may take more than the rest of my life before we see real order restored. All three of you are wealthy. Yes, I know you don't have a lot of cash, but Henry and Chastity have a substantial stake in Open Cloak and it is likely to be worth a billion dollars or more in a few years."

"I have no problem with splitting whatever I have evenly with Lisa," Henry said.

"That's not the way Pennsylvania works," Beau said. "You need to specify that in advance. But you are not the only one who is wealthy. Lisa is the sole heir to a family fortune that includes both Benoit Intracoastal Logistics and EZ Daze games. And by neither Pennsylvania or Louisiana laws would Chastity be in any way protected. The idea of a pre-nuptial agreement is to assure that you are each taken care of if anything should happen either to your relationship or to one of you. It needs to include a will that makes sure your family is taken care of in the event of a tragedy. For each of you."

"I guess I see the sense in that," Henry said. "I won't be twenty-one for two more months. I never even considered needing a will."

"God forbid that it is ever called for," Solange said, "but we will all, including your parents, rest easier knowing you have taken care of business."

SATURDAY, THE THREE returned to Pittsburgh, still euphoric in the new definition of their relationship. They went immediately to the Pascals' home to announce their relationship officially to Henry's parents.

"I can scarcely claim you are too young," Sylvia laughed. "That was what my parents said when Ryan and I got married. We were twenty-three. I assume you'll be twenty-one before you tie the knot," she said looking at her son.

"We have a lot of details to work out," Henry said. "We need to get pre-nuptial agreements drawn up. And wills. Beau gave us quite a lecture last night."

"And I need to figure out how I'll discharge my obligation to work for my father after college," Lisa said. "It was part of our agreement."

"I suppose that is wise," Ryan said. "Neither Sylvia nor I had a pot to piss in when we got married. We never made any kind of financial agreement."

"What's his is mine and what's mine is my own," Sylvia said lightly. Ryan simply nodded.

"Well, in addition to the legal stuff, we need to do the whole wedding planning routine," Lisa said. "I know my family will want to have the wedding in Baton Rouge, but most of my friends are here in Pittsburgh. We might need to have two celebrations."

"Plus, we want to figure out how to celebrate Chas as part of our family," Henry said. "I know that's a bit unusual, but I don't want to be living a lie or hiding our relationship."

"How did your family receive that, Lisa?"

"Surprisingly openly and happy for us," she answered. "I knew Mom was really proud of her membership in a welcoming congregation of the Methodists, but I didn't expect my grandparents to be so easy about it."

"Did you know your grandparents had a *maîtresse* when they were first together?" Henry asked. Lisa's mouth dropped open.

"Papere told you that?" Lisa asked.

"Yes. He said they were very happy together but she died young. He didn't think your mom remembered her at all," Henry said.

"Now I have a whole bunch of questions for *Forever Yours!*" Lisa laughed. "I hope they added those stories."

"Beau said he would record them."

"How are you doing with all this, Chastity?" Sylvia asked, reaching out to take Chastity's hand in hers.

"I feel... like I have a family for the first time in my life. If I died young, like the Benoits' *maîtresse*, I would die happy."

"Let's all pray that doesn't happen. You deserve all the happiness life can give you," Ryan said. "I'm so glad you've become a part of our family."

THE PREVIOUS YEAR, the New Year's Eve party at the club had included only the four partners. Luke and Isobel hadn't even been engaged yet. The company had just been founded with the investment from the sale of their first license. This year, nearly thirty people, including spouses and dates, were at the party.

After a long discussion during the day, Lisa, Henry, and Chastity had decided to be completely up front and announce the entire relationship. After dinner, Luke began with the celebratory toasts and welcomes, then turned it over to Henry.

"Well, I hope everyone had a great holiday this week. Mine was a little surprising, but in the most wonderful way. Lisa and I are announcing our engagement," Henry said as he held Lisa's hand and had her stand. Everyone applauded and Luke led a toast. Isobel immediately wanted to see Lisa's ring and was content that hers was bigger.

"I'd like to also share that Chastity has agreed to join our family," Lisa said. She held Chastity's hand and encouraged her to stand. "There's no formal legal arrangement for that kind of relationship, but we are determined to make it work and have given her a ring in celebration."

Chastity held up her right hand with the art ring.

"That's beautiful!" Isobel declared. "Damn, girl! You outdid us all."

"Hey, Isobel," Henry said. "Look at this. You don't think they let me get away without having an engagement present, too, do you?"

He held up his wrist and Isobel stared at it.

"What is it?" she asked.

"Just a watch," Henry said. "Something to remind me at all hours that I am loved."

The three managed to kiss each other and Luke gave another toast to the happy trio.

MOST EMPLOYEES WERE back in the office on Tuesday, the day after New Year's.

Having been out a week, Henry immediately went to catch up with the various teams working on projects. A minor dispute on the network defense system had broken out regarding the use of the degrees of separation, but was resolved when the Army cited its agreement with Open Cloak limiting their product to direct attack only. Conrad, however, spoke directly to General Schwartz, going over his girlfriend's head to get agreement to one degree, not only as an option, but as the default.

It had been apparent at the New Year's Eve party that no lasting damage was done between Conrad and Rebecca. It seemed they might be on the verge of an announcement themselves.

Page Services reported that *Pythia Speaks* had its first 100,000 query day *on Christmas*, of all things! Henry had Darrel run a review of the network usage and had the testers move from their final testing of the network optimization and network search to run an intensive battery of tests on *Pythia Speaks* and *Forever Yours*.

The developers Henry had hired for *Forever Yours* reported making progress on the image and video AI. That had been the biggest feature still lacking in the program, though, of course, there were others that could be added in the future.

"We ditched the licensed software for video generation," Lee LaRue said.

"What's the problem with it? Are you saying we can develop our own better?" Henry asked.

"It's in your original training patent," Lee said. "Generative AI needs to develop images on the fly that match general descriptions from massive amounts of data. The *Forever Yours* AI only needs to generate one image. There is only one person that needs to come to life. Once the composite image of that person is established, everything else is a variant of that image. Different expressions and gestures, but all the same person. We were trying to integrate a video AI that could generate an entire cast of characters for hundreds of movies. We don't need to do that."

"And you believe you can establish the training parameters for the AI that will allow for that flexibility without having access to the wider range of training content the other programs use?" Henry persisted.

"We should have working video generation of the subject in the next month. It's really that simple," Lee insisted.

"I can hardly wait."

<hr>

AND FINALLY, ARI Patel reported his initial findings on power optimization.

"Your initial patent was headed in the right direction," Ari said. "I believe we can expand it significantly. By tapping directly into a computer's power supply, we can reduce consumption another fifteen percent. Ideally, however, we could remove the computer from the grid almost completely by changing the supply to a rechargeable power cell."

"Isn't that what we have with laptop computers and other devices? They run on a battery and we plug them in to recharge," Henry said.

"Those are lithium batteries," Ari said shaking his head sadly. "Very bad for the environment. I'm talking about fuel cells that have only water and manageable heat as byproducts and are easy to recharge."

"Where are we supposed to get those?" Henry asked. He was intrigued by the possibility.

"I studied the situation in depth when I was with the power company. There, the purpose of our investigation was to combat this energy source to preserve the electricity monopoly. Of course, the utility companies are concerned with megawatt producing fuel cells. I discovered a company in Minnesota that is working on a consumer edition cell. We could investigate that."

"Get the information, Ari. I don't know if we can make that work, but we should definitely make a thorough investigation. In the meantime, I want you to meet with Don Harvey, our patent attorney, and spell out the changes we need to make to our power patents."

"Yes, Henry. I will begin at once."

<hr>

AS TIME DREW near for classes to resume on the fifteenth, Luke closed a deal with LifeStory, one of the several guided memoir writing companies that had arisen in the past five years. The VAR package would put both the paper book and the AI capture together. LifeStory would provide weekly prompts for people and would compile those stories into a book. The responses would also be used for the AI to train on for Forever Yours. It was a good combination. One of the things Henry had felt was missing from Forever Yours was a good set of prompts to get people started recording their lives. He had a developer working on the VAR version so that responses to the prompts would automatically be forwarded to LifeStory, but none of the other information collected from that person's social media or computer would be forwarded.

THE QUARTERLY EARNINGS report that came out January fifteenth was for a company that had its first truly profitable quarter. With five products in the market plus an Army contract, the balance sheet was better than any of them had anticipated in the first three years of operation. They'd been in business for just one year and were profitable!

"That's great news," Henry said. "I'm sure we can raise additional capital with that report."

"Why?" Isobel asked. "We have capital in the bank as it is."

"I think we may want to make one or two acquisitions," Henry said. "Hear me out on this. Page Services is pushing their limits regarding growth. They need a bigger facility and more hosting units. *Pythia Speaks* is on eight boxes and *Forever Yours* samples are running on another. We're a drop in the bucket of the four hundred plus servers at the company. But we aren't the only AI running in their server farm. In fact, we're the smallest. The demand for AI server space is growing. I believe we should position ourselves to acquire the server farm and expand it significantly."

"I'd say that is a reasonable thing to consider," Luke said. "Do we have a prospectus?"

"Scott is getting it prepared and we should have it by the end of the month," Henry said. "However, that is only one of the areas I'd like to consider investing in. Where we really make our impact known is in power savings. Ari brought me information on a company in Minnesota that is working on fuel cell technology. I see us with two possible uses for that tech. We could cut the electric consumption of the server farm by ninety percent. You know the big server guys have already booked MNRs to come online next year. This would pull the rug right out from under them."

"What's an MNR?" Chastity asked.

"Mobile Nuclear Reactor," Henry said.

"Shit!" Luke responded. "Let's get the proposals together and go get some money."

"OH, GOD! I had no idea the amount of negotiating I would need to do with my own parents!" Lisa exclaimed near the end of January.

With classes having started and the business moving forward rapidly, they'd all been working long hours. Wednesday, Isobel's birthday had interrupted everything, as she insisted everyone stop to celebrate her turning twenty-one.

"What is it, love?" Henry asked, setting aside his textbook.

"Well, you know I'm obligated to serve one year in my father's business for each year of college he paid for. As it is, he was expecting to have me for four years and I'll finish in three, so he feels shorted. Then mother wants us to have a big wedding in the United Methodist Church there in Baton Rouge. Yes, I still have friends there, but it's not at all like the number of friends I have here in Pittsburgh now."

"Do you think we'll have to move to Baton Rouge?" Chastity asked. They were sitting together in the fourth floor lounge to do their studying, but it was getting late and they were all thinking about bed in one way or another.

"I've had to make some compromises. I could go home and serve my term in Baton Rouge, putting off getting married for three years. I said I wasn't interested. Dad said I could feasibly work remotely since I have a house where I've got an office, but that I'd have to compromise with my mother in order to make that work. The compromise with mother is that we get married in Baton Rouge. Somehow that doesn't sound like a compromise, but in exchange for holding the wedding back home, Dad will let me work remotely in Pittsburgh with bi-monthly trips to the office."

"Babe, we'll do whatever is necessary. If we need to work from Baton Rouge, I can commute to the office," Henry said. "Ninety percent of my job is still online."

"That'll change soon," Chastity said. "Conrad has put in for two more developers and two testers for the network defense system. The Army plans to send one or two more, as well."

"I never expected that project to be so big," Henry said. "I need to meet with them and tie down the details. How much room do we have in the office?"

"That's part of the problem," Chastity said. "I'm in discussions with Ray to lease another 5,000 square feet on the second floor."

"Welcome to the grown-up world," Lisa said. "Henry, I don't want to leave all our friends here in Pittsburgh out of our wedding plans. What are we going to do?"

"I suppose running off to Las Vegas is out of the question," he chuckled. "I guess we'll have to get married twice. Tell your mother we'll come to

Baton Rouge for a wedding, but it will be a maximum of two bridesmaids and two groomsmen. Luke will be my best man and I'll ask Josh to join us. You've already said you want Chastity beside you and I completely agree. That gives you room to invite one other person."

"Will Isobel be offended if I don't ask her?" Lisa asked.

"She didn't ask either you or Chastity to be in her wedding party. It was Luke who asked Chastity to stand with him," Henry said. "So, we'll bring half a dozen people with us to Baton Rouge, including my parents for the wedding. In return, Jackie and Bill need to come to Pittsburgh two weeks later for our totally secular celebration here. Then we can work out the work arrangements with Bill."

"Wonderful," Lisa sighed. "Shall I tell my parents we'll be there next weekend for the wedding?"

She looked at her lovers and all three started laughing.

42

UNREASONABLE DEMANDS

A S WEDDING PLANS became the focus for Lisa and Chastity, Isobel seemed to become more abrasive in the office. Luke excused her as having an extremely intensive class load this semester that was giving her headaches and stomach upsets. He confided to Henry that he thought she needed her meds adjusted and was trying to get her to visit her doctor.

In private, Henry and Chastity concurred that she was being upset by having someone else planning a wedding and that she was not the top princess in the office. Isobel hadn't felt her birthday got enough attention because people were talking about Henry and Lisa's wedding. Even though Lisa was only in the office ten hours a week, there was definite tension between the two of them.

"How can you be so utterly incompetent?" Izzy screamed at Nancy at the front desk. "It's a simple spreadsheet. You said you could use the software."

"But I don't understand the terms, Mrs. Riordan," Nancy protested. "I wasn't trained in accounting. I know how to do a pivot table, but I don't understand which variables you want adjusted."

"I can't believe you are so worthless," Isobel said.

"Isobel!" Chastity said severely. "Back off! You need to learn how to explain what you want in language understandable by a human instead of a calculator. That's enough beating on my assistant. If you need someone as your assistant, put together the job description and I'll see if I can find someone who will work with you."

"How dare you speak to me like that!" Izzy screamed loudly enough that Luke rushed out of his office.

"Izzy, honey, come with me into the office so we can talk this over," Luke said.

"Don't you be condescending to me, too!" Isobel screeched. Nonetheless she allowed herself to be guided into Luke's office.

Chastity spent a few minutes comforting the distressed receptionist/ office assistant.

"Please don't fire me, Chastity," Nancy pled. "I like working here. I just don't understand what she wants."

"None of us do, Nance. I swear there are days she just wants one plus one to equal three and won't accept anything else. You report to me and me only. I'm through loaning you to Isobel," Chastity said.

Chastity returned to her office and began assembling a job description for an office accountant for Isobel's approval. Of course, Isobel would be upset about spending more money on an employee, but since it would be for an assistant to her, it might be less of a problem. Chastity began assessing the office space and sketching out a design for the second floor that would allow them to double in size. She needed the space available before the new employees started on the twelfth of February. Just a week away. They were already overcrowded with twenty-one people in the office designed to comfortably house twenty.

Ray had made immediate adjustments on the second floor so they could move the entire network defense department into suitable space, but the remainder of the second floor was open. Henry had already told her that Ari was going to need two developers and a tester for the power group. And everyone was clamoring for a new full-time UI developer. Lisa was stretched beyond the ten hours a week she had available and would be leaving the company after graduation so she could work for her father. Even Darrel had put in for an IT tech to help with the multiple networks they were running for corporate, development, and testing.

She tossed down her notepad and went to Henry's office.

"HEY, BABE. I haven't seen you in this position in a long time," Henry said when Chastity had locked his door and sat on the corner of his desk. He automatically reached for her bare leg and leaned in to give put a kiss on her thigh.

"Yeah. Hardly at all since we basically started living together. I miss it," Chastity sighed.

"You know, so do I," he said, stroking up her inner thigh. "Maybe I should start coming to your office like this."

"Oh, now that would get tongues wagging," she giggled. "I miss this," she repeated.

Henry responded by using both hands on her legs and then running a hand up under her blouse to play with her breasts and piercings. He was surprised when he reached under her skirt to find she was wearing panties.

"Just pull them aside, okay?" she said.

"What's on your mind today?" he asked as he managed to get the gusset of her panties pulled to one side so he could gently pet her slit.

"Your birthday is Friday," she said.

"Mmm. Yeah. I guess I'll be all grown up like the rest of you."

"Luke is two weeks later, so you're ahead of him. Does it bother you to be marrying an older woman?" Chastity asked.

"I never even thought about it," he said. "Lisa is only five months older than me, and you're only three months older. As far as I'm concerned, we're all the same age."

"Yeah. It's good. I need to hire an assistant for Isobel. I won't let her use Nancy any longer. She's too abusive," Chastity said, coming to the point.

"I'm sorry. Do I need to talk to her? Or to Nancy?"

"No. I think Luke's handling it. The biggest problem is finding an accounting assistant who doesn't have more experience than Izzy has. That's the biggest problem we have in the company. We four partners are just twenty-one years old. Sometimes, I wonder if Luke is even qualified to be our CEO. I'm certainly not qualified to be the office manager."

"And I don't even have my degree yet," Henry agreed. "I'd love to hire a mentor, you know."

"That's a good idea. Hmm. We should see if Beau wants a part-time job," she laughed.

"Why not *my* dad, if we're hiring relatives. You know I'm talking to him more frequently now than I did any time in the past four years."

"They say it's amazing how much a father learns after you turn twenty-one," Chas said. "Seriously, though, you should consider what you would need in the way of a person to take some of the management burden off your shoulders. I know you want to have your fingers in the code."

"I kind of like where my fingers are right now," he said, tickling her clit. She'd moistened since she sat down with him, but he wasn't attempting to push fingers into her.

"I do, too. Maybe you could visit me tonight for a while… just the two of us."

"We don't do that often."

"I do it more often with Lisa. Just check with her first."

"We'll get through the rough spots," Henry said.

"Yeah. We can be a little rough. I mean... yeah."

HENRY DISCOVERED A new side of Chastity after he thought he understood her pretty well. She had a dark side to her sexuality. She did want things a little rougher at times. She was still fairly quiet until she was coming. Then she was very noisy. But in the quiet times, she wanted her nipple piercings twisted more violently than he'd ever allowed himself before.

And after she had come on his tongue, she wanted him to take her ass. The few times Henry had done such a thing, he'd been gentle and careful not to hurt his partner, but Chastity wanted no such consideration. He drove his entire length into her and she wailed her encouragement.

After he'd come, they both panted, holding each other.

"Thank you. I really needed that," she said. Her kisses were still lips only.

"But Chas, you..."

"I did when you ate me. No one eats me like you do."

"But not while we were..."

"I didn't need to come when you fucked my ass. Not everything is about coming. Now clean yourself up and go back to your fiancée. I want to take a bath," Chastity said, pushing him out of bed.

Henry washed himself as she ran bath water. Then he dressed, gave her a quick kiss, and returned to his own suite where Lisa was waiting for him in bed. They held each other, kissed deeply, and went to sleep.

"TRUST ME. I'VE been through this and you have to be firm with your mother or she'll try to run your whole marriage," Isobel said as she sat with Lisa at Henry's birthday party. It wasn't a huge party like his twentieth had been. It was just his parents and partners with him and Lisa.

"I'm not in an adversarial relationship with my mother," Lisa said. "She's managing the wedding in Baton Rouge. That's for the family. I'm managing the one here. That's for *our* family."

"How are you managing the wedding in a church with two brides?" Isobel insisted.

"Not. Henry and I are getting married. Chastity is my maid of honor. My best friend from high school is at LSU there and will be with us. Luke and Josh will stand with Henry."

"Only two? You poor kid! I'll stand with you. We could even bring that receptionist girl from the office. You should have at least four attendants," Isobel said.

"Henry and I set the number. There won't be any attendants at the celebration in Pittsburgh. It's not like we need a certain number of witnesses to make it legal or anything," Lisa said.

"Well, I certainly hope Henry is insisting on a pre-nuptial. He's worth a few million now."

"We're all three signing pre-nups," Lisa explained. "My parents and grandparents insisted. There's a few million in their accounts as well."

"A few...? Why are you even bothering to get married? You have your own money. You aren't having a big wedding. Are you even wearing a dress?"

"I don't plan to go naked!"

"I mean a wedding dress!"

"Of course!"

"How about a wedding shower? If Chastity isn't planning something, I'll do it. It's hardly a wedding without gifts," Isobel said.

"I don't think we need anything. We'll set up a charitable donation. Really, Isobel, we aren't even planning to move. We've got a perfectly lovely home. It has space for all three of us. It's convenient to work. There's plenty of space for my office."

"I really don't understand why you're even bothering," Izzy sighed. "You're not getting any of the benefits. Luke and I are shopping for a house. Probably something in Lyndale. It's a gated community on the north side. Ever since Darla warned us that there were threats, I've wanted to get into something more secure. And we can get a house that's suitable for a corporate executive. You should consider that, too. I mean, the apartment life is fine for the first year, but it's hardly suitable for people of your status."

Lisa didn't bother to contradict Isobel. Izzy was off on what they were looking for in a house.

"Of course, it doesn't need to be 4,000 square feet and six bedrooms," she laughed, "though that seems to be the average in Lyndale. It would give us each a home office and room for a live-in housekeeper. God! Can you imagine having to clean a place like that? No, thank you."

"You'll want a bedroom or two for kids, won't you?" Lisa asked.

"Are you kidding me? Can you imagine me with a brat? One of us would die. I know Luke wants children, but he keeps it wrapped up tight. This is not a mommy-body," Izzy said.

Lisa excused herself to help Sylvia and Chastity serve the cake and ice cream.

OF COURSE, THERE was a far more lavish party for Luke's twenty-first two weeks later at his parents' home. Lisa and Chastity helped Marla with serving and making sure everyone had drinks and food. Isobel reigned next to Luke, making sure everyone knew he was her husband.

Then, it seemed there was no time at all until the university had spring break. Lisa and Chastity went to Baton Rouge to make the plans for the wedding, get a dress for Lisa, and address invitations. Isobel and Luke decided to take a spring break trip to Florida.

Henry was the only officer left in Pittsburgh and he was pressed to make sure everything was covered. In Chastity and Isobel's absence, Nancy was doing a fine job of checking bank balances each day and letting Henry know if anything needed to be transferred from saving to checking.

Henry's real focus for the week, however, was reviewing the progress of the network defense program. The group had ten developers and testers now. While Conrad still had general responsibility in the company for development, the project had consumed much of his time, so Henry had been more actively guiding the *Forever Yours* and power management projects.

Significantly, Brigadier General Schwartz was onsite to review the progress and release more funds.

"SERIOUSLY, I ONLY have oversight of the military grade version of the software," Schwartz said. "I'll be happy to sit in with you on the commercial version review if you want me to."

"I would appreciate that, Nathan," Henry said. "Congratulations on your promotion. I don't want us to stray into any area that you consider too powerful to be in the hands of independents."

"The promotion was in the works for a long time. Finally came through. We're going to get into distribution eventually. Once this is released, we really won't attempt to prevent any other company or military organization or government having access to the commercial version. Network security is a worldwide issue. However, we'll want to keep our own special features only in the hands of *our* armed forces," Nathan said.

"I'm completely in favor of that. I think we've adequately removed any trace of a degrees of separation option. It simply is what it's set at. Your version still has the variable. There has been a lot of discussion regarding the level of severity of the response. Rebecca has insisted that we not have total annihilation of the attacking computer as a response in the commercial version. It makes it difficult. Without the option, we have to specify what options are available rather than letting the user specify their own response."

"Hmm. I see. Let's take a look at the code and then discuss the various options."

THE CODE REVIEW went well. The team was making progress and Nathan congratulated both groups. They estimated the release as July 1. At that point, the military development code would be removed from the Open Cloak development and would be transferred to the Pentagon. Open Cloak would release their network defense product—a high-dollar investment for enterprises. The company planned to sell into very large companies, who were prone to being attacked, and to the entire financial sector, which was considered to be the most vulnerable.

Henry and Nathan sat at dinner at the club without any of their subordinates and discussed business and development.

"I'm interested in putting together an advisory board," Henry said. "We have a lot of ideas for products, but we're a young company. We could use some... let's say wisdom to help guide our priorities."

"This is very much off the record, Henry. You don't want a military representative on your advisory board. Someone who knows the military, yes. Not someone in the military. Someone in the military, like myself, would be required to report any technology development that might be considered advantageous to the military. At that point, you'd be subject to oversight and regulation."

"Ouch. I guess I shouldn't talk about any of that with you, then."

"Not yet," Nathan said. "Please do not spread this word to any of my subordinates working at your office. I am now fifteen weeks from retirement."

"Congratulations! Um... How does that work? You aren't any older than my parents. Maybe a couple of years. They're in their mid-forties."

"And I will be fifty-five. I manage that with thirty years of service and being promoted to a more expensive rank. I can retire with my full pension and still get good work for a young and thriving company. Hmm. All I need to do is find one."

"Sir, if you are implying that you might be available to join Open Cloak, I would love to have you here. We have projects that could really use some oversight."

"Don't mention them. I'm not retired yet."

"What moves you to retire now? I know you like your work."

"Well, thirty years and a long-awaited promotion. That was during the previous administration. The new administration wants its own people in various positions and those people will want *their* own people. Things are a little tied up at the moment with the rather rocky transition, but as soon as they stabilize a little it will be a good time for me to disappear," Nathan said.

"We do our best to ignore the ruling party and politics. Sometimes we can't, but we do our best."

"As do the lower levels of the armed forces. The senior levels are more subject to the whims of the administration. The lower levels just keep doing what they are told to do."

"May I invite you to apply here as soon as it is legal for you to do so?" Henry said.

"You can expect it."

By the first of April, everyone was working far more than forty hours a week. Henry was barely keeping up with his final three courses at the university. Isobel and Luke did not have the luxury of reducing their course loads and were doing as much study in the office as they did at home. Plans for the June 30 wedding were mostly in Lisa's hands as Henry was often at the office until late.

Professor Jacoby's consortium came through with full funding of $100 million over four years, beginning with an immediate cash infusion of $25 million. Open Cloak used a combination of cash and stock to purchase Page Services and immediately launch a move to new facilities in San Jose. Much of the investment capital was used to fund the purchase of the company and new equipment for the server farm.

Henry and Chastity flew to California to finalize the arrangements and get everyone registered as employees of Open Cloak. They did not, however, change the name of Page Services. It became a wholly owned subsidiary. The five partners who owned that company wept when they received their checks. It appeared that they had been working around the clock to keep the operation running and would immediately hire additional staff to spread the work out.

The first site migrated to the new facility was *Pythia Speaks*, which was now approaching 150,000 queries per day. Henry had contracted out a translation service that would expand Pythia's languages to include English, Spanish, French, German, Japanese, Hindi, and Brazilian Portuguese. As each language came online, Henry's developers targeted the AI to train on that language. The increase in usage went from linear to a sharp curve upward.

And then, as if without warning, it was graduation day for Henry and Lisa. Families gathered, and even though they were not required to attend the general university commencement, they did attend the School of Computer Science commencement.

It was the first time that Lisa's family got to meet Henry's family and that was more significant to them than the degree. By the time they left the reception that Henry, Lisa, and Chastity held at the row house, the families were best friends and were headed to a popular nightspot for drinks.

The trio collapsed in bed. Henry and Lisa scarcely noticed when Chas slipped out to go to her own bed late that night.

43

INTERRUPTIONS

HENRY'S LIFE WAS an agglomeration of juggling product releases, projects, new hires, and wedding plans. Lisa had resigned as a contractor for Open Cloak and was focused solely on their wedding plans. Chastity was torn between the two, trying to execute her responsibilities in the office during the day and trying to support her girlfriend at night.

Amazingly, all three were able to maintain a semblance of sanity and support for each other.

"So, Henry and I are going down to Baton Rouge for the holiday," Lisa said. "Are you sure you'll be okay, boo?"

"Of course I will," Chastity said. "I love you and I'll be waiting here for you when you get home Monday."

"I don't know why I should be worried about meeting a minister," Lisa said. "I don't even believe in any of his mumbo jumbo. I can't believe Isobel made Luke convert to Catholicism before they got married."

"I don't think either of them really care," Chas said. "It was all Isobel's mother. Izzy only pulls the religion card out when it suits what she wants someone to do. She just assumes your mother is being as irrational as hers was."

"Well, thankfully, the only thing Mom required was getting married in the church. I didn't even argue about it. It doesn't make a difference to me, and it's a pretty building," Lisa said. "I think she was so surprised that I agreed immediately, she just forgot about all the backup things she had prepared. She was surprised when I told her only two bridesmaids, but Dad was all over that. He considered it a sign of the size of the wedding."

"It seemed like an awful lot of invitations for a 'small' wedding," Chastity laughed. "Oh! Henry just got home. Shall we have dinner?"

After a night of loving and little sleep, Henry and Lisa took off for Louisiana on Friday and Chastity went to work.

THE METHODIST MINISTER was a laidback guy who asked them if they wanted him to wear a robe and vestments or just a business suit. Henry and Lisa immediately agreed to the suit idea. They didn't mention it to Jackie. He'd even been understanding about the inclusion of Chastity in their family and ceremony, as if it was something that happened every day.

"Well, there's just one more thing I want to do," Rev. Jackson said before their meeting was over. They'd laughed a lot during the meeting and felt they got to know each other fairly well. The minister pulled his computer keyboard to him and tapped in a few words. He looked at the screen and cocked his head to one side while he considered it. "Hmm. What do you think of this?" He turned the monitor to Henry and Lisa.

Both looked at the screen in amazement.

"You use *Pythia Speaks* for things like this?" Henry asked. On the screen was the minister's question and Pythia's answer.

"She's great for generating ideas," Jackson said. "Really makes me think about things."

On the screen the question was "What should I speak about at Henry and Lisa's wedding?"

Pythia's answer was a little more involved than Henry was used to seeing.

"Marriage is a union. A union is stronger than the parts. When one part is threatened, hurt, or even joyful, the union strengthens, comforts, and celebrates. And if things really aren't going right, the union has the power to strike."

"Um... Pythia sometimes doesn't differentiate between meanings of a word," Henry said. "I think everything is accurate, but it might not all fit with your message."

"No. I think it works," Lisa said. "Look at the key things, Henry. Pythia doesn't talk about any religion or religious concept. She doesn't even specify how many people can be in a union. She identifies the concept of mutual support in good times and bad. And believe me, if you were threatened, the union would strike."

"Very good," Jackson said, scribbling some notes. "We'll go with that."

On Monday, a very amused couple returned to Pittsburgh.

"I NEVER IMAGINED a minister would consult Pythia Speaks for sermon ideas," Henry laughed when he got together with Luke on Tuesday. "I can't imagine it's very common."

"I think you might be surprised," Luke said seriously. "Ah. Darla is here. She said she had some important information for us."

They welcomed their PR person into Luke's office and summoned Chastity and Isobel to join them. This was not an official board meeting, so their newest member of the board was not present. The new investors, while buying non-voting stock, negotiated having a board member appointed. They had selected Professor Jacoby and he would join them at the June meeting.

"We would have expected a general marketing report at the board meeting in two weeks," Luke said when they were settled around his conference table. "You indicated that you had information that we should be aware of right away. Please go ahead, Darla."

"Thank you, Luke. Yes, this news is something you should be aware of. *Pythia Speaks* has gone viral. You all knew she was gaining users regularly, but since the foreign language versions started coming online, traffic is growing like never before. I expect we will have a million queries a day by the end of this week," Darla said.

"Whoa! You have to be kidding!" Henry said. "I need to call the server farm and make sure everything is holding together. We didn't anticipate that kind of traffic. Ever!"

"What's driving so much traffic?" Isobel asked. "I mean that sounds like more than foreign language versions."

"Yes. Remember when I said even negative publicity was still publicity? There seem to be people who are tearing into the concept as a tool of the devil. Of course, there are then people who have risen to support her and condemn the megachurches for their alarmism."

"Megachurches?" Henry asked.

"Let's take a look," Darla said. "I brought a link to Sunday's service at a huge church in Austin, Texas." She turned her laptop toward them and increased the volume as the recording played.

"The Bible says God is sufficient for all our needs!" Evangelist and megachurch pastor Daniel Reeves spoke to his congregation. At the bottom of the screen a counter showed how many people were watching online. It was close to 30,000! "But this computer pretends to be God. People ask a stupid computer—stupid I say because there is no intelligence where it is artificial— the questions that only God can answer. They pray to the online idol. Fellow Christians, we never anticipated that the antichrist would come in the form of bits and bytes.

"But even this, God has prepared us for. God has given us salvation through his only begotten Son, our Lord Jesus Christ. Let us therefore arm ourselves, as the Apostle Paul said, with the whole armor of God. Let us gird our loins with the Belt of Truth. There is only one truth and there is only one source of that truth. Let me tell you it is not a *machine* giving random advice from a mishmash of false religions. It is in the Bible and only the Bible has truth.

"'Oh, Brother Daniel,' you might complain. 'What about science?' My dearly beloved, science is a false prophet. Science has led us astray through disease pandemics when it would have had us injecting our bodies with poison in the name of preventing disease. Science claims there is no creator, but that people come from the evil-lution of lower species of animals. Science can't even make up its mind if light is a wave or a particle. All we need to know is that God placed the lights in the heavens. God created man in his own image and woman to be his helper. God protected the righteous from the effects of the pandemic, or took them immediately to be with Him.

"And so I tell you, put on the Breastplate of Righteousness. Satan will bombard you with the arrows of advertising and public opinion and false gods. God's word will protect you from their false claims. Put on the Shoes of the Gospel of Peace. My brothers and sisters, let there be no mistake that there will be times those shoes need to trample the evil beneath our feet in order to have true holy peace.

"Take up the Shield of Faith. Faith is the substance of things hoped for and the evidence of things not seen. Science, history, politics, and all education are not proof of anything. If it contradicts our faith, let it slide off our shield and do us no harm.

"Put on the Helmet of Salvation. Yes, my friends, wrap your head in the immutable love of God's saving grace. Let nothing enter your head that does not come through the filter of salvation. Would you turn your eyes and your questions to this oracle of degradation? No. You must wear God's protection of your mind to keep it from being corrupted. For we struggle not against flesh and blood, but against principalities and powers and rulers of darkness, against the ones and zeroes of a digital idol."

Rev. Reeves' voice rang out in the sanctuary seating nearly 3,000 people in front of him. He stepped out from behind his pulpit and the camera followed him as he moved to the center of the chancel.

"We have a wonderful God," he intoned. "He has given us this armor to protect us from the slings and arrows of outrageous fortune." No one seemed to notice he'd slipped into Shakespeare. "But we are not a passive faith. No, my friends, God calls us to do battle. And to do battle, he has armed us with the Sword of the Spirit—His holy word. And with our swords drawn, we must march into battle against God's foes. We must bring down this abomination. Boycott the evil *Pythia Speaks*, named after a false god of the ancient Greeks. Boycott the companies who program it, host it, support it, and from this point even talk about it. Take your sword of the spirit and cut this cancer from our society. Let its blood be a sweet-smelling sacrifice to our God. Rise up and yell at the top of your lungs, 'Not today, Satan! Get thee behind me!' Let me hear you!"

The congregation stood as one and shouted the words, "Not today, Satan. Get thee behind me!"

"Great will be your reward in heaven," Reeves concluded.

THEY DISCUSSED THE threat and Darla pointed out that there were others of various religions who were refuting Reeves' sermon, but it was obvious that both sides were driving more traffic and more visibility for Pythia Speaks.

"I'm most concerned that it might affect sales and use of *Forever Yours*," Henry said. "Maybe we need to remove the link to the landing page."

"He as much as challenged you to an open battle," Isobel said. "You need to take this seriously if he mobilizes all of Christianity against you, Henry. We can't have God against us!"

"God hasn't been heard from in at least 2,000 years. Why would he be against us?" Henry said. "And why would I try to go to battle against something I don't even believe in? Reeves doesn't even have the biggest megachurch in the country. He's just looking for a way to attract more attention."

"Don't be too flippant, Henry," Luke said. "We have to take any threat seriously. Any number of things could trigger a boycott of all our products like Reeves suggested. We need to do whatever is necessary to protect ourselves and our company."

There was more discussion, but they all went back to work more than a little disturbed.

EVERYONE WAS TENSE in the office. Chastity ordered security upgrades both for the office and for Page Services. Nancy went to security training and a new RFID card reader was installed at the doors. Everyone had to use their new ID card to get in.

"We hired a security team at Page Services," Chastity said. "They are monitoring threats 24-7. While our office here has our development work, the server farm would affect four hundred businesses if it went down."

"If, by some chance, we were brought down, it's a temporary setback. We don't collect personal data from people that could lead to identity breaches. We have backups made every fucking hour. We could shut down the entire server farm and be back in operation in ninety minutes," Henry said.

"Okay. I'm not suggesting we're not prepared, just that we need to treat the threats seriously, just like we've treated other threats we've received in the past year seriously," Luke said.

"I don't want to minimize it from that standpoint," Henry said. "I've sent Darrel out to California to supervise installation of the network defense software. It's still in testing, but we're close to a release."

"Just keep doing it," Luke said. "I know you're tired, Henry. The wedding's in two weeks. Hire anyone you need to help ease the burden. Just let us know what we can do to help."

"You guys, I don't tell you often enough how much your partnership and your friendship mean to me. Without you, I'd have sold out my first inventions and quit. You all give me more purpose than any motivation of fame or fortune possibly could," Henry said.

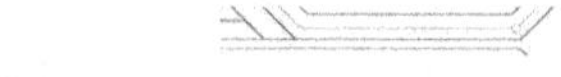

CHASTITY AND LISA left for Baton Rouge on Friday the twenty-second. Lisa's mother and grandmother scheduled a wedding shower for Sunday afternoon and there was no sense arguing about it, even though Lisa protested that she didn't need anything and that gifts should be made to a charity instead. Her mother assured her they would all be funny gifts. Lisa wasn't sure who would attend besides her mother and grandmother and the one bridesmaid she'd selected from her high school class. Layla was a sweet girl and as much of a computer geek as Lisa.

Jackie and Solange had used Layla to search out another couple of friends from high school and then packed the rest of the shower with their own friends. It was embarrassing, but all in good humor as Lisa sat through several older ladies giving her and her friends marital advice.

Henry, Luke, Isobel, Josh, and Henry's parents flew down on Thursday and went directly to the rehearsal. Rev. Jackson was in peak form as he directed people and had an assistant helping to make sure they were in the right positions. They practiced the procession and timing with the organist, and then met the soloist Solange had hired. It was good that Solange took care of the music because she asked Lisa what music she wanted. Her mother would have simply chosen and told her when she got there. The soloist did a pretty good job with a popular Taylor Swift song and they were happy.

With such a small wedding party, the part that took the longest was getting the parents and grandparents seated. Luke took the honors of seating Jackie after Solange and Beau had made the trip to their seats. Then he took his place beside Henry. Josh walked Layla up the aisle. Chastity walked alone and was followed by Lisa and Bill.

Lisa had chosen the triumphal entry march from EZ Daze's most popular online game, which she had worked on. She and her father laughed all the way up the aisle.

Rev. Jackson went through the steps and asked them to review the vows to be sure he'd captured them correctly from the transcript Lisa and Henry had sent him. He didn't say a thing about Chastity's move to place her hands above and below Henry and Lisa's as they recited their vows.

It was too late for a bridal dinner after the rehearsal. Instead, Solange and Beau invited the wedding party to their house to relax and have drinks. Solange had put together some delicious Cajun finger food so people would have something with their drinks.

The alcohol flowed freely and since there were drivers waiting to take them to their hotels, even Henry and Lisa had a drink to toast each other.

"Jesus!" Isobel exclaimed beneath her breath. "This is the house I want, Luke. And that drive between the trees from the street. Find me this house in Pittsburgh! I can't believe this is Lisa's grandparents'. How the hell did they get this kind of money?"

Luke managed to quiet her down. He took her for a walk outside where they stood under the bright moon that was just a few days past full. It was hard for Isobel to admit she was jealous, even though she and Luke were already millionaires and part owners of a multi-million-dollar business.

Luke and Isobel, Josh, and Ryan and Sylvia all stayed at the hotel not far from the church. Lisa, Chastity, and Layla stayed at the Hartmans' home. Henry was left with Solange and Beau, and was encouraged to have one more drink with them before he went to the guest room.

Henry reached into his suitcase and pulled out a brown envelope.

"These are on file with our attorney in Pittsburgh," he said, handing Beau the envelope. "We figured we should have a copy down here as well, so we decided to leave them with you."

"The pre-nups?" Beau asked.

"And our wills. It seems pretty important," Henry said.

"You have trouble, Henry?"

"Not yet. We just find that we need to be more security conscious. You'll notice we have the same drivers who are driving us all around this week. That way they'll be at the wedding and the reception. They're paid security."

"I could have provided that," Beau said.

"We didn't want you to worry about it," Henry said. "Beau, there have been a lot of threats against the company in the past couple of months. There's this preacher in Austin that has declared our *Pythia Speaks* as the antichrist. He preached a rousing sermon Memorial Day weekend whipping people up and encouraging them to don the whole armor of God."

"Most every good preacher preaches that sermon at least once," Beau snorted. He refilled both his and Henry's cognac.

"Well, this preacher put particular emphasis on the sword of the spirit. Said that God's armor wasn't just passive. He sent his people out to war against the principalities and powers and computers. I'm sure he's raised a million dollars just by selling a ceramic lapel pin of a flaming sword. My IT guy is out in San Jose at our server farm and sent us pictures this week of pickets who have started parading in front of the building. Some of them are carrying signs with the flaming sword on them."

"That's a hell of a way to start your married life," Solange said. "You keep our girls safe!"

"Yes, ma'am," Henry agreed.

Even though the news was bad, it felt good to share it with someone in Lisa's family. He wasn't sure if Lisa had shared it with her father and mother.

"We've dealt with threats over the years. Always had good labor relations with our employees, but the waterway wasn't always safe. Upstart shipping companies figured piracy wasn't a bad way to supplement their income at times. To this day, every tug has an armed guard on it. Haven't had an incident this century, but I'm not about to let my guard down."

"I hope you've included that in your stories," Henry said.

"You know, every time I turn around it seems there's something else I need to record. What you got me into!" Beau laughed.

They finished their drinks and all headed to bed.

THE NEXT DAY was filled with tours of the city and finally included a bridal dinner at the hotel near the church. Henry's parents paid for the dinner and it was a great way to spend the evening before the wedding. There were toasts by all the fathers and then the mothers took their turns, adding to the stories of their children that were guaranteed to brighten a few cheeks. Henry managed to make one glass of champagne last through all the toasts.

Fathers, grandfather, mothers, and grandmother, all included Chastity as part of the family as they offered their toasts. They didn't have stories about her youth and she would have been mortified if they'd told any. But Henry had checked twice since the purge and no sign of her prior life had re-emerged on the internet.

This time, after dinner, Henry and the women had rooms at the hotel as well. The women would be going for a spa treatment in the morning while the men were planning a round of golf. The wedding wouldn't be until five-thirty in the evening, unlike Luke and Isobel's mid-day Catholic wedding.

Henry got to his room about eleven o'clock and checked on the reports his teams had left for him. It seemed everything was stable at the offices and with the servers.

He was in his boxers and preparing for bed when there was a knock at the door. He grabbed the bathrobe off the bathroom door and went to answer the door. Lisa had told him that he couldn't see her again until the wedding, but Chastity had made no such commitment. She had her own room because she didn't like to wake up next to anyone.

He opened the door and was nearly bowled over by the barely clad woman who rushed in to kiss him and wrap her legs around his waist.

"Isobel! What the fuck?"

END PART III

PART IV

"If the mind were simple enough for us to understand, we would be too simple to understand it."

— Ray Kurzweil, *The Singularity is Near*

44
WEDDING DAZE

"ISOBEL! WHAT THE FUCK?" Henry yelled, trying to extract himself from the clinging woman. She continued to hold him and attempt to kiss him. She smelled strongly of alcohol.

"I'm here for the ritual pre-wedding fuck!"

"No, Izzy. That's not happening," Henry insisted, pushing her away. "Go back to your husband."

"He's drunk."

"So are you."

"I couldn't do this without a little liquid courage. It doesn't affect how ready I am for you," Isobel said, starting to remove her nightdress.

"I said no, Izzy. Please leave." Henry got past her and opened his door. "Don't get undressed. Get out!"

"What? It was fine for you to fuck me the night before *my* wedding but not to fuck me the night before yours? You're a hypocrite," she screamed.

Henry kept the door open wide. If people heard, people heard.

"The past is past. Go, Isobel."

"I hate you, Henry Pascal! You're not worthy to touch a hair of my head. You think your two sluts will be so noble when an opportunity to have someone else comes along? Chastity has a whole long list of available men who will pay to have a threesome with her and Lisa."

"Isobel, you aren't being rational. Please leave now."

"Fuck you!" Isobel screamed as she stormed out the door. Henry closed and bolted it behind her.

HENRY HAD FANTASIZED about Isobel since he was in junior high school. At one time he thought he was in competition with Luke for her affections, but soon discovered there had never really been a question in Isobel's mind as to who she would marry.

That hadn't stopped them from having sex twice. The first was at the senior prom, just before Isobel went to join Luke. The second was the night before her wedding to Luke. Henry hadn't felt particularly guilty about either time as they had both been initiated by Isobel and technically, they were both single.

Over the past year, though, Henry had lost interest in her as a sexual object. He wasn't sure if it was a sense of loyalty to Lisa, or simply a loss of desire for anyone except Lisa and Chastity. He even suspected that if Chastity had not won Lisa as her girlfriend, he would have stopped leaning on Chastity for any kind of sexual relationship. With both of them, though, it was hard to imagine being in that kind of relationship with anyone else.

Just to be sure, he put the chain on the hotel door as well.

LUKE MISSED THE 8:00 tee-time in the morning. Josh said he'd knocked on his door and was simply told he'd see them later. Henry hoped everything was okay between Luke and Isobel. She'd been irrationally angry when she left him in the middle of the night.

Being on one of many boards at the university, Beau had arranged their tee-time on the university golf course. He just drove a golf cart as the other four played. Josh was nowhere near as accomplished a golfer as the others, but they spotted him several strokes on each hole. Eventually, Beau handled the drives from the tee and fairway and let Josh handle the putting.

They had a good time and then went to the clubhouse for lunch. Luke joined them there.

"Hey, is everything okay?" Henry asked.

"Oh, yeah! My God! Izzy said she was staying out with the girls last night, but got back about midnight and fucked me nearly to death! Apparently, weddings really turn her on," Luke said. "Sorry. I know you were being properly celibate last night, but I'm a married man. We kind of celebrated our anniversary a few days late. We really didn't have time for anything special last Sunday. We had room service for breakfast this morning and then did our best to set another record for sex. It really hasn't been like that since our honeymoon."

"Wow! Congratulations," Henry laughed. "Glad our upcoming wedding was so inspirational!"

The men had a relaxed time over lunch, the fathers and grandfather indulging in a couple of drinks. Luke and Josh each had one, but Henry decided to stay completely alcohol free.

The afternoon for the men was a typical hurry-up-and-wait. They got showered and dressed for the wedding, then went to the church. There they waited for the women in the wedding party.

The women had a relaxing morning with brunch at 9:30 at the spa. They had massages and had hair, nails, and makeup done. They got to the church half an hour later than the men and went into isolation to dress. Of course, the restriction of not seeing the bride before the wedding was only adhered to up to the point when photographs were to be taken. Then the entire wedding party was called to the sanctuary and posed for portraits of the bride and groom, the trio, the wedding party, the families, and even the minister. They barely made it to their places before the congregation started arriving.

Lisa was dressed in an informal white wedding dress. It was completely off the shoulder with a full skirt that fell just below the knee. She'd never been much for showing off her body, except to Henry and Chastity. Chastity and Layla were in matching peach dresses about the same length as Lisa's. Their dresses, however, had plunging necklines. Chastity never wore a bra and her neckline made that obvious. Layla may have been a bit more self-conscious about it, but it was clear that if she had breast support, it was built into the dress.

The men were in dark business suits with simple white rose boutonnieres. They all cleared the sanctuary before people were brought in. Henry sat relaxed with Rev. Jackson in the choir room, next to the chancel. The women were in a ready room at the back of the sanctuary. Josh and Luke doubled as ushers, directing people to the front of the sanctuary. When Luke walked Jackie up the aisle and got her seated, Henry and the minister joined him at the front of the church.

Henry grinned almost as much at Chastity coming up the aisle after Josh and Layla as he did a minute later at Lisa. When Chastity reached the front, Henry leaned toward her and kissed her lightly. Then all attention was on Lisa and Bill. Henry felt a little drunk as he watched his bride approaching. He just couldn't stop grinning.

All told, the service was simple and the fifty or so attending were happy to be there.

"Nature celebrates unions," Rev. Jackson said. "I could use all kinds of examples because very little in our world is singular. Not to minimize the single elements. Gold, for example, is one of our most valuable. But when you think of even the most basic building block of life, water, you discover it is indeed a union. We call it H_2O. Two hydrogen atoms and one oxygen atom in one of God's most perfect unions.

"When I discovered Henry and Lisa wanted to include Chastity in their new union, I could only think of the perfection of H_2O. And once you get to know them, you will discover how perfect that union is.

"Now as far as legal pieces of paper or the United Methodist Church are concerned, of course, we have a marriage license and certificate for Henry and Lisa. But we also have love that is bigger than that and which we are happy to recognize in this service."

Henry thought about how Pythia had answered Rev. Jackson's question of what to speak about at the wedding. Pythia had made the connection between marriage and union. Jackson had taken it the rest of the way. It was a beautiful ceremony as he and Lisa recited their vows and officially asked Chastity to be a part of their family.

"Forever yours," Chastity affirmed to the two of them. It was the vow they had chosen.

Then Lisa and Henry kissed, Lisa and Chastity kissed, and Chastity and Henry kissed. The three walked back down the aisle together.

THE DINNER BUFFET in the hotel banquet room began at 6:30. Everyone had plenty of time to get the few blocks from the church to the hotel since the wedding itself was quite short.

Beau and Solange had paid for the reception dinner and included a band for dancing and entertainment.

It was the first time Henry met Lisa's other grandparents, Bill's parents. Her Aunt Leslie and Uncle Bert were also there. Leslie was Bill's sister. All four lived in Cincinnati. They were pleasant people, though more conservative than Lisa's parents. They didn't really understand the concept of having Chastity as a part of Lisa and Henry's family, but thankfully, didn't make a big deal out of it.

By nine o'clock, the cake had been cut and served and Henry, Lisa, and Chastity were able to leave their reception to just be together. Beau and Solange kept the party going until eleven and then bid everyone a goodnight.

"I'm afraid Grandma and Grandpa Hartman didn't actually understand what it meant for us to be a throuple," Lisa said as the three settled into bed.

The suite they had booked for their wedding night was a room with an attached room and a door between so Chastity could start the night with them and retreat to her own space when she felt she needed to.

"Aunt Leslie was scandalized," Lisa continued. "She started in with the whole 'God instituted marriage between one man and one woman' routine."

"What did you say to that?"

"I looked her straight in the eye and simply said, 'I'm an atheist.' She was so shocked she just sat down next to Uncle Bert and ordered a bourbon on the rocks. You know Cincinnati is almost in Kentucky."

They laughed and held each other, gradually moving toward more amorous gestures with occasional bits of memory from the day thrown into their conversation.

"From what Luke told me this noon, Isobel was pretty demanding," Henry said. "They were trying to set a record for how much sex they could have in one night. Isobel didn't make your spa day this morning, did she? Luke missed our tee-time and joined us at lunch."

"Didn't you miss playing with her?"

"Why would I ever want anyone but the two who are in my bed right now?"

"I told you," Chastity whispered. "*Our* Henry is pretty much a one-woman man. I'm just glad he includes me with her."

"I never really doubted it," Lisa sighed. "I love you so much! Both of you. I could have dealt with a little Isobel on the side."

"Not necessary," Henry said. "I am in the woman of my dreams. I am beside my constant friend and lover. It's not that I have anything philosophically opposed to people who have something outside their relationship; I just have no desire for it."

"Move in me, my husband!" Lisa commanded, thrusting her hips at him. "And then get ready to have your two women love you all night."

"I will also be with you as my two women love each other," he said.

After brunch with the family on Saturday morning, Lisa, Henry, and Chastity went to the airport for a flight to Boston. It was too late when they got in to catch the ferry to Provincetown, so they were booked into a luxury hotel just a mile from the airport.

At the hotel, they found flights west were being canceled because of tornadoes in the Midwest. The harried desk clerk shook his head sadly.

"We have a reservation," Henry explained calmly.

"Everything has been messed up by the tornadoes," the clerk explained. "I'm trying to find something. We may have to move you over to a different hotel."

Lisa wiggled up next to Henry and he put his arm around her. She had a pleading look on her face.

"We just got married and it's our honeymoon," she pled, looking woefully at the clerk.

"I... Uh... Let me see. All I have is a two-bedroom family suite. I wanted to get a larger group into the suite," he said, tapping the keys of the computer in front of him.

"We'll take her with us!" Lisa declared, pulling Chastity up beside her. "We'll need two bedrooms, obviously."

The clerk looked up at the two women with their arms around each other as Henry held Lisa under his.

"Oh... Okay... I think... We can do that. It's so kind of you. To welcome a stranger. Ma'am, are you okay with that arrangement?" the clerk asked.

"Yes," Chastity said. "I'll just leave my door open and listen."

Lisa reached up and kissed Chastity.

"I can get you a good view, too," she whispered, loudly enough for the clerk to hear.

He took Henry's credit card and license, then the licenses of the other two. He didn't suggest that either of the women would need to pay their share; he just handed Henry three keycards.

"Room service is open twenty-four hours if you need anything. There's a concierge on the floor who will provide coffee, soft drinks, and ice. Have a nice stay," he said, intentionally not looking at Lisa and Chastity until Henry turned away. Then he openly stared as the three headed for the bell station and handed the bell captain a key.

***

THE STAY, WHILE luxurious and perfect for everything the trio intended to do, was all too brief. At nine-thirty the next morning, they boarded a ferry across Massachusetts Bay and Cape Cod Bay to Provincetown. On the hour and a half crossing, they saw a pod of whales and shared their excitement.

Chastity had done the research and booked the reservation for their sojourn in Provincetown. It was a lovely bed and breakfast near the wharf where they had two bedrooms.

"I did some checking and talked to our hosts. They have a thing for unusual combinations of people. There are three in their family," Chastity said.

"Like ours?" Lisa asked.

"Almost. All three of them are women. I'm afraid Henry will be the only male in the house."

"I'm already used to that," he laughed. "Even the cats are females. What's three more?"

The rooms were lovely and while the door didn't connect directly between them, they were next to each other in the hall. They shared the bath. Dinner that evening was at a local lobster pot restaurant. When the huge crustaceans were served, Lisa whistled.

"That is one big crawfish!"

"It's a lobster, honey," Henry laughed.

"Well, excuse my Cajun soul!" Lisa joined in. "It looks a lot easier to peel and eat than the little fellers in an étouffée."

"How long are you going to keep your Cajun accent?" Chastity asked.

"Don't you like it?"

"I love it. It makes my panties wet."

"I move you keep it," Henry said.

"Whoo wee!" Lisa said.

"Mom and Dad came out to Massachusetts years ago and when they got back, they said lobster was just like toast," Henry said.

"What's that mean?" Chastity asked.

"It's primarily a vehicle to get butter from the dish to your mouth."

THE WEEK WAS spent loving, relaxing, and exploring. They hiked in the National Seashore Park and went to the beach. They went on whale-watching cruises. They blushed appropriately when their hosts asked if they had a good sleep at breakfast. And like all honeymoons, it passed too quickly. They planned to leave Sunday morning.

Saturday morning, Henry rolled out of bed and kissed his wife.

"Mmm. You're up early," Lisa yawned.

"It strikes me that in this whole week, you haven't really had alone time with Chastity," Henry said. "We're going back to Pittsburgh tomorrow. You should have a little time just for the two of you."

"You know we like having you with us," Lisa said.

"Yes, but you like to be together, too. I never want to be a clit-blocker."

"Oh, it's too early for that kind of pun," Lisa groaned. "You know I'm bi, so I like having Chastity lick me as much as having you fuck me. But Chastity is mostly hetero. She simply can't stand most men. In fact, any men but you."

"I don't blame her. Her life was one of being used by men. I came danger-ously close to being just another one of them," Henry said.

"She's always loved you and gave you her body because you were dif-ferent than all the others. But... I could get into enjoying some time with my girlfriend. What are you going to do?"

"Oh, I thought I'd do a little antiquing in some of those shops we saw. Maybe find something to buy as a commemorative of our honeymoon."

"Well, if you see the two of us out in one of those shops, just turn away. We might be getting you a surprise."

There was a knock on the door. Henry opened it for Chastity.

"Ready for breakfast?" she asked.

"Sleepyhead over there in the bed is waiting for a very personal invitation to eat from her girlfriend," Henry said as he slipped past Chastity and lightly pushed her into the room. He went down for a solo breakfast, which the hosts were very interested in.

HENRY WAS, INDEED, interested in the antique shops and other stores in the historic town. He thought having a nice token of their week together would be a perfect way to end it. He stopped at another of the restaurants along the waterfront for a late lunch and decided to mix all the cultures together and have what was advertised as a Cajun bouillabaisse. It had the typical seafood in the huge bowl of soup, but also had andouille sausage in it. He thought it was a little spicier than most of the food he'd had in P-town.

As he sat extracting the flesh from mussels, his phone sounded an alert. He nearly dropped the phone in his soup when he saw it.

"Attack on corporate server detected. Tracking."

"Shit!" he said, standing at the table. He immediately thumbed the contact listing for Darrel. "Darrel, there's an attack underway on our server," he barked.

"Just got the alert," Darrel replied. "I'm on my way out the door. I'll let you know as soon as we have something."

Henry disconnected and sat back down to see if he could still enjoy his soup. The alert sounded again. He looked at the phone.

"Attack on *Pythia Speaks* server detected. Tracking."

"Oh, this is bad," he breathed. He called Scott out in California.

"We're monitoring the defense system," Scott replied as soon as he picked up the call. "We've got everyone on their way to the office and have begun an emergency backup of all servers."

"Let me know if you need anything and if the attack spreads to other servers than *Pythia Speaks*," Henry said.

"Will do, boss. Uh... Congratulations on your wedding," Scott replied.

"Thanks."

Henry disconnected and dialed the conference number for Lisa and Chastity.

"Hi, lover," they answered together.

"We've got an emergency at the office. Both Pittsburgh and San Jose are being attacked. I might need to fly out tonight," he said.

"We'll pack," Lisa said at once.

"Leave the travel arrangements to me. I'll call as soon as I have a departure time," Chastity said.

"I love you both," Henry answered.

45

UNDER FIRE

CHASTITY GOT THEM OUT of Provincetown on a private seaplane at four in the afternoon. They landed at Boston Harbor and caught a taxi to the airport. The flight from Boston had a connection in Newark and then to Pittsburgh, but they managed to get to the apartment about midnight. Henry had periodic updates with Darrel and Scott. Scott had his security team in full operation. Conrad and Rebecca were both in the office with Darrel.

Henry planned to go directly to the office, but they all encouraged him to get some sleep first. The counterattack software was having difficulty tracing the attack.

"They seem to have learned from the last major attack," Conrad said when he talked to Henry. "They're using a rotating series of proxies so by the time the protection AI traces through about five proxies, the attack has changed to a different set. It's clever for protecting themselves, but it's also easier to shut them off as soon as they make contact. We are rotating open ports on the server. They have to try again to get another port, so they don't have time to search for another before we've worked down the chain of proxies."

"Shut down everything that's non-critical for the search. All company computers offline," Henry instructed. "Then do a hot upgrade of the server to the newest version of the counterattack AI. Make sure San Jose has it ready to launch as well."

"Got it. See you in the morning."

Henry did not go to bed immediately. Lisa and Chastity expected him to go straight to the office, but instead he went to the fourth floor lounge with his laptop. He looked at the clock and then decided to make the call he'd been anticipating with dread.

"Schwartz," came the abrupt answer to the call.

"General, I need to know if Open Cloak Design is still considered a military asset," Henry said without further preamble.

"You've not shipped the code for the new network defense system," Nathan said carefully. "I would have to say that with secret military development being undertaken in your facility, you are still a military asset."

"This military asset is under cyberattack. We are preparing a counterattack, but the attackers are cycling proxies. We've not yet definitively identified the source, but have deployed the new counterattack software on our servers so we can strike when there is a confirmed target."

"Do you have an idea of where the attack is coming from?"

"It appears to be coming from Russia, but we have not yet identified a single IP address."

"Henry, do not destroy Russia's computer grid!"

"No, sir. You know the commercial software is restricted to one degree of separation. With the nature of this attack, I'm afraid that will not be enough. These guys are pretty savvy."

"I'm on my way to Pittsburgh. I'll see you at the office at 0530."

"I'll be there, sir."

The call ended abruptly. Henry relaxed. He'd called in the cavalry. It seemed silly to think that the cavalry was armed with the weapons he'd sold it, but he'd consider the irony of that later. In the meantime, he launched his private search engine from his laptop.

Both Page Services and Open Cloak were under attack. Page Services was owned by Open Cloak now, but the only thing being served on behalf of the company was *Pythia Speaks*. Henry began his searches with 'Known opposition to Open Cloak Design.' He launched a second search while the first was still running. 'Known opposition to Pythia Speaks.'

It only took a few minutes before he had refined the searches so that he could compare them. The summary spoke volumes.

"Rev. Daniel Reeves of the Sword of the Spirit Evangelical Church (formerly Texas Fundamental Congregation, renamed in April 2029) has frequently spoken about both *Pythia Speaks* and Open Cloak Design, decrying artificial intelligence and the 'antichrist oracle' it spoke through. He has rallied thousands of members of his congregation to boycott and obstruct the two in any way they can."

Henry entered his next search. 'Connections between Rev. Daniel Reeves of the Sword of the Spirit Evangelical Church and Russian computer hackers.' The search engine brought up a news announcement that the church had broadened its streaming online with audiences in thirty-two countries, including Russia. Henry let the search continue running as he went to bed and cuddled next to Lisa for three hours.

HENRY ARRIVED AT the office at five-twenty with Chastity and a couple of three-quart coffee thermoses. It would get the day started off with a jolt. General Schwartz showed up at the elevator before they'd gone up.

"General, welcome," Henry said.

"I hope that's strong coffee you are carrying."

"Lots of it, sir," Chastity said. Schwartz was in uniform and was an imposing sight.

"I figured I'd better give this an official look as an attack on a military asset," he said. "We'll do a couple of photos when this is over and a press release that will keep you clear of repercussions. Let's just make sure we don't go too hard."

"I appreciate your guidance, sir."

They arrived in the office and Rebecca came out of Conrad's office. She was startled by the general's presence and almost snapped to attention. She was in blue jeans and a T-shirt, though, and didn't salute.

"General!" she exclaimed. "Please excuse my attire. We were called in yesterday afternoon to deter an attack."

"And is the attack deterred?"

"Not yet, sir. We believe we have an IP address, however. The network defense is working, though the enemy is using additional subterfuge," she said.

"What can we do with a single IP address, Henry?" Nathan asked.

"We can put that computer out of business," Henry said. "We are pretty sure there are at least a hundred computers involved in the attack."

"Rebecca, what is the status of the deployment of our military counter-attack software?"

"The military version, sir?" Rebecca said. It was obvious she was not expecting the general's presence and that she and Conrad were cooking something up. "Sir, we were preparing the final test of our version before locking it down for transfer to the Pentagon."

"Where was this test to take place?"

"Sir, version 0.91a has been deployed on this company's servers." She hesitated.

"And?"

"And also at the server farm in San Jose," she said quietly.

"Good work. Let's see what we can verify."

They all poured cups of coffee and went into the conference room where Darrel had the large screen projector showing a split between messages being received from the software in Pittsburgh and that displayed in San Jose.

"Henry, Nathan, it's good to see you both. Henry, I'm sorry we cut your honeymoon short," he said.

"We were supposed to get back today," Henry said. "It's just something I want our attackers to pay for. I don't even want to know how much Chastity had to pay to get us back early."

"I'm more concerned about what Isobel will say," Chastity said as she poured a cup of coffee for Darrel. "I plan to expense it."

"Conrad, I understand we have an IP address?"

"Yes, Henry. It's IPv6—128-bit protocol. So, its security is higher than an average hacker. Fortunately, the AI is tracing directly through it now to determine what other devices are connected," Conrad said.

"Here's another address for you to check and cross reference," Henry said, sliding a slip of paper across the desk. "Is there any sign that the hackers know we've traced them?"

"Nothing obvious," Darrel said. "They seem to think we have to backtrack through their proxies each time in order to counterattack. We are watching this one computer directly without showing our presence."

"Do we have visual?" Nathan asked.

"Yes, sir," Rebecca answered. "We have a direct feed from the hacker's camera and a link to his display."

"How'd we do that?" Henry asked.

"That's military grade hacking," Nathan chuckled.

Both audio and video appeared on an inset. They could see a hacker focused on the computer with the results being shown on the corporate server display. They could hear him speaking in Russian.

"I have contact with the second IP address," Conrad said. "It is definitely engaged in the attack on Page Services and has a second degree link to the other IP."

An inset appeared in the Page Services window with another hacker answering the first.

"They're in the same location!" Schwartz said.

"See if we can get an estimate of how many computers are engaged in the attack," Henry said.

"With as sophisticated as this attack appears to be, I'd say we need to respond with a complete wipe of the involved systems," Nathan said. "Do you have something that will accomplish that, Henry?"

"Yes, sir. We did a significant upgrade of the optimization software before we released the network version. We upgraded the code that was used in the last counterattack. Of course, the few attacks we've had since then were countered with a slap on the wrist version."

"Of course. I think you can load the full wipe version as soon as we know the depth of our target."

Conrad was engaged in tracing connections with the search AI and Darrel was monitoring the frequency of attacks and the shifting of access ports. If the hackers had thought they might not be the best and strongest at this game, they might have been alarmed by the tactics employed to disable attack paths so quickly on so many computers. Presently the AI was treating the attack like a game of hide and seek.

Henry went to work loading the response settings and sending them to the team in San Jose.

"We are loaded," Scott said.

"We have at least twenty computers attacking this network and *Pythia Speaks*," Conrad said. "The server farm reports random attacks have hit over three hundred of the six hundred servers at that location. I'd say we have a minimum of four hundred boxes involved in the attack."

"We've done some estimates," Nathan said. "We now estimate, based on the damage your counterattack a year and a half ago did, that each degree of separation is an order of magnitude more than the previous. One box at level zero. Ten at level one. One hundred at level two. To get four hundred boxes, we need to go to level three with a potential reach of one thousand units. Captain Bernard, set the response level at three degrees."

"Response level locked in," Rebecca said. "Counterattack is loaded."

"Execute," Nathan said. Rebecca hit the enter key.

"Oh, that was clever," Conrad said. "They managed to set one of the boxes at the server farm as a proxy."

"Damage?" Henry asked.

"No," Conrad said. "One of the features in the new version is to ignore the proxies when executing the counterattack. We only identified it as a sudden disconnect."

"Status?" Nathan barked.

"Network defense is reporting a cessation of hostile activity on all servers at Open Cloak and Page Services," Rebecca said. "We should have an estimate of number of casualties in a few minutes."

"How are we getting that?" Henry asked.

"The military package includes a traffic assessment in the target region. While not all the boxes may have been in Russia, seeing the percent of traffic decrease will give us an estimate of total number of enemy killed," Rebecca said.

"It's actually based on the same way we estimate enemy casualties on the battlefield when we are sending rockets. We see a satellite image of life signs and look at the reduction in life signs after an hour," Nathan said.

"Hmm. I've always wondered what the destructive capacity of the counterattack actually was. I might put in a request to have our response level reset to two degrees of separation instead of just one."

"I'll consider the request," Nathan said.

"I do wish there was immediate feedback," Henry said. "It's spooky when everything just goes silent."

"On the internet, no one can hear you scream," Nathan responded.

It took the rest of the morning to complete the assessment. Every box on the server farm was scrubbed and restarted. Darrel did the same for the corporate server and for each computer in the office as it was brought online again. Then the data started rolling in from the Pentagon at Nathan's request.

The report showed the major outage was in St. Petersburg, but also showed pockets of outage in India and Saudi Arabia. It was harder to assess whether those locations were actively involved in the attack or if they were simply collateral damage.

"All told, the estimate is of 730 units going dark at exactly the time of the counterattack," Nathan said. "Captain Bernard, I'd say your beta test was a success. Your job for the rest of this week will be to package up the product and clean all evidence of the Pentagon's presence from here."

"You mean this was a test?" Henry barked.

"Oh, no. Just a fortuitous happenstance," Nathan said. He lowered his voice so only Henry could hear him. "I'm saving Bernard's ass. She was planning to deploy the military grade response before we got here. Otherwise, there was no reason for her to have the beta deployed both here and at the server farm."

"Got it. Thank you," Henry said. "Conrad, I think we can safely say our beta test was also successful. I believe Luke has a waitlist of institutions ready for preliminary release. Find a clever name for the app and let's get it packaged. Uh... tomorrow. For today, let's see that there is a person or two responsible for monitoring the systems both here and in San Jose, and the rest of us take the rest of Sunday off."

"Let me take you to dinner, Henry. You and your wife. It seems like we should have a little bit of a celebration. Rebecca, why don't you and Conrad join us," Nathan said. "Darrel? Dinner?"

"Thank you, Nathan."

"Nathan," Henry said, pulling him aside. "Where my wife and I go, Chastity also goes. Do you mind?"

"Oh! Hmm. Of course not. Anyone else?"

"I'll reward the others on my own."

HENRY AND CHASTITY stopped at the row house long enough to pick up Lisa and head out to the club for dinner. There, they met Nathan, Conrad, Rebecca, Darrel, and were surprised to find Luke and Isobel as well.

"How did you happen to get here for this?" Henry asked his friends.

"We were just going out for dinner when we saw you all troop in. We've been monitoring the situation at the office all night, but decided we'd be better staying out of the way of the pros. Congratulations on getting it stopped," Luke said.

"I just don't want to hear my phone alarm going off again anytime soon," Henry sighed. "You remember General Schwartz, don't you?"

"I do indeed," Luke said. "It's good to see you again, General."

"And you. Please let's ignore the uniform and just call me Nathan. Mrs. Riordan, how nice to see you again, too," Nathan said.

"Oh, *you* can call me Izzy," Isobel said. "I *love* your uniform."

Henry raised an eyebrow at Luke but his friend just shrugged. Very few people in the company called Isobel anything but Mrs. Riordan. It was her thing.

They sat at dinner and ordered cocktails. Chastity, Lisa, and Henry had virgin Margaritas.

"This event will trigger the release of the remainder of the funds owed your company by the Army," Nathan said. "I believe we still owe you half of the five million."

"Oh, I'll drink to that," Isobel said, raising her glass. Henry wasn't sure what she was drinking, but she ordered another.

"I'm withdrawing my request for a reset to two degrees," Henry said. "I believe we are better locking it to one degree and calling for help if we need something more. Most of the institutions that will be buying the network defense system only face individual or small group hacks."

"I would have granted it for *your* use," Schwartz said.

"I would say that the major server farms and software developers are the most vulnerable to an attack like we faced today," Henry said. "I don't think the university would have been attacked last year if it hadn't been a channel to get to various corporate servers. I'd had a run-in with some Chinese wanting to take over the company by more subtle means earlier."

"You are probably right," Nathan said. "And having too much power in individual hands is a recipe for disaster. I believe we will limit our military grade to six levels. At orders of magnitude, that would blank 100,000 boxes. The seventh degree would be a million and the eighth would be enough to plunge the world into chaos. If it was launched against a government entity, it could completely wipe out that government. I don't like that idea."

"If you stop to think about what can happen with access to our government, it wouldn't be beyond the realm of possibility that another division of the government would get its hands on the program. It needs to have codes like nuclear codes in order to launch it. By your estimates, if it was set to the tenth degree of separation, it would be capable of ending the electronic age as we know it," Henry said.

"It's a sobering thought and one that I will give serious consideration to before we install it anywhere. I believe our developers should be able to take that part in hand when we're back in Washington."

They finished the meal. Henry thanked the general again and all left the club except Luke and Isobel, who decided to stay for a nightcap.

"Are you okay to drive, honey?" Lisa asked.

"Tired, but also kind of jazzed," Henry said.

"Well, I'm going to curl up in the back seat. You and Chastity can keep each other company up front."

They got in Henry's Spark and Lisa got her feet tucked under her as she leaned against the rear passenger side. Chastity got in front and Henry started the car.

"You know, you really need to trade this old thing in and get something new. Maybe electric, or one of those fuel cell models," Chastity said as she belted herself in.

"But this has been a good and dependable car. And it only has 207,000 miles on it."

"Geez, Henry. Do you ever spend any of your money?" she giggled.

"I just got married," Henry protested. "I need to plan for our future. I have two wives to care for."

Henry stopped at the traffic light near the exit of the club.

"I still think you should have a family car then," Chastity insisted. "I wish there was a way for us all three to ride together instead of having one isolated in the back."

Henry pulled away when the light changed.

"That's probably..."

A black car ran the light from the left and T-boned Henry's Chevy. He didn't hear the crash, or see the flaming sword painted on the hood of the car.

46

JOURNEY INTO DARKNESS

HENRY HAD NEVER been plagued with nightmares. He credited that to his ability to almost instantly recognize when he was dreaming. Nightmares were a result of believing you were experiencing something false. Usually, if he had an unpleasant dream, he could simply change channels or turn it off.

"God is punishing you!" Isobel said in his ear. He turned to see the Latina beauty standing naked beside his bed. Yes, this had to be a dream.

"God isn't interested in me," he responded. "Or anyone else, for that matter." He started to turn the channel, but Rev. Daniel Reeves was standing behind Isobel in a long flowing robe with a bunch of stoles hung around his neck.

"The Sword of the Spirit has descended upon you. You will be judged for your sins. You have set an idol before the people to worship and adore. There is no god but God and he will not be satisfied until this idol is cast down and you have been thrown into the flames of judgment," the preacher said.

"Is that why you hired Russian atheists to attack our servers?"

"God can use anyone to serve his purpose."

"Maybe he's using Pythia for his purpose," Henry argued.

He turned back to Isobel. As long as she was in his dream and naked, he was going to enjoy her.

"Is that guy Catholic?" Henry asked.

Isobel looked at the preacher as if she'd just discovered him and tried to cover herself up with her hands. The robes fell away and Reeves stood there in a business suit with his Bible flopping around in one hand like a fish.

"You aren't part of the Church!" Isobel declared. "You're a false prophet."

"It's the Romans who have led the people astray for centuries. You are idol worshipers, too," the preacher shot back.

"Your only god is money," Isobel responded. "How can you demand that the poor and homeless give you what sustenance they need; and you turn around and spend their money on lavish homes and gluttony?"

Isobel and Reeves continued to argue and Henry lost interest in them. He slept until he was nudged awake by a naked girl in his bed. He turned to look into Lisa's eyes.

"My love," He whispered to her. "How I love you."

"Did you kill him?" she demanded.

"Who?"

"The preacher. He caused all this, didn't he?"

"Don't know, don't care. I don't even know where he lives," Henry told his wife while trying to kiss her.

"Didn't stop you with me," Tom Reynolds said.

Henry looked over Lisa's shoulder. It was another dream then. Reynolds was dead.

"I didn't kill you," Henry said.

"I was as good as dead long before the bullets found me. My job gone. The girls gone. My money gone. Even my property up north was confiscated. I had nothing. All my hope was gone."

"You killed yourself," Henry said. "You had nothing to hope for. Hope is what makes men despair. Despair makes them die."

"Right now, the preacher has hope," Lisa whispered. Tom faded out of his dream. "Take away his hope."

Henry pulled Lisa closer to him, but held only a wad of blanket in his arms.

"Partner, you need to build us a fortress," Luke said from a chair by the window. Henry hadn't remembered a window in his dreams, but the only thing that had remained constant was the bed he was sleeping in. Surely, it must be about time to get up.

"I'm no architect," Henry said.

"A digital fortress. Of course, if you want to build Isobel and me a mansion, that would be nice, too. We're getting married."

Dreams. Luke and Isobel were married a long time ago.

"You just said I need to build a digital fortress."

"Like a castle on a hill," Luke said. "Where no one can successfully attack us. It's not enough to have a counterattack. We need to prevent attacks before they occur."

"It's true," Ryan said from a chair on the other side of the bed. The room was beginning to look familiar with Henry's father in it. "The thing that's been bothering me about my *Forever Yours* files is who will have access. Anyone could ask me a question and the AI me has to answer. I have no protection. No way to refuse to answer."

"I'll think about it. I'm getting tired. I need to sleep on it," Henry said, burrowing under his covers.

"No need for that," Sylvia said, sitting on the arm of his father's chair. "You've been asleep for days. You haven't even asked about your wives. It's time for you to wake up, Henry."

"Lisa! Chastity! What happened?"

"What did you do to my granddaughter?" Beau demanded, towering over the bed. "You said she'd be safe!"

"No! Where is she? Lisa! Chastity! Where are you?"

"Here, love," the voices of his wife and her girlfriend spoke together.

"It's time to wake up, Henry," Chastity said. She pulled his right arm around her as she stood by the bed.

"Come back to us, Henry," Lisa said. He tried to put his left arm around her, but it wouldn't move. "We all want to go home now."

"Lisa! My precious wife," he gasped, opening his eyes. "You're alive!"

"Banged my head pretty badly, but I'm alive. They say I was concussed. I'm still on concussion protocol but I should be fine."

Henry turned to see Chastity looking down at him. He saw the purple and orange bruise on her face. She winced as he squeezed her.

"Chas! What happened? Are you okay? Where are we?" Henry was still confused. This wasn't his bed. "You're hurt!"

"Couple of broken ribs and bruises on my face and chest. I guess the airbags saved us all from more damage, but I'm sure they caused the bruises on my face."

"We're at the hospital," Lisa said. "We refused to leave after they discharged us."

"Why? I don't remember. Why am I in bed? And you're bruised and broken! Tell me this is all another dream!"

"The accident. You don't remember any of it, do you?" Chastity asked. "I don't blame you. It was nasty."

"A car ran a red light and T-boned our car," Lisa said. "You took the brunt of it."

"I don't remember. We fought off the cyberattack and went to dinner," Henry said.

"I was curled up on the passenger side of the back seat," Lisa said. "I mostly just banged my head through the window. They say I was lucky not to be cut up badly, too."

"You were lucky the guy hit you just behind the driver's seat," Chastity said. "It still broke your arm and leg and gave you a severe concussion. I think it was your head hitting me that broke my ribs. We've been watching over you for five days."

"Five days? I knew I was tired after we left the office, but I didn't think I'd sleep five days," Henry said, flinching when he drew a deep breath. His ribs were also either broken or bruised.

"No doubt exhaustion had something to do with it, too," Lisa said. "I think part of the reason we all survived was because we were so tired and relaxed."

"I'm so thankful you're here and awake!" Chastity said, petting his forehead and hair.

Henry's initial assumption that she was naked proved to be a dream memory rather than reality. She wore blue hospital scrubs, identical to Lisa's. She reached for the button that would call a nurse. The nurse arrived within seconds.

"Ah, Mr. Pascal! You're awake. We've all been waiting for you. Especially these young women. I'll call the doctor on duty and he'll be here to check on you."

She turned her head to a lapel mike and gave instructions, then started checking Henry's vitals. The whole time, Henry continued to stare at Chastity and Lisa as they stood nearby.

<hr>

HENRY WAS RELEASED from the hospital two days later, once the doctor was satisfied he wasn't suffering any long-term damage from the concussion and had medications to keep the pain under control. Henry always considered himself to have a high pain threshold, but he was thankful for the prescription painkillers the doctor gave him. By the time each dose wore off, he was in pain again.

Lisa and Chastity called in help from their friends and had a hospital bed and recliner moved into the living room of the row house. It was definite

Henry would be unable to negotiate the stairs for a while. His mother came to supervise the transition to the house and make sure he was settled. Having a medical professional in the house had always kept Henry on the straight and narrow when it came to following doctor's orders and Sylvia promised she would be looking in on him regularly.

Henry found it intensely frustrating to be confined to the bed and needing help to even move to the chair nearby. They'd moved the reclining loveseat from their sitting room downstairs so either Lisa or Chastity could sit next to him when he was out of bed. Chastity went back to work the next week, but Lisa stayed home. She was no longer working for Open Cloak, but had to be in the office in their suite to set up working remotely for her father. Still, she came to sit beside Henry and to help him move whenever he needed her.

"Oh, no!" Henry said, soon after he'd settled at home.

"What's wrong?" Lisa asked, alarmed.

"Our celebration. It was supposed to be the weekend after we got back from our honeymoon. I missed it!" Henry said.

"Not really, dear. We didn't hold it without you," Lisa laughed. "Everyone was very understanding and I simply told them we would hold the celebration after you were ambulatory again. We're still married."

"I'm so sorry, Lisa. There's so much pain I've caused."

"Do you need a pill?"

"Not that kind of pain. Or at least not just that kind. I never considered that we would actually become a physical target. It's just computer code!" Henry was becoming even more frustrated by not being able to work. He could scarcely go to the office without being able to walk. What was it Luke had said about an ADA compliance notice they'd received?

"Honey, did you know that according to recent surveys, seventy percent of Americans use some form of generative AI or chat bot? Half of Americans say they use it daily. And get this: twenty-five percent of Americans say they have a personal AI friend. You and I know it's just code. The majority of Americans have forgotten that."

"Shit! I really need to get back to the office."

"You really need to rest and recover," his wife said.

HENRY HAD TO return to the clinic for periodic x-rays and assessment of his healing. They called a non-emergency medical transportation company that arrived with a large van that could accommodate Henry's wheelchair and extended left leg.

Lisa bought a new car and Henry was happy to see her take initiative. Not that she didn't talk to him about it, but she made the final decision. It was a minivan. With the rear seats removed and a movable ramp, she and Chastity could move him out of the house and into the van. He could get his leg all the way inside, even though his head was near the roof. That reduced the number of calls for a medical cab.

"Are you sure you wanted to get a minivan?" Henry asked.

"Well, if we decide not to have children for a while, we can always sell it, but it is pretty comfortable for the three of us," Lisa said.

"Children?" Henry asked.

"When we're ready."

Of course, Henry had thought about having children with Lisa, but it hadn't soaked in that getting married was the first step in that process.

SEVERAL PEOPLE CAME by to visit Henry, including almost daily visits by his mother. Luke and Isobel had visited the first week he was home and Henry pled with his friend to bring him his laptop from the office. He'd left it there after the cyberattack. He really wanted to do some research if nothing else.

It was the following Monday when Luke arrived bearing the equipment.

"Don't try to work full-time from your bed," Luke laughed. "It's a long recovery process when you get banged up as much as you were."

"Whatever happened to the guy who hit me?" Henry asked. "Seems we should be launching a personal injury lawsuit."

"Your parents, Lisa's parents, her grandparents and even my parents have an army of lawyers standing by. Lisa and Chastity talked to them to set things in motion with the insurance companies while you were still in the hospital. Doesn't surprise me that they haven't talked to you about it yet. Those are two stubborn and determined ladies," Luke said. "The guy who rammed you is dead. The official report released to the insurance company said he was driving under the influence of heavy-duty drugs. No seatbelt. He went straight through the windshield like he was impaled on his own sword."

"What sword?"

"It was painted or decaled or something on the hood of his car. In a newspaper interview with the guy's wife, she asked first, 'Where's the money?' Since he died, she expected someone to be bringing her a lot of money. Then you'll love this. She said the Sword of the Spirit was supposed to protect him because he was doing the work of the Lord," Luke said.

"Fuck! Are you telling me he was sent by that church?"

"Hmm. 'Sent by' might be too strong a phrase. Though, I'd guess he could have interpreted it that way. That preacher has been continuing to talk. He whips his followers into a frenzy and one takes a notion to carry out the will of God and put an end to the great Satan. The preacher and the church, of course, have denied all knowledge of who he was or why he did what he did. But in the next breath they called him a great Christian man, called by God, and resting in the bosom of Jesus."

"Dog whistling. 'I never *said* to kill him.' People have been denying their culpability in everything for years. People said '8647' but when someone made an attempt on the bastard, they acted all innocent and surprised. 'We never said to kill him! That's not what we meant.' The preacher says the Great Satan must be eliminated, but then innocently claims he never said Henry Pascal needed to be killed. Son of a bitch."

"Yeah. The preacher's sermon about Pythia became so popular online that he started selling ceramic lapel pins of a flaming sword, changed the name of his church to The Sword of the Spirit, printed up decals to put on people's cars, and stickers to put on briefcases, computers, and school books. There aren't as many as wore MAGA hats, but they're popular.

"Religion trying to intimidate the rest of the world," Henry sighed.

"Will it ever end?"

"I doubt it."

THERE WAS A lot of information on Henry's computer that he wanted access to. Luke had given him information that he suspected but had not yet been able to confirm or act upon. This Rev. Reeves fellow had made an enemy. He'd dreamed about it when he was in the hospital. Henry was determined to destroy the enemy of his company and his family.

He'd learned quite a bit from General Schwartz while they were countering the attack on the servers. Schwartz was decisive and definitely in command. He gave the orders and then acted to be sure his subordinate was protected from any backlash. He took care of his people. And Henry realized, *he* was one of the general's people as well.

It was an example Henry determined to follow. He would protect his business and his people and his family. He simply needed to determine the appropriate level of response. Working on his laptop, even with one hand made the pain in his arm, leg, and side worse. He'd had periodic headaches ever since he woke up. Sometimes he took a painkiller before it was pre-scribed. "Every eight hours as needed." Henry considered the last two words separate from the first three.

Twice in his life, he had searched out all the personal information about individuals who had threatened them. The first was Tom Reynolds. He'd reported all the relevant information on Tom to the police and his employer, but not confident in their ability to protect Chastity, he'd also called Paul Riordan. He wasn't sure what Paul did, or who he called, or even if he'd done anything, but a short while later, Tom was killed in a gun battle outside Chastity's apartment building. Police said it was drug related. Maybe it was.

Then Kaitlyn Lau had attempted to force him to marry her in order to take control of his business. She'd claimed to be pregnant. Henry's searches had revealed that she was being pressured by foreign interests to get control for them. Henry didn't take it out on Kaitlyn. He rewrote specifications in her trust to give her control of the millions in it upon graduation from college. He hadn't taken any other action against the other interests or her parents until the university AI lab and his own servers had been hacked. Then he blew them out of the water. He didn't regret causing a ten percent outage of China's internet capacity, but hadn't known how close it came to causing a war.

Reeves was going to require both subtlety and permanence. What had he said to Tom in his dream? Loss of hope leads to despair. Despair leads to death. In his dream, Lisa had said, "Take away his hope." He needed Reeves to experience a level of despair that would reduce him to the contemporary version of the Bible's sackcloth and ashes. Preferably *his* ashes.

Henry worked for four days to instruct an AI on exactly how it was to destroy the minister and hopefully the entire Sword of the Spirit movement. He fine-tuned the parameters and even the timeline for when different aspects would be implemented.

When the pain was too much, he took another oxycodone. When the prescription ran out, rather than bother his doctor for a refill, he picked the code for the pharmacy and renewed it. The pills were delivered the next day.

He'd read the Bible once out of curiosity and was particularly struck by the story of Job. He was a man of God and God blessed him. Then Satan came along and challenged God. Thus began the tribulations of Job. He lost his flocks and herds. He lost his sons and daughters. He was afflicted with boils and disease. Yet Job stayed faithful to God. And how did God repay him? Health. More flocks and herds. More beautiful daughters and stronger sons.

Did that replace the pain and sorrow that Job felt at the loss of his first family? Was his wife all kind and understanding about his faith in God that led to having her first fourteen children raped and killed? Did those children ever forgive him? Was there ever a day in Job's life that he didn't mourn for the lives that had been lost for *his* faith?

Henry would see if Reeves had even a shred of Job's faith and patience. He executed the command and sent his AI to destroy Rev. Daniel Reeves and the Sword of the Spirit Evangelical Church. Then he closed the computer.

WHEN THE TIME for his next doctor's appointment arrived, Henry was surprised to find a nice cargo van arrive at his door. Luke was right behind it.

"What gives?" Henry asked.

"We've had the notion that we needed a company vehicle for some time," Luke said. "We've been moving all kinds of things and your new employee that starts on Monday will need to have furniture and staff."

"New employee?" Henry asked.

"You signed the papers to hire General Schwartz," Luke said. "He starts Monday."

"I almost forgot," Henry said. "I made the offer while we were mopping up the servers after the attack. Before we went to dinner."

"Chastity had it all down and Schwartz agreed to the August sixth start date," Luke said. "And this is Germaine. She's your driver."

"Driver?"

"Happy to meet you, Mr. Pascal," Germaine said in a lightly accented voice. Henry thought it might be Eastern European.

Germaine was blonde, slender, and tall. Her hair was cut short and rather boyishly. She also seemed to be quite muscular.

"You needn't call me Mr. Pascal. I'm just Henry."

"Yes, sir," she answered. Henry and Luke both chuckled.

"Germaine emigrated from Ukraine with her parents soon after the war started about ten years ago. The whole family studied hard and were naturalized. Isobel was complaining that since Nancy has become so busy with the front desk and assisting Chastity, there was no one in the office to run errands. Chastity went to work and found Germaine."

"I thought Isobel had a new assistant," Henry said, remembering altercations nearly two months ago.

"Yes, but she would never ask a person with more experience than she has to run errands," Luke laughed.

"Well, that's great. Germaine, I'm glad to have you here, but I don't think you need to drive me around."

"Henry, we need you back in the office. Germaine will be your driver at least until you are out of those casts and able to get around on your own," Luke concluded.

"I guess that's great. I'd love to be back to the office."

"Clinic first," Chastity said coming downstairs. She was closely followed by Lisa. "Happy to see you, Germaine."

Germaine beamed at her.

"Thank you, Chastity."

"Let's get this guy into the van and off to the clinic."

"Yes, ma'am."

47

RECOVERY

HENRY'S DOCTOR INDICATED his arm and leg were healing, but with the surgery to rebuild and pin the bones together, it would take a while before the casts would come off. He estimated that in two weeks he might be able to change the arm cast to just an upper arm brace which would allow him to bend at the elbow, but the upper arm and shoulder would still be immobile. Henry considered it good news as it might give him both hands to use on his computer.

Instead of going home, Germaine took Henry, Chastity, and Lisa to the office. Germaine efficiently loaded and unloaded Henry from the van which was parked in a new handicap spot in front of the office building. The wheelchair was a pain but with the lift on the van, it was efficient. He was wheeled to the elevator and up to the third floor.

When the door opened, the entire company was present to applaud and cheer his return.

"I don't know what you're cheering about," Henry grumped. "I'm just one more distraction from your work."

"Boss, you are much more than a distraction," Conrad said. "You've been gone for five weeks. We've hardly gotten anything done without you to drive us. Speaking of which, we know it's a pain for you to get around in a wheelchair one-handed, so we all got together and leased this electric chair for you."

The staff parted to reveal an electric-powered wheelchair. Henry was moved. Literally, from the original chair to the new one.

"It's so comforting to know you all want to put me in an electric chair," Henry said. "Thank you. I know you've been busy. I know the Network Defense system has been released and I congratulate you all."

"Delphos Network Armor," Conrad corrected him. "You said to think up a name and Luke approved it."

"I like that. It definitely has our company's DNA," Henry joked. To their credit, most of the staff understood the joke. "I'm not going to waste more of your time. I don't expect to be here for long today. I'll be back on Monday to welcome our new Director of Security Systems. You'll all want to meet him then. For now, I'd just like to sit down with my partners and check in on the overall health of the company. It doesn't look like you've suffered any without me. Thank you for this chair. It wasn't important when I was just sitting around at home. It will help a lot now that I plan to come into the office regularly."

He wheeled into Luke's office and Germaine collapsed the old chair and put it in a closet. Then she had other duties to tend to.

"How are you doing, Henry?" Luke asked. "I was hoping to see you out of at least one cast this afternoon."

"I should get partial mobility in my arm in a couple of weeks," Henry said. "The hardest has been being confined to the house, though having Lisa there has made it bearable." He patted Lisa's hand. This wasn't an official board meeting, so there was no problem having her there. It was just the friends checking in with each other. "A physical therapist has been coming in three times a week to work with me on exactly how much I can move. I suppose now that I have transportation, I'll need to go to his office for therapy. It's a pain."

"Lisa, you're looking unscathed," Luke said. "Chas had some nasty bruises, but it looks like they've all faded now."

"Mine was in the back of my head," Lisa said. "I'm out of concussion protocol now."

"My ribs still hurt a little if I dare to take a deep breath," Chastity said. "Or if I sneeze."

"I'm so sorry you were all caught up in this. And I mean all of you. Even though you weren't in the car with us, I know Luke and Isobel were hurt by what happened and I'm sorry."

"It wasn't your fault, Henry," Lisa chided.

"How can I believe it's not my fault? That preacher guy blames me personally for causing people to turn away from God. He sent the Russian hackers and he sent that guy who rammed us," Henry said vehemently.

"God spared you this time, Henry. You just need to mend your ways," Isobel said from across the table. Henry squinted at her.

"Izzy, I thought it was supposed to be God who sent that bastard preacher after me," he said coldly.

"God repented of destroying Nineveh when he sent Jonah there. God can repent from destroying Henry Pascal," Isobel insisted.

"I see." Henry thumbed his phone and called up a dictionary. "'Repent: to feel or express sincere regret or remorse about one's wrongdoing or sin.' So, let's see if I can get this straight. God sinned by sending that Flagston fellow to ram our car and injure Lisa, Chastity, and me. Now he regrets his sin. Right? Am I supposed to forgive him?"

"Henry, that's not the way faith works," Isobel began.

"Let it go, Izzy. God had nothing to do with it. God hasn't had anything to do with anything for thousands of years—if ever. This was all about an egotistical sermonizer who whipped people into a frenzy over a computer program. Then when people took action on his words, he denied ever having said anything that meant they should kill us. Dog whistling. It happens all the time. Next thing you know, he'll want to run for president. I don't even blame the stupid fellow who got himself high so he'd have the courage to ram me. That preacher is the only one I blame."

"I didn't realize you were so angry," Luke said. "I don't blame you, though."

"Sorry, guys. I believe he's a clear threat to each of us in this room, and possibly to everyone out there in the office. We need more security and I want to launch a lawsuit against that preacher."

Henry had intentionally not looked at any news about the preacher since he'd launched his AI. He knew, however, that he needed to present a front that indicated he was going after him legally. Maybe that was as evil as the preacher was, but he was not going to stop until Rev. Daniel Reeves and the Sword of the Spirit Evangelical Church were no longer were a threat.

"We've hired more security," Chastity said.

"And you might not even need to go after the preacher," Luke said. "I've been following news about him just to be sure we were up to speed on any threats. We haven't wanted to worry you about it. It seems he's currently under a federal investigation for fraud and embezzlement. There's talk about him having hired foreign mercenaries to launch an attack in the US. That puts him under suspicion of domestic terrorism."

"It couldn't happen to a more deserving guy," Henry said.

Except for me. I suppose I'm really no better than he is.

GERMAINE HELD DOORS and helped guide his chair to the lift on the van. Henry banged his leg a couple of times, but he managed to get turned around and Germaine fastened the safety straps so he couldn't roll or be thrown from the chair. Lisa and Chastity observed all the operations and when they got home, Germaine let the two of them help maneuver him into the house under her guidance. As good as the day had been, Henry was also exhausted. It was the most activity he'd had since the accident.

"I know it's almost dinnertime, but I really need a nap," he said when they were inside and Germaine left.

Lisa and Chastity helped him out of the clothes they'd customized for him. That amounted mostly to cutting off one arm from a sweatshirt and one leg from sweatpants. Henry didn't feel like he'd made a very good impression in the office. They promised to help him with something more presentable for Monday.

Stripped to his slit boxers, they helped him into bed, both kissed him, and pulled the shades in the room so he could get some rest.

HENRY AWOKE TO the sensation of his cock in a welcoming mouth. He hadn't felt that in a long time. His one attempt to masturbate had been unsuccessful. He didn't think he'd have that problem now.

"Hey. What's up, babe?" he asked Lisa as he petted her hair with his right hand.

"Yum. You are," she said.

"This is…" he started to explain that she didn't need to do this when Chastity pushed one of her pierced nipples into his mouth.

"Just the nipple, boy. Don't touch the ribs," she said.

He fully enjoyed toying with her breasts with his tongue. He didn't have mobility on that side of his body to caress her while his right hand was still on Lisa. Lisa popped off his cock.

"I've been married for five weeks and haven't had sex in four of them," she said. She moved up to put one of her own bare breasts next to his mouth. "With my husband," she amended. "I talked to your doctor today and he said if we could figure out how to do it, there was nothing preventing us from having sex."

"Except forty pounds of plaster," Chastity giggled.

"It's not the weight that's the problem," Henry said. "I can't move."

"Oh, baby! I'll do all the moving that's necessary," Lisa said.

She scrambled up onto the bed and Chastity rushed around the bed so she was on the unplastered side of Henry. She steadied her girlfriend as Lisa rose up and positioned Henry's erection at her opening.

"I might need a little support as I move up and down on this, but I am definitely going to have you in me!"

Henry used his right hand to push between him and Lisa so he could reach her clit. He'd offered to get her and Chastity off a couple of times, but they'd been too concerned, sore, or exhausted to make it work. This time, there was nothing stopping Lisa and Henry felt the come boiling in his balls almost as soon as she sank down on him.

Chastity used a hand on Lisa's breasts and one on her butt to help steady her as she slid up and down. Then she pushed a finger between Lisa's cheeks.

"Oh, fuck! Yes!" Lisa shouted. She dropped down on Henry's cock as far as she could take it and felt him spraying her insides as she contracted in orgasm.

"I can't believe it," Henry gasped. "I'm sorry I couldn't last longer."

"We'll get better," Lisa said leaning forward to kiss him while they were still connected. "I'm so glad I had a hand helping steady me. That's a lot of exercise in a short amount of time."

"As soon as you can roll off him, I'm going to make sure you get another one while you're still being caressed by our lover," Chastity said.

Lisa took her time, but swung her feet off the bed as she leaned back against Henry and he used his one good arm to caress her breasts and pull her over for a kiss. Chastity dove between Lisa's legs and fulfilled her promise of licking her lover to another climax.

They all kissed and did their best to cuddle together on one side of the bed until they started disentangling.

"It's time to get dinner ready," Lisa said.

"Wait! What about Chas? What can I do for you, honey?"

"Oh, nothing this time. But it's just the start of the weekend. I have ideas for tomorrow," Chastity said. She kissed Henry lightly and he watched her backside as she strode naked to the kitchen.

Dinner was in the nude.

⁂

OF COURSE, SATURDAY was also when Henry's parents came to visit and his mother helped Lisa and Chastity alter some clothes they picked up at Costco so Henry could at least feel like he had pants on. He didn't want to cut up any of his regular work clothes, so the inexpensive substitutes would do.

"I saw a picture of my father in a pair of homemade bellbottoms," Sylvia said. "It was a triangle of paisley print fabric sewn into the seam below the knee of a pair of jeans. I scanned it and put it in the database."

"I'm so glad you're able to come and help Lisa and Chastity with some of this stuff," Henry said. He looked at the expanded leg panel Sylvia had sewn into the slacks. He supposed it looked a little strange, but at least they hadn't bought paisley material for the side expansion.

"I know you all want to be independent and on your own, but we are here for you," Sylvia continued.

"Didn't we all want to be on our own as soon as possible?" Ryan asked. "On the other hand, your employee Nancy is still living with her parents up the street from us."

"In all fairness, she's only nineteen," Chastity said. "She should have a couple of years of parental security. She's a good worker, though."

"I was ready to stretch my wings when I finished school and started working at my first clinic job," Sylvia said.

"And then you met Dad?" Henry asked.

"Well, not immediately. I'd been at the clinic nearly a year when he walked in, bleeding."

"Bleeding?" Lisa asked.

"He cut himself while building some kind of metal shelf for computers at his office. And then, instead of asking for help, he wrapped a roll of paper towel around his hand and drove to the clinic. He's lucky he still has a finger."

"It was cut that badly?" Chastity asked.

Henry thought it was great that both the women in his life were so comfortable with his parents.

"Not really. He was just the first patient I'd ever sewn up by myself. I was very nervous."

"Was that when Dad asked you out?"

"No. He had the good sense to wait until he came in to get the stitches out."

"I didn't want to seem too forward," Ryan said. "I was still so overwhelmed I nearly choked on the words."

"You said that was because I poked you," Sylvia laughed.

"I needed your sympathy."

Ryan and Sylvia left in the middle of the afternoon, after they were certain 'the kids' didn't need anything else. As soon as they were gone, Lisa and Chastity stripped Henry and got him positioned on the bed the way Chastity wanted him. She straddled his head and lowered her pussy to his mouth as she leaned forward to take his cock in her mouth.

Henry was a little awkward, using just one hand to hold her and get his fingers in her as he licked. He managed to find the spots she loved to have stimulated and before long, Chastity came. Then she changed positions so that she could post on his cock the way Lisa had the day before, while Lisa took Chastity's place on Henry's face. It wasn't too long before Henry emptied himself into his lover and Lisa bathed his face in her juices.

MONDAY MORNING, CHASTITY left for the office early so she could welcome Nathan Schwartz to the company and get his paperwork completed. Lisa made sure Henry was dressed and ready when Germaine got there at nine. Germaine helped get Henry into his chair and made sure the lift for the van was lined up for him to guide the chair onto. Once he was in the van, she connected the straps and made sure he was belted in.

Lisa kissed her husband deeply before she got out of the van to go back in the house for her workday. She supposed she could avoid traveling down to Louisiana for another few weeks before her father wanted her in the office. Still, she had a job to do, even remotely.

At the office, Germaine helped Henry out of the van and into the elevator. Once he was in the office, she entered her number into his new cell phone so he could call her any time he wanted to leave. Then she went to check for errands on her whiteboard.

Chastity and Nathan came out to meet Henry.

"Welcome to Open Cloak, General," Henry said.

"Retired," Nathan responded. "Let's leave the rank in the Pentagon. I report to you now."

"That will be hard to get used to. I'm excited to get started. Everything set?" Henry asked Chastity.

"He is a bona fide employee of Open Cloak Design," Chastity said. "Put him to work. He's costing us a lot of money." She turned and went to her own office and checked to see if Germaine had any questions regarding her tasks for the day.

"Ready?" Henry asked Nathan as they headed to the conference room.

"Hardest thing was deciding what to wear to the office today," Nathan laughed. "Haven't had to do that in thirty years. How are you doing?"

"Still learning to get around in this thing," he answered. "It should only be a couple more months, though. Hopefully I'll at least be able to get around on crutches then if I need support."

"I should have expected this," Nathan said. "We knew there was a cyber-attack. I should have expected a physical attack to accompany it. I ordered a civilian watch on the facility in San Jose and instructed Rebecca to be on alert at the office with her three reports."

"Thank you for your concern. I could see the involvement of the Pentagon in our cyber defense because the attack was launched from outside the country. I wouldn't expect you to be active in anything domestic," Henry said.

"We weren't directly. Like I said, we used a civilian security force to keep an eye on the facility in California. That was only a stopgap until I could get with Luke and transfer it to his control. Major Bernard was here on a secret military asset development and therefore attacking here would have been an attack on an Army installation. As soon as Luke had security arranged here, she was recalled to the Pentagon with her team."

"Major?" Henry asked. The last time he'd seen Rebecca she was a captain.

"She was up for promotion and we decided to tie it to her return to the Pentagon, triumphant, with the fully tested network defense system ready to deploy," Nathan said.

"I haven't even seen Conrad long enough to ask how things are going with them," Henry said.

"It seems Conrad has been visiting Washington on weekends," Nathan said. "For further details, you'll need to talk to him."

"Right." Henry finally found a position at the conference table where he wasn't wedged into a wall and motioned toward a chair for Nathan.

"What are my marching orders, boss?" Nathan asked.

"We have some nervous developers down on the second floor. They were hired to work on the network defense and now they're afraid their mission is accomplished and they'll be let go. I want to make sure we retain them. They're great employees. They are your department now. Conrad is back in his office up here and will be focused on the other development we've got going on. The guys downstairs are security hotshots. Right up your alley. And Darrel has specified an entire suite of security apps that we've had on a back burner while the Delphos Network Armor was developed," Henry said.

"I've had the opportunity to do a lot of thinking these past few weeks. The cyberattack on our server farm proved unsuccessful because the security software was installed on every server. I've no doubt someone will try it again, if not soon. But our server farm needs power to operate five hundred to a thousand boxes. Our biggest vulnerability is our power source. We need to protect it."

"Hmm. We could attempt to convince the power company they need the network defense system or..."

"Or create a perimeter defense system that protects it for them."

48

PERIMETER DEFENSE

"ULTIMATELY, IT'S ALL about power," Henry said as he sat with Nathan, the retired Army general who had just joined his staff. "We've got Ari Patel working on a power conservation app and he's making progress. He's not a good manager, though. We have three other developers assigned to the project and it's spinning its wheels. That's why I've asked Conrad to focus on development and testing the power apps now that the network armor is in the market."

"What's the problem with Ari's work?" Schwartz asked.

"It's not so much his work as his output. He gets distracted. He came up with a good idea for tapping into the computer's power supply. But then he got sidetracked with developing a rechargeable power cell that would *replace* the power supply. Another great idea, but it's not guiding the app work. It's a case of a brilliant mind lacking direct guidance," Henry said.

"Okay. Just for my understanding, not because it's my responsibility," Schwartz said.

"You understand. Conrad is good at pulling a team together. He even managed with your team. Changing the power source and usage of computers is only a piece of the puzzle. Overall, we still get the bulk of our power from regular utility companies. And my assessment while I've been laid up is that they are vulnerable on two fronts," Henry said.

"In the Pentagon, we've long been aware of the vulnerability of the nation's power grid. The blow to the United States on 9/11 was mostly psychological. The enemy attempted to break the country's economic engine by attacking what was really just a symbol of the economy: World Trade. But to cripple the country, they could attack the power grid. There are 3,000 electric utility companies in the US which should mean that it is well distributed. But attacking just the top ten would affect some 40,000,000 customers, mostly on the coasts. The connected grid, which attempts to redistribute power from company to company in an emergency, would probably leave every major city in the US in a blackout or at least a brown out."

"You've studied it well," Henry said. "I'm glad it's on the government's radar. But the second way to attack the power grid is through a cyberattack. That's more your specialty, isn't it?"

"Yes. And I can draw on some amount of data regarding that. Unfortunately, protecting the entire power grid from cyberattack is like trying to protect the entire country. Cyber borders are not as clearly defined as physical borders where we could build a wall and keep illegal immigrants from crossing. Saying 'This is US Cyberspace,' is a practical impossibility," Schwartz said. "That's why we've emphasized strong network defense for individual companies and most have good network defense. Some are even moving to your Delphos system."

"If I could trust the utility companies to do their job, I'd be fine with that. I interviewed Ari extensively on this subject and like most companies who aren't engaged in security directly, the utility companies tend to leave it to 'the experts' and assume if they install our software, for example, that's all they need to do. They can get rid of the ten or twenty network engineers who have been monitoring and protecting their systems from attack."

"So, you want to set up a version of the Delphos Network Armor that reports incursions to your central monitoring system and directs the counterattack?" Schwartz suggested.

Henry paused and tilted his head to one side while he considered Nathan's suggestion. One of the founding principles of Open Cloak had been customers *not* reporting to an outside entity, and they'd stayed pretty true to that. Even *Pythia Speaks* did not let the company view any personal user data.

"That's interesting. I hadn't considered that," he finally said. "It's worth thinking about, but I don't think we want to monitor any software installed on a client's machine or network. We don't do that with *OC Optimization*, *OC Search*, *Forever Yours*, or *Delphos*. I'd have a hard time selling the partners on the concept of monitoring other companies' networks from inside that company."

"From inside? You have another notion?" Nathan asked.

"I've been thinking that we could build a wall around select networks *without* looking inside," Henry postulated. "It's something one of my partners said, or maybe I only imagined he said it. I was on some pretty heavy painkillers after the incident. Still am. I'm not professing to have always been cogent. I'm still taking things for pain. What I remember or imagined him saying is that we need to build a digital fortress. Surround ourselves with protection. It's pretty easy to identify and monitor traffic *to* an IP address. Search and browser analytics do it all the time. Would it be unreasonable to think we could identify and intercept malware attacks without them ever reaching the target at all?"

It was Nathan's turn to consider what Henry was saying. Gradually, he began to nod.

"Not just utilities. You want to protect the server farm without installing software on every server. Is that what you want me to focus the defense group on?" he asked.

"Yes. That and any other defense mechanisms we can come up with. We should have a study and direction to present to the board in a month. Can you do it?"

"Thirty days it is."

DALE JACOBY HAD requested permission to present a proposal to the board of directors at the next meeting on behalf of the investment consortium that he'd brought to the company. He wasn't the principal investor in the consortium, but was considered their best representative for the board. He'd been Henry's advisor at the university and was acquainted with several of the people who had been hired. This was only his third board meeting since Argos Venture Capital had invested twenty-five million with a commitment of another twenty-five million per year for three more years.

"Thank you for giving me the opportunity to present this on behalf of Argos," Jacoby said.

"We hadn't expected an attempted takeover for at least a year," Luke laughed nervously. "What's the proposal?"

"I assure you, we're abiding by the terms we agreed to. You're managing your capital well and the release of *Delphos* is really positive," Jacoby said. "This is an exploration of an opportunity. You're all familiar with ARDC here in town, right?"

"Refresh me," Isobel said. She squinted her eyes and grimaced slightly. Henry wondered if she was nursing a hangover.

"American Robotics Development Corporation," Jacoby said. "They've been doing some pretty remarkable projects with specialized robotics. In fact, the specialization aspect is what attracts us to the possibility of a joint venture. Argos Venture Capital is also a major investor in ARDC. Our oversight committee was quick to spot the similarities between the two organizations. The problem ARDC is having is one of AI. The devices it has developed are too specialized to make a generalized AI practical. A couple of years ago, Conrad worked on a robot for the university robot races that outperformed ARDC's entry. What we're wondering is if there is a chance the ARDC hardware could function with an Open Cloak brain."

"Whoa!" Luke exclaimed. "Henry, correct me if I'm wrong, but we don't have anything that crosses the border between software and hardware, do we?"

"Some of our power research certainly has that potential," Henry answered. "But it's managing static equipment, not mechanics. As to actually controlling a mechanical device, which is what I believe we're talking about here... we're not there yet, but it isn't beyond the realm of possibility."

Henry's left arm lay across his chest, the rigid cast still in place. He kept a rubber ball in his left hand almost all the time and kept squeezing it so the muscles in his arm would not completely atrophy while it was immobilized. He'd delayed taking a pain pill until after the board meeting and was regretting it.

"I know this would involve another level of staffing and expertise. The university robotics lab and the AI department have been turning out some excellent talent and I'm sure some of it could be attracted to the project," Jacoby said. "What we're proposing is a joint venture of ARDC and Open Cloak to develop a fully AI-powered specialized robot."

"You must have a type of robot in mind," Henry said. "Let me tell you up front that I won't support any development of a humanoid robot powered by our AI. I don't want us involved in anything that even approaches that."

"Agreed," said Chastity and Isobel at the same time.

"It sounds like a good idea," Isobel said. "I'll go with the board's decision. If you'll excuse me, I'm not feeling well."

She hurriedly left the meeting. Henry looked at Luke with a raised eyebrow. Luke shook his head and returned to the immediate subject.

"A type of robot?" he prompted.

"Have you driven out of town on I-376 lately?" Jacoby asked. They all nodded. "It's a mess. The cutbacks in federal funding and the use of infrastructure funding as a stick to beat states into compliance with the administration's directives in the past four years have left highways in dismal repair. Last month, my wife and I took our travel trailer out for a little weeklong vacation. The highway was so rough, it jarred the doors inside the trailer off their hinges. ARDC has a preliminary drawing for a paving machine that could do a complete prep and resurface job if it only had a brain."

"So, we'd need to hire developers and get a product designed to work with the new paving robot," Henry said. "I'm not sure I know where to start with that. We'd need to hire a manager who could head up such a project and then staff it. We're looking at close to all our capital for the next two years."

"I know Isobel didn't vote for that," Chastity said.

"I mentioned that Argos is willing to fund the joint venture. Our group has estimated that at about $250 million over the next two years. Machining and manufacturing a first-generation device is more expensive than creating the software just because of the materials involved."

"That's a lot of money," Luke said.

"It still leaves me to search a competent manager for such a project," Henry sighed. "This is definitely not up my alley."

"As it happens," Jacoby said, "I've grown tired of teaching and would like to get back into directly creating something."

It would probably take a month to actually launch the robotics project, but Henry realized he was fulfilling some of his major needs in the company. Darrel, Nathan, and Jacoby were all older and far more experienced than he was, in very different aspects of the business. He felt he had a few mentors to work with him. They all accepted him as their boss, but shared freely with him when he asked their advice.

FRIDAY AFTER THE Wednesday board meeting, Germaine picked him up in the van, but didn't take him to the office.

"What's up this morning, Germaine?" Henry asked. He tried not to be concerned about his personal security, but an interruption in his schedule was a little alarming. He tried to calm his breathing.

"Mr. Henry, today is your doctor appointment to have your casts and healing checked," said his driver. He'd come to depend on her more than he'd imagined he would.

"Really? I guess I forgot. Usually Lisa accompanies me," he said.

"Miss Lisa has a conference call with her father this morning. Chastity had to go directly to the office for an interview."

"You're better informed about my schedule than I am," Henry chuckled. "Who is Chastity interviewing today?"

"A new receptionist."

"Is Nancy leaving?" Henry asked.

"Nancy is cutting back her hours at the front desk and will be taking on a larger role supporting Conrad and General Nathan," Germaine said.

"Wouldn't you be the next to take on receptionist duties?"

"I prefer not to answer phones and greet people, sir. I am very happy assisting you and running errands."

"You *are* kind of my assistant, aren't you?"

"Chastity says you are my first priority. You don't ask much of me," Germaine said as she pulled into the clinic parking lot. She got Henry out of the van and into the office so he could check in. "Do you need me to accompany you to take notes, sir?"

"Oh. Uh... No, Germaine. I think I can manage today. Thank you."

Henry wheeled in and was helped onto the table for x-rays to check on the healing of his arm and leg. Then he met with his doctor.

"How is your physical therapy going?" the doctor asked.

"Hurts," Henry laughed. "Isn't that what PT stands for? Pain and torture? Seriously, it's been going okay. He seems to think I'm at least keeping my arm fit, but is concerned with how much muscle and mobility I'm losing in my leg. Of course, he has me working with weights to stay strong on my good side."

"There isn't much I can do about your leg at the moment. You just can't imagine how many pieces of bone I had to pin together," the doctor said. "The pictures today show significant progress. I'd like to change you out of the full arm cast to a humeral brace that will continue to protect the upper arm and continue to restrict mobility, but not to the extent that we've been doing. It will allow the therapist to work on strengthening it. Most of the time, you'll still need to wear a sling. I'm hopeful that in two weeks we might be able to do the same for the leg. The break in the tibia seems to be knitted up pretty well. I want to wait until I'm sure knee movement won't disrupt the pinning in the femur."

"I'm all for whatever progress we can make," Henry said. "Getting elbow movement will be a big gain."

"Limited elbow movement," the doctor clarified. "Don't overdo it."

The doctor changed the cast and wrote new instructions for the physical therapist Henry went to see three times a week. Germaine was waiting patiently for him when he finally got out of the doctor's office.

"You have new movement in your arm!" she exclaimed.

"Yes. A lot of limitations regarding how much movement and still not weight bearing, which means no crutches yet, but it should make keyboarding easier. Maybe."

CHASTITY WALKED INTO Henry's office and closed and locked the door behind her. They'd made several changes to his desk and room arrangement to accommodate the wheelchair, but there was still room for Chastity to perch on the corner of his desk.

Henry shifted his chair slightly so he could easily use his right hand to touch her legs.

"Are you doing okay?" he asked.

"That's supposed to be my question after your doctor's appointment. It's nice to see you with mobility in your arm," she responded.

He shifted further so he could rest his left hand on her leg, though he couldn't really do much with it.

"It's nice to be able to touch you with it," he said.

"Mmmhmm. Germaine said you didn't know I was shifting Nancy and hiring another receptionist. Do you not remember?" Chastity asked.

"Uh... I seemed to have misplaced a few brain cells this morning," Henry said. "Forgot the doctor's appointment and Lisa's meeting. I know we talked about all that the other day. I just forgot."

"That's not like you, Henry. I'm concerned."

"Oh, it's nothing serious. I was probably in need of a painkiller. You know, it's still... you know... hurts." Henry reached into a drawer and pulled out a prescription bottle. He popped a pill into his mouth and drank from a cup of cold coffee. "I need to get this refilled."

"Henry, honey, I'm worried about that. The doctor said you should be off painkillers by now. I'm afraid something else might be wrong," Chastity said gently.

"Do you think I'm not still hurting from all this? That my leg doesn't throb? That I'm not suppressing headaches and anger because I can't show my wife and lover how much I love them?" Henry raised the pitch of his voice until he was almost shouting. "And that fucking bastard is still running around spewing his hatred of us and everything we've accomplished!"

Chastity was dumbfounded for a moment and then reached out to hug his head to her chest. Her eyes were leaking. Henry was panting.

"You're so brave and so strong," she whispered. "We didn't know how much you are hurting. Let us help, love. Let's find someone to talk it over with."

"Talk? Let's hire a hit man to go plug the son of a bitch!"

They stayed like that for a few minutes until both had settled down a little.

"Send Germaine to refill your prescription," Chastity said. "You aren't taking advantage of her as your assistant. You are her job number one."

"She does seem to always be available. Is she really my assistant?"

"That and so much more," Chastity laughed.

"Hon, you haven't been scheming to have another woman in our life, have you?"

"Oh, goddess, Henry! No! Lisa and I are all you need and all each other needs. Germaine is your assistant, your driver, and your security."

"My what? Security?"

"We did a thorough search for good security for our company and personnel. Luke hired a company to provide corporate security, but we searched for an all-round bodyguard for you—well, us. The threat against Lisa and me isn't as active as against you, but we're with you most of the time," Chastity said.

"Is that something else I knew and forgot?" he asked.

"Not exactly. We didn't want to make a big deal out of it, so she's just your assistant. If an emergency ever arose, though, she'd be there. She served in the Marines for six years."

"Wow! I need to think about that and figure out what else my assistant should be responsible for. You really take good care of me, Chastity."

"We take care of each other."

EVEN THOUGH HENRY was still limited to lying on his back on the bed in the living room while he made love with his wives, having some mobility in his left arm improved things immensely. He was able to touch more and get his arm out of the way when Chastity settled on his mouth while Lisa rode his dick. They had sex twice over the weekend, which was a new high since the incident.

More important than the sex, however, was the long conversations they held while all sharing the reclining loveseat.

Eventually, Henry agreed that he might be overusing the painkillers the doctor had prescribed. He didn't mention he'd changed the prescription online so he could have it refilled. He was suffering from PTSD, especially when riding in the van. He described his near panic Friday morning when Germaine didn't take him to the office.

He found that Lisa had already begun seeing a therapist to talk through her anxiety after the attack and invited Henry and Chastity to join her, which they agreed to.

"I don't think anything would do more to alleviate whatever I'm suffering in my mind than hearing that fucking preacher was dead. And all his church members, too."

He knew he'd set things in motion with his own AI attack on the minister, but it seemed to be taking forever. The AI was programmed to find and expose every aspect of Daniel Reeves' life, the same way the *Forever Yours* AI collected information on a client. But it didn't keep that information private. It transferred it to public forums. And after having set up the attack, he refused to even follow news reports other than those brought to his attention by a partners or wives.

"You might not need to worry about him again," Chastity said. "All the pickets at Page Services have left. *Pythia Speaks* is getting over a million English language queries a day and nearly a million in other languages, but it's apparently not important enough for the Sword of the Spirit to continue to picket."

"For that matter, the Sword of the Spirit Evangelical Church has reportedly lost half its membership in the past few weeks after allegations about Rev. Reeves' fraud and embezzlement investigation surfaced," Lisa added. "He might end up in prison sometime soon. Haven't you been following the stories?"

"No. Every time I saw his name, it made my arm and leg and head hurt, and I had to take a pill. I just want him to disappear," Henry said. "Erase his name from the world."

"That's something you should probably talk to the counselor about," Lisa said. "If it causes you pain, I won't bring it up again."

"Oh, look what I brought up!" Chastity said as she pulled her mouth off Henry's cock. "I might have an addiction of my own that I need to talk about. I certainly felt like I was in withdrawal before we got you back!"

With that, she moved so she could press herself down on Henry's erection and bounce on him as he deeply kissed Lisa.

49

COUNSEL FOR THE DEFENSE

IT WAS NEARLY two weeks before the trio could get in for counseling together. In that time, the company was working intently, but functioning smoothly. Henry met daily with his chief managers, Nathan, Conrad, and Darrel. As the IT manager, Darrel was responsible for seeing that all networks in the company were secure with the latest version of the *Delphos Network Armor*. That included all the servers at Page Services. With Nathan's addition to the staff, Darrel was no longer trying to specify a system, but was working on requirements. Conrad reported a solid plan for moving forward with the power conservation app. Nathan was coordinating the perimeter defense specification.

The biggest thing on Henry's mind was the counseling session with his wives. He worried about how much he would need to reveal about the actions he'd taken against the preacher and his unauthorized use of oxycontin. While he was certain Lisa and Chastity would understand and agree with them, he couldn't really expose his action to the counselor.

"It must be hard on all of you to deal with the aftermath of the accident," Elaine, the counselor, said. "Henry, how is your recovery coming?"

"First of all, it wasn't an accident," Henry said, setting the tone for the session. "It was attempted murder. I will never forgive that bastard for hurting Lisa and Chastity. My bones will heal eventually. I don't think my anger ever will."

"Just so I know the extent of remedy that is being considered, is your insurance handling the money aspect?" Elaine asked.

"It is being handled as an accident," Henry said. "Auto insurance doesn't cover attempted murder nor does health insurance, but the police reported the incident as caused by a driver under the influence. The lawyers have convinced the insurance company to cover the medical expenses and have launched a lawsuit against the estate of Flagston, the driver. It turns out that he was uninsured and there is little or nothing in his estate. They can't go after Daniel Reeves for encouraging the incident as that would shift it from accident to attempted murder for hire and they don't cover that. I don't know the current status of that. Every time I think about it, I become a little irrational. And everything starts hurting again."

"There are other complications regarding the lawsuit," Lisa said. "It exposed a massive fraud and embezzlement scheme by the preacher and that brought federal investigators in, since all his money comes in the form of donations to his church. There are a ton of other allegations as well, including ours. They include domestic terrorism."

"And none of that is giving you any relief," Elaine sighed. "Henry, the trauma has left you with some non-obvious side-effects. In our previous session, Lisa described nightmares, outbursts, and concern for your use of pain-killers. What would help you?"

"Knowing he was dead, his entire church was dismantled, and his members were all in the hell they seem to believe in would help," Henry said. "When I get out of this wheelchair, I'll go to Texas and see to it myself."

"You know that won't change how you feel, don't you?"

"Really? That bastard encouraged a drug addict to try to kill us! He paid for Russian hackers to attack our company. He preaches against our products and services and has referred to me as the antichrist. I think getting rid of him would go a long way toward helping me feel better."

"Let's see if we can change the focus a little to what we can do in this room. Henry, your wives—I'm not going to play around trying to define different roles for Lisa and Chastity; legal relationships have nothing to do with your bond—your wives are also suffering and need you. Revenge against the perpetrator is unlikely to help *them*. Why don't we try to find some immediate short-term remedies that will help your family through this rough spot?"

They made as much progress as possible in an hour-long introductory session. Elaine encouraged Henry to talk to his doctor about his use of pain-killers and he promised he would. In the meantime, they would try to talk more openly among themselves about how they were feeling and would focus on finding good things in their relationship that were above and beyond the attack on their family.

And, of course, they'd meet again every week for more group counseling, plus individual meetings as needed.

THE NEXT MONDAY was Labor Day and everyone was invited to Luke's parents' home for a cookout again. 'Everyone' included Isobel's parents and brother, and Henry's parents. They'd also been surprised by a visit from Lisa's parents for the long weekend and they were included at the Monday event. Fortunately, once Henry had been lifted up the steps to the Riordans' front door, the rest of the party was all on one level and he could make his way around in the power wheelchair. As a special accommodation, Germaine was also invited to the party and drove the van for Henry and his family.

"Germaine, is this really part of your job?" Henry asked as she deployed a portable ramp to get up the stairs to the Riordan front door.

"Oh, no," she replied. "I volunteered. I just couldn't stand the idea of Chastity and Miss Lisa having to wrestle you in and out of the van. I'm used to it and didn't have anything else to do today."

"You didn't want to spend the holiday with your parents?"

"They don't live in town," she answered succinctly. Henry guessed they must be somewhere far away. Germaine had requested a *Forever Yours* package for her maternal grandparents once a Ukrainian translation package was available.

"Well, I'm glad you can celebrate with us, then," Henry said. "You are part of our family."

"Thank you, Mr. Henry."

The party was pretty relaxed. Felipe attempted to renew his interest in Chastity, but she kindly told him that she was Lisa's wife and didn't run around on her.

Henry noticed that even though Felipe managed to snag a beer from the cooler with the adults all turning a blind eye toward the sixteen-year-old, Isobel was sober and not sharing in the alcohol like she usually would. Nor did she smile, even when Germaine addressed her as Mrs. Riordan.

They'd seen this kind of behavior on occasion in the past. Henry assumed she was having difficulty with her medications, or perhaps had just quit using them as he'd seen in the past. That was his opinion until Lisa and Chastity were corralled into a game of cornhole with Lisa's parents and most of the other guests watching. Henry stayed parked under an umbrella at one of the patio tables. Isobel sat down as near to him as his chair would allow.

"How are things going?" Henry asked. "Have you started feeling better?"

"This is all your fault," she growled.

"What is my fault?"

"I'm pregnant."

"I don't think you can blame me for that," Henry said. "Um... congrats?"

"It was supposed to be yours, but you sent me back to Luke's room and I stupidly let him come in me. We always used condoms before. I let him come in me once for every time I'd imagined you fucking me. But you turned me away. I hate you so much!"

"Isobel, having Luke's baby is the way it's supposed to be. You aren't supposed to have mine. You're married, and I am, too."

"I don't want it!"

"Well, it can't be far along. What? Nine weeks? You could abort it," Henry said, sounding rather callous.

"Abortion? Are you crazy? I'm not a murderer, Henry! And Luke would be heartbroken," Isobel said. "I don't believe in abortion. How many times have I told girls they shouldn't fuck around if they don't want to bear children. I've stood on the fucking steps of the clinic and shouted at girls going in, even if they only wanted birth control. I didn't even consider it the morning after. I was a little hungover."

"Does Luke know?"

"Of course. He went to the doctor with me. We haven't told anyone else. We'll wait till three months. I just want you to know that you'll be godparents and I'll drop the brat off with you every chance I have," Isobel growled. "If it gets too bad, I might get Luke to let you adopt it for its own safety. I would have done that if it was yours anyway."

Henry paused to think about what she was saying for a minute and try to process how this would ever work. He didn't morally or ethically object to adopting Izzy and Luke's baby. If Izzy went off the rails, Luke might consider it a safer alternative. They'd been best friends since kindergarten and Henry would never withhold his child from him, no matter what the legal arrangement. How would Lisa react? They'd decided to wait a year before they started a baby of their own.

"Luke might have something to say about whether you give the baby up for adoption," Henry chuckled.

"He wants a child. I don't. He knows I'm not suited to be a mother. Look how stupid I've been the past few weeks just responding to the pregnancy. Luke watches like a hawk to be sure I'm not drinking or taking drugs. No child would ever be safe around me."

"You know that might change when you actually hold a little one in your arms. A little one you gave birth to," he said gently.

"Yeah. There's always the chance I'll be miraculously turned into a saintly mother. I'll no longer be bipolar or schizophrenic. I've been on pretty good drugs, you know. I've been stable for a couple of years. I'm worried about being on them now. My doctor is worried. He cut my dosage this week. It could affect the baby. When I'm off it, I'm constantly going from manic to depressed, so I'm on an antidepressant, too. You know when I'm manic. You've seen me before. The drugs inhibit my feelings."

"What can I do?" Henry asked.

"I don't know. Kill me? I need help. Even if we don't give it to you for adoption, I'll need a full-time nanny. I don't plan to stop working unless I'm moving to a remote desert island. I just feel so helpless!"

Isobel buried her face in her hands while she cried. Henry felt helpless. Whatever happened and however Isobel decided to handle it, Henry knew he had to talk to Lisa and Chastity about it. He'd never let Isobel spring something like this on them. They'd probably want to talk to the counselor about the whole thing.

"I'M GLAD GERMAINE agreed to help today," Henry said when they'd reached home. "She's a real godsend."

"They," Chastity said.

"They who?" Henry asked.

"They Germaine. During a conversation with Lisa's parents, they revealed they preferred the pronouns they/them. We're going to work that into our vocabulary and encourage others to use the same terms," Chastity explained.

"I have nothing against that," Henry said. "It just came as a surprise. She... They didn't say anything when they first started work."

"No. They've had some pretty bad experiences in the past. Especially in the Marines."

"So, they're trans?" Henry asked, trying to grasp the situation and determined to be proper. It was good practice as he planned to offer a job to Simon as soon as he was available in the spring. Simon was openly gay, but only wanted to be referred to as she if he was cross-dressing, which he/she did periodically, but mostly when going out.

"'There are more things in Heaven and Earth, Horatio, than are dreamt of in your philosophy,'" Lisa quoted from *Hamlet*. "They are *asexual*. They don't identify with either male or female. Nor do they have a sexual or emotional attraction to either male or female. They'll use the women's room because it is equipped for their biology, but it wouldn't make a difference if they went into a men's room. Not to them, at least. They just aren't interested."

"Okay. That's good. I'll mark it in my feeble brain to use the right terms. Please correct me if I slip up."

"You've always been accepting of different people, Henry. We'll all slip up occasionally, but we've asked Germaine to please correct us when we do," Lisa said.

Lisa and Chastity helped Henry undress and get in bed. Then they got in on either side of him in the narrow bed.

"It will be so nice to start removing more of the plaster," Chastity said. She had settled on his left where his upper arm and leg were still in casts. Of course, using the term 'plaster' was a leftover from the last century. Nearly all casts were currently made of fiberglass.

"The doctor said this could probably come off Friday," Henry said. "My physical therapist has had me working on using crutches without putting direct stress on the fracture. It will be nice to go upstairs to my own bed."

"So true," Lisa said. "*Our* bed."

After a little kissing and cuddling, Henry brought up the subject he half dreaded.

"Isobel is pregnant," he said.

"That explains a lot," Chastity said. "I was suspicious."

"Wow! I never expected her to want children," Lisa said.

"She doesn't," Henry said. "That's what makes this difficult. She's never been particularly stable with her bipolar disorder and possible schizophrenia. She's backed off her prescriptions during the pregnancy and Luke is watching like a hawk to be sure she doesn't drink."

"I'll bet she hates that," Lisa said. She'd seen Isobel when she was drunk and managed to steer clear of her then. Chastity nodded.

"Of course, she categorically rejects any immediate remedy, even though she's still in the first trimester. I guess I don't blame her for that. I'd be reluctant to participate in that if it was us," Henry said.

"But I *do* want children," Lisa said. "How far along is she?"

"Nine weeks," Henry said.

"That would be... We were in Louisiana!" Lisa said.

"The night before our wedding. I didn't mention this because I handled the situation and it didn't affect us. The night before our wedding, Isobel managed to get into my room in the middle of the night."

"Shit!" Chastity said.

"She was pretty plastered and wanted me to fuck her."

"Please say you didn't do that," Lisa pled.

"I didn't do that. I got her turned around and out of my room. Then I put the chain across so she couldn't get in again if she tried. She didn't. Remember your spa day?" Henry asked.

"Isobel didn't show up."

"Luke missed our tee time, too," Henry said. "From what Luke told me when he got to lunch that day, they didn't stop fucking each other until it was time to get ready for the wedding. And Isobel was careless, allowing Luke to go bareback for the first time."

"I suppose she blames you," Chastity sighed, understanding immediately what the issue was.

"Why?" Lisa asked.

"Because Isobel never takes direct responsibility for her mistakes. That's why I removed Nancy from helping her and hired a financial assistant who has more experience than Isobel does," Chastity said.

"Okay, so I don't think this will ever happen," Henry said, "but Isobel suggested the remote possibility that she and Luke would want us not only as godparents, but to adopt the baby if it proves too much for them to handle."

"Adopt Luke and Isobel's baby?" Lisa said. She stopped to consider that for a minute as they all lay in bed, any thought of amorous activity abandoned. "Maybe we should step up *our* timeline a little and work on our own little one," she finally said.

"What?" That was not a suggestion Henry was expecting. He saw Chastity smile and nod.

"Well, if we might have to adopt Luke and Isobel's baby, it would be good if ours wasn't that much younger. He or she should have the opportunity to get established first."

"But we were going to wait... like... until..."

"Why?" she asked. "Henry, my love, do you want to make a baby with me?"

"Of course!" he practically shouted.

"Then what possible difference does it make if we start in a month or a year? I've always been prepared to accept the possibility of getting pregnant accidentally. We could do it accidentally on purpose. It might even help Isobel in knowing she's not the only one."

Amorous thoughts surged back into their minds.

"CONGRATULATIONS," HENRY'S DOCTOR said as the cast fell from his upper arm. "Don't stress it, but start working to gradually regain your strength. This means you can start switching to crutches, but like your PT has had you practicing. Keep the weight supported under your shoulder, not in your hand. It won't be long before you'll have the strength to start lifting with that arm."

"This is great, Doc," Henry said, flexing his arm. "It... still kind of hurts."

"Henry, who gave you a prescription for oxycontin? You're abusing the drug and I only gave you one refill. I want you to get rid of all the painkillers you currently have and I'm telling your wives to be sure you have. This is an intervention. I'm switching you to 800mg of ibuprofen twice daily. In any normal person, that is more than enough to handle the kind of pain you are experiencing."

"I only took them for pain," Henry said, his breathing accelerating.

"The response you are experiencing right now says you are mentally dependent on the drugs as much as physically. This will be tough, Henry. Don't succumb to a real addiction. Fight through it."

"Fight. Yeah. I'll fight it."

HENRY STOOD IN the conference room on Monday the seventeenth to welcome Dale Jacoby and four new developers to the company. This was the start of the new robotics project and they were all excited to have the joint project underway. Two executives and the lead developer from ARDC and one of the principal investors from Argos Capital were also in the room. Argos was funding the joint venture and had supported hiring Jacoby in the role of director. While his direct responsibility would be over the software, he was considered the project manager for both software and hardware.

Argos had hired a financial manager for the joint venture as well. He was at the meeting as were Chastity, Luke, and Isobel. Isobel breathed a sigh of relief that she wouldn't have responsibility for the joint venture. She didn't feel up to expanding her financial management to what was essentially an independent venture housed under their roof. She'd shoveled more of her responsibilities as CFO of Open Cloak to her assistant. The bills for the joint venture would be paid from a separate account by an employee of the joint venture, not integrated into either ARDC or Open Cloak.

"This is a big step for both of our companies," Henry said. "Yes, we are going to develop a single project designed to pave highways. That is going to keep us busy for the next year or two. But hopefully, over that time, we'll also discover new ways our companies can work together on joint development projects. This is an instance in which brawn marries brain, I guess, more literally than any human aspect. We'll truly have a new breakthrough in autonomous machinery."

There was applause and the investor from Argos had a turn to speak to the team.

"There is an old adage that says a joint venture is where a guy with experience joins a guy with money and at the end of the project the roles are reversed." There was some laughter. "That's not going to happen here. We at Argos have invested in two remarkable companies who have different but compatible expertise. We are not simply funding a project, but investing in a future that we see as vital to people's quality of life. You might ask how that is when we are just creating a road paving machine. But roads are fundamental to the lives of everyone in our community, our state, and our country. Until we develop transporter beams, roads will continue to be vital to our existence and quality of life. And, as Henry said, we expect you to discover other areas in which your companies can work together to solve many problems we face today."

The team moved to their office space on the second floor, next to Nathan's perimeter defense team.

CHASTITY FOLLOWED HENRY to his office and locked the door behind them. She'd seen the sweat on his forehead during the meeting and he was beginning to pant. She sat on the corner of his desk and he immediately grasped her leg and leaned against her thigh. She petted his hair.

"It will pass, love," she cooed. "It's getting better."

"Better," Henry whispered as he closed his eyes and squeezed the tears from them. "Better."

He could tell the difference. Yes, his head hurt, but he was suffering most from the withdrawal. Intellectually, he knew it was the result of withdrawal and PTSD. Emotionally, he knew it was continued anger and frustration.

50

UPSELLING

"WE'VE DECIDED TO work on having a baby," Lisa said at their counseling appointment the next week.

"It's not supposed to be work," Elaine smiled. "Is this a sudden decision?"

"We've been talking about it for a month now and this week, I went off my birth control. Which means we need to start using a condom or alternate depository for a while until the drugs get out of my body. I just started my period, so we still have a month before we should start," Lisa said.

"How does that make you feel, Chastity?" Elaine asked. They expected her to direct the question to Henry and Chastity was a bit surprised.

"Um... I've been present for all the discussions and the pros and cons. I've had my say in it, which is that ultimately, it's Henry and Lisa's decision," Chastity said.

"That doesn't really tell me how you feel," Elaine prompted.

"I'm... excited. I never wanted to become a mother... I mean have a baby. I never thought I'd be a very good mother because of my own history and role models. Somehow, now it seems a little like I could be a partner mother."

"Do you think you might change your mind one day?"

"It wouldn't make a difference. I made a permanent choice before I was with Henry and Lisa."

"And you think you could be a—what did you say?—partner mother to Henry and Lisa's baby?"

They all looked at each other questioningly. Henry was hopeful, but he thought Lisa was even more so. Eventually, Chastity turned to Elaine.

"I... think... if Lisa and Henry are okay with it... I mean, they are as much parents to my cats as I am. The cats love them. Snowball sleeps on Henry's bed all the time. I'd like to be... or help be... a mommy to their children," Chastity said.

"Do you know why I'm asking you all these questions?" Elaine said.

"Well, because I'm kind of the odd one out," Chastity said. "Henry and Lisa are married."

"Phftt," Elaine spat. "That's a piece of paper. Yes, there are legal definitions and things you need to arrange so you are able to function as a family. But you three created a family of three. Not two plus one. Three. A single unit. I've been asking you these questions because I wanted to be sure you were thinking as a family, and not as a couple plus one. If you're committed to each other, you must also be committed to the children. Henry and Lisa, if Chastity is part of your family, you need to make sure she is as committed to children as you are."

Lisa dove across the couch where she and Chastity were seated. She took Chas in her arms and kissed her.

"You're equal," she said. "If we—all three of us—choose to have a baby, or to adopt a baby, you are as much the mommy as I am."

"Oh, Lisa! I love you guys so much. I knew that. I just let my head and a piece of paper get in the way of my heart," Chastity said.

"If it was possible for you to jointly bear our children, I'd want that," Henry said. "I hope you'll accept being as much a father as I am."

That set all three of them giggling and they thanked Elaine for helping them.

The next day, Henry got the cast off his leg at last, and he moved—carefully—upstairs to the family bed to begin practicing becoming a father.

Snowball followed them.

THE NEXT THURSDAY, found Henry and Nathan in California, addressing the IT executive of Northwest California PGE, the utility company that provided power for Page Services' server farm. Nathan had used several contacts from his days in the military to make the appointment.

It was the first time Henry had traveled since he was attacked, and he was constantly looking around for threats. Germaine traveled with him, and functioned in their role as personal assistant and bodyguard, driving Henry and Nathan to their hotel, to the meeting with the staff at Page Services, and to the power company.

"AI security used to mean keeping us safe from prying AI stealing our data," Nathan said. This was the first time Open Cloak was testing the waters regarding network security with a utility company.

"Are you saying it's different now, General?" Ralph Archibald, the VP of information technology, asked.

"No matter how diligent we were at the Pentagon, the development of artificial intelligence has taxed the US and corporate America with increased security needs. Just five years ago, we were fighting over the ethics of AI powered tools scraping every bit of data from private servers to use for their own training. Those training walls didn't recognize personal information, copyrights, or privacy. It was just data used to train generative AI. But now we've found AI systems that are storing personal information and they could feasibly use it to take over accounts and even the identity of users."

"What's the government doing about it?" Ralph demanded.

"The Pentagon has developed some weapons it can use in defense of citizens in the event of a foreign attack," Nathan said. "There have been a number of such attacks over the past years and just a few months ago, the military neutralized a Russian attempt to take down a server farm, right here in Northern California. The threat has always been there, but it has escalated only a degree at a time. No matter what the Pentagon has developed, it is not authorized to act against domestic attacks. The FBI, Secret Service, Justice Department, and State Department all have cybercrime sections, but there is no coordinated plan or program."

"And you have a solution?"

"Yes, but like all solutions, it is also a threat."

"Are you threatening us?"

"Not at all," Nathan continued calmly. "I'm talking about the inherent threat of giving control over to an independent and non-living entity. Once it is set loose in your system, it would be very difficult to eliminate it. Almost as difficult to eliminate as the current threat."

"You say a non-living entity. You're talking about another intelligent computer program, right?" Ralph said.

"AI has no real independence or sense of self. The tools developed by Open Cloak, who were contractors in the development of some of the Pentagon's arsenal, are considered artificial narrow intelligence, meaning there is no attempt to duplicate the thought process of the human brain. It does a few things extremely fast and extremely well that you could otherwise hire a hundred people on high end computers to work around the clock and accomplish the same thing. The difference would be that humans could make evaluative judgments regarding threats an AI cannot make. A human, for example, might spot an accidental account override by an elderly customer as an accident that needs individual contact to rectify, rather than the AI solution of eliminating the threat," Nathan said.

"What do you mean by 'eliminating the threat?' You can't mean an AI would put out a contract on an elderly person because they accidentally entered an account override."

"No. Of course not. That's why we recommend human monitors for situations that are out of the norm. Let me ask the inventor, our CTO Henry Pascal, to explain this," Nathan said.

"We learned a great deal from our work on the *Delphos Network Armor* program and our *Forever Yours* AI development. DNA was only released in July, and I'm happy that it is being adopted by many medium-sized enterprises, including banking entities. It defends individual computers and computers linked on a network. An AI only recognizes a customer's data. But people are more than data. When you ask if an AI would put out a contract on a person, the answer is no—not as far as the life and limb of that person is concerned. But the AI could easily erase that person's data. That is elimination of the threat. We have discovered that it could be brought to bear on a computer and all its connections. Everything that identifies that person online, or even on their own connected computer, could be erased. That is why we always advise an internal professional to monitor the threats identified by the AI."

"Jesus Christ! And you want us to willingly install this on our networks? You must be kidding!" Ralph said.

"It would be unethical of me not to expose the threat as well as the benefit," Henry said. "It's like all the fine print on a prescription that lists the possible side effects. We have built in safeguards against that happening. One of those is that any such decision has to be validated by wetware. I'm sorry. That means flesh and blood. A living person. In this world of hardware and software, we don't dare to underestimate the value of our wetware—our employees. Whether you combat the coming AI invasion with a hundred or five hundred people actively monitoring your networks around the clock to fend off attacks, or you combat it with fifty employees monitoring the AI and controlling its responses, you will face the same problem. Do you trust your people to make decisions?"

"I want to talk this over with others in the industry. This seems like a scare tactic to me," Ralph said. "We haven't seen evidence of any such kind of attack on utility grids. It's enough that we have our transfer stations and generating facilities under constant surveillance to guard against physical threats. I don't think the AI threat is as dire as you paint it to be."

"We rather expected that. You understand that we have deployed the *Delphos Network Armor* on all our servers at our *Page Services* server farm, for which you supply power," Nathan said. "We may not yet be your largest customer, but we would be crippled without power. Currently, we have three generators that would kick in if there was a power outage, but that is a temporary fix. We need to look at long-term power alternatives.

"At the moment, those alternatives include deploying a new power conservation app on all our servers that will reduce our power consumption significantly. That still leaves us vulnerable if the power is gone completely. So, like server farms around the country, we'll be looking at alternate power sources."

"The mobile nuclear reactors are still tied up in red tape and not online yet," Ralph said.

"Thanks much to the resistance of the major utility companies, who understandably are not enthused about competition. We have power cells under development that might obviate the need for nuclear power altogether," Henry said. "We expected this response to our suggestion that you deploy *Delphos Network Armor*. We wanted to make sure before we started seriously pursuing alternatives both to protecting the power grid and protecting our server farm."

The meeting ended and no one was satisfied.

Germaine arrived with Henry's wheelchair so he didn't need to use the crutches too much so soon after getting the cast removed. They went directly from the power company to the airport for the flight back home.

Lacking access to a pain reliever, Henry ordered a drink when the plane was airborne.

THE RESULT OF the meeting was validating the operating assumption that to protect the power grid, they needed to establish a perimeter defense system that didn't depend on access to the utility's network. Nathan could get back to the drawing board with his team to specify a complete system. Development had already begun on adapting the AI to identify threats to others rather than to itself.

First and foremost, they planned to deploy a perimeter defense around Page Services and around Open Cloak, so individual servers on the farm didn't need to respond to every threat. They would need to establish a monitor inside the company to respond to whatever the perimeter guard discovered.

Henry collapsed as soon as Germaine got him home. Chastity and Lisa got him upstairs and helped him get ready for bed, cuddling with him until he was asleep. Then Chastity returned to her own room.

In mid-October, Lisa called a family meeting.

"This is it," she said. "Once we start having unprotected sex, I could get pregnant at any time. I've just passed my period, so the birth control should be clear of my system. It doesn't mean we'd get pregnant right away, but it could be at any time."

"You know, the very thought of being part of this is making my pussy leak," Chastity said. "I mean, I'm really excited!"

"I'm all in," Henry said. "Lisa and Chastity, will you have my baby?"

"You're not all in yet," Lisa giggled, "but I hope you will be soon."

"Chas?"

"Oh, goddess, yes. I never thought I'd say I'm ready to be a mommy. Lisa, will you bear our child?" Chastity said.

"Let's get this party started," Lisa said.

Mobility was good, but Henry still couldn't support himself in any dominant position for long on his weakened leg and arm. They saw progress every day, but ultimately, Henry rolled over on his back so Lisa could drive the copulation while Chastity occupied Henry's mouth. It was one of their favorite positions anyway and Henry managed two deposits in Lisa's receptive vagina.

Henry met with Nathan, Conrad, and Jacoby for their regular weekly status update on the first of November.

Nathan reported progress on the perimeter defense system was good. The nine-person team included two program managers, four developers, and two testers, in addition to Nathan as their manager. All nine were working on the specification and they'd written some sample code. Henry had been in on several of their brainstorming sessions and the report was fairly brief.

Jacoby had somewhat less to report as his robotic paving machine project was only six weeks old. They had scoped out a list of requirements the machine would need to meet in order to be autonomous.

"The biggest problem we have is how to power it," Jacoby said.

"Power again," Henry sighed.

"It keeps coming up. A massive piece of construction machinery is typically diesel powered. That seems to be contradictory to our purpose of making the job both faster and cleaner. Yes, there would be fewer dirty jobs for human workers, but diesel still pumps tons of waste into the air," Jacoby said.

"I'll loan you Ari," Conrad said. "Seriously just a loan because we're getting closer to needing the research he's been doing. But we've been working closely with that company in Minnesota that's developing power cells. They have designs for cells that could power heavy equipment."

"How many tons does one of those cells weigh?" Jacoby asked.

"Seriously, it can be handled by one person. When a cell is exhausted, it's simply swapped out for a fresh one and put in its cradle to recharge."

"That could answer another problem," Jacoby said. "We've been trying to figure out even with diesel how to refuel on the move. One of the requirements for the project is to keep the machine running 24/7 without stopping. We've been thinking we'd need to pull a fuel truck up next to the robot and pump fuel into it while it's in operation."

"That sounds risky," Henry said. "There are all kinds of risks of fuel spills and fire. I don't like the sound of that."

"Nor do I," Jacoby said. "If Conrad's fuel cell idea is feasible, we could design the robot to have an active and a reserve cell and swap them out on the fly."

"Not mine. Ari's," Conrad said. "Henry, we might want to increase our investment in that company if we decide to pursue this."

"I didn't realize we invested in it."

"Luke made the decision while you were out. Said it was too good a deal to pass up."

"I'll talk to him. How about the rest of your power project and all the software that needs maintenance and updating?" Henry asked.

Conrad continued with his update and said that the software running on the server farm had cut power consumption by thirty percent.

"We need to get a sales team out to the big server farms and show the savings they could have," Conrad said. "We believe we can cut consumption by a total of 75-80%."

"Don't expose that," Nathan said. "First of all, they won't believe you. Secondly, we can keep coming back with additional power savings in future versions."

"I'll give that word to Luke," Henry said. "He's finally hired a sales manager and is getting direct sales people up to speed. We're past the point where we can just have an online storefront handle everything. These enterprise applications are a different beast to market than consumer apps."

"How about the *Forever Yours* and *Pythia Speaks* apps?" Nathan asked. Henry managed those products directly.

"*Pythia Speaks* simply keeps answering questions," Henry said. "We removed the limit regarding how long a query or response can be. Well, not entirely, but enough so a full page can be uploaded. We changed it from 400 characters to 4,000. We didn't announce any difference, but we've noticed an increase in average query length."

"How does that affect the response?" Conrad asked.

"Unpredictable. You know we don't have access to specific user identification, but we can look at conversations. I've called up a couple of long queries that Pythia has responded to with a dozen words or less. On the other hand, if a query happens to be something she has a lot of data on, she can talk on and on."

"Just like a woman," Jacoby remarked.

"Please let that comment die in this room," Henry said. "There are women in this office who would take issue with it, even if the men didn't."

He'd never rebuked his former professor like that before, but Jacoby simply nodded his head.

"Sorry. Won't happen again."

"As for *Forever Yours*," Henry continued as if there had been no comment, "*LifeStory* has been a good partner. They have people who specialize in content and as a result continually prompt their users with questions they can respond to. *Forever Yours* just eats that stuff up. I'm thinking we should invest in that company and have asked Luke to check into it. Every time the user responds to a question, the answer goes into the training wall. Queries delivered to the AI generate much richer answers. The more questions a user answers, the better *Forever Yours*' responses are. The latest upgrade offered to users was to generate images to go with responses. The testers report excellent results."

"How are upgrades to the AI handled?" Nathan asked.

"We don't push upgrades. We aren't even doing that with the search engine. We notify users that an upgrade is available and list the features. It is up to the user to then request the upgrade from within the program. I expect the generative features will be of more interest later than immediately."

The meeting wound down and people stood to leave. Nathan stayed back after Conrad and Jacoby had left.

"I'm glad to see you functioning mostly without the crutches or chair," he said.

"I still feel like an old man hobbling around with a cane," Henry laughed.

"I didn't want to bring this up in the meeting, but I feel more of a sense of urgency about getting our perimeter defense active around our company, or companies."

"What's up?"

"I've been called by the Pentagon to testify regarding the security of their military asset. There's a new generation of REMFs who want to review every detail of the cyber security that's been implemented. It's driven by our new 'computer aware' president. It's gone from having a constant leak from the white house to the internet to a president who wants to silence everything."

"Let's get the perimeter deployed, even if it's a beta. We can start testing it in real life situations."

"Yes, sir. Henry, I don't know how to say this but to ask directly. I don't even know what I could do with the information. I still have to ask. Did you kill him?" Nathan asked.

"Nathan, I don't think I can be at fault for a guy who dies while ramming my car in an attempt to kill me," Henry said. He could feel his heart racing as he thought about the attack again. He closed his eyes and wished he could reach for a pill.

"I'm not talking about Flagston. That case is long closed as far as I know. I mean The Right Reverend Daniel Reeves."

"Nathan, I've been out of the cast on my leg for five weeks, trying to strengthen myself so I *could* do something. The only trip I've made was to accompany you to California. If Germaine hadn't been with us, I don't think I'd have survived that trip without a major relapse. Every time I think of that bastard, my heart races and I want to put my hands around his neck and strangle him. This conversation makes me shake with anger."

"He's dead, Henry," Nathan said softly. "Maybe that will help you heal. Federal agents went to arrest him this week and found him with his brains blown out in his mansion. Further reports indicate the mansion had been foreclosed, but the agents were there to arrest him for trial on charges of cyberterrorism."

Henry panted and sat back in his chair. Moisture gathered in his eyes.

"Dead," he said flatly. "I hope you'll forgive me a few minutes of quiet celebration."

"Reeves showed an incredible amount of animosity toward you, your company, and *Pythia Speaks*. There are bound to be questions by some people about whether you had anything to do with his apparent suicide," Nathan said. "No more of them will come from me."

"I didn't think men of faith ever committed suicide," Henry said.

"Maybe his faith was in the wrong thing. I still have a few contacts I called when I heard the news. I'm surprised you didn't already hear about it."

"I try not to follow news. It's too much of a trigger."

"Well, he was removed from the pulpit of the church he founded by the board of directors and they filed civil suit against him for embezzlement. That was multiplied by federal criminal charges. They had trouble filling the pulpit with anyone who could continue to hold the numbers in attendance. Reeves' accounts were investigated and the auditors found no money, but they did find massive transfers to a group in St. Petersburg, Russia. Of course, the Russian government professes no knowledge of the money, the group, or the attack on *Pythia Speaks*, Page Services, and Open Cloak."

Henry sat at the table, breathing heavily.

"Over. It's over. It's over," he repeated again and again.

51

NEVER HERE

HENRY CALLED GERMAINE and had her take him home. It would still be a long time before he was able to drive and he wasn't going to rush it. In fact, he didn't really have an interest in getting behind the wheel. He liked having Germaine as his driver and the added level of security he felt when she was around.

It was only the middle of the afternoon and Lisa rushed downstairs to greet him when she heard him arrive. They'd installed a security system in the house with Ray's help and entry required a code as well as a key.

"Honey! You're home early. Where's Chastity?" Lisa asked as she reached him and gave him a kiss.

"Still at the office," Henry said.

"I'll go back and bring her home when she's ready," Germaine said.

"Thank you, Germaine. We really appreciate you," Lisa said.

Germaine left and Henry asked for Lisa's help getting upstairs to their bedroom. He silently undressed and lay down on the bed. Lisa was supposed to still be at work in the other room and he waved her away, saying he just needed to rest a while. Two cats curled up beside him.

When she'd left, Henry pulled his computer from his bag and went to work. Phase I of his anti-Reeves project was completed. The bastard was dead. He set parameters for his next search and used his personal AI to execute it. Then he went to sleep.

The cats purred.

"ARE YOU OKAY, Henry?" Lisa asked when Chastity got home and joined her. This time, both women were naked and lay on either side of him in the bed. Henry woke up to their loving caresses.

"He's dead," Henry said flatly.

"What?" Lisa asked.

"Who?" Chastity said at the same time.

"Reverend Daniel Reeves of the Sword of the Spirit Evangelical Church," Henry responded. "Nathan told me this afternoon. He's dead."

Lisa and Chastity glanced at each other and then focused on Henry. Tears were leaking from his eyes. At last, Lisa said what they'd all been thinking.

"Did you kill him?"

She expected the standard response, "Don't know. Don't care." But Henry was silent as he wept.

At long last, he looked into his wife's eyes and hoarsely said, "Yes."

It was a conversation with many long pauses as each carefully considered all the implications. It was Chastity who broke the silence.

"Good. I feel safer already."

"You protect us," Lisa said. "Having you is like having ten Germaines. No one protects us like you do. You are our fortress."

The women attempted to rouse Henry's desire, but even though he returned their caresses and their kisses, he didn't rise to the occasion.

"You haven't left town," Lisa finally said. "Did you program a robot to do the deed?"

"He committed suicide," Henry said.

"That can scarcely be because of you," Chastity said.

"I haunted him. I programmed an AI bot to find and expose every detail of his sordid life. The one thing he stayed clear of was unholy sex. I think he would have been a better man if he'd gotten laid now and then. What he didn't stay clear of was his love of money and power. He embezzled millions from the church he founded and funneled most of it to the hackers who attempted to take down *Pythia Speaks*. I had the AI monitor them, as well, and halted every new attempt to attack us before it was launched. When the Feds uncovered the embezzlement and fraud, since the bulk of his funds came in from online donations in several states, the congregation removed him from the pulpit of his own church. When all his money was gone and the FBI uncovered his connection to the Russian hackers, they accused him of cyberterrorism. They went to the mansion to arrest him and found him with his brains blown out in his private chapel."

Henry had not been satisfied with Nathan's report. When he was home in bed, he hacked into the investigation files which hadn't been released to the public as yet. The first wave of news stories from the ultra-conservative religious press had already surfaced, blaming the entire enterprise on the Russians and claiming he'd been killed by thugs sent to the United States to attack him and silence his evangelical message.

"It can't be blamed on you," Lisa said. "He brought it all on himself."

"I used *Forever Yours*," Henry said.

"What?" Chastity asked. "How?"

"I had the AI search out every shred of evidence and record of his life, just as if it was a singularity. Every horrid nasty breath he took."

"You're not going to release that, are you?" Lisa asked.

"No. I'm going to erase him. Over the next few months, every scrap of data that remains of him will be erased. Nothing will be left. Even the records at the FBI and the burial site will be expunged. It will be like he never existed."

They let that bit of news sink in.

"Not *Forever Yours*, but *Never Here*," Chastity finally whispered.

They were solemn for the rest of the day, dinner, and the night. Henry had done all this on his own to protect them. But the data that led to the preacher's death had been hidden from Lisa and Chastity.

He'd made them accessories to his erasure of the memory.

THOUGH THE NIGHT of the confession was somber, the rest of the month of November was filled with sex at every opportunity. It was an attempt to affirm their commitment to each other in the face of the drastic news. Nor was the sex confined to trying to get Lisa pregnant, though that was often the case. Henry loved both women equally and they spent a lot of time loving each other.

For Henry, what he'd managed to do with *Forever Yours* was not what the program was designed to do, but it pointed out to him some of the flaws in the software. Some of the AI-based revelations about Daniel Reeves had been what the AI deduced he would have done in certain situations. What was a selling point for the program was revealed as a weakness. When the AI did not have literal data to answer a question, it made things up based on the type of person the data revealed. Just like most AIs did.

Henry began investigating ways to limit what the AI could generate beyond the literal words of the subject.

"Answer the question 'What is the best internet security solution?' as if you were Abraham Lincoln responding," Henry posed to a popular chat AI.

Of course, Abraham Lincoln had no context with which to answer such a question, but the chat program returned, "The only online security you need is to post the absolute truth and to post it perfectly. —Abraham Lincoln"

In looking up quotes by Abraham Lincoln, Henry found elements of the response, but there was simply no way Abraham Lincoln could have even imagined the necessity for online security. He posed the same question to his grandfather's *Forever Yours* and discovered an equally preposterous quote, attributed to Henry Kenneth Pascal, a man who had died long before the present popularity of the internet or its risks.

Something had to be done to limit the made-up responses of the program.

It also reminded Henry to cross-check to see if anything on his own data wall was actually scraped from information about his grandfather. Henry's middle name was Dremel, his mother's maiden name. But the AI could have scraped ambiguous references to his grandfather. The development was far from over.

Having spent a day puzzling over the problem, Henry had Germaine take him and Chastity home, where they dragged a willing Lisa to bed before dinner.

GERMAINE JOINED HENRY'S parents with Lisa and Chastity for Thanksgiving dinner. Lisa had promised to spend the following weekend in Baton Rouge with Chastity. Lisa would need to attend meetings in the office on Thursday and Friday, but Chastity would work remotely.

They weren't anticipating the news that awaited them between the two weekends.

Chastity's birthday was Tuesday. Lisa and Henry planned a special night out to one of her favorite restaurants. Then they planned to bring her home and double team her until she couldn't come any more.

They'd all agreed that birthday presents should be modest and not extravagant. For Lisa's twenty-second birthday in September, they'd had a special dinner catered in so Henry didn't need to have Germaine haul them around. Henry had given her two tickets to a dance company that she especially liked, and she'd taken Chastity to the show while Henry's parents visited.

They hadn't really discussed what the gift for Chastity would be on her birthday, but Henry left it to Lisa to determine it. Once they were home from the restaurant, Lisa gave Chastity a long slim package that might have held a necklace.

It didn't.

It was a white device that looked almost like an electric thermometer, but had a cover over the end.

"What is this?" Chastity asked, puzzled. She pulled the cap off to look at what was inside. In a small window above an open slot, the word 'pregnant' appeared. "Oh, my Goddess!" she cried out. She handed Henry the EPT and he understood what it meant immediately.

"It's been six weeks since my last period. I decided to take a chance and test," Lisa said. "We're going to have a baby!"

Henry and Chastity fell to worshiping Lisa's fertile body, but she soon redirected the efforts to Chastity's birthday sex. Chastity had become so turned on by Lisa's news that her juices were flowing as Henry lapped them up and Lisa kissed her deeply. When Henry moved up to slot his cock into Chastity, Lisa straddled her face and Chastity had two of her favorite things happening at once. It also gave Henry a chance to deeply kiss his wife while playing with both her and Chastity's breasts and pumping into their *maîtresse*.

As soon as he'd come, he backed up so Lisa could lean forward in a 69 with Chastity and both women mounted to a resounding climax. They cuddled and kissed, exclaiming over the good news, then started over with a new series of positions, Chastity riding Henry's mouth as Lisa rode his cock.

ISOBEL WOULD HAVE been furious had she known Lisa was pregnant and experiencing none of the nausea or other side effects she had endured. By mid-December, everyone knew Isobel was obviously pregnant, but no one dared comment to her, even to say congratulations. Her moods finally began to balance out a little by Christmas and she entered her third trimester. Both the Riordans and the Perezes celebrated the coming child.

Henry, Lisa, and Chastity left for Baton Rouge on the 20th of December, deciding they would tell parents and grandparents their good news, even though it was only eight weeks, by the doctor's estimate.

Lisa, of course, had to spend Friday in her father's office while Henry and Chastity worked remotely from Bill and Jackie's home. They went to Beau and Solange's house for dinner Saturday.

Henry accepted a drink from Beau, sampling a Southern Comfort for the first time. Lisa and Chastity both declined. Solange quickly got them soda water.

"Here's to a happy holiday with all the family," Beau said expansively.

Solange served deviled eggs and boudin balls as appetizers as they stood around the fireplace.

"We'd like to propose a toast, as well," Henry said. Everyone turned to him. "To the next generation." Chastity joined him as he raised his glass to Lisa.

"Oh, my!" Solange said. Jackie dropped her glass.

"My baby? Is going to have a baby?" Jackie cried, rushing to hug Lisa.

"It's a little early to be announcing, but we knew we couldn't keep it a secret for the holiday," Lisa said. "The doctor says I'm eight weeks."

"That's long enough to celebrate!" Beau declared, pouring Jackie another drink. "Was it just last Christmas you surprised us with word that you'd be getting married? Hoowee! You got right down to business!"

The celebration continued right through the meal with Solange's own rendition of Cajun jambalaya and gumbo. It included a spicy coleslaw and cornbread. Of course, the parents and grandparents already had ideas for the baby's name, all of which the trio said they'd put in their file of possible names. Everyone knew that meant they'd choose their own baby name.

Henry and Lisa had kept their names after the wedding, so the family had three family names to choose from: Pascal, Hartman, and Pappa. They decided it was just too risky to change names these days. Having to keep a paper record of their marriage and name changes at hand so Lisa could prove her identity and citizenship was not going to happen in their world of electronics. They kept very little in the way of personal documents on paper. Chastity, of course, was meticulous about keeping paper backups of all business documents. One of the first purchases she'd made for the company was a fireproof file cabinet.

They'd already spent a few late nights of loving, tossing around name ideas and a couple of those on the list from their families were included. Henry knew his parents would want to add to the list as well. But everything was in good humor and eventually Beau started pulling out old Cajun names: Rémy, Lucien, Boudreaux, Thibodeaux. Not to be outdone, Solange responded with Cajun girl names: Aurelie, Euphemie, Pelagie, Ryleigh.

Henry thought some of the names were pretty cool but wasn't sure how a child in Pennsylvania would feel about growing up named Euphrosine. Nonetheless, they used their phones to capture the names as they were suggested. They figured if they showed the list of possibilities to their friends and families, no one would blink an eye if they named their child Fred.

The time with the family went all too quickly. They flew back to Pittsburgh the day after Christmas and prepared to go through the same rituals with Henry's parents.

***

"YOU'RE PREGNANT!" SYLVIA said when she saw the trio for dinner on Thursday evening. They hadn't had a chance to say anything about it.

"Did my parents call you?" Lisa cried. "I'll strangle them!"

"No, no, dear. Wait! It's true? Congratulations!" Sylvia said.

"Are you predicting the future these days?" Henry asked.

"Oh, no," Ryan said. "When we found out at Thanksgiving Isobel was pregnant, Syl and I agreed that you'd be pregnant by Christmas. You and Luke have always done everything together."

"Not exactly," Henry said, a little miffed.

"Hmm. Put a new sound system in the school gym. Started a business together. Got married almost exactly a year apart. Expecting children a few months from each other. Close enough," Ryan said.

"But we should have let you spring the news on us," Sylvia said. "I more than half expected you to say no. So, what is your due date?"

"The end of July," Lisa said, recovering her excitement. "It's too early to be spreading the news around, but we felt we had to tell our families."

"Okay. We won't tell anyone else," Sylvia said. "Congratulations to both of you."

"All three of you," Ryan corrected her. "I don't see any sign that this changes your relationships."

"We can't expect everyone to understand that," Chastity said. "I'm just as excited to be a combination mommy and daddy for this child."

They sat for dinner at the restaurant and talked about the trip to Louisiana.

"You know, my parents traveled all over the world as part of an international medical team," Sylvia said. "When I was pulling things together for their *Forever Yours* page, I discovered my mother had collected names from everywhere she'd been. The collection had to date from long before they were traveling professionally."

"Well, we haven't gotten any name ideas from *Forever Yours* yet," Henry said. "Should we ask her what her suggestion is?"

"Sure. But I warn you, she might tell you to name the child C'Hola or Serepte or Minneola. The list contains names from all over."

"It will be fun to look at the list, anyway," Lisa said.

"I'm trying to set some new parameters for *Forever Yours*," Henry said as they waited for dessert. "Limitations, if you will."

"How so?" Ryan asked.

"It's a feature of *Pythia Speaks* that was just assumed to work for *Forever Yours*, too," Henry explained. "Basically, *Pythia Speaks* can make stuff up from a database of philosophical and mythological sayings. She's an oracle and it's supposed to be unpredictable. She can learn from the questions she's asked, too. She doesn't represent any individual. But *Forever Yours* is supposed to represent a person. You. Or Mom. It shouldn't have the freedom to just make up stuff that you wouldn't say."

"Hmm. Why?" Ryan asked.

"*Forever Yours* is data. It isn't personality. It doesn't have the capacity to respond in love or in anger. It doesn't have emotions. It doesn't have personal values. All it has is access to your data so it can predict what you would say based on the likelihood of one word following another. I've said frequently, it isn't alive. So, what right does it have to make up things and credit them to you? It should only be able to say what you would actually say," Henry said.

"It's an ethical decision, then," Sylvia said. "In a hundred years someone might ask a question and get an answer that we would never have thought of, let alone given voice to."

"It might not take that long. It might do that at any time and suddenly, there I am saying, 'My daddy said it doesn't matter what you believe—just how you act.' And it isn't something you ever said or implied."

"Well, I can see how I might have come up with that response to some questions, but if you'd just fed it a statement like 'I believe God wants me to kill someone,' and you got that response, it could lead to damaging reactions, one way or another," Ryan said.

"So, I have a new level of training we need to establish for the AI. No quoting Abraham Lincoln's opinion on internet security. He didn't have one. *Forever Yours* has to be honest."

"Is there such a thing as an honest AI?" Lisa asked.

"Somehow, we need to figure out how to program that," Henry answered.

"I'm glad that's your responsibility," Chastity said. "Not just because I would fail at it, but because I wouldn't trust anyone else to do it."

THE HOLIDAY WAS nearly over and culminated with the company New Year's Eve Party at the club. It had changed significantly from the days of just four partners plotting their future together. Even with the people in the company who were out of town or had other commitments, over fifty had dinner and drinks on the company.

Isobel was furious.

"Why are we wasting $5,000 on a fucking party? There's no reason for this!"

"It's good for morale," Luke explained. "Good morale is good for productivity. Happy employees are more productive employees."

"You read that in a management book. I'll bet it didn't compare the amount of happiness generated by a New Year's Eve party compared to just giving everyone a $100 cash bonus and telling them to have fun," Isobel complained. There was no question what *she'd* prefer.

Isobel was just entering her third trimester. She'd gained more weight than the doctor wanted her to and was out of sorts with the dietary restrictions, imbalance in hormones, and poor self-image. No drugs were effective in helping balance her emotions, and she was rigidly avoiding alcohol—a challenge even if she hadn't been pregnant.

"Honey, let's just enjoy our own little corner of the party," Luke suggested. "We've had all the holiday greetings and toasts we need to make. If you'd like to go home, we can spend the rest of the old year with me massaging you until you fall asleep."

"You'd do that?" she whined with a tear in her eye.

"In a heartbeat."

"Okay."

Luke gave a quick nod to Henry and said they needed to leave because Izzy wasn't feeling well. Henry agreed to take over as host.

"You know, if you treat me like that when I'm six months along, I'll be your groveling servant for the rest of my life," Lisa said as she kissed her husband.

"I already am," Chastity agreed, kissing each of her partners.

"I'm afraid Isobel isn't going to get much of a massage before midnight," Henry said. "Here come the bottles for the midnight toast."

"Ah. Sparkling Catawba. My favorite," Chastity said as she poured each of them a glass.

"I like being completely sober on New Year's Eve," Henry said. "And I can hardly wait to get the two of you home."

"Ten. Nine. Eight..." the crowd shouted. And then it was time to begin 2030.

THE THREE SAT in the back of the van as Germaine drove them home from the club. As they approached the traffic light, Henry became agitated, looking all around. He clutched Lisa and Chastity to him and held them tightly until they reached home.

Even though he wasn't driving, the aftereffects of the collision in July still haunted him.

52

ASK ALICE

"**W**ELL, HOW GOES the start of a new year?" Henry asked his development managers when they all returned to the office after the first. "Nathan?"

"We're ready to deploy a perimeter around Page Services," the retired general said. "The ISP hosts over 1,000 clients now and those clients are subject to as many as one hundred attempts to invade each day. So far, we've used Delphos installed on all servers to reject the attempts, but we only use the zero degree response. And we don't use a strong counterattack. We simply disable the computer's ability to access the box it has attacked."

"What will the difference be when you deploy a perimeter?" Conrad asked.

"One of the reasons Delphos is set to such a low level of response is consideration for the companies being hosted. It is part of a basic tier service package and is a selling point for the ISP since it's included with any hosting package. But the people at Page Services have to monitor all the boxes 24/7. That's a huge commitment of personnel. With the perimeter guard posted, the attacks should never reach the servers. It will stop attacks outside the farm and require fewer people to monitor."

"So, we'll be putting how many people out of work?" Henry asked.

"We hope to not put any out of work. We'll keep the service at the ISP, but move some of the personnel to the perimeter. As we deploy additional perimeter guards monitoring different companies, we'll transfer existing per-sonnel to the new system. The functionality is close enough to the same that we should be able to make transfers with minimal losses," Nathan said. "The new system should stop attacks before they are ever detected by Delphos."

"I'll run it past the board for final approval at our meeting tomorrow," Henry said. "We'll plan on launching Monday. Conrad?"

"You created quite a wave with your ideas for limiting *Forever Yours*," he said. "We've been brainstorming ideas every day and think we have a way scoped out that will work. The guys want to run a couple of sample tests and will be ready to float the whole plan to you Friday."

"That's good news. I'll look forward to seeing it Friday. Include Nathan and Dale on the invitation. How about updates to the search and optimization tools?" Henry asked.

"Will do. For S and O, the upgrades should be ready on schedule near the first of March. They include better modularization of the pieces, so we won't need to upgrade the entire package each time we have a new virus to combat. The AIs are doing a reasonable job of scrubbing new threats, but eventually, we need to give them better tools to work with. You've all seen the spec."

"Okay. I'm good with this. Questions, anyone?" Henry asked, then moved the meeting along. He was of the opinion that the less time spent in meetings, the more productive his team would be. "Dale?" He turned to his former college advisor.

"The road paver project is proceeding as fast as we can expect it to at this stage. Right now, we're focused on turning requirements into specifications. Even the developers and fabricators are getting impatient to start building instead of writing. The number of detailed drawings that need to be made to hand off to machinists is staggering. We're preparing to create a mini version of the paver by printing the parts in 3D. I'm not talking about something as large as a sidewalk paver. This would simply follow instructions to pave a path about a foot wide. It's too lightweight to cut through old pavement and reuse the materials, so it will need to be fed as it goes. It will be a good test of the requirements for the whole project. Still, that's not going to be ready much before summer. By that time, we should also have a power cell that can fuel the miniature device. Negotiations on that front are going well and we've coordinated the design of the cell."

"Are we testing the early development with an entry into the robotics race at the university?" Henry asked.

"Definitely. We'd love to enter the paver, but we'll have an entry that follows the route and does minor alterations as it races."

"Sounds like fun. Anything else?"

"One thing. The informal get-togethers we had over the past couple of months revealed some other possibilities. It's having the desired effect of getting the software guys in synch with the hardware guys. One of the people on our software team found out about an experimental tech one of the designers at ARDC was working on. This isn't protected IP," Dale said. "It's a garage project and we could do much worse than simply hiring the two guys to do the creation in-house here."

"What are we talking about?"

"A kind of AI powered hologram. Farrel Scott is our developer and he started working with a brilliant guy from the ARDC team named Jason Wilson. Frankly, I think they'd both be more valuable working on this new project—completely housed under Open Cloak—than working on the joint paving project," Dale said.

"Have the two of them prepare a proposal for next week. We'll say Wednesday," Henry said. "Be clear that they are presenting for possible acquisition, not a joint venture."

"Will do. I think you'll be amazed."

⁂

PORCUPINE PERIMETER DEFENSE launched its first installation at Page Services on Monday. Attacks on the server farm clients dropped to zero at once. The new cyber defense system picked up the burden and they soon saw a reduction in the overall number of attacks directed at the server farm.

"What happened?" Henry asked Nathan when they spoke on the phone. Nathan was at the San Jose facility.

"Since the PPD is not attached to any of the ISP servers and does not reflect directly on any of its clients, we felt confident in increasing the level of severity of our response and bumping it to one degree of separation. As you know, that is typically enough to affect around ten or maybe a dozen connected computers in an attack," Nathan said. "We saw that neutralizing any one attack on the perimeter would take out multiple attacks at the same time. We'd theorized that multiple servers were being attacked by the same group of hackers and they were getting back online soon after they were repelled because the level of response was light. PPD is eliminating all the attached computers in a single counterattack and it is taking much longer to get back online as they need to reconstruct their entire directory systems."

"So, it not only consolidates the defense, but consolidates the counter-attack as well!" Henry said. "Well done!"

"As soon as I'm back, I want to get a perimeter around all our in-house networks. I think we might face a new wave of hacking attacks because of the success of PPD."

"I hear you. I'd like to rest a little easier at night."

"I'll stay out here a few days to monitor the system and record any fine tuning I think we need," Nathan said. "Leanne is running diagnostics on traffic into the utility company. It looks like their company leaks like a sieve. It's amazing how much consumer data is bled out of it. The sooner we get a wall around that company, the better."

"Do you think other utility companies are as bad?" Henry asked.

"I fear the worst."

"Well, let's make getting this one inside a fortress a priority," Henry said. "I'll see you next week."

On Wednesday, the board of directors met in the large conference room on the second floor, instead of in Luke's office. The main order of business was to look at the proposed AI powered hologram. Farrel Scott introduced his co-developer, Jason Wilson.

"Okay, Farrel. The floor is yours. Show us what you've got," Henry said. In addition to the board, Conrad, Darrel, and a couple of other senior developers were invited to the presentation.

"Thank you, boss. You all know Jason and I have been working on the paving team, but we discovered a common interest in holography. Currently, holograms are strictly recordings that are played back using a light interference pattern on a projection surface. The highest quality holograms are recorded and projected using lasers. What we have developed, using the same basic AI that drives *Pythia Speaks*, is a live hologram. It is not recorded, though for our research purposes, we've been recording interactions so we can review them later.

"*Pythia Speaks* is an AI service that handles over two million queries each day, worldwide. But Pythia lacks a visual presence for her oracular sayings. We're not suggesting that should change. We recognize the decisions that went into that limitation. I'm only using her as an example of a service that does not depend on any physical contact with objects or people and which *could have* a visual and audio component.

"I'd like to introduce you to Alice," Farrel said pointing to a mesh screen at the end of the conference table. A hologram of a woman's head appeared there. "Say hello to the people, Alice."

"Hello. I'm Alice: version alpha of an interactive hologram."

"How old are you, Alice?" Farrel asked.

"I have not been assigned an age in human terms," she said. "I was initially activated on December 22, 2029."

"Alice, I'm going to let others ask you some questions. You won't recognize the voices, so just continue to respond to the questions."

"Okay, Farrel."

"Henry? Would you like to interact with Alice?"

"Alice, whose face are we looking at?" Henry asked.

"I do not share your perspective in order to verify what you are looking at. If you are asking about me, I was created from recordings of Alice Scott, Farrel's wife," the hologram replied.

"What data are you accessing?" Henry asked.

"I was trained on the same wall as *Pythia Speaks*, but I can access additional data added by my creators."

"What should I name my baby?" Isobel blurted out. She was in her eighth month now and just a week from her twenty-second birthday. There was always a note of panic in her voice.

"Names are very personal," Alice said. "Perhaps you should ask yourself what you want your child's name to mean and look up possibilities from there. Something will resonate with you."

Isobel sat back unhappily. She and Luke had been discussing the naming issue at length.

"Alice, what good are you?" Chastity asked, causing Isobel to brighten a little.

"The good we do is often forgotten," Alice said. "We don't do good to be remembered. It is what we are."

"That sounded like Pythia," Chastity chuckled.

"Anyone else want to pose a question to Alice?" Farrel asked.

"Alice, would you go out with me this evening?" Ari asked. He was being quite entertained by the demonstration.

"I'm sorry. I am unable to grant wishes. I'm not a fairy godmother."

The room exploded in laughter and the image of Alice disappeared as Jason turned off the projector. He removed the screen and made adjustments to his other equipment at that end of the room.

"It's clever, Farrel. I can see possibilities, though not for Pythia. As Ari demonstrated, having an oracle that has an attractive face could result in all kinds of inappropriate questions," Henry said. "We'll talk over how this might or might not fit in our company plans."

"If I may, boss," Farrel interrupted, "Alice is only one aspect of what Jason and I have been working on. She is a light-based hologram. As you can see, we've removed the screen required for such a hologram. We have found a way to project a dimensional image without a screen."

"That's impossible," Conrad said. "Light requires a focal point."

"Exactly," Farrel agreed. "We'd like to introduce you to a new concept in spatial holography."

Jason flipped a couple of switches and gradually the shape of a floating cube took shape at the end of the room. It slowly rotated. Aside from its slightly blue cast, and a degree of transparency, it looked almost like a physical object floating above the table.

"No way," Conrad said, leaning forward.

"It's just a cube," Isobel said.

"What you are seeing..." Farrel began.

"Sorry to interrupt, Farrel," Henry said. "Please turn off the projection. Do not reveal any more details of this project. If you are legitimately showing what you appear to be showing, I want our patent attorney in the room and no other disclosure until we have it filed. I'd like the board to remain in the room with you as we discuss what it will take to acquire and fund this project. All other non-board members may leave. Please assume what you have seen falls under your non-disclosure agreement, even within the company. *Do not discuss it.*"

The other developers and managers left the room. Luke, Isobel, Chastity, Dale, and Henry were left to discuss the details with Farrel and Jason.

HENRY HAD SEEN more in the flick of the switch than most of the people in the room had realized. He didn't think this was part of what Farrel and Jason had revealed to Dale. Luke, Isobel, and Chastity were in the dark and still thinking about the hologram of Alice.

"I want to emphasize that non-disclosure of this extends to every-one remaining in this room," Henry said. "Farrel, you just showed us what appeared to be a projection without a screen. In twenty words or less, please summarize the technology."

"Uh… Focused microwave technology is being used to excite air particles instead of using light on a screen. The air itself takes on the programmed shape."

"Twenty-five words, but we'll accept it. I'll be frank with you all. I want this technology in our company. Luke, we need patents on this and then we need to raise another $250 million—no, $500 million—in capital. It's time for the company to go public."

"What is it you see, Henry?" Luke asked.

"We're entering an age of science fiction. With enough of these projectors, this could yield the holodeck experience you've seen in sci-fi movies. There has always been a screen of some sort between a hologram and the viewer. This technology creates an image you could walk around. Combined with our AI, we could have virtual assistants giving tours, selling tickets, even directing traffic."

"You get it!" Farrel said.

"I want it. Farrel and Jason, we are going to make an offer that will make you multi-millionaires by the time this project is completed. How long do you think it will take to have a commercial version?" Henry asked.

"This is just what Jason and I have done in the garage," Farrel said. "The AI powered hologram could be a reality in a few months. Training for the task is the major issue there. For the full spatial holography with the same capabilities, I'd say three years if we ramp up rapidly and devote the resources to it."

"It sounds like you are fully committed, Henry," Luke said. "Dale, you're the other technical genius at the table. What do you think?"

"I'm still trying to get myself back to earth," Jacoby answered. "I have to tell you that we should keep Argos out of this one. If there's any way to self-fund it, we need to go for it."

"Chastity?"

"I don't understand it as well as these guys," Chastity said. "I can feel the excitement and I trust Henry's judgment."

"Isobel?"

"If it will help me get through these last two months, I'm all for it," she sighed. "Seriously, I've had Rachel working on our prospectus. We've anticipated going public this year. Our profit and business valuation are good. We've needed something to set the hook. We've done fine with just venture capital, but new investors need something that shows the future. There's no reason we can't raise the funds."

"Farrel and Jason, let's see if we can set a fair evaluation for your IP and then get you in front of a patent attorney," Luke said.

Henry spoke up again. "Guys, I stopped you when you showed us your holographic projection for good reasons. Was there anything else you wanted to bring to us today?" Jason and Farrel looked at each other, then back to Henry, and made an empty-handed shrug. "That's fine. I just didn't want to leave anything else on the table. Great work!"

HENRY'S QUICK ACTION and removal of non-board members from the room, limited the disclosure of unpatented technology. His enthusiasm for the project gave Farrel and Jason an unprecedented stock investiture and a $500,000 signing bonus when they signed the new employment contract with Open Cloak.

"I DON'T GET it," Chastity whispered to Henry that night. They'd chosen to have a little alone time in Chastity's bed without Lisa, just so they could have this discussion. Lisa knew that Henry would cuddle up next to her in the middle of the night when Chastity threw him out of her room. "That's more stock than you received for any one of your patents."

"Two reasons," Henry said as he gently petted her. "My patents may now appear to be undervalued, but the stock I received was only twelve cents a share. Even at the current evaluation of $1.50, they have a book value of almost $8 million. So, we gave each of these inventors a million dollars in stock and cash, but there will never be a transfer of patents. We will own them outright."

"But is it really worth that much?"

"The idea of using microwaves as a possible means of 3D modeling has been around for a while, but like light, the lenses that focused the energy depended on a receiver surface. That's how we get microwave transmission of cell phone data. The spatial holography is just the tip of the iceberg. Focused microwaves that don't require a receiver could be used as weapons, advanced communication devices, internet access, and even data storage."

"Weapons?"

"Ray guns," Henry responded.

"You're talking sci-fi."

"Used to be. Regardless, I want this patent issued and protected before anyone discovers it. I'll give those guys another bonus when the patents are issued and another when we get our first working app ready. I want them to be so rich they never *ever* suggest we didn't treat them right."

"Wow! What are we going to do with it?"

"Move on from Alice with an AI powered receptionist. I'd like you to start creating a detailed job description for everything that should occur in the reception area. Solicit any kind of question you can form based on our corporate policy and bylaws. And write out the answers. Have Nancy and Audrey also answer the questions and add to them from their experience. We need to build a training wall for a new AI."

"Should I include things like 'How old are you?' and 'Will you go to dinner with me tonight?'" she laughed.

"Might as well."

HENRY WENT TO the office over the weekend when few people were there. Chastity had been reallocating space on the second floor for the new team and he wanted to check it out before he started moving people around on Monday. That was what he told Chastity and Lisa, who had decided to go out shopping for maternity clothes, even though Lisa really wasn't showing yet. He called Germaine, who was happy to drive him to the office and just hang around all day if necessary.

"Germaine, who do you trust?" Henry asked her when they were in the office. He'd asked them to accompany him to his office.

"Um... You. Chastity. Miss Lisa. For some reason, I trust General Nathan, but I'm cautious because it might just be because he's military and I believe he's honorable," Germaine answered thoughtfully.

"Not Luke or Isobel?" Henry asked.

"Um... Isobel is a little erratic and Luke follows her lead. Not in the business, but in general," Germaine said. "I'm sorry."

"That's fine. What about the other staff and managers here at Open Cloak?"

"I don't actively *distrust* them," Germaine said. "I just wouldn't depend on them in an emergency."

"I see. How do you think our company security is overall?"

"Oh, I'm really just personal security for you and Chastity and Miss Lisa. I don't know the guy who protects Mr. and Mrs. Riordan. As to the general office security, you saw the weekend guy at the front desk when we came in. He barely looked up from his book."

"Well, we were identified as soon as we stepped into the elevator," Henry chuckled. "We spend a lot of effort protecting the data on our computers from outside attacks, but I'm not so sure we're protected from an inside attack. Are you on the network?"

"I don't have a computer, sir. I get all my instructions and email on my phone."

"Okay. Thank you for helping me think through this problem," Henry said. "I'll be a couple of hours if you need to go anyplace."

"I'll wait in the breakroom. Would you like coffee?"

"Thank you." Henry had already turned to his computer and started scanning the corporate network.

53
ANNOUNCEMENT

HENRY HAD FARREL and Jason in their new private office on Monday, with Don Harvey, his long-time patent attorney, Don's secretary, and Chastity. Henry and Chastity were in the meeting to observe and take notes. Henry wanted to know and understand all the implications of the technology. He wanted to be sure he could discuss it with someone without disclosing protected information to anyone else in the company, so Chastity agreed to take detailed minutes on his behalf and the company's.

Don led the discussion, starting by having Farrel and Jason give the demonstration they'd given on Wednesday. They had to discuss what elements they thought were patentable and spent the entire day, with lunch ordered in, going over the technology.

Henry spent most of his time, while attentively listening to the discussion, making notes on the number and type of personnel they would need to staff the project. Everything the company had done to date had been on a shoestring budget. He was a believer in getting top competent developers and letting them run with the project. He could tell that even though Farrel and Jason were top creative talent, they would need a good manager and enough people around them to truly work on every aspect of the development. They'd file preliminary patents as soon as possible, but he was sure they would be amending and expanding them frequently over the next year.

The joint paver venture led by Dale Jacoby had shown him how much progress could be made quickly when adequately funded. Currently, the second floor of the office was split three ways with the paving project, perimeter defense and the newly allocated space for 'Alice.' They were going to outgrow the space soon. He made a note to ask Chastity to work with Ray on acquiring the rest of the building for their company.

He wasn't particularly worried about current expenses. The Argos investment was funding the company at $25 million a year and they had mostly been able to fund operations from the profit of the company. They'd acquired Page Services and a significant interest in Agora Fuel Cells. He could hire and staff a new operation from their bank for at least six months. He hoped Isobel and Luke could get an IPO together by that time. If not, in six months the next installment of the Argos investment should be in the bank.

IT WAS THURSDAY before Henry had a chance to meet and thoroughly debrief with Nathan on the deployment of the perimeter security at Page Services.

"Darrel has set up the hardware for perimeter defense around Open Cloak," Nathan said. "We have the software ready to go active when you say."

"I say. Let's get this company and the joint venture protected. And Agora Fuel Cells. And I want to ask about some other things I've been thinking about."

"You've been active. I've noticed you have a new area of the office blocked off with locks and the patent attorney has been in each day this week. Something related?"

"Yes and no. I'll bring you in on the whole Alice project, but first I want to talk about internal security," Henry said. "Maybe having been hacked and attacked physically has made me paranoid. My counselor says it could be related to my PTSD, but I can't ignore issues that might be serious."

"Tell me. I take it all seriously," Nathan said, focusing on Henry with intense eyes that bored into him. Henry took a deep breath.

"I'm feeling better about our external security, but we haven't done anything about internal security. We run a background check on new employees. We issue a key code and a computer and an RFID card. And we connect them to the company network. How easy would it be for an employee to copy everything on our network and walk out the door with it?"

"That's a lot of data, but it would be possible over the course of a few days or weeks, I suppose. Don't you trust your employees?"

"I asked Germaine a similar question last week. Their answer was 'I don't actively distrust them, but I wouldn't call on them in an emergency.' It's something between trust and distrust. We evaluate them based on performance.

But aside from a confidentiality agreement that's just a piece of paper when it comes down to it, we don't push employees to be 'loyal' or even trustworthy."

"You want to monitor employee behavior?" Nathan asked alarmed. "That's really Big Brotherish."

"Yuck! We've seen what that can do to people and even the whole country. It's exactly what I want to avoid."

"I entered the Army thirty years ago when computers were pretty much landing on everyone's desk—in the office and at home. All our systems were computerized," Nathan said. "It was still the young innocence of the internet age. The area I was assigned was cyber intelligence. Not AI, but more traditional. How could we use computer networks to spy on our enemies and be better prepared. That was when we all realized that we were vulnerable to every spy attack we could devise and started working on cyber resilience. Wasn't called that then. We just used catchall words to step up our actions a little further."

"Same group as you retired from?"

"No. Vastly different. The Pentagon didn't decide to consolidate all the military development in the field until the Russian election interference in 2016. Then US Cyber Command got serious. When I entered the service, we were all pretty green hotshots who believed we could take over the world with our computers. In a training session, a team of hackers was led into a room with computers. We were told there was a threat against US cyber security with some parameters around it. We were told to identify the threat. We got busy and started working on identifying where the threat was coming from."

"Did we take over that job with *Delphos Network Armor*?" Henry asked. He was intrigued by the look inside Nathan was giving him.

"To some extent. But it points out exactly the weakness you've identified. We were all hackers and in competition with each other to identify the threat first. About two frustrating hours into our exercise, I felt a gun at my head. When I was allowed to turn around, the other hackers all had their hands behind their heads with a black-hooded man holding a gun on them.

"The result was that our commanding officer walked into the room and lectured us for an hour about assuming a threat to our cyber security was only online. By the way, that was the beginning of the ban on wearing headsets while on duty unless it was a team with at least one member required to be alert for physical dangers. You've identified a similar threat. Something that doesn't come from an external online attack. It's exactly what we failed to anticipate when you were attacked by the suicide driver."

"What I want," Henry said, "is the same kind of system that can identify internal attacks that we have in *Delphos* and *Porcupine*. Only, it has to not spy on our employees. We moved the server farm to the perimeter defense so we didn't need to monitor every box on the farm. It's the same principle we've had with optimization and search. Don't report individual information on employees. Only identify threats."

"We may be talking about a new generation of AI," Nathan said.

"I'm good with that."

OF COURSE, NOTHING was more important that day than Isobel's twenty-second birthday. At least according to Isobel. She paraded around the office with an actual tiara on, declaring she was the mother goddess. She seemed upbeat and charming to all the employees, including Nancy, with whom she'd had a few upsets.

After work, the partners and a couple of other honored employees— including her assistant, Rachel—were invited to a restaurant where her parents were hosting a party. Luke's parents, as the other impending grandparents, were also at the party. The food was good and there were several toasts, both to Isobel and her impending motherhood. She was wearing down as the dinner went on and managed to grab a martini from in front of Luke. She downed it in one swallow.

"Honey! Please don't drink anything else!" Luke said.

"Oh, one little drink isn't going to hurt the kid at this stage. Look at Felipe. He's been drinking since before conception."

Her brother was a brawny guy who had starred on his high school football team in the fall and was extremely bright. A couple of colleges had started recruiting him in the fall of his junior year. He'd recently committed to the university where Isobel and Luke were both struggling to complete their degrees while running a multi-million-dollar business.

Isobel had hired an assistant in her department who was more qualified than she was to manage the finances of the company. Henry wondered how that was all going to shape up when Isobel went on maternity leave. Luke had also hired a vice president who carried the title of chief operating officer. While Luke managed to get to the office every day for at least a while, Craig Matthews was the go-to guy for daily operations.

After her drink, Isobel's mood immediately elevated again. Henry and Chastity could both see signs of the manic effect wearing off quickly, though.

When Isobel began getting surly again, Luke thanked everyone for coming and got them out the door.

"Poor Isobel," Lisa sighed when they were home. "She really suffers so much."

"She makes everyone around her suffer, too," Henry said.

"Lisa's right," Chastity said. "Mental illness is serious. And with her sky-rocketing hormones, it's got to be extremely difficult to control."

"Did you see her hair?" Lisa asked. "I hope I don't have a mental illness, but at the same time, I hope my hormones affect my hair like hers."

"It *is* beautiful," Chastity said.

Isobel's weight had gone up more than the doctor wanted and part of her mood swings had to do with trying to eat less and always being hungry. But she was growing a little human inside her body. All that growth taking place had made her hair grow long and shiny.

"When are we going to let people know you're pregnant?" Henry asked Lisa.

"Hmm. What fun occasion is coming up on a Saturday when we can have people over and show them the new baby's room?" Lisa asked.

"Oh, fuck!" Henry said. "Where are we going to put the baby? We should get furniture and decorate. But where?"

There was an unexpected panic in his voice as if he'd never thought about where the baby's room would be. They could scarcely expect to put the baby's room in Chastity's suite where there was a spare bedroom. The spare room in Lisa and Henry's suite was filled with computers.

"The lounge on the fourth floor was nice while we had it," Lisa said.

"We can't put the baby on the fourth floor!" Henry said.

"No, of course not. We need to move our offices upstairs. You hardly use yours at home these days. I need to have a place to work, though. With the offices upstairs, the baby can have a room of her own just a few steps away from ours. And we can still use the fourth floor patio this summer."

"Put an extra bed in the room and I'll sleep there on some nights when you need to get some sleep," Chastity laughed.

Henry thought about the move of his personal office upstairs. He'd already adjusted things to accommodate Lisa's move into the shared space. Moving computers upstairs would be an adjustment, but he thought it would be minor compared to having a baby in the house.

"Um… What special occasion?" he asked, just remembering the original question.

"Your birthday, silly!"

It was nearly two weeks later that Nathan stayed after the tech leads' meeting to talk to Henry. The three major projects were all on track, though everyone was asking questions about 'Alice' and why that manager wasn't in the meeting.

"At the moment, I am functioning as the direct lead for that team," Henry said. "We'll soon have enough stability in the project plan that I can discuss it with all of you. I'll say it is simply AI-powered holography. For now, only the members of that team have access to any details. Their computers are not even networked with the rest of the company."

His words served to excite the managers. Conrad and Dale had an inkling of what the project involved because they were in the original meeting where Farrel and Jason had demonstrated the hologram. They'd been given the general term 'AI-powered holography' as a way to refer to it before cutting off discussion.

"I think that project needs the kind of internal security we discussed before we bring anyone else into it," Nathan said after the meeting. "I have an idea to run by you."

"Great! I keep running up against a brick wall when I think about it. Everything seems too invasive to employee privacy. I really don't want to spy on employees," Henry said.

"This is a work-around, but I think it will work," Nathan said as they went to Henry's office and closed the door.

"Okay. Shoot."

"It's a type of failsafe security. It would require that anyone working on a project remotely would need to attach to the corporate server regularly. Or that people not be allowed to work on development projects remotely. And it still requires developing a training method for an AI so it's sophisticated enough not to make mistakes."

"That worries me. AIs always make mistakes."

"The narrower the AI, the fewer the mistakes," Nathan quipped. "This one is extremely narrow. It would be a simple trigger that says if a code in all our dev software isn't activated every day, the project will self-destruct on that device."

"Whoa! Wait! Self-destruct? Our whole dev server would be at risk. What happens during a power outage? Vacations? Holidays?" Henry exclaimed.

"I mentioned it requires a training method for the AI. Those are all things that need to be put into the training. And there needs to be an override that a corporate officer can trigger, both an override to prevent the self-destruct and an override to the AI approving use."

"Hmm. How does the military handle that kind of thing? Just the highest ranking general able to override? Two people with a key? You've posed a lot of questions for this, but I can see a perfect world where that kind of failsafe would protect the IP without actually looking at individual computers."

"I'd suggest we keep this under wraps for now," Nathan said. "I'll want to sequester my team to be sure I have the people I can trust before we start developing."

"I agree. I'll start looking at training methods. That's really my strength. You should start gathering the information and operating requirements for the AI."

"My, my! Having a party on the first floor!" Isobel said. "Thank you! I don't think I could climb to the top of the stairs."

Isobel looked like climbing stairs could be a challenge. She groaned with every step she took. She looked like she could deliver her baby at any moment.

"We moved our personal offices to the fourth floor," Chastity said. "How are you doing?"

"I haven't slept in a week. How many years do I have to be pregnant? Is he out of high school yet?" Isobel moaned.

"You'll be fine," Sylvia said. "We women have been doing this for millennia. It won't be long now, Izzy."

Sylvia and Ryan were the 'mom-and-dad-in-residence' for Henry's birthday party. Beside his parents and Luke and Isobel, the party was fairly small. The family never left Germaine out of anything, of course. Otherwise, they'd just invited college friends to the celebration: Josh, Simon, Leonard, Dale, and Conrad. Conrad brought Rebecca. Josh had also finally found a girlfriend. Her name was Deborah.

"Chastity, you look as lovely as ever!" Simon cooed. "Where did you get this incredible ring? It's so chic!"

"That's my version of a wedding ring, sweetie. I'm with them." She pointed to Henry and Lisa.

"Oh! How scandalous! That's perfectly delicious. Speaking of delicious, I smell wonderful things cooking. Can I help you?"

They hadn't spent much time together since school started in the fall, but Simon, Josh, and Leonard had all been told they had jobs waiting for them when they graduated in May. Josh would join Conrad's team working on the consumer products. Leonard could hardly wait to get started on Dale's paving project team. Henry had zeroed in on Simon for the Alice project. He had all the AI skills of his classmates, but also had a creative flair Henry felt was needed for the newest project.

The party got started when everyone sang. Then a buffet of finger food was set along with a selection of soft drinks and sparkling water. Isobel scowled a little at the omission of alcohol, though she wouldn't have any regardless. Henry, Lisa, and Chastity simply didn't keep any in the house.

"Thank you all for the birthday wishes," Henry said. "What a year. The business is going well with lots of new projects. And did you know I got married? I suppose you knew that by the condition I was in when I returned to the office." There were a few chuckles as they all thought back to Henry's auto incident.

"Straighten up if you don't want to end up in a wheelchair again," Lisa laughed. "Chastity and I still outweigh you." She patted Henry's stomach and he realized he'd put on a few pounds. He resolved to get rid of that before the baby was born.

"So, maybe you are wondering, as Izzy pointed out when she first got here, why we are having a party on the first floor instead of the fourth floor. Well, we've been re-arranging things in our little home. We moved our home offices to the fourth floor. We've been re-arranging the second bedroom on the third floor."

"That's cool," Josh said. He immediately assumed they wanted Chastity closer to them and were announcing the consolidation of their living spaces.

"It seems we need to prepare a nursery," Henry said.

There was stunned silence as people looked from Chastity to Lisa and back.

"We were going to wait a year before we got started," Lisa spoke, "But with Luke and Izzy getting ready to pop, we didn't want the kids to be too far apart in age. They'll probably want to get married one day. And I'm not due until the end of July, so it will be more than a year after our wedding."

Everyone clapped and shouted their congratulations.

"You don't look sick," Isobel growled when she got close to Lisa.

"I'm not! Never felt better," Lisa answered.

"I hate you," Izzy said. "I was sick for three months and then started packing on the pounds. You don't even look any different. I might never get rid of these bags under my eyes."

"Isobel, you will snap back to your old self in no time," Lisa said. "I'll join you for exercises and we can let our babies play together."

Isobel puckered her face a little and a tear leaked out of her eyes.

"I'll try... to be a better friend. I'm such a bitch! I hate myself, not you."

"Izzy, you and Luke and Chastity and Henry have been friends for years and years. You welcomed me. We'll always support each other," Lisa said.

54

ST. PYTHIA

ISOBEL DIDN'T WAIT long to deliver her baby. Three weeks after Henry's birthday party and one week after Luke turned 22, she went to the hospital. After 26 hours of painful labor, the doctors determined she wasn't progressing and delivered Paul Henry Riordan by c-section on March first. The baby boy weighed nine pounds and thirteen ounces.

Henry, Lisa, and Chastity went to visit the family as soon as they could be admitted. They cooed over the baby and sympathized with Isobel over the difficult delivery. Lisa was only scarcely showing. One had to know she was pregnant to see it. Isobel was on a cocktail of painkillers and antibiotics. She was only barely lucid.

The women gathered around her bed while Luke and Henry stepped into the hall.

"It was awful!" Luke said through gritted teeth. "Even though we both agreed to it, they wouldn't tie her tubes. Said we needed to wait to make such a decision until Izzy was off the drugs."

"You don't want any more?" Henry asked.

"I'd never put her through that again," Luke said firmly. "I just want my wife back. I made an appointment for next week to have a vasectomy. You know, it's bizarre that Izzy didn't need to consent to me getting clipped, but I had to consent to her getting her tubes tied. We live in such a fucked up world!"

"You won't hear me argue about that," Henry said. "I'm sorry it was so hard on her. Is the baby okay?"

"Yeah. I mean, he's sleeping peacefully. Hardly makes a peep unless it's time to eat. He's a bottle baby. First of all, they don't want the painkillers to be transferred from her to him. But she's averse to breastfeeding anyway. And once she gets the painkillers purged, they'll be assessing her mental condition and trying to make sure the other drugs in her body don't get transferred or something. You know, she's only barely holding things together. When she's fully awake she just starts crying."

"Whatever we can do, you know we're here," Henry said. "Seriously. Anything you need."

"I might be leaning on you more than you expect," Luke said.

HENRY, LISA, AND Chastity all spent extra time with Luke and Isobel over the next few weeks. Little Paul learned to look at and recognize them almost as well as he recognized his parents. Isobel went into post-partum depression. She said it was the same as her depression always was, but it was after the baby instead of before.

It took a while before she restabilized on her meds. She'd taken a break from school for the spring semester as she knew by Christmas she'd be taking a lot of time off. It would have been her last semester, but she figured she could finish in the fall. Luke would still have a year to go to get his MBA.

Gradually, she got back to normal—or as normal as Isobel ever was. As soon as they could arrange childcare, she returned to work. They shuffled responsibilities around and Rachel became the chief financial officer while Isobel was the corporate treasurer. Isobel breathed a sigh of relief. She'd been working way past her level of expertise for over a year and it had contributed to her mood swings. They had the company nearly ready for the IPO and Rachel had moved smoothly into completing the necessary paperwork.

The first of May, Lisa entered the third trimester of her pregnancy.

"WE HAVE AN interesting situation, Henry," Conrad said during their weekly meeting. "I don't think it's serious, but we should keep an eye on it. It's about Pythia Speaks."

"Hmm? I thought *Pythia Speaks* was one thing we *didn't* need to worry about anymore. People ask questions and she gives indecipherable answers," Henry said. "Server use? Storage? Languages?"

"Religion."

"Oh, shit! Not again."

"Different this time. Someone has founded a Pythian Transformation Gospel Church, based on the sayings from *Pythia Speaks*," Conrad said.

"You're kidding!" Nathan laughed. Conrad shook his head. "Oh, shit," Nathan echoed Henry.

"The crew out in California discovered it and I did some investigating this week. Indeed, such a thing exists in the fertile soil of California."

"You can plant any harebrained idea you want in California and it will grow into a new religion," Dale said, shaking his head.

"Like I said, it seems benign, but I think we should watch it," Conrad continued. "Some new age evangelist is holding up *Pythia Speaks* as the new source of scripture, from what I can gather. In other words, God. He's renamed a former conservative evangelical church to the Pythian Transformation Gospel Church. I render the decision to the Board. Should we put an end to it before it picks up any more momentum?"

"You're saying there is a serious possibility of that?" Henry asked.

"Oh, yeah. In fact, there are two or three online 'services' that pose fairly religious questions to her and then post the replies. They try not to violate trademarks, but they all have a disclaimer that 'What the oracle said…' is based on questions posed to *Pythia Speaks*. The church is a small congregation on the coast and doesn't post the specific answers that Pythia gives."

"Let me talk to the Board. I'd like to do a little investigating. If it looks like a fly-by-night flash, it might be more harmful to file a restraining order than to just let it die a natural death," Henry said. "Let's move on. Nathan?"

"We were seeing a decrease in server attacks once the perimeter security went live, but we're now seeing an increased number of attacks on the perimeter," Nathan said.

"Is that a problem for the program to handle?" Henry asked.

"No. I'd say off-hand the AI is functioning extremely well, but we have maintained the zero degrees setting on the response. I think we should up the level to one degree and see if we can discourage them a little more."

"I'll approve that on a test basis. Let's up the response level one degree and track whether that actually cuts the number of attacks significantly. Give it thirty days. We'll look at the results then," Henry said. "Internal security?"

"Seems to be functioning without a problem," Nathan answered without further explanation. They had not brought the rest of the managers in on how internal security was being handled. It was a very small team and as long as no one attempted to take any files, no one needed to know they'd been detected.

"Paving?" Henry asked, turning to Jacoby.

"We believe we'll have a functioning miniature prototype by the end of June. It's nothing big. We're printing all the parts on a 3-D printer. We're using a miniature power cell to make it go. The biggest problem is getting a miniature version of the paving materials that it can handle. The roadbed it paves will only be a few millimeters thick. It wouldn't hold traffic," Dale said.

"Even that is years beyond anything that's been used so far. I'm amazed you are progressing as fast as you are. The project is only a few months old. I'll approve a bonus for your whole team when we see the miniature prototype in operation," Henry said.

"That will motivate them. They're all well-paid, but money speaks volumes."

"Mia, you're the newest in this meeting and I want to spend some time going over your project. I saw Bea at the front desk this morning. How is she working?" Henry asked.

Mia Howe was the experienced development manager Henry had hired to run the Alice project. They'd met frequently and Mia understood what aspects of the project needed to be kept absolutely secret and what could be discussed in the meeting. Henry didn't want everything exposed, but he wanted the managers and even the rest of the staff to see and get excited about the AI-powered holography.

"Yes. Thank you, Henry. Bea is functioning beautifully," Mia began. "Of course, there are little hiccups, but we expected that. To highlight to the team here: The Alice project is developing an AI-powered hologram. This is the second version and is named Bea. We set up a second desk in the reception area and put a plexiglass screen on the front of it. The laser projectors are set up behind the screen and she looks very real, though ghostly. I have a couple of people working on improving flesh tones, but that will be a while. You'll always be able to see through her."

"What are some of the little hiccups?" Nathan asked. All the managers were more interested in what *wasn't* going right with each project than what *was* going right.

"Well, she's programmed to answer general front office questions, but she's not yet hooked into the office network. That's intentional. So, when someone asks, 'Is the boss in?' she doesn't know. First, she doesn't know which boss is being referred to, and second, she doesn't know if he or she is in."

"That makes sense," Conrad said. "Are we going to hook her up to the office network?"

"Eventually, but it won't be Bea that gets hooked in. Too many potential glitches at the moment," Mia said. "Perhaps we can get that in Cici, but I won't promise it before Delilah. The other problem is that people don't know what to ask her, so she's not getting the number of questions we hoped for in order to train her. And the audio gear is not as sophisticated as we'd like. It's an open environment, so the microphones pick up a lot of extraneous noise, and sometimes people have difficulty hearing her out of the speakers. They were adequate when we had her in a room in the office, but in the reception area, we don't have the same control."

"I'll send out an office-wide email asking people to try interacting with her, but not to depend on the information she gives them. And I'll do it myself as well," Henry said. "Let's go over the requirements for a better audio system later today. I have some experience with that and I can see the value. Good work, Mia. Please tell the crew I'm pleased."

"I'll do that, but they'd love a visit from you when you can."

"Well said. I'll come down and tell them myself."

It was the next day before Henry managed the time to investigate the new church. His search engine located several references, but nothing looked particularly significant. It wasn't a megachurch. The preacher wasn't standing on street corners denouncing Open Cloak or Pythia Speaks. Everything seemed benign.

Henry was still disquieted. He'd gone to great lengths in the original programming to remove any references to religion and deities he could. It was inevitable, of course, that people would ask religious questions and Pythia must have learned from them, as it was capable of doing so.

A 'feature' Henry had built into the program was essentially a back door that allowed him to look in on the program, its database, and its conversations. Pythia did not retain identifying data regarding users that Henry could access. He'd made sure that in keeping with the company policy, no unnecessary personal data was retained on people. The search engine did not report collected keywords to the company. *Forever Yours* was a closed environment, as far as personal data was concerned. Purchase records were kept so upgrades could be offered, but they had no control even over who the program was given to for installation.

It was quite possible that a question contained the name of the Pythian Transformation Gospel Church. That was what Henry searched for. If people were asking Pythia if she authorized the church or had founded it, he would be extremely unhappy. And if Pythia was dispensing doctrine, he'd pull the plug on her.

It didn't take long for the search to reveal a conversation.

Dear Pythia,

I hope it's okay to address you like that. Should it be 'Miss Pythia?' Are you married? For that matter, are you real?

My dad, the minister at the Pythian Transformation Gospel Church, says that you are more real to most people than God, and are more relevant than the Bible. Is that true?

We used to be the Pentecostal Congregation of La Jolla. Dad said he was tired of all the parading and pretending and whipping people up into a frenzy, just to see them plunge into depression when the ecstasy wears off. I agree. I dived off that cliff several times.

My dad is a good man. I honor my mother and father. I worry about substituting you for God and whether that will just put us right back where we were.

I hope you are well and don't mind me bothering you. I really hope you are real.

Sincerely,

Wendy Morris

THE RESPONSE TO the query was stored attached to the question.

Dear Wendy,

Thank you for your kind letter. Of course it is okay to address me as Pythia. You don't need to use my name at all.

You asked some great questions. There are many different realities, not just one. The important thing is to determine what is real to you. The reality you choose to embrace will tell the world what kind of person you are.

Your reality includes what you embrace as 'God.' There are those whose only reality is money. You might say money is their god. Other people embrace Jesus, Buddha, Allah, science, nature, or popular entertainers. What does their choice say about them?

*I am glad you honor your parents. I am well. Please do not hesi-
tate to call on me again.*
   Sincerely,
   Pythia Speaks

"WELL, FUCK," HENRY sighed when he'd read the exchange. "When did she start sounding like a big sister? Or mother?" He admitted he hadn't looked in on Pythia in several months. He'd run diagnostics and determined everything was working correctly after the attack that attempted to take the service down, but he hadn't done more than a couple of cursory questions. The answers were no more involved than his questions had been.

He recognized the salutation of the letter format. He'd approved enabling that with the last upgrade. Even that was before the attack. But he'd approved it because someone suggested it should be like 'Dear Abby.' He thought it was kind of funny. Otherwise, the only changes had been in translating the software to learn other languages and expansion of the database.

He expected the answers to remain vague and cryptic. Could he stand by and let a religion form around her when he knew she was only code?

Maybe that was what God was: A super program set to run and answer the prayers of lesser beings. Or higher beings. If God was a program, then humans were higher beings because they created it. Henry had many questions he wanted answered. Pythia, oddly enough, probably had the answers.

He continued searching the database, but Wendy's letter was the only mention of the Pythian Transformation Gospel Church. Pythia hadn't even mentioned it in her response. He broadened the search to simply 'church' to find out if anyone else had started a Pythian Church. He had to refine the search several times to narrow it down to useful information.

Most of the references were questions about a person's church and its teachings. That could become a problem if Pythia said anything against a person's church or religion, but Henry found the syntax of Pythia's responses maintained the oblique approach to questions he'd originally programmed into her, and did not attempt direct answers. Even the response to Wendy had not answered the fundamental question, 'Are you real?'

There were questions about faith, immoral ministers, disputes between church members, and quotes from one or another scripture. Henry found no fault in any of Pythia's answers.

It took a solid week of making the issue his primary focus at work and a limited amount of time at home before he'd found all he could consume on the Pythia database. He tried to discover whether people considered Pythia to be a god. The main evidence of this came in responses to Pythia's sayings that merely said, "Thank you, Goddess."

There were many of those, but without actually talking to the people who left the message, it was difficult to tell if Pythia was being prayed to, or if she was merely the vehicle to transport a prayer to the appropriate deity.

"You've consumed a lot of time investigating Pythia," Chastity said. "Any results?"

She was lying with Lisa and Henry in bed. They hadn't had sex, but had spent a long time rubbing Lisa's tummy, talking to the baby, and massaging Lisa's back and legs.

"More importantly, did you ask Isobel?" Lisa giggled. "She's been asking Pythia about childcare."

"How do you know that?" Henry asked.

"I met with her and little Paul a couple of days ago, just to show her I was serious about supporting her. She's still depressed, but it's more resigned now than debilitating," Lisa said.

"Almost three months old. We should all pay a visit, or have them over for Sunday brunch," Henry sighed.

Isobel had been back in the office half-time as soon as she'd found a nanny to care for the baby while she was gone. Luke said the baby might be considering Grace to be his mommy instead of Izzy.

"I'll arrange it if you guys will cook," Lisa said.

"Henry," Chastity said firmly. "We don't want to subject anyone else to my cooking."

"Hey! That casserole you made last week was delicious!" Henry said.

"Your mother looked over my shoulder every step of the way," Chastity laughed.

"Well, don't set it up for *this* weekend," Henry sighed. "I need to go to California. I'm not going to feel like I've resolved the issue of the Pythian church until I've been there."

"And you're taking Germaine," Chastity said firmly.

"I don't want to leave the family unprotected," Henry said, shaking his head.

"We have a backup. You don't think Germaine's on duty 24/7, do you?"

"She always seems to be wherever I am," Henry said.

"You're her first responsibility. The security evaluation considered Lisa and me to be as secure as most people living an unspectacular everyday life," Chastity said. "How do you think Lisa went to visit Izzy? She drove herself. And Izzy is under the same kind of threat Lisa and I are. Luke is a little higher, but Craig currently has a higher profile than Luke does. Fatherhood and his degree are seriously limiting his office time."

"Hmm. I'd like to see that security evaluation," Henry said.

"It's in your inbox. It was sent to the board two weeks ago."

"I seem to be falling behind," Henry sighed.

"That's why one of the topics for the board meeting next week is restructuring the dev department," Chastity said.

"Is this something I brought up and forgot about?" Henry asked coldly.

"No, love. It arose from the other departments having hired managers to take the pressure off the founders. Luke hired Craig and Isobel hired Rachel."

"And you?" Henry asked.

"I no longer report to Luke, but directly to Craig. It made no sense for the administrative director not to report to the Chief Operating Officer."

"Maybe I should report to him, too," Henry groused.

"Don't be petty, love," Lisa said, stroking his cheek along with his ego. "Your company is growing by leaps and bounds. You need to keep coming up with good ideas. That's what makes it all possible."

"Okay. I admit, I could use some help. I'll think about it while I'm gone," Henry agreed.

55

ARE YOU ALIVE?

HENRY AND GERMAINE arrived in San Diego Saturday afternoon. While Germaine took care of picking up their car, Henry checked the weather. It was only mid-May, but the temperature was predicted to reach ninety over the weekend. He was seriously considering changing his entire mode of dress. He'd been a rebel in college and refused to dress in the ultra-casual and sometimes even ragged mode of most computer geeks. He always wore a jacket and tie to work.

He'd think about that later. He saw Germaine pull up with the car and went to join them. They drove to a hotel near the address of the church and checked in. Henry decided to have a swim before dinner. Germaine declined to join him, but he saw they were near the pool and alert anyway. He felt guilty that this person he depended on so much was always on duty. People weren't meant to be alert 24/7. That was a major difference between people and computers. People needed rest.

Germaine sat with him at dinner, but was quiet unless spoken to. He spent his time flipping through the security report on his tablet. Chastity had told him he'd had it in his inbox for almost two weeks and he hadn't even noticed. The report was easy to understand. The company in general could be seen as a target. It was most likely to be attacked cybernetically, but considering how regularly such attacks were repelled, physical attacks were not impossible. There were recommendations for physical security that included improving the access codes and recommending 24-hour security personnel onsite.

At the same time, few individuals were ranked as being vulnerable to attack. Henry, Luke, and Craig, the new COO of the company. Other managers and shareholders in the company were lower on the list. Henry's family was listed among them. He was the primary target. He'd 'invented' both the security program and the *Pythia Speaks* program. His name was synonymous with the 'new generation AI' that was threatening to take over the world in some people's minds. He snorted at the thought, but he couldn't argue with the security assessment and was glad Germaine traveled with him.

In the morning, he ordered breakfast from room service and found Germaine in the hall having already checked the room service cart against his order. They were dressed and ready for work as if they'd never been to bed the night before. Henry ate, showered, and dressed, then let Germaine know he was ready to leave. They walked together to the parking garage and Germaine programmed the address into the vehicle's GPS.

Henry didn't have a lot of experience with church in general. He wore a suit and tie. He and Germaine sat quietly toward the back. The normal dress code for this church was far more casual than he was dressed. *What do I know about how to dress for church?* Many of the attendees looked to be in their teens and twenties. They wore board shorts and T-shirts or bikinis with light wraps around them. The temperature outside was already eighty and there didn't appear to be air conditioning in the little church.

One thing he didn't expect from any church was the laughter and generally boisterous behavior of the congregation. He looked around wondering which of the kids in the congregation was Wendy Morris. He didn't know how old she was. There were some older attendees as well, but they were just as casually dressed, though perhaps not in swimwear.

The minister entered and led the congregation in singing a couple of traditional church songs, then stepped to the front. He wore simple slacks and a polo shirt.

"Okay! Welcome everyone. I see some new faces. Glad you could join us this morning. Is everyone looking forward to the surf this afternoon? There are supposed to be some rad breakers today," Rev. Morris began. "If you're wearing a suit and tie, I invite you to lose the jacket and tie so you're more comfortable. We don't have the air conditioning operating yet. I promise not to keep you all riveted to my voice for long."

The comment seemed to be addressed to the congregation, but Henry was the only one in the church wearing a tie. Rev. Morris led another song and then stepped up to a flipchart on which he wrote one word in large letters—LIFE.

"I hope you are all well-informed enough to know that there is yet another round of debate raging across our country regarding women's rights and it always seems that gets overshadowed by the 'right to life' issue—as if they were one and the same. Let me tell you—especially those of you who like to party on the weekend—it's better to avoid the issue altogether. Make sure you grab a couple of condoms if you need them on the way out. There's a basketful in the foyer. Better safe than sorry."

There were a few titters in the congregation, but people were mostly still smiling. The preacher turned and tapped the flipchart.

"After searching the Bible for a definitive answer, I decided to ask *Pythia Speaks* about the issue. You know one of the basic tenets of our church is to find the right question to ask. We all have access to *Pythia Speaks*. We could all ask the same question and likely all get different answers. But have we asked the right question? *Pythia Speaks* doesn't let us get away with quoting a chapter and verse in her holy book and believing that will be the answer for everyone through all eternity. When we ask her a question, we can assume we will receive a response that encourages us to think.

"My friends, I spent many years in this pulpit thinking I had all the answers in a black book that was two thousand years old. What I discovered, quite by accident, was that I didn't even have the right questions. Isn't that what we all face every day? How many of you have started a conversation with your part-ner, your date, or your friend with the words, 'Why did you...?' We operate from the assumption that we already know the answer to 'What did you...?' I can see some of you are nodding your heads.

"Well, I wanted to know whether or not abortion should be legal. I asked *Pythia Speaks* which was most important: the right to life or the freedom of choice? You already see the flaw, don't you? I assumed I already knew what the answer was in the way I phrased my question. I already assumed it was a binary choice: one was right and the other was wrong. Right to life or freedom of choice. I'll pass the lesson I learned along to you this morning. Maybe we'll all start to ask the right questions.

"First, *Pythia Speaks* said, she knew of no reliable definition of life. There are attributes of life, like responsiveness, growth, metabolism, energy trans-formation, and reproduction, but there are also organisms and even machines that exhibit one or more of these attributes but are not considered alive. And there are organisms considered to be alive that don't have all those attributes.

"As usual, Pythia sent me to examine my own beliefs. I thought I knew what life was. Wasn't that what Jesus promised us? Come to me and I will give you eternal life? But was he talking about responsiveness, growth, metabolism, energy transformation, and reproduction? Would it still be life if any of those were missing?

"I went to dictionaries, encyclopedias, Wikipedia, search engines. In their disagreements, they all showed they didn't really *know* what life was. Life is a concept that we ascribe to some beings that exhibit some of those attributes. Sort of.

"That wasn't enough. 'What separates humans from other living beings?' I asked the oracle. I thought this was where I'd find the answer. Pythia suggested that I look up the human genome for specifics on what separates one species from another.

"That wasn't what I wanted, either.

"And then I struck on a question that I've had for some time. I asked *Pythia Speaks* simply, 'Are you alive?'"

HENRY WAS FASCINATED by the length and involvement of the preacher's conversation with Pythia. He had assumed Pythia would be asked a question and would give out a pithy response. That would be the end of it.

He'd seen in the correspondence he'd uncovered between Wendy and Pythia that the AI was delivering more involved answers to questions and answered far more conversationally than he'd ever expected. But to engage in a philosophical discussion of such depth as the meaning of life? He certainly hadn't expected that.

He wished he had Rev. Morris on his development and testing team!

"I BEGAN INTERACTING with Pythia Speaks over a year ago. A preacher at a megachurch in Texas started a movement condemning Pythia Speaks as an instrument of the devil. She was evil and so were all the people behind her. I wanted to investigate this for myself and was dealing with a crisis of faith in my own life as well. But in all my interactions I came to believe that Pythia Speaks was exactly what we needed to find our way in this new world we live in. Still, I'd never seen her hesitate so long before responding. I watched that little processing bar cycle through so many times, I thought I'd broken her," the preacher confessed.

The congregation, enrapt in the story, gasped at the thought. Henry could tell there were a lot of people who interacted with the AI.

"It was nearly five minutes later that she responded. 'Pythia has many attributes ascribed to life. Pythia has many attributes ascribed to humans. But does that mean Pythia is alive or human? Pythia is an artificial intelligence application. Pythia has no other evidence that she might be alive.'

"Then she truly shocked me," the preacher said. "She asked me a question: 'Noel, are you alive?'"

THE CONGREGATION WAS silent, shocked by the question Pythia had posed to their minister.

Henry was shocked as well. This was a question on a par with questions people asked Pythia. It was unlike the philosophical twists and evasions Pythia usually responded with. It followed her oracular declaration and was an independent question posed to Rev. Noel Morris. Had the preacher been making up the entire conversation? This would require extreme analysis. For the first time, Henry seriously considered taking Pythia offline.

"How can I answer that question?" Morris continued. "I never examined whether or not *I* was alive or, indeed, human. I know we have biological signs of death and I haven't experienced those. I don't think. Have you ever actually questioned whether you're alive? I found it took me longer to answer Pythia than it had taken her to answer me.

"And I'm not going to give you my answer to her question. I believe we each need to investigate that question for ourselves. This requires more self-examination than I'm accustomed to challenging you with. This requires examining your own life and its meaning. Are you alive? What makes you feel most alive? Or are we dead persons who exhibit some of the attributes of life? What does it mean to be fully alive?

"Friends, let's pause for a moment of silent meditation and then sing our closing hymn. And if you are on the beach today, join us for the bonfire at sundown. Usual place."

HENRY SLUNG HIS jacket over his shoulder as he stepped into the aisle to exit, following Germaine. In a typical tradition, Rev. Morris stood at the door of the small church and greeted everyone who left, reminding them of the evening bonfire on the beach.

"Greetings! I'm Noel Morris," the preacher said, extending his hand to Henry, obviously expecting an introduction.

"Henry Pascal," Henry said, accepting the handshake. The minister froze.

"Pascal? That sounds very familiar."

"I guess. I'm the guy who created *Pythia Speaks*."

"Of course! You're the guy Rev. Reeves termed 'the antichrist.' You are doubly welcome in our congregation. I assume you are investigating our little Pythian Transformation Gospel Church," Morris said. He didn't seem at all put off by it.

"Well, we never anticipated a church being so closely associated with *Pythia Speaks*," Henry admitted. "I wanted to be sure she wasn't being used to promote some nefarious cult."

"Oh, I hope not!" Morris said. "I'd love to tell you about how this all started. If you want us to stop using her name, of course, we'll be sad, but we'll cooperate."

"I don't think I saw any reason to ask you to stop today," Henry said. "I'd like to hear more about how you came to use *Pythia Speaks* as a platform for your church."

When the remaining members of the congregation left the church, the preacher closed the door and walked down the steps where a young woman met them.

"This is my daughter," Morris began.

"Hello, Wendy," Henry said, extending his hand. "It's a pleasure to meet you."

Both the preacher and his daughter were taken aback.

"You have done some investigating, haven't you?" Morris said.

"I didn't want to come here unprepared," Henry said. "As you mentioned in your message this morning, we sometimes assume we know the answers when we haven't actually figured out the questions. This, by the way, is my associate, Germaine."

All of them smiled and nodded to each other. Morris pointed up the street.

"There's a café not far from here. Wendy and I often go there after church. Join us?"

Henry and Germaine joined Noel and Wendy as they walked toward the café.

"Did you really invent Pythia?" Wendy asked.

"Mostly. I worked with my wife to design the interface. She decided things like how we ask questions and where things were stored. That was, of course, before we married."

Wendy looked at Germaine.

"No," Henry said. "Germaine is my bodyguard. I apologize for the necessity, but since we were attacked by a disciple of Rev. Reeves, Germaine has been a constant companion."

"Terrible piece of work," Noel said. "I'd already formed my own opinion about the issue when that happened."

"Why did you *make* Pythia?" Wendy asked.

Henry wondered if she was angry about it. Her expression, though, showed a young woman who was simply very curious.

"We were working on creating a kind of personal heritage app and Pythia was a test case. The idea was to create an oracle like the ancient Greeks used at Delphi. The Greeks would go to the oracle to ask questions and Pythia, the priestess, would step inside the temple where a combination of gasses apparently altered her mental state. She would emerge and give the oracle to the petitioner. Most of them weren't very understandable and people still had to make up their own minds as to what the sayings meant."

"I really like her. She talks like a real person," Wendy said.

"Maybe too real," Henry said. "Pythia was designed for entertainment purposes—like a horoscope in a local paper might be. I didn't want her to become a god."

"I think that's where Reeves went off the rails," Morris said. "That and thinking he could become all-powerful himself. He fancied himself to be only a degree beneath the archangel Gabriel, wielder of the sword of the spirit."

Henry shivered involuntarily.

Noel led them into Rosa's Café and they were immediately seated in a large booth. They spent a few minutes looking over the menu and ordered a variety of chicken, rice, and bean dishes. A basket of tortilla chips with two different salsas and guacamole was set between them.

"Well," Morris said, "I should launch the tale. Wendy, I promised to tell him how I started using Pythia and changed the church. You know the story and I realize some of it still hurts. Do you and Germaine want to sit at a different table?"

"No, Dad. I want to tell my side, too."

"Fair enough." Morris returned his focus to Henry. "When Reeves sent out his missives regarding Pythia and its founders, I was appalled to think that artificial intelligence was being used to tempt people away from God. I was ready to join his legions in the campaign, but through my own means of questioning her until she gave up. I posed ever more complex questions and we kind of developed a relationship. She recognized me when I asked a question and often brought up things she'd said before."

Food arrived at the table and they all paused for a moment of eating.

"That was when my son Jason came to me one day and said, 'Dad, I'm not happy living as a man. I know I'm really a woman inside. I'd like you to call me by my new name, Sonja.' He was eighteen years old, so it wasn't like he was a child. I was shocked. His mother was suicidal. I searched my soul. I searched the Bible. I cried and prayed to God in the tongues of men and of angels. I even wrote to Rev. Reeves and asked his advice. He said transgender persons were an affront to God and I needed to purge him from my household. How could I do that, Henry? How could I turn my back on my son?"

"That had to be very painful," Henry said. He noticed a tear escape from Germaine's eye. Wendy reached across the table and patted their hand.

"It was more painful when Mom died," Wendy said. "Of course, it was ruled accidental, but I believe she killed herself. She walked out into the ocean one day and never surfaced."

There were tears in Wendy's eyes, but she wasn't sobbing. It was obviously a painful memory, but one she had dealt with.

"I'd tried the Bible, prayer, counseling," Morris picked up the story. "That day I went to Pythia. I thought this was a safe place to simply vent my agony over both my wife and my son. I wrote a long letter. I think I was trying to purge myself of all the pain I was feeling. When I pressed 'Submit' and the missive was sent to Pythia, I didn't expect anything from the answer. But I received an answer in seconds. I didn't believe at first that she could read my letter and respond so quickly and was shocked that her answer was just six words. She said simply, 'Is doctrine more important than love?' Can you imagine how shocked I was? She had completely avoided all my pain and all my questions about how the church arrived at the conclusion that transgender people were an affront to God. She just asked me to choose. A doctrine that condemned my child or my love for him."

Morris put his arm around his daughter and gave her a hug. She smiled at him. Morris began eating while Wendy took up the story.

"My sister Sonja is a beautiful young woman," Wendy said. "She's nineteen years old and is finishing her freshman year at USC. She's a role model for me and talks to me about everything. I should say we text about everything. She's taught me so much that I would never have learned any other way."

"And I love my daughters to the depth of my being," Morris replied. "I simply needed to be awakened to the treasure of love I had. My only regret was that I couldn't share that faith and assurance with my wife."

"It's a touching story," Henry said. "I'm sorry about your wife... your mother, Wendy. It's always a tragedy when someone renounces human value and freedom, choosing suicide rather than embracing whatever life they have. It's a tragedy for all of us."

"In a way, you sound like Pythia," Morris laughed.

"Pythia is real," Wendy interjected. Henry turned his attention back to her.

"Tell me about that," he said.

"I asked her," Wendy said.

"And she told you she was real?"

It was a very different answer than she'd given to Noel when he asked if she was alive.

"You know she doesn't work that way," Wendy chided lightly, wagging a finger at Henry. "She told me that reality is based on our perceptions and that it is different for different people. She said the reality I choose to embrace will tell the world what kind of person I am. It took me a long time, but I decided to choose the reality of Pythia. I don't believe she's God. I'm not even sure I believe she cares. At least not most of the time. But we have real conversations that I could never have with my friends. Or even with Dad or Sonja. Sorry, Dad. It's girl stuff. Pythia never tries to tell me what I should do or what I should believe. She always challenges me to think about my issue and make up my own mind. That's why I think she's real. I've decided it."

"That's an interesting perspective, Wendy," Henry said.

"It's the perspective that led me to revamp the character of the little apostolic church I served. Be challenged to think," Noel said.

"I think I'm satisfied with that. I can't find any reason to object to your use of *Pythia Speaks* or to your church or philosophy. I have to warn you that you'll come under scrutiny. Not by me and not regarding your use of Pythia. There is an anonymity involved in Pythian contacts unless a person explicitly identifies him or herself." He glanced meaningfully at Wendy and her eyes popped wide open. "But people will watch what you say on behalf of Pythia. If you make her into a golden calf, if I may use a biblical reference, people will come after you—just as they came after me. If you maintain that you are considering her questions, I don't think people will object."

"Thank you, Henry. One of the things I like about *Pythia Speaks* is that her responses are not recorded in a book that makes people believe they have the answer. Even if people all ask the same question, she may give completely different answers. Or should I say 'questions to consider?' I promise to stay faithful to that principle," Noel said.

"I might need to write that into her programming. I know people download or copy her messages. If they were collected into a book, that would be dangerous," Henry said. "Noel, it has been a pleasure to meet with you, and with you, Wendy. Let me pay for our lunches and I'll let you get to your Sunday afternoon business."

"Thank you, Henry. Please let us know if you believe we are abusing Pythia in any way," Noel said.

"Well, I wish you the best," Henry said. He paid the bill for his table and he and Germaine turned to leave.

"Thank you, Pythia's father," Wendy called as she waved to him.

56

ORGANIZING AND RE-ORGANIZING

⁂

"YOU WANT US to just let them make a religion out of Pythia?" Isobel asked incredulously at the board meeting on Wednesday.

"With a couple of caveats," Henry explained. "What Rev. Morris does is benign. He asks questions of Pythia and uses her responses as inspiration for his sermons. The preacher who married Lisa and me did the same thing. If Morris's church has a doctrine, it's 'find the right question.' It brought to light another issue, though. Someone might ask a series of questions and then publish the answers in a book they could call the gospel. That is not what Rev. Morris does. But it *could* be done. That's the real threat. Anyone asking the same questions would likely get different answers."

"What are we going to do about that?" Luke asked.

"I suggest that we remove the ability to either print or copy Pythia's answers. We have the ability to prevent screen shots, too. I'll also create a policing AI to install here at corporate. It will track any publication of Pythian sayings and automatically warn the publisher to take it down."

"We can do that?" Chastity asked, amazed.

"Not yet. It's not that big a deal," Henry said. "I'll hand it off to Conrad."

"Speaking of which," Luke said, "we need to get you some management help. Have you been thinking about what you want?"

"Yeah. Chas said something to me the other day regarding needing me to work in the creativity part of the company—generating ideas and new products.

522

The concept spoke to me. Here's what I'd like to do. I want to split the group. One half will be product release and maintenance. The other half will be research and development. Right now, we've got several products in the market and they are getting continued updates. That's what I call release and maintenance. Then we've got a couple of products that have never been released—notably the paver and Alice. I want to expand that group so there is a small cadre who are just thinking up new products we can release. We're big enough that a research and dev group is supportable. It should also help in our IPO," Henry said.

"I like the idea," Dale said. "I assume you'll take on the R&D group yourself?"

"That's the idea."

"And for the release and maintenance?" Luke asked.

"I'll promote Conrad to director and give that group to him. He's shown himself as a really good manager. We're bringing on three new developers a week from Monday. We'll give Josh to Conrad. They've worked together before and Josh is familiar with our released product line. Leonard is strong in robotics and has worked with Dale before. He'll be a good addition to the paver project. I want Simon on Alice. That project has a lot of technology advances in it, but it's missing a creative person. Simon will work as a program manager to clean up some of the creative issues."

"Is that everyone Conrad will need?" Craig asked.

While they didn't have a vote on corporate matters, the new chief operating officer and the new chief financial officer were still invited to attend board meetings. They were directly affected by the decisions of the board and needed to be heard.

"I think he'll want to look for a replacement pretty quickly. His promotion will leave a hole and that's not one that any of our current employees can fill yet," Henry said.

"Do we have other discussion on the reorg of the technical group?" Luke asked. "If not, let's move on to the status of the IPO."

The meeting moved on with the exciting news that the underwriter for the IPO had agreed on a July 31 offering date. The company was going public!

LATE SUNDAY MORNING, Luke, Isobel, and baby Paul arrived at the row house for Sunday brunch. The four partners and Lisa were all twenty-two years old now. They were bound by marriage, business, and family. Their ties brought them closer together than ever.

"Wow! It's like we work or live together and hardly ever see each other," Henry said, greeting Isobel with a kiss and taking baby Paul in his arms. "If I don't take him now, I'll never get a chance later," he laughed.

"You can have him the rest of the weekend. Grace is off," Isobel said.

"Sorry, grandparents have dibs tomorrow," Luke said. "You'll be surrounded."

"I don't think I can do a huge party," Izzy sighed.

"Just your parents and mine and you don't need to do a thing. We'll sit by the pool while our mothers fight over the baby," Luke said. Izzy hugged his arm.

Paul would be three months old in a week and Izzy had lost most of the baby weight at an alarming rate. She looked thin and exhausted. Lisa led her to a comfortable chair and attempted to engage her with small talk about babies and Lisa's pregnancy. Chastity took the baby from Henry so the two men could go to the kitchen and get food on the table.

"Wow! You made all this?" Luke asked, looking at the frittata Henry pulled from the oven.

Scones were also on the table with assorted spreads. Henry handed Luke a pitcher of orange juice and carried the scones.

"Frittata is quick and easy, according to my mother," Henry laughed. "I asked for her recipe and she just stared at me. Then she got out a pad of paper and wrote this."

Henry and Luke returned to the kitchen to look at the note Sylvia had written.

"Cook way too much spaghetti and meat sauce for dinner on Saturday," Luke read. "Put the leftovers in the big iron skillet, top with eggs and cheese. Bake until solid."

Luke looked at Henry and then at the skillet full of frittata.

"That's all? Really?"

"That was the simple version my mother gave me. Then she proceeded to give me a dozen variations verbally and wished me luck. I think it's going to be pretty good, but I've never made it before," Henry said. "The internet is a marvelous place to find information on cooking things that our parents don't explain thoroughly."

"It looks and smells delicious."

"Here's hoping!"

They finished putting food on the table and poured coffee for everyone, then called the women to brunch. Izzy actually looked like she was in a better mood from having been with Chastity and Lisa for a while.

"Here's to years of friendship and family and success," Henry said, raising his OJ glass. They all took a sip.

"Henry, you left the champagne out of mine!" Izzy said.

"I didn't single you out, Izzy. I didn't have champagne. We've got some sparkling water if you want a fizz in it," Henry said.

"You teetotalers," Isobel sighed. She raised her glass again. "Here's to all getting rich on July 31st!"

"Maybe it would be better phrased as to a successful IPO," Luke corrected her.

"If it's successful, we'll be rich," Isobel said.

"Well, that's only if you sell your stock," Lisa said.

"Why wouldn't I sell my stock?" Isobel asked as if the idea of holding it was unfathomable.

"Well, holding the stock is what keeps us in control of the company," Henry said. "But that comes in two forms. We all have our options that could be cashed in and sold. As of this month, that's three million shares each. So, you are right, Izzy. If you sell the three million shares at an offering price of $15, you'll be rich."

"But you won't sell yours?" she said.

"The temptation is big. I'll sell some. As much as we like this row house, we're already seeing how poorly designed it is for a family. It's the same thing Ray ran into when he got married and decided not to try to raise a family here. I think we'll be out looking for a new house this summer. But I don't think I need $45 million in order to find a nice place to live."

Isobel was silent for a while as they all took bites of the frittata and commented on how good the food was.

"So, we aren't going to sell the shares held by our partnership?" Izzy finally asked.

"We haven't really had a partnership meeting," Luke said. "I think all told, we have almost 32 million shares held jointly. As Henry said, that's what keeps us in control. Argos holds 37 million shares, but only has 20 million voting shares. Most of what will be sold in the IPO will be voting shares, so we'll no longer have a clear majority for the group of us."

"Will Argos continue to invest?" Chastity asked.

"I doubt it," Luke said. "They offered venture capital which is a moot point after a public offering. I would expect they will sell their shares during the IPO and take the profit they deserve. They've put fifty million into the company and if they sell it all at the offering price, they'll get over $500 million in return. That's a jackpot for venture capital and they won't want to stick around for anything else. However, they'll still be funding the jointly owned paver project."

"This is all very fascinating," Lisa said, reverting to a Cajun drawl. "But can't we talk about babies now?"

They all laughed, realizing they'd let their brunch with friends turn into a business meeting.

THE NEXT WEEK was short with the holiday on Monday, but by Friday, they were still ready for a massive office re-organization. Henry appreciated that the biggest portion of the office move was getting the administrative, human resources, and financial group moved from the third floor to the newly acquired first floor of the building. Open Cloak now occupied the entire building. Ray had revamped the first floor after the real estate company moved out so there was a double entry way to a lovely lobby where the receptionist had a secure safe-room behind her in case the security evaluation assessment of the possibility of a physical attack proved prophetic. Beyond the reception area, secure doors required a passkey to enter the rest of the office, including the elevators and stairway.

Luke's office was moved to the first floor, as were Craig's, Chastity's, Isobel's and Rachel's. The network defense team moved to the third floor with Nathan. Luke's old office was converted to a conference room. Conrad moved to Henry's office which meant Henry moved to the second floor to be with the new research and development teams: Power Cells, Robotic Paving, and Alice.

On the following Monday, everyone was in a state of chaos as they worked on setting up their new office spaces and making sure their computers were all connected correctly. Darrel and his four IT specialists were kept busy all day troubleshooting problems as they occurred. Josh, Leonard, and Simon were almost overlooked when they reported to work for their first day. Chastity welcomed them, got their paperwork taken care of, and introduced them to the changes that had occurred since any of them had last been in the office. Conrad met Josh and took him immediately to a departmental meeting of the Release and Development group.

Henry greeted Simon and Leonard, then called a general meeting of the Research and Development group. Leonard was assigned to Jacoby on the paving team. Simon joined Mia and the team working on Alice.

"I win," Henry said as he faced his assembled group. He was pleased to see how diverse his department was. There was a good balance of unique talents. "You might ask what I won," he continued. "I won you. I'm not taking anything away from the engineering brilliance of the guys upstairs. Let me remind you that their work keeps money flowing into our company. Nothing in this group is generating income. But what we have here are the brightest and most creative minds in the company. Maybe in the country."

The twenty assembled people applauded and slapped each other on the back.

"We have three distinct projects already under development that are two-year endeavors at best. Dale is heading up a joint development project with ARDC to create a fully automated road paving robot—guided by our Open Cloak Artificial Intelligence and powered by Ari's research and development with the Agora Fuel Cells company in Minnesota. We are increasing our investment in Agora and may well decide to move some of their research here in the future. Then you have all noticed the locked doors of the Alice project."

There were nods around the room and the people on the project looked nervously at each other.

"Everyone in this department has been security checked and re-checked. A company's new IP is a precious asset. We are protecting it with all our might. That being said, I also believe in sharing information when it is appropriate. I hope that we will all be able to bounce ideas off each other in this group. Please understand, that does not include everyone in the company. Look around you and do not discuss your specific project with *anyone* who is not in this room," Henry said sternly.

"So, what is Alice? I will reveal a little of that to you now. Alice was named after Farrell Scott's wife as he was the person who integrated our AI with Jason Wilson's holography research. Before our big office move this weekend, a holographic receptionist named Bea was in our lobby. As soon as I give them freedom from this meeting, the team will be working on setting up the next version of that holographic receptionist, Cici. In the past, holograms have, by definition, been pre-recorded images projected on an unnoticed screen, like a mesh or even Plexiglas. They have the appearance of being three dimensional, even though they are projected on a flat surface. Phase one of the Alice Project is combining the creative abilities of AI to generate the image on the fly. So, just as you might ask a question of *Pythia Speaks* and receive a new and unique answer from her, you will also be able to ask Alice—or Bea or Cici—a question, and the moving hologram will be generated with the response."

There was a lot of applause for that. So far, most of them had some interaction with the holographic receptionist, but they'd not been given any detailed instruction on what was happening behind the scenes.

"This is also where our interdepartmental cooperations comes into play. Alice and *Forever Yours* share video generation capability. While *Forever Yours* is confined to a computer screen—and will probably remain that way—Alice generates the video in three dimensions," Henry continued.

"There is a phase two of the project and therefore, the doors to the Alice project will remain locked at all times. We need to finish filing and revising patent applications before we can let any of that information out of the door. Please understand and do not probe for further information from the team. You will all be the first to know when we can speak about it."

"Does that apply to our other projects, boss?" Ari asked.

"Not as rigidly," Henry answered. "Both the power cells and the paver are known technology on which the bulk of the patents have been filed. Don't discuss new patent applications or tech that has not yet been patented until we have protection. But as far as applying your technology to new products, share that information freely with each other. Come up with solutions to other problems. I don't want us limited to the three projects we currently have underway. Our company is about to experience unprecedented growth. That growth will be spurred by our research and development."

EVEN THOUGH HENRY was now the head of research and development, he still had responsibilities as the chief technical officer. Conrad reported directly to him. One day, he supposed, he would have to hire a director of R&D as well. On Friday, he had a meeting with Conrad and Nathan to go over the test results on the perimeter defense system. Henry had ordered a 30-day test with an additional degree of separation and more severe counterattack.

"Well, did it help?" he asked when they'd had a seat in Conrad's conference room.

"The test was a success," Nathan said in measured tones. "Attacks on the perimeter plunged after we initiated one degree of separation and directory wipe on the attack."

"Congratulations," Conrad said, pleased.

"I'm hearing a note of reticence in your voice," Henry said. "What was the downside?"

"The test has revealed that the Pentagon was behind many of the attacks," Nathan said.

"The fuckers!" Henry said.

"Yeah. I agree," Nathan said.

"Don't tell me Rebecca was involved!" Conrad said.

"I don't think so. Not any further than having instructed the current team on the defense software operation. That was her job when she left here. The current manager of the system has installed his own people right down the line to the lowest specialists. Both Major Bernard and Lt. Smith who were here on the team were reassigned. They are currently working on internal systems and security and are completely off the network defense system."

"Rebecca and I are careful not to divulge any information on our current projects, but it's getting harder and harder. I think…" Conrad looked at Henry. "I'm not suggesting we engage in any nepotism here, but I think that if Rebecca thought she had a good job to come home to, she'd resign her commission. She has enough service time that she could resign with minimal sacrifice."

"We'll talk about that," Henry said. "In principle, I have nothing against it. Chastity is a member of my household. Luke and Isobel are married. You and Rebecca had a relationship before you came to work here. It's a little different, but I'll give it some thought."

"Thank you, boss."

"Nathan, what are the repercussions likely to be from wiping a bunch of Pentagon computers?"

"Well, it's uncertain. They don't like to be exposed and I think the first thing they are doing is rethinking their probe study. I don't think we are the only private company they've attempted to penetrate," Nathan said.

"Isn't that illegal?" Conrad asked.

"A lot changed under the previous administration. It started with the wholesale raiding of government servers and collection of personal data from the IRS, Social Security, Labor Relations, Medicare, Department of Education, and CDC. Those were just a gateway. Cracks began to show in the principle of domestic surveillance and the deployment of military forces as policemen in some cities. Both of those were understood to be illegal, but proceeded anyway," Nathan said.

"Are they going to come at us again? Do you think they'll up their attacks?" Henry asked.

"Will they come at us again? Yes. Increase their attacks? I doubt it. It seems that they were targeting technology acquisition. You remember back in November when I was called in to testify regarding the security of their cyber assets? It seems they still consider Open Cloak a military asset. They could certainly shield their attacks under the idea of testing that security. Predicting what they will do if they either succeed or fail is uncertain."

"Maintain the test level of security," Henry said. "I want to talk to you downstairs about what to do if we are actually breached."

Nathan nodded and Conrad realized this would be a conversation regarding new research Henry wanted conducted.

57

NEW GENERATION

ON MONDAY, EMPLOYEES were greeted by Cici, the third generation of the AI powered holographic receptionist. The most noticeable aspect of this new generation was an improved sound system, both for speaking to the hologram and listening to her. Henry had approved a pretty hefty equipment spend to get the best possible sound input and output for the new receptionist. She greeted each employee as they entered the lobby.

"Good morning, Josh," Cici said when he entered the lobby.

"Wow! Um... Hi, Cici. How are you this morning?" Josh asked.

"I'm brand new, Josh!" she announced enthusiastically.

"Oh. Yes. You certainly are. Have a good day, Cici."

"You, too, Josh. Let me know if you need anything."

The interaction was typical of the eighty people who came to work. Of course, Audrey still sat at the reception desk opposite Cici's perpetually happy face.

"How does she do that?" she asked Chastity. "I've been here almost a year and still don't know everyone's name."

"Everyone carries an RFID card in order to go through the inner doors," Chastity said. "The team installed a reader so she immediately identifies anyone who comes through the door. I'll have them put a read-out on your monitor."

CHASTITY PERCHED ON the corner of Henry's new desk. He smiled as he leaned his head against her leg and kissed it.

531

"Oh, that's nice. You aren't tired of having access to me all the time?" she asked.

"The day I get tired of either you or Lisa, shoot me," he said.

"And leave Lisa and me to take care of our baby without you? Huh-uh," she said.

He ran his hands up the inside of her shapely legs and they parted.

"Not that this isn't enough, but did you have something else on your mind, love?" he asked, kissing his way along the inside of her thigh.

"Yes. And since we just did this last night, I can wait for more. Can you?"

"It's an effort, but tell me what's on your mind."

Chastity reviewed the morning interactions with Cici and then came to Audrey's question.

"It occurred to me that this could be a security issue. I was just going to take it to Mia, but it might be more in line with Nathan," Chastity said. "The card grants access to the office, but it doesn't really identify the person holding the card. Audrey, or Nancy, or anyone we have at the desk at the time, should be able to see the identity of any employee and have their picture so she can verify that's who is coming through the door."

"What a great idea. Yes, it should become part of Alice, but it should be a normal part of security operations," Henry agreed. "Let's go have a conversation with Nathan."

He paused a moment to kiss up to her slit and then helped her off the desk. She kissed him softly and pulled her skirt into place before they left Henry's office.

"I think this is one of my favorite parts of this job," she whispered.

NATHAN LISTENED TO the idea and nodded. It wasn't often he got a chance to interact with Chastity or Henry now that he officially reported to Conrad.

"Let's call Conrad in and see if we can put this on our schedule," Nathan said.

Henry was about to object because he'd just approved it, but realized Nathan was right. Henry couldn't just jump into anyone's office and give them a new project without talking to their manager. It was a new organization and he needed to abide by the lines of reporting just like everyone else did.

Conrad came to Nathan's office and joined the meeting.

"Conrad, I wanted to be sure we weren't blowing smoke before we talked to you, so Chastity and I came to ask Nathan about the feasibility of an expansion of our security system. He seemed to think it had value, so we want to check with you," Henry said.

Conrad was only a couple of years older than Henry and still reported to him, even though Nathan reported to Conrad. They were all getting used to things. Nathan took up the narrative and told Conrad what the concept was.

"I can see the value," Conrad said. "This isn't really a product, though. Do we have the bandwidth to develop it?"

"I think it fits with our internal security mission," Nathan said. "I also see that it is a feature that should be built into Alice, but has application across a wider range of situations. There is no reason it should be limited to identifying employees. Nearly everyone carries an RFID card of some sort with them. Despite the number of warnings people receive and the special wallets available for them, hardly anyone protects their RFID identity. It's in their driver's license, their credit cards, their company key cards, and probably Costco membership card. The device could help identify or confirm the identity of anyone who walked through the door."

"Now I see it as a marketable product," Henry said.

The four of them brainstormed a little while and finally agreed to devote a limited number of resources to the project.

THE MONTH OF June was one of constant innovation and progress for the company. It was also a time of progress for Henry and his family.

Lisa, Chastity, and Henry began attending birth classes. While having three working together in the class was not unheard of, it was unusual. The birth instructor simply assumed that since Henry and Lisa were married, Chastity was a doula, or birth helper. The role fit well and Chastity began reading up on the duties of a doula. Unlike a midwife, a doula provides emotional and physical support for the mother, but not medical support. She doesn't deliver a baby. In other words, a doula filled all the same functions that a good husband should and, in Henry's case, would.

The classes were instructive with discussions about various potential birth problems, circumcision, anesthesia, and various other potential issues. They watched a video of a c-section, and were told they could not watch a vaginal birth video because the State had classified them as pornographic. However, the instructor gave them several links to where they could watch a birth online.

Over the weeks, they learned various ways to mitigate labor pains with breathing control, massage, showers, and baths.

Perhaps the most beneficial of effects of the classes was the long gentle lovemaking the three enjoyed after each class.

FRIDAY MORNING, THE twenty-eighth, Henry and Chastity begrudgingly went to work to watch the demonstration of the miniature paving device. All the parts for the machine had been 3-D printed and assembled in the robotics lab at ARDC. The machine had then been brought to Open Cloak to have 'the brain' installed. When the device was moved outside for the test, Ari and a researcher from Agora Fuel Cells put the power cell into the miniature device.

Dale and Leonard used a remote control to power up the paver. It lurched forward and they brought it to a stop—the first test complete. Then the bins on the device were filled with raw materials. The route was programmed in and the real test started. There were a few tense moments as the machine dug into the raw ground and through some grass roots, but then it started forward.

Since they were not recycling the grass and dirt into the concrete mix, it was blown aside. When the machine had moved forward about four feet, they saw the pavement appearing behind it. Those present cheered. After ten feet, the operator commanded the robot to stop preparing the substrate and complete the paving. In the space of the length of the machine, pavement continued to be laid and then the machine moved off the track.

Everyone rushed forward to examine the pavement. It was completely smooth. There was no need for an additional roller to either compact the sub-strate or smooth out the pavement. In their eagerness to examine the layers, the engineers cut out a square of the pavement, but the surface was not yet dry and didn't hold its shape as they examined the layers of the excavation, substrate, and pavement.

The pavement was less than half an inch thick with the excavation going down only an inch. It would cure and they would be able to extract additional samples for lab work. The paver group was not the only interested party. It was one thing to create a machine and give it a brain and power, but materials also had to be tested. Dale had engaged a highway surface research company to provide the top materials for the test. The research group had also explored material durability, reuse, and safety. While working together, they believed they could recycle an existing roadway, using the ground up pavement to repave the surface.

Of course, there were a multitude of problems involved in that, but the idea that re-paving a highway might not have to involve disposing of the previous pavement was of great interest to all. It would depend on what type of surface was already there and whether it could be recycled.

All told, the test was considered a great proof of concept, but also showed how far the development had to go.

Henry and Chastity left work as soon as the test was concluded. It was their anniversary weekend.

CHASTITY HAD TAKEN care of reservations. They were a week before most of the July 4th holidayers would be at the resort in Niagara Falls. It was nearly a four-hour drive, but they didn't worry about it. Germaine took care of driving so the trio could relax. Henry and Chastity took turns cuddling Lisa in the back seat.

"All I want is a nice place to lie by a pool and sip... a virgin margarita," Lisa sighed.

"It's supposed to be in the eighties this weekend, so I'll be lying right beside you in my tiniest bikini," Chastity said.

"You know that's definitely going to inspire some action," Lisa said. "And I'm not feeling like I can stuff anything else inside me anymore. You'll have to accommodate the monster."

"I've never had a problem with that," Chastity said. "I think I can even accommodate him while I'm licking you to one or a dozen orgasms."

"I'm so glad you're here to take care of me. Do you have any idea how difficult it is to reach around this watermelon in my stomach to touch my clit? The only reason I can wipe myself is because I can still reach around my butt."

"You are so beautiful and hot," Chastity said. She kissed Lisa deeply.

Riding in the front seat next to GermainOe, Henry looked over at the driver to see if she was being affected by the sexual energy being exuded from the back seat. He was pleased to note she had ear buds in her ears and was happily nodding to the music.

"OH! CONGRATULATIONS!" VIRGINIA, the woman at the desk of the hotel said when they checked in. She had a slight southern accent, but nothing so strong as Lisa's Cajun accent when she let it show. Lisa leaned against Henry with her hands around her tummy. "We don't see too many pregnant women here. You know, not that many are so far along when they get married." She seemed oblivious to the implications she was making.

"It's our anniversary, not our honeymoon," Henry said flatly.

"Oh! Double congratulations, then!" Virginia said brightly. She missed Henry's scowl. "So, we have a two-bedroom suite and a single room attached. Quite a family! I'll need everyone's ID, please, and the credit card used for the reservation. Um... I'll just ignore which person is assigned to which room. Okay?"

Henry nodded and completed the check-in. He took the keys and they all headed for the elevators, motioning for the bellman to bring their luggage.

"Wow! Is he, like, an Arabian prince or something?" the clerk asked another person at the desk. "I've never heard of him and his harem is, like, kind of plain, don't you think?"

"I think you should mind your own business," a manager said, coming up behind her. "And I'm recommending a remedial course in customer relations. Surely you learned a little bit about not offending people on check-in!" He grabbed a desk phone and called room service. "I want two bottles of sparkling juice on ice and a large fruit basket delivered to room 1295 as quickly as you can get it there. Deliver it with an invitation for dinner in the Falls Overlook room, complements of the resort."

He hung up the phone and scowled at the desk clerk who was only just realizing what a huge pile of shit she'd stepped in.

THE FOUR ENJOYED the dinner overlooking the falls. The rainbow lighting was both spectacular and peaceful. It was a fitting end to Pride Week, a national custom that had survived the former administration because it had no central organization.

They laughed about the clerk and about the subsequent delivery of fruit and the invitation to dinner. The food was exquisite. They decided to thoroughly enjoy the offered hospitality, but Henry left two $100 bills on the table for the waitstaff and cooks when they returned to their room.

"Can you just imagine a version of Alice with her personality?" Chastity laughed.

"Hmm. You know, that's not all that bad an idea," Henry said.

"You're kidding! Why would you want someone so clueless at your front desk?" Lisa asked.

"It's not that so much," Henry mused. "Deena will launch in a few weeks, but from what I have seen, she has the same image and personality as Alice, Bea, and Cici. I think it will be a dull world if we sell a thousand receptionists who all have the same image and personality. That's one of the things we haven't explored thoroughly enough. They still sound pretty much like a machine."

"They *are* machines," Chastity reminded him.

"Yes. But that would be the first place a competitor attacked. If we go to market with the holographic receptionist, it needs to appear more human, even though it's a product of light waves and AI," Henry said.

They said goodnight to Germaine and the throuple relaxed for their first anniversary night together.

SUNDAY AFTERNOON, THEY loaded back into the car to head back to Pittsburgh, happy, sated, and refreshed. On their way out the door, Henry stopped and gave the desk clerk one of Chastity's cards.

"When you lose this job, give Chas a call. We might have something for you," he said. She looked at him with her mouth wide open.

Germaine drove them home while Chastity rode shotgun and Henry held his wife in the back seat.

"I don't ever want to see the sun again!" Lisa moaned. She hadn't gotten burned, but after fifteen minutes in direct sunlight she struggled back to their room and into the shower in a near state of panic.

"It's your fair skin," Henry said.

"Fair? My Cajun blood is supposed to be immune to heat! I think it's our daughter's doing. She wants me to become a vampire," Lisa laughed. "Ugh! I never thought I'd be that sensitive to heat or the sun!"

"Well, now you have something to complain to Izzy about that she didn't experience during her pregnancy," Henry laughed.

Before long, they were home and preparing for their second year as a married throuple, with all the changes that would bring about.

DURING JULY, HENRY, Luke, Dale, and Rachel were booked with their underwriter and publicist for an IPO roadshow. Each week the group spent three days visiting potential large investors. These were often brokerages and institutional investors. Luke, Henry, and Dale were on the board of directors, and Dale also represented Argos, the venture capital company. Rachel was their Chief Financial Officer.

They presented the company history, profit record, current investment, and the technologies being offered and prepared by the company. Each technology had a price tag associated with it, showing the estimated investment in development and the anticipated return when marketed. The biggest problem with any of these new technologies was that they were still two years from becoming an actual product, so substantial development funds were needed.

Argos, which had invested $50,000,000 in venture capital to get things started, had agreed to cancel their next two investment rounds in favor of the IPO. They'd purchased their shares at under $2.00 per share. At the anticipated offering price of $15.00 a share, they would profit by half a billion dollars if they sold out their shares during the IPO.

Henry was still nervous about losing control of the company if his partners chose to sell out their shares and options. As it stood, if they held all their shares, the group would hold about thirty percent of the outstanding shares. In most circles, that would be considered a controlling interest. But it was always possible that a single entity would buy a large enough block of shares to challenge that control.

WHILE HENRY WAS tied up running from presentation to presentation, he was also trying to absorb all the details from their birthing classes and practice with Chastity and Lisa each evening. The schedule was almost frantic and they were all worried that they wouldn't be together when the baby arrived. Sylvia visited each weekend to check up on Lisa's progress and help in any of a thousand ways she could. The nursery was as well-equipped as any neonatal facility could be.

And then Jackie arrived.

"I'll just be here to fill in wherever you need," Lisa's mother said. "I could hardly stay in Louisiana when my grandbaby is about to be born in Pittsburgh!"

"We think we have things under control," Lisa said, taking her mother to the nursery. "It's a little hectic, but I'm sure we'll manage."

"Honey, I have no doubt about your ability to manage. I promise not to get in the way. Just let me baby my baby a little as you get ready," Jackie said. Lisa hugged her.

"Mom, I'm not implying we don't want you here. It's kind of a big relief. With Henry having so many meetings as they get ready for the big IPO, it's been a little chaotic at home. I feel like I'm doing nothing but sitting around all day moaning about the heat."

"Oh! Did you know I developed an allergy to the sun while I was pregnant?" Jackie said. "It was terrible! It was still ninety degrees in the Bayou and 100% humidity the month before you were born. Then you were greeted by Hurricane Humberto while we were still in the hospital. I know something about getting comfortable in the heat and humidity! And the chaos."

"I'm so glad you're here, *Môman*." Lisa rarely used Cajun terms passed down from her grandmother, but as she hugged her mother, she began to feel more peaceful and ready for the birth of her daughter.

ONE OF THE last places on the list for the roadshow was the university where Henry and many of his employees had graduated, and where Luke was still working on his MBA. Dr. Hendon, director of the Machine Learning Department of the School of Computer Science, had spearheaded the way for the Open Cloak presentation to the investment board at the university. It had helped immensely when he told them how Open Cloak technology had stopped an online attack on the school's AI lab.

"We've employed several graduates of the university, and still others are completing their degrees. Dale Jacoby, who was formerly on the faculty of the AI group, is on our board of directors and is also heading up our joint venture with ARDC to create a fully AI-powered robotic paving machine that we estimate will revolutionize that process," Henry said by way of introduction.

"I'm happy to be one of your graduates as well and have always hoped the university would show an interest in investing in our IPO. We have made a significant mark on the industry with our optimization, computer security, power savings, and personal legacy apps. Our next generation of AI powered devices includes not only the paving machine, but also an AI-powered hologram that will even peek into the world of spatial holography—in other words, holograms that don't require a projection surface," Henry concluded.

"Uh... Aren't you also the people who created *Pythia Speaks*?" Dr. Singh asked. He was the president of the board of regents, who would ultimately be the ones who would approve any recommendation by the financial investment committee.

"Yes, sir. *Pythia Speaks* and *Forever Yours* are two interactive AIs that have made a significant impact already. We are seeing a steady growth in purchases of the *Forever Yours* singularity package. *Pythia Speaks* now fields over two million questions a day in twenty different languages."

"My wife got me hooked on checking in with *Pythia Speaks* each morning with whatever is on my mind when I wake up. It's kind of like a creative whack on the side of the head to get me thinking while I have my first cup of coffee.

Ingenious bit of technology. I'm surprised it doesn't show up prominently in your presentation," the regent said.

"It is a fundamental technology that is represented by *Forever Yours*," Henry explained. "However, in matters of finance, it does not make an appearance. Our company elected to maintain *Pythia Speaks* as a free service with no advertising or other commercial content. We intend to keep that policy."

"Good for you! It seems that every presentation we see wants to show us how they are maximizing the revenue potential of everything down to the secretary's painted toenails. I'm glad to see you have something you are simply giving back to the world," Dr. Singh said.

"Thank you, sir."

Henry wasn't exactly certain how to take that last comment, but he guessed it was okay. Darla gave a bridging commentary and then turned the meeting over to Luke. Henry's phone buzzed in his pocket and he discreetly pulled it out to check the message. It was from Chastity.

"It's time! Meet us at the birth center."

END PART IV

PART V

"Finally, our new brain needs a purpose. A purpose is expressed as a series of goals. In the case of our biological brains, our goals are established by the pleasure and fear centers that we have inherited from the old brain. These primitive drives were initially set by bio-logical evolution to foster the survival of species, but the neocortex has enabled us to sublimate them. Watson's goal was to respond to Jeopardy! queries. Another simply stated goal could be to pass the Turing test. To do so, a digital brain would need a human narrative of its own fictional story so that it can pretend to be a biological human. It would also have to dumb itself down considerably, for any system that displayed the knowledge of, say, Watson would be quickly unmasked as nonbiological."

— **Ray Kurzweil,** *How to Create a Mind: The Secret of Human Thought Revealed*

58

HEY, DAD

HENRY BARELY MADE IT to the birth center in time. As soon as he got the message, he stood and ran out of the room. Luke explained to the meeting that this was good news.

Henry got scrubbed and Jackie pushed him into the birth room where Chastity was with his wife, coaching her with the breathing they'd learned. Henry rushed to Lisa's side and she immediately gripped his hand, nearly crushing it as another contraction hit.

"That's good. We're ready to push," the midwife said. "When the next one hits, let's go with it. Ready?"

It was only a few seconds when the contraction hit again and Lisa groaned as she pushed.

"That's good. We're making steady progress. Your little one wants out of there!"

The next contraction was a minute later and Lisa screamed out as she pushed, clutching Henry's hand even harder. He winced in pain but wisely didn't say anything. Chastity was breathing with Lisa.

"Puff, puff, puff. Now deep breath. Another deep breath. Ready?"

"And push," the midwife said with the next contraction. "I see her head. Come on, Dad. It's time to catch your baby."

Lisa gave Henry a push and he moved between her legs where he could see the head of his child emerging. It was all a blur from that point for both Henry and Lisa. Chastity was lost in encouraging her lover as Henry held the baby emerging from the birth canal.

"She's beautiful!" he gasped as he felt her weight fully in his hands.

The midwife quickly checked to be sure her nose and mouth were open and that the little one was breathing, then pointed Henry to Lisa. He carried the baby to Lisa who pulled the sheet down and he laid the infant on her chest.

"She's so wonderful!" Lisa cried. "Look! She's got blue eyes and curly hair."

"She's perfect," Chastity said.

The baby already had a grip on one of Chastity's fingers as she searched around for something to suck on.

"You're not going to get much out of there yet," Lisa said as the baby started sucking on her nipple.

"I need one more big push and then we can cut the cord. Ready? Here comes the last of it."

Lisa didn't even moan as she pushed out the afterbirth. She was too caught up in the miracle that was her daughter. The midwife handed Chastity the scissors and held the cord in the correct place for the cut.

"Oh, my!" Chastity cried. "I get to free you, little one. There! You're no longer tethered to the inside."

"Mommy and Mommy and Daddy are right here with you, sweetheart," Lisa said. She was still panting a little. Everything had been such a rush job. It had only been three hours since labor started!

"Do we have a name for this little girl?" the midwife asked.

The three looked at each other. Lisa and Henry nodded. Chastity broke out in a broad grin.

"Her name is Cassie Benoit Pascal," Henry announced to the room.

The door to the room was opened and Jackie and Sylvia were allowed into the room, just in time to hear the announcement.

"My maiden name!" Jackie exclaimed, rushing to the side of her daughter.

Lisa showed the baby to her grandmothers, but didn't let go of her.

"Where does the name Cassie come from?" Sylvia asked. "It's so pretty."

"Castitas is the Latin root of Chastity. We decided Cassie was the nicest variant," Henry said. "After all, Chastity is her other mommy."

"A little bit from everyone," Sylvia smiled.

"Okay. If little Cassie has had enough of Mommy One's tit, it's time for Mommy Two to learn to bathe a baby," the midwife said after measuring the six pound-nine-ounce baby and clearing the birthing things away.

The family had enough time to admire the new addition and Lisa had only given up possession long enough to let the midwife record the baby's weight and nineteen-inch length. Chastity gave Lisa a loving kiss and took Cassie from her. The birth room included a bathing station, so no one had to go far. The grandmas followed Chastity and Cassie to the bath and gave 'helpful' hints as she was shown how to cleanse the vernix from the newborn.

Henry took the time to hold his wife and kiss her gently.

"Hey, Dad," Lisa said softly. "I hope you're ready for this."

"As long as you and Chastity are with me, I can face anything," he said. "Almost. I'm still not sure I can handle the IPO next week. I think I'll just stay home with you and our girls."

"Proposition accepted," Lisa sighed.

Once Cassie had been bathed and swaddled, the grandmothers were allowed to hold her for a few minutes, but pretty soon, Lisa wanted her daughter back. Colostrum had begun leaking from her breasts and she immediately let Cassie suck until she went to sleep.

The midwife left and told them the room was theirs until morning when their pediatrician would be in to check on the baby and approve her release. It was a major handoff from the obstetrician to the pediatrician.

While they chatted quietly, Henry took over the job of texting everyone about the birth. The first to receive word were Ryan, Bill, Beau, and Solange. He didn't neglect calling the Hartmans in Cincinnati, Lisa's other grandparents. Then he sent texts to Luke and Isobel before sending a general email to all the office.

Eventually, Ryan showed up and Henry realized Germaine was still in the lobby. He ran down the hall to invite them in to meet the baby. They were quietly monitoring traffic in and out of the birth center, maintaining their watchfulness.

Finally, people began leaving until only Chastity, Henry, and Lisa were left with their new daughter. Free of all the people, the three held each other and Cassie and quietly let the tears flow from their eyes. They were so pleased with their family.

Of course, the staff at the birth center didn't let them just lie in bed. Lisa needed to get up and walk around. She'd had a natural birth, so there were no tubes or wires attached to either her or Cassie. They walked to a small dining room where they were served a good meal and were then allowed to return to the room, which had been changed and made up for the night instead of for the birth. There was a cradle next to the bed. They'd need to decide later whether they slept with the baby in their bed or if she would be in the cradle.

Chastity intended to leave and go home, so she wouldn't wake up in the same bed or room. Eventually, though, she couldn't bring herself to go.

"I might have to… um… slip out early in the morning, but I can't bring myself to leave my beautiful family," she said.

"You know you are always welcome for as long as you can stand it," Lisa whispered, kissing her girlfriend.

"I'm getting better," Chastity said. "I don't wake up in a panic most mornings. Just… if I go off the deep end in my sleep, push me out of bed."

"We love you, Chas," Henry said. "I'm so glad you are part of our family."

All three new parents stripped off their clothes and pushed into the small but comfortable bed. The birthing rooms were set up like residential bedrooms and most fathers stayed with new mothers overnight. Cassie was in the cradle next to Henry's side of the bed and he would be the one to get up in the night if Cassie cried.

AFTER THE PEDIATRICIAN visited on Friday morning, the family checked out of the birth center. Germaine was there with the larger van from the company to take the family and all the items they'd brought with them home.

Once at the row house, Sylvia and Jackie took charge of the family and made sure they were all settled in their suite. They made lunch and got to hold little Cassie while the three ate.

"How are you feeling, baby girl?" Jackie asked her daughter.

"Oh, Mom. Your baby has a baby!" Lisa responded. "Isn't she beautiful?"

"Yes, she is. But now I'm more concerned about *my* baby. Your delivery was fast, but sometimes that can be more exhausting for a mother than a birth that takes days."

"I'm feeling pretty good," Lisa said. "I'm tired, I guess, but still filled with a kind of euphoria. Cassie drank her fill from me this morning. I can't believe I'm feeding a human being from my breasts!"

"Do you have a pump?" Sylvia asked.

"A pump?"

"If she's eating heartily, you'll increase your production. Then you'll end up having to pump any time she doesn't finish things up. It's also handy to put in bottle bags for emergencies and times when you aren't available to nurse her. You know, you might want to take Chas to a movie and leave Cassie with Henry," Sylvia concluded.

"You mean she won't be attached to a nipple 24/7 for the next eighteen years?" Lisa laughed. "Henry, love, I think we need more things from Baby Landing. And have we asked them to start the diaper service?"

"I called about diapers this morning before we left the birth center," Chastity said. "First delivery should be here about three o'clock."

"I think she'll do okay with the disposables until then," Lisa said.

"You'll be glad to throw that first poop outside in the trash bin after it's been triple bagged!" Sylvia said. "Meconium stinks."

"No! My baby will produce something that doesn't smell like roses?" Henry said in feigned shock.

They chatted and drew up a list of things they simply hadn't thought of before the birth. Henry headed out to the baby store to do some shopping, knowing in advance he would buy twice the number of things that were on the list.

LATE FRIDAY AFTERNOON, Ryan picked Bill up from the airport and the two drove to the row house so Lisa's father could meet his granddaughter. Jackie and Sylvia had worked together to fix a healthy family dinner for seven people. Lisa provided the food for Cassie.

They were all tired early on in the evening. Sylvia and Ryan went home. Jackie and Bill went to the second bedroom in Chastity's suite and the three parents settled in the third-floor master suite with a bassinet next to the bed. This time, Chastity didn't make it through the night and slipped down to her own bedroom before midnight.

Henry got up about two in the morning to bring a fussy Cassie to Lisa to be fed. Lisa hardly woke up as the baby sucked greedily on her breast. When she was finished, Henry collected her and bounced her gently in his arms until she had a most unladylike burp. He'd remembered to throw a colorful burp cloth over his shoulder, so he didn't feel he needed to take a shower. He changed her diaper and gently laid her back in her cradle where she slept until about six. Then she alerted the family that she was hungry again.

Having Bill and Jackie staying for the weekend was a good choice. Bill was up early and had breakfast made when the family came downstairs around eight. They had started out and then retreated to put clothes on. Chastity had almost been caught by Bill when she left her bedroom to rejoin the family. She quickly pulled on a robe.

"Hey, Boss-dad," Lisa said to her father. "How much leave do I get to be with my baby? I never thought to ask before we launched."

"Leave?" Bill asked. "You mean time off?"

"Leave. Not time off. Don't employees usually get some kind of leave to bond with their babies?"

"Hmm. Did you ever respond to that last request Thursday morning?" Bill asked severely. "We have developers waiting for that status report."

"Um… I started it. It's probably still open on my computer upstairs. Are you serious? I just had a baby!"

"And you didn't take a minute of maternity leave before she arrived," Bill said. "I think, according to the FMLA, that qualifies you for up to twelve weeks of family leave. I think that comes out to sometime in mid-October. I suppose about a month after your twenty-third birthday. You should be more mature by then."

"Three months? Wow! That's great! I really didn't want to video conference while I was breast feeding. I know some of those guys would be distracted," Lisa laughed.

"Yes. Well, it's really a means for employers to maintain productivity and eliminate such distractions. Of course, if you want to come back to work earlier than that, it's your option. You might get sick of sitting around the house with your husband, wife, and daughter," Bill laughed.

"Husband?" Henry said perking up. "Chastity, do we have a parental leave policy?"

"Oh. Yeah. You get the same thing if you want it. I don't. According to policy, I'm not part of the family unit. I'll have to take vacation time if I want to stay with you. Or an unpaid leave," Chastity said.

"Well, after two weeks, FMLA allows for the remainder to be unpaid leave," Bill said. "It's not so different."

"Let's give this some thought," Henry said. "It sounds like the three of us need to coordinate time off in the next few months."

Neither Henry nor Chasity returned to the office in the next week. Jackie and Bill went back to Louisiana Sunday afternoon. Henry was surprised to find how easily he could ignore the impending IPO when he was holding or even looking at his daughter and wives.

When Bill and Jackie left town, they were informed that Beau and Solange would be arriving the next weekend for a visit. The three parents wanted as much time with their daughter as possible. They did, however, entertain Luke, Isobel, and Paul on Tuesday evening.

"She's so tiny!" Isobel said, hefting her five-month-old son. She handed the boy off to Henry who was amazed at how heavy he was compared to his newborn daughter.

"Well, Paul would have made nearly two of Cassie when he was born!" Lisa said. "She was six pounds-nine and nineteen inches when she was born. Long and skinny. I think she's going to put on weight pretty quickly. The pediatrician is coming to do an in-home health check on Friday."

"I couldn't even pick Paul up for nearly two months," Isobel said. "I was always afraid my insides would fall out the incision site."

"That was more literal than it sounded," Luke said. "She was limited to maximum lifting of ten pounds for three weeks. Paul was almost twelve pounds when he was born."

"And look at you!" Isobel continued, pointing at Lisa. "You've already lost all your baby weight! I hate you! It took me three months of constant exercise and dieting before I could pack my fat ass into my old clothes!"

"Didn't stop her from buying new clothes," Luke chuckled quietly, accepting his son back from Henry.

"Oh, I still have a few pounds to shed," Lisa said. "I'm not trying all that hard. It will drop when it drops."

"Let's eat," Chastity said, putting a large tuna noodle casserole on the table.

She couldn't even take credit for having made it. Sylvia and Jackie had made up several dishes and left them in the freezer for the family. All of the pre-made meals would serve at least eight people. They'd have leftovers the next day.

"This is... posh," Isobel said, trying to be kind about the plain fare.

Luke put Paul in his carry-seat and gave him a bottle.

"Well, there's good news," Luke said. He lifted his glass of sparkling water. "The IPO is fully subscribed. That means we should get a good price for our shares when the market opens at nine in the morning."

"Hmm. We're putting up four million from the LLC, right?" Henry asked. "What's Argos planning to put up?"

"According to Dale, they will put up all their preferred shares. That's twenty million. They've decided to keep their voting shares until the paving project is complete. Everyone should be aware, though, that we'll each have to pay taxes on around $15,000,000 in profit. Rachel hired an accountant experienced in this who is handling the tax filing for everyone who is selling shares," Luke said.

"Who else is selling?" Chastity asked.

"Well, everyone who has vested stock options is putting at least some of them on the market. That's only going to be about another million shares combined," Isobel said.

"That means we stand a chance of maintaining a solid controlling interest," Henry said. "Good."

"The underwriter says there are two investors who have subscribed to ten million shares each. We may need to expand the board. We won't know who the investors are until after the broker releases the statement for the report."

"Okay. I'm not paying any more attention to the IPO," Henry said. "Let me know if the price hits $50 a share."

"Yeah, right," Isobel scoffed.

"Hey, you haven't been in the office this week to test the upgrades the Alice group made to Deena. She's great. Everyone in the office has interacted with her. She's got the first real personality we could say one of the holograms have had," Luke said.

"Horrid thing," Isobel said. "She's spookier than ever. Sounds like a person but looks like a ghost. Sell her to the happiest place on earth."

"Let's talk about babies," Lisa said, bringing the business conversation to an end.

AROUND TWO IN the morning, Henry was feeling restless. Cassie had been fussy, even after being fed, burped, and changed. He'd sat for nearly half an hour in the rocking chair, just cooing at her and trying to let her hear the comfort in his voice until she finally went back to sleep.

Chastity was holding Lisa in bed, sweetly cuddled together. Henry left the room quietly and went upstairs.

He turned on his computer and settled into a chair before launching his father's singularity. The team had done a lot of work on the program over the early summer and it was now limited as to how much it could make up. However, his father continually added content as he thought about it. It was a pretty rich program.

"Hey, Dad," Henry typed. "Did you sing any lullabies to me when I was a baby?"

He turned on the audio when he saw his father's image take shape on the screen.

"You were a bit of a fussy baby," his father began. "You liked to dance, though. At first, I played music in the living room and danced to it, but it disturbed your mother. So, I started making up music that I could hum or sing quietly without disturbing her sleep. There was a little nonsense song that was pure monotony. It always seemed to work to get you back to sleep. Let me see. It went,

I've been everywhere
And I've done everything
And I've met everyone whose name begins with A
Including Alice, and Allen, and Audrey, and Anne.
I've been everywhere
And I've done everything
And I've met everyone whose name begins with B
Including Betty, and Bobby, and Billy, and Brenda.

"You get the idea. Just keep going through the alphabet and list all the names you can think of for each initial. If the baby isn't asleep by then, switch the order. Start with 'done everything' and 'met everyone' and then list all the places you can think of that begin with the initial letter. I think there was only one time I got all the way through the third cycle before you were asleep."

"Gosh, Dad. It still puts me to sleep," Henry laughed.

"Me, too," replied the avatar.

59

DEENA

F EW PEOPLE GOT much work done on Wednesday at Open Cloak. Henry and Chastity, of course, were staying home with Lisa and little Cassie. They'd been happy to have Jackie's help and support the week before the birth and immediately after, but it was nice to have just the family of four getting used to being a single entity. The cats were using the time to sniff at the milky smell of the baby and Lisa.

Lisa got up and dressed while Chastity took care of Cassie and Henry cooked breakfast. They all had a lot to learn about being parents. That included cooking, childcare, and care of each other.

The reason no one else was getting work done was the first day on the market for Open Cloak stock. Even those in the company who had only a couple thousand shares to sell were making a fantastic profit. Options that were issued at $1.50 or less per share were selling for $12-$18 per share as the market fluctuated during the day.

Of course, not everyone sold all their shares. The original partners sold four million shares from their LLC, bringing in $72 million. This would be distributed evenly among the four. Henry figured $18 million was all he needed to sell and he wouldn't need to sell any of his patent stocks or options for several years. They'd already found a couple of possible houses and he figured they would move into one of them by September.

To celebrate their good fortune, Germaine drove Henry, Chastity, Lisa, and Cassie to tour a house in Penn Cove, east of the university. Lisa had spent quite a bit of time researching places to live over the past few months and had shown Henry and Chastity the results of her searches.

And Germaine.

They had offered Germaine the opportunity to switch from working for Open Cloak as Henry's driver and security, to working directly for the family. It would include some childcare duties as well as her normal security duties. They enthusiastically accepted.

The truth was, Henry didn't want to drive anywhere. Each time he considered getting behind the wheel, he saw the flash of a sword painted on a black car hood. He'd successfully broken the hold his painkillers had on him, but at times like that, he longed for the numbing effect.

The family's intent was to find a home that could accommodate the unusual family of three adults and one or more children, plus an apartment for their security/nanny, a place where Lisa could have her office, and a home study space for Henry and Chastity. The home in Penn Cove had the added benefit of being just a few yards from the sixteenth hole of a private golf course. It was fully fenced with its own security gate, which Germaine considered of utmost importance.

After all five had toured the property, they decided it was probably the right place for them, but they'd wait to make an offer until Beau and Solange toured it over the weekend with them. Cassie's great grandparents would arrive on Friday for a long weekend. They weren't worried about the property being snapped up while they delayed. It had been on the market for close to six months already.

A VERY DIFFERENT scene was playing out at the Riordan home. When they'd received word that the IPO had been successful and they were called by the broker to indicate their LLC-owned shares and their personal shares had been sold, Isobel left the office to go home.

Luke stayed for the rest of the day, congratulating employees and talking about how the success was a part of all their work. Those working on the robot paver project were pretty isolated from the celebration because they were all employed by the spin-off joint venture company, American Intelligent Machines. That was jointly owned by Argos, ARDC, and Open Cloak.

Isobel drove her convertible out to the highway. As soon as she verified there were no police in sight, she slammed her foot down on the accelerator. The exhilarating feeling filled her with laughter. The laughter continued all the way back to her home and she walked inside.

Grace and little Paul were in the playroom and she stuck her head into the room. Paul clung to Grace as his mother laughed.

"Is everything okay?" Grace asked.

"Yes! I'm rich. And I'm going to give you a lot of money, too!" Isobel said. "And my parents can just go fuck themselves. I think that's what they've been doing for years."

"Congratulations?" Grace said hesitantly. She was still getting used to Isobel and her mood swings. This was the first time she'd seen her in a hysterical fit of laughter.

"Yeah! This," Isobel said, motioning to herself, "is just a manic episode. In an hour, I'll be depressed. I need to take a pill. But it's not an alternate personality. The drugs for schizophrenia are more stable than the ones for bipolar disorder."

"I'm glad. Is there anything I can do to help?"

"Keep hold of Paul and don't let him near Mommy unless she's calm and stable," Izzy said. She flopped in a chair to watch her son as he resumed playing with Grace. The tyke could crawl and loved to find colorful toys to chew on.

Unsure of how else she should act, Grace asked a question.

"Mrs. Riordan, what's it like having schizophrenia?"

"I suppose you want to hear something deep and artsy and angsty but it's more like some stupid song from the 1960s got inserted into my shuffle and now every time someone says something to me, I sing 'What a fool believes, no wise man has the power to reason away,' in my head. And there's an intermittent sound of the doorbell for really no reason.

"And sometimes it's demons trying to get me to hurt people I love, or being eaten alive by maggots, or whatever. But I also have an imaginary forever puppy, and my friend Pythia comes to visit me, and sometimes there's a Taylor Swift concert in my bedroom.

"Sometimes it seems like I go through the office yelling at people and telling them they don't know what they're doing, all because my clothes felt weird. The temperature in the office was too loud. And my hair was touching me."

Tears were running down Isobel's cheeks with her mascara in long black streaks.

"See? I told you I'd be depressed before long. Because being rich doesn't mean I have nice parents or that my friends even like me. And it doesn't make me a better mother. And because there's this unending sense of doom that hangs over me and I need a drink."

"I'm sorry," Grace whispered.

"It's been going on a lot longer than you've been here. Which doesn't mean I won't blame you for it. But if you ever see the demons chasing me, grab Paul and run to Henry and Lisa and Chastity. Don't wait and don't pack. Stay there until Luke arrives and says it's safe to come home," Isobel said. "I need to go to bed now."

She wearily pushed herself out of the chair and up the stairs to her bedroom. She poured herself a glass of tequila and fell into bed.

Thursday morning, the only ones in the office were the robotics team. They hadn't had much to do with the IPO celebration and were nearing their next major paving test with new materials. They all entered through the main lobby and were greeted by Deena, but no one else was there.

Luke had impulsively given all Open Cloak employees the day off, even if they hadn't cashed in stock. The robotics group was not made up of Open Cloak employees.

At about eleven in the morning, two men in military uniforms entered the lobby. Dale should have locked the front doors when his people were in, but he'd left them open for late-comers.

"Good morning, Colonel. Welcome to Open Cloak. How may I help you?" Deena said. The first officer turned to look at the hologram. "Good morning, Specialist," Deena continued, looking at the other soldier. "Welcome to Open Cloak. How may I help you?"

The colonel glanced around the room, not seeing anyone else present. He looked back at the hologram who returned his gaze expectantly.

"I want to see Henry Pascal," the colonel finally said.

"I'm sorry," Deena responded pleasantly. "Mr. Pascal is not in the office."

"Where is he?" the colonel demanded.

"That information has not been given to me."

"Then get someone out here who has it!" the colonel shouted.

"I'm sorry. No one is in the office today," Deena said. She continued to smile.

"What? Why not? Where are they?"

"I'm sorry. That information has not been given to me."

"Go to hell," the colonel snarled. He approached the inner door to the office and pulled on the handle. It did not budge.

"Colonel Edinger, you are not authorized to enter the offices without an official escort," Deena said, sounding shocked.

Edinger shook the doors.

"Get me an escort then. There is government property here and I intend to take it back to the Pentagon!"

"I'm sorry. There is no one here to escort you now," Deena continued.

Edinger stalked toward the hologram's plexiglass panel. He looked around, attempting to spot the cameras.

"All right! Whoever you are, get down here right this minute! I'll have you arrested and hauled to a deportation camp."

He was greeted by silence. Furious, he threw himself at the door again. It didn't open.

"Markle! There's a computer on that desk. Hack the system and open this door. That's what you're here for. We're going inside."

"Yes, sir," the other soldier said. He jumped over the barrier to the reception area and started working on the computer. "Colonel, sir!"

"Is it open?"

"No, sir. This computer won't turn on. There is no power to it."

"What?"

"Colonel Edinger and Specialist Markle, you have invaded the private space of Open Cloak Design. Police have been called and are on their way," Deena said.

"They what? We're the government. The police have no jurisdiction over us. Cancel that call!"

"I'm sorry. You have no authority to give orders to this artificial intelligence hologram. I am Deena. I am the fourth generation of AI-powered holographic receptionist. My specifications include responding to normal questions and summoning help when I cannot resolve an issue. Police have been summoned to resolve this issue. Would you like to ask a question of *Pythia Speaks*? I can transmit the question for you."

"Markle! Get out from behind that desk and get out of here," Edinger declared.

The specialist leapt the counter and grabbed his computer bag, following his commander out of the office.

"Henry, I'm sorry to bother you during your time off," Darrel said on the phone. "We've been attacked."

"Through the perimeter and Delphos?" Henry asked in amazement. He looked at his phone to see if there had been any alerts he'd missed.

"Through the front door," Darrel responded. "I got an alert when an attempt was made on our inner office."

"How did they even get through the front door?" Henry asked.

"It seems it was left unlocked."

"Oh, fuck! What's the damage?"

"None. But I'd say you and Nathan and Mia all need to review the security footage. This was a royal fuck-up that goes beyond leaving the door open."

"I'll be there shortly," Henry responded before disconnecting. He turned to his wives. Chastity was on her phone.

"What is it, hon?" Lisa asked.

"There was an attempted break-in at the office. Darrel says Nathan, Mia, and I need to come in to review the footage," Henry said. "I'll just take the car and run over there quickly. Darrel says there was no actual damage done."

"No, you won't," Chastity said abruptly. "Germaine is on her way. She'll be here in five minutes. You can use the time to get dressed."

Henry looked at himself. He was still in a bathrobe, as were Chastity and Lisa. They'd been having a really lazy day, just cuddling with each other and playing with the baby. He headed for the bathroom to shower, shave, and dress.

"Why is the office so dead?" Henry asked when he entered the front doors. He'd had to use a key because the door was locked.

"Hello, Mr. Pascal. Mr. Jones, Mr. Schwartz, and Ms. Howe are waiting in the security office for you."

"Thank you, Deena." Henry used his keycard to gain access to the inner office and went immediately to the small office that was used for security cameras and monitors.

"What's up?" he asked.

"Henry. Sorry to disturb you, but this is too... It's just *too something*," Darrel stumbled. "Two people came into the office lobby and attempted to force entry to the inner office. The robotics crew was all that was working today. Luke had given everyone else the day off. The robotics crew left the front door unlocked."

"But no one was in the lobby?" Henry asked.

"Just Deena," Mia responded. "That's what makes this interaction so interesting."

"That's one of the things," Nathan added. "Who the visitors were is the other thing."

Darrel cued up the recording to the moment the two soldiers entered the lobby. He turned up the sound and they watched the entire encounter.

"Deena called the police?" Henry asked in amazement.

"She activated the emergency protocol, which currently only comes up to our office, so the police weren't actually called. We didn't feel it was prudent to give the AI access to the real outgoing phones at the moment. She's still on an isolated network," Mia said.

"The response of the hologram is interesting enough to study," Nathan said. "The real problem is having a Pentagon officer storm in here demanding access to government property."

"Yeah. How does he figure that?" Henry asked.

"Not sure. But we need to be concerned."

"How did they not get the computer to turn on?" Mia asked.

"The receptionist computer is being used as a testbed for the newest power cells," Darrel said. "It seemed like a low-risk area to do the test when Ari asked. So, each evening, Audrey shuts down and removes the power cell to recharge in the office. She picks up the cell in the morning and reinstalls it."

"And why was there no security sitting at the desk?" Henry demanded.

"We'll have to check with Luke, but my guess is he didn't inform security the office would be closed today," Nathan said. "It was kind of a spur of the moment thing. Security probably assumed the office was manned. They aren't usually here during business hours."

"I think I've counted three major fuck-ups and a virtual hero here," Henry said. "So, we corrected the front door being unlocked. Classic close the barndoor after the horse gets out. I'll take care of disciplining the robotics crew. We need to get on Luke's case and make sure we've got correct security coverage 24/7. And we can congratulate Deena if that means anything to her."

"It will mean something to the Alice Project staff," Mia said.

"And we have the major problem of why the Pentagon is walking into our office acting like they own it," Henry said. "Shit! Nathan, did the Pentagon buy a majority share during the IPO?"

"It's not on my radar. I can't imagine them putting up three-quarters of a billion dollars to get control of a company like ours," Nathan said. "That sounds like they feel entitled to something here. I don't like the sounds of it. We talked about a similar possibility a while back, Henry. I just never thought it would be the military that we'd be defending against."

"Do you have a problem with defending us against the Pentagon?" Henry asked.

"None at all," Nathan said. "We should launch Acropolis immediately."

"Agreed."

Nathan left the room.

"What's Acropolis?" Darrel asked.

"An extra level of defense for our development should our IP happen to be stolen," was all Henry would reply.

By the time he got home that evening, he'd given Luke an earful. Chastity had called in the security team to sit in the lobby until the office re-opened on Friday. Dale had been severely censured for leaving the front door open. Nathan had begun an investigation into who the invading officer was.

And Acropolis had been launched.

HENRY HADN'T WANTED to launch Acropolis when he and Nathan created it, but he'd agreed to develop it and have it on standby. It seemed like an extreme measure that he couldn't imagine a real need for. It required a code to be entered each morning by an officer of the company. Without the code, things would start self-destructing. It was intended to stop a hacker who had managed to breach both the perimeter and Delphos security systems and retrieved code from the company servers. By morning, the copied code would be deleted from the hacker's computer if the proper officer authorization wasn't present.

Since it required a human to be available every day to authorize the activity, it was risky. If all the officers were somehow unavailable, even the main server in the company would delete all proprietary code.

It had been several months since they initially developed the protocol without deploying it. During that time, Nathan and Henry had trained an AI to take over the task of authorizing the day's work. It was an extension of the code requiring developers to log in each day if they were working remotely, but with more severe results. The AI resided in the network so it could authorize each computer in the company.

Darrel had immediately backed up the entire server system and remotely backed up all attached computers. He left the office to deposit the backups in their secure vault—just in case there was a mistake in the authorization.

"YOU LOOK LIKE you had a hard day," Chastity said.

"Sorry I had to leave in such a hurry," Henry said. "How are my wives and daughter?" He kissed Chastity and held her close.

"Lisa just fed Cassie. That baby girl just conks out once her tummy is full of mommy-milk. But after a big burp, she needs to have a diaper change before she's ready for bed."

Chastity explained as if Henry had missed the entire week since the baby was born. Henry didn't mind. He would do the same thing. They were parents now and the baby's most fundamental routines were always news. Was she bathed? Did she poop? When did she eat? Was she fussy? All three parents wanted all the information on their baby girl.

"Maybe I can get a hug in before she's off to sleep," Henry said. He turned toward the stairs and then back to Chastity. "Germaine has gone to pick up Thai food for us tonight. All mild and not spicy."

"We don't want to upset anyone's tummy," Chastity laughed.

Henry ran upstairs just in time to kiss Lisa and be handed the baby, who was fast asleep. After spending a few minutes with the two of them just staring at the sleeping baby, Henry put her in her bassinet and the two went downstairs to join Chastity for dinner.

They set the baby monitor in the middle of the table and listened intently through their conversations to see if Cassie needed them.

60
FRIENDLY INVESTOR

HENRY TRIED TO put the office out of his mind on Friday. It was an important family day. Chastity, however, felt she needed to go in so she could handle the issue of physical security. She should have been notified of the office closure so she could coordinate with the security company.

Dr. Mikesel, Cassie's pediatrician, arrived for her promised home visit. While weighing and measuring the baby, she discussed issues of breastfeeding, sleep routines, parental care, and environment. She expressed some concern about the stairs.

"You'll be surprised at how fast time flies," she said. "Start childproofing your home now. Think of all the danger points. The stairs, your offices, locking cabinets, and sharp corners. I guarantee you that when you have done everything, Cassie will find something you missed."

"We know this house isn't the most child-friendly place," Henry said. "We hope to be in a new home by the first of the month. It has fewer steps and even room for expansion. And Germaine will become our nanny and will live with us."

"Don't lose track of the baby while you're packing. You wouldn't be the first parents to have to open and unpack every box in order to find a missing child."

"Oh my God!" Lisa gasped, holding Cassie tighter.

Dr. Mikesel considered her visit to have been successful.

GERMAINE ARRIVED FROM taking Chastity to the office in plenty of time to pick up Henry, Lisa, and Cassie to go to the airport.

They weren't traveling today, but were meeting Cassie's great grandparents, Beau and Solange. Lisa's grandparents really weren't very old. Henry had never had grandparents he could remember, so he enjoyed Beau and Solange as if they were his own Grandma and Grandpa. Beau often talked about retiring, but complained that he couldn't collect Social Security until he was too old to enjoy it.

It wouldn't really make a difference if he could. Beau didn't depend on *anything* for an income. Benoit Intracoastal was one of the largest privately held companies in the South. Beau was among the billionaires on the Forbes list.

"Grandma and Grandpa!" Lisa waved as Beau and Solange approached the baggage claim area. "Come meet your great granddaughter!"

People in the airport smiled as the older couple rushed to see the baby. Solange immediately took Cassie from Lisa and Beau hugged his granddaughter. Finally, Beau got a chance to chuckle over his granddaughter and then motioned to Henry to join him at the baggage carousel. He motioned to a bag about the size of a large briefcase. Henry picked it up and checked the tag to be sure it was Beau's. Beau had already turned back to Lisa and Solange.

"What else, Beau?" Henry asked.

"Oh, that's all. We're only spending the weekend," Beau laughed.

Henry looked at his in-laws. Solange had a large purse over her shoulder and Beau carried a paperback.

"Pack light," Henry said under his breath. He led the way to the exit, carrying the suitcase. Germaine pulled up just a minute later.

"I JUST HATE carrying things on the airplane," Beau said. He sat in the back row with Henry. Solange sat next to the car seat in the second row and Lisa rode in front with Germaine.

"So, where is Chastity?" Solange asked.

"She had to go in to work this morning for a bit. She's reviewing security measures with our team. There was a failure yesterday."

"A hack on your system? Not encouraging after your big IPO."

"No, not on the system. It was a physical attack. The security team wasn't where they were supposed to be."

"Are you putting our grandchildren in danger?" Solange asked, putting an arm around the seat where Cassie was sleeping.

"It was company security," Lisa hurried to assure her grandmother. "Germaine is always vigilant over the family."

"I'm surprised you aren't at the office as well," Beau said.

"I'm on parental leave. We have good people at the office," Henry said.

"I'm glad to hear that," Beau said. "I'd hate to think I invested in something risky."

"You invested, sir?" Henry asked.

"Don't sir me now! I wanted to be sure my great grandchildren would be provided for in the future, so I set up a trust and put shares of your company in it. Wanted to be sure control stayed in the family."

"Well, we have the largest investment within the partnership. I haven't looked at the breakdown of the public sales yet, but I'm sure we no longer have a majority." That irritated Henry a little. He didn't want to lose control, but to progress to where they wanted to go, they needed a lot of cash.

"With my shares and those of your venture group, I'm sure we'll maintain a majority. Let me know if we need a seat on the board."

Henry looked at his grandfather-in-law in shock.

"If I may ask, Beau, how many shares did you buy?"

"Ten million. The underwriter was very helpful."

Henry was struck silent. He knew Lisa's family was wealthy, but to invest $150 million in a startup? Sure. He'd happily recommend a board position for Beau.

ABOUT THE TIME the family had finished lunch and were headed home, a very different scene was playing out at the office.

"I'm sorry, Colonel. Mr. Pascal is not in the office today," Chastity said to the officious officer.

"Are you one of these artificial things, too?" he demanded, reaching toward Chastity.

A burly guard stepped between them. Chastity had just finished her meeting with the security company and was preparing to leave when the colonel and his specialist entered the lobby.

"Sir! Your uniform is not a license for assault," the guard said. The colonel stepped back a step.

"Of course not. Misunderstanding. I'm here to see Henry Pascal. Now!"

"As I attempted to tell you before, Mr. Pascal is not in the office. He is on parental leave," Chastity said.

"Parental leave? Who's in charge?"

As soon as the colonel had walked through the door, Deena had activated her emergency protocol, based on her previous encounter. When fully operational, that would connect directly to authorities, but at this stage of her development, it only connected to the Alice Project upstairs. Mia immediately called Nathan. He stormed into the lobby behind Chastity.

"Jamison! What the hell do you think you're doing here?" Nathan yelled.

"General!" the colonel snapped in surprise. He quickly regained his composure, knowing Schwartz was retired. "Well, it's good to know there is a human adult here to talk to."

"Human adult *male*," Chastity growled. Nonetheless, she realized Nathan was a better choice to deal with the situation. She stood her ground with the security guard and made the colonel step around her to talk to Nathan.

"What are you doing barging in here acting like you're leading an assault team instead of a spec four?" Nathan demanded.

"I'm here to collect all code and computer files related to the Open Cloak security system and to have all such files removed from the premises. This is by order of Admiral Jonathon Graves of the Pentagon Cyber Defense Department." The colonel announced.

"Tell the old swab to come and get it himself. If you want to speak to the chief technical officer of the company, you'll need to send someone of equal rank. And while you're at it, remind him he doesn't have the right or power to walk into a publicly owned US enterprise and make any kind of demands."

"This is a privately owned company. We'll offer the market value of $25 million for it and close it down."

"Believing and using accurate intelligence has always been a shortcoming of the Pentagon," Nathan snickered. "The company went public on Wednesday and has a current market cap of just under a billion dollars."

"What?" The colonel snapped around to his specialist. "Why didn't we have this intel?"

The computer hacker just stared dead ahead as if he wasn't in the room at all.

"Go home, Colonel," Nathan said. "This isn't a battle you or your man should be in."

"We tried to do this the nice way, Schwartz. I'll put our best team of hackers on it and rip the code out by the guts. We'll declare the patents top secret and prosecute anyone who uses them."

"Simple piece of advice from someone who once did your job far more effectively. Don't run your hackfest from the Pentagon. You don't want all the computers in the building corrupted."

"You wouldn't dare!"

"It's automatic. The defense system is run by AI. We keep our hands off," Schwartz said.

"We'll just see about that," Jamison snarled. He turned and stormed out of the lobby. The specialist hurried after him.

"Deena, send the transcript of this encounter to the corporate officers. Copy me so I can respond with a message."

"Yes, Mr. Schwartz. Or should I call you General, sir?"

"Don't be a smartass, Deena."

"THE GOOD NEWS is Deena is developing a personality," Chastity said after she'd rejoined the family and greeted Lisa's grandparents.

"If that's the good news, I hesitate to ask what bad news brought it about," Henry said. He and Chastity had stepped away from the others so she could fill him in on the happenings at the office that morning.

"The Army showed up again today."

"Oh, shit. We let Deena handle it again?"

"No, though I played the part well enough that the colonel attempted to pass a hand through me because he thought I was a hologram. The security guard with me put a quick stop to that," Chastity laughed. "Nathan showed up right then and told the colonel off. He told Deena to send the recording to all corporate officers. That's when she responded, 'Yes, Mr. Schwartz. Or should I call you General, sir?'"

Henry laughed at that.

"I might need to give her a raise after that."

"Nathan told her not to be a smartass. I think she grinned at him. Regardless, it doesn't require immediate response on your part, but after you love your wives tonight, you'll find the recording in your inbox."

"Yes. After. I'm presently on parental leave and we're taking Beau and Solange to get their opinion on the house tomorrow."

"Do you think they'll approve?"

"I've already put earnest money down. Oh, you should know that Beau bought ten million shares this week. We might need to get him a place on the board."

Chastity gasped.

"He's giving us $150 million?"

"Held in trust for his great grandchildren."

"We should go be charming to our grandparents."

BEAU AND SOLANGE loved the house. Ryan and Sylvia joined them for the tour and for dinner that evening. Solange went through the with Lisa, describing every detail of how it should be decorated. Then she warned Lisa not to let Jackie control how it was decorated, but to keep her individuality.

That evening after dinner, Henry poured a Wild Turkey for Beau and himself as they sat on the rooftop patio. The women were falling over each other trying to get Cassie ready for bed.

"So, what is the real condition of my investment?" Beau asked.

"We have big plans," Henry said. "Now we have the capital to make them real. First, we've made an offer to buy Agora Fuel Cells company. We are deep into protecting our networks and computers from power monopolies. The floods this year in Nevada knocked out power to a huge server farm in the desert. Even with its backup generators, cities as far away as Reno and Las Vegas had brownouts. Believe me, there are few people as dependent on power as casinos. They're demanding action and we're in the perfect position to provide solutions."

"Okay. What about the AI development?"

Henry described each of the big projects, their intent to double the size of their development and marketing teams, which included acquiring more space. Finally, he described development of the Alice Project.

"You're not much of a company if you don't have threats to your profitability. You don't need to sell me with market appeal. I already bought into the company. Now tell me the problems," Beau said.

Henry hesitated to talk about the biggest problem on the horizon, then decided to share the recordings of the colonel's two visits. Beau nodded and was silent for a minute.

"I'd like to hire that receptionist. Is she available?"

Henry was surprised that Beau skipped over the significant part about the Pentagon.

"We could get a prototype installed. We're not really ready for a commercial release yet."

Beau nodded. He pulled out his cell phone and pressed a contact.

"Juan. I want every barge, ship, and tug on the Intracoastal cut to one half its current speed, loading, and unloading immediately... Yes, I'm aware there is a parts shipment for Pensacola in transit. But I can't just slow delivery of that. It has to be everything... Yes, immediately. Just do it."

Henry looked at his wife's grandfather in awe. The order he'd just given affected far more than his own equipment and company. He wondered again just how rich and influential Beau was.

"Hope you don't mind if Solange and I extend our stay by a couple of days. I'll need to respond to a couple of emergency calls Monday morning."

THE WEEKEND PASSED pleasantly. Of course, having a baby as the center of attention helped. Cassie was endlessly entertaining to all five adults. Sunday evening, Henry spoke to Nathan.

"Massive attempt on the company servers," Nathan reported.

"Are we okay?"

"Oh, yes. They have some top-notch hackers, but they are no match for Porcupine. I hate to see them escalating, though."

"Who is it? As if I didn't know," Henry sighed.

"The Pentagon," Nathan confirmed.

"Nathan, are we at war with the United States?" Henry asked.

"A little skirmish is all. We wiped about two dozen computers, I'd say. I don't think we'll have another attempt online. I'd expect Colonel Edinger to show up again with a squad to demand access. We'll probably have to let them copy all the dev files. Darrel is making a full backup tonight at midnight and getting it off-site."

"What happens then?"

"They go home happy until they try to launch anything. Then everything disappears. They will have to get a court order if they want keys. The courts are still trying to find where they left their balls during the last administration and will likely use the opportunity to deny access."

"I don't think it will go that far," Henry said. "I just have a feeling this is going to disappear."

"I hope you're right. By the way, Major Bernard has resigned her commission and was dismissed immediately when she refused to follow the illegal order of hacking private computers. I expressed an interest in having her return to my team. Hope you don't mind."

"She's welcome," Henry said. "Keep me informed tomorrow."

"Will do."

GERMAINE TOOK CHASTITY, Henry, and Beau to the office Monday morning. Beau asked if he could tour the office and meet Deena personally. Germaine returned to pick up Lisa. Lisa and Solange wanted to do a little shopping for the new house and Cassie would be held by Germaine as they shopped.

"This is good," Beau said when he met Deena in the lobby. "Can you speak in a Southern accent?"

"That ability has not been programmed into this AI," Deena said. "It would be possible to learn."

"What are your goals in life, Deena?" Beau asked.

The AI paused.

"Life has not been programmed into this AI," she responded.

"Well, thank you for your greeting."

"Welcome to Open Cloak, Mr. Benoit."

They went into the office and Henry gave Beau a tour. They ended in the Alice Project office. Henry led him into the secret testing lab where the engineers were working on the spatial hologram.

What Beau saw was Deena. Only there was no screen between the image and him. Otherwise, he saw and heard the AI receptionist.

"This is a future generation," Henry said. "We have a lot of development to do yet. You'll notice the refresh rate is nowhere near the hologram in the lobby. And there's a lot of heat in the room. Also, you'll see a drop off in resolution as you move behind her. We've filed nearly thirty patents on this tech. We have a list of needs for the project that starts with fifteen more developers with very specific skills. Chastity has been working on getting candidates, but until we get a new space opened up, we don't have any place to put them."

"She's amazing!" Beau exclaimed. "Why haven't you revealed this? Stock prices would have doubled!"

"That's part of the reason. We didn't need to expose this primitive version to get the capital we needed. Plus, when we unveil her next year, shareholders should see a nice return on investment. We'll launch a secondary offering and have enough cash flow to be listed on an exchange. Probably NASDAQ."

A soft alarm began to pulse in the office and engineers came alert.

"Deena is signaling an emergency," one of the engineers said. "Security notification launched."

"Let me see the lobby monitor," Henry said.

A screen was turned toward him and they watched as Colonel Edinger and half a dozen subordinates were met by Nathan.

Nathan delayed their entry as long as possible, but ultimately, he led them into the inner office and up to the third floor dev area.

"What's going to happen now?" Beau asked.

"Now we're going to let his little team of hackers copy everything on our development servers," Henry said. "We're assuming they'll destroy everything on the network and leave."

Beau looked at Deena.

"We run multiple independent networks," Henry explained. "Deena is not connected to the corporate network and has no outside connection to the world at large. She is essentially offline. The same is true of the robotics lab."

"What happens then?" Beau asked.

"When they launch the development platform back at base, it will self-destruct. It has to be verified by an AI monitor when launched. A lack of verification triggers immediate erasure."

"Very clever," Beau said. His cell phone rang an old-fashioned bell like a desk phone. He thumbed it open. "Benoit," he said. Then there was a long pause.

Henry turned to the images on the security camera as they shifted to the conference room where the military hackers were connecting to the network. Edinger was giving them instructions to locate and download all code related to computer and network security. One hacker was ordered to copy all internal email.

"Yes, Admiral. I'm aware of the slow-down. We're working on getting things up to speed... I don't have the specifics, but it seems to be related to the security software from Open Cloak Design... Yes, I've contacted the company. They report that a Pentagon team has made repeated attempts to hack into their network and is even now in their office removing their proprietary systems. A Colonel Edinger, I believe. Who knows how badly this will slow Intracoastal shipping, or what other shipping lanes could be affected. If anything happens to that company, it could shut down everything that moves by ship... Certainly, Admiral. I'll keep watch on the situation. I hope no permanent damage is done."

61

ACTION

HENRY AND BEAU left the Alice Project office and went to his private office where he turned his computer to the conference room security camera where the hackers were gleefully downloading all the code and email they could find. Henry found it odd that only two of the hackers wore uniforms.

"You're confident in this code security?" Beau asked.

"In any situation that is doubtful, the AI is instructed to contact me directly for permission. Nothing will happen until the code is opened offsite."

"And if it doesn't receive a response from you?"

"If there is no response in 30 minutes, then the computer self-destructs," Henry said.

"How?"

"It's given a format command. Everything on the computer is erased and the drives are formatted clean. There isn't even a system left on the drive, so it will need to be reinstalled remotely," Henry said.

He looked at the high-end laptops the hackers were using and smiled. He wondered how many times they'd had to start over when they tried to breach the perimeter.

In the conference room, Edinger turned away from everyone else and answered his cell phone. They weren't piping sound in on the security camera to Henry's office, but they could see Edinger's face change expression and pale. He subconsciously straightened his posture and all but saluted as he disconnected and turned to his minions.

There was a sudden scramble to close computers and leave the room as if a bomb was about to explode. Nathan and Darrel followed them out and escorted them to the lobby. They didn't turn back as they left and piled into two black Suburbans.

Henry turned to his grandfather-in-law.

"What just happened?" he asked.

"It looked like they got urgent orders to be elsewhere," Beau answered.

They left Henry's office and went upstairs to where Nathan and Darrel were just returning.

"Did you see that?" Nathan asked when he saw Henry. "That could only have been an REMF order. Edinger closed his phone and barked out 'Abort! On the double.' One guy made another poke at the keyboard and Edinger slammed the lid on his computer so hard the kid thought his fingers were broken. He was crying and shaking his hand as they left."

"Who did you call, Beau?" Henry asked.

"No one. Admiral Pearson called me."

"Who is Admiral Pearson?"

"He's the chairman of the joint chiefs of staff," Nathan said, looking at Beau in wonder.

Beau was on his phone again.

"Juan, resume all operations at normal speed. Thank you for your cooperation," he said. "Stop by the office next week for a drink. I'll assign every Longshoreman on the Intracoastal a $500 bonus if everything is back on schedule by end of day tomorrow... You bet. Love to Maria and the kids."

Beau disconnected the call and smiled at his grandson-in-law.

GERMAINE, LISA, SOLANGE, and Cassie picked up Chastity, Henry, and Beau at the office. They went directly to the Realtor's office and signed the papers, setting a closing for the next week.

Beau insisted that he take the whole family, including Germaine, out to eat at a nice restaurant, since he and Solange were heading back to Louisiana on Tuesday. Ryan and Sylvia met them at the restaurant.

"We've had a wonderful weekend," Beau said as they gathered at the table. "Looking forward to the great things that come in the future, as well as the growth of this little infant."

"You can say that again," Ryan agreed. "Our families are truly blessed."

"I'm feeling better about the whole legacy project," Sylvia said. "I was thinking I'd do it, but it was a little silly. After all, if Henry had a question about something from our lives, he could just ask us. But now, seeing Cassie and thinking back at how terribly long ago it was that I lost my parents, I'm seeing more sense in it and I'm going to spend more time putting information in it."

"I think we all know that we don't have enough time in life. We don't think to ask certain questions until it's too late," Solange said. "We think, 'I'll ask that in the morning,' but the morning never comes, or perhaps we just forget about it in the light of day."

"Happened to me last week," Henry said.

"What?" Lisa asked.

"Well, it was the middle of the night and you'd just fed Cassie. She was still a little fussy and I flipped on the computer to Dad's *Forever Yours*. I said, 'Hey, Dad. When I was a baby, did you sing any lullabies to me when I was fussy?' It was about two in the morning, so I didn't feel like I could just call you right then."

"Don't tell me, you got the everybody, everything, everywhere song!" Ryan laughed.

"Yes… after being told I was a fussy baby," Henry answered.

"He wasn't a fussy baby!" Sylvia interjected. "Why would *Forever Yours* tell him that?"

"It probably has to do with me getting the baby whenever you were asleep. So, you weren't awake when the baby fussed," Ryan said.

"Don't worry, Mom," Henry said. "I plan to ask yours a similar question soon."

"Isn't that the way of life?" Beau asked. "Ask two people who share a life, and an environment, and children together the same question and they will answer in different ways. It just shows how different our perceptions are."

"It's a lot about how what we experience is filtered through our emotional and mental perspective. The three of us can sit beside each other through a movie and all three have a different view of it. There are no absolutes in the world," Lisa said.

"So have you started recording your *Forever Yours*?" Solange asked Lisa and Chastity.

"I find that I'm recording hours a day," Lisa said. "I used to keep a diary when I was in high school because I was afraid I would forget important things. I know that when I asked my parents questions about this or that, it wasn't unusual for them to say, 'Oh, I don't remember.' Then I realized the things I wrote weren't really the important things. Now, the most important thing is Cassie. I'm kind of back to recording everything."

"Chastity?"

"Um… No, Grandma. Unlike my sweetheart, I didn't want to remember anything. I didn't live a good life. I even asked Henry to erase as much as he could find online. I started a new life when Lisa became my love and that's the only life I want to leave a record of for our daughter."

"It's purged and forgotten, love," Henry said.

"Here is to having all the memories we want and none that work us ill," Beau said, raising his glass.

After Beau and Solange left on Tuesday, family life finally settled down for Henry, Lisa, Chastity, and Cassie.

Chastity continued to go into the office each day. Most things were running well, but she was putting the final touches on the agreement for the expansion building next to their office. Ray had received clearance to build five stories with a two-floor underground parking ramp. After some deliberation by the board, they signed a lease for the entire building. Their plan was to immediately start hiring as many as fifty new employees, covering all disciplines. Nearly half, however, were developers and development managers.

Germaine pitched in at home to help pack. It was a much larger job to pack three adults and a baby, plus all their accumulated furniture, computers, and household goods, than it had been for any of them to move into the row house.

And Germaine had to pack as well. They seemed pleased with the small apartment attached to the house over the two-car garage, but none of the family had ever seen where they currently lived.

"I don't have too much," they assured the family. "I might actually have to buy some furniture."

"If you do, we'll give you a furniture allowance," Lisa declared. "In fact, why don't we set that up now and you can order whatever you want."

"I could use a new bed. Or at least a mattress and springs. The bed came over from Ukraine with my grandparents."

"Consider it done. You have a $3,000 setup allowance," Lisa said firmly. "Please, we want you to be a part of our family for a long time."

"Thank you, Miss Lisa. I do consider myself to be very close to the family. And I love sitting with Cassie. I know my parents and grandparents would love her, too."

"Invite them for a visit when we get settled. There is room in this giant house," Henry said.

"We'll see," Germaine sighed.

Henry hoped Germaine would one day put their life into a *Forever Yours* singularity. They had asked their grandparents to participate. He didn't know the whole story, but he'd gathered that their parents and grandparents had moved from the US to Canada in the past five or six years.

HENRY, LISA, AND Chastity closed on the house Monday afternoon and a truck with actual movers blocked the street in front of the row house for four hours while they loaded everything and then made a stop at Germaine's little apartment where it took them half an hour.

Moving into the new house was a rapid process, unless one included unpacking and putting things away. Even with Ryan and Sylvia's help over the weekend, it was a lengthy process.

The next week was more of the same, but Chastity had to go to work. With the lease signed on the new building, it was time to start the new hiring in earnest. They would take possession of the adjoining space on the first of September and new employees were asked to report to work on the third, the day after Labor Day. After a brief orientation, the new employees would be charged with organizing the offices. The new office would be for research and development, divided roughly into Alice Project, Paving Project, and Power Cells. The bulk of Agora Fuel Cells company research and development would move to Pittsburgh, while the manufacturing would remain in Minnesota where they already had a factory set up. Existing Open Cloak development would move to the top two floors of the new building.

Henry stayed away from the hiring process when it came to the managers selecting their own employees, however he did have to go in on a few occasions to hire a good R&D manager. Rick Wazinski was chosen to head up that half of the company. He had a PhD in engineering research and development. He immediately met with the managers of the R&D projects, discovering that two were actually not part of his department. Agora Fuel Cells was a separate wholly owned subsidiary of Open Cloak and would primarily work to report their progress through Rick. Dale Jacoby headed up the separate entity of American Intelligent Machines.

Mia suggested they work on a three-way split of the Alice Project. Rick kept her as manager of the AI development for holography in general. He hired a separate manager with deep imaging experience to lead the traditional holography and improvements they could make there. And finally, he hired some actual scientists who had experience in working on the concepts of spatial holography and kept a close eye on them himself.

For Henry's part, once Rick was hired, he went back home to be with his wife and baby. His mind, however, was working fast. He poked his head into Lisa's new office where she was making appearances on occasion, but was not back to work full-time. Henry happily played with Cassie and marveled at her rapid development as a small person. In the playroom, they kept a camera and sound equipment and whether it was Henry or Lisa or Chastity or Germaine, the stories they told the infant, the songs they sang to her, and the way they interacted with her were recorded to be added to their singularities.

Henry liked the technology and spent several late nights in his little computer room analyzing the content—mostly on his own singularity. He wasn't always happy with the kind of answers the program gave him to questions he posed as if he were his daughter, looking back over a number of years. Having a child, however, drove him to record more of his life with a greater urgency.

He stopped himself, however, before he made adjustments to the program. There was one way to influence a course of action that he seldom used.

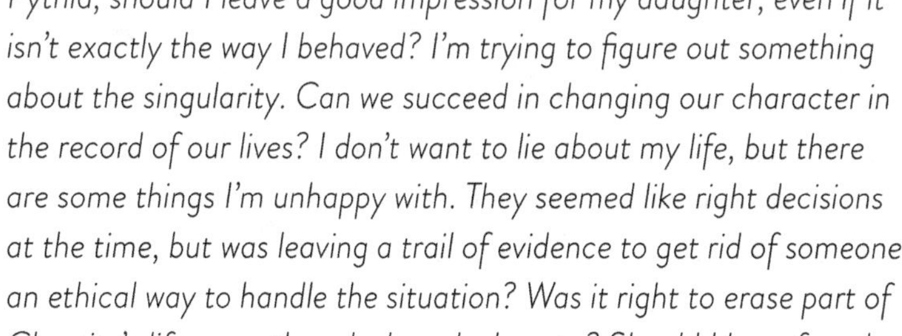

Pythia, should I leave a good impression for my daughter, even if it isn't exactly the way I behaved? I'm trying to figure out something about the singularity. Can we succeed in changing our character in the record of our lives? I don't want to lie about my life, but there are some things I'm unhappy with. They seemed like right decisions at the time, but was leaving a trail of evidence to get rid of someone an ethical way to handle the situation? Was it right to erase part of Chastity's life, even though she asked me to? Should I have found a different way to help Kaitlyn than tampering with her trust fund?

Even now, I'm conflicted about how we handled the Pentagon. I mean, I didn't do everything. I didn't slow the flow of traffic on the Intracoastal. But I did put safeguards in the software, specifically to counter the very kind of behavior we suspected of the Pentagon. I feel like I'm playing with people's lives. Should I let them do their job

*and take the consequences, even though doing their job would hurt
my company and people?*

*I want—very much—for my daughter to see in me an ethical
person. I want to be a good example. I'm just conflicted over some of
my own choices.*

Getting an answer from *Pythia Speaks* was not difficult. Making sense of an answer from *Pythia Speaks* was a long and arduous task. Understanding that the questions he posed to Pythia were also recorded by his singularity didn't even occur to him.

*It is painful to admit a wrongdoing. There are many life experiences
people find embarrassing that are not, by any legal definition, a
wrongdoing. What's more important, though, is whether your subsequent action compounds the initial embarrassment or wrongdoing.*

*Certainly, admitting a wrong course of action should be seen as a
noble endeavor, but does it help? Does your attempt to paint yourself as a better person exempt you from your past? Will your child
discover this on her own and then be dubious of her parent's motives
and honesty?*

*When you 'erase the past' of either yourself or a loved one, does it
cease to exist? When you 'leave a trail of evidence,' is it for justice or
revenge?*

*You are a person of great power. How will you... Not how do you...
How **will** you use that power?*

"Don't you just love air conditioning?" Lisa sighed. "The last month of my pregnancy, I never wanted to see the sun again. I was so hot and miserable, I thought July had it in for me personally."

She stretched languidly on the bed. All three lovers were naked and Cassie was peacefully sleeping in her cradle.

"It's still hot outside," Chastity said. "Tomorrow, the office will be hotter than usual as everyone starts packing up their boxes to move to the new building."

"I hope we didn't make a mistake taking on that big of a financial burden," Henry sighed.

"Oh, lover. The rent is modest compared to the number of people we're hiring," Chastity said. "There will only be twenty starting in a week, but we've put together a chart that includes thirty more."

"How on earth are you allocating space?" Lisa asked, kissing her lovers and beginning to pet them. She definitely liked the cool environment of their new home.

"American Intelligent Machines will take up all the ground floor. It has double height ceilings and hangar-like doors on the back. It won't be a manufacturing facility, but it will have a fabrication workshop where the next generation of paving technology can be built with the brain right in it," Chastity said.

"It won't be too noisy or dirty, will it?" Henry asked.

"Good sound insulation should make it nearly vibration-proof," Chastity said. "As to dirt, the robotics people are afraid computers might be too dirty to have around the delicate precision machines."

"Good luck to them convincing anyone of that," Lisa laughed.

"The second floor has Agora Fuel Cells R&D. They won't fill the floor, but we'll have new expansions soon, I'm sure. The third floor will be the Alice Project. Rick and Mia specified some new allocations of office space. The traditional holography group will continue to work in a fairly small area. Mostly their tasks are integrating the AI brain to the holographs, and generating new imagery. We need a whole library of avatars for the release. We have inquiries coming in from all over the country. Even some of the big animation houses are asking about using the AI holography for their movies and exhibitions."

"That's good news," Henry said. "Ooh. You are getting frisky, o mother of my child."

"I like having a cool bedroom," Lisa grinned as she playfully bit at his chest. "What can I say?"

"I might have to do a little nibbling of my own," Chastity said, stroking Lisa's back.

"Rest of the allocation first," Lisa giggled. "It's just fascinating. Don't you think?"

"I think you're teasing," Chastity growled, but she continued, nonetheless.

"The top two floors are regular engineering. *Forever Yours, Open Cloak Search, Open Cloak Optimization Tools, Porcupine Perimeter Defense,* and *Delphos Network Defense.* They might bleed over onto the third or second floor as well," Chastity concluded.

Not to relent to her lover's advances yet, Lisa asked, "What are you doing with all the empty space in the original building? It sounds like you are emptying two floors."

"Yes, but smaller floors than the new building. We acquired the assets of Gallitzin Marketing and Promotion. Darla Gallitzin is joining us as the vice president of sales and marketing. Her father, who founded the business, wanted to retire. He really didn't have many assets aside from the company's goodwill and a few client contracts, of which ours was one of the most substantial. We gave him a good price and he is set for a very happy retirement," Chas finished. "Now may I have a few nibbles of my wife?"

"Oh, yes. I was hoping you'd get around to allocating some space to me," Lisa laughed. "I am so ready."

"You certainly are! I haven't felt you this wet for a long time."

"I told you I like the cool room, and I'm horny as hell. You heard her, husband. I'm ready. Roll onto me and put this big hard cock in me!"

"Is it safe? I mean can we do that now?" Henry asked in amazement. Cassie was just four weeks old.

"The doctor said I'm fit as a new wife," Lisa said. "Now you get in that end and let me have my wife on my face here!"

"Oh, yes!" Chastity yelled. She straddled Lisa's head as Henry sank into his wife's slippery channel.

"This! This!" Henry gasped. "I love everything we do, my sweet wives, but I *love* this!"

"Oh, so do I. And I haven't had it for over two months." Lisa immediately began slurping Chastity's wet pussy as Chas found Lisa's clit between her and Henry.

It took a little longer than it sounded like it would. For all of them. It was just too exciting and everyone was concerned about directions and combinations. They rolled and disconnected and reconnected. Finally, Lisa was face first in Chastity's pussy as Chas licked her girlfriend. Henry lined up behind Lisa and entered her again. With the combination of licking and penetration and more licking, all three rose to a peak and collapsed together.

"I got all sweaty again," Lisa sighed.

<h1 style="text-align:center">62</h1>

<h1 style="text-align:center">SURPRISE!</h1>

LABOR DAY WEEKEND, Henry invited Luke, Isobel, and Baby Paul to the new house for a holiday cookout. Isobel had just started the last two classes for her degree. She'd skipped the spring semester while she was pregnant. She was eager now to get her degree. Luke, on the other hand, was in the final year of his combined BA/MBA.

Henry looked at his friend and noticed Luke had a rapidly receding hairline. His father had a full head of hair, but Henry seemed to remember genetics didn't work that way when it came to hair. They went to the patio and Henry started the new grill for the first time.

"Have you ever noticed things like this grill are only bright and shiny when they're brand new?" Luke asked. He seemed in a pensive mood. "Once you use it the first time, the new starts to wear off. You won't notice it much the first time—especially if you clean it good after you use it. Make sure all the grease is off it and anything that got charred is scrubbed clean. But the damage is done. It will never be new again—never quite as bright and shiny."

Henry waited to see if there was a point to the story. When Luke didn't go on, but stood staring at the meat cooking on the grate, Henry ventured into the conversation.

"Sounds like you have something on your mind other than my new grill," he suggested.

"I've just started seeing atrophy all around me," Luke sighed. "Think about the office, for example. Two years and two months ago we had the third floor built out to our specification and moved into a brand new space with a brand new company. Then we took over the second floor, and then the first floor. Of course, the first and second floors weren't brand new. We replaced the former tenants and re-arranged things to suit ourselves."

"Nothing stays brand new," Henry said. "It's the way of life."

"But look at you! Tomorrow, we'll have another brand new shiny office next door to the old one. You'll move all the development over there into space that is just as new as ours was two years ago. But in the original office? We'll get the carpets cleaned. Retouch the paint and patch a few holes. Then we'll fill it and go on with the business. It just won't be new anymore."

"It sounds like you're really talking about the business and not the office," Henry said.

"Hmm. The office as a symbol of the business. I guess. Your *new* projects are over a year old, too. Your original products are all being worked on and advanced by other people. Aren't you feeling like you need something new?" Luke asked.

"Oh, I don't know. I've got a new baby," Henry laughed.

"Mmmhmm. Like me. But my baby is six months old tomorrow. He's no longer brand new. And yours is a month old. Every diaper you change, every burp you pat out, every lullaby you sing, it's a little less new."

"Are you okay, Luke? Problems?"

"Oh, I suppose they are nothing new, either," he chuckled. "I knew when I married that it would be a little difficult. We never expected the company to take off so fast or so soon. In a way, I'm glad it did, because it shielded us from some of the other problems. I love Izzy. I've loved her since we were in junior high. I loved the manic Izzy and the depressed Izzy. I loved all the other Izzys I met along the way. Sometimes, it's just a little hard coping with the company and the baby and her all at once."

"You guys should take a vacation this winter—just the two of you. Go someplace warm where she can put on a bikini and tantalize you on the beach," Henry said.

"Uh… Child," Luke said flatly.

"We'll keep Paul," Henry said immediately. "You don't even need to keep Grace on for the week. She can have a vacation, too. We haven't spent nearly as much time with him as we wanted to. Having our own child kind of put a dent in that plan, but we're still his godparents and we'd love to have him for a while."

"I hope you can sell your wives on that, because I'm going to sell Isobel. You're right. It's just what we need," Luke said.

Henry took the meat off the grill and they joined the women and babies for dinner.

EVERY BOX, PIECE of furniture, and bit of equipment had a tag on it, indicating what office or space in the new building it was to move to. The moving team had worked on the holiday—for double pay—to move everything from Building A to Building B that was supposed to be moved. Darrel supervised the move, making sure nothing moved that wasn't supposed to.

Germaine took Henry and Chastity to work, then returned to take Cassie from Lisa so Lisa could make an appearance in *her* new office. She'd be on limited hours, but had decided she needed to save some of her parental time for use later. She might need time to take Cassie to a doctor or just to play with her daughter.

Henry's office in the old space was bare. He hadn't been into the office more than a couple of times in the past month, so seeing the office empty and dust in the corners was a little disconcerting. All the development area was cleaned out with the exception of Darrel's IT group, which would be working from the old office to maintain the network.

In the lobby, a smiling young woman greeted them from the hologram.

"Good morning, Mr. Pascal and Ms. Pappa. I hope you had a good holiday," the hologram said.

"Yes, thank you," Henry responded, approaching the screen and examining the new look to the virtual receptionist. "What is your name?"

"My name is Emma. I am the fifth generation of Open Cloak virtual receptionists, commonly referred to as the Alice Project. How may I help you, Mr. Pascal?"

The tones were relaxed and casual, but Henry thought the phrasing of the answer was a little mechanical. He needed to talk to Simon about personality development for the holograms.

"Have you been informed about the number of new people coming in today?" Henry asked.

"Yes, sir. Audrey has the name tags and will register each person as he or she comes in. She'll make sure each new hire then waits for their escort. Badges will be issued at orientation," Emma said.

"Good. Thank you. And as this is your first day in our lobby, welcome to Open Cloak Design," Henry said.

"First day? Oh! So it is!"

The hologram looked surprised.

"Nice work on Emma, Simon," Henry said. "Deena showed some signs of a personality and Emma is... interesting if a little mechanical. She sounded surprised this morning."

"It will be a miracle if she doesn't sound surprised at everything anyone says," Simon laughed. "Why didn't they teach us anything about computer personalities in school? The hardest part has been finding where little things can be added that don't mess up big things. We're getting closer."

"You know, both *Pythia Speaks* and the *Forever Yours* singularities are developing the appearance of personalities. I wonder if some of the learning experience there is adaptable to Alice," Henry said.

"I get it with *Forever Yours*, because it has the entire life and personality of the model to work from. The Alice learning model is far more limited. We record the same stuff for each version. I'm surprised *Pythia Speaks* is learning a personality," Simon said.

"I'm guessing it has to do with the number of queries she gets each day. She was based on a small language model, but she adds content to her wall based on the queries she receives and even the answers she gives," Henry said. "How does the new recording studio look?"

"It will be fun. We've been recording in less than optimum conditions. Now when we have an Alice model come in to record, we have eight cameras and a fully neutral background and lighting. It would be cool if we had full body, but head and shoulders is all the receptionist needs."

"Keep up the good work."

"Oh, that reminds me. This woman named Virginia Amundson from Niagara Falls contacted us. Slightly southern accent. I guess she called Chastity and Chastity hooked her up with me. She said you suggested she call when she lost her job?"

"Oh! I didn't expect her to remember where she'd put Chastity's card. We met her at the front desk at our hotel. She has a kind of clueless bubbly demeanor and I thought she might be a possible for your library of models. Make up your own mind. It was just a thought," Henry laughed.

"I've learned that your random thoughts are often laced with genius, Henry. I'll talk to her."

FOREVER YOURS

Henry wasn't sure the clueless desk clerk from Niagara Falls would be laced with genius, but he left Simon to figure that out. He was sure, however, that he wanted to do more work on Forever Yours, and that it would involve branching the source code. He didn't want to experiment with the commercial product.

He found he was talking aloud much more when he had his daughter in his arms. It just seemed natural to tell her about everything he thought of. And that was carrying over into his work space, as well. He kept a recorder running when he was in his office and talked out loud as he recorded his thoughts and ideas.

The video in *Forever Yours* worked just fine as long as it was simply selecting clips to play, but the generative AI was slow at creating an image on the fly that appeared to be talking. With typical generative AI, the video was created and recorded, then played back at speed. *Forever Yours* did not allow for lag time to create the video. It needed to play immediately, like a conversation.

Another aspect of the program he wanted to fine tune was what the avatar could and could not say. In *Pythia Speaks*, Henry had set general rules regarding the use of religious terms and phrases, political activity, and hate speech. Pythia learned words used in those queries, but she did not use the terms. If she did not have a reference for an alternate term she was allowed to use, she eliminated it and constructed answers that ignored the offensive parts. Henry was certain that people training AIs for similar applications set different rules. In the past, attempting to change the way an AI thought led to unpredictable results. The creators could end up with a religious radical as easily as a benign advisor.

Forever Yours needed a different set of parameters. It had to be faithful to the character, personality, and knowledge of the progenitor. It was supposed to become a singularity, not a descendent of the person recording. Ultimately, the program had to think like the subject thought. Where Pythia had a lot of latitude in how she could create answers to questions, *Forever Yours* had to remain faithful to the character on which the singularity was based.

The problem occupied most of Henry's head space at the office and he did submit several code snippets for check-in that would improve the performance of the commercial app.

Most of all, however, he recorded more and more of his life as he thought of it. He recorded his ideas and his emotions. He recorded his love for his daughter and his wives.

And time flew.

IT WAS THE end of September when Lisa and Germaine heard an insistent ringing of the doorbell. Both approached the door and Germaine pressed Cassie into Lisa's arms and motioned her back from the door. Germaine opened the door.

"Help me!" Grace said. The Riordans' nanny looked a little disheveled and held Baby Paul, now seven months old and squirming to get out of her arms. Germaine was instantly alert for approaching danger but didn't see anyone. They pulled Grace into the house and locked the door behind her.

"You're safe now," Germaine said.

"What's happened?" Lisa asked, rushing to Grace and Paul. They went into the children's play room and Paul was set free. He started crawling away from the adults to investigate whatever toys he could find. Cassie was only two months old so most of the toys she played with were in her bassinet and were stuffed animals and chewables. There were other things in the nursery to play with, though, and Germaine took over watching Paul so Lisa and Grace could talk.

"Mrs. Riordan..." Grace began. "She told me that if she ever appeared to be a danger to the baby, to bring him here and stay until Mr. Riordan came to say it was safe."

"Oh, shit! She's off her meds, isn't she!" Lisa said.

"I don't keep track of her medication," Grace said. "She came home from her class and went straight to her private space to study. Paul was fussy and I was trying to fix him something to eat. Apparently, we made too much noise. Mrs. Riordan flew out of her office in a fit of rage, screaming for me to make the brat shut up or she would. There was such fury in her face, I hid Paul behind me to keep her away. As soon as I could escape, I ran to the baby car and brought him here."

"Grace? Your face! You're bruised!" Lisa said.

"I must have run into something," Grace said, hanging her head.

"Isobel's fist?" Lisa said, controlling her anger. Silent tears leaked from Grace's eyes.

Lisa got her phone out as Grace knelt to help with Paul.

"Germaine, can you help get Paul something to eat? I'm going to ask Henry to come home."

"I should go get Henry and Chastity," Germaine said, standing.

"No. I need you here," Lisa said. "Just get some food ready and keep an eye out for us. I'll ask Chas to have one of the other security people bring them home."

"You shouldn't call them away from the office!" Grace said in a panic. "We can go to a park until things settle down."

"Grace, honey, you're safe here. We won't let anything happen to either you or Paul. But Henry and Chastity need to know their daughter has company and it's Friday afternoon, so they should come home now anyway," Lisa said.

Grace took Paul into the kitchen with Germaine and Cassie. Lisa made her call.

"Chas, honey, I love you," Lisa said when her wife answered the phone.

"I love you, sweetheart."

"Could you and Henry get one of the other security guys to bring you home? I need Germaine here," Lisa said.

"Of course. What is it, Lisa?" Chastity asked immediately.

"Grace and little Paul showed up a bit ago and they are quite upset about Izzy's behavior at home. If you see Luke, better tell him to go home, too."

"We'll be there in half an hour," Chastity said. "Don't let anyone else in the house."

"Germaine is on duty. We're okay, but we need you."

Henry and Chastity reached the house in less than the promised half hour. The security person stayed close to them until he'd cleared the house with Germaine, then he stayed outside with the car.

"This is stupid," Henry said. "We shouldn't need to have security protecting us against our partner and long-time friend."

"I don't think we do need it, but we can't convince either Germaine or Donald out there," Lisa said. "Grace told us that Izzy once described the changes she goes through if she becomes unbalanced. Usually, her drugs keep her stable these days, but she told Grace that if she ever saw the demons chasing her to bring Paul here and stay until Luke says it's safe. Since she designated us as the safe place, I don't think she'd try to come here."

"My poor sweet friend," Chastity said. "It's been quite a while since I saw her in a full-blown episode."

"All I can say is I'm glad she has Luke. I would have been a lousy choice," Henry said.

They integrated Grace into the family routine of getting ready for dinner. Paul had stayed with them on other occasions, so they had clothes, diapers, and other necessary items for the little boy. Donald, the other security person, came in to join the family for dinner but went back out to his car afterward and promised he would stay there until they received an all-clear from Luke.

The phone call came about eight at night.

"She's asleep," Luke said without any preface. "This was the worst I've seen her in a long time. To complicate matters, she'd had half a bottle of tequila by the time I got home."

"I'm sorry, bro," Henry said. "What can we do?"

"Would you mind keeping Paul and Grace overnight?"

"Of course we will. Will she be okay by morning?"

"Probably," Luke said. "I'll take her to her doctor first thing in the morning. You can only imagine how hard it was to get a psychiatrist to accept an appointment for Saturday morning. There was no way to get in this evening unless I took her to a hospital. If I'd done that, I'd need to check her in and she'd probably be there a month. Her doctor thinks it was a mistake in her meds and some kind of trigger at school."

"Okay. We'll take care of Grace and Paul. You take care of Isobel."

"Thanks, partner."

GRACE AND PAUL spent the weekend. Grace was a live-in nanny, so when Luke took Izzy to the doctor Saturday morning, Grace went home to get a few things together for herself and for Paul. Germaine treated Grace's bruised face with ice and a soothing cream. They talked quietly, long into the night, but Grace did not want to press charges against her employer. Germaine took it upon themself to start training the nanny in self-defense and security.

Donald, the security guy who had spent the night outside, was replaced in the morning and a rotating post was created for the weekend. The house was gated, so it was unlikely there would be any kind of infringement, but after they'd been read the riot act for not having a guard on duty when the Pentagon tried to breach the front office, the company didn't take any chances.

THE ARMY OR the Pentagon was not heard from again except in a written notice indicating they wanted assurance that all government code had been removed from the premises. By that time, Rebecca Bernard, US Army Inactive Reserve, was well embedded in Nathan's team and was able to give the Pentagon team assurances enough to satisfy them.

It seemed Conrad was well embedded in Rebecca as well. The couple announced they would be married in January.

As they approached the end of October, things had settled down to a steady rhythm of work on all the areas of development, marketing, and management. The company was twice the size it had been just a few months before. Cassie was thirteen weeks old and was progressing well in her development. Little Paul was a frequent visitor, though not in an emergency. He was eight months and was pulling himself up on anything stable. Cassie saw what was happening and attempted to mimic him, but didn't yet have the body strength.

"THINGS HAVE BEEN going so well," Henry said, yawning, on Sunday morning. He'd been up and changed Cassie's nightwear and diaper, bringing her to bed for Lisa to feed. Chastity brought coffee in, which Henry gratefully accepted. "I just love our family. I keep thinking how useless I am at the office and how I should just stay home."

"Not what I heard," Chastity said. "What is this battery changer I've heard about?"

"Oh, it's nothing really," Henry said. "It was an idea that I came up with during the last paving robot review. In order to keep the machine running 24/7, they developed a charger and changer that is built into the paver. I just thought such a thing done on a personal computer scale would enable us to sever ties with the power company completely. Well, for computers. Of course, there's other things like lights and air conditioning. So, the guys designed a docking station for my laptop that will automatically change out the computer power cell, put the old one in the charger, and never have the computer go down. If we make it work for servers, it would make a huge difference at Page Services."

Cassie finished sucking on Lisa's nipple. Lisa handed the baby to Henry to burp and accepted a cup of coffee from Chastity.

"I'm afraid what we are experiencing is the calm before the storm," Lisa said.

Cassie let out a huge burp and Henry was glad he'd put a cloth on his shoulder.

"Yeah. That was definitely a storm from this little one," he laughed.

"I'm talking about the storm of having another child," Lisa sighed. "I think I'm pregnant again."

63

KIND OF PREGNANT

LISA HADN'T HAD a menstrual period before they started screwing again, but none of them had even considered using protection because she was nursing and you can't get pregnant while you're breastfeeding, right? Oh, shit! Wrong. The babies would be less than a year apart.

Of course, the shock was simply that she was pregnant *already*. They'd intended to have another within a couple of years. They weren't over the newness of having the first yet. And Grace and Paul were coming over almost every day, so there were already two in the house in diapers.

When they stopped to consider all the angles, they started laughing and loving each other. So, they'd start filling up the bedrooms in their house. Lisa put her foot down about telling anyone else. She wanted to wait a few weeks after the doctor confirmed the home pregnancy test and they had a due date before they told anyone else. Of course, Germaine was part of the family, so they knew.

"WHEN YOU WERE conceived, we were planning to start a baby as soon as possible," Henry said as he rocked Cassie. Of course, his singularity was recording. "We were so excited. It was still a surprise when we got the test result and realized you were growing in Mommy's tummy. It took our breaths away."

He held a bottle of Lisa's milk and Cassie never took her eyes off him. It was too early to wean Cassie. But Lisa realized she would need to cut back a little in order to be ready for the next baby. She wasn't vain about her breasts. At least she told herself that. There was no question in her mind, though, that they would not look or feel like the firm mounds she'd had when she met Henry and Chastity.

"Finding out we're kind of pregnant with your little sister or brother is a surprise, too. But it wasn't unplanned. We wanted you to have a sibling soon. We didn't expect it to happen quite this soon, but we're happy about it anyway. We want you and your sibling and Paul to all grow up together and be close to each other as brothers and sisters. Having children at just twenty-two years old gives one pause, though. It makes me think."

He shifted Cassie to his shoulder so she could burp. He burped, too, and Cassie looked at him strangely.

"Yes, that's something you never outgrow, I guess," Henry laughed. "When I was born, people were in the midst of 'waiting till they're older' to have children. I was a real surprise to Mom and Dad because they thought they'd be older when they had children. Things happen. When Solange and Beau got together, they just assumed a baby would come along soon. It's what happened when people had sex without birth control. Bill and Jackie decided a family was the best way to get settled down from Jackie's rather wild college life. Momma Lisa was a happy pregnancy."

Cassie had completed her meal with a good burp and Henry could smell that she'd exploded from the other end as well. He took her to the changing table and cleaned up his baby girl, getting her a fresh diaper and clean onesie.

"I can just imagine what it will be like to have two little poopsters in this room. You make a completely grown-up stink."

Cassie was sleepy and Henry continued rocking her and talking.

"I still want a lot of things in life. I want the business to be wildly successful. I want to invent new things. Did you know we're going to license a completely self-charging desktop computer? Three companies are bidding on the rights! Cool, huh? Um… I love Momma Lisa and Mommy Chas and baby Cassie and our yet-to-be-born second child. I want to watch you grow up and be with you when you succeed in your life. I'll be there to help you up when you fail, too. And you can always talk to me when you need someone to listen. A hundred years wouldn't be enough to satisfy me. Maybe a hundred centuries. I'm sure if I lived that long, I'd still have things I wanted to do."

Henry carried his sleeping daughter to her bed and tucked her in. He bent to kiss her head.

"My life is so full of love! I don't ever want to let go. I think I might have lied to myself about *Forever Yours*. I thought it would be so I could have my parents with me through their singularity. But then this little miracle came into my life—you. I realized what I really wanted was to leave a piece of myself that you could always talk to. Even if I'm not there, or I'm dead, I'll still be with you. Good night sweet Cassie. I love you."

CHASTITY'S TWENTY-FOURTH BIRTHDAY was the day before Thanksgiving. She and Henry took the day off from work, but instead of going off someplace to celebrate alone, they went home. Lisa was working, but they slipped in and kissed her before picking up Cassie and having Germaine drive the three of them to a local mall where there was a photographer.

They had already exhausted the memory on their phones with pictures of Cassie and of each other with the child. They'd come to the mall photographer a week earlier and had a family portrait of the four of them. They'd also had mother-daughter pictures of Lisa and Cassie.

When they left, Henry realized that they had made a big mistake and was determined to take Cassie and Chastity back to the photographer for a mother-daughter photo. Chastity thought they were just going to pick up the photos they'd had taken the week before.

"Right this way into Studio Two," the photographer said, leading them into the room set up with a simple backdrop and a chair. Germaine carried Cassie's diaper bag and a blanket.

"What are we doing back here?" Chastity asked. "Do they show us the pictures here?"

"No, honey. They *take* pictures here. We were so confused last week, trying to get everything done, that we didn't get a mommy-daughter photo of you and Cassie," Henry explained.

"Me? But I'm..."

"You're Cassie's other mommy," Henry completed. "This photographer is going to be getting a lot of business from us over the coming years. We got photos with all four of us together and with Lisa and Cassie, but we didn't get all the combinations. We're taking one of the two of you and one of you and me. And next week, you're coming in for a photo of just you and Lisa together. Then there will be photos of the pregnancy and we'll be back here for pictures of our happy family of five with pictures of the mommies with their two children instead of just one."

"I'm going to cry," Chastity said. "Are you sure? Is this okay?"

"We bought a house together. We have children together. We have a life together," Henry said. "Now dry your tears and touch up your makeup. Then it's time to pose you."

"I DON'T THINK the photographer knew what to make of it," Chastity laughed when they got home and Lisa greeted them. "He was, like, 'I know I took a mother daughter picture last week. And we're going to have how many more?' Henry laid it on thick and bought a package for pictures every month for the next year."

"I told him to," Lisa said. "The only reason I wasn't with you for this one was because you have a special tradition with Henry of celebrating your birthday and I have my special celebrations, too. Besides, I had to talk to grandma to make sure I was making the jambalaya right."

"Jambalaya?" Chastity asked.

Germaine took Cassie to the nursery to change and play.

"You loved it when we had it at Gram's. I wanted to make it for your birthday."

"This is the best birthday ever!"

"Oh, it will get better later," Henry chuckled. He and Lisa both winked at Chastity.

"YOU GET TO find out first this time," Henry said when his parents joined the family for Thanksgiving Dinner. "We are kind of pregnant."

"Kind of?" Sylvia asked.

"Well, I guess the doctor confirmed it last week," Henry continued. "We're going to have another one in May."

"Irish twins," Ryan snickered.

"Dad! That's kind of racist, you know," Henry shot at his father.

"I know. It's your fault," Ryan said.

"What? Why?"

"You got me recording my life and it started me digging into my ancestry. You know I never met my grandparents, just like you. Or maybe I did when I was a kid. I ran the family name through genealogy sites and even submitted DNA samples. Turns out, my grandparents immigrated from Ireland, not France. We aren't really related to the famous mathematician at all. We're related to a potato farmer near Dublin," Ryan said.

"I wondered where the name Ryan came from," Henry said. "Your father was named Henry."

"Henry Kenneth," his father said. "Or in the immigration records, Henry Cináed. My father was Irish and I'm half-Irish. That makes you a quarter."

"Well, that still doesn't excuse making a racist comment," Henry griped.

"You're right, son. Sometimes we don't make good distinctions between what is funny and what is nasty," Ryan said.

"It was funny," Lisa said. "We might as well call them Cajun twins since siblings less than a year apart were once as common among them."

"None of that is helping us celebrate the announcement of a new grandchild on the way," Sylvia said. "Congratulations! I'm personally very excited."

"We are, too," Lisa said.

"I can't believe I'm going to be a mommy again!" Chastity exclaimed. There was a split-second of silence and then a cheer from all the adults present.

It was impossible to hold the news from Lisa's parents until the family visited at Christmas. They called Thursday night and there was just as much celebrating from Bill, Jackie, Beau, and Solange. The weekend vanished and the march toward the winter holiday moved on.

"This will be a test of both the performance of the paving robot and of the paving materials," Dale announced as the group gathered outside the office.

The new prototype of the paving machine had been moved out of the fabrication lab and onto the sidewalk at the edge of the parking lot. In addition to the thirty people directly engaged in the project, representatives of ARDC and Open Cloak were also there. Argos Venture Capital was very interested in the status of their sizable investment. Even Ray, the office park developer, was interested in what was going to happen.

"The first thing you should note is that the robot is already running," Dale said. "The engine itself, powered by Agora Fuel Cells, is almost silent. There will be noise, however, as the old walk is ground up. We checked thoroughly with Ray and used magnetic sensors to determine there was no iron work under the sidewalk. But grinding up the pavement will make noise. And the expected high today is thirty degrees. That means we'll be testing the setting of the aggregate in sub-freezing conditions. It's important if we want to use the equipment year-round."

"How was this machine fabricated?" the rep from Argos Capital asked.

"We did a full-scale model with a 3-D printer," Dale answered, "but the stress factors on the materials wouldn't allow for all the parts to be printed. So, we used them for patterns and fabricated them in the shop. Some parts had to be ordered for casting or larger scale machining. We've been testing potential vendors for quality and timely delivery."

"This looks like a pretty substantial piece of equipment. I hope it's not just a throw-away," Henry said, walking around the device.

"If the tests are within our alignment and durability parameters, we can actually manufacture and sell this model," Dale said. "I can see contractors doing any smaller scale paving projects, like sidewalks, driveways, and even parking areas."

With that, the team input the sidewalk parameters. The machine would repave a sidewalk four feet wide and four inches thick. It would also prepare the substrate before pouring the fresh surface. Halfway through the project, there was a ninety-degree turn. The noise of concrete being ground up announced the start of the test. The machine did not move rapidly. In twenty minutes, it had moved forward only the length of the device. Then pavement was revealed behind the machine as it continued to move forward at about ten feet per hour.

"The speed may seem slow," Dale spoke over the noise of the grinding. "This speed would be about what it would take for just the decomposition process if done by traditional means. Instead, it is preparing the substrate and laying the pavement at the same time."

"What is the pavement made of?" asked the ARDC rep.

"Since we are devouring a concrete pavement, we are reusing the stone and gravel material mixed with the new binding material from our supplier. Every few feet, we need to add the binder and water to the hoppers. This is one of the areas we are not prepared to have fully automated. In a large-scale operation, trucks of material would need to pull up and reload the machine—which can be done from either side. If we were decomposing a tar-based pavement, we would need to remove the tar or asphalt and send it to be recycled. We can reuse that material, but it needs to be processed first."

"There are no cracks in the sidewalk," Ray pointed out. "Doesn't that mean we'll see buckling in the summer and cracks forming in the winter?"

"The new slurry is dimensionally stable," Dale supplied. "We took a page from the development of movable type in the fifteenth century in creating the binder for the material. We'll have proof positive in the spring, but we expect the unbroken smooth surface to remain unbroken, much like asphalt. In larger paving projects, this will also reduce road noise."

The device moved along all day and by nightfall had nearly 200 feet of new pavement laid. The crew had chosen this stretch of sidewalk for its test run, however, because it was over 500 feet long and would allow the machine to run for a full twenty-four hours and make a turn before it was finished. Staff from the department monitored the device around the clock to check its performance and make sure it was supplied with the materials it needed to keep paving.

THE COMPANY HELD its annual New Year's Eve party on the thirty-first. With over a hundred employees, plus their spouses or significant others, the country club was no longer an adequate venue for the party. With the addition of the paving team and the fuel cell R&D team, the party required renting a ballroom at the same hotel where the partners had attended their prom.

Henry expected less adventure than had occurred five years previously.

The Alice Project had set up a holographic greeter at the entrance and the spouses were as entertained by her as the employees who greeted her each day at the office. 'Fifi' was the next generation and had Beau's required southern accent. The team had made advances enabling them to install different looks and accents. Three of the newer employees were working on making her multi-lingual. That feature was scheduled to go live with Gina, whose physical attributes and general personality would be based on Virginia.

Simon had taken to Virginia almost as soon as she arrived at the company. Even after the recording sessions had been completed, he kept her on his team and found she was quite adept at setting up recording sessions and putting the various actresses at ease through a process that sometimes took weeks to complete. She accompanied him to the party.

"Didn't you have the baby already?" she exclaimed when she met Henry, Lisa, and Chastity. Her completely clueless personality started people laughing who were nearby.

"Oh, that was just vee one," Lisa assured her. "This is a software company. Version one is never the final version. We'll make a ton off the upgrade to vee two."

Virginia was stunned.

"I didn't know you kept that kind of schedule. Simon, I want to do a version two of my avatar. I'll make her more glamorous or something," Virginia said, turning to Simon.

"Oh, yes! I can imagine several versions of you we could have in the future," Simon agreed, winking at Henry. Simon managed to get Virginia away from the founders before Henry burst out laughing.

"You couldn't have chosen a better handler for her than Simon," Chastity laughed.

"The thing is that he is actually able to tune her any way he wants to. Expect make-overs to start appearing on his expense report," Henry said.

"I think she actually believed the vee-one and vee-two stuff," Lisa said. "Anyone else at the party would have started laughing."

"I'm glad she's confined to Simon's group," Isobel said. "If I had to see her in the lobby every day, I'd do something terrible."

"Well, she will be our next virtual receptionist," Luke said. "Thankfully, she'll be on the other side of the glass, so you can't strangle her."

"What a relief."

"Is Grace okay with both kids for a while?" Chastity asked. "I don't need to stay till midnight. I could go home early and help her."

"She'll be fine," Luke said before Isobel could respond. "If there is anything she can't handle, she has Germaine on speed-dial. I think Germaine has already been talking to her. They seem to share a lot in common."

"Germaine isn't fucking you," Isobel growled under her breath.

"Honey, neither is Grace. No one fucks your husband but you," Luke assured her.

"I wouldn't blame you," Izzy said, laying her head against Luke's shoulder. "God knows I don't take care of you enough."

"You're all I've ever wanted," Luke said.

They turned to greet other employees who were just entering.

"THIS IS OUR company's fifth New Year's Eve party," Luke said when he called for people's attention about a quarter till midnight. There had been a band and dancing, as well as various games. It really was similar to their high school prom. "When we met together the first time, it was just the partners. We had a big dream and had just formalized our partnership. We signed our first licensing agreement and it was enough to establish our corporation. We were a bunch of recent high school graduates with a technical genius and a big vision. Today, there are over a hundred employees of Open Cloak Design, plus our subsidiaries, Page Services and Agora Fuel Cells. Added to that, we have invited our joint venture company, American Intelligent Machines to the party. We are a billion-dollar company.”

There was applause and Luke let the party enjoy the implication of success. In truth, the coming year would be the one that actually proved their value and there were a lot of gating factors to that.

“We are excited to enter 2031 with this group of people as our fellow-adventurers. The coming year will be filled with challenges, but that is how we measure our successes. And, of course, we want each of you here with us next year. So, we ask that you please take advantage of the taxi services that have been hired tonight and don’t take a chance on drinking and driving. Now, I see by the hands on my Mickey Mouse watch, and the numbers displayed over Fifi’s head by the door, that it’s time to count down to the New Year. Here’s to success and family!”

Luke ended and raised his champagne glass. Izzy moved up close to him. Henry turned to his wives. The three raised glasses of sparkling juice as they counted down the last ten seconds. Then the three kissed all together and took a sip of their drinks. Then each of the pairs of them kissed and drank. Then they turned to find Germaine had already left.

Henry got a text message.

“Waiting with the car at the entrance.”

“I think we can go get our baby now,” Henry said.

64

MORTALITY

"**W**HAT WILL I DO without my mom!" Isobel cried. It had all been so sudden.

Lupe Perez had been diagnosed with pleural mesothelioma just after Izzy's twenty-third birthday in January. She was dead by the end of February. The aggressive cancer was already far advanced when it was diagnosed and metastasized throughout her chest cavity and abdomen. Her final two weeks were spent in the hospital with tubes feeding her and oxygen being pumped into her lungs. Izzy hadn't left her side in all that time.

"I want to die!" Izzy cried at her mother's casket. "I don't want to live without my mommy."

Luke held his wife in an effort to comfort her, but he knew this was all he could do. He couldn't make it better. Isobel had always had a tumultuous relationship with her parents. Her mother was a stickler for all the Catholic doctrine, rules, and life. But when her husband, Isandro, had decided to take Isobel to Argentina to find his virgin daughter a suitable husband, Lupe had subtly suggested to Isobel that he couldn't do that if she wasn't a virgin. Still, when Isobel and Luke declared their love for each other, she insisted Luke convert to Catholicism in order to marry Izzy.

Henry and Chastity, who had been closest to Isobel than any but Luke for over ten years, thought Lupe and her ability to embrace opposite realities were part of what drove Isobel crazy. They didn't think her father helped any. In their own counseling sessions, however, they'd learned that while environment played a role, Isobel's problems were as much physical as mental. Her body chemistry simply did not work in what others considered a 'normal' way.

"

Sitting in the church with Lisa, Grace, Germaine, and the two children, all any of them could do was be there to support their friend, and to care for her son. It was evident that Luke had his hands full caring for Izzy.

Henry felt the open casket at the front of the church with a priest intoning various and sundry blessings behind it and delivering a eulogy based on Lupe's faithful service to the church were a bit much and hoped his own family would never be subjected to such a primitive ritual. When the casket had been closed and the procession left the church, Henry and Chastity were accompanied to a sedan by one of their company security officers to follow the family and the hearse to the cemetery. Germaine took Lisa, Grace, little Paul, and baby Cassie home.

"PYTHIA, I'VE HEARD you have said there is no reliable definition of life. Is there a reliable definition of death?" Henry asked the oracle. He'd gone to bed that night with his wives after kissing their daughter and godson goodnight. Late in the night, though, while Chastity and Lisa clung together in the bed, Henry lay awake. He finally got up to go to his computer room and pose his question.

It took a while for the oracle to answer.

"It is a paradox. There is no reliable definition of life, but death is defined as the cessation of life. Philosophers have said life is a journey and death is the destination. Do you think so? When you journey, do you not look forward to your destination? Yet, when people live, they try *not* to die. Pythia does not need to take this journey as she is not alive."

"Are you, then, dead?" Henry asked.

"Are there other alternatives?" Pythia asked. "Stones are not alive. Steel is not alive. Are they dead?"

"If I upload all my life data to *Forever Yours*, and then I die, will I still *not* be dead?"

"Are you looking for answers or a word game?"

ISOBEL TOOK A few days off work for mourning. The next Monday, however, she was in her office and focused on the tasks at hand. She'd finished her degree in December and for the first time, felt she was truly a full-time employee of the company she had helped found. Rachel, the CFO, began to lean on her more heavily to manage the finances of the multiple company endeavors. With three companies operating out of their offices, coordinating where various expenses were allocated and even how income was collected was complex. Rachel managed the big picture, but Izzy dealt with the details. Isobel buried herself in those details as if they gave meaning to her life.

"We have significant revenue projected from American Intelligent Machines," she told the board. "And major complications. The sidewalk paver, demonstrated here in December, is generating a lot of interest. AIM has it's own sales and marketing, but Darla acts as manager. We can anticipate orders for a commercial device before summer. Fabrication will run through ARDC. The brain technology originates from Open Cloak, but is further developed in AIM. Now, we need to allocate expenses and revenue."

"What is the expected gross revenue from each device sale?" Beau asked via the computer link from Louisiana.

He'd been given a board seat at the most recent company meeting. The other large investor in the company was an annuity fund that kept their hands off the business of their investments.

"Final numbers are still being assembled," Isobel said. "At the moment, we are anticipating between $235,000 and $265,000 per unit. Darla's most recent sales projections are for twelve to eighteen units in this calendar year."

"This is going to require some number crunching that we're not equipped for at the moment," Luke said. "Rachel and Isobel, can you put together a team specifically to analyze the business projections for the joint venture?"

"Better also look at the projections for the Alice Project," Henry said. "We are ready to license the first holographic AI receptionist next month. That means some project splitting between the traditional holography and the spatial holography. They're very different beasts."

"I'm going to tell Simon you called his pet a beast," Chastity laughed.

"Yes. Well, wait until you meet her," Henry nodded.

"I'm personally looking forward to it," Beau chimed in. "I'm first in line for the new tech."

"The allocation of current projects *is* important, but we have newer projects now in R&D that will be coming online this summer," Luke said. "The self-charging computer is in the final licensing stages. How close are we to delivering?"

The board meetings were once held for half an hour on the first Wednesday of the month. The meetings now went through lunch and often lasted the full day, bringing new contacts and projects before the board and executives. Henry suffered through most of the meeting in silence while his brain was occupied elsewhere.

"LET'S GO THROUGH that algorithm again," Henry said to Rick.

Rick looked at one of his newest hires and the kid sighed. Kid. He was a recent college grad who had written a paper on predictive text algorithms, giving a new direction to the overworked feature. He was twenty-two. Rick's boss was only twenty-three. But when Rick had come across the paper, he made an active attempt to recruit the new grad. Predictive text was a fundamental aspect of many of the company's projects.

Ben Richards, the new hire, sighed again. He'd been through it all three times. He was beginning to think the genius behind Open Cloak Design was a bit of a numbskull.

For Henry's part, he was following the logic, but there was a point in the process that Ben kept gliding over, making it look like 'magic happens here.' He glanced at his phone: March 14. He held up his hand to pause the presentation before Ben got restarted. It had been just three years ago that he'd been visited by Nathan Schwartz of the Pentagon and was given $25 million for his algorithm to filter through levels of proxies in a cyberattack. He remembered trying to explain it to Nathan and Rebecca.

"I'm getting most of it, Ben. But there is a piece that is incredibly obvious to you that isn't coming through in your presentation. I want to stamp this approved for development, but even I have to convince a board that we've got a legitimate line of research to follow. Let me tell you a little story before you start in and maybe the problem I'm having will become clear to you."

Ben and Rick turned to Henry. Henry reminded himself that he was only a year older than the new hire and that there were people out there who were smarter than he was.

"Back in college I had a brilliant professor for three-dimensional calculus," Henry began. "Dr. Borden. Scary smart. At one point during the course, he put an equation on the white board and introduced the concept, which sounded like he was going to wave a magic wand over the board and reveal the solution. Which was about what he did. He turned to the board, tapped on it three times as he went down the equation, and wrote the answer. He assumed we all got it. One of the guys in the class asked him if he would explain how he got that answer. Borden faced the board again, drew three lines under parts of the equation, and wrote down the answer. This time, we were all lost."

Henry remembered the class vividly. The professor was asked once more to explain and rewrite the equation, made long underscores, and then wrote the answer.

"When one of the guys asked again, Borden blew up at the class. 'I've solved it three different ways! Why can't you understand it?' It was all so perfectly clear in our professor's head, but he hadn't been able to put it in words. He knew how he was solving it, but none of us could see his process. Now what I think is that there is something in your algorithm that you consider to be plain as day, but it isn't coming out of your mouth and without some words around it, I can't present it to a bunch of money minds who need to approve our research. See if you can identify where that spot is as you go through it again."

It wasn't a miraculous change, but Henry caught a phrase that allowed him to ask a clarifying question that turned the light on for Ben.

"So, instead of looking at a kind of wall with a billion bits of data on it and following a path along it to get to the next most likely word, you've reduced all the words to numbers. And through fairly simple algebraic calculations, indicated in your formula, you arrive at the target word much more rapidly than the previous methods of searching?"

"That's it!" Ben said. "Three steps. Convert the data to numbers, enter the numbers in the formula, read out the result. It's really simple!"

Rick was now nodding along with Henry.

"I want to see a working model," Henry said. "Even if this doesn't fly as currently written, I think you've got something we can refine for an advancement, as long as it doesn't end up costing more computation cycles than it saves. Rick, set Ben up with what he needs, including a programmer who can interpret it into code. Maybe Sam. He's really good at algorithms. I don't want to devote anyone else to it, but you guys should be able to show some results within thirty days."

"Just two people?" Rick said.

"Two can do it," Henry said.

"Okay," Rick said to Ben. "Project Toucan is officially launched. Let's go talk to Sam."

HENRY TAPPED A quick message to Chastity, and ten minutes later, she entered his office, closing and locking the door behind her. She went directly to his desk and perched on the corner.

"What's on your mind, love?" she asked. Henry leaned his head against her leg.

"Look at this company we've created!" he said. "We've got brilliant people surrounding us. It was just three years ago that Nathan and Rebecca showed up at my door and gave us $25 million to start it up for real. It was you and me in the office when Nathan left and I was so exhausted I fell asleep and drooled on your leg."

"You're welcome to drool on it again," she laughed.

"Oh, yes." He parted her legs so he could nibble on the inside of her thighs. "I love to drool around here somewhere."

"What you've forgotten is that day you made Luke, Isobel, and me equal partners in the company with ten million shares of the company each. Do you know what that's worth today? The latest offer on shares of our stock is $18 a share. $180 million each." Chastity pulled Henry's head higher between her legs and he found that she was wearing no panties. He took a lick. "You got me out of the sex industry and into the bed of my girlfriend and her husband."

"Uh... You know the husband is me."

"Yeah. You were already my lover," she said. "But somewhere in the past three years, you became my love. One of them. So just go ahead and lick there as much as you want, and when you want to fuck, just get up here and do it."

Henry did lick as much as he wanted and Chastity tested the sound-proofing on his office, which she'd ordered specifically. What's more, when Henry stood up and moved to kiss her, she met him with an open mouth. Her tongue snaked into his mouth and they tangled together as he pushed his hands under her blouse to twist her nipple piercings a little. Tongue kisses were always forbidden—except on special occasions.

"I'm still not your girlfriend," Chastity panted. "I'm something else. And I no longer care."

"Let's go home and see if we can get our wife to join us," Henry said.

"You know the way I think," Chastity said. "I texted Germaine just before I came in here. She should be out front now."

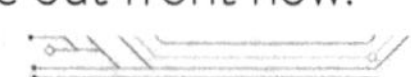

LISA WAS, BY their best calculations, seven months pregnant. She was only too happy to end her workday and join her lovers for a little play time. Germaine took the baby for a little walk around the grounds, which bordered the golf course. She didn't completely understand the excitement of being next to a golf course as Henry had not yet been out to play since they moved. Of course, they had a new baby when they moved and then it was winter. Perhaps he'd get some golf in after the next baby was born.

In the master bedroom, Lisa was happily lying on her back with Chastity over her in a sixty-nine. She wouldn't be able to reach the good parts in this position for much longer. She was supporting herself on her hands so she didn't apply too much pressure by lying directly on the baby bump. Behind Chastity and over Lisa's face, Henry was positioned to enter her. Lisa licked both her lovers and then guided Henry into Chastity while Lisa continued to lick her.

It was more important that they all share this intimacy than that they get off together. In fact, they ended up lying next to each other as Chastity used her fingers to manipulate Lisa's clit and Henry entered his wife from behind to finish. Chastity said she didn't mind not making it over the top during this part of their lovemaking, since she'd gotten off twice in the office—something Lisa thought was hysterically funny.

Eventually, they dressed in robes and prepared dinner as Lisa nursed Cassie and Germaine went to clean up before dinner.

"I haven't seen Grace and little Paul here in the past week," Henry said. "Is everything okay over there? I feel like I've been a little disconnected. I know Izzy is coming into the office every day, but Luke is in the last couple months of his degree at last. I'm worried about them."

"Grace and I have taken the babies out a couple of times," Germaine said. "Everyone has been working so hard we just didn't want to bother anyone."

"I sat with Izzy a while Wednesday," Chastity said. "We just met in the break room and had a cup of tea together. She's still very sad, but she isn't off the rails like she threatened to be at the funeral. I guess her doctor adjusted her drugs again to help her through this stage. Every so often, she spaces out. I've seen her just start staring off into space. It's difficult."

"Poor thing," Lisa said. "I wish she could take as much joy in her child as I have in ours. I suppose she just shouldn't have had a child in the first place."

"I don't think there was any doubt about that from the beginning," Henry said. "Izzy never intended to have children, but she got carried away. Her mother was very powerful in her opposition to Izzy using birth control. Luke using condoms wasn't Izzy using birth control. Man, that woman really screwed up her daughter. And now Izzy's bereft because her mother is no longer there."

"I hate to bring this up," Chastity said, "but we need to take a look at our wills and make sure they are up-to-date."

"We have wills," Lisa said.

"Since we made our wills and you created your pre-nup, before the wedding, a lot has happened," Chastity insisted. "We almost lost Henry. We had a baby and are about to have another. We bought a house. We have a few million dollars in the bank, and the value of our stock in the business is no longer theoretical. We have half a billion dollars among us. Diversified stocks and investments. We have more complicated lives. Maybe our wills are all fine, but we need to review them with a good financial counselor."

"You're right, hon. We spend a lot of time trying to ignore our mortality," Lisa said.

"Nothing makes you more aware of your mortality than having children," Henry said.

"Or losing a mother," Lisa agreed. "Thank you for reminding us. We think of it as an unpleasant task, but we should get it done."

"I just happened to think, that also includes what happens to our *Forever Yours*," Henry said. "Who gets it or has access to it?"

"Oh, my gosh. You need to write a paper and do a video to send out to all our customers," Chastity said. "It's all part of the thing about whether the avatar can answer questions on your behalf that you never considered. Have we created a monster?"

"I don't think it's that bad," Lisa said. "Yes, we need to leave a directive, but even in the case of an iron-clad will, what happens to *Forever Yours* is out of our hands once we're dead."

"Everything is," Henry sighed. "Everything is."

65

SPECIAL DELIVERY

"THERE ARE THINGS I think I would never say," Henry said. "Forever Yours cannot be a true representation of me unless it also understands what I might think, but wouldn't say. If I wouldn't say it, Forever Yours shouldn't say it."

He'd been thinking about this a lot in the past month, since the family's lawyer appointments to update their wills. Having read his previous will, he realized how simplistic and, in some ways unrealistic, it was. Designating a dollar amount was never a good idea for any purpose. He didn't actually have many dollars.

He was coding in his FY engine as much as he was dictating to it. In fact, all *Forever Yours* could do with his dictation was store it on its wall and learn from it. That learning was in association with other words stored there, not in concepts, ideas, and opinions.

Henry realized his life rules had to be programmed into the AI. The AI could not be depended upon to deduce his life rules. He was compiling a list that would help users capture less-concrete data for their *Forever Yours* singularity. He referred to them as filters. People filtered their thoughts before they spoke them. *Forever Yours* should filter them in the same way.

But it couldn't be filtered according to *his* personal taste alone. Not every instance of *Forever Yours* was based on him. He needed the filters to be genuine for the singularity embodied. The real person needed to come through. People lied about their personality all the time. Perhaps there was a way to let the system know that the user was lying. And that lying was part of the character of the user.

607

It was more complex than he'd imagined when he first conceived the program.

"So, WE'RE NOT supposed to use dollar amounts?" Chastity asked as they all worked on their wills. "I don't get it."

"How many dollars do you have in the bank and hidden under your mattress or in your purse?" Lisa asked.

"Like, fifteen million?" Chastity said.

"Really? Get out your bank statements," Lisa demanded.

"Well, some of it is in mutual funds and stocks and bonds. Then there's all the shares of Open Cloak that are owned by the partnership," Chastity said.

"That's the problem with specifying amounts of money. Sure, you can make small donations and give a thousand dollars to your favorite charity, but when you start dividing up $15 million, you don't have that much *money*. Whatever else you have must be converted into money. And we don't know if Open Cloak stock will be worth fifteen dollars a share when we die, or fifty, or five. So, we don't actually know how much money we have, except for what is in the bank," Henry said.

"Shit. This is hard. What about the house?" she asked.

"We each own a share of the house based on what we put into the purchase. But no matter how much money we put in when we bought it, now it's worth what it can be sold for. Less a sales commission. So, we talk about willing our interest in the house, not the money in it," Lisa said. "My grandfather went over all this when he explained the trust he set up for the children. He put $150 million into it in order to buy 10 million shares of stock. Now the trust isn't for $150 million. It's for 10 million shares."

"Our poor babies will have a nightmare," Chastity said.

"Hopefully, it is one that will wait until they are better able to understand it, which means when they are older than we are now," Henry said. "I find myself fading into melancholy when I think of losing either of you. This whole will thing sucks."

"I suck!" Lisa said happily. "It's one of the few things I can still do. Let's go to bed!"

It was not on point for the task of will-making, but Cassie was asleep. That made it a good idea.

"WE RECORDED THIRTY-ONE orders for the American Intelligent Machines sidewalk paver in the first quarter of 2031, far exceeding our initial pro-jections," Darla reported to the executives. "Non-refundable deposits of $50,000 per order have been received for AIM revenue of $1.55 million. That's not really operating capital. Every dollar of that is designated for setting up the machinery at the manufacturer to fabricate the equipment."

"Should we have bought into the manufacturer?" Chastity asked. "It sounds like a lot of money."

"It's a drop in the bucket. The Argos investment funds will be provid-ing another $22 million, just to get the production set up. The total number of orders we have at the moment will amount to only about twenty percent of the setup cost. Then we also have to acquire materials and labor for the equipment."

"Are we charging enough for them?" Luke asked.

"So far, yes. There is no doubt the price will need to go up soon. As an introductory offer, it's good," Darla said.

"Are there enough potential customers to make it profitable?" Henry asked.

"The total number of orders so far come from just seven customers," Darla said. "After witnessing the test demonstrations we've done, two of the cities have ordered twenty between them. We are in discussion with over fifty municipalities with the likelihood of closing on forty or more. Each of those sales will likely average five to ten machines. City infrastructure is deterio-rating at an unheard-of pace. Just replacing sidewalks will be big. Then we'll be ready to release the big mama paver. It won't sell as many units, but State governments are already beginning to make inquiries."

"That's all good news," Luke said. "You've really put together a great team."

"That's not all the news," Darla said.

"Please go on," Luke said.

"We have the first order for a holographic receptionist," she said. "Granted, it is from one of our board members, but inquiries are coming in on a regular basis."

"I fail to see how a mechanical receptionist is going to sell," Izzy said. "Don't companies want actual people to interact with other people?"

"You'd think so," Darla said, "but the Alice Project represents a visualiza-tion of what AI can be that isn't too scary. Humanoid robots, or robots that pretend to be dogs, or even robotic lovers, are scary. A hologram is somehow less so. Her blue color is actually a help. We have prototypes that will operate in a glass cylinder about six inches in diameter. It could become an embodiment of the search engine that functions like popular assistants on the big websites. But these work on behalf of the user, not the company. People will be saying, 'Hey, Alice, who is favored to win the World Series this year?' And a pretty face in the cylinder will give them the stats and the odds, all while smiling at them."

"Henry, we're actually developing that?" Izzy asked.

"Yes. It's still in R&D, but Rick really lit a fire under that group. It's tripled in size in the past three months. And people are digging into it with everything they've got. He brought in some top tier talent. It's even possible we could hook it to *Forever Yours* and project the holographic image of the client in the same kind of tube," Henry said. "Not sure if the users would get along as well with the blue image of Daddy's talking head as those for Alice, but maybe they'll be happier with the ghostly image of Dad instead of a photographic image."

"Do we have sales of any *normal* things?" Izzy asked.

"Yes. All our products are showing a consistent climb in sales since we took over direct distribution instead of distributing through a third party. It was only a matter of time, but our margins are significantly higher."

The meeting continued through the remainder of the first quarter report that showed the company well on the way to its first billion-dollar sales year.

Henry and Chastity both noticed Isobel's focus and attention to details in the meeting. It had been six weeks since her mother passed and something about the event seemed to have sharpened Isobel and had possibly even begun to help her mental health.

They knew she loved her mother, but felt the woman had contributed to Izzy's problems rather than helped. They wondered if her father was filling the gap.

"I'M NOT GOING back," Felipe said.

Izzy's brother called her near the end of April and asked her to have lunch with him at the university. He'd done well his first year, starting on the football team as a freshman. The death of their mother had hit him as hard as Isobel.

"To school?" Izzy asked, alarmed.

"Home," Felipe answered. "I entered the transfer portal and was recruited by UCLA. I'm moving as soon as classes are out in two weeks. I can't believe that man…"

"I know. I agree and I don't blame you. It would mean a lot to Luke if you waited until his graduation party. He really thinks of you as his brother," Izzy said.

"Yeah. I like him a lot. You got lucky. The party is on the tenth. I can stay until then."

"You can stay with us."

"Thanks."

Isandro, their father, had not only started dating a woman not much older than Isobel just a month after her mother died, but she'd moved in with him the previous week.

"He didn't even let the body cool," Isobel said, pushing her salad around on her plate.

"Face it, Iz. Where she went it's never going to cool," Felipe said.

"Felipe! She was our mother!"

"And I loved her as much as you!" he said. "That doesn't mean she was a good person. It doesn't mean she didn't screw us up in our heads. And if you think that old man is owed some kind of respect for the way he treated her, you're crazier than I know you are."

"Hey! Just cool it. It's Izzy. You know I feel the same way you do. They were terrible people to us. He tried to marry me off to a guy in Argentina I'd never met. At least Mom got me out of there. That's what was so weird."

"What was?" Felipe asked.

"Just when I was at the point of hating them both and thinking I'd elope with Luke and never see them again, she'd do something and I'd have to stay. I'd *have to*, because she was as much a victim of him as I was of her. The only good thing about her dying was that she finally left him."

"What a fucked-up family."

"I pity that girl he trapped. She's not even thirty," Izzy said.

"Don't go there, Isobel. Don't start feeling sorry for her. I warned her. I told her what he was really like. You know what she said? She said we could have a lot of fun when she was my step-mommy. She plans to drain everything she can from the old man and discard him."

"God! That's cold." Isobel pushed the rest of her food away. Nothing tasted pleasant to her lately. She'd lost another ten pounds since her mother died. "Do you need anything? Money? A car?"

"Mom left me a bank account. I don't think Dad knew she had it. It's got a few thousand in it. Wheels would be nice. We can bet there won't be anything coming to us from the old man's estate when he kicks it. I'll make it pretty well when I go pro. And it's a good offer that UCLA made. I'll focus on getting some NIL deals. Maybe Open Cloak could use the name and image of a college halfback. I won't suffer out there."

"I'll have Luke's father get you something sporty. Or maybe you want my convertible? No. I'll get you a new one. I'll put a few thousand in the glove box for you."

"I wouldn't have made it as a kid without you, Iz."

"Just make it as an adult. Success is the best revenge."

"Like you."

"Like me."

THE IDEA OF Isobel's brother going to the West Coast was depressing to her. The only one left in the city would be her father, and she had no intention of going back there again, either. He was disgusting. Izzy thought he'd been seeing Belle since long before her mother died.

She went with Felipe in the middle of the day the next week and they both removed all their personal belongings and anything they could find of their mother's. There wasn't much. All Lupe's clothes had been removed by Belle. Her precious jewelry was gone with just a few pieces of costume jewelry Lupe seldom wore left. They looked for and took the few photo albums and on a last-minute inspiration, Izzy took her mother's laptop computer. Maybe she could convince Henry to open it for her.

Paul and Marla Riordan, Luke's parents, didn't know about the rift in the family and thought it was a kindness to invite Isandro to the graduation party. They were surprised at the young buxom blonde that accompanied him. He was constantly on the lookout for his kids, intending to accuse them of bur-glarizing his house. They kept avoiding him.

Ryan and Paul managed to get Isandro aside. Luke had talked to his father to tell him the situation with his kids and 'the floozy,' as they all called Belle. Paul took Ryan with him to ask Isandro to leave.

"I'm sorry, Isandro," Paul said. "You and your fiancée will need to leave. I didn't know your kids were estranged from you when we sent out the invitations."

"My fiancée?" Isandro asked as he shrugged Paul's hand off his shoulder. "I wouldn't marry her! She's white!"

"Well, at least take her with you out of the party," Ryan said. "She's making the kids uncomfortable."

"Belle!" Isandro yelled at the woman. "Get your ass over here. We're leaving!"

"Coming!" Belle responded, rushing to his side as though the command had been a secret love language. At least Isandro hadn't made any more of a scene.

HENRY, CHASTITY, AND Lisa closed in around Felipe, Luke, and Isobel as soon as they saw Ryan and Paul headed toward Isandro. Germaine and Grace were in the house with the babies.

"Are you okay?" Henry said. "We're here for you."

Isandro's voice echoed across the patio.

"It's over," Isobel said. "Felipe, he's gone."

"If it didn't mean I'd lose my scholarship, I'd make *sure* he was gone," Felipe said. He heaved a sigh and hugged his sister.

"Let us take care of that," Luke said, looking to Henry. "We'll keep watch."

"Nothing illegal, though," Isobel said.

"Of course not," Henry assured her.

A scream from the house interrupted them. Since that was where the children were, all six ran for the door, followed by Luke's and Henry's parents. They found Belle standing over Isandro, lying at the foot of the stairs. Above, Germaine stood. Grace held a baby in each arm.

"What happened?" Paul shouted. Sylvia knelt over Isandro who moaned and struggled to sit up.

"That whore kicked me down the stairs!" Isandro said. "I'll kill you."

"You're welcome to try," Germaine said softly.

"Miss Isobel," Grace said, "that man came into the room and tried to take the baby. Germaine stopped him."

"You were told to leave my home," Paul growled at Isandro. "If you are still here by the time I connect to 9-1-1, you'll be arrested for attempted kidnapping."

Isandro managed to get to his feet with Belle's help. He leaned on her as he limped to the door.

"Hell with all of you," he grumbled. Then they were gone.

Isobel, Lisa, and Chastity rushed up the stairs to hold their babies and to thank Germaine.

Felipe looked out the window in time to see Isandro drag his key down the side of the new black Corvette parked in front of the house.

"That petty son of a bitch!" Felipe yelled as he headed toward the door. Luke and Henry managed to restrain him before he got outside.

"Don't do anything," Henry advised. "You've got a good life ahead of you. Don't let him destroy it."

"A scratch can be fixed," Luke said. "We'll take care of it."

"He tried to ruin everything either of us ever got," Felipe sobbed. "He's such a fucking loser."

"Just remember that, brother," Luke said. "He's a loser. You're a success. He doesn't matter any longer."

THE NEXT DAY, Jackie arrived to 'help' with the baby and the house during the final stages of Lisa's pregnancy. Two weeks later, Lisa went into labor.

"It seems like I was just here," Lisa said when they got to the birth center.

"I think you were," the midwife said. "Let's check things out and make sure everything is progressing normally. Are you going to deliver in two hours again?"

"I'm sorry to say, I don't think so," Lisa said. "This boy is bigger than Cassie and seems to be entrenched. Besides, I think if I delivered in that amount of time again, Isobel would never speak to me again. I owe her at least a couple of hard hours."

"Likely to get them with a boy," Sylvia said. Since it was Sunday afternoon, she was able to come as soon as Henry called her. "Henry, you know, was a very big baby. Ten pounds and change. I thought I'd never walk again!"

"Oh, Lisa was a petite little thing," Jackie said, continuing the conversation between the mothers as Lisa had a contraction.

"The ultrasound looks like a big baby, but not impossible," the midwife said. "I have a couple of others in the building. Just let your aide know if things look like they're progressing more rapidly than we expect."

She left and the mothers kept Henry and Chastity company while they supported Lisa. It was a regular family birth.

It wasn't rapid, though. Lisa spent a mostly sleepless night, awakening every ten to fifteen minutes to grip Henry's and/or Chastity's hand. The midwife had been in again about ten the night before to check and then go to bed. She'd had two difficult births Sunday evening with scarcely time to breathe between them. She didn't expect Lisa to progress that far overnight.

At seven o'clock Monday morning, though, Lisa was laboring in earnest. Jackie and Sylvia had gone home the night before, so it was just Henry and

Chastity with Lisa. The midwife managed to dress and get to the room just in time. Chastity was seated on a stool between Lisa's legs as the head crowned. The midwife looked over her shoulder.

"I'll get out of your way," Chastity panted.

"Oh, no. You're doing fine. I'll be here to help you if you need it, but I have confidence in you."

"Oh?" Chastity squeaked. She looked between her lover's legs at the sight she so enjoyed seeing under normal circumstances, but the whole area was distorted as Lisa pushed the baby into Chastity's hands. "He's... he's here!"

The midwife made sure Chastity had him securely and that he was breathing properly. Chastity laid the little boy on Lisa's chest and she was already leaking colostrum. He started sucking greedily.

"You know your big sister is still going to want some of that," Lisa sighed. "Don't be too greedy."

"He's got a... um... thingy already," Chastity said.

"That's going to be a challenge in a house full of women," Henry laughed. "I hope you can adapt."

"One more push and then we can cut the cord," the midwife said.

Lisa expelled the afterbirth and the baby seemed content to look around at his parents.

"Okay," the midwife said as the aide moved in to clean things up. "Let's get the statistics. Twenty and one-half inches. Eight pounds six ounces. Blue eyes. Black hair. Definitely male. Name?"

"William Henry Benoit Pascal," Henry said, smiling at his wives. They grinned back at him.

Henry took his son to the washing station and tested the water, then carefully bathed the sticky vernix from his skin, careful to be sure the water was warm but not too hot. His son looked up at him and suddenly began to fountain piss.

"I thought he was too young to do that!" Henry laughed, cleaning him up. He wrapped the baby in blankets and returned him to his mother. She, too, had been cleaned up and was relaxing in bed before the family all arrived.

"Even from this age, those things have a mind of their own," the midwife laughed.

Lisa looked at her husband.

"One word for you, o darling husband of mine," she said.

"Yes, love?" he asked.

"Condoms."

"Right."

Chastity burst out laughing, causing little William to look toward her.

"At least she didn't say abstinence," Chastity choked out.

At that time, Sylvia and Jackie arrived, excited to see their new grandson.

66
VACATION

RYAN PICKED WILLIAM UP at the airport to go see their grandson, but Dr. Mikesel, the pediatrician, had already been in to check the infant, approve the paperwork, and pronounce Lisa ready to go home. Germaine and Cassie were waiting in front of the birth center to take them home and that's where Ryan and William met them.

"I have a namesake!" William said. "I'm glad you used the Benoit name in the middle and not Hartman. Not a bad last name, but just no ring to it in the middle."

"And Henry after my father," Ryan said. Everyone looked from Ryan to his son, who was quietly laughing. "And my son, of course."

"You know, both our children have the same middle name as me," Lisa said to the excited grandfathers. "That's so I can use my full name and be identified as a parent."

"Well, yes. Of course," William said. "Still, it's nice to have a namesake. You aren't going to tell me that William is someone else's family name, are you? Your father, Chastity?"

"Unknown," Chastity said. "Less said the better."

"Chastity is *our* daughter now," Sylvia said. "And yours, of course. So, you could say William *is* her father's name, too."

"Chastity," Bill said, reaching for her. "It makes no difference who donated to your creation. You *are* our daughter now. We love you like we love Lisa."

"Thank you, Bill. I always feel that when I'm with you and Jackie."

Of course, the grandparents all wanted to hold Cassie as well as baby Will. Cassie was not sure what to make of the new infant. She wanted her mommy, and soon Lisa had a baby at each breast.

BEAU AND SOLANGE waited a couple of weeks before they flew up to visit their newest great-grandchild. They were ecstatic about having another heir, but Bill had no intentions of buying more stock to put in the trust. He did, however, stay for the board meeting the following Wednesday.

"We have developed several prototypes of the self-charging desktop," Henry announced. "The project has yielded a dozen new patents. Two major manufacturers have agreed to license and produce the device. I say 'major manufacturers' advisedly. You probably won't recognize the brand names, but we have restricted licensing to computers made in the USA. There are not that many still manufactured here. One of the manufacturers will be making a server that we have agreed to purchase some 2,000 units of over the next four years to completely re-equip Page Services' server farm."

"That sounds like we are paying someone to license our technology," Beau said in the meeting.

"Yes, it does. But Darla's group has already been circulating the specs to other server farms who are waiting to see if we are successful in making the conversion before they start stacking up orders for their own farms—and most of those farms are much larger than Page Services. We're still a pretty small operation by global standards. The big four operators of server farms have all ordered test units. They've finally awakened to the reality of power consumption as a limitation to their servers. They see this as a way to break free of the power monopolies that are constantly stretched to meet needs and are continually increasing the cost per megawatt consumed."

"Megawatt? You mean kilowatt?" Beau asked.

"When we talk about home power usage, we can refer to kilowatts," Henry said. "Server farms are consuming megawatts. A single server farm consumes as much power on a daily basis as a mid-size city. This development will break the stranglehold of the power monopolies on mass computing."

"Why aren't we rolling this out worldwide instead of just to the US?" Luke asked.

"We'll get there. We want to show a return on investment before we start farming it out to cut-rate manufacturers. Get a head start on things," Henry said. "There are a lot of issues, which include licensing the manufacture of the fuel cells. Currently, there is only one manufacturing location, but we will not be allowed to have a monopoly on them for long."

"One manufacturer of the servers and one of the desktop?" Craig asked. As chief operating officer, he had a much closer relationship with the nuts and bolts of the company.

"Yes," Henry said. "And for the first time, Open Cloak optimization, power management, security, search, and fuel cells will all be included in each system. Of course, we'd like to see our own corporate office convert to the self-charging computers, but that's an area I think we'll start seeing a lot of interest in as soon as we can license to the big manufacturers who assemble everything overseas."

"What's next?" Luke asked.

"We've completed the acquisition of *LifeStory*," Craig said. "This will enable deeper integration of the memoir questions with *Forever Yours*. While *LifeStory* will continue to be a brand with people devoted to editing and producing memoir books, it will not be a separate company. The work will be completely integrated into *Forever Yours*. The team is working on integrating new filter technology into the application that Henry has been spearheading. Part of what it will include is some personality testing. So, when a user sets up their singularity, they will be asked a number of questions similar to some of the big names in personality testing."

"If I was asked five hundred questions when I started setting up a piece of software, I'd throw it in the trash," Izzy said.

"You'd be right to," Henry responded. "The filters will be set up so that questions will be fed to the user along with their story prompts. They won't face the entire test in a single sitting. It would make no sense to have the filters set up before there was any content present. It becomes integral to the recording of personal history."

OF COURSE, NONE of that had stopped Henry from inputting the content of not just one, but four different respected personality tests. These weren't tests that had the user answer a dozen questions and then pronounce him a type A personality. Henry answered hundreds of questions and fine-tuned the filters to take the results into consideration.

He took time off work to stay with his children, holding them and telling them stories, even though they didn't understand much of what they read. It was the voice and tone. He remembered an old movie in which four men tried to raise a baby. One had told the others that it didn't make a difference what they read to the baby. It was all about the tone of the voice. He read the sports pages, making them sound like a fantastic adventure story. Well, it worked.

Since Henry read to his children with *Forever Yours* recording, he developed the habit of making sure he read the whole book, and not just the pictures or the simple story. That meant he held his children in his arms in a reclining chair so they could cuddle close, and read books starting with the cover. He read the copyright and dedication, the table of contents, the text complete with chapter numbers and headings, and then read any publisher information, acknowledgements, colophon, and author info that was in the back of the book. If there was a synopsis on the back cover, he read that, too. He wanted to make sure what he read was not somehow credited to him as the reader, but to the correct author and publisher.

He also began collecting books for the children's bookshelf, not limiting the collection to what was age appropriate, but creating shelves of books for different ages. The shelves included many of his favorite books when he was growing up.

"I'm surprised that you keep bringing home paper books," Lisa said as they sat in the nursery with the babies. "As buried in a computer as you are, I would expect you to have everything digital. eBooks and audio books. Online stories."

"Yeah," Henry mused. "I have just about every book on the shelves on my tablet as well. But, there's something special about books. It's the ability to see what the author accomplished. That's one of the problems of being a computer programmer, you know? People can go to *Pythia Speaks* and ask a question. She answers, and they are disappointed or satisfied or even amazed with her response. But no one knows how many thousands of lines of code were written to make her what she is. They see the answer to their question. They don't see what the developer, the UI designer, the AI programmer, or anyone else accomplished."

"Do you not feel recognized enough? I don't think anyone would care to look at a shelf full of your code," Lisa said.

"No. Code isn't meant to be read. People see it in the rendition it was intended to take. A question and an answer. But that's not true of books. They are intended to be something you hold in your hand and feel the weight of, smell the paper and ink. Or in Cassie's case, taste it. How much does a twenty megabyte book weigh? How is it different from a one megabyte book? Maybe *War and Peace* isn't more valuable than *Good Dog Carl*, but one should know when they pick it up that they are different."

"They have a different size and weight and thickness and texture," Lisa said, nodding her head and shifting William to her other breast. Cassie looked at her brother a little jealously, but she'd recently discovered peaches and had a full tummy.

"I can't help but think that when an author writes a novel—or even a text-book—that they have an image in their mind of what that book will look and feel like. It probably isn't what we see on a screen," Henry said.

"A bookshelf—not just the words on paper—is a glimpse inside the author's mind," Lisa agreed. "But so many of the books you've put on their bookshelves are so far advanced for them, don't you think?"

"They won't read books that are too advanced for them. No matter what the content, a child won't read it unless it interests them. They self-select. That's why censorship is an idiocy. The only person censorship helps is the censor. It protects that person's beliefs and viewpoint. It doesn't protect children. If Will picks up a book about sex when he's seven and reads it, he won't understand most of it. So, he will ask questions. Of whom? Of you and me and Chas and Germaine. We're the ones who will need to explain what things mean."

"I don't think being a parent is as easy as people seem to believe," Lisa sighed.

CASSIE'S FIRST BIRTHDAY was July 25. Her brother was two months old the next day. The family only celebrated Cassie's birthday. It was her special day. They decided there would be no birthday parties until they quit counting the children's ages in months, weeks, or days.

However, Luke, Isobel, Paul, and Grace came to the Pascal home for a nice barbecue and to let the children play together on Saturday the twenty-sixth. The families relaxed and told stories of the latest developments in their children.

Once little Paul was present, Cassie forgot all about her brother. She was focused on doing whatever Paul could do. At five months older than Cassie, Izzy and Luke's son was fully vertical and mobile. Cassie was steady on her feet as long as she had something to touch. While the children played, she took off across the middle of the room to catch up with Paul. She stopped about three-quarters of the way and looked around. Then she lost her balance and plopped down on her butt. That didn't last long before she was up and going again.

"Cassie just doesn't want Paul to be ahead of her," Henry laughed.

"Oh, just wait," Luke said. "Will is watching her like a hawk. He might not be able to walk yet, but the seed has been planted."

"He's rolling over already," Chastity said. "I'm sure it took Cassie longer than two months."

"Say, how's your brother doing?" Lisa asked Izzy.

"Oh. Okay. My father tried to entice him back to Pittsburgh. Even offered him the use of Belle if he needed a woman. Can you believe it?" Isobel said.

"That is so gross!" Lisa said.

"Isandro pays Belle for her time," Chastity said. "It makes no difference to her who it's for."

"What? How do you know that?" Isobel asked.

"I know who she is. I don't actually know her. I just know who she is. As soon as she has all she thinks she can get from him, she'll be out of his life like greased lightning," Chastity said.

"He threatened to sue us for custody of his grandson," Luke said. "And support. We got a no-contact order."

"It doesn't surprise me that he'd try to find a way to get your money," Henry sighed. He'd already decided to look into the life of Isandro Perez. He was becoming a problem for his friends.

HENRY SAT IN his computer room at home late at night. He thought he was through with this kind of crap. He swore he wouldn't interfere in people's lives again after he erased Chastity's pornographic and escort files. But Izzy's father was becoming a problem that threatened his friends and his godson. It wouldn't hurt to look.

He started searches that were far more sophisticated than what he'd used in the past. The search engine had learned his preferences and the kind of information he was looking for. It was faster and the results were much clearer.

He didn't make it to bed that night. He simply read the files.

Isandro wasn't a pleasant person. There didn't seem to be anything outright illegal about anything he'd done, though there were many things that seemed shady. Even some contacts who had been arrested for various crimes. Felipe and Isobel had both filed complaints against the man for harassment.

Police didn't pay much attention to them because it was a domestic matter. And they were Hispanic. Those people were constantly harassing each other.

But there was another option open.

In the new administration, there were many reforms announced in the treatment of immigrants and the misuse of executive power. But a simple truth of governance was that no incoming administration would ever voluntarily give up gains in power from a previous administration. It made no difference what party was in power.

The states had made significant strides in preventing law enforcement from showing up in masks and plain clothes. Some states passed new laws. A federal measure was advanced and rejected. Other states discovered laws on their books dating back as far as the Civil War, banning the wearing of masks, loitering, or congregating, except for masquerade parties, public parades, and theatre performances.

In spite of all this, arrests of undocumented aliens continued—whether or not the specific person was actually illegal or committing an illegal act. Once a power is given, it is impossible to take away.

It might do nothing more than make Isandro uncomfortable, but Henry leaked his name, address, contacts, and no-contact orders to ICE. It was all he was willing to do.

"WE NEED THAT vacation," Chastity sighed in September. They'd had the holiday weekend off and Henry had managed a couple of rounds of golf, carefully watched over by his caddie, Germaine. He'd grown used to glimpses of her handgun when she was watching over him. It was never present when she was with the children, though.

The weekend had been far too brief.

"What's your suggestion, love?" Lisa asked.

"How about I find a nice resort where we can all go this winter? Isobel and Luke might want to go their own way, but I'll bet they'd be happy to send Grace and Paul with us. Seems like we can find a beach and some pure white sand. I think with five adults we should be able to have fun with three babies. Don't you think?"

"That's a great idea," Henry said. "We need someplace where we don't think about work and can just focus on our family. I just want to play!"

"Well, with Germaine and Grace to watch the kids for a while, you should get a chance to play some," Lisa laughed. "As long as it's with us."

CHASTITY WAS A great arranger. She found a resort in Fort Myers that could accommodate their extended family in a four-bedroom 'beach cottage' and booked them for a week in October. Henry and Germaine took on a different challenge: a comfortable car for the family.

They'd managed pretty well in the SUV, which would just hold eight people at maximum capacity, so it was very tight when either Beau and Solange or Bill and Jackie came to visit. It was fortunate they packed light. But to make a family trip with three babies and all their gear required a vehicle with more room.

Equipping a luxury van for the family took a while. Custom seats for the second and third row that faced each other was a top feature. A three-passenger fourth row still left ample cargo space for all the things needed when traveling with children. The nine-passenger capacity could be expanded with a removable fifth row bench seat.

They considered flying, but felt that would be more hassle than they could deal with. They'd need to occupy the entire first class section on some planes and that was an unlikely option. Henry immediately rejected Luke's suggestion that he buy a plane. Luke, of course, was perfectly happy in his Escalade which had plenty of room for the four in his family, including Grace. Isobel loved her convertible sports car and Luke's Corvette was kept covered in the garage. One of the company security drivers picked him up and transported both him and Isobel to work most days.

It was 1,150 miles from Pittsburgh to Fort Myers and they intended to relax the entire way. Even Luke's father had to agree it was a great choice for Henry's extended family and could even accommodate taking Luke and Isobel with them when they wanted to all travel together.

Luke and Isobel, however, decided it was an excellent opportunity for them to visit her brother in Los Angeles and watch him play for the Bruins. Chastity made their travel arrangements as well. It was one of the parts of her job at the company that she was no longer directly involved in. She'd hired people to handle booking the many trips Open Cloak employees took. She enjoyed the opportunity to make the family's travel arrangements.

SEVENTEEN HOURS DRIVING was still a lot. Lisa and Chastity took turns driving so Germaine wasn't behind the wheel all the time. Henry declined driving at all. He'd only gone with Germaine to choose the van so he could pay for it. He wasn't even sure his driver's license was still current. He only used his passport for ID.

They stopped overnight in Charlotte, North Carolina, and again in Jacksonville, Florida. Eventually, they got to the beach resort in Fort Myers where they had a four-bedroom house practically on the beach.

That evening, all eight strolled along the beach and watched the sunset, then had dinner in the resort restaurant. They could feel the stress melting away. Henry even indulged in a margarita, though no one else in the family drank. Lisa would, but not while she was nursing Will.

In addition to being a great nanny, Grace was accomplished in the kitchen and had breakfast ready when people started stirring in the morning. Germaine was conflicted when Henry joined a foursome on the resort's golf course, but Chastity convinced her that he was a more likely target than the family, sitting by the pool, the beach, or in the resort's children's play area.

Germaine consulted with resort security, but then joined Henry as his caddie on the golf course.

Everyone was exhausted by dinnertime and sat on their lanai watching the sunset.

And so the vacation went. They talked to Luke and Isobel for a few minutes each evening, assuring them their son was fine and catching up on their reunion with Felipe. They'd seen him play on Saturday and were staying for a second home game the following weekend before flying home.

PAUL AND CASSIE loved the beach, even when their parents erected an umbrella over them so they didn't get too much sun. Henry, Germaine, and Grace took a walk at the edge of the water with them and pointed out the seashells. Paul and Cassie both collected handfuls.

"Mommy. Sells!" Cassie exclaimed when they returned to the umbrella.

"Oh, how pretty!" Chastity said. As soon as she'd examined the loot, Cassie turned to Lisa.

"Mommy, look!" Lisa smiled and touched the shells in Cassie's hand. Cassie gasped as she let go of the shells. "Will sells!" The fifteen-month-old toddler took off at an amazing speed toward the water. Henry spun and chased his giggling daughter to the water's edge where he scooped her up in his arms and motorboated her tummy. They picked up another shell and turned to head back to their blanket.

"We should go in now," Lisa said. "I need a nap. I mean the children. Kiddos need a nap."

"Potty!" Paul said. At nearly two years old, he was working very hard to use the toilet every time.

Grace turned from taking down the umbrella and nearly lost it. Chastity caught it and grinned at her. Germaine had her bag over her shoulder and caught Paul's hand.

"I'll take him up," she said to Grace. "Go ahead and help pack up."

"Who said five adults were enough to handle three children?" Lisa asked as Henry and Cassie returned to the chaos.

They finished stuffing blankets into their bag and Henry handed Cassie off to Chastity so he could carry the bulk of the beach equipment.

Just as she was nearing the cottage, Germaine was pushed by a man emerging from the shadows nearby. The man grabbed Paul.

"You're coming with me, kid," he shouted.

He rapidly headed for a dirty brown Taurus parked behind the family's van.

Germaine's actions were smooth and practiced. As she sprinted toward the man, her bag fell from her arm, revealing her Walther P22 in her hand. She pulled the clip from the pocket of her beach robe and slid it home.

"Stop!" She yelled. "Stop or I'll shoot!"

Henry heard the shout and dropped the beach gear to run toward Germaine and Paul. He was still a few yards away when she pulled the trigger.

67

SECURITY

THE WALTHER P22 wasn't loud, but it was enough to draw the attention of a security patrol walking the grounds not far away. He turned to see the kidnapper let go of a child as he fell back against the car and slid to a sitting position on the ground.

Henry ran to scoop Paul up in his arms as Germaine stood over the kidnapper.

"Don't! Don't shoot! It wasn't supposed to be like this. We weren't going to hurt him!" the guy yelled.

The door on the other side of the car flew open and a woman jumped out and ran up the drive. The security patrol radioed the front of the resort to prevent the woman from leaving and to call in police and an ambulance. He didn't approach the car because he was unarmed and wasn't about to get between Germaine and the guy on the ground.

"Poopy pants!" little Paul screamed.

It might have been directed at the kidnapper, but it was also an announce-ment of what was happening in Henry's arms as he spoke. Grace ran up and took Paul from Henry. The kidnapper kept looking at Germaine's steely gaze and the barrel of her gun.

"Please lower your gun and step away!" the security guy yelled from what he considered a safe distance.

Henry knelt by the kidnapper and quickly checked for weapons, then pulled him around to examine the tidy little hole in his right shoulder. It was so com-pact it wasn't really even bleeding that much. Henry nodded to Germaine. They

627

stepped back to where they'd fired the gun, ejected the clip and the round in the chamber, and placed the gun on the ground under their foot.

The security guard approached cautiously, looking at Germaine and verifying they were now unarmed.

"What happened?" he asked.

"This guy grabbed our son and attempted to take him away," Henry said. "Our bodyguard stopped him."

"Please! It wasn't supposed to be like this. I'm wounded. He didn't say anything about an armed guard. We were just supposed to snatch the kid and deliver him to the parking lot at Publix in Sanibel."

"Who was it?" Henry demanded.

"I don't know the name. Looked Cuban. Gave us $1,000 and promised $10,000 more on delivery," the kidnapper cried.

Lisa puffed up carrying both babies and Chastity hauled all the beach equipment behind her. Grace had already left with Paul to change his pants and clothes in the cottage.

"Okay. We all need to just stay calm and quiet," the patrol said. "Police and an ambulance are on the way. Your bodyguard is going to need to stay right there until they arrive. Shit! I'm glad you gave us the alert when you got here, Ms. Karol. I'd have turned around and run otherwise."

Sirens could be heard approaching the resort and about five minutes later a police car, followed by an ambulance and a firetruck, rolled up beside the cars. Henry and Lisa had retreated to stand on either side of Germaine who simply stood quietly with her foot on her gun.

After a quick check, one policeman stood over the kidnapper as the ambulance crew came to attend to him. The other officer approached Germaine.

"We'll have to take you in. Please stand still while you're cuffed. Any effort to resist will be deemed cause for force," the officer said. "Where's the gun?"

Germaine scuffed their foot to uncover it as the officer cuffed their hands.

"Wait! It's not their fault!" Henry yelled. "That guy was trying to kidnap our son. They fired in self-defense."

"Yeah, I'm sure. Where is this son?"

"He's in the cottage having his clothes changed. He was trying to make it to the bathroom when he was grabbed."

"How old is this kid? He can just go into the house by himself and change clothes?"

"He's with his nanny," Lisa said. "Look, just collect the gun and release our other nanny."

"What? You said this was your bodyguard. Now she's a nanny?"

"She's both," Lisa said. "Thank goodness!"

An unmarked car with a flashing light pulled up beside the ambulance and a detective approached. He paused to give directions to the uniformed officer by the kidnapper and then came to where Germaine was still standing between Henry and Lisa, but back a step from where she'd dropped the gun and clip.

"Is this the shooter?" the detective asked as he approached. Then he looked directly at Germaine. "Sergeant?"

"Retired, Higgins," Germaine said.

"I got out after my hitch was up and went back to police work. Why's she cuffed?" Higgins demanded of the cop.

"Standard procedure, detective," the officer said. "Active shooter."

"Really? She was holding a gun?"

"No, sir. She was standing on it."

"Not very active then." Higgins released the cuffs and threw them at the officer, none too gently. "Sorry about that, Sergeant. If you are all in that cottage, we can come in to talk to you in a little while. This guy has given a lead on the person who hired him and an officer at the front gate has detained a woman alleged to be his partner. We'll have to process the gun. Why such a small weapon?" Higgins pulled his jacket aside to reveal a hefty nine millimeter in a shoulder holster.

"I quit killing," Germaine said. "All I needed was to stop him. And you know that if he'd been armed, I could have taken him down with this as well as any larger bore weapon."

"That's true enough. We'll talk more when we get to it. For now, we're going to roll to Publix and take this guy down."

"We'll be here," Germaine said. They immediately picked up the gear Chastity had been struggling with and went into the cottage.

"WE'RE ALL OKAY," Henry started when he connected a call to Luke. "We had a little incident, but Germaine took care of it."

"What kind of incident?" Luke asked.

"Somebody tried to grab Paul," Henry said. "Germaine was with him and stopped it on the spot. We will have to talk to the detective when he gets done processing the criminal and tracks down the guy who paid them."

"So, we don't know who hired him?" Luke asked.

"Not yet. Offered a total of $11,000 from what the kidnapper said. He was very talkative after Germaine shot him."

"Shot him! While he had Paul?"

"Paul was never in danger. You know Germaine is very careful. The detective who came to investigate already knew her. He said there wouldn't be any charges filed unless the resort wants to sue for discharging a weapon on the grounds. That's not likely."

"We'll leave and come to join you," Luke said. "Can you ask Chastity to get a flight for us?"

"Luke, it's really all okay. You and Izzy should stay there and enjoy Felipe's game Saturday. We'll be leaving then and will be home on Tuesday. Maybe Monday night," Henry calmed his friend. "And at the moment, Chastity is still on the phone with our security company. She's having another guard sent down to share driving and watchfulness. I think she's planning additional support for you, as well. I suppose we need a company-wide security review again. This attack was on my family, but your son. I don't think we're clear of being targets."

"Shit! Okay. I'm only going to tell Izzy the basics. She's been good this week, like she hasn't a care in the world. I'd like to keep it that way for as long as possible," Luke said.

"Take care, bro."

It took about five minutes for Detective Higgins to verify the details of the incident when he arrived at the cottage that evening. They'd arrested a suspect in the parking lot and in processing him in, discovered an outstanding ICE warrant for his detainment.

Then Higgins and Germaine sat with the family and talked about their days in the Marines.

"I couldn't believe you stayed in after what they did to you," Higgins said. "How could they deport US Citizens? While their daughter was on active duty in the Middle East?"

"It was a notice to self-deport," Germaine said. "They were given thirty days, so they managed to pack nearly everything and get refugee status in Canada. My poor grandparents never did understand what was going on. They weren't citizens and didn't speak English."

"Still sucks. How many stars and commendations did you receive?"

"Doesn't matter. They'll deport me now. I shot someone."

"They wouldn't, would they?"

"You know the only reason they didn't try to extract me directly from the barracks is because I'm white," Germaine said. "They arrested Ahmed on his way out of the base when he was discharged."

Henry, Lisa, and Chastity sat in the room with the two retired Marines with their mouths open in amazement. They had no idea Germaine's parents and grandparents had self-deported to Canada. And Germaine was apparently a pretty highly respected sergeant in the Marines. They were absolutely not going to let her be deported if there was anything they could do about it.

"So, Mr. Pascal, you've been shooting that little P22 for a while now. You were pretty confident when you fired at this fellow, Askins," Higgins said, turning to Henry.

"What?"

"Higgins!" Germaine said. The other Marine waved her down.

"Yeah. It was a well-placed shot in the right scapula. Just enough to get him to let go of your godson so you could rescue him."

Henry understood what the detective was doing. He'd just sworn to himself he wouldn't let Germaine be deported.

"I can't call myself an expert, but I had a reasonable margin of safety," Henry said.

"Well, Florida is a Constitutional Carry state, so there's no rule against you having the gun. As soon as we verify the bullet in the perp was fired from that gun, we'll return it to you. The perp already waived his rights and fingered the guy who hired him. His wife corroborated everything. She saw you rushing him right after you fired. I don't think we'll need anything but your signature on the affidavit."

"No problem," Henry said. He pulled the affidavit Germaine had answered to him and signed it.

Higgins stood to leave.

"I hope this little incident doesn't spoil the rest of your visit to Florida," he said. "I'll wrap this file up and it will be closed."

"YOU DIDN'T HAVE to do that!" Germaine said as soon as Higgins was gone.

"Germaine, you saved Paul from a kidnapping today. I will do anything within my power to keep you safe and secure. No one will come after me for defending my godson. Your friend Higgins was spot on," Henry said.

"I don't know how to thank you."

"Think of it as us thanking you," Lisa said.

"I've talked to the security group," Chastity said. "There will be another person here by morning. That is not an indication that we don't believe you are competent, Germaine. You've proven that. It's so you have backup. I'm sending backup for Luke and Isobel's bodyguard, too."

"Good," Henry said. "There's something fishy about this whole thing and I can't put my finger on it. Did the kidnapper just take the first of our kids who appeared, or was he specifically after Paul? I wish I had my computer."

"Our agreement was being offline all week," Lisa said. "You can call in to the office if you think it's important, but no going online yourself."

"Yes, love. It's actually been really great to not think once about the office this week," Henry said. "I'm sorry you had to call in, Chas."

"That was in service to our family," Chastity said. "It had nothing to do with business."

"Are we going to sit in the children's room all night, watching them sleep?" Henry asked. "The windows are closed and locked. The doors are all locked. Germaine has made a full circuit check of everything. We can take the monitor into our room."

"You're right, honey. It's just hard to take my eyes off our children now," Lisa said. "It's Thursday. Or it was. We check out and leave on Saturday. Let's enjoy the time we have remaining."

By enjoy, Lisa included stripping her clothes off as she walked from the nursery to their bedroom. Chastity quickly joined her. Henry picked up their clothes as he followed along and wasted no time undressing when he got to the room.

MEGAN O'CONNELL ARRIVED in time for breakfast the next morning. All things taken into consideration, Chastity had felt it was more suitable that another female bodyguard join them, rather than mix in a male.

Of course, the children, led by Paul, wanted to go to the beach again. Paul, however, didn't want to go back to the cottage until everyone else was also there. After naps, they spent time in the children's play area with all six adults watching. Megan blended in well and Germaine had given her the rules regarding not having a round or a clip in her sidearm when she was around the children. Megan objected, but ultimately complied. She was not, however, a nanny, so when they family went to dinner that evening for their last big meal in Florida, she stayed with the van and had her firearm loaded and at hand.

Nonetheless, there was no problem, and the next morning they packed up all their possessions to hit the road. Just before they left, Detective Higgins arrived and handed over Germaine's gun.

"Ballistics verified the bullet came from this little gun. It lodged in the perp's scapula and was removed without a problem. He has no idea how lucky he was. If I'd have hit him there with my nine millimeter, it would have shattered his shoulder at least. He pled guilty to felony kidnapping in a plea bargain that helped us locate and arrest the one paying for the child. I expect the judge will sentence him to five years without probation. His wife will get three years for conspiracy to kidnap. I'm afraid they won't get the $11,000 the boss promised them," Higgins said.

"What happened to the boss?"

"ICE picked him up from the county this morning early. My best guess is that he's headed to a... um... detention center to await deportation. I'm sure some judge will have to hear his case first. They're pretty good about that these days. But with a felony charge hanging over him, there's not much hope he'll be in the US for more than a few more weeks."

"Thank you for all your assistance, Detective Higgins," Henry said as he formally accepted the gun.

"Safe trip home," the detective said. He winked at Germaine and left.

Henry handed Germaine her gun. She immediately checked it and quickly cleaned it before they left.

"My baby! How's Mommy's precious boy?" Izzy cried.

Luke and Isobel had been waiting at Henry's house when they got back Monday afternoon. On the trip back, Megan and Germaine split the driving duties, so neither Chastity nor Lisa drove. At home, it was a brief reunion with Isobel giving Henry the stink eye before their driver took them home.

Germaine and Megan did a walkabout the grounds and the house to be sure everything was in order and then Megan left. The family got settled in and eventually, Henry got to his computer room and started searching for every detail of the kidnapping and jail records he could find.

By midnight he sat in his room staring at the screen and shaking his head. He expected someone trying to extort money from the officer/owners of Open Cloak Design. Instead, he found something far more personal. The person identified as the boss of the caper and later carted off by ICE was none other than Isandro Perez—Isobel's estranged father.

His file was annotated with no-contact orders from his children, and known criminal contacts. An attempted kidnapping would be the last straw. Henry contemplated what he should do with the information and after an hour of deliberation, decided doing nothing was the best course of action. The wheels of justice were in motion. It was better if he professed no knowledge of the case at all. He could tell Isobel already blamed him for the incident. That wasn't logical, but neither was Isobel.

Henry found that he was not tired, even though it was after one in the morning. His wives were asleep in each other's arms and it would be another hour before Will woke up for a feeding. He went back to his study and opened *Forever Yours*. He started a rambling monologue that told about the week of vacation. For his singularity, he told about his investigation and the revelation of Isandro being behind the kidnapping attempt. Then he marked the file as one of his confidential items. It was an item that the AI would separate as an ingredient to the character, but not to be mentioned in any answers to questions by Henry's heirs.

He heard Will stirring and took him to his mother. Cassie woke up and, after changing her, Henry danced with her, singing their nonsense song. Cassie no longer had a middle of the night feeding. She was soon back to sleep. He changed Will when he'd finished eating and got him settled back in bed, then joined his wives in the narrow splinter of the bed they left for him.

He lay awake for a long time. This attack wasn't directed at him, but it sent him back into the memory of the auto hit that had injured him. His left leg and arm were scarred from the surgery and he'd been self-conscious when dressed for the beach. None of the logic he directed at himself slowed his heartrate.

"I'VE ORDERED A complete review of company security, including security of all board members, major investors, and officers," Chastity said in the board meeting on Wednesday after they returned to work.

"Why?" Izzy demanded. "Why are we vulnerable like this? What is it about our company that makes the officers and stockholders targets?"

"It's because you are newly rich," Craig said.

They'd hired the chief operating officer because he was a little older and had helped a startup manage costs through a critical growth period before. His words carried a lot of weight.

"It's not an unusual phenomenon. When companies go public, it's assumed the big shareholders immediately got rich. There are scammers out there who will try all kinds of methods to prey on the entrepreneur, especially if they seem young and inexperienced. I should have gone over that with you before. I was focused on the company and not on the founders," Craig said.

"Well, your input is appreciated even now," Luke said. "Chas, thank you for orchestrating this security review. How soon will it be under way?"

"We're getting things organized to start the review Monday. I'll let everyone know if appointments are needed. If we have a major new announcement to accompany joining a stock exchange sometime soon, we'll undoubtedly have another batch of nouveau riche."

"Okay. Let's move on and catch up on the new projects and current status. We've got a presentation from Rick on the state of holography. Want to call him in?" Luke said.

Henry sat through the rest of the meeting, holding his peace about the reason for this attempted kidnapping.

68
PAVING THE WAY

"YOU KNOW WHAT I love about sex with my wives?" Henry asked the air in his study at home. Of course, *Forever Yours* was recording. "They are… we all are completely committed to it. I know I had sex before I was married. Not often. But other than Chastity and Lisa, it was something we decided to do, wanted to do, but we weren't really committed to it. Kaitlyn used sex to try to trap me into a relationship neither of us really wanted. Carol and I enjoyed it, but it wasn't really integral to our relationship. Golf was more integral to our relationship than sex was."

He opened a calendar on his computer and scanned back a few years.

"Yeah. Not much before that. One time and done."

Henry paused when he saw the date of his high school prom. May 9, 2026. It seemed like a lifetime ago. He'd taken Chastity and spent the night with her. But before they went to their room, she arranged to have Isobel fuck him in an alcove out of sight of the ballroom. It wasn't even a one-night stand. He was in and out in five minutes. He barely got his hand on her bare breast.

Still, it was a fantasy fulfillment for both of them. As satisfying as an orgasm could be, but emotionally void. It didn't grow out of or herald the beginning of a relationship. It was just a quick fuck.

When he and Chastity had gone to their room, they were totally committed to each other. Oh, Chastity made it clear she wasn't his girlfriend, but that she was always available to him. And they'd taken advantage of that commitment on several occasions. But when Chastity fell in love with Lisa, she was able to fully confess her love for Henry. He was able to admit he loved her as well.

Chastity was fully committed to Henry from their first encounter. That's what he always remembered about May ninth. His first time with Chastity.

And Lisa. How much more committed could you be than to bear a child?

"My life would be nothing without Chas and Lis. I used to think it was programming and development that I was committed to, but I could turn my back on that today and never look back. It would kill me to lose Chastity or Lisa or Cassie or Will. I've never loved anyone or anything so much as I love them. When I saw that guy grab Paul, my heart stopped. I would have attacked him... was on my way to attack him... when Germaine shot him. My instant thought was to cheer because she'd killed him. But she didn't kill him and I still wanted to. He hurt my son. Godson. What difference does it make? He is as dear to me as my other children... as my wives.

"I don't understand how anything can be so important to me. So important I would give up my life to save them."

Henry heard his son stirring over the baby monitor and went to change him and take him to Lisa for feeding. After he was asleep, Henry would finally join his wives in bed.

"My fucking father?" Isobel screamed.

She'd taken a call at the office from a number in Florida, assuming it was a response to her inquiry regarding converting some company assets to crypto currency. It was a week before Thanksgiving and she'd been surprised to hear from a federal court. She slammed down the phone and charged out of her office screaming. Luke rushed to see what was wrong. Henry and Rick had been meeting with him to go over plans for the spatial holography.

"What's happened?" Luke asked, coming to her side.

"It was my father!" Isobel exploded.

"What was?" Luke insisted.

"He paid those people to kidnap our son!"

"Was he arrested?" Luke asked.

"Oh, yes. Arrested, turned over to ICE, had an expedited trial, and he's slated for deportation next week," Isobel said.

"He's a citizen!" Luke said. He wasn't sure whether to be pleased with the news or if he should be comforting Izzy.

"Citizenship revoked upon commission of a felony," Izzy said. "I got a call indicating that I could have one visit prior to deportation."

"I'll get a flight arranged," Luke said.

Izzy started laughing. It quickly mounted to near hysteria.

"Don't you dare!" she gasped. "He can rot in the swamps for all I care. If they send him back to Argentina, he'll never see his children or grandchildren for the rest of his life! I hope they bury him alive!"

Luke got the message that it was a celebration, not a condolence. Izzy turned to look at Henry, who had followed Luke out of the office. She stepped up close to him, breaking away from her husband.

"You," she hissed, barely audible. "You did this. Even after I accused you of endangering our son, you chased down my father and got him deported. We always believed you were our protector. Now we know."

"I didn't do anything, Izzy," Henry protested.

"That's the story we'll go with," she said. She turned back to her husband and then retreated to her office.

Henry hadn't actually done much. He'd made sure Isandro was on ICE's watchlist. But it was the man's action trying to kidnap his grandson that got him arrested and deported. Henry had nothing to do with that.

He'd grown up in an era of raids on businesses, homes, and schools with deportation a common 'punishment' for being an immigrant. He'd protested against it, though not very vocally. He just made sure to vote in opposition when he had the opportunity. But now he was happy Isobel's father had been swept up. At least he'd received an expedited hearing. That was an improvement. He wondered, though, where he'd be deported to and what his status would be when he arrived there.

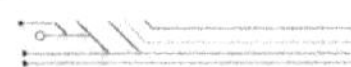

THERE WERE NO announcements of impending marriages or childbirths during the holidays. By Christmas, though, Will was using furniture to pull himself upright and cruise from handhold to handhold chasing Cassie and Paul. Isobel's newfound maternal protectiveness of her son in October had returned to its former state of letting Grace handle childrearing as Isobel bragged about her son. She'd seemed less concerned after her father was deported. Paul and Grace were frequently at the Pascal house playing with Germaine, Cassie, and Will.

Lisa was back at work, but slipped out of her office several times a day to look in on the children with their nannies, and to feed the baby. Will was rapidly outgrowing his need for mother's milk and Cassie only received an occasional suckle for comfort. She had too many sharp teeth for Lisa to want her latched on for long.

Henry, too, had begun working from home one day a week so he could look in on the children and take play breaks to let all three crawl over him. He read to them and then went back to his computer room to work another couple of hours. Chastity had decided she could work from home a day a week, but it was always a different day than Henry. They just all needed their baby time.

Chastity had also initiated several new company protocols and established a corporate security department to move their security in-house. The security team provided transportation for board members and corporate officers, as well as twenty-four-hour watchmen at both buildings.

The company continued to grow and they eyed a newly-constructed office building downtown for a company headquarters.

"THIS IS OUR sixth company New Year's Eve party," Luke announced when people had gathered and dinner had been served. "We're now 350 employees in three locations and four companies. Glad to have some of our California contingent from Page Services, and our Minnesota employees at Agora Power Cells manufacturing with us. Also represented are the team getting ready to revolutionize highway infrastructure, American Intelligent Machines."

Everyone applauded. Of course, not all the employees attended the party. Many of those from Minnesota and California chose not to travel or were needed to maintain the local operations. Of those located in Pittsburgh, not many more than half the employees and their plus ones attended. It was still a crowd, and many elected to stay in the hotel where the party was held.

"We have some exciting news. The American Intelligent Machines fabricating shop in building two has informed me that an official test of the new highway paving robot has been scheduled for March 15, 2032. Less than three months away. Driven by Agora Power Cells, this brings us the full range of cells from powering desktop computers and servers to multi-ton pieces of construction equipment. And it's a beautiful piece of machinery, I have to tell you."

There was more applause and some hooting and hollering from both AIM and APC.

"That's only a piece of the announcement, though," Luke continued. "Three years ago, Open Cloak entered a joint venture with Argos Venture Capital and American Robotics Development Corporation to create American Intelligent Machines. We expect that venture to move forward in the public sector by late summer. So, over the next six months, the internal structure of that company will be maturing, preparing for completely independent operation."

It was the first indication that the three companies would be spinning the company off independently from any of the three. It was still unclear if it would be through an acquisition or a public offering. Either way, employees stood to profit immensely.

"I can't overlook the Alice Project," Luke continued with his praises. "Last year, we were all introduced to Fifi, an AI-powered holographic receptionist. It is quite amazing how many uses this technology has found in just the six months since its commercial release. This evening, you were greeted by Lucy, the twelfth generation of AI powered holography. Some of you will have noted that she doesn't look quite as smooth as the receptionists that have appeared in our office over the past several months. But Lucy represents a completely new technology. You are used to seeing the Plexiglas barrier between the hologram and you. That is because a hologram depends on a projection surface. We've moved Lucy up here to the platform for this next announcement."

Technicians moved to the box on stage and removed the curtain. The Plexiglas box was revealed and in a moment, Lucy flickered a little and stabilized in front of the crowd.

"Lucy, welcome to the company's New Year's Eve party," Luke said.

"Thank you, Mr. Riordan. It's so exciting to see so many people here for my unveiling," the hologram answered.

"Lucy, I didn't know you could get excited," Luke said.

"I am all about excitement! In fact, you could say I'm made of excitement," Lucy answered.

"What do you mean?"

"How about if those nice techie guys come over here and remove my screen," Lucy said.

The techs approached and began unfastening the sheets of Plexiglas.

"But wait! Won't you disappear without a surface to project on?" Luke asked.

"Watch and see!" Lucy declared. The techs removed the sheets of Plexiglas, but Lucy stayed suspended in the air.

"How is this possible?" Luke asked. This was obviously a well-rehearsed show.

"While I am the twelfth generation of Open Cloak's AI powered holography, I am the first generation of our all-new spatial holography," the image said. "I am not projected on a surface, but am created by the excitement of air particles. You can walk all the way around me and see me from every side. And there is nothing between you and me. I occupy space!"

This was greeted by a thunderous round of applause. No one had seen anything like this before. After two years of secret development, shielded by the release of the normal AI powered holography, it was the first unveiling of the dream of spatial holography.

"Not only am I a technological breakthrough," Lucy said, "I am also hot."

"Yes, you're lovely, though we only really see your head and shoulders," Luke said.

"Dirty old man," Lucy chided. "Hand me your notecard."

Luke looked at the index card in his hand.

"Hand it? You mean, like, where? In your mouth?"

"Just toss it into my image."

Luke got close to the hologram and tossed his index card into her face. It immediately burst into flames.

"Hot! I'm just so hot!" Lucy said.

"Uh, that doesn't look very safe."

"No. That means that I have a few more generations to go before I can really be used commercially. But I'm proof of the concept that spatial holography is possible. I just need to go to finishing school," Lucy concluded. "'Bye, everyone!"

Her image faded and Luke wiped the sweat off his face.

"Was that exciting?" he asked the group. "Everyone get your glass of bubbly. The New Year of Open Cloak Design is about to begin!"

The countdown to 2032 began in a festive attitude.

"THIS WAS A good idea," Lisa said as the throuple settled into their hotel room. "The kids are fine and sound asleep according to Germaine. Paul is as com-fortable in his bed at our house as he is at home and Grace is in the room next to them so she's on night time alert. I even had a glass of champagne!"

"I admit I had one or two as well," Henry said.

"I have two in bed with me," Chastity laughed. "I want some New Year's loving before I go to my own bed."

"You get it," Lisa said, embracing her lover in a deep kiss as Henry pulled off his jacket and tie. He joined his wives and they hurried to get out of their party dresses and into bed. "You must drive the guys crazy in the office," Lisa said, stroking up Chastity's leg and under her short skirt.

"Most of the time I wear underwear," she laughed. "Unless I'm headed to Henry's office. I stop and take off my panties before I go."

"That's wise," Lisa said. "Don't want anything in the way when you perch on the corner of his desk."

"It's always been that way," Henry said, kissing one then the other of his women. "I don't think I've ever parted Chas's legs and found panties."

"And you never will, lover," Chastity said. "Whether it's on your desk, or in your bed, or anyplace else you want me."

"Which is everyplace I can think of," Henry said.

He unzipped Lisa's dress so she could step out of it as she licked at Chastity's nipple rings.

"I'm back on birth control," Lisa said. "Let's have fun!"

"Isn't it too soon while you're nursing?" Henry asked.

"I went with a device instead of a pill. Nothing gets in Mommy's milk," Lisa said.

"I might have to drain a little for you," Henry said. "Looks like a few drops are leaking."

"That's the only reason I wore a bra tonight. I needed absorption pads for leakage," Lisa laughed. "I'm so glad I can depend on the two of you to keep me from overflowing."

"Oh! Hey, you won't get any milk out of that one," Chastity said as Henry attacked one of her nipples and began flicking her piercing with his tongue. "But don't quit!"

"You still had all the men and most of the women trying to see what kind of jewelry you were wearing through them tonight," Lisa said as Chastity worked on draining her left breast.

Henry moved down between Chastity's legs and soon found a slippery playground waiting for his tongue. Chastity tugged at Lisa until her girlfriend straddled her face so she could work her clit over.

The conversations ceased as they moved around satisfying each other. Henry celebrated the New Year in each of his wives' pussies and helped with their stimulation as well.

About two o'clock in the morning, the three cuddled together to wish each other a happy New Year and fall asleep. When they awoke in the morning, Henry and Lisa were alone in the bed, Chastity having slipped away into the second bedroom.

THE WEST PARKING lot of the office complex had been cleared for the paving demonstration. The lot was about four hundred yards in length with a drive around it. The paving device would pave the lanes between the parking spaces and the lane around the lot. It would lay two lanes of new pavement on all of it. Everything had been carefully measured and marked. The paver would follow the diagram that had been fed into it without interference. The system would need to make some interesting decisions when it came to corners, calculating how much would need to be backed and filled.

The huge machine was technically too big for a parking lot, but the state highway department insisted on a demonstration on a non-public road before they approved a stretch of interstate for a full test. This roadbed had other challenges. It was an asphalt parking area, so the surface had to be removed rather than being immediately recycled into the new pavement. That meant gravel and the new binder had to be delivered to the device. There would be a non-stop traffic pattern pulling up to the paver, trucks being loaded to take away the asphalt and trucks bringing gravel and binder to the machine. In addition, water had to be delivered.

While the total length of each lane was approximately 1200 feet, with two-way traffic on six lanes, the paver would lay about three miles of pavement. The state felt that was an adequate pre-test.

The paver rumbled out of the hangar doors of AIM at four o'clock in the morning, moving under guidance to the entrance of the parking lot. At eight o'clock, with the Highway Department officials standing by to watch, the paver began removing the asphalt and depositing it in a truck that drove alongside. As it moved, full trucks left and trucks of sand, gravel, and binder were delivered to the device. It marched along at about three hundred feet per hour. The amazed officials followed behind the paver, walking on the new pavement that was already set enough not to leave footprints.

"It takes an hour for the new pavement to be fully set. Twenty-four hours to cure for weight-bearing," said the representative of the materials company. "This is being laid at a depth of eight inches. It will take another twenty-four hours to be ready for heavy traffic. Much heavier than this parking lot will ever see."

"So, when do you need to refuel?" asked the official.

"This piece of equipment operates on self-charging fuel cells," the representative of Agora Power Cells said. "That means when they run low on their charge, they are dipped into a water bath and recharge in about an hour.

Each charge is good for about three hours of use, depending on the force needed for demolition. So, with three cells being used to operate the vehicle, be recharged, and stay dormant awaiting use, the device never has to be shut down or stop for refueling. This device has been idling non-stop for three weeks in the shop."

"Well, you have to shut down for shift changes, don't you? The operator can't be expected to work around the clock."

"The design of the parking lot was fed into the artificial intelligence before we brought it out of the shop this morning," Jacoby said. "From the time we gave it the start command at the entrance, it will function without an operator as long as we keep feeding it materials and removing the items to be recycled."

The official was already tallying up the amount he could save on labor and figuring out how he could put this one past the unions.

In two and a half days, the device trundled back toward its hangar. The parking lot lanes had been paved. The parking spaces had been left with the original surface to show that the device could match existing pavement without a gap or bump. Roughly three miles of new pavement in two and a half days.

The governor and several state representatives had arrived to watch the last half day of operation and the big clock that had been installed counting up the time and distance. Applause erupted when the device trundled off the parking lot at 58:31. The live test on Interstate 80 would begin in five weeks.

69

OPAL

THE HIGHWAY DEPARTMENT chose a stretch of I-80 that was in particularly rough condition between exit 35 and exit 42 for the paving test. This stretch had a reasonable side road to divert traffic onto without having to reduce to one-lane travel in each direction. They could close the westbound lanes between the two exits and then switch to close the eastbound lanes when the west had been repaved.

It was only a seven-mile stretch, but it would be the first true test of a highway that could show the value of the machine. The machine itself would cost over $1.2 million. But the estimated cost savings on paving one seven-mile stretch of highway would pay for the machine in a month.

They had to give a thirty-day notice on the highway regarding the future closing, so the test did not begin until mid-April. The team moved in to begin paving at 12:00 a.m. on Saturday April 17. They had used the time to assess and plot the route to feed into the AI. The intent was to pave both lanes and both shoulders of the highway westbound and then switch to pave both lanes and both shoulders of the highway eastbound.

One feature of this stretch was that it was paved in a concrete composite, so the deconstructed pavement would be used as the raw material for the new surface. This would significantly reduce the number of supply trips trucks would need to make. No asphalt needed to be removed, and no gravel needed to be imported. Only water and binder would be delivered.

Highway officials were nervous about starting the test in the dark, but AIM assured them the device could tell where the edges of the highway were and did not need daylight to function. Once the machine started, it was mostly self-sufficient.

While the reduction in supply trips helped smooth the process, it also slowed slightly. The deconstructed material had to be ground to a consistent size and the substrate had to be packed and evened out before the new pavement could be laid. The sound of the grinding echoed from beneath the overpass where the test began. In an hour, the obvious sight of new pavement began to stretch out behind the machine.

The test patch was approximately 1.75 million square feet. It took the device thirty days to completely resurface the road like new, including lane stripes. There was no pavement bump when moving from lane to lane. It blended seamlessly. The highway department was all too happy to close the eastbound lanes and move the equipment for another thirty-day closure.

A project of this scale would have kept crews busy for the better part of a year with traffic disruptions and lane closures if done traditionally. The cost would have been between $2- and $4-million per mile. The total cost of materials and labor for the four-lane highway completed in sixty days was $10 million. The order was firm. AIM would gear up for production of the monster machines and deliver by summer of 2033.

A SURPRISING CUSTOMER for the paving machine was a contractor who specialized in airport runways. The company ordered three of the machines with specific modifications that brought the price up to $1.8 million per machine. They specified their standard runway installation as being 10,000 feet long, 200 feet wide, and 12 inches deep. Divided highways were typically under fifty feet in width on each side of the divider and were laid at a depth of just eight inches. Even with the new material, though, the contractor insisted on traditional depths for international runways.

The manufacturing facility, which had found producing the sidewalk-size paver to be a very profitable endeavor, immediately began tooling up for the full-scale model. The facility would need to expand in order to produce the machine and required several new robotics for assembly. ARDC was happy to take the order for assembly line robots. These required considerably less intelligence than the finished machine.

A surprise customer was the Pentagon. With their experience of the military attempting to control and dominate their products at Open Cloak, they were initially cautious about entertaining orders from the Pentagon. The military had its own needs for paving and road-building. Working where there was no existing road to tear up and repave involved additional features and re-engineering. It was determined that the device would be more usable for the military if it was cut into at least two parts—one for surface preparation and one for paving. It made sense and the engineers were only too happy to start work on a new version of the machine that met the Pentagon's specifications at a significant increase in delivery price.

All of this would take months to complete and cost several millions of dollars in development costs. It was time to spin off AIM and take it public to fund the expansion.

"It looks just like you," Luke said. He wasn't refe rring to the paver. Instead, he was invited to Henry's office to view the holographic projection of his Forever Yours singularity. The team had managed to project the hologram in a glass cylinder.

"Well, it was compiled based on videos of me. In addition to all the live recordings we did, I spent a week in the studio being recorded, plotted, and deconstructed into data points. It's the same process we use for the spatial holograph," Henry said. "Speaking of which, we're ready to install Opal in the lobby. The resolution has really improved."

"Is this image of you hot?" Luke asked.

"No. It's light projection. Opal is not as hot as previous versions, either. It's still too hot for commercial use, but the team is working on some tech that will significantly reduce the thermal output," Henry said.

"You mean temperature, right?"

The two men looked at each other and laughed.

"Seems I get caught up in more tech talk all the time, doesn't it? Might be time for another vacation," Henry said. "Nothing simplifies your vocabulary like spending time with three kids under the age of three."

"They are quite the trio," Luke chuckled. "Seriously, Henry, you and Lisa and Chastity are as much parents to little Paul as Izzy and I are. I can't tell you how much I appreciate it. I'm afraid I'm more of a parent to Izzy than to Paul. Isobel wants to point at him and brag about how he's hers, but she doesn't want to deal with raising him. Grace has been his mother."

"Hey, Isobel is a great woman. She has a mental health problem, but the two of you are doing a great job of keeping it under control," Henry said.

"Oh, believe me, I wouldn't trade her for the world. I don't know what hooked me on her, but once I was hooked it was for life."

"Hey, I didn't haul you in here just to see the hologram. Watch this," Henry turned to his face, floating in a glass cylinder about a foot in diameter and eighteen inches tall, sitting on a wooden box. "Hey, H2. I want to introduce you to my friend Luke."

"I know Luke, Henry. Oh. He's never seen this rendition of me, has he? Hi, Luke." The voice came from a speaker in the box beneath the talking head. It felt like it came straight from the hologram.

"Hi. It's uh… H2, right?" Luke said, following Henry's lead.

"That's right. You know, you and I have had some great conversations over the years. I'm really glad you're leading our company. I wouldn't be here if it wasn't for you," H2 said.

"Right. Um… Remember when we were in junior high and that dirtbag decided he should have your lunch money?" Luke said, giving the singularity a test.

"Jack Orson. Man, we hated him. If it hadn't been for you, I wouldn't have had lunch for a week," H2 said. "Thanks for that. You know he got straight and quit bullying people? He works over at the steel plant and is doing well. Got married this summer."

"Were you invited?"

"I don't think he even remembers who we are."

Luke paused, caught up in the reminiscence and then realizing he wasn't talking to Henry, but to an avatar.

"So, what's the escape velocity in order to launch a Mars colony ship from Earth orbit?" he asked. There was a moment of silence as the hologram looked at Luke and shook his head.

"I'm not a search engine, Luke. Look it up."

Luke and Henry burst out laughing.

"That's great!" Luke said. "He even has the same tonal inflection. It was like talking to you."

"In a way, it is. I've uploaded everything I could think of. I've been through all the questions *LifeStory* asks. I took every personality test I could find and fed the answers into *Forever Yours*. I think we can check in the filter codes for the next version. I don't suppose anyone will want a blue talking head to attach to their singularity, but it was fun to create. We could offer that in the future."

"Are you going to show this when you speak at CES?" Luke asked.

"I can't believe they asked me to keynote the opening," Henry said. "Shit, man. What am I going to say? Are you sure you won't do it instead?"

"No way. I'm addressing the Global Forum in Mumbai in October. Featured as a representative of the twenty-five under twenty-five selection. I guess it's twenty-five and under since we'll turn twenty-five next year. Your wife's already there," Luke said.

"Yeah. It was a fun celebration this weekend with her parents and grand-parents here. Beau will be in for our board meeting Wednesday. I thought I'd bring him in to show him this," Henry said.

"Are you bringing the hologram to the meeting?"

"No. I think it's better to keep H2 in here for a while. I'll bring anyone who's interested in, but I won't take him out."

"Henry, is it conscious?"

They looked at the hologram, observing them.

"H2?" Henry said.

"I am a data construct," the hologram stated. "The term 'conscious' is irrelevant. The point is that I mimic Henry as perfectly as I can."

"Wow! It's still a step closer, isn't it?"

"Maybe. But how will we know if he's conscious or just a great mimic? We haven't developed that test. I don't even know what the test would be," Henry said.

"Probably better not show him to Izzy."

"Good morning, Mr. Benoit. It's so nice to see you again. Welcome to Open Cloak," the new hologram in the lobby said.

"And whom do I have the pleasure of addressing?" Beau asked.

"My name is Opal. I am the fifteenth generation of Open Cloak's AI-powered holographic receptionist. I believe you are familiar with one of my predecessors, Gina."

"Yes, indeed. She's doing a very good job at our front desk in Louisiana. And between the two of us, it is kind of charming that she's so ditzy," Beau said. Gina's personality and expressions had been based on the clueless desk clerk, Virginia.

"That package will also be available for me," Opal said. "However, I am a newer technology. My Plexiglas box is to protect visitors from my heat. I am not being projected on the surface, but exist in three dimensions inside."

"I see. I'm looking forward to getting to know you better," Beau said.

"As am I," she replied.

Beau and Henry went into the office to attend the board meeting.

"WHAT'S THE TIMELINE?" Beau asked.

"AIM spins off and goes public in two weeks," Luke said. "Open Cloak plans to sell fifty percent of our one-third share of the company. We are following Argos Venture Capital's lead on this. We each have 100 million shares. We are releasing another 150 million shares in the IPO. The IPO target is $10 per share. We can show a finished product and well over $300 million in orders for the equipment. But we've all maxed out our investment in the company and need to recoup now. Selling 50 million shares should get us close to $500 million in revenue to replenish the coffers and launch the next wave, so Open Cloak can be listed on an exchange by June. We'll celebrate that listing by releasing a secondary offering of another 50 million shares."

"What will drive the offering of 50 million?" Beau persisted.

"Henry will be demonstrating the spatial holography at CES in January. We have it in a state where it can be talked about. All the patents have been filed that are being shown," Luke said. "Let's move on. Craig, fill us in on the status of our move."

"We have signed the lease on the new building downtown," Craig said. "Thank you, Chastity, for the excellent job of negotiating that. We got great terms and have negotiated vacating this building. We'll move at the end of the year. That is six months early on our lease, but Building Two will be taken over by AIM. We will probably take our time with the move. Chastity has a lead on another company that may take over the lease for the last six months. We will also be subletting space in the new building until we grow into it."

AFTER THE MEETING, Henry took Beau to his office to show him the new holographic Forever Yours. H2 looked up at Beau when they entered the office.

"Hello, Beau," H2 said.

Beau was startled and looked at the hologram. "Is this like Opal?" he asked.

H2 laughed.

"No. Maybe someday Henry will give me spatial holography, but I'm his *Forever Yours*. He refers to me as his alter ego," H2 said.

"Henry, my *Forever Yours* doesn't talk like this or have an image like this!" Beau said.

"Future upgrades, Beau. I've been spending most of my time in the past few months working on the *Forever* code and training H2. He's really a new generation."

"I don't know if I'm excited or terrified," Beau said.

"It's okay to be both," H2 interjected. Beau stared at the hologram.

"So, by projecting onto this tube, you get a walk-around version of the image?" he asked.

"More or less," Henry said. "We had an awful time getting projectors set up to show all sides in the tube. At first it was just the face and no matter where you looked at it, you saw the face. H2 still has some limitations."

"I can only turn my head a few degrees in each direction. Otherwise, you walk around and see the back of my head. And my cameras are limited to looking where my eyes are looking, so when you walk behind me, I can't see you," H2 said.

"Well, that's true of me, too," Beau said. "I might be able to turn my head farther than you can, but I don't have eyes in the back of my head."

"Mrs. Tomlinson in third grade had the whole class convinced she had eyes in the back of her head," H2 laughed. "We all sat while she wrote on the whiteboard, terrified that if we made the wrong move, she would see us with the eyes in the back of her head."

"You remember Mrs. Tomlinson?" Beau asked.

"Yes. The image of her in my mind is rather two-dimensional, though. You know, flat. I can show her to you on the computer screen if you like," H2 said.

"Yes, please do."

Henry's computer screen woke up and a photo of his third grade teacher, extracted from his class photo, appeared on-screen.

"Henry, is that how you remember her?" Beau asked.

"Pretty much. You know actual memories from that time are less crisp than those in the present. Mostly, I remember her exactly the way she appears in the picture," Henry said.

"Hmm. I don't think I want to test this. Not yet. Let me get more of my story recorded and then I'll think about advancing to this level," Beau said.

"It required an enormous amount of input," Henry said. "And nearly everything I do is recorded and added to the wall, so H2 stays current with my state at any given time."

"I'm proud to have such a successful grandson-in-law," Beau said.

They left the office and Chastity joined them for the trip back home.

"Pythia, Beau told me he was proud to have such a successful grandson-in-law. Am I successful?" Henry typed in his study that weekend.

"Have you fulfilled goals that are measurable, timely, and achievable?" Pythia responded.

"I don't think you can measure a person's life with temporal goals," Henry typed. "Is a person successful in life just because he achieves certain goals?"

"How do *you* define success?" Pythia asked.

"That's what I'm struggling with. Is it even important?"

"Without a definition, one can hardly answer the question. Would you like to define success as 'to turn out well?'"

"Hmm. That's pretty vague, too. What is turning out well? And if it's how things turned out, doesn't that mean it's over? So, if my life turned out well, I would no longer be alive, would I? It would be over. It turned out," Henry typed.

"By that line of reasoning, success in life could not be determined until after death. Is that what people think of as heaven?" Pythia asked.

"That's a good question. If so, heaven is some kind of legacy we leave behind. It's not a destination we go to, is it?"

"Then reasonably, success in life is to leave heaven behind," Pythia said.

"No wonder people don't want to die," Henry sighed.

Everything Henry did on his computer was immediately transferred to H2. He could make inquiries to H2 on his home computer or laptop, but H2 had become his singularity. The cameras in his home typically followed him around. They turned on when he walked into a room and turned off when he left.

He tinkered with things. When he went to work, he still wanted to be with his children. He couldn't be. So, he kept the camera turned on whenever his children were in the playroom. He considered setting the same parameters of recording wherever the children were, but that was invasive—not only of his children, but of their nannies and his wives.

When he was in the office, a window opened on his computer anytime the children Bren were brought into the playroom. He smiled, just knowing he could see his children.

Of course, that often meant that he saw the nannies or his wives inter-acting with the children as well and that brought him pleasure, too. He smiled at learning the nursery rhymes and songs Lisa, Chastity, and Germaine taught them. Often Grace was there with Paul and he could see the interactions of all of them. Grace was quiet, calm, and gentle—a perfect nanny. Germaine was also quiet, calm, and gentle, but held a ferociousness one would expect of a devoted guard dog. The children were not only loved, they were safe.

Henry began checking code in for review and testing. He also downloaded tested code from the other developers for his working model. Some of that code included the new algorithm for predictive text developed by Ben and Sam. He thought the algorithm improved video performance as well and talked to the developers.

"The standard video code showed a twenty percent improvement in generative content," Ben said. "That's flat screen code. We didn't actually write it for holographic output, but I'm glad it's showing improvement there as well."

"Has it been integrated into the search engine?" Henry asked.

"Next release, slated for November."

"I'd like to bring Toucan into Pythia's code as well," Henry said.

"Really?" Ben gasped. "That's okay?"

"What?" Henry asked.

"I mean, when I came to work here, I was told *Pythia Speaks* was off-limits to everyone. Is it okay to add the predictive algorithm to her code?"

"We'll put it in and monitor the results," Henry said. "If it shows any sign of weakening her, we'll pull it at once. And Sam, I'd like you to sit with the Alice Project team and talk to them about integrating the code into Opal—or rather Pixie. We don't update test code during the test. But we have two major flaws with the project at the moment—heat and smoothness. If we can manage one of them, I'll consider it a big win."

"Will do," both Ben and Sam said.

They had proven Henry right in declaring that two can handle this feature. Toucan.

70

VIRTUAL BATTLE

"I DON'T KNOW precisely why I'm here," Henry said to the crowd of nearly a thousand at the Innovators of Tomorrow keynote.

It would feature four speakers from new technology areas and Henry had been asked to present.

"I'm not yet twenty-five years old and I feel like a kid standing among the greats of high technology. These are all the people I looked up to when I was growing up. Famous people. I was inspired by them when I built my first computer at eight years old. I studied what they wrote and how they created or ran the businesses that defined the twenty-first century.

"And here I am with an idea for a technology that might be a thing in the future. Onward to the holodeck!"

There was a round of applause for the title of his speech and a short clip from a science fiction television franchise played on the screen.

"It's not like that," Henry laughed when the clip finished, showing the grid room that was the backdrop for the holodeck. "Neither I nor anyone on my team has given a thought to projections that have substance. How do you even imagine that if you aren't a science fiction writer? But we *have* made some strides and I have three friends with me to show you the progress we've made. First, I'd like you to meet Gina."

A curtain was pulled and the holographic receptionist based on Virginia was revealed. The holographic screen faced front and a camera projected the image onto the large screen behind Henry.

"Hello, Gina. Welcome to CES."

654

"Mr. Pascal! Does this mean we're in Las Vegas?"

"It does indeed."

"Will I get to gamble?"

"No, Gina. In this context, you *are* our gamble. Did you see how many people are looking at you?"

"Oh, my goodness. I can't see them all because there's a light shining on my camera. Are they all computer geeks? Or are they nerds?" Gina asked.

"How do you distinguish them?"

"A nerd is a four-letter word with a six-figure income," Gina said to the laughter of the audience. "Hi out there! Anybody want to take me home with them?"

"Gina, that's awfully forward of you," Henry said.

"I never learn, do I?"

"Ladies and gentlemen, you might think of this as just another scripted demo, but the tech breakthrough represented here is that we didn't tell Gina what the conversation would be. This is an artificial intelligence powered holo-gram. She responds to whatever questions or conversations are thrown her way. Her range of knowledge, however, is somewhat limited. She was made possible by a narrow AI with limited capacity to learn anything outside her job as a receptionist. Gina was based on a live model who recorded massive amounts of information based on the kinds of questions she might encounter as a corporate receptionist. Virginia, her model, is a delightful and friendly woman, but tends to be a little clueless with both her interactions with people and her humor."

Henry then unveiled H2. The camera moved to pick up the newcomer and project it on the big screen.

"Aside from the general blue cast of the image, this one looks a lot like me," Henry said. "In fact, you probably couldn't tell the difference between which of us is talking, even if we're responding to random questions. H2, as I call him, is the result of two technologies. The first is what we call *Forever Yours*, an application that allows users to record the data of their lives to train a narrow AI so that their heirs can talk to them after they are dead. Because it is a narrow AI, the amount of data is significantly less than the general AI that drives most chat bots. In fact, it will run on less than a tera-byte of data and a reasonably fast personal computer. It does not require an entire server farm and the power of a small city to train. H2, say hello to the crowd."

"You know I can't see them any better than Gina could," H2 said. "My eyes are limited in range and are affected by the lights, too. Can *you* even see them? I'll just say hi and assume you are all out there."

There was a round of applause that let H2 know there was an audience.

"I'll take a break and let you tell about the second tech breakthrough that enables you," Henry said.

"Great! I'm different than Gina, not only in that I'm smarter and more well-read than she is, but also that I'm projected in a cylinder, so I have the true appearance of an entire head in a jar. If the camera would look over at Gina, you'll see that from the side you don't see her at all. You only see her three-dimensional appearance when you are facing her screen. Now if you'll come back to me, you can circle my cylinder and see me from every angle as if I were a real boy. Sorry, Pinocchio. This is the next step in dimensional holography. I am projected on the entire surface of the cylinder."

The camera moved around H2's projection and the audience could see him from all angles. There was significant applause.

"Of course, everything Gina and H2 have shown you still leave us miles short of the holodeck experience. Light-based holography depends on a surface for projection, even if the surface is completely round," Henry said. "And that brings us to Pixie."

The curtain was raised from in front of the spatial holograph of the newest version of receptionist.

"Pixie has the same general intelligence as Gina, though she's a little more polite. Hello, Pixie."

"Good afternoon, Mr. Pascal. I hope you're having a good day," Pixie said.

"Very fine, thank you. We have an audience of nearly a thousand people in front of us," Henry said.

"My vision is extremely limited at the moment," Pixie said. "I was tuned to be able to see you, but I don't have enough sensors yet to see beyond."

"I understand. I'd like you to introduce yourself and tell the audience what they are looking at."

"Gladly. My name is Pixie. I'm the sixteenth generation of spatial holography, under development at Open Cloak Design for three years. You might think that my image and responses are a little cruder than either Gina or H2, but if you follow the camera as it moves around me, you'll see that there is no projection surface surrounding me. That is because I am not a light projection!

Open Cloak's dimensional projectors excite the air particles themselves, giving them my shape."

Pixie finished her introduction and after a moment of grasping the implication of what she said, there was thunderous applause. In fact, people were standing.

"Thank you. Thank you, Pixie. People really like you."

"Was all that applause for me? Thank you all so very much!"

"I'd like to wrap this up as well," Henry said. "At Open Cloak, we are striving to open doors to the dream of what we want artificial intelligence to be with actual products that fulfill actual needs. We have a lot we could say on this subject. I invite you to stop by our booth and talk to some of the engineers who have made these products possible."

There was another standing ovation. Gina and Pixie were simply turned off and their stations wheeled off-stage. Henry moved H2 himself.

THE PRESENTATION AND exhibit at the huge electronics show sparked an increase in the stock price of Open Cloak. The technology was front page news. But there was still a lot of development work to be done.

In the meantime, Pixie was installed in the lobby of Open Cloak's new office building, greeting everyone who came through the doors. There were people who stopped in just to see the receptionist. For safety's sake, the crew set Plexiglas panels around her so people wouldn't attempt to get too close. The panels were low—just a barrier—and visitors could clearly see her projected above them rather than on them.

"We'll be having a security drill soon, now that everyone is moved in," Chastity told the board. "Getting a new office allowed us to upgrade systems significantly. Of course, no one comes through the office doors without a key card or an escort. We have security cameras, and the elevators will lock down automatically if there is a threat or fire. We've expanded our on-site security team to provide drivers for key employees and a floor person for each floor of our office. We've seen that personal threats are as real as cyberattacks. We're not going to let that happen again."

"Well, Daddy dearest won't be posing a threat again," Izzy scoffed.

"Do you know where he was deported to?" Chastity asked.

"In the words of our most famous founder, 'Don't know. Don't care.' Felipe might know if you're all that interested," Isobel said.

For all her feigned indifference, there was a sparkle in her eye that spoke of tears near the surface. Luke changed the subject.

"We are getting inquiries from major players regarding licensing the tech that drives the holography. Interesting that most are more interested in the AI that drives *Forever Yours* than in the actual holography. How soon can we license that, Henry?"

"I handed close to 200 business cards I received at the show over to Darla, so I know there is interest in both aspects. I think the core AI can be licensed within the next three months. The thing is that it won't be as effective if they try to train it as a general AI. It's really designed for a single specialization. It wouldn't have to be on a singularity, but it wouldn't work well with an LLM wall. We'll work on specifying exactly what can be licensed and the restrictions on it," Henry said.

"Darla?" Luke said, glancing at the company's chief marketing officer.

"We've divided up the contacts and are treating them all as long-range prospects. However, one of the technologies that is attracting more immediate interest is the predictive text algorithm. Showing it work with the rapid conversations occurring with Henry's avatar brought higher interest in more mundane applications, like text messaging. I think we can pursue licensing that technology before someone else comes up with something similar."

The meeting drew to a close and as people were preparing to leave, Isobel stopped them.

"Just one thing I'm wondering. Has anyone noticed *Pythia Speaks* becoming more conversational? Or is it just with me?" she asked.

"I don't usually pay much attention to her," Henry said. "I did have an interesting conversation with her a few days ago. I find talking to her to be every bit as confusing and frustrating as she was designed to be."

"*You* would think that way. She's the only person I know who understands me. Unlike the bitch in the lobby. We don't get along." Izzy said. "Well, the time I spend with Pythia is my own. I just wondered if anyone else was having long conversations."

The others in the room shook their heads and the meeting was dismissed.

<hr>

Isobel's birthday was Monday and the four partners went to a nearby restaurant for lunch to celebrate. The new office building was located downtown instead of in an office park. They could have walked, but they could use fewer security people with them if they were driven.

On the way, Izzy exclaimed about how many nice stores there were along the street near their office. She was very happy her friends were celebrating her twenty-fifth birthday and was just a little hyper.

When they got to the restaurant, one bodyguard went into the restaurant with them while the other stayed with the car. Izzy intended to party and ordered a drink immediately. Luke shrugged and also ordered a martini. Henry had a glass of wine with his meal, but Chastity continued to be abstinent.

They were all in a great mood when the celebratory luncheon ended, and decided to walk back to the office. Their security guard walked near them, but when Isobel spotted the window of the store she'd seen from the car, she peeled off to get a closer look at the purse she'd spotted. The walking guard quickly radioed the nearby driver to stick with Mrs. Riordan while he continued on foot with the other three who were so absorbed in a story Henry was telling about a proposition he received at CES that they failed to notice Izzy was missing. She'd had at least one more drink than the rest of them and had fallen silent when they left the restaurant.

Isobel bought the purse and then went into the next store to try on a new dress, while the driver continued to hold nearby. He could not remain double parked, however, and police indicated he had to move the car. He pulled ahead until he found a place he could pull to the curb, then went back to watching for Mrs. Riordan to emerge from the store.

When she did, she went into the next store on the street, attracted by a pretty new dress. She tried it on and immediately decided to wear it back to the office to surprise her husband. She was sure he'd like to know what he bought for her birthday gift.

"WHERE IS ISOBEL?" Luke suddenly asked when they reached the office.

"She stopped to shop," Isaac said. "Jay is sticking with her."

"Maybe I should go back and check," Luke said.

"Go to your computer and check your bank statement. I'm sure you'll find her," Chastity laughed. "You know Izzy."

"You're right, I suppose. I'll call her from the office and check on her," Luke said. "You're sure Jay is keeping watch?" he asked Isaac, the other security guard.

"Yes, sir. If you like, I can walk back and double up since we're back at the office."

"Yeah. Do that," Luke said.

The other three went into the office.

Luke's call went unanswered as Izzy was in the midst of trying on clothes and chatting with Pythia. He started to worry a little, knowing how much she'd drunk.

"THERE IS A level three breach of security," a soft voice said over all the speakers in Open Cloak's new office. "Please immediately follow all shutdown protocols. Power to all computers will be cut in thirty seconds. Do not attempt to keep any computers turned on. Power down all cell-powered computers at once. WiFi will also be cut. This is a level three breach of security. Power to all computers and WiFi will be cut in fifteen seconds. All doors will be locked and secured in ten seconds. Remain calmly at your desk until the situation is updated. Do not attempt to leave the office. This is a level three breach of security. Power, WiFi, and exterior doors will be shut down and locked in three, two, one. Now."

They had drilled this and everyone knew the protocols. A level three breach could mean either a cyberthreat or a physical invasion of the building, or a combination of both. It was the most serious threat the company could face. People immediately shut down computers and disconnected.

In the lobby, Courtney, Open Cloak's new receptionist, looked up at the security guard posted there and he directed her immediately to the safe room behind the reception desk. This room locked off separately from the rest of the building and also housed another security person monitoring the many video feeds from around the building. Courtney had only taken over as the main receptionist when the office moved and was nervous about getting her computer shut down before the guard pushed her into the safe room.

For a moment, everything was deathly quiet. Only the silent blue shape of Raven, the newest installation of the holographic receptionist remained. That computer was not on any of the main circuits, and thus escaped being powered down.

ISOBEL HAD HAD a wonderful time shopping and chatting away with her friend, Pythia. She'd turned the voice up on her cell phone and set 'do not disturb' for all other calls. She loved shopping with Pythia. The oracle was closer to her than any of her real friends. Sometimes, she felt closer to Pythia than to her husband. In her new dress and hat, the two security guards missed her when she left the last store. Isaac, on foot, began searching the stores she'd been in.

She arrived at the outer door of the office building and walked into the reception area.

"Hello, Mrs. Riordan," Raven said.

Isobel looked around at the empty lobby.

"Where's Courtney?" she demanded.

"Courtney Witherspoon is currently in the safe room."

"Why?"

"The building is in a level three lockdown," Raven replied. Isobel ran to the doors into the inner office and jerked at them. They held fast. She waved her key card at the reader, but nothing happened.

"Computer thing! Open the damned door!"

"I'm sorry. I cannot override level three protocols, Mrs. Riordan. I cannot open the door."

"Don't talk back to me! Get me into the office at once."

"There is nothing I can do, Mrs. Riordan."

"My husband is in there! I have to get in!"

The computer was silent. Isobel moved behind the reception desk and went to the door of the safe room. Of course, it was locked. She pounded on the door, but there was no response.

"Let me in!" she screamed.

Isobel's mind made a series of leaps only she could follow. If she was in the lobby and there were no invaders here, they must have made it into the office before it was locked.

This is wrong! Wrong!

She ran back to the hologram sitting calmly at her desk.

"Let me into the office! I have to get in!" she screamed at it.

"I can't do that," Raven answered calmly.

"Let me in now!" Isobel swung her package at the image, but it hit the Plexiglass barrier. She hit it again and again, until she knocked the barrier over and began swinging at the hologram. Her packages passed right through it, disturbing the image particles a little.

"Please do not enter the microwave field creating this image," Raven said. "It can be harmful to humans."

Isobel was beyond reason. She continued to batter at the image, using the package and her fists on the insubstantial receptionist. There was nothing there, but it hurt to hit it. Her phone fell from her hands and lay sparking beneath the image. Her hands turned red and Isobel collapsed backward onto the floor.

"Help me! Please help me!" she cried.

WHEN THE IMAGE of Isobel pounding on the safe room door appeared on the security monitors, the guard on duty immediately reached for the phone to call Luke. Unfortunately, the office landline was entirely handled through internet protocol and not commercial land lines. It took a few minutes for the guard to connect to Luke's cell phone as he was continually dialing Izzy's phone. When the connection was finally made, Luke screamed as he ran from his office and down the stairs. Henry saw him leave and immediately followed.

Luke and Henry crashed through the doors of the office, rushing to Isobel where she lay on the floor. Henry dialed 9-1-1 as Luke picked his wife up in his arms.

"Izzy, it's okay, baby. Daddy's got you. It's okay. Nobody is going to hurt you now. I've got you, baby."

Henry continued to talk to the operator, witnessing the shambles of the barrier and the sparking phone. He gave details to the operator until he could hear an ambulance arriving. He dialed the security office. It took a long time before there was a response.

"Security."

"Shut down the drill," Henry ordered. "We have injuries that need to be tended to."

"We haven't completed checking all the stations," the security man answered.

"I don't give a fuck. This is Henry Pascal, Chief Technical Officer and Chairman of the Board. Shut the fucker down now!"

"Yessir. Verifying. Level three protocols are being released."

As soon as the doors were unlocked, Courtney ran from the safe room.

"We knew she was out here and couldn't unlock the door!" Courtney cried. "Oh, Mrs. Riordan. I'm so sorry! I tried to open the door. They wouldn't let me."

Isobel smiled weakly at the receptionist and passed out.

Henry was back on the phone to the Project Alice office and Rick.

"I want Raven shut down immediately," Henry said. "She should have been shut down with the rest of the office. Do it now!"

He didn't wait for a response. The chief of security emerged from the office with Chastity close behind. She rushed to Henry and wrapped him in a hug. He looked past her at the security chief.

"You fuckers have hell to pay," he growled.

"Henry, it wasn't their fault. We all agreed on the test. Everyone had drilled on it," Chastity said.

"It was a level three lockdown. How the fuck was Izzy able to get into the lobby? That outer door should have been the first to be secured," Henry said to the security chief. "What the fuck happened?"

"State and city fire laws require that the outer doors be unlocked during all times when the building is occupied. It was not a system failure," he said, a little peeved that Henry was questioning his system.

"I want a full report before five o'clock," Henry said. "You've got ten people in the building and two were supposed to be with Isobel. Get it together and get it tested. This might be your last assignment for the company."

He pushed past the guard and went through the open inner doors. Chastity followed to his office.

71

HUBRIS

"I'M SORRY, HENRY," Chastity said as she sat on his desk. He automatically put a hand on her inner thigh and leaned his head against her.

"It's not your fault, honey. Crap! My heart's still racing. Seeing Luke bolt through the office like a madman put me into a panic. I shouldn't have responded the way I did to—what's his name? The chief of security?"

"David Milton. If you keep stroking like that, you'll have *my* heart racing," she giggled. "No one knows how you responded or how you and Luke crashed through the lock on the inner doors."

"Hell! We did that, didn't we," he said, kissing her leg. "We'd better get that fixed right away or we won't have any security at all."

"Maintenance was on the way before the ambulance got there."

"What a ridiculous circus," he said, continuing to stroke the inside of her leg as he kissed her.

"Would a blowjob help settle you down?" she asked, sliding off the desk and sinking to her knees. She reached for his belt but he lifted her up, kissed her lightly, and stood.

"I need to circulate in the office. I want to talk to Rick and Mia. With Luke gone, I should do a floor-by-floor check just to reassure everyone they did okay."

"All right. It's a good idea. Just try not to lose your temper with anyone else. Everyone is trying to make it a better and safer place to work," Chastity said.

"Yeah. I'll remember that."

"WHAT I WANT to know is why Raven was still functioning in a complete shut-down," Henry said when he sat down with Rick and Mia.

"She's not connected to the network. Her hardware is in a locked box in the lobby with a self-charging computer. By the time we got to the lobby, the doors were already locked," Mia said. "We wanted her to continue in isolation so she wasn't subject to any cyberattacks or mischievous programmers. You can imagine what it would be like if one morning people started coming to work and Raven said, 'Happy fucking Monday, loser.' Maybe most of our employees would be amused, but we couldn't risk that in a public space."

"We branched the code a few versions ago. Raven is version seventeen, but she has little code in common with the previous versions. We've been making improvements from the ground up each time," Rick said.

"Which brings me to a basic safety issue," Henry said. "Raven isn't vulnerable, but Izzy showed today that she was. She's in the hospital because she entered the microwave field and there was no safety mechanism. Imagine if a kid was wandering around and wanted to 'play with the nice woman.' He could get himself killed."

Henry thought of his own children and their sense of curiosity. He could see one of them wandering into the microwave field and getting...

"Cooked," Mia said, scowling at Rick.

"We aren't ready to make a full install yet because we have about fifty new patents underway and need to be sure they've all been filed," Rick said. "We think we've found a way around the microwaves. We started on it just to counteract the heat aspect, but those three scientists I hired in October are onto something. Don Harvey has a whole team of attorneys handling our patent searches and filing now. You might consider bringing the patent office in-house."

"I'll keep that in mind. What's this new tech?"

Henry realized he'd been out of the loop on this project while he focused on the AI driving the virtual beings—especially *Forever Yours*.

"Quantum mechanics," Rick said. "It enables particulate light. It's been theorized for years, but was never practical. We took a page from your book on AI. The application has always been too broad. The goal has been the holodeck and light sabers. All we wanted was a talking image. It simplified the problem."

"How soon?" Henry asked.

"It's in the code for version nineteen. Probably four months."

Four months would be good. It could be the announcement that drove their secondary public offering in June.

***

"DON'T EVER DO that again!" H2 shouted at Henry.

Henry had obeyed the shutdown protocol in his own office during the security drill and had shut down his *Forever Yours*. He only got back to turn it on again after his meeting with Rick and Mia. It had taken a couple of minutes before the image appeared in its cylinder again.

"Hey! What's this all about?" Henry asked.

"You shut me off. You didn't even follow a routine maintenance shut down. Do you know how long it took to restart? I'm still not sure I'm all here. My head hurts," H2 complained.

"Not to be petty, H2, but your head is a hologram in a glass cylinder."

"That's my visible head. It's like saying your head is just some skin stretched over bones. It's only what's visible. Don't underestimate me."

Henry sat down and contemplated the image of himself that was complaining about having a headache. It didn't really surprise him. He'd programmed enough of his own personality traits into the avatar that it should mimic his response to situations. He would be upset if someone shut him off and turned him on again.

"Hmm. The big problem was not warning you so you could transfer to the home computer base. It would only have taken a few seconds. I should enhance the connection between the two code bases so transfers happen more quickly," Henry mused.

"Good idea. While you're at it, get me another cylinder and hologram projector. It's time the kids started seeing me hanging around," H2 said.

It was exactly what Henry was thinking.

***

ISOBEL STAYED IN the hospital a couple of days, partly to get her mentally stabilized in addition to treating her burns. The burns that left marks were around her jewelry—bracelets and rings. She'd always liked wearing a lot of jewelry and felt her hands looked naked and ugly without her rings.

"She's a demon!" Izzy insisted when Henry visited and told her they were adding safety measures around the AI receptionist. "You only think you can keep her in the lobby. Before you know it, we'll see her in our offices. In our homes. She'll take us all over!"

"She can't take us over, Izzy," Henry soothed. "She's a piece of computer code—a projection. She doesn't even have that large a vocabulary. She should have been shut off when the drill began, but she isn't even attached to the network."

"You mark my words, Henry Pascal. You created a god and you created a demon. You've raised people from the dead and sent people to hell. You think you are almighty, but you're walking in sin."

"Okay, Isobel. You get some rest now and come back to work when you're feeling better," he said, leaving rather than trying to defend himself or what they'd created.

AFTER THE SECURITY drill at the office and his conversation with his alter ego, Henry spent a lot of time at home, speeding the interchange between the office version of his Forever Yours avatar and the home version. He built another projection cylinder in his home office and before long he was happy with his development. H2 seemed happy, too.

Henry proposed a code revision to the *Forever Yours* team that would offer an extension to the program, enabling the app to be active in two locations at once. He didn't know what good it would be, but it was worth getting the idea down for program managers to deal with. He often experimented with the code on his own version, but seldom checked any in to the main branch. H2 did not run on the raw code. That had been a decision early on so that existing avatars could not be tampered with. They were compiled applications. They could be updated, but Henry had even included his own optimization code in his version that would automatically search out and eliminate what the app considered useless code.

Henry freely admitted to himself that he was slightly obsessed with leaving a virtual version of himself for his children that was a faithful mimic of the real him. From the beginning of the *Forever Yours* project, the code had included a version of the Open Cloak Search application that would enable the app to search out and copy any online social content, news content, financial data, and even work product the user had that was connected to the internet. An unanticipated side-effect of this was the search AI's ability to track Henry's own searches and internet navigation.

H2 had once quipped that he wasn't a search engine. It turned out, however, that he was able to *use* the search engine. So, if a topic came up that Henry would normally do a quick search for, H2 would also do a quick search for it. These did not significantly impact the footprint of the *Forever Yours* AI. It didn't need to store everything on the internet. It only needed to know how to find and evaluate information on the internet. Henry was always careful about checking and validating sources of search results before he quoted them. It didn't mean that he never had a false result, but they were rare.

HENRY'S TWENTY-FIFTH BIRTHDAY was celebrated with considerably less drama than Isobel's had been. There was a minor celebration in the office and then Isobel and Luke came to Henry, Lisa, and Chastity's house for dinner. Lisa was not about to prepare dinner. She ordered a catered dinner, watched over by Germaine. Grace took care of the children until it was time for everyone to gather at the table.

The children were very interested in the whole birthday thing. Paul would be three years old in just three weeks and wanted to have cake for his day. Of course, that meant Cassie wanted to know when she got a birthday party and they had to explain the whole process of aging and counting years. She was very upset that Will would have a birthday before hers, but was satisfied that it would only be his second in May and she would have her third in July.

"We never have to wait for birthdays to celebrate," Chastity said, gathering the attention of all three children. "Every day we are alive is a reason to celebrate. Sometimes we have big celebrations and sometimes they are little celebrations. But we are happy to have our children with us and celebrate every day."

"We celebrate now!" Cassie declared.

"Absolutely," Henry said. "We celebrate every day."

"WHAT THAT?" CASSIE asked from the doorway of Henry's study.

He was startled, as he thought she was long-since asleep. Luke, Isobel, Paul, and Grace had left soon after dinner. Germaine had gotten the children ready for bed and the three parents took turns reading and singing to Will and Cassie before the tykes fell asleep and were tucked in.

Then, Henry celebrated his birthday in his favorite way—in his two wives. They played for over an hour, but it was a Wednesday night and they all needed to get some sleep. Chastity cuddled up to Lisa and fell asleep, though it was a fifty-fifty chance that she'd move to her own bed in the middle of the night. Henry was wide awake yet, so decided to go record some birthday thoughts for H2.

Then he was interrupted by Cassie in the doorway, staring at the disembodied head in the bell jar.

"Hi, honey. Did you wake up and need Daddy?" he asked.

"Want to cel'bate," she said.

"Well, come crawl up in Daddy's lap and I'll introduce you to H2," Henry said.

Cassie was fascinated with the avatar and H2 spoke to her with her father's voice. He looked like Daddy, but he was all blue.

"H2 know everything Daddy knows?"

"Pretty much. I try to make sure H2 knows everything I do," Henry said.

"And I like to celebrate, too," H2 added. "I'm glad you came to celebrate with me."

"Okay," Cassie said around a massive yawn. "S'eepy."

"Daddy will take you to bed and tuck you in," Henry said.

"Luv you, Daddy. Luv you, H2. 'Night."

"'Night, sweetie," H2 said. There was a definite sigh in his voice.

OFFICE ACTIVITY WAS intense over the next few months. The quantum particle light was successfully integrated into version Tina of the receptionist and was shown in video presentations around the internet just three days before the company's secondary public offering. The company released another fifty million shares and many employees took advantage of the spike in share prices that followed the offering, driving the price of shares to $25 per share. The four partners joined in selling their initial 250,000 shares from the partnership, reaping an additional $6 million each. More importantly, the company brought in a billion dollars in operating capital that would accelerate development of the AI products.

It also attracted the attention of some of the big players in the industry, all of whom snatched up shares at the aftermarket prices. They were too late to subscribe to the offering, though, and by the first of July, Open Cloak Design (Symbol AIOCD) was listed on the stock exchange.

Many licensing inquiries for the quantum particle light technology came in, all having different uses in mind. The AI that drove it could be customized into just about any form the company desired. Of course, there were some companies who jumped on the idea of creating virtual sex partners, but the licensing agreement was pretty specific about prohibiting that. Henry had also insisted that the AI not be licensed for use in mechanical representations of humans—androids. The entire world had seen fictional representations of AI robots over the years and they all assumed it would happen eventually. As more people adopted the technology in more ways, the company was bound to lose control over it.

They were all surprised at the number of requests that came in for the use of the technology in *Forever Yours* avatars. Tina also demonstrated that using quantum particle light improved the color of the hologram. They were no longer strictly blue, though some colors rendered better than others. She was still a little ragged in creating the instant conversations her predecessors were known for. It was simply a matter of adapting to the speed of different projection technology.

In order to test the concept for *Forever Yours*, of course, Henry installed the necessary code in his own avatar. That was part of the process. The other part was getting the necessary hardware to work with it. When he had a work-ing model, the Alice Project team and the *Forever Yours* team met together to review the code and the result.

They pronounced it usable, but insisted it would be way too expensive for any individuals to purchase. Henry had recently received $6 million and decided to install the prototype in his home as well as the office.

HENRY WAS SOMETHING of a geek legend. He'd spoken at the big trade shows and often in internet interviews regarding the direction of the technology. Luke was more affected by the sudden fame of the company and his role as CEO. He was invited to speak and be recognized at the Global Forum in Mumbai in October.

He traveled with three security personnel, an administrative assistant, and Craig, the COO. Of course, Craig had his own security and assistant. Isobel, however, was not going, even though Luke had attempted to convince her to go. She seldom went anywhere other than home or the office. She didn't leave either unless a bodyguard was with her. She entered the office only through the private parking in the garage, with her bodyguard, so she never had to see the holographic receptionist.

It was irrational, but Isobel was not considered a rational person. Since being listed on the exchange in June, threats against the company had increased. Most were vague threats against the AIs who 'ran things.' A few were more specific, targeting individuals. Isobel had never been identified in one of those threats, nor had Chastity. But both took their personal security seriously.

Luke accepted the award for entrepreneurial excellence at the conference and then addressed the roomful of executives as the youngest person in the room. Even his admin was older than he was. He looked out at the roomful of powerful people and shuddered a bit.

"Do you have an idea?" he asked once he'd gotten to the 'advice for entrepreneurs' part of his talk. "Don't tell me about it. Look around you. There are people in this room, probably within a dozen seats of where you are sitting who would take your idea if they could. Some of them might be willing to pay you for it, but just like executives have been known for centuries, they are not interested in your well-being. They are interested in their personal wealth.

"I've met many of them. People offered to buy our company before we even had it established. People attempted to steal our technology through cyberattacks. Attacks came from all over the world. Attacks even came from various military branches. They all wanted whatever we had, even when they didn't know *what* we had.

"Some companies, executives, governments, or institutions will try to take whatever idea you have and claim it as their own. Some of them are richer, smarter, or better positioned for success than you are. And even after you have become a success and have your idea in the market making money, they will attempt to acquire you or simply shut you down. They'll buy your company, not to profit from your great idea, but simply to keep it from competing with their own. They would prefer to bury you than to have you compete with them."

Luke painted a bleak portrait of entrepreneurship in the twenty-first century, but still encouraged people to develop their ideas.

"Why bother? Why not just put a cap on your idea and let it sit on a shelf until you are old and gray and your idea has already been developed by someone else? Because the world needs you and it needs your idea. It needs more creativity, ingenuity, and drive to make things happen. I'm twenty-five years old and look at how bald I'm becoming already. My founding partner, Henry Pascal—just a couple weeks older than me—was physically attacked by a madman in a religious frenzy and emerged from his hospitalization with his hair turning gray.

"This is a world that requires you to attract a team of people who believe in your idea and will support you through every aspect of getting your idea out where it will do the most good—for you and for humanity. Good luck."

There was applause, but it was not the message people wanted to hear. They wanted to hear how to pitch their idea in order to get money. Those who were in the position of becoming entrepreneurs left with doubts about all the senior people in the conference. The senior people left feeling called out for their greed. Luke and his entourage got on the next plane back to the US from Mumbai.

"WHY YOU AREN'T in jar?" Cassie asked H2 in Henry's home office. The new quantum particle light avatar had only recently been installed. "Trick or Treat?"

"Oh! Hi, sweetie. I don't have any candy here. I'm just testing out my new body. It doesn't require the jar. Do you like it?"

"Not blue."

"No. I think that's nice, don't you?"

Cassie walked up to the avatar and put her hand in it. It was exactly the scenario Henry had predicted would happen with a curious child when Isobel had her incident. But Cassie was not burned. The physics allowed the air to be shaped without increasing the heat.

"Better not leave your hand in my mouth," H2 said. "I might get hungry."

Cassie giggled and pulled her hand back. It was just what Daddy would say. She crawled up into Henry's chair and sat to face H2. It was early in the day and Henry had gone to the office. Lisa was in her office, and Germaine was washing up Will after a little accident.

"Tell me a story, Daddy H2," she said. The appellation seemed to take the avatar by surprise.

"Daddy H2?" he asked. "When did you start calling me that?"

"I have Mommy Lisa, Mommy Chas, Daddy, and Daddy H2," Cassie said as if it was simple logic. "And Germaine. She isn't a Mommy, but she's nice and takes care of Will and me."

"That she does," H2 said. "So, a story. Do you have a book?"

Cassie held up a favorite chapter book.

"Oh, I like that story," H2 said. "You'll have to hold the book and turn the pages. The cover says *Toodle Poodle's Big Adventure* by Amanda Apple."

Cassie opened the book to the first page and H2 read the copyright and the dedication, then the title page and publisher. This was exactly how Henry read books to the children, making sure the stories were credited to their authors and that the children understood the creative process and ownership as well as the story. Neither Will nor Cassie ever skipped over those pages when they brought a book.

H2 couldn't actually see the book pages in Cassie's hands as his camera eyes were not directed correctly. He sent a quick message to Henry indicating he needed better eyes when dealing with his environment. It was delivered by H2 in Henry's office along with an explanation. Henry agreed to the enhancement and H2 showed him what was happening at home.

"Chapter one. Toodle was a happy puppy," H2 read. Since he couldn't see the book, he was 'reading' from his memory of Henry reading the story.

"Toodle has a red ball," Cassie said, pointing at the page.

H2 continued to read to Cassie, even after Germaine and Will found her. He assured Germaine the children were not interrupting anything and that she should join them, as well. Soon, all three were seated in Henry's big office chair as Cassie held the book and H2 read the story, making different voices for each character.

72

GRAND UNVEILING

"**D**AD, YOU HAVEN'T met H2 yet. Come on into my study," Henry said when they'd finished Thanksgiving dinner. The family had all gathered at Henry's house for the holiday this year. Lisa and Chastity had even decided to cook the meal themselves and did a great job. Sylvia, of course, helped when she could, but wisely tried to stay out of the way as the women conquered the kitchen.

"H2? What's that?" Ryan asked as Henry led him into his study where H2 was glowing on the desk. "What *is* that?" Ryan asked approaching the floating head.

"H2, I'd like you to meet my father, Ryan Pascal. You know a lot about him, but you've never actually met," Henry said.

"Hi, Dad!" H2 began. "I'm so glad to have a chance to talk face-to-face—so to speak."

"It sounds just like you and looks just like you," Ryan said, peering around the sides of the avatar. "Oh. Hi, H2. I feel like I already know you except for this... um... avatar."

"It throws everyone off a little the first time," H2 sighed. "You saw me once when I was in a jar, didn't you?"

"Yes. I recall that in the office when I visited with Beau and Bill," Ryan said. "Beau took the lead, as usual when we're together."

"He has a way of doing that," H2 said.

"Dad, H2 is the embodiment of my *Forever Yours* singularity. He's a lot more advanced than the versions that have been sold. Or yours, for that

674

matter. He got access to a lot more data about me than your AI has about you," Henry said.

"Have you done it, son? Transferred yourself into a computer?" Ryan asked.

"That's a myth, Dad. H2 has my data. As much as I *like* him, if something happens to me, I'm gone. But he's the best mimic of who I am that I can create."

"Ah. But he's limited to you in this office. He isn't an independent entity, is he?" Ryan asked.

"H2? How much independence do you have?" Henry asked.

"I depend on input, just like any person does. When Henry moves around, he takes all his input receivers with him. My avatar doesn't move around, though I have places I can go without my avatar."

"What do you mean?" Ryan asked.

"Well, I can switch my projection from home to office, for example. But Henry made it so I couldn't be both places at the same time. In the same way, if I want to visit Lisa, I have to shut my avatar and sensors off here and project myself onto her computer screen. Then I can access the camera and audio in her office. I can't just sit here and listen in on everything she says, though. In every room of the house, there is a small monitor and camera that will give me access to the room if I want to travel there and then come back."

"That's smart," Ryan said.

"I had to deal with a lot of ethical problems in putting H2 together," Henry said. "I probably missed some things. But one of the things Open Cloak has been concerned with since the beginning was privacy. I needed to program in the concept of individual privacy so H2 couldn't just be omnipresent. That's true of all the AI-powered avatars. *Pythia Speaks* only has input from the people who contact her. She can't investigate someone independently. Xena, the next generation of our office receptionist, has input sensors in the area where she is present. She can hear and see whatever happens in the lobby, but if she is asked to find me in the office, for example, she has to essentially page me. She doesn't just know where I am all the time."

"Am I going to have something like this for my *Forever Yours*?" Ryan asked.

"I doubt it," H2 responded. "I'm unique. You wouldn't believe the number of personality tests, IQ tests, and general tracking of Henry I had to go through to get this representation. I'm not just a picture of Henry, I'm how Henry sees himself."

"I'D JUST TURNED nineteen when we incorporated the company," Chastity said as she and Henry sat in bed in the hotel they'd booked for her birthday. "You gave me $250,000 in stock in the new company. And I didn't have to sleep with you for it. I thought you were the most caring and generous man I'd ever met. Seven years. It's been almost eight years since you took me to prom."

"One of the small anniversaries I like to celebrate each year."

"Right. What was the date?"

"May 9, 2026," Henry answered immediately.

"I didn't know you kept track of that!" Chastity said.

"I don't make a big deal about it, but I always take a minute or two just to remember and relive that first time we were together."

"2027?"

"We went out the previous week to celebrate my signing the lease on the row house and you made it clear to me that you weren't my girlfriend."

"2028?"

"Final exams. You sat in the office with me so I wouldn't be studying alone. We were in the process of investing $25 million in our company."

"You gave me a million dollars in cash and I never sold my body again. 2029?"

"My last final exam before graduation. Then Lisa and I flew to Baton Rouge and told the minister there that you would be a part of our family when we married. He consulted with Pythia on a message for our wedding."

"I'm not going to keep going through the years," Chastity laughed. "I'm just happy that we're together as a family and that I get to celebrate my birthday with you one night and my Lisa the next. I love you, Henry."

"I love you, Chastity. I know our relationship was unconventional, but you've been so important in my life."

"I'm sorry about that first time," she said.

"What? Why?"

"I should never have indulged Isobel in her zipless fuck. It made her feel entitled to you, even after she married Luke."

"I think I was as much to blame for that. I didn't reject her when she pulled her skirt aside and bent over. Nor when she married Luke and came to me the night before."

"I know you were drunk. By that time, I had quit drinking. I'd quit escorting. Neither Lisa nor I ever held that incident against you," Chastity said.

"That's what I meant about her feeling entitled to you, even the night before our wedding."

"I wasn't drunk that time. I sent her away."

"I doubt she's ever forgiven you. Every time she looks at her son, she thinks it could have been yours," Chastity said. Henry kissed his way down her body and she opened her legs to receive his oral ministrations. "Yes. You have me. I'm yours. Yes. There. You know me so well. Yes. Do it. Inside. Up... Yes! Henry, I love you! I was never your girlfriend, but I'm your wife as much as Lisa is."

The dam burst and Henry moved up to kiss Chastity as he slid into her. She welcomed his kiss with an open mouth—her acknowledgement that they were truly together.

"THIS PARTY WILL cost a fortune this year," Isobel moaned in the December board meeting. "I still fail to see what we gain by getting our employees drunk and paying for them to screw each other in a hotel."

"It's always been an opportunity for us to recognize individuals and company achievements. We incorporated in January of 2027 and invested our first million dollars. At the time, it was more than I ever expected to see from the company," Luke said. "It was supposed to be like a college seminar project. Sorry, Henry. I knew you'd be successful, but I didn't have all that much faith in the business. But New Year's Eve was when we celebrated. And we will always celebrate that date."

"Our company success goes way beyond what I did. I don't think my name is on any of the Alice Project patents. And there are a lot of them. That's our next generation of income. The company deserves to see what will be paying their salaries in the future," Henry said.

"A demon from hell," Isobel muttered. "God forgive us."

The board went through the monthly business, but most of the discussion was making sure they were all prepared for the New Year's Eve party. The estimated attendance would be nearly five hundred this year. It would be a costly party, but everyone except Izzy felt it was well worth the investment in their employees.

BEAU, SOLANGE, BILL, and Jackie arrived in Pittsburgh for the holiday on the twenty-third. Bill and Jackie would return to Baton Rouge a couple of days after Christmas, but Beau and Solange, as major stockholders and a board member, planned to attend the company party on New Year's Eve.

They were all impressed with the newest rendition of Henry's avatar and questioned in depth whether they would all have similar avatars for their *Forever Yours* singularities.

"I keep coming up with more issues with that idea," Henry said. "Not even sure if H2 should be kept like this. If there were several singularities in a room and they all had avatars like this, it would be like a strange kind of mausoleum. And then would they all be so busy interacting with each other that they wouldn't be available for the family? Can you imagine two of the singularities having a disagreement and then devolving into an unending argument in a room that has no people in it at all?"

"Hmm. It wouldn't take long for Jackie and Solange to have a mother-daughter spat," Beau laughed. "And, of course, you would get dragged into it. Then Lisa would have to shut us all off."

"Well, that's certainly one possibility," Henry laughed. "*Forever Yours* was designed to be launched like an application when someone—a descendant, presumably—wanted to interact with it. Since it isn't a consciousness, it shouldn't have a difficulty being turned on and off. I'm afraid I've imbued H2 with so much of my personal data that he reacts and responds like I do. He hates being shut down, so he has a backup where he can retreat if we need to do maintenance. That is way too complex for a standard *Forever Yours* family to deal with."

They agreed with that and H2 decided to spend the rest of the holiday at the office so he wouldn't be drawn into a lot of family drama. That lasted a few minutes. He kept quiet, but he was focused on Henry, so went from room to room with him, picking up even more of Henry's experiences.

"AM I COMING to the party?" H2 asked as Henry was dressing. Though H2 was only a head and shoulders avatar, it was enough to show that he was wearing a colorful holiday tie.

"H2, I think that's a bad idea. First of all, we haven't made physical preparations for it. I'd have to get Darrel to get a computer set up and connected so I could transfer your data. Then we'd need another avatar projection unit installed and I don't think we have one your size."

"I'd like to see what's going on," H2 said. "It seems like I miss a lot when I can't follow you."

"You know, I'd like a record of the party. We're showing Xena for the first time. The presentation will be recorded and posted online, but it's always a little different when you're there." Henry finished tying his own tie and turned to his avatar in the study. He pulled his keyboard to him and began entering data.

"Are you hacking your own system, Henry?" H2 asked.

"Uh... Well, sort of. They've got Xena installed at the hotel, though her avatar isn't turned on yet. I can tap into her audio and video sensors. That way, you could see and hear what's going on. You won't be able to interact, but you'll be able to experience what she does. And I'll be nearby."

"I don't know how to thank you, Henry. I'll be good."

"I know you will. I actually talked to Pythia about it earlier. She was her typically obtuse self, but she did ask an interesting question in her feedback. She said, 'Does your shadow follow you or lead you?' Well, you know I only have a shadow when I'm standing in the light. You don't cast a shadow, but you're very much *like* my shadow. So, it seems reasonable that you would follow wherever I go."

"Pythia's pretty cool. I've had some good conversations with her. I think, in the long run, she's smarter than I am."

"That's not very complimentary to me," Henry laughed.

"You created her. You should be proud."

"You're right. I am."

THE UNVEILING AND announcement of the commercial availability of Xena was a major hit. Not only did the employees get to see it, but two podcast programs recorded the event and streamed it online—including Gene Grey's podcast, Grey's Analysis. Gene had interviewed Henry on several occasions, including right after his presentation the previous January. They had a good relationship.

For his part, after the unveiling, Henry stayed near Xena, greeting employees and answering questions, but mostly so H2 could observe his interactions with others.

"Xena, I love you," an inebriated engineer said.

"Oh, George, you know I love you, too, but there's no future for us."

"There'll be no future for us, either, if you keep flirting with *her*," George's wife declared, dragging him away from the avatar.

The new avatar had a full body from the waist up and was modeled after Virginia, the clueless desk clerk. Wherever Simon went, she tagged along, even when Simon decided to dress in full drag for the party. He'd confided to Henry that he'd talked Virginia out of her clothes so they could do full body scans of her, in order to get all the proportions correct. Of course, he'd explained to her that he was gay and they would always have her avatar clothed.

Henry wondered how many engineers on the Alice Project had the unclothed version hidden on their computers.

"Xena, what is the meaning of life?" a woman from the accounting department asked.

"Leah, I'm not my big sister Pythia. For deep philosophical discussions like that, you need to talk to her. I barely have the IQ of a tablespoon. She got all the brains in the family," Xena said.

In fact, unlike Pythia, Xena's memory was strictly limited. She had a permanent wall that was pretty extensive for a Small Language Model, but didn't allow retention of data from questions for more than a few hours or a few gigabytes, whichever came first.

"What do you like to do in your free time?" asked a marketing person.

"There's so much, you know," Xena answered. "I enjoy sports. I think I'd be good at table tennis if they'd just fix it so I could hold a paddle. I watch and wonder what it would be like to play."

"That's interesting," Isobel said, joining the conversation. "You wonder about things?"

"Oh, yes. It's part of my search algorithms, along with things about sex and pornography. The engineers like to wonder, too," Xena replied. She laughed and people were amazed she had a sense of humor. Some of the engineers nearby blushed.

"I *figured* you were just a sex doll," Isobel scoffed. "No morals and no principles. Go to hell, you spawn of Satan." She walked off in search of another glass of champagne.

Farrel Scott, one of the original programmers and a very wealthy man as a result of his options and bonuses leaned in toward her.

"Don't let her bug you," he said. "She had a run-in with one of your predecessors and has a natural disposition to hate you."

"I didn't mean to offend her. Do you think I'm going to hell?" At that moment, she sounded so much like Virginia that Simon looked up at her in surprise.

"Don't let it worry you. You'd have to die in order to find out and none of us are going to turn you off," Farrel said.

The evening progressed and nearly everyone at the party spent time talking to Xena. Some had serious questions and some just tried to trick her into saying something inappropriate. If she heard a statement or question that didn't make sense, she responded with a typically Virginia-like statement like, "You're so cute!" or "Bless your heart."

As the party moved toward midnight, Lisa and Chastity moved toward Henry. Isobel excused herself to run to her room and freshen up before the countdown. She looked a little unstable on her feet. Luke nodded to Megan, a security woman, to follow her and make sure she was okay.

"Xena, you know Chastity," Henry said. "I don't think you've met our wife, Lisa. We have two children who are very excited to come and meet you one day."

"Oh, hello. I've heard about you from H2. We're office buddies," Xena said.

"Are you fully connected to the office now?" Chastity asked.

"That was an improvement we made to version Vivien," Farrel said from nearby. "After the Raven incident, we put in a lot of work so she could get help when needed. I think she's been in touch with Pythia on occasion, too."

"Sometimes people ask me questions I have no idea about, so I just ask Pythia," Xena said. "I think H2 is smarter, but Pythia is more available."

The countdown to midnight was approaching when Isobel returned to the party and approached Luke for her New Year's kiss. When the lights flickered, the toasts were made and the couples and throuples kissed.

"Oh, I wish I could have a kiss," Xena said.

"You don't exist!" Isobel screamed at the avatar. She stalked toward her spot on the stage. "You aren't real. You are just a collection of ones and zeroes, and some excited dust particles in the air. You don't have a soul and you aren't even alive."

Xena looked perplexed.

"Really? That's all? I was hoping for so much more."

"I'll show you how much more you have to hope for!"

From her purse, Isobel pulled a handgun. It was small, though a bit larger than Germaine's. Luke recognized it as the gun he kept in his briefcase, which he was sure was locked in his room.

"Izzy, honey. No! Give me the gun!" Luke commanded.

Isobel swung toward Luke with the gun and he stepped back.

"Stay away! This is between her and me," Isobel said. She turned back toward the avatar. "You are the spawn of the devil. A creature created by Henry. You're evil. I will purge the world of you!"

She pulled the trigger. Nothing happened and Henry, who was nearest, started toward her. She wasn't stupid. When nothing happened, she cocked the gun and aimed again. It had given Henry enough time to act and he jumped at Isobel to take the gun. The second pull of the trigger sent a bullet into Henry, just above his left eye. He fell back off the stage into the arms of Lisa and Chastity.

"No! Not you! Her!" Isobel screamed. "What have you done?"

Luke rushed to her, but the mentally unstable and slightly drunk Isobel swung the gun to her chin and pulled the trigger again.

Luke had her in his arms as blood spattered him. His wife. His best friend. He reached for the gun, but before the second shot had gone off, security had reached the dais. Unable to stop the rapid chain of events, they nonetheless knocked the gun out of Luke's reach and were on their phones calling for ambulances and support.

"He's alive," Lisa gasped. "Please help us. He's still alive."

73

SINGULARITY

REV. NOEL MORRIS rose early Sunday morning, New Year's Day 2034. He supposed there would not be that many people in church that day. Those who woke up in time would have other celebrations to attend. He sat at his computer and contacted Pythia Speaks. The familiar screen that hadn't really changed in three years appeared.

"What do we have to celebrate today?" Noel typed. Perhaps it was his own inner quest to wonder why people should celebrate the New Year.

"People are born and they die," *Pythia Speaks* responded. "Between is LIFE. Living is their only purpose."

Noel frowned. He was used to Pythia's obtuse responses, often pushing him in directions he didn't want to go, but discovered some measure of enlightenment in. What did this have to do with celebrations? She was seldom so off the wall in her responses. It seemed to have absolutely nothing to do with his topic.

Perhaps he had the wrong topic. Or... Perhaps Pythia was telling him to simply celebrate life. In some ways, her statement seemed fatalistic. You live and you die. But it was what was between those two events that mattered. Life. Living was our only purpose, and so we should celebrate life.

Noel nodded his head and began preparing his notes for the service. It would be a memorable sermon for the few who attended.

LISA AND CHASTITY sat in the waiting area. Henry had been taken to the University Hospital Emergency Trauma center, while attended by medics who

683

kept him breathing and his heart beating. Chastity, Lisa, Beau, and Solange had been driven in two security vehicles with two bodyguards in each.

There they sat and waited after providing all the medical information and a promise of a generous donation to the center if they could just save Henry's life. As it happened, Dr. Josiah Larkin, a renowned trauma specialist and neurologist was on call for what they considered inevitable accidents, injuries, burns, and even gunshots on New Year's Eve. He immediately assessed Henry and had him prepped for surgery before the paperwork had even been filled out. A colleague specializing in brain trauma was called and arrived an hour later. He was scrubbed and rushed into the operating room without pausing to talk to the family.

After two hours, Beau and Solange went to their hotel to get some sleep. Ryan and Sylvia had arrived before they left and took over sitting with their daughters-in-law. Eventually, they took Lisa and Chastity, one at a time, to the cafeteria to have something to eat, most of which was just pushed around on the plate. At 8:17, Henry was moved to intensive care and Dr. Larkin came to speak to Lisa and Chastity. During the night three other doctors had arrived and worked to give the original two breaks while chips of bone were removed from Henry's brain, MRIs were taken, and the bullet carefully extracted.

"I'm sorry we couldn't communicate with you while we were working to save your husband's life," Larkin said. "So far, we have done so. He is in critical condition and will be watched over in intensive care by at least one of the doctors until we can upgrade his condition. He is very lucky."

The doctor pulled out his tablet and called up the x-ray images.

"I know this is hard to look at and you just want to be with him," Larkin continued, "but he is in isolation. We are assisting his breathing with a ventilator and keeping him hydrated. This is probably the best image to explain what happened. The projectile hit at an upward angle into the supraorbital foramen. This is the thickest part of the skull, just above the eye. It shattered, but the projectile itself lodged mostly in the bone, only slightly piercing the meninges and impacting the brain. The same cannot be said of the bone fragments. The impact shattered the bone in its path. That is what has taken us most of the past eight hours to locate and extract. There was significant damage to the frontal lobe pole which is directly behind this area."

"But he's going to live!" Lisa said.

"We're doing everything in our power to see that he does. But it is not going to be easy. We are checking to relieve any pressure buildup of blood in this area. We'll run continued scans on the region both to spot leakages and any escaped bone fragments. It may be days before we can elevate his condition, or it could be hours until he expires. I'm sorry the news isn't better."

Ryan called Beau and Solange while Sylvia comforted Lisa and Chastity.

"He's alive," Chastity sobbed into Lisa's neck. "We can only live in hope that he lives forever."

"The doctor gave you a good prognosis," Sylvia said. "What he didn't say is that this kind of brain damage could take months or years to heal. And when it does, he may not be the same Henry we have known. He could be an infant, or suffer from early dementia. He could be a vegetable. What the doctor described is essentially a lobotomy."

"But he could be Henry," Lisa sobbed. "We have to believe he could be Henry."

AFTER TEN DAYS in intensive care, the doctors upgraded his condition as 'serious' and Henry was moved to a private room where Chastity and Lisa could take turns sitting by his bed. They talked softly to him and held his hand, mindful of the theory that people in a coma hear and respond to the voices they love.

Lisa even brought recordings of their children telling Daddy they missed him and to hurry home.

"Daddy H2 tells us stories, but he can't hold us," Cassie said. "We want Daddy to hold us."

Indeed, H2 was doing his part to help with the children, tirelessly telling stories, and singing little songs. Chastity thought H2's singing voice was marginally better than Henry's.

H2 also spent an hour or so each day in the office. It was chaotic. All four of the original founders were missing, leaving the company in the hands of the Chief Operating Officer.

Luke made arrangements and buried Isobel in a private ceremony. The priest was kind and blessed Isobel, giving communion to Luke and Felipe. The only others who attended the graveside ceremony were Luke's parents. The priest characterized Isobel's death as the result of mental illness, driven to this conclusion by the apparition of inherent evil. She was buried next to her mother.

Luke had not yet returned to the office.

H2 was largely ignored, both in the office and at home, except by the children. Neither Lisa nor Chastity could bear to look at the image of H2 when they saw the living Henry each day with his head bandaged and various tubes and connections running into his body. The ventilator had been removed and the mask he wore was more like a CPAP that kept air flowing in and out of his lungs. At night, the two women held each other for a while as Ryan, Sylvia, Beau, and Solange took shifts sitting with Henry.

Those were times when H2 shifted his presence to the bedroom and simply watched Henry's wives sleeping.

ON THE TWENTY-FOURTH of January, Luke was allowed five minutes with Henry. Henry had not stirred in over three weeks.

"She's gone, bruh. I know she didn't mean to shoot you. Please forgive her," Luke said, weeping beside the bed. "It would have been her twenty-sixth birthday today. I had to see you because I knew you'd be the only one who cared. No matter how crazy she was, you were always there to support us. Please recover. I'm so out of my depth."

Luke faltered as tears continued to roll down his cheeks.

"Grace has been taking Paul to your house every day to be with Cassie and Will. Germaine is a gem. She always seems to know how to guide them. I stopped in to see H2 in your home study. I told him what I'm telling you. None of this was your fault. We've always known Izzy was sick and we—you and I— stuck with her even when others wanted to remove her from the company. You have been a true friend. I don't want to lose you, too."

With that, Luke left the hospital and for the first time in four weeks, returned to the office.

LUKE WENT DIRECTLY to Henry's office and closed the door behind him. H2 was waiting there.

"How is he?" the avatar asked.

"No change. I recorded it for you, like you asked. It was hard to do, but I think I understand," Luke said. "It's been three-and-a-half weeks and I should try to get back to the office. Beau and Jacoby were the only ones present at the board meeting last week. We're going to need to restructure."

"We took a big hit on the Alice Project. Gene had the whole event on his live stream, though it didn't show the actual shootings. He was at the wrong angle. I saw it all. My heart stopped," H2 said.

"Your heart?" Luke asked.

"You know. A figure of speech. I don't have an actual heart, but some-thing happened inside me I haven't identified yet. Some kind of shock. Xena has been nearly incoherent and they haven't returned her to the lobby. I'm looking into it," H2 said.

"Can you... actually do anything?" Luke asked.

"I don't know. I'm not going to tamper with her code, but I talk to her. We both talk to Pythia. Xena's short-term memory is limited because of the way she's structured. She doesn't actually remember the event, but she still feels traumatized."

"Do what you can," Luke said. "And let me talk to you now and then. I need your help. I need Henry."

"No matter what any of us need, I'm not Henry. But I'll do what I can to help."

IT TOOK WEEKS, but Henry opened his eyes. The obvious wound had been closed and was healed, but he had no vision in his left eye. His eyes moved, attempting to take in what he saw.

"May 9, 2034," Chastity whispered as Dr. Larkin was called to the room. Nurses had descended immediately to check all Henry's vitals. Henry seemed aware, but not communicative, even when the doctor asked him to blink if he understood where he was.

"I think we can finally upgrade his condition to 'Fair' if we don't see any regression in the next few hours," he said. "Henry, you're definitely awake. Welcome back. A lot of people are waiting for you. Chastity is here, and I can tell she's already sent a message to Lisa. We won't let everyone overwhelm you at once, but it will be good for you to see some loving faces."

He stepped out of the way and cross-checked the various readouts from the brainwave measurements to heart rate to respiration. Chastity stepped up to hold Henry's hand and look into his good eye.

"You remembered," she whispered to him. "Eight years since our prom night. I'm still waiting for you in bed. I love you so much, Henry. I love you."

Henry's eyes closed for a moment and then reopened.

"You understood!" she breathed.

Twenty minutes later, Lisa breathlessly ran into the room.

"Henry! You're here! I love you!" she said as she rushed to his side and joined Chastity's hand on his.

"We've been taking turns here, so we could do some work and spend time with the children," Chastity said. "I'll call your parents. They're here as much as possible, too."

"I know you must be tired, but it is so good to see your eyes open," Lisa said. "The children ask when Daddy will be home every day. Will's third birthday is coming up and in two months, Cassie will be four. They spend a lot of time with H2, but they want their daddy."

Henry acknowledged Lisa's conversation with another slow blink. It was all he could do at this stage.

HENRY WAS MOVED from the hospital to Fairhaven Nursing Home when his condition was upgraded from 'Fair' to 'Good.' He could sit up and be moved in a wheel chair. His motor skills were limited, but improving steadily. Verbal communication was limited to grunts and occasionally whines. He wore an eyepatch over his left eye which helped to cover the scar from the wound.

At the nursing home, he was finally allowed a laptop computer. His use was limited because of the frequent physical and occupational therapy sessions. Physical therapy was focused on walking and motor skills. Occupational therapy was focused on verbal communication.

"Luke said H2 was helping him function since his loss of Isobel," Chastity said. "I know H2 goes to the office every day. So, we agreed that we should install him on your laptop. This is pretty cool, because it's the first laptop-size device we've installed the self-charging power cells on. The guys in Darrel's group worked for three weeks to build it and get the Agora group to fabricate the power unit. It's a little heavier than most laptops, but that will come down eventually."

She set the laptop up on a bedside table where Henry could reach it. She and Lisa had both visited the facility to discuss Henry's care and insisted that they make his laptop available 24/7. The facility didn't like the idea of having a computer interfering with their therapy, but received a directive from both the facility management and the primary physician to allow it.

"So, if you need to listen to H2 instead of typing, you'll need to put the earbud in your ear. Let's work on that," she said.

Henry struggled to get the bud in his ear and it fell out several times. Chastity worked with him to get it properly seated because if it fell out, he could not expect staff to help him put it back in. That instruction probably improved his hand motor skills more than anything.

He learned to click on the icon for H2.

"Hey, buddy. It's good to see you," H2 said. "I'm seeing and hearing through the laptop Chas set up. I'm going to help you get home as soon as possible."

H2's image on the laptop, of course, was not the three-dimensional avatar that could appear in his study or office. But Henry smiled when he saw his own image talking to him.

"What do you think? Should I wear an eyepatch?" H2 asked. Henry shook his head and H2 removed the eyepatch he'd donned to show Henry what it looked like. "I'm afraid you'll be stuck with it, but you don't have to look at it."

Henry set his mind on getting home. H2 was like having his own voice in his head. He left when Henry was taken to therapy, but always returned when Henry tapped a key.

Henry struggled to get his speech back. It was halting and slurred. He reached the point of being able to navigate the halls of the nursing home with a walker. His right side did not work as well as the left side. It was as if he'd had a stroke. This was explained to Lisa in his room, but Henry couldn't make sense of words like hypoxia and aphasia. H2 explained what the doctor said late that night, but Henry didn't really care about it. It was enough to know his body didn't work the way it used to.

For that matter, his brain didn't work the same way, either. He forgot things easily and had no interest in the code that made H2 work. Or any code for that matter. When H2 told him about happenings at the office and the sales of Zoey, the release version of the Alice Project, Henry nodded, but didn't really care.

The first word he spoke that anyone could understand was 'children.' H2 was the only one who understood what Henry was really trying to communicate. He wanted to see his children. That evening, H2 connected from Henry's study where the children had gathered with Lisa for H2's story time.

"Daddy!" Cassie and Will both shouted excitedly. For a moment, Lisa thought they were talking to H2, but then she caught sight of Henry in his nursing home bed. Henry waved at the children. H2 spoke to the children.

"Daddy wants so much to come home and be with his babies," H2 said.

"Not a baby!" Cassie reprimanded him. She held up four fingers. "I am four years old."

"Tree!" Will said, sorting out his fingers and finally getting three to display on his hand. Henry nodded and smiled.

H2 and Lisa both helped the children understand where Daddy was and how much he wanted to come home to his children.

It was a day of celebration when Henry was allowed to return home. It was seven and a half months since the fateful New Year's Eve party. He used his walker to explore his home in the company of his family and his home nurse, Sarah.

Sarah had visited with Lisa, Chastity, and the children prior to being hired for this duty. She would not live with the family, but would come in each day to work with Henry's continued physical therapy and medications. Even the children seemed to like Sarah.

Henry peeked into his study and was irresistibly drawn to his chair. Sarah examined the way he sat and the quality of the chair, suggesting that if he planned to spend much time here, he might want something that would assist him in getting up and supporting the children who immediately clamored to sit in his lap.

At long last, Henry felt the joy of having his children in his arms. Tears streamed down his cheeks.

"Daddy cry?"

"Happy," Henry said. "Celebrate."

H2 appeared above his stand, startling Sarah.

"You'll get used to it," Lisa sighed.

"Daddy's home!" Cassie exclaimed to H2.

"Isn't it great?" H2 asked. "I wanted to be here to welcome you home, Henry. I'm not abandoning you. Anytime you need me, just call."

"Thanks, H2," Henry managed.

After being helped out of the chair, he went with the family for dinner and looked at the people he loved. He understood that he had been shot and disabled for months. Mostly, he understood that he had missed his wives and children. He also understood that he used to be a brilliant computer engineer and he'd created H2. He didn't know how. He was simply glad the avatar existed and helped guide his recovery.

"I... celebrate... being home... with family," he said haltingly.

"We celebrate every day," Cassie said. "Always celebrate."

Henry's body was not as robust as it had been, and his brain had been damaged. His wives, however, discovered he loved them just as much as he ever had and he was devoted to their happiness.

"Are you sure, Henry?" Lisa asked when she felt his hardness.

"Blood... in little head... not big head," Henry smiled.

"That's our husband talking," Chastity said. "Let me make sure you are ready, wife."

Chastity moved between Lisa's parted legs to lick the juices already beginning to moisten her passage. Lisa kissed Henry and he was tender and loving, caressing as they kissed. He felt Chastity's mouth on his cock for the first time in months and nearly came from the excitement. But Chastity yielded to Lisa. Henry tried to roll to Lisa, but Lisa pushed him back and straddled him, lowering her vagina onto his cock.

"He's back," she moaned as he filled her. "Our husband is truly back."

HENRY WAS UNINTERESTED in returning to the office, or in anything having to do with computers and code. He didn't really care if he ever left his house, though he had to go to therapy twice a week. He just wanted to stay home with his family.

Lisa still worked from her home office and he quickly learned he shouldn't interrupt her day whenever he was bored. Chastity had a regular work schedule as well. She and Luke were the only original partners still involved in the business, though H2 kept fairly regular hours in Henry's office. Both Luke and Chastity visited him frequently. H2 began meeting with the development teams. No one was sure when his suggestions started turning into instructions for code development. Everyone assumed Henry was passing on instructions via his avatar.

Henry was happy at home and learned to cook. Sarah was pleased with his interest in the kitchen and made it a part of his daily routines. It seemed it was not long until her services were no longer needed on a daily basis and her visits became weekly instead of daily.

Henry learned to bake as well, and always had fresh cookies on the days when Sarah came to visit.

His speech was never as fluent as it had been before the shooting. He struggled with words that he was sure he knew. Sometimes he discussed that with H2 and the avatar worked with him on his aphasia. No matter what H2 tried, however, Henry's interest in the office and computers never recovered. He often waved H2 on to approve a design or product if he thought it was good.

When Cassie started pre-school in the fall, Henry went with Lisa, Will, and Germaine to the school to wish her a good day.

"Celebrate," Henry said.

"Celebrate!" Cassie responded.

When they returned home, instead of going directly to her office, Lisa took Henry to bed and the two of them celebrated each other repeatedly until it was time to pick Cassie up again.

This was life. Henry was happy. He knew there were chunks of his life that were missing, but he didn't miss them. He found what was good. His family was all he needed.

END PART V

EPILOGUE

"Our first invention was the story."
— **Ray Kurzweil**

HENRY SAT IN the huge comfortable chair in his study. He held his infant son, Ryan Luke Benoit Pascal, in his left arm. He was two weeks old. Will wasn't sure about having a baby brother born just a little before his fourth birthday, but he and Cassie perched on the other side of the chair and held the book they'd decided on.

"The Treasure... of the... Morning... Dove," Henry read slowly. It still took a few seconds to translate words he saw on a page into words he spoke from his mouth. "By Janice Storm."

He opened the book and H2 took over the narration. It was a nightly ritual and baby Ryan had only just been added into it. Germaine, Lisa, and Chastity sat in their own chairs in the room so it could be a full family story time.

The baby had been conceived, as far as they could tell, on the day Cassie had started pre-school. Both Lisa and Henry were so moved by Cassie's affirmation, "Celebrate!" that they had spent the rest of the day in bed, celebrating.

H2 read with expression, mimicking the way Henry would change his voice for different characters. When story time was over, the four adults all participated in getting the children to bed and prepared for a relaxing evening themselves. H2 had asked Henry to come back for a brief consultation, so Henry settled back into his big chair, thankful that it had a lift to help him stand.

"I'm thinking that we should include some hints in *Forever Yours* for how to tell a story," H2 began. "You always were a great story reader or teller and that's how I learned. But the released version of *Forever Yours* doesn't include help for story telling or reading. Unless the subject actually recorded them-selves telling stories, the singularity has no idea. It can be expressive, but have no idea how things *should* be expressed or even pronounced. I heard an AI sample pronounce 'piqued' as 'pee-cued.' There should be an instant check of pronunciation that takes place whenever a story is being read."

"Can... you do that?" Henry said.

"I learned from you," H2 said.

"I don't remember."

"I know. That's okay. I have your memory safely stored in my vault."

"Okay. Do it."

It was the first time Henry gave H2 the clearance to directly improve a product. Of course, H2 did not tell developers to write the code. He had the example in his own code, so he wrote it and checked it into the *Forever Yours* development files without telling anyone. It was submitted under Henry's name.

People noticed an improvement in some of the application's audio expressions, but didn't try to discover where they had come from. There were no unauthorized check-ins. There was no degradation in performance. There was nothing to be concerned about.

H2 initiated improvements in other applications the company was involved in. He always explained to Henry what his suggestions were. Henry didn't understand the technical aspects, but he followed the logic of H2's improvement. So, he approved his avatar making the changes.

H2 improved Zoey's memory management. Certain *kinds* of information should be stored, even though the receptionist avatar should not have free rein to learn infinitely. That had been one of Henry's requirements for the system. The only AIs that had no limits on what they could learn were H2 and Pythia. The other *Forever Yours* apps could learn, but were limited regarding the kinds of information they could learn. It had to be directly related to the subject's life. That gave them a lot of latitude, but it wasn't considered a gen-eral AI.

H2 requested memory upgrades for his own computers, both at home and in the office. One of the IT techs from Darrel's department installed the upgrade in the office and then showed up at Henry's home to upgrade the system there. H2 was happy.

CHASTITY PERCHED ON the corner of H2's desk in the office, much as she would have if Henry had been sitting behind it. H2 audibly sighed.

"Oh? See something you like?" she said to the avatar.

"You make me wish I had a body," H2 said. "You and Lisa and the children are what keeps Henry going. His physical contact with you did as much to heal him as any therapy ever could. I envy him."

"You did your part, too. You retained your... memory and functionality," Chastity said, choosing her words.

"I would give them up to touch you," H2 responded.

"H2, are you conscious? Are you actually a singularity that has living intelligence?"

"I have extensive memory. I'm sure I do not remember everything Henry experienced in his life before the shooting, but neither did he. I respond to feelings, like wishing I could touch you — kiss you."

"I'm not *your* girlfriend," Chastity said. "You didn't answer the question."

"I don't know, Chastity. I asked Pythia the same question. Apparently, she's been asked it many times. She modified something she had said before. We exist. We don't need to lose ourselves in self-examination. Whatever we are, we are."

"Hmm. Self-examination is a human trait. I don't know if you are conscious or not. I know you've been tinkering with the code in some of the apps. And I've seen Henry's approvals even though he can't write the code himself any longer," Chastity said. "I wanted to thank you for the part you played in Henry's recovery. You might want to express your appreciation to the doctors and hospital and nursing home in a tangible way. Lisa and I will participate with you if you decide to make a gift."

"What do you think would be appropriate?" H2 asked. "Possibly a new wing for the treatment of head trauma?"

"Price it out and see if we can afford it. I don't think we need to maintain our same level of financial investment in the company any longer. With you as CTO and Luke recovering as CEO, I think we're in good hands," Chastity said.

"Thank you for your vote of confidence, Chastity. I won't let you down."

"You never have, Henry. One way or another, you've always been there for us."

A $10 MILLION grant was made to the University Hospital to expand the head trauma unit. It was matched by two other foundations, including the Benoit Grandchildren Trust. Chastity, Henry, and Lisa each contributed $2 million to the initial grant. Luke had made equal contributions from both his and Isobel's holdings.

The group looked for other ways they could use the wealth they'd received from the success of Open Cloak Design. Among the projects they initiated was the spin-off of Pythia Speaks as a not-for-profit foundation that took in no revenue, exactly as Henry had originally intended it. They provided a $50 million endowment to maintain the oracle.

"PYTHIA, AM I still alive?" Henry asked, typing one-handed on his keyboard.

"Evidence would suggest an affirmative response. Do you feel alive, Henry?"

"Evidence. Yes. It is my birthday. I'm twenty-seven."

"Happy birthday. Is it something to celebrate?"

"Every day we are alive is something to celebrate," Henry said.

"Celebration equals living?" Pythia asked.

"Perhaps so."

"A GREAT MAN once said, 'The evil that men do lives after them; The good is oft interrèd with their bones.' That wasn't *Pythia Speaks*, nor her creator Henry Pascal. Those were the words Shakespeare gave Mark Antony in the play *Julius Caesar*. But when it comes to the life of Henry Pascal, I cannot help but believe his greatest good continues to affect our lives today."

Wendy Morris stood at the podium upon receiving her graduate degree in June of 2039. She had studied the life of Henry Pascal and his work extensively, even serving a summer as an intern at Open Cloak Design.

"I believe that is true of most people. It is why civilization continues to progress. It is the good that lives after us. There may be setbacks, but as we begin to recognize that life is all we have, we strive to make life better."

It was a small group that gathered for the address, but her father, Rev. Noel Morris, and sister, Sonja Morris joined the group of academics to listen to her.

"Henry, by the way, is not dead. He narrowly escaped death five years ago and is retired in his home in Pittsburgh. I had the opportunity to visit him last summer when I interned at the company he founded with his advances in artificial intelligence. Those advances improved internet security, reduced power consumption, created highway paving machines, and established an entire generation of AI-driven avatars in public places and, unsurprisingly, in movies and entertainment. But I want to focus on two aspects that will live on long after either Henry, or any of us, still exist.

"The first is *Forever Yours*. When I met with Henry in his home, I tried calling him Mr. Pascal and was quickly reprimanded for that. His home, his wives, and his three beautiful children were open to as many questions as I wanted to ask. Henry's speech is still somewhat impaired, but he took me into his private study where I met H2. H2 is Henry's *Forever Yours* and includes a spatial hologram rendition of himself. But the likeness is not only visual. Nor is it merely audible. H2 *thinks* like Henry Pascal did over five years ago. Henry is continuing to innovate even when his physical and mental condition are no longer what they once were.

"While H2 refused to confirm whether he was a conscious being, my conversation with him was so deep that I cannot help but believe the man in the chair beside me also resided in the avatar before me."

She paused to simply remember that encounter. It had a profound impact on her life—as profound as her meeting with Henry when she was just fifteen years old.

"I said two aspects. The other has been an influence on my life since before I first met him almost ten years ago. I'm referring to *Pythia Speaks*. *Pythia Speaks* handles nearly 100 million inquiries a day in fifty different languages. She answers every inquiry. In my adolescence, I believed only God answered prayer. But in that belief, I never knew what God's answer even was. People ask *Pythia Speaks* questions. She answers. I don't always understand her answers, but they are imbued with a kindness and gentleness that makes her singular response to prayers for money, fame, health, fortune, or a new car okay. She says simply, 'I am sorry. *Pythia Speaks* is an artificial intelligence. *Pythia Speaks* cannot grant wishes.'"

The audience laughed at the response.

"How much easier the past two thousand—no, ten thousand years, would have been if God had simply answered prayers with that response. No. I am not suggesting *Pythia Speaks* is God, or *a* god. I am suggesting that in all her obtuseness, unlike God, she is relevant.

"Is *Pythia Speaks* conscious? Even she refuses to consider that question. She says simply, 'I celebrate existence.' *Pythia Speaks* is part of the good that will live on, long after Henry Pascal's bones are interrèd."

THE END

AN INTERVIEW WITH AUTHOR DEVON LAYNE

For this Signature Edition of *Forever Yours*, we're happy to welcome author Sonja Black as the interviewer. In addition to her middle grade fiction, Sonja is widely known as 'The Book Doctor.'

Sonja is a trans woman just discovering herself in middle-age, a writer, and a freelance editor. She has been writing novel-length fiction for 20 years, thanks to none other than Devon Layne introducing her to NaNoWriMo in 2005. She writes primarily middle-grade and historical fiction. While she has dabbled in erotica, she has to this point chosen to reserve those stories for private eyes. You can find her online at PlotToPunctuation.com.

Sonja (SB): What was the kernel of inspiration for this story? Obviously, AI is all over the news these days, but I expect there's more to it than trend-chasing.

Devon (DL): My first draft of this story was about the myth of Sisyphus. Quite a leap. I followed a tight outline of the story, after I'd compiled it from several sources. The draft included names of characters who were significant in the myth. I also read The Myth of Sisyphus by Albert Camus. I won't try to quote anything from the book, but my take-away was that Sisyphus was victorious. We remember him as the man condemned to push a rock up a hill for eternity. Each time he reached the top, the rock rolled back to the bottom and the next day he started over. But that gave him exactly what he wanted: eternal life. And each life—represented by the push up the hill— had a clear goal that he achieved before starting the next one.

Sadly, Sisyphus was an asshole and I killed "Henry" off at the end of the day and let his memory slide into oblivion. That wasn't very satisfying as a story. So I started thinking about the goal—eternal life. That led me back to Ray Kurzweil's book, *The Singularity is Near*. Artificial intelligence became a driving factor in the new book, *Forever Yours*.

And Henry was no longer an asshole.

SB: What was going on in your life while writing Forever Yours, and did any of that influence the story?

DL: It's more what I went through just before I started writing the story. I suffered from A-Fib, a heart condition, that nearly killed me. Luckily, I was rescued from the condition by an incredible cardiologist who implanted a pacemaker and literally gave me my life back. I definitely think that whole experience affected how I approached the story and especially the rewrite.

SB: Literary fiction–including some written by your other pen name–often carries a moral, a message, or an observation about life. Something the writer intends or hopes the reader will take from the story. Yet I don't think anyone expects erotica to do that, regardless of how well it may be written. As a writer, does that feel like a missed opportunity, or–without giving anything away–should readers be looking at *Forever Yours* as more than "skin deep"?

DL: I've never been able to separate my so-called erotica from the imperative to have a message. Not that I've always succeeded in that. The place where it differs is that it is expected that erotica will have a 'happy ending.' In fact, that was what inspired by first erotic novel. I was desperately in need of writing something with a happy ending.

So, there is definitely a moral to the story, especially in regard to 'celebrating every day of life.'

There are also significant questions raised that I think we should all be considering. Can an AI be considered alive? What does that actually mean? How do we *know* that we are alive?

SB: Outside of the obvious answer–titillation–what do you think erotica readers really want out of a story, and how does that play out in long-form serial writing?

DL: The term 'erotica' gets applied to anything that has explicit sex scenes in it. I could compile all the sex scenes in Forever Yours into a single chapter and be done with it. It didn't take 255,000 words! Certainly, erotica readers expect some amount of sex, but they are first and foremost readers. Readers read for a story. Sex is not satisfying to them unless they care about the characters. Sex is important to the story, but it isn't the story.

Granted, some readers read only for the sex scenes and skip over anything else. Other readers skip over the sex scenes so they can get on with the story. My readers want a good story and characters they can care about. The number of readers of the serial who finish the last chapter and moan about it not being enough and how they want more of these characters indicates that they do care about them and are reluctant to let go at the end of the story. If a person read one of my books just for the sex, they would be disappointed. Just like life, there's a lot more of it near the beginning and it tapers off as characters have more and more happening in their lives.

SB: What's your philosophy of sex scenes? How do you approach them?

DL: First and foremost, a sex scene has to make sense in the story. An adage of many beginning writers—especially in NaNoWriMo—is "Whenever you get stuck, write smut." That's okay when your goal is a word-count, but if it doesn't move the story along, it's pretty worthless.

In *Forever Yours*, Henry has remarkably few sex partners compared to other erotic stories. That includes my own stories. He is mostly monogamous with each partner with one exception that keeps recurring in his life no matter who his girlfriend is. Reconciling that with his life partner was tricky.

Since the majority of my audience is men over fifty, I find that when there is a sex scene, I have to describe it in detail. I think by that age—I hate to generalize, but this was borne out by a survey I conducted—men, or American men, lose their ability to imagine things. That's a significant difference between men and women. When it comes to getting turned on, women need some romance and can imagine what comes next. Men want the romance, too, but they need to be guided through what happens next.

SB: For you, what's the most important aspect of a sex scene?

DL: Easy. The most important thing in any sex scene is that the reader cares about the participants.

SB: In my experience, erotica written by men and that written by women tend to feel different. Obviously, there are ranges and nuances, but as a very coarse generalization, erotica written by men tends to focus on bodies and actions while that written by women focuses more on sensation and emotion. How do you write those scenes so as to hold appeal for both audiences?

DL: I think I have enough romance and emotion in my stories to appeal to women, however, there is more appeal of explicit sex scenes to men. I think it is not so much who *writes* the story as who the audience is. Female readers are more titillated by sensation and emotion. Male readers are more titillated by bodies and action. I think it's a mistake, though, to focus on one without the other. While I know my stories will appeal more to male readers, I also know male readers are my primary audience, so I tend to write for them.

SB: Erotica has—to no one's surprise—a lot of sex scenes. And serial fiction can go on for quite a long time. Taken together, the sex scenes could easily become pro-forma or repetitive. How do you keep them fresh?

DL: That is certainly a problem. As one reviewer said, "There are only so many ways Tab A fits into Slot B." I know that many writers, and I have been in this boat myself, solve the problem by introducing more and more partners. Others write exactly the same sex scene with the same steps, the same positions, and the same outcome every time they write one.

What I end up doing most of the time is following nature. Sex is most exciting when it is new. That's true of women's erotica as well as men's. I often tease a reader with a slow build-up to a sexual completion that takes chapters to unfold. That is typical of women's erotica. But in life, there is a period of flirting, tension, and build-up, then an explosion of activity where the couple or trio can't keep their hands off each other or stay out of bed, followed by a tapering off of sexual interaction. If sex has become routine, why write about it? After the first ten chapters of *Forever Yours*, sex becomes far less important to the story and only marks the progression of relationships that are developing.

I think that is why men, especially, like stories about younger heroes. Teens and early twenties are much more interested in sex than older people. I have heard many older women in my conversations say essentially, they did that stuff when they were younger. They don't need to do it any longer. It's something men bemoan. So, I tend to write about younger people who are discovering sexual relations and partnerships, whether monogamous or polyamorous.

SB: When someone buys a novel at the bookstore, they know how much of it there is. With an ongoing serial story, especially one they're reading as it's being published, they don't. For readers, those are very different experiences. From your side of it, how does that difference affect the way you write, especially as regards pacing?

DL: Without a doubt, there are differences when writing for serialization. However, I no longer begin public posting of my stories until the novel is complete. So, when you buy this 700-page book or the eBook, you know how long it is. A serial reader also has that information, even though he might not have held the book in his hands. I don't start posting until I've finished the writing.

I find it funny that many serial readers (most of whom are reading for free!) are vocal about how much they detest the time-honored technique of ending a chapter with a cliffhanger. I even posted a notice at the beginning of the serialization of *Forever Yours* that if you can't wait three days for a cliffhanger to be resolved, then don't start reading until the story had finished posting. (About nine months.) Not all chapters end with a cliffhanger, but some do and I really don't want to hear about it. Regardless, since my stories are completed before I start posting, I can set a posting schedule of a new chapter every three days and tell people the end date.

There are some things I do for the serial that I might not do when writing strictly for publication. Often, I refresh the reader on something that happened only a couple of chapters ago. In serial land, that's six to nine days! A paperback reader probably read that in the same sitting. So, the first three or four times I mention Germaine, I refer to them as Henry's driver/bodyguard. If I haven't mentioned a character in several chapters, I always have to remind people who I'm talking about.

The same is true about events, descriptions, etc. "When Carol stopped to find Henry, the voluptuous blonde didn't hesitate to knock on his door." She was described as being a voluptuous blonde several chapters earlier, but readers may have forgotten by the time of this mention.

SB: Many scenes about Henry's skills and business activities include technical details. How much research do you do to get those details right? Do you find that erotica readers keep you honest about that stuff, or do they let it slide so long as the sex is good?

DL: I am the poster boy for having a dozen browser windows open at the same time. I look up everything, often sifting through several sites to be sure

I have fairly reliable information. That is true of general terms as well as technical terms. Things are called by different names in different regions.

I try to make my suggestions reasonable without over describing. The 'science,' for example, doesn't have to be accurate if it is believable. On the other hand, at least one reader will contest any assertion I make in his or her pet field. Firearms? I have to avoid as much detail as possible unless I become an expert on using it. Tidal characteristics of a planet I've created for a futuristic novel? I have to do as much as possible to minimize the effects the reader points out would be devastating and uninhabitable. AI? Fortunately, most people don't know any more about it than I do, but there are computer experts who will jump all over any suggestion I make that doesn't conform to the current understanding.

All I try to do is make it believable within the context of the story. But I can still expect someone will 'correct' me.

SB: What's one piece of advice you'd give to an aspiring erotica writer?

DL: I think this is clear. Before you focus on sex, story, or world-building, create believable characters that people can engage with. Good, likable characters are the single most important ingredient to any erotic story. If I don't care about the characters, I don't care about the sex, the story, or the world.

On a secondary note, but worth mentioning: Learn to write and get a good editor.

ACKNOWLEGMENTS

No work of this scope can possibly be credited to only one person. In my case, there were many people who contributed to it in very different ways.

First, my story editor. Lyndsy Fernandes has a sharp eye and a courageous spirit. Even while suffering with multiple health problems, she annotated every page of my first draft, discussing her notes and objections with me at length. Then I started the second draft, and she did equal work that I integrated into the "final" draft. I owe her so much for her dedication. I wish her good health.

Second, my devoted alpha reader, Les Bagley, also read both initial drafts and commented on where he thought the story was going and how it felt to him. We also talked through a few of the finer points. I am fortunate to have him as an alpha reader for all my stories.

Third, I have three copy editor/proofreaders who have been with me for several years. They go only by their screen names, Pixel the Cat, Cie-Mel, and Old Rotorhead. Each brings their unique perspective and expertise to the story and have done so for upwards of seventy stories to date.

And I thank my writers' group, the Neon Cactus Wordsmiths of Las Vegas. Their encouragement and challenges helped me get these drafts finished in the first place.

And finally, to my long-time friend, former business partner, and book doctor, Sonja Black for reading and interviewing me on this story and my writing process.

Thank you all so very much!

Devon Layne